BLACK LIGHT: ROULETTE WAR

LIVIA GRANT   RENEE ROSE   MEASHA STONE

SUE LYNDON   GOLDEN ANGEL   ERIS ADDERLY

KAY ELLE PARKER   JENNIFER BENE

Black Light: Roulette War
Jennifer Bene, Livia Grant, Renee Rose, Sue Lyndon, Measha Stone, Golden Angel, Eris Adderly, Kay Elle Parker

Published by Black Collar Press

EBook ISBN: **978-1-947559-22-6**
Print ISBN: **978-1-947559-21-9**

Cover Art by Eris Adderly, http://erisadderly.com/

This book is a work of fiction. Names, characters, places, and incidents either are products of the author's imagination or are used fictitiously. Any resemblance to actual persons, living or dead, events, or locales is entirely coincidental.

ROULETTE WAR: INTRODUCTION

By Jennifer Bene & Livia Grant

DECLARATION OF WAR

ELIJAH

*unway West*
Mid-December

ELIJAH PULLED up to the front gate of the Runway/Black Light property thirty minutes later than he'd wanted. Waving his ID card in front of the reader on the pedestal, the gates started to open, and he nodded at the security guy in the guard shack as he drove through the gate. The poor schmuck had pulled the unlucky shift of working while the rest of the employees would be taking the night off to party.

The Runway parking lot was half full, telling him the turnout for the annual holiday party his bosses were throwing was strong. He rolled out of his sports car with effort, not for the first time thinking about how it was time to trade it in.

He was distracted with the thought, accidentally dropping his keys to the dark pavement.

"Damnit."

His lower back cracked as he crouched to the ground, feeling around until he found his keyring. He hated how old he'd started to feel, courtesy of his much-abused body.

Ignoring the aches, Elijah took the front stairs to the Runway mansion two at a time in a show of defiance against his own body. He rarely came in the front door, usually entering the property through the secret entrance leading directly to Black Light in the bowels of the building. He'd forgotten how impressive the grand foyer was with its double staircases leading up to the opulent suites.

The mansion was especially beautiful at this time of year, courtesy of the more than a dozen Christmas trees dispersed through the property, each beautifully decorated with twinkling lights and sparkling ornaments. He passed several of them as he made his way toward the mammoth Runway party room where that night's event was being hosted.

"It's about time you got here. I was about to send out a search party for you." His number two, Tyler Darden, greeted him as soon as he rounded the corner just outside the main club room. The holiday music was loud enough he had to speak up to answer.

"Be glad I came at all. I'm not really into the dance scene, and even less into Christmas parties."

"Bah humbug. I'll just call you the grinch for the rest of the night. Maybe you should start with a visit to the open bar."

"Maybe you're right," he offered as he passed his co-worker.

He spent more than enough time in clubs these days. It had been tempting to just stay home, yet it was events like this that reminded Elijah of how lucky he was to have fallen into his second career. As he looked around the room full of revelers, many of whom he now considered close personal friends, he was grateful the Cartwright-Davidsons had given him a chance when they'd opened the club almost two years before. Considering he'd had no experience in running a BDSM club, they'd taken a risk.

"Elijah!"

Avery, the mansion's chef, ambushed him from behind. When he turned to greet her, she leaned in for an extra-long hug.

"Hey there. Looks like everyone's having fun."

Avery's eyes twinkled with mischief as she replied. "You can say that. We're burning through alcohol faster than food. At this rate, I worry we'll have a lot of people either sleeping over or calling an Uber later."

Elijah chuckled. "Well, I'm not planning on drinking much tonight so I'm happy to give rides home to anyone who needs them."

"Funny. I never thought of you as the *designated driver* type," Avery added.

He didn't take her bait. She didn't need to know he'd just started a new round of medicine in the hopes of finding something that could help his broken body not feel like it had been run over by a truck half the time.

They spent a few minutes chit-chatting with a group of groundskeepers and security guards before moving deeper into the room toward the large crowd gathered around several tables near the patio door. Jaxson Cartwright-Davidson was tall enough to stand a head above everyone else in the pack.

Elijah was almost to the group when he stopped dead in his tracks. What the fuck? If he didn't know better, he could swear that was…

"There he is! I was just asking about you, old man."

"What the hell are you doing here, Cook? You decide to visit the real Black Light looking for pointers on how to up your game?"

Despite his antagonistic words, Elijah reached out to shake hands with his East Coast counterpart, Spencer Cook. Only after the men were shaking hands did he notice the attractive woman moving closer to the men.

"I see you're still hanging out with this jerk, Klara. Isn't it time you come to your senses and ditch him?"

The men had dropped their handshake in time for Elijah to lean in to place a platonic kiss on the Black Light East head bartender's cheek as she chuckled.

"I think it's too late for that now. We just got hitched."

Elijah looked back at Spencer who had a shit-eating grin on his face.

"That's right. Better be careful there, Keaton. I don't like you getting handsy with my wife."

"Holy shit. Spencer Cook married. That's something I never saw coming." Elijah grinned at Klara, teasing, "Here I thought you were a smart woman."

She played along. "I know, right? Although I did finally convince him to take a few weeks off at least for a vacation over the holidays. Too bad I had to get hitched just to get time-off."

Elijah razzed Spencer. "Wow, what a cheap bastard. Since when is attending a complimentary Christmas party considered a honeymoon?"

"You're an asshole, you know that?" Spencer countered before turning to his wife. "Are you going to let that stand without telling him the truth?"

Klara grinned as she reached out to pat her husband's chest as if to placate him. "What's the fun in that?"

Spencer groused as he was forced to set Elijah straight on his own. "We're just in town on a two-day stopover between Vegas and Hawaii. Silly me, I thought coming to the party would be fun, but I clearly forgot you'd be here, Keaton."

Elijah laughed off the insult. Spencer Cook was a certified asshole, but he didn't take it personally since he was pretty much an equal-opportunity asshole, treating everyone, including the club's owners, like shit.

"Well, I'm sorry to hear you're off the market, Klara. Especially since you decided to marry a grumpy old man. I've been hoping you'd move out here to the best Black Light," Elijah joked.

"Are you fucking kidding me? You have a watered down version of Black Light going on out here with your fancy celebrities and the throngs of fans who just come to watch. You don't have a clue how to run a real BDSM club," Spencer spat, clearly not realizing Elijah had been goofing around.

"Hey, can you keep it down? I don't think the shoppers down on Rodeo Drive heard you talking about our completely private and secret club." Jaxson had walked over to join them, toddler Alicia wiggling in his arms. "And for the record, I'd appreciate it, Cook, if you'd stop cussing in front of my kids. In fact, I think everyone here for the Christmas party would prefer you left your f-bombs at home."

Elijah had to hide his grin at watching the owner setting Spencer in his place. Jaxson was about the only person who usually got away with it. Well, him and Klara, of course.

Spencer wouldn't let it drop. "I was just explaining to Elijah that his club isn't really a BDSM club. It's just a private sex club where a few BDSM scenes may occasionally happen."

He couldn't let the diss stand. "Are you kidding me? The level of kink is way heavier here than in D.C. You guys are just a bunch of stuffy politicians and uptight government officials."

"Are you fu... um... I mean, are you kidding me? Not only is the East Coast way more hardcore into the kink scene, but we have more members and bring in more membership fees every month."

Elijah could feel his blood pressure rising. He hadn't come to the party expecting to have to defend Black Light West. If it was just him, he might just laugh it off and walk away, but it suddenly felt like the music volume had been turned down and the group of his dungeon monitors that had been hanging out by the bar had walked over to stand behind Elijah, forming a nice line of defense.

"First of all, you may have more members on your membership roll, but I pay attention to the numbers too. Your attendance has been declining in the last year and you have less than twenty-five percent of the number of educational classes that we do out here."

"Like I said, that's because no one is really experienced out here. Just a sex club."

"That's bullshit." Only after he said it did Elijah remember, glancing up at Jaxson and adding, "Sorry. I meant that's crap." He then turned back to Spencer to continue. "More importantly, our membership numbers are growing month over month and our food and beverage revenue has never been higher."

"So what? That just means you're turning into a restaurant instead of a *real* club."

Madison and Avery had joined their group, as had all of the security guards hanging out with Miguel and his wife. Elijah had to stifle a smile when he realized Spencer was literally surrounded by the whole West Coast family. They'd gathered around to watch the showdown.

He didn't want to disappoint them.

Stepping closer to Spencer, Elijah resisted bumping chests like a caveman. "You have a lot of balls, I'll give you that. Coming into our house and throwing shade. But you've got your head up your ass if you think the East Coast club is better in any way.

"We are growing. Both our revenue and bottom line income outpaces you. Hell, we've raised more for charity in the last year than you've taken in for profit."

Spencer's face was getting more red by the minute as he stepped forward to bump chests, knocking into Elijah hard enough that he almost fell backwards. He steeled himself to hold his ground.

"The fact that you spend time raising money for charity instead of for the bottom line just proves my point. You're running a glorified country club out here. Admit it. You're no more a BDSM club than Runway is."

His DMs started to crowd in, and Elijah threw his arms out to hold them back. Cook clearly had a death wish coming into their house and picking a fight like this.

He wasn't going to let Spencer's hotheaded temper drag him into a physical fight. He took a few deep breaths before he replied up in Spencer's face.

"First of all, not everyone in this room is a Black Light employee, so you should absolutely know better than to be picking this particular fight with me up here at Runway. But for the record, we raised a ton of money *and* hosted an epic Roulette event last year. You see, we can talk and chew gum at the same time.

"More importantly, we've already started planning for the upcoming Valentine's Day and once again, like last year, we're gonna blow your numbers out of the water!"

"Oh yeah, well money isn't everything. Our Valentine's Day is going to be epic. We have a waiting list a mile long for Roulette participants and we haven't even opened enrollment yet."

"That doesn't make any sense. And anyway, of course we're both going to have plenty of participants. This isn't about quantity anyway, it's about quality. Our scenes from last year were hands down the best ever. People are still talking about that night, months later."

"That's only because they don't know any better. The few West members who have visited us on the East coast always say they wish their club could be more like ours."

"Oh really. That's funny. They all come back home and tell me how glad they are I'm not a raving asshole like you are."

"Alright, alright, I think that's just about enough…" Jaxson tried to step between his two DMs to break things up. He had gotten rid of Alicia at some point, which was a good thing.

Klara was grabbing her husband's forearm, pulling him away and berating him for embarrassing her.

Elijah took a few deep breaths, determined not to let Spencer's sunny nature drag him down.

But the visitor was determined to escalate things by shouting, "I'll bet you anything our event will blow yours out of the water this year."

"What does that even mean? Do you hear yourself?"

"It means our members will have the most fun, and our participants will spin the edgiest kinks."

"Oh, and just how do you propose we measure this?" Elijah countered, sure the idea was stupid.

"We get the members to vote, that's how."

"Say what?"

"You heard me. We add a voting component to the event. The spectators each get a ballot and get to vote for their favorite couples and kinks. They can rate us on other things for the event as well. We tally votes at the end of the night to declare a winner."

"You're insane. First of all, we hold an auction for our celebrities so it isn't even apples to apples. I'm not giving up on making money for charities just because you're so insecure you need to pick a fight."

Jaxson surprised Elijah by piping in again. "You know, we've talked about changing things up out here this year. I'm worried we'll have trouble finding enough celebrities to sign up."

Elijah shot his boss a look that could kill a lesser man. Whose side was he on anyway?

"See! Even Jaxson agrees you guys can't pull this off."

Jaxson turned on Spencer. "Don't you dare try to pull me into this pissing contest. We're all one family, so you two need to drop the antagonistic shit right away. This is a party, goddamnit. We're here to have fun."

Spencer dared spar back. "I thought you said there was no cussing in front of the kids?"

Jaxson pointed at him. "Really? That's how you want to handle this?"

"It is if you aren't going to have the balls to tell Keaton he's wrong."

Jaxson growled in frustration. "You can be a real pain in my ass, you know that? You don't have a clue what the hell you're talking about Spencer. The event out here was every bit as epic as the Roulette events on the East Coast. One isn't better than the other."

"Oh yeah, well I'd like a chance to prove you all wrong."

Behind him, he could hear his guys talking about who was going to throw the first punch to put Cook in his place. Things were about to escalate. He glanced around at the wide eyes of the other employees gathered around for the spectacle. This was not how they should be celebrating Christmas.

Chase had come forward along with Madison and Avery. Everyone was talking at once. The room was devolving into chaos. He needed to get things back under control, and there was only one way to do that.

"Fine. I accept your challenge. One night. Valentine's Day. A Roulette event on each coast. Each of us get three hours, fifteen couples and two roulette wheels. We'll let the spectators vote on their favorite scenes and couples, but…"

Elijah hesitated and the room seemed to hold their breath waiting for him to finish his thought.

"But, we need impartial judges to choose the final winning club. East versus West. Winner takes all."

Spencer looked surprised that Elijah had agreed to his challenge. "And what exactly is it that we are taking if we win?"

Elijah scrambled to think of what he wanted. "For the winning club, the employees each get an extra three days of paid vacation for the year."

He loved the 'hell yes' and the 'we're gonna kick their ass' he heard behind him from his dungeon monitors.

Elijah then added, "And you and me, we go not only for bragging rights, but we'll put our own personal money on the line. I'll wager…" he paused before finishing with, "ten grand. Winner collects ten grand from the loser."

Spencer's eyes grew wide. It was Klara that spoke up.

"No fucking way. You are not gambling away my new kitchen renovation money for some stupid bet because you can't keep your mouth shut." When she realized what she'd said, she looked up at Emma and apologized. "Sorry, I shouldn't have cussed in front of the twins."

Emma smiled. "It's okay. I think I might have said worse in your shoes."

When Spencer stood looking conflicted, Elijah took pity on the newlywed. "Fine. The last thing I want to do is hurt Klara. After all, she has to put up with your sorry crap every day. I'm not going to deny her a new kitchen too."

"Pretty confident you're gonna win, aren't you? When I win, I'll be able to take her on a second honeymoon with your ten grand."

Jaxson held his arms out to separate the men again. "That's enough. No money will change hands. You want to bet, that's fine. But it'll be for bragging rights only. I'll pitch in a Roulette trophy that we'll award to the winning club. They'll keep it on display until the next event. And I'll go along with the extra vacation time for the winning employees, but one day, not three. We're not running a damn charity here."

Chase surprised Elijah by stepping into the fray next to his husband. "The competition is fine, but I'm not willing to give up on making money for charity again this year. It felt good to give so much last year and anyway, after the whole Ainsworth debacle last year, we've already been talking to a sexual abuse victim group to receive our donation this year."

After what their friend and coworker Nalani had gone through just weeks after last year's roulette, Elijah couldn't agree more.

"Fine. I'll give up the celebrity auction part, but we keep the silent auction. And the East Coast has to add that to their event starting this year. At least then even when they lose, something good will come out of it. I'll even let them choose their own charity for the auction proceeds. The club that gets the highest donations for the night will get bonus points toward the overall competition."

Spencer looked like he'd swallowed something sour. "This is bullshit."

"Take it or leave it," Elijah dared.

"Oh I'll take it. And I'm gonna win. I just have one more question. Just who the hell is going to be the impartial judge considering we are on opposite sides of the country?"

Chase jumped in again with a solution. "Jaxson and I will be the judges. One of us will go to the East Coast. The other the West. We'll tally spectator votes and auction totals and then confer together to name the final winner."

Emma spoke up. "Wait a minute. I object. Does this mean I'll have to spend Valentine's Day without one of you? You gonna make me and the kids choose who to be with?"

Jaxson reassured her. "Don't worry, baby. We'll figure something out. There's no way in hell any one of us will be spending Valentine's Day without the other two."

Pint-sized Madison had been standing on the sidelines, taking the challenge in, but she'd clearly had enough, stepping into the middle of the group and declaring, "Okay, now that's enough talk about Valentine's Day. It's not even Christmas yet. We're all here to have fun with each other, so no more arguing. It's time to really get this party started."

Elijah watched as the group dispersed. His mind was already racing, realizing he had just declared war.

Well, hell.

THE WAR IS ON

SPENCER

*B*lack Light East
February 14th, 3:00pm

"You've got to be fucking kidding me," Spencer growled, turning around in front of the bar to observe the chaos still unfolding around him. A pair of dungeon monitors were securing a spanking bench to one of the raised platforms, which should have been done an hour ago, and that meant someone was about to get their ass handed to them.

"Don't even think about it," Klara's voice drawled from behind him, and he spun around to point at her.

"I will absolutely spank your ass when—"

"When we get home," she finished, nodding, her red lips turning up into a smirk that showed just how little that threat meant to his little masochist. "But right now, you need to not jump down the guys' throats. They're working on it, and we've got a while to go before anyone shows up."

"I told them to get this shit done hours ago."

"Yes, and they're doing it," Klara answered, sighing as she gestured out toward the floor. "That to do list you and Maxine came up with isn't exactly a short one."

"Where the hell is Maxine anyway? Isn't she the one that pestered the fuck out of me to be involved in this shitshow?" Turning, Spencer scanned the floor of Black Light again, trying to ignore the flurry of activity that confirmed just how *not* ready they were.

No Maxine.

Dammit.

"If it wasn't Roulette night, I'd pour you a glass of whiskey... but I know you won't drink it." Klara laughed under her breath, and when he looked back at her again those honey brown eyes were lit with mischief. Just how he liked her, when he could bend her over his knee — but now was definitely not one of those times.

"It's tempting," he conceded, crossing his arms as he leaned back on the bar. Klara kept moving as he brooded, cutting limes without pause, and it was one of the things he loved most about her. She had his work ethic, and was always cool when his blood boiled, which made her the perfect partner in all things. Hell, it was why he'd broken his promise to himself to never get married. Walking away from a woman like Klara Eriksson would have been incredibly stupid, so he'd put a ring on her finger.

"Here." The glass smacked down on the bar top with a distinct *clack*, but Klara kept her fingers around it until Spencer met her gaze. "It's one drink, four hours before the party even starts. You'll be fine, and trust me you need it."

"Not happening, Klara," he replied sharply, but he couldn't help eyeballing the shallow pour of amber liquid lurking in the glass.

"Sure," she said on a laugh. "When are you going to finally admit that I'm always right?"

Spencer laughed, a short sound as he leaned across to get close enough to smell her shampoo. "That is never going to happen."

"Happy wife, happy life," Klara answered, winking at him before she picked up the knife to continue cutting limes. "Don't be a little bitch about it and take the drink."

"I swear, Klara. I'm going to turn your ass bright red tonight."

"I look forward to it." She glanced up at him and tilted her head toward the glass. "Until then, do everyone a favor and drink it. You're going to get everyone so freaked out that you're going to lose, and then you'll be sleeping on the couch because I am *not* putting up with you when you're whiny."

Gritting his teeth, Spencer reached across the bar to catch her by the back of the neck, reveling in the way her breath caught for just a moment as her eyes widened. "That mouth of yours... I'm definitely going to put it to work in other ways after I *win* this shit."

"Okay," she whispered, and he had to fight the urge to kiss her. Getting coated in red lipstick was not going to do his image any favors, and she'd be pissed about having to fix it, so he just squeezed her neck once more before letting go to snatch the glass and take a swallow. It burned sweet and warm down the back of his throat, landing in his stomach with a soothing heat.

"Wow, drinking on the job, Cook?" Maxine asked a little too loudly as she approached from the side, and Spencer didn't miss the flash of an amused grin on Klara's face before she turned away to pull more glasses.

"Taste-testing," he answered her through clenched teeth. "But at least I've *been* here, at my job, where I'm supposed to be. Where exactly have you been?"

Maxine waggled the tablet in her hand before tucking it against her side again to tap away at it. "I've been working, asshole. I thought you wanted to win this whole Roulette War thing?"

"Obviously, but I told you I needed you down here. At two. It's three o'clock, Maxine, so how the fuck is—"

"First of all, do you know how many guests we're going to have tonight? Two-hundred and forty-eight tickets have sold. That's almost fire code capacity for Black Light"—Maxine waved her hand—"And I know you don't give a shit about that, but it's the most successful night this club has had. It's not just going to be busy, it's going to be *packed* and since I'm the only one here with any idea how to manage a club that busy, then I thought I should do some planning for crowd control, backfilling food and beverage, and handling parking. Plus I've got Runway all squared away so I can babysit you. So, yeah, I've been working Spencer, what have you been doing?"

The irritation that always accompanied Maxine's rants was even worse tonight, and it was the last thing Spencer needed — even with a half a shot of whiskey in his stomach. Taking a slow breath, he crossed his arms and stared down the short little pitbull of a woman. "Well?"

"Well, what?" she snapped.

"Did you get all of that situated, because I've got more important things we need to handle down here."

"You're an asshole, Spencer."

He couldn't help but grin as her cheeks turned ruddy with the same irritation that was burrowing deep under his skin just by sharing the same air as Maxine Torres. "Absolutely. Now, are you ready to go through the checklist?"

"Fine," Maxine grumbled, bringing her tablet back to life with a swipe of her finger. "I see your employees are setting up the equipment list, but we need to grab one of them to setup the ballot box and bring the roulette wheels out of the office."

"They can do that *after* all of the equipment is installed—"

"Did you want to get this done now, or do you want to be a jerk and lose tonight?" With a flick of her eyebrow, Maxine drove the issue home once more and Spencer sneered at her.

"We're not going to lose this war, because there is no way in hell I'm going to congratulate Elijah Keaton tomorrow." Turning away from the annoying GM of Runway, Spencer whistled across the floor. "Muscles! Get over here."

Terry was carrying a wooden pony on one shoulder across the floor, but he stopped instantly and set it down beside a platform to jog over. The man was built like a brickhouse and the black dungeon monitor shirt he wore seemed close to snapping across his chest, which was exactly what the man wanted.

At least the subs enjoy the view.

"What's up, boss?" Terry asked, nodding at Maxine before his eyes swiveled back to Spencer.

"Need you to help us out with a few things. Follow me," Spencer said, immediately turning to walk past Maxine toward the stage. "There's a big black box on a stand in storage, I need you to bring it out and put it here."

"Actually, we need it to the right of the center stairs," Maxine interrupted, moving to point at a spot a mere four feet to the right. "We can't have people impeding traffic up to the stage when participants want to roll again."

"Fine. Put it there." Spencer could feel his jaw creak as he swallowed the shit he wanted to say to the woman. "Then we need you to bring the roulette wheels from the office and set them up on that black table we always use. Center stage."

"I can do that. May need to grab someone to get the table up there." Terry twisted to look out over the other dungeon monitors at work and then he shrugged. "Don't worry, sir, I'll get it done. Anything else?"

Waving his arm at Maxine, he stared at her, waiting for her to mouth off again, but she was tapping away at the damn tablet in her hand. Grumbling under his breath, he shook his head. "I think that's it for now, Muscles. Just get on it. We've got a lot of shit to do."

"You're not kidding. All that violet wand shit is breakable as hell, and Chad is trying to secure it over by the massage tables." Every word out of the man's mouth was making Spencer tense even further, and — although he'd never admit it to Klara — he wished he'd finished the damn shot she'd poured him.

"Fine. Just don't fuck anything up. This is our name on the line."

Terry laughed and spread his arms wide. "No one is going to take this win from us, or that extra vacation day. We're the fucking best, and they're all a bunch of West Coast pansies. Jaxson will see that for sure."

Jaxson. Fuck.

"That's a great attitude, Terry. Thank you for your help," Maxine finally chimed in, smiling at the dungeon monitor as he walked away to start moving shit into place. When her eyes swung back to Spencer, the smile disappeared. "So, where did you end up putting the silent auction?"

He didn't even bother answering, just turned away from her to march back across the club toward the costume rental and naughty gift shop. The long tables had been set up earlier in the day, with Klara's guidance, on the very edge of the bar area. The two tables were separated enough to allow people to walk between them and still enter the shop if they wanted, but the location at least meant that non-participants would have the chance to check out the auction items while grabbing a drink.

"This looks good," Maxine said, and Spencer was just about to acknowledge the compliment when she continued with, "Klara really knows her stuff."

Biting back a retort, Spencer managed a smile that was probably closer to a grimace. "Yep."

"Don't forget Jaxson is going to be looking at the silent auction proceeds just as hard as he is the actual play that will go on tonight. It would be a good idea to have the bar staff and the servers pushing people toward the tables as much as possible, and—"

"People will bid on whatever the fuck they want to bid on, Maxine. They're coming here for Roulette, to enjoy the scenes, not to pick up another strap, or a secluded cabin getaway, and shoving them toward this thing isn't going to make them spend more."

"Still butthurt that this little addition came from Elijah's club, are you?" Maxine didn't even try to hide her smile, and Spencer had to bite his tongue before he pissed off Klara's buddy. Again. For the ten-millionth time.

"Look, I'm fine with supporting the people in the community who make this stuff. Hell, I'm fine with all this charity donation bullshit! But I'm not fine with taking up more space for this on a night like tonight when we're already, as you said, going to be fucking packed."

"Yet, it still matters to Jaxson and Chase and Emma, and therefore it matters to us."

"Yeah? Well, if it matters so much, where the fuck is Jaxson? I know they wanted to have their little Valentine's morning fuckfest in Colorado, but when does he get his ass here?" Spencer snapped, glancing back at the stage to see Terry and Garreth setting up the roulette wheels on stage. *At least someone is getting shit done.*

"You do realize Colorado is two hours behind D.C., right? He left as early as he could, on a chartered plane from what Emma said, and he'll land about 4:30."

"Four fucking thirty?" Spencer groaned and scraped his fingers through his short hair. "With traffic it could be six o'clock before he's here from the airport. That's barely before Roulette starts!"

"Then it's lucky for us that Jaxson isn't the MC for tonight," Maxine replied with an almost motherly tone, which somehow grated his nerves worse than her normal sharp banter.

"Yeah, *Elixxir*." Spencer huffed. "That kid hasn't done anything like this before, and he won't be able to just turn on some music if he forgets his lines."

"He's great with the crowd, Cook. Everyone loves him already and he's got a great personality — which you'd know if you ever gave him a chance." Maxine gave him a pointed look over the top of her tablet. "You need to take a breath, finish that drink Klara poured you, and relax. Jaxson will be here in time to do his little welcome comments, DJ Elixxir will be fine, and if you can keep your head out of your ass long enough to keep the fun going for Roulette then you might actually win this little pissing contest with Elijah."

"We are going to win," Spencer ground out through his teeth, and Maxine just smiled.

"Of course you are." Tapping her tablet once more, she dropped it to her side and reached across to smack him on the arm. "Try not to rip everyone's heads off. Save the badass routine for the members when they arrive, alright?"

"Don't you have things you can be doing?" he asked, crossing his arms as he stepped away from her.

"I absolutely do. I'll be upstairs, but feel free to send one of your minions after me if you need me to hold your hand."

"Fuck off, Maxine."

"I think there will be plenty of that tonight, don't you?" she quipped, laughing to herself as she turned to walk back toward the stairs up to Runway.

Growling under his breath, Spencer marched back to the bar where Klara was already setting another whiskey on the bar top.

"Did you play nice with Maxine?" Klara asked, leaning on the bar to give him an excellent view of her cleavage and those sinful red lips she wore every time she tended bar.

"No." Grabbing the drink, he tipped it up and let the burn roll down his throat.

"Well, that's good. Wouldn't want to confuse her into thinking you're not an asshole."

Spencer's head snapped up and Klara just grinned at him.

"But I love you, and everything is going to go just fine tonight. Elijah and Black Light West won't know what hit them." Reaching over, she squeezed his hand and he didn't brush her off. No one in the world got him quite like Klara Eriksson-Cook, but tonight wasn't something she could guarantee. Fierce little Swedish bartender or not, tonight was going to come down to the couples playing and whether or not Jaxson liked what he saw.

Maybe I should have been nicer to the cocky prick all these years.

Finishing the drink, he set it down with a *thunk*. "I'm going to go find someone to yell at."

"That always makes you feel better," Klara answered with a grin, giving his hand one more squeeze before she let him go.

"Love you," he said, and she winked at him as he turned to march out onto the floor to see who was fucking up — and God help the first idiot he found being lazy. He'd put the freshly cleaned whips into practice before he lost this war without a fight.

SHOWTIME AT BLACK LIGHT EAST

ELIXXIR

Black Light East
February 14th, 6:30pm

ADJUSTING HIS HEADPHONES, MARVIN 'ELIXXIR' Washington shifted on the plush couch, flicking through his notecards one more time. Chase had given him tips for the MC gig tonight, but even after they'd talked about it... he didn't feel confident. Sure, he performed in front of hundreds of people almost every night of the week, but this was different.

It wasn't a bunch of drunk club kids listening to his music. No, this was politicians and rich people and doms and subs that he respected listening to him — just him — talk while running the most important event of the entire year.

No pressure.

Sighing, he leaned forward again to peek down three stories to the dance floor of Runway. The club wasn't open yet, but it would be soon, and he could already see the giant inflatable coyote attached to the second floor DJ stand. That asshole DJ Fullmoon was going to make Runway look like a fucking joke on Valentine's Day, and he was using *his* DJ booth to do it.

"Fucker," Elixxir mumbled under his breath, sagging back against the couch to stare up at the dimmed lights in the ceiling. Music thumped steadily in his ears, blocking out whatever noise was rising up from below, but it wasn't helping him focus like it usually did.

When Chase, Jaxson, and Emma had asked him to MC for Valentine Roulette, he'd jumped at the chance. Ever since he'd found out about the club, he'd been going on his off nights to enjoy it. He'd even played with some of the subs, and he liked it, but he was still a newbie.

Everyone knew he was a newbie.

And now he was leading the fucking event that people scrambled for every damn year.

Tonight could either be awesome for him, or a complete and utter fuck-up, and which way it was going to go would be down to fate... but he'd always had a knack for sneaking by on wit and charm and he'd just have to use that skill to *make* it a success no matter what fate had in mind.

"Marvin!" Maxine snapped from the doorway, her face flushed with fury, and he jerked to attention, ripping his headphones off as she huffed. "You've been hiding way up here all this time? I swear I've been over every inch of this damn club! Do you have any idea what time it is?"

"Shit!" Standing up, Elixxir glanced at his watch and groaned. "I've been reviewing my notecards for the welcome speech, and—"

"I don't care what you've been doing! Spencer is going to skin you alive if you don't get downstairs right now!" Muttering under her breath, Maxine marched toward the elevator and he followed quickly on her heels. "I can't believe you were up here on the third floor, Marvin."

Cringing, Elixxir tucked the notecards away. "Come on, you know how much I hate that."

"Yeah? Well, when you act like a child, I'm gonna call you by your name. *Elixxir* is supposed to be a professional who doesn't hide in a damn lounge three floors above where he's scheduled to work!"

"I'm sorry, Max. Come on, you know I wouldn't have been late for real, and I've been stressing because that fuck DJ Fullmoon is messing up my area and—"

"No!" Maxine raised a finger in his face just as the elevator arrived. "You don't get to complain to me right now. Get inside."

Moving into the elevator, he tried his best charming smile and spread his arms wide. "Max, when have I ever missed a gig?"

"Don't look at me with your cute face, *you* don't get to use cute face right now. Spencer has been on my ass all day, and I had to step away from Runway stuff to track you down." Huffing, Maxine swept her bangs off her forehead as she pressed the button for the first floor.

"I'm sorry?" Elixxir offered, still working his smile, and eventually he saw Maxine's lips twitch at the corner.

"Ugh, I hate how much I like you sometimes." Her shoulders relaxed a bit as she rolled her eyes. "Fine, you're forgiven, but that isn't going to mean much when you face Spencer and Jaxson in a minute."

Fuck.

"Jaxson is here?" All the wit and charm in the world wouldn't mean jack shit in front of Jaxson Cartwright-Davidson. The dude was serious as fuck, and always more intense when Emma and Chase weren't around.

"Yep," Maxine replied with a crisp pop of her lips, and all Elixxir could do was groan. "But he's not who you should be scared of, Spencer is on the warpath today with his little pissing contest against Elijah out at Black Light West."

"Right, the whole voting thing the non-participants are doing."

"Well, yeah, but we all know that Jaxson and Chase are going to make the real decision on which club wins overall. It's war, and we're right in the middle of it."

"Lucky us," Elixxir muttered as the elevator opened.

"Go head downstairs, I have stuff to handle up here," Maxine said, already walking in the direction of the bar.

Even though he should be hurrying to Black Light, he couldn't move from his spot because the ten-foot-tall inflatable wolf was now blinking on and off in a variety of colors. It looked cheap, and stupid, and instead of apologizing to Maxine he should have pointed out this crap and told her exactly why he would have preferred *anyone* other than DJ Fullmoon filling in for him tonight.

"Fucking fullmoon asshat..." Elixxir grumbled as he marched to the hall to sneak down the hidden stairs to Black Light. Just as he opened the door into the locker room, Danny started laughing.

"Oh, man, you're in for it."

"That bad, huh?" Elixxir asked, grinning at Danny as the man shook his head.

"I'm not sure if you've had your ass whipped before tonight, but if you don't find Spencer ASAP you're gonna find out." Danny pressed the button to let him into the club, and Elixxir hurried inside to search for Spencer — not that it was hard to find him.

Spencer Cook was standing in front of the stage with Jaxson and neither of them looked happy. Breaking into a jog, he came up to them just as both men turned to face him with their arms crossed.

"Decided to show up?" Spencer asked, his face a mask of enraged stone.

"We've got plenty of time," Elixxir replied, grinning as he shrugged his shoulders. "Plus, I've got this."

Fake it till you make it, right?

"Ignore Spencer, he's always wound tight." Jaxson offered his hand, and Elixxir shook it with a chuckle.

"Yeah, but without him this place wouldn't run, so we still like him."

"Sucking up doesn't make you less of a fuck-up, *Marvin*." Spencer put more emphasis on his real name than necessary, but Elixxir managed to grin at the grouchy Dungeon Master.

"Love you too, sir."

Jaxson chuckled a little before running a hand over his face. "Look, I'm already dealing with one pissing contest between you and Elijah, I'm not in the mood to referee for you, Spencer. I had to schedule sex this morning and then spent a goddamn fortune to fly here on a chartered plane *just* to be here for your Roulette war today — so cut it the fuck out."

"You had to schedule sex?" Elixxir asked, confused.

"I can tell you don't have kids. Between the flights Chase and I had to be on today, and the risk of the twins needing us, we were all up at the crack of fucking dawn to have time to celebrate Valentine's our way." Shaking his head, Jaxson looked up at the ceiling and sighed. "I swear, next year I'm not agreeing to this insanity."

"Well, thank you for being here, sir," Elixxir answered just as Spencer scoffed and rolled his eyes.

"Get on stage for sound check. Now." Snapping his fingers, Spencer pointed up the stairs and Elixxir gave Jaxson a quick salute before marching up the steps.

It took longer than Elixxir expected for the sound system at Black Light to get adjusted. They didn't use the microphone setup in the club very often, and that meant it wasn't as well-tuned as the booth in Runway, but after almost twenty minutes they got it done.

Just a few minutes before Spencer might have *actually* killed him for delaying it.

People were already pouring into the club, crowding the tables and chairs near the bar, and the additional seating set up temporarily in front of the stage. He'd heard that a lot of tickets had sold for non-participants, but *this* was more people than he'd ever seen downstairs.

Of course, it's not like he ever got to come on the most popular nights. Wednesdays and Thursdays weren't exactly the hottest nights for any club, which is why he got to come down in the first place.

Several men had already begun to line up to the side of the stage, and a few women were gathered near the steps looking nervous and excited in equal measure. Hell, Elixxir was starting to catch it too. The energy in the room was vastly different than the dance club, but no less intoxicating. Sex and curiosity and lust and adventure all rolled into one.

Or rolled on the roulette wheels at least.

"You ready for this?" A man's voice asked, and Elixxir turned to see Chad, one of the dungeon monitors, positioning a cage against the wall.

"Yeah, I'm good, man."

Chad grinned as he sidled up to him, his eyes scanning the room like the watchful guy he always was when he was working. "Have you been upstairs? There's a fucking wolf—"

"I saw that shit. I told Maxine not to hire DJ Fullmoon and she did it anyway. That asshole hauls all that weird shit with him wherever he goes and it's going to take me hours to get the booth back the way I like it."

"You regretting this whole MC thing?" Chad asked, eyebrow raised.

"Fuck no, I get the best seat in the house tonight!" Elixxir laughed and Chad slapped him on the shoulder, squeezing.

"Well, you'll get to see a lot of fun shit tonight. Keep your eyes open, newbie, and maybe we'll find something new for you to try." Grinning, Chad gave him a friendly punch on the shoulder and then rushed down the steps to take up his post near the group shower area.

Newbie.

Dammit, was everyone thinking that? Elixxir turned his back to the audience just so he could drop the smile for a second and breathe. This was final countdown time, no more room for anxiety, and that meant no bullshit like second-guessing himself or his decision.

The lights dimmed, flashed, and then he felt the heat of the spotlight on his back.

Showtime, Elixxir. Work your magic.

Turning around, he held his arms out and the music he'd set up with Owen started to play. The heavy bass hit hard even in the flat space of Black Light, and as his track continued on people rapidly pulled closer to the stage. He swayed just like he always did in the booth, losing himself in the music, and when one of the women in the audience cheered at him he lifted up his shirt to show off his abs — and the feminine cheers and screams were *exactly* what he needed to get his confidence back on track.

He fucking had this. He performed for a living, and this was just a different stage.

"Welcome to Black Light!" Elixxir called out, the mic amplifying his voice, and the crowd roared, a wall of sound just as powerful as Runway on its best night. Owen lowered the music a little, letting it fade into the background as he paced the front of the stage. "I know we're all anxious to get this show on the road, and — trust me — I can't wait either. This is the fourth annual Valentine Roulette here at Black Light, and it's going to be dirtier, naughtier, and sexier than ever!"

Another cheer rolled out of the crowd like a wave, and he rode it with a grin as he made eye contact with Jaxson and tilted his head back.

"Of course, before I review our rules for the night, and introduce you to our participants, my man Jaxson Cartwright-Davidson is going to say a few words."

Jaxson was chuckling and shaking his head as he climbed the stairs, raising an arm to wave at the crowd when he joined him at center stage. "Good evening, everyone!"

There was no choice but to pause as applause thundered through the room for one of the owners that made the club possible, but Jaxson took it in stride. Smiling and waiting for the noise to die down.

"Yes, I'm just as excited for tonight to get going as our MC is, and for those of you who haven't heard him upstairs at Runway, this is DJ Elixxir! He'll be leading us all through Roulette tonight, and I'm very glad to be here as just another guest, enjoying a drink and all of the sights." A few wolf whistles cut through the room and laughter followed. "Oh yes, it's going to be a great night, and I want to wish all of our participants good luck and thank them for joining us! Without these brave souls, we'd never be able to run this amazing event each year for all of you."

Jaxson smiled at the audience, and Elixxir wasn't surprised he'd been a model before all of this — the guy knew how to look charming and suave as fuck in a suit that easily cost as much as his rent each month.

"Anyway, I'm not going to take up any more of your time. Thank you all for coming, and let's hear it for DJ Elixxir!" Jaxson clapped him on the shoulder, nodding his head at the crowd as they applauded, and then he headed back off stage.

"Thank you, Jaxson!" Elixxir called out before pointing at the audience. "Now it's time for the fun stuff. All of you are here to either participate in this naughty game of chance, or to watch it, and that means we need to remind everyone exactly how this game is played."

Turning around, he spun one of the wheels to send it clicking before facing the audience again.

"Our dominants for the evening will draw to see what order they'll be spinning this first wheel, which will tell them which lovely submissive they'll be playing with. Then," he paused to set the other wheel spinning with a grin. "The sub will join us on stage and spin the second wheel for their first kink of the night. We've got a lot of fun stuff on here, and a few that might make this Roulette extra interesting."

Laughter and shouts echoed back from the darkness beyond the spotlight, and Elixxir laughed along with them, shaking his finger in an animated way as he moved to the edge of the stage.

"Now, now, you're all getting ahead of yourselves. We're a civilized group of depraved kink-lovers, and that means we always follow the rules." Winking at a woman in the front row, he spread his arms again. "Roulette goes until eleven o'clock tonight, and couples who stay together through the whole night will win a free month of membership here at Black Light, worth a cool twenty-five hundred bucks."

Gesturing to the club beyond, he added, "We've got our expert dungeon monitors strategically placed all around the club, so if any of you doms have any questions, or need some tips on some of the more creative equipment, all you have to do is speak up. We might get a little weird tonight, but we're all gonna be safe. Speaking of safe, the official safe word of the night is 'red' and use of the word by any of our participants will — as always — cease play immediately, but it will also disqualify you from winning your prize. That means you can push your sub's limits, but you gotta pay attention."

A few of the men in line beside the stage nudged each other, laughing in a friendly way, and Elixxir gave them a quick salute before turning back to the audience.

"For each kink you spin, you have to spend at least thirty minutes in the scene. There's always time for aftercare, and any necessary clean up"—Elixxir winked at the audience and heard a small peep from the group of submissives in front of him—"but you're going to want to keep the party going, and so whenever you're ready come back to me to spin again."

Holding his hands out, he grinned. "Now, I know it might be tempting to play along, but if you're not here to play the game, remember that tonight Black Light equipment is for Roulette participants only. But that doesn't mean you won't get to have fun! We've got an awesome bar staff, and some tasty snacks to keep you entertained... and you'll want to be paying attention to our participants because each of our guests tonight will be voting on their favorite couple of the evening."

Elixxir hopped down a couple of the steps at center stage, stopping near a few surprised subs as the spotlight landed on them and the ballot box. "Whenever you've decided you've seen the hottest scene of the night, the dirtiest act, the best Dom and sub in the game, just fill out your ballot and drop it in the box here to the right of the center stairs!"

Spinning on his heel, he marched back up the stairs and waved the line of dominants onto the stage as he continued. "The couple who receives the most votes will each win an additional free month of Black Light. That's right, *two* free months! I know I'd appreciate that in my pocket!"

The crowd applauded as the doms finished filing onto the stage, and Elixxir grabbed the handful of labeled sticks from the cup on the table. Approaching the line, he let each participant take one, until he got to a dom that just stared at them.

"This is going to be your number," Elixxir said away from the mic, waiting for the man he recognized as Mister M to take one. "Here."

"I, uh"—Mister M cleared his throat—"I can't touch that." Jerking his chin toward the stick on one side, he said, "Just— that one. I'll remember my number."

"Okaaay..." Plucking the stick out, he turned it over. "Seven."

"Seven," the dom repeated. "Got it. Thanks."

What the hell?

Elixxir was hella confused, but he didn't have time for this, and he quickly moved down the line to distribute the rest of the sticks, keeping the number seven in his other hand. Once he was done, he moved back to center stage to drop the errant stick on the table before he clapped his hands.

"Alright, everyone, who's ready to get this party started?" he called out, enjoying the rush as the crowd cheered and whistled. *This* was what he'd always been meant for, it's why he loved being a DJ.

Performing was in his blood, and he had no plans in screwing up tonight. "Dominant number one, please step forward!"

The fire-loving dominant, Elliott, stepped forward with a serious expression on his face. Handing him the marble, Elixxir set the wheel to spinning and watched as the first dom of the night dropped the ball in. It bounced, spun, and as the wheel slowed it settled on the man's partner.

"Lovely Lisa!" he announced, turning toward the submissives. The pretty blonde marched up the steps with a look of determination on her face, and he chuckled as he handed her the marble. Elliott moved in close, saying something to her about whether or not she wanted to do this, warning her that he wouldn't go easy on her.

"I'm not asking you to," Lovely Lisa snapped back.

"Oooo… I'm sensing some tension. Be careful with this one," DJ Elixxir teased, tilting his head at Master Elliott as he remembered the man's profile. "He doesn't have any hard limits listed on his card."

The sub's mouth dropped open for a moment before she composed herself, straightening her spine. "I want to remove mine also."

"I— uhh…" Glancing down at the cards he'd tucked behind the roulette wheels, he saw that she'd chosen all four hard limits, and he looked back at her, confused as hell. "I'm sorry, what?"

"I don't need any either," she confirmed. "I only put them because I thought we had to."

Why was the night starting off like this?

Glancing over at Jaxson, he saw the man shrug, waving him on with an amused expression that looked a lot like 'it's her funeral.' Still, Elixxir felt uncomfortable with it. The last thing they needed in their competition with the West Coast club was to lose a couple right off the bat due to a safe word. But, it wasn't his choice. "Alright. That's… up to you, of course."

The wheel spun and Lovely Lisa dropped the marble in with a look of defiance as Master Elliott shook his head, wearing a similar amused expression to Jaxson.

"*Fire play!*" he called, and Lisa seemed *very* happy with that idea as they moved off to the side.

Fortunately, the next several couples paired off without any issues or spontaneous removal of limits. Most of the pairs seemed happy, but one submissive looked downright irritated when the older dom spun her name. *Yikes*. As they stomped off stage, Elixxir felt sorry for the man, but 'the show must go on.'

Glancing at the row of men, he saw the very tall dom who was up next and called him to the wheels, "Master Finnegan!"

The man had a small smile as he glanced out at the audience before joining him at center stage. Handing him the ball, he gave a quick wink and set the wheel to spinning.

"Master Finnegan, the wheel has paired you wiiiith…" Elixxir dragged out the word as the ball bounced and the roulette wheel slowed. "A very lucky lady indeed! Could Ava make her way up here?"

Glancing at the stairs, he saw that one of the DMs was helping the girl up the stairs. She looked utterly terrified, and Master Finnegan seemed to notice as he moved to meet her. Ava straightened her shoulders and took a couple of brave steps toward the wheels, when a loud *crack* echoed across the stage and she stumbled toward the steep drop at the edge. Instinct had him lunging from behind the wheels, but Master Finnegan grabbed her, yanking her back from the darkness beyond the stage lights.

Applause exploded in the audience as the dom lifted her in his arms and carried her the rest of the way to center stage. When he put the girl back on her feet he dropped to one knee, removing her shoes to the soft sounds of the audience's "Aww."

They spoke quickly, and then the large man stood behind her, nudging her toward the wheel as Elixxir offered her the little white ball.

"Spin," Master Finnegan ordered her, already getting into the game, and Elixxir couldn't help but chuckle.

"Looks like you two have hit things off already," he said, winking at her as she took the marble. "Now, you both have *humiliation* down as a hard limit, but let's see what the wheel has in store for your first scene." He sent it whirring, watching the small submissive as she stared at the spinning kinks. "Anytime, Ava."

Finally, she dropped the ball, and a moment later their destiny was revealed.

"*Impact play!*" he announced, watching as Finnegan led the pretty Ava away.

Glancing down at the table, he saw the abandoned popsicle stick that Mister M had refused to touch.

"Aaand number seven!" Elixxir called. The dom hesitated at the side of the stage, but after an awkward moment he started moving, and he announced the man's chosen name. "Mister M!"

With a flick of his wrist, he spun the roulette wheel and offered the marble to the dom, wondering if he'd refuse to take it as well. But, he didn't. Mister M took the marble and let it drop into the blur of names. *Tick, tick...*

"Miss Payne!" he announced, watching one of the submissives push forward from the back. As she climbed onto the stage he saw a fox tail peeking out from the bottom of her short, black dress, and he grinned as someone in the audience let out a cheer. The new pair were watching each other with surprise.

"I... I just saw you. The other day." Her hair was incredibly long as she tilted her head, letting it flow off her shoulder.

"I was," Mister M confirmed, and Elixxir felt awkward as the two just stared at each other. One looking stiff, the other like a wild earth child. *Interesting matches tonight.*

"Miss Payne?" Elixxir interrupted their moment, holding the marble out for her as he spun the wheel of kinks. "Would you like to roll?"

"Um, yes." She took it and let it roll fluidly off her hand, bouncing and spinning as the wheel began to slow.

When it finally settled, he couldn't help but chuckle to himself. "And Miss Payne has rolled *latex!*"

"After you," Mister M said, nodding toward the stairs with the manners of an old-world gentleman. If he didn't have to be on stage all night for second and third spins, *that* would be a couple he'd be interested in watching, if just to see how the two polar opposites would mix.

But, he'd have to settle for second-hand accounts from the DMs, and there were still over half of the participants to match up before the clock struck eight. Welcoming the next man to the wheel, he finally got back into a routine. They moved quickly from one to the next, only concerned by the submissive who seemed like she was carrying her own play bag on her shoulder. It was a big purse, but Elixxir had thought they weren't allowed to bring things in.

Surely someone searched it.

Either way, not his problem, and as the pair headed off the stage he looked toward number thirteen. The blond man was huge, his muscles bulging under a fitted black t-shirt that stood out among the suits and button-downs. Everything about him screamed 'Don't fuck with me' and Elixxir felt a little sorry for whichever sub the tattooed dominant spun.

"Lucky number thirteen. Master R if you'll come spin?" *Please?* Elixxir toned down his normally playful tone, keeping it short and sweet so that he didn't piss the man off. The dom didn't even look at him as he took the ball and scanned the wheel. When it started to spin, he dropped the ball almost immediately and turned to look at the last few submissives, apparently not interested in watching the wheel choose for him. Then the ball stopped and Elixxir had to stifle a laugh.

Irony must be having a field day tonight.

"Master R will be paired with Lady Luck!" he called out, watching as a pretty woman in a red dress climbed the stage. Surprisingly, Master R marched toward her, touching her back as he guided her the last few steps to the wheels.

The huge man was looking at her like he might tear off the dress center stage and take her without the formality of their spin, but Lady Luck didn't seem to feel the same way. She was stiff, tense, and Elixxir's discomfort ratcheted up a notch as he slid the cards in front of him to find hers.

"Lady Luck's hard limits are: *ABDL*, or *adult baby diaper lover*, *blood play*, *needle play*, and *fisting*," he clarified, as if being aware that there were limits tonight might make the man back down a little before he scared the woman into a safe word before she'd even spun the wheel.

It didn't work.

If anything it seemed to make the man more aggressive as Elixxir, and the whole audience, watched him lean down and lick her neck.

Well... this will either be explosively awesome, or a dramatic catastrophe.

Spinning the wheel, Elixxir offered the trembling submissive the ball. She barely touched it before she threw it into the wheel like it burned her. It bounced high, almost rocketing straight out of the roulette wheel before it finally calmed and caught the spin.

A moment later it lands, and Elixxir released a breath he hadn't realized he was holding. "*Wax play!*"

Not so bad, not as intense as many of the things on the wheel, which meant it would hopefully contain the intensity of the intimidating dom. Elixxir couldn't resist watching them leave the stage, and it seemed the rest of the audience was just as curious.

Two more.

Unlike scary tattooed dom, the next man was in a suit, and his submissive seemed relieved to have been paired with him after Master R left the stage. Elixxir definitely understood, but who was he to judge? People looked how they looked on the outside, but that didn't *always* mean their actions corresponded to it.

Some of the most sadistic assholes he'd seen inside Black Light had shown up in a three-piece suit and two-thousand-dollar shoes.

The last pair was their only domme and only male submissive that had signed up. The brunette was tall, beautiful, and Elixxir thought it might be fun to try that... sometime. Just to see. *Maybe.*

They spun *flogging*, and as the final couple left the stage, Elixxir returned to the front to spread his arms wide for the audience, letting his grin flash as he winked at a submissive on her knees in the front row. "Everyone's paired up, and you know what that means! It's time to start Valentine Roulette!"

The crowd cheered so loud that he felt the vibration of the noise in his chest. Giving a signal to the guy running the sound, they brought the music back up and Elixxir spun around, dancing a bit to the heady beat as the participants wandered off to claim their play spaces.

Roulette was officially started, for the East Coast anyway, and as Elixxir caught Spencer's eye near the stairs he knew what that really meant.

The war is on.

PRELUDE

A Black Light: Roulette War Novella

By

Renee Rose

CHAPTER 1

RAVIL

*W*hy anyone would *pay* to whip a woman is beyond me.

But then, Valdemar is not Bratva, like me. He's a diplomat. Dignified. Interested in closed-circle events that convey both prestige and sex appeal. Plus, he doesn't have the opportunities that those of us who live by the Code of Thieves have.

"So, you will enter Valentine Roulette with me?" he persists. We're in his house in Georgetown, and he pours me another two fingers of his favorite Russian vodka, Beluga Noble.

I imagine he considers himself some kind of nobility.

I shrug. "Why not? *Da.* Of course."

I don't make a practice of kissing ass, but Valdemar is key to our network's smuggling trade and I've been ordered by the Moscow *pakhan*—the Bratva boss—to keep this wheel greased.

The Valentine Roulette is some kind of event at his sex club. A gameshow pairing of dominants with submissives and three activities rolled for the scenes.

I like sex. I like dominating women. I certainly don't need to pay good rubles to do it, but whatever. For Valdemar, I will.

Valdemar loves his exclusive Black Light club in D.C. where the rich and elite spank asses together.

I thought he had important business to discuss, but it's fine. He likes me as his wingman. Or perhaps he's actually mine. I suppose he believes my tattoos and dangerous air give him an extra edge in an arena where alpha manliness is required. He knows women find me attractive and hopes they will overlook his birthmark the size of Leningrad if I'm with him.

The last time we went together, he kept me at his elbow the entire time, swapping and sharing women with me, inviting me to wield the crop for him. Making a big show about discussing techniques. As if there was one right way to do it. No, you dominate the woman until she begs for release or screams in pleasure. Or breaks and then screams in pleasure.

I didn't mind. The women we played with found it hot to be objectified. They tolerated Valdemar. I made sure they both got off.

"You must fill out the application." He opens a laptop and finds the necessary screen. "This information, here." He pushes the computer in front of me. "I know they will take you because I already called and used my diplomatic sway. They said so long as they have even pairings, you may join."

I quickly fill out the entry form and click submit. "Done."

He smiles at me. "Good. Now we will have our entertainment next week."

Now I'm making a second trip to D.C. Either that, or I have to stay and lube Valdemar all week. "Is that why I'm here?"

He shrugs. "Partly. Also, I have need of your services." He switches to Russian. "Someone I need you to teach a lesson."

I barely manage not to roll my eyes. Seriously? Does this fuck not know I have a hundred men back in Chicago working under me who do that kind of shit? I am the Bratva boss. The mastermind. I don't bloody my own hands anymore.

I could've sent a *shestyorka*—someone in the lowest rank of the organization—to fly to D.C. and do such a task. Or if it's sensitive, I would've sent my best muscle, silent Boris, over to do the job.

I release my clenching jaw and spread my hands amiably. "As you wish."

He beams at me. "Good. We go now."

I stand up and crack my neck.

Fine.

But only because we need this man to keep things running.

Lucy

"I'M DEFINITELY HAVING second thoughts about this thing." I shake out my hands to stop wringing them.

I'm with Gretchen, my former roommate and best friend during law school. She never left D.C. after we graduated from Georgetown. Now she's a hot shot in the Attorney General's office and I'm...

Completely lost.

I shrug off the devastation that's been hitting me square in the chest lately. This is not how I pictured my life at thirty-five.

"Nope," she says, as if telling me *no* will erase my doubts. "This is exactly what you need to forget Jeffrey and move on."

Says the woman with no long-term relationships to speak of. Even back in law school, she preferred the one-night-stands while I was searching for 'the one.'

And dammit, I thought I'd found him. But last month I finally had to face the fact that my Jeffrey, my seemingly perfect boyfriend, had no intention of ever sealing the deal. Eight years as my boyfriend and he couldn't commit. Didn't want to put a ring on it, let alone help me out with creating the family I've always longed for.

So, I finally let go.

Which was harder than it might seem.

It's easy if a guy cheats on you, or offends one of your friends or family, or does something concrete to convict him. No, Jeffrey was a perfectly nice, handsome guy who cared about me... but not enough.

Oh well.

Thank you, next, as the lovely Ariana Grande would say. But I don't feel that *fucking grateful.*

No, I feel like I just got mowed down by an asphalt truck.

So, when Gretchen came up with this crazy idea of me joining her for a special event at her BDSM club, I agreed.

But now I'm definitely having second thoughts. I'm not the adventurous one. And *Rocky Horror Picture Show* always confuses me.

"What are you going to wear?" Gretchen demands, pretending I'm not still on the fence about this thing. She unzips the garment bag I hung in her guest room closet and stares at my options.

"Um..." Apparently she finds them lacking.

"The red dress," I say without enthusiasm.

She unhooks the hanger and holds it up. It's a slinky wrap-around dress made out of soft, clingy fabric and a low-cut neckline. "This would be nice—*for a date with a lawyer.*"

"I *am* a lawyer," I point out unnecessarily.

"Not tonight you're not. Tonight you are a sex slave. A submissive." She tosses the red dress on the bed and takes my hand, leading me to her bedroom. "Tonight you're going to learn to surrender control. As soon as you surrender, the universe can deliver the perfect man to you. The guy who will be so honored to be your man and make beautiful blond babies with you, and..."

"I don't see how offering my body up for torture is surrendering to the Universe."

She opens the bottom drawer of her dresser where, apparently, she keeps her dungeon gear.

I recoil at the tiny, latex clothing items she pulls out.

"Well, it's not. But you'll find the joy of surrender. It's a practice session. You give up control for three hours. Let someone else take the reins and be in charge of your pleasure."

"What if I don't find pleasure?" I hold up a pair of shiny red latex booty shorts that lace in the front. Super hot—for a stripper. "I'm sorry, I just don't think I could wear anything like this."

"A dom is responsible for your pleasure."

"He's also responsible for giving me pain."

A wide grin stretches across her face. "That might be *his* pleasure." She shrugs. "And it might be yours."

Gretchen is a switch—someone who likes to play both top or bottom. Not at the same time, obviously.

Tonight, she'll be going as a domme, because that's what Black Light—the exclusive BDSM club she's a member of—requested of her after she submitted her application for Valentine Roulette. They hold a special event every year. Gretchen told me about it last year, only back then I'd been listening with the avid interest of a voyeur, never imagining I would throw my own name into the hat to participate.

The event involves a roulette wheel which is used to select one partner for the night and up to three 'scenes.' On my application, I was only able to select four hard limits, which nearly killed me, because I pretty much wanted to hard limit out of everything on the list except for intercourse.

No, that's not true. I've been fascinated by Gretchen's lifestyle from the beginning. I'm just getting cold feet now that I'm considering dipping my toes in.

"Well, wear the red dress if that makes you feel more comfortable. Just tell me you have sexy panties to wear underneath."

I make an attempt at being brave. "I was thinking no panties." I wink.

"That's my girl!" She slingshots a thong at my face and I splutter as I catch it. "This is going to be fun. Promise me you'll let yourself have fun?"

I suck in a deep breath and nod. I'm not a wimp. I am a hard-ass lawyer who defends ruthless criminals without letting *anyone* see her sweat. Hell, I manage the account of one of the most powerful crime families in Chicago. I can certainly handle whatever the Black Light wheel throws at me.

I hope.

CHAPTER 2

RAVIL

*B*lack Light is a secret club, hidden beneath a dance club. The guard knows Valdemar, but I have to show my invitation and I.D. to get in.

Valdemar stops to greet everyone he knows, so I slide past and head to the bar.

"Wild Turkey on the rocks," I tell the pretty bartender.

I nod appreciatively when she brings it and slide a large tip across the bar.

Valdemar gives me a wave from where he's flirting with a couple of women and I lift my chin. I'm not going to trot over there and introduce myself, which I know is what he wants. If they want to meet me, they can come over here.

I'm content to sit and observe.

Two women enter and the energy in the room shifts. Women and men alike blatantly check out the newcomers.

Both are tall. One blonde, one with long dark brown hair. At first, I think both are dommes because they wield that kind of power. They seem to carry the control and confidence necessary to dominate another.

But then I realize the blonde is too stiff. The confidence is put on —more of a defense mechanism than an internal resonance.

For some reason, that makes my dick go stiff. I like recognizing weakness in another. And this one is absolutely delicious.

Her clothing is all wrong. She's not in a role-playing costume or something revealing with easy access.

She's in a red dress that clings to her curves—which are slight. She's too thin, as if she keeps her body to the same rigorous standard she holds all others to. Her neck is long and stiff like a ballerina's. Her hair is pulled up in a twist.

If she were my partner, the first thing I would do would be to take that hair down and wrap my fist in it.

Tug her head back and bare that throat.

Flick my tongue in the hollow of her neck and taste her.

I suddenly want very much to have her as my partner. Especially because I am quite certain she would hate such a thing. A woman like her wants one of the diplomats. A man in a suit and tie. The kind who makes a show of removing his cufflinks to roll up his sleeves to spank her.

Not a tattooed Russian cur dressed in a black t-shirt and black jeans.

And because I am a man outside the law, one who lives by the Code of Thieves, I instantly slide off my stool to make it happen.

"Who do I pay to get the right girl?" I murmur in Russian to Valdemar.

He breaks off his conversation with the enthusiastic women to raise his bushy brows at me. "You cannot."

I scoff. "Of course I can. Someone will always take payment. Who do I pay? Who runs this place?"

He shakes his head, insistent. "No, you cannot. It is a roll of a ball. I told you this. A game of chance. No one can fix it."

My jaw flexes as I look around. I believe Valdemar, I just don't want to accept his answer.

I want the blonde. She looks like so much more fun than the eager women begging to be hurt by me.

She needs to be taught to let go.

Taught to receive pain.

Taught to yield.

Only then should she receive pleasure.

Only then *can* she receive pleasure.

Because I seriously doubt that woman has ever had a decent orgasm in her life.

She and her gorgeous friend head to the bar. I'm tempted to take up my seat again, to get close enough to hear their conversation, but I hold back. I'm the sort of man who never shows his hand too soon.

There's a reason they call me The Director.

Besides, I need to consider my move. If I don't win the roll for this woman, what other options are available to me? I could pay the man who does win her to swap with me.

Da. This is a good plan.

I will not allow him to refuse. I can be very persuasive.

I finish my whiskey and set it on a tray nearby. It's settled.

One way or another, the woman will be mine for the night.

Lucy

"Everyone's looking at you," Gretchen murmurs when we sit at the bar at Black Light. I order a red wine, which makes Gretchen roll her eyes.

"Because I'm not dressed right?" I ask. Of course it's because I'm not dressed right, I don't know why I'm even asking.

"No, because they're curious. It's almost too bad tonight's the Roulette event, because you could probably have your pick of the men here on an ordinary night." She looks around. "Which one would you pick?"

I sip my wine and swivel on the bar stool to look around. The truth is, I hardly saw anything as we came in. I was too worried about projecting my courtroom bad-assery so no one would know how much I'm freaking out.

There are men of varying ages—many older than we are, which makes sense considering how expensive this club is. The few younger men I see look like playboys spending their trust funds. Many appear screwable.

"That one," I murmur, directing my gaze at a man with dark hair in an expensive suit.

Gretchen smiles. "Nice choice. You didn't hear it from me, but that's Trent Joyner, the CEO of McFennel Holdings—the company that owns half the coal mines in this country. Unfortunately for you, he's a bottom. I've had the pleasure of topping him once and it was very fun."

Damn. I try to picture myself topping someone like Gretchen does. I believe I could do it—maybe even be good at it. I play the bitch role to perfection, when necessary. But the truth is, it's just a role. A persona I put on because that's what is required of a woman practicing criminal law. But it doesn't turn me on.

No, I may have never allowed it in real life, but my darkest fantasies are of a man taking control. As a teenager, I used to read Viking romance under the covers at night. They always started with some strapping young Viking warrior carrying off the heroine as his war prize. And I always rooted for him eventually winning her over.

Gretchen's right. She knows me better than I know myself sometimes.

"How about that one?" I ask, directing my attention to an extremely good-looking man in a suit, looking like he's charming the panties off the group of women standing around him.

Gretchen rolls her eyes. "Master Lancelot. Yes, everyone wants him and, unfortunately, he knows it."

"He calls himself Master Lancelot?" I give a derisive snort. "Okay, yeah. I'll skip him."

"You don't get to decide," she reminds me. "Surrender, remember? Ask the Universe to pair you with the perfect dom and it will happen."

"Uh huh." Gretchen has always been into positive thinking strategies to get ahead. And I have to say, for her, they work. Being here with her reminds me how much I miss being around her infectious outlook on life. Like anything is possible.

She was right. This is exactly what I need to get over Jeffrey and the reality of being single at thirty-five, with my biological clock blaring that it's getting late—way too late—to find a man and have the family I always dreamed of.

I want to keep playing the game of pointing out guys and having Gretchen give me the dirt on them, but the MC—a hot young black DJ who goes by the name Elixxir—calls all the participants to the stage.

I down the rest of my red wine all at once and slide to my feet. "Here goes nothing," I murmur to Gretchen.

She hip bumps me. "Knock 'em dead, counselor."

We hook arms and walk toward the stage.

"I take it back. That was the wrong thing to say. *Surrender.* Remember—just let go of control. Trust someone else to take care of you."

I'm shaking all over, but I nod my head.

Right. *Trust.*

Easy for her to say. She gets to be the one holding the leash tonight.

We separate when we get to the stage—she stops to stand with the dominants, and I continue to the submissives. I scan the dominants so I can put in my order with the universe. If I'm going to be following Gretchen's quasi-spiritual manifestation beliefs, I might as well be specific.

Not him. Not her. Not him. He's a maybe. Maybe. I'd take him. Maybe. No way. I stop on a blond man in a fitted black t-shirt. He looks like an Instagram-ready bodybuilder, covered in tattoos, except the tattoos aren't pretty. They aren't the colorful swirls of dragons or designs you see on the arms of young men these days.

His are done in black and dark blue ink, the markings distinctive, and what I see chills me to the core.

I've seen markings like that before.

On photos of dead bodies the D.A. sent over to me when they wanted to question one of my clients.

They're a type of gang symbol, but very different from your usual American street gang.

These are Russian markings.

Which means this man is a member of Russian organized crime.

The Bratva. It means *brotherhood* in Russian.

I shudder.

Not him, Universe.

Definitely not him.

Ravil

I DON'T BELIEVE in luck. I make my own fortune. When you grow up on the streets of Leningrad, when you've spent time in a Siberian prison—you learn there's only one person you can rely on to change your fate.

Yourself.

Some believe the brotherhood can be trusted, but I know there's always someone waiting to stab me in the back. Especially now that I've climbed as high as I have.

I don't ask for luck when I draw my number to choose the order of pairing. I don't ask for luck when I'm called forward to spin for my submissive.

I have no expectations of my ball landing in the groove for the woman in the red dress. I have my plan to get her another way. I don't even pay attention to the spinning wheel, or the name they call out when my ball settles. I glance with disinterest at the group of submissives, not allowing myself to even look at my prey.

"Master R will be paired with Lady Luck," the DJ calls out.

I don't plan to watch my lovely target, but it's the startled reaction that runs through her body that snaps my focus to her face.

Our gazes tangle. Hers is charged with alarm before she blinks a few times and steps forward.

She's Lady Luck?

I lose my breath.

So easily? I didn't even have to work for it.

Lady Luck, indeed. Maybe I do believe in good fortune. I stride forward and place my hand at her lower back, claiming her with a light but possessive touch.

I listen as the DJ reads out the important notes, "Lady Luck's hard limits are: *ABDL,* or *adult baby diaper lover, blood play, needle play,* and *fisting.*"

I take it in without any reaction. She turns her head to look up at me, but doesn't quite manage eye contact. She smells like red wine and fruity shampoo. The urge to lick her neck returns with a sudden tightening of my balls.

I decide not to resist. Primarily because I can tell she's not happy about our pairing and I need to establish that it's my will she bows to now, whether she likes it or not. I dip my head and brush my lips across the place where shoulder meets neck.

She doesn't breathe at all.

I flick my tongue over her skin and a shiver rips through her. A stronger shiver than the light trembling I already detect.

"Come, Lady Luck. You must choose our entertainment," I murmur in her ear.

Another shiver, but she straightens her spine even more—which seems impossible—and allows me to lead her to the wheel.

Her fingers visibly tremble when she picks up the ball, and she throws it so wildly it barely stays within the confines of the wheel, bouncing erratically and taking some time to settle.

"*Wax play,*" the DJ announces.

"Ah, another fortuitous choice for Lady Luck," I murmur.

She sends another darted glance in my direction. This time I catch her gaze. Her eyes are wide-set and a soft brown, like a doe's. It's a lovely combination with the blonde hair, which appears natural. Her skin is pale and ice-princess smooth. She has high cheekbones and one of those dimples in the center of her chin.

She could have been a model, this one, when she was in the full bloom of youth. But she's too smart for that. Intelligence radiates from that gaze. I read it in her wariness, her quick checks of her surroundings. Her mind is working hard.

I'll have to work even harder to get her past it.

"Come, kitten. Let's find some wax."

～

Lucy

I'M GOING to tell Gretchen this whole surrendering to the Universe thing is bullshit. She's the one who picked the name *Lady Luck* for me because she said it helps to affirm what you want to believe.

But this is the opposite of luck.

I specifically said *not him.*

Although it occurs to me that she might have told me once you never ask for anything in the negative because the subconscious—or the Universe—or whatever mental gymnastics Gretchen was programming at the time—doesn't hear the negative, it only hears what you're focusing on. In this case, it was the Russian.

Damn.

Master R leads me off-stage and it's a good thing he's holding my elbow because my knees are so weak I can barely walk in the stilettos I usually strut in with ease.

I can't tell if he's noticed how scared I am or not. He's pretty inscrutable.

Because he has a lot to hide, the lawyer in me notes.

We stand beside the stage until the rest of the spins finish. Then Elixxir announces that Roulette starts and he guides me to the costume shop where a pretty young attendant helps him. He requests the wax and a lighter and he also picks up a leather flogger. Despite my trepidation and my total reluctance to be intimate with this crim-inal in any way, I can't deny the flicker of interest that runs through me at the sight of the flogger. It's the one implement I wanted to expe-rience, mostly because Gretchen said it can be used in a sensuous and gentle way in addition to inflicting pain.

I realize I haven't said a word since we've been paired, and the lawyer in me forces her way to the surface. "Why the flogger?" I ask as he takes the items and leads me out. "I didn't land on *whipping.*"

"Hmm."

Huh? What kind of answer is that?

He stops and takes my chin. "I think I liked it better when you didn't speak."

My mouth drops open in shock. The *nerve.*

"Let's say this: no speaking unless it's to safe word. You remember of the Black Light safe words announced at the opening ceremony, I'm sure?"

I grit my teeth. Now I'm kind of pissed.

Amusement dances over his expression and I realize that was his goal. His gaze dips to my breasts and I follow it. I didn't wear a bra and my nipples stand up in stiff peaks. As if I *like* him being a dick and saying I can't speak.

Grrr.

"I do require your answer now, *kotyonok.* Tell me you remember the safe words."

I narrow my eyes. I want to not speak just to spite him. But I'm too out of my element to push. There are implements of torture all around me and he could pick any one of them. Not that I couldn't just safe word out of it.

Actually, *I could safe word out of the whole thing right now.*

All I have to do is say *red* and the night is over. We both 'lose' officially, but I don't care about that.

Except, I sort of do.

I'm one of those highly competitive type-A personalities who can't stand losing.

Dammit.

I force the words across my lips. "I remember."

He touches them. "Less venom, kitten. I know you're scared. You don't have to—"

"I'm not scared," I cut in, forgetting I'm not allowed to speak.

To my surprise, he agrees. "Of course not." He starts to crowd me. "You're very strong."

I step back and he follows, backing me up against a nearby wall.

"But with me, it's all right to show the fear." He brushes my cheek with the backs of his fingers. "I'm in charge of you. I need you to show me everything so I know how far to push. Otherwise, I can't show you pleasure."

A shudder runs through me. It seems every time this man speaks to me, I shiver, only this time I register a lick of heat with the shiver, not the ice-cold fear I felt before.

Goosebumps stand up on my arms. He's talking about pleasure, like Gretchen promised.

He tugs my hair out of the updo Gretchen told me was all wrong. Then his hand drops to my thigh and slides up, bringing the fabric of my dress higher and higher until it's at my waist. His brows shoot up in surprise. "No panties?" His smile is feral. "Nice choice, kitten." He slides one fingertip around to the back of my thigh and traces the inner curve of my butt cheek.

"It's your first time here, no?"

"Is it that obvious?" I don't know if he's going to let me speak, but he didn't call me on it last time.

He shakes his head. "Not to anyone but me," he promises, which I doubt is true. I grudgingly appreciate that he's trying to protect my pride here. It surprises me, considering the name of this game is supposed to be humiliation.

"Here's what we're going to do, *kotyonok*. I'm going to help you focus. Help you let go. Close your eyes."

I don't want to.

I *really* don't want to.

I stare at him defiantly, but he's confident. Patient. As if he knows he will eventually get what he wants.

Fine. I close my eyes.

The moment I do, he unties my wrap-around dress and tugs it off me. My eyes fly open. I'm wearing nothing under the dress, so now I'm buck naked in front of everybody!

"Eyes closed." The command is nothing like the coaxing way he spoke to me a moment ago. It's a harsh, guttural order. One that demands immediate obedience. My body responds even before my brain agrees. I squeeze my eyes shut.

He wraps the sash of my dress around my eyes and ties it in the back.

For a moment I stand there, waiting for something else to happen.

Nothing does. I sense him in front of me, hear his easy breath, feel the heat of his body. He touches me and I jerk in surprise. His hand connects with my ribs—lightly. Very lightly. He slides it slowly down my right side until he reaches my waist. Then he strokes across my lower back down to my ass.

"It's easier this way, no? Your attention is on me and me alone. You must trust me to guide you."

"I don't like it."

His laugh is soft. "I know, *kotyonok.*"

"What does that mean?" I demand.

"It means *kitten*. An endearment, not an underestimation of your fierceness." He brushes a digit across my lower lip—his thumb, perhaps. You'll keep your claws in for me, though, won't you, beautiful lioness?"

I don't know where he gets all these ideas about me. They both insult me and assuage my anger at once. But that's stupid. He probably says the same thing to everyone.

And for some reason, that really pisses me off.

He traces a fingertip around my right nipple. My shivering grows.

"You are not cold, Lady Luck?"

I shake my head. They have the heat turned up in this place—I imagine it's to ensure the scantily-clad submissives are warm enough. I'm not sure the men in three-piece suits love it, though.

As much as I hate having my eyes covered—and I absolutely detest it—Master R was right about what it achieves.

I am highly attuned to him now. His proximity. His voice. And especially his touch. Every time he makes contact, a shock of heat rushes through me.

And the fact that every contact is feather-light, sharpens my awareness. I'm now searingly aware of his every breath. The distance between our bodies. The space between them.

He shifts his touch, connecting the backs of his knuckles with my breastbone and lightly draws them down. My belly shudders as he strokes over it, down my freshly waxed mound.

I embarrass myself by letting out a tiny mewl when he strokes down my labia.

"Spread."

A single-word command. No *please*. No *thank you*. Total certainty he will be obeyed.

I swallow. Shift on my heels to widen my stance by a half-inch.

"More."

One finger strokes lightly over my slit.

My pussy clenches. Belly tightens.

"Not ripe, yet," he comments. "Soon."

"Soon what?" I'm still expecting him to punish me for speaking one of these times, but he hasn't yet.

"Soon she'll be weeping for it."

"*She*? Did you just personify my pussy?"

His lips brush my collarbone and I jerk at the sensation. "No more speaking, kitten. Not unless it's to tell me *yellow*."

"Yellow." I'm so damn stubborn. I know I am. That's how I made it through law school and made damn sure my dad's partners respected me when I joined the firm.

"Speak, kitten." There's a note of indulgence in his tone. Like I'm a preschooler testing him and he'll allow it to show me the rules work as intended.

"I don't like the blindfold."

He adjusts the fabric. "Is it pulling your hair? Too tight?"

"No," I admit.

"Then it stays." When I open my mouth, he repeats it with a *don't-fuck-with-me* tone. "It stays or you say *red* and end this. But I don't believe that's what you want." He takes my left nipple between his fingers and squeezes, gradually increasing the tension until I gasp. "Is it, kitten? You may answer."

"No."

"*No, Master*," he corrects.

Fucker.

"No, Master."

He releases my nipple. "Good girl."

Ravil

SHE'S EXQUISITE. Lovely and strong but also fragile. I love playing with her.

It's a long game. I'll have to work slowly. And while I understand the Roulette event is one of chance and entertainment, I'm inclined to use multiple stimuli to create an experience. So, for my Lady Luck, wax play alone probably won't get her wet. I need to start with sensory deprivation. Get her bonded to me. Heighten her senses. Make her ache for my touch.

Only then will the hot wax be sensual enough to turn her on.

Bondage would help, too. I need her to feel as vulnerable and exposed as possible.

"I see a place for us to play," I tell her. "Would you like me to lead you, or carry you? You may answer, now."

Some women, you take away all their choices. Dictate everything. With her, I'm offering a small sliver of control for her to cling to. It's not real, of course. The only real control is her safe word, but I'm willing to provide the illusion.

"Lead me."

I knew that would be her answer. Too bad. I'd love to have those slender arms wrapped around my neck and feel her weight in my arms. Later, perhaps.

I wrap one arm snugly around her waist and take her elbow with my other hand so we're closely joined at the hip. It's easy to steer her this way, despite her hesitant steps.

Stripping her completely naked was to help her head space. It does nothing beneficial to mine, however.

I issue a death-glare to everyone looking on with interest and appreciation as I guide my beautiful Lady Luck through the audience. I'm not usually a jealous man. Something about this one inspires a fierce protectiveness in me. Perhaps it's because the women we played with in the past enjoyed the attention.

This one, I believe, would not. Or at least not yet.

I bring her to a padded table, then turn and push her until she sits. "On your back, *kotyonok*." I guide her into position, cupping my hand behind her head to lower it.

Moving swiftly, I buckle her ankles and wrists into the cuffs. She immediately tests them, turning her wrists and tugging against the leather cuffs.

She's a lovely captive—pale skinned and nervous, not lusty, like the rest of the submissives here. There's desire underneath the uncertainty, but it will have to be coaxed.

Her breath shudders in and out, making her flat belly quake with each inhale. Her lips part and she turns her face slightly to the right, as if listening for me.

"I'm just looking, kitten," I tell her and she snaps her unseeing focus in my direction. "You are a beautiful sight. Angelic, really."

Her lips move, start to form a word, then drop open again. Perhaps she finally remembered my rule not to speak.

I pick up the flogger and trail it from the hollow of her throat and down between her breasts. "You were interested in this."

Surprise flickers over her face—whether she's surprised I noticed her interest, or wasn't aware of her own interest, I can't say. A flogger is an excellent instrument for a beginner. The leather strands can feel like the softest caress when used sensually. And even their bite can be warm and diffused, when applied correctly.

I take my time, tracing over her breasts, down her sides, tickling her ribs. Up the undersides of her outstretched arms. I stroke down the side of her face, slowing my movement and watching her breath match my speed.

I flick my wrist and snap the tips of the strands across the side of one breast. She cries out, jerking in surprise. I know it didn't hurt—maybe a momentary sting—but I have her completely in my thrall now.

I reward her by trailing the soft strands down her belly and between her legs. Her shiver gives away her excitement. I follow down her inner thigh and tickle the bottom of her foot, then work my way to the other foot and up her opposite leg.

I give a quick flick to her pussy and she bows up off the table. Her cry is more erotic this time. She's falling under my spell.

My dick pushes against the fabric of my jeans, but I ignore it. Another submissive here might get into the head space by being forced to her knees and having a cock stuffed in her mouth, but not this one.

Long game.

Her pleasure first.

I have to convince her to receive from me before I can expect anything back.

I trail the flogger strands between her legs again. I see the glistening of her juices gathering there. I want to test with my finger, to taste with my tongue, but I hold back. Fingers and tongue would be jumping ahead.

She requires more priming. Flogger and wax.

Then her next roll. Then her third. I have this creature for three hours. I can take my time with the seduction.

It's odd how much satisfaction this game is giving me—I'm actually glad Valdemar dragged me along. I suppose it's the challenge. I haven't been challenged by a woman in years. Even American women throw themselves at my feet now with the wealth and power I've amassed.

So, this one presents a challenge and The Director in me—the engineer of possibilities, the mastermind behind the Bratva's success in North America—loves a problem to solve.

I continue my slow exploration of her skin with the falls, stroking, flicking, engaging her body as I tease her mind.

"This is a change for you."

I have to hide my irritation at hearing Valdemar's voice. He's standing across the table with an adorable schoolgirl submissive cuddled up to him.

"What is?" I grit out.

"I'm not accustomed to seeing you so gentle with a woman. Where is the crop? The tears? Is this one made of glass?"

Mudak.

Really, what a dickhead. For a diplomat, Valdemar seriously lacks delicacy.

I want to bitchslap him right now.

"Lady Luck requires a slower approach. Not every submissive loves pain. Does yours?"

The pig-tailed schoolgirl giggles. "Only when I'm a bad girl."

My tactic worked, because Valdemar's attention moves to his submissive and they move along.

"Forgive my friend," I murmur, trailing the flogger across her breasts. "I have no intention of making you cry."

Her lips part, then close. I slide a soft leather tassel across them.

"Thank you," she says finally as I drag the strands down her neck.

I mark that concession from her. Maybe Valdemar's remarks helped more than harmed. That's good.

I fall into the zone. She deepens into the space I've created for her. I want to start flogging her in earnest, but that would warm her skin up and detract from the shock of the hot wax, so I set the tool aside and give her a moment to cool down.

For a long moment, I don't move. I watch her tilt her head, seeking me with her senses. Last time I reassured her. This time I let her wonder.

Her lips open, as if she's going to speak, but she stops herself. I give it another few beats, then circle one of her nipples with my fingertip.

She jerks and a tremor runs through her body.

"These are pretty," I observe, circling the other beaded nipple. I pinch both at once and squeeze. "They would look good in clamps. Would you like that? Nod your head if you would."

Her head rolls in an indeterminate direction. Not a nod or a shake.

I lightly slap her breast. "Yes? All right. I'll get some later. I won't leave you here unattended."

I don't know what makes me reassure her that way. I should be keeping her more on edge. Playing both sides of reassuring and making her guess.

"Have you felt hot wax on your skin before?"

She shakes her head.

I light the candle and let the flame burn a pool of wax. "It's nothing to fear. A bit of heat, then it cools. This wax is made to burn at a lower temperature so it won't damage your pretty skin. It's where I choose to use the wax that can make you plead *mercy*."

She shakes her head.

"That's cute." I touch her nose. "You don't get to tell me no. Not unless you safe word. But I doubt you will. You're not a quitter."

She shakes her head again, as if agreeing.

I swirl the wax around in the candle and then hold it over her belly, letting a drop go.

I love watching her belly contract, her breath expand on a gasp. She's too skinny, this one. If she were mine, I'd make sure she was kinder to her body. Didn't hold herself to such strict standards.

I wonder what she does for a living. Drug rep? No, she has the looks, but she's not a pleaser. She's more of the CEO type.

My curiosity is strange. I never want to actually know my partners. I prefer to keep exchanges like this impersonal. The mystery lends to the excitement.

Besides, Black Light is about anonymity. A place where the rich and famous, the influential people in the world, indulge in their kinks without fear of being outed.

I allow another droplet to fall, then another. I circle her belly button, making a pattern around it. Then I move to her nipples. She jerks and hisses at the first droplet, but her nipples grow longer, swelling and hardening beneath the wax.

Her breath shortens, comes in little pants. She stirs restlessly, tugging against the bonds.

"I want to hear your voice now," I tell her. "Tell me what you need."

"Need?" She's breathless. Sounds confused. "I-I need..."

"What *kotyonok*? Does your pussy need some attention?" I drip some wax on her mound and she gasps.

"Yes—*no!*"

Another drip. It lands on her labia. "What do you need?" I let another drip fall, and another. "What is your pleasure, Lady Luck?" I drip wax onto her inner thighs.

She whimpers.

If she were ready, I'd make her beg for release, but I haven't won her over yet. She's proud and reserved and asking her to beg might make her stubborn. Simply demanding she make a request is the first step.

"Tell me, kitten."

"Will you… touch me?"

"Here?" I bring my thumb to her slit and find her clit. I drip a bit of wax on her nipple at the same time.

Her hips buck off the table. "Yes! Um… yes, there. And…" She tosses her head back and forth.

It's fucking beautiful. Like I'm witnessing some rare and exotic creature in her native habitat. The snow leopard of the Himalayas. My fierce and sensual lioness.

Keeping my thumb on her clit, I rub her entrance with my index and middle fingers. Her folds are swollen and wet and my fingers slide right in.

I ditch the candle. "Is this what you need?"

"Yes, please."

There, I got a *please* and I didn't even demand it. "Yes, Master," I correct her.

I rub along her front inner wall, seeking her G-spot. When I find it, her muscles contract around my fingers and her legs jerk.

I take my time. Slow strokes over the sensitive tissue. I could finger-fuck her hard right now, hit that spot with each thrust and she'd come in less than thirty seconds.

But I want to edge her.

See how desperate she gets when she really wants release. Break down that resistance a little more.

I keep at it, waiting until she starts making little noises, until her body quakes and trembles, right on the precipice. Then I slip my fingers out.

She gasps. Lips part, waiting. When I don't move, don't make a sound, she begs. "P-please, Master?"

My dick gets rock hard.

I unbuckle her ankles, then her wrists.

She sits up. "Wh-what happened?" She's bewildered.

"On your knees, kitten," I say softly. "Show me how much you want it."

It offends her. I can see in the rigidity that straightens her spine. The way her shoulders spread and stiffen.

But she does want it. Her cheeks and neck are flushed, the heat from her skin radiates between us.

I tug her elbow and she drops to her knees in front of the table.

I unbutton my pants and free my erection. "Find pleasure giving pleasure, *kotyonok*," I advise.

She opens her mouth willingly and I feed my length in.

It's a slow start. Takes her a few moments to sink back into the head space I'd created, but she does.

And when she does, it's magnificent.

Her hands come to my hips and she hollows out her cheeks to suck hard. Her knees spread on the floor, her back arches. Her enthusiasm attracts the attention of the people around us and the collective energy sparks.

I want to tell them to go fuck off, but that would alert my beautiful submissive, and I can't have her inhibited. I pick up the flogger and flick lightly down the sides of her thighs as she sucks, which makes her moan around my cock.

I let her go off-leash for a while, let her run the show, until I start losing control. Then I grip the back of her head and drive. She stiffens at first, then relaxes her jaw and lets me pump into her mouth.

"That's it," I praise. "Good girl."

Her tongue swirls along the underside of my cock. My balls draw up tight. I want to make it last forever, but I also need this to take the edge off so I can enjoy mastering my Lady Luck.

I close my eyes and succumb to the delicious sensation of her hot, wet mouth, the little sounds she makes around my cock.

"I'm coming, kitten," I warn her. "Suck it hard and swallow every last drop like a good girl."

I give it a fifty-fifty chance of her complying, but it seems she is Lady Luck, because she obeys.

I tug the sash of her dress off her head because I want to see her eyes. She blinks in surprise and pops off, sitting back on her high heels.

"Good girl." I hold out her dress and sweep it around her shoulders like a robe, then grip her elbow and help her to stand.

Confusion flits over her face.

"I'm going to make you wait for yours," I explain.

~

Lucy

HE'S GOT to be kidding.

All that pent-up need turns to fury when I realize he just made me suck him off with no intention of giving me my hard-earned orgasm.

Okay, maybe not that hard-earned, but I feel like I've been through the ringer. The wax play and flogging wasn't painful, but the whole experience was intense.

He must see my anger because he catches my chin with his tattooed fingers. His touch has been nothing but gentle, but I still flinch every time he reaches for me.

"I wouldn't say whatever it is you're thinking about saying. You're still mine for two more scenes. You'll get your reward when I decide." His accent is growing on me. Maybe because his voice was the only thing I had to go by when he had me blindfolded.

I shake off his hold and pull the fabric of my dress around me now, then tie the sash. The hardened wax still clings to my skin, bringing continued awareness to my most sensitive places.

Everything's buzzing. My core is hot and activated. Almost uncomfortable. This must be the female version of blue balls. I didn't know it existed. I've never been so wound up in my life.

I guess I'm a high-stress kind of person. Tightly wound. I can count the number of times I've actually achieved orgasm with a partner on one hand.

And I was so damn close.

And the Russian—Master R—had to pull back.

Seriously, if I don't orgasm tonight, I will never forgive this man.

Not that I'll ever see him again. But he will have to bear the weight of a lifelong stranger-grudge.

He studies me coolly.

I want to kick him in the shin.

All these gentlemen in the room and I ended up with the Russian street thug.

But that's not fair. This guy is actually very much a gentleman, despite the extremely rough appearance.

That doesn't mean I believe he's not dangerous with a capital D.

I represent one of the biggest Italian mob families in Chicago. I know better than to confuse charming with safe. I should talk to Gretchen about getting this guy's membership to Black Light revoked.

That thought gives me a pang, though. He's done nothing wrong. And there's nothing to make me believe he will. Still, I keep thinking the reason he's so good at this is because he's perfected his skills at every form of torture.

Across the room, a woman yells "It's not alcohol! Give it back!"

I see one of the dungeon monitors confiscating a water bottle from her. Her dom leads her to the bar. Hopefully not for more liquor.

"Would you like a drink?" my dom offers politely, as if this is a date.

My first instinct is to refuse because my defenses are back up, but the fact is a nice glass of wine might take the edge off.

I nod stiffly. "Yes, please."

He slides his arm around my waist, his palm lightly molding to the upper curve of my buttock.

If this were a date, I'd elbow that hand away, but my body's still aflame, and the touch feels good. My body has no idea that I don't like or trust this man.

At the bar, the dominant of the woman with the alcohol is speaking to her in a low tone, offering her a bottle of water.

I order a merlot. Master R asks for water.

He stays in my space, pinning me against the bar, one hand lightly at my waist. Now that we're up close, I can see the black jeans are designer. His t-shirt is soft and expensive. He may be dressed as a thug, but he has money.

Not at the bottom of the Bratva ranks, then.

He's good-looking, beneath the tattoos and scars. Ice-blue eyes. Sandy blond hair cut short and rumpled in the front. His muscles bulge beneath the t-shirt. I must be ovulating because all I can think about is how it would feel to be under him.

How pretty our babies would look.

Not that I'd ever choose a guy like him to be my baby daddy.

A stab of pain runs through my heart. Damn Jeffrey for taking all those years from me without ever sealing the deal.

"This is a rebound," Master R says and my gaze flies to his face in shock. "You're getting over someone?"

I consider myself a good read of people, but that's just uncanny.

My face grows warm. I take a sip of wine to gather my composure. "How can you tell?"

He runs his thumb lightly over my cheekbone. "A trace of sadness in your eyes. The unsuitability of this place for you."

I blink, trying to decide if I'm flattered or offended that he finds Black Light unsuitable for me.

"Why do you say that?"

He shrugs but leans in close and brushes his lips across the side of my neck. He smells of soap and light aftershave. It's a pleasing mixture. "You're uncomfortable. This isn't your scene. You want to be dominated, but not this way."

He's not wrong.

I take another sip of wine. "How do you think I want to be dominated?"

His smile turns feral. "You want to have control taken *from* you, so you don't have to think or be right. You already do too much of that. You might like it rough, but you'd have to trust the man. You're not there yet with me."

I note he said *yet*. As if he thinks he's going to get me there tonight.

The excitement that elicits in my body tells me he's right. I *would* like it. And now I'm already fantasizing about it being with him.

But rough probably isn't just a scene for him. This man gets rough for real.

My next sip misses and I dribble wine down my chin like an idiot.

Without missing a beat, the Russian grips my hair in the back and uses it to tilt my head back and expose my throat. Then he licks the droplets from my skin with little flicks of his tongue.

My pussy clenches.

"H-how do you know so much about being a dom?"

I just can't stop myself from interrogating the defendant.

Another casual shrug. "I make it my business to know what people want. What they're willing to do for it."

I drain the last of my wine and set it on the bar. "I'll bet you do."

He indicates my glass. "Would you like another?"

I shake my head. Gretchen explained it's a two drink maximum at Black Light. They don't want people playing inebriated, which is why the submissive had her contraband liquor taken away.

"I would like to see you intoxicated," he observes.

I lift my brows. "Why?"

"You keep yourself under tight wraps. I wonder what might come out if you let yourself loose."

His words hit a little too close to home and I'm unnerved at how much he seems to see. "Well, it's not going to happen," I tell him.

"Of course not." Always the easy agreement. "Ready for the next roll?"

I stubbornly refuse to move. "Are you going to let me come?"

I see amusement dancing in his eyes. "We'll see, kitten."

Grr.

CHAPTER 3

LUCY

I'm grateful I can see and wear my dress to return to the stage. I throw the ball into the spinning roulette wheel. It bounces off the walls and finally settles in a slot.

I hold my breath. *Please don't let it be something horrible.*

"*Anal play* for Lady Luck," DJ Elixxir announces.

My anus contracts at the pronouncement.

Oh God.

I'm so not up for this. I am a total anal virgin. But who am I kidding—I have zero experience with almost everything on that wheel.

At least I didn't get fisting. Oh, but that was a hard limit, so it would've been thrown out.

Well, at least I didn't get all the other things that were not quite bad enough for me to pick as my four hard limits, but still scare the bejeezus out of me.

I steal a glance at my dominant, but as usual, he shows nothing in his expression. Just the same cool indifference.

"Are you into… ass play?" I ask as he leads me off the stage. I don't know why I'm trying to make conversation. I guess I just crave more information—any information—about what to expect.

He shrugs. "It's good. Good for you. You'll like it."

I arch a doubtful brow and one corner of his mouth ticks up in a lopsided smile. "You don't believe me yet?"

"I'm beginning to," I admit. He does seem to not only know what he's doing but understand me and my needs far better than I do.

My response elicits a genuine smile from him. "Don't be afraid, *kotyonok*. I know how to make it good."

We return to the costume shop where he buys an anal plug, lube, and a vibrator. She gives it to him in a drawstring bag with a re-sealing packet of disinfecting wipes.

I find that somewhat reassuring. I notice most of the doms are carrying their own bags of implements, but mine came empty-handed.

"You don't bring your own toys?" I ask as we stand at the counter getting checked out.

He shakes his head. "No." Single syllable. No elaboration.

I try again. "Do you come here often?"

I catch another lift of his lips. "Is that a pickup line, kitten?"

"Dream on, my friend."

He turns to face me. "Oh, I wouldn't call us friends." His smile doesn't reach his eyes. "Not yet, anyway."

My heart starts beating faster as we lock gazes. He looks down at me impassively, his blue eyes showing nothing but clear-minded intelligence. Heat races along my skin.

Dammit.

I'm finding this man more and more attractive.

I can't decide if it's his mysterious nature or his skill as a dominant. Or is it just all the masculine attention he's pouring into me?

It's not something I've had much of. Jeffrey wasn't the most sexual of boyfriends. I suppose that's why Gretchen thought this experience would kick start my new love life. Open me to a new world of possibilities.

"Come, beautiful." He takes my elbow and leads me out of the costume shop, scanning the large room.

It seems noisy and distracting now. I find myself almost wishing for the blindfold. The chance to shrink my world back down to the man beside me and what he's going to do to my body. As off-putting as I found it, I have to admit, my dom actually knows what he's doing.

He heads for one of the scary spanking benches, but another couple claims it first, so he takes me to a couch instead. "I'll have you over my lap. It's more intimate, no?"

I cringe just a little at the word intimate.

Maybe intimacy isn't really my thing. Maybe if Jeffrey and I had more intimacy we wouldn't have gone on for so many years without really getting anywhere. He would've known how important children were to me. Or I would've recognized he wasn't that interested.

The blindfold worked for me because it kept me from intimacy. I was in my own little world. I didn't have to think about the man touching me. About his tattoos or scars. About what illegal things he probably does for a living.

He sits on the sofa and tugs me face down over his lap, taking his time to arrange a pillow under my head and shoulders.

"Are you comfortable, *kotyonok*?"

I nod my head.

"Yes, Master," he prompts.

"Yes, Master." I don't even grumble it. Maybe it's the growing sense of appreciation I have for this man's care of me.

He pushes my dress up to my back and runs his hand over my ass. In my mind's eye, I picture those tattooed knuckles. The muscled forearms. His brutal face.

As much as I wanted him least as my partner because of those things, I get damp between my legs thinking of them. He's scary.

And some part of me finds that thrilling as much as the other part wants to run the other way.

But he's proven himself to be a thoughtful and attentive partner.

He pulls my arms behind my back and ties my wrists together with some soft fabric. It immediately puts me back in that helpless space. I still wish my eyes were covered, but I can turn my face toward the pillow and block everything out.

Everything but his hand slowly caressing my ass.

Crack!

I nearly leap off the couch when he smacks one butt cheek.

So much harder than I expected.

He smacks the other side, then repeats right and left.

Holy wow. Um, yeah. That hurts. I scramble on his lap, trying to dodge the spanks, but he wraps an arm tightly around my waist to hold me in place.

I roll my lips together to keep my cries in and smash my face into the pillow. He continues, spanking me hard and steady until my entire ass burns.

"Ow," I finally moan.

"Pain invites pleasure," he tells me, resting his palm on my heated skin.

I'm tempted to say any number of things that aren't ladylike, so I keep my mouth shut.

He slides his fingers between my legs and I'm shocked to feel how slippery wet I am. Apparently, he's right. Pain does invite pleasure.

He rubs lightly, his touch unambitious, soothing almost. Sensation blooms into more heat.

But then he parts my cheeks and I clench in response. It's embarrassing. Exposing.

Not. Right.

I hear the rustle of plastic and smell the slightly astringent scent of alcohol wipes. He's cleaning the toys he bought.

I flinch at the dollop of cool gel that lands on my anus. I expect to wait—the way he made me anticipate the wax, but the rounded tip of the buttplug immediately prods my back entrance.

I squeeze everything closed—my eyes, my butt cheeks, my anus.

He slaps the back of my thigh, which hurts fifty times worse than his spanks on my ass.

"Ouch!" I protest.

"Open for me."

I don't want to. But I already know there's no point in refusing. I don't plan to safe word, so I might as well concede.

I draw in a deep breath and slowly exhale, willing my body parts to relax. To open.

He presses the bulbous head of the plug against my anus and waits.

What for, I'm not sure.

But then the tight ring of muscles relax on their own and he presses forward, like he expected that moment and was waiting for it.

Again, I find myself relieved to be with an experienced partner.

I hate the feel of the plug. The intrusion. Not because it hurts, although there is a bit of stretch. But it's more the humiliation of the thing. The sense of wrong-ness.

The fire of the stretch grows the more he presses forward.

I start to tighten, but he makes a negative sound.

"Take your plug, kitten."

I whine a little as it goes in, but once it's past the widest place it settles, and the burn is gone. Now I just experience the sensation of being filled. And the stimulation around my anus where the neck still holds it open.

"Good girl."

I exhale again. I don't hate it. I don't love it, either.

But then he begins to spank me again. The plug jostles in my ass, providing more stimulation.

I reflexively squeeze my anus, but with the plug, I just get more feedback.

And dammit, I am finding it arousing.

Which feels terribly wrong.

He slaps one side, then the other, making me bounce over his lap. Every wiggle, every movement moves the plug inside me. Moves me around the plug. It becomes intense. Not painful—I hardly notice the sting of the spanks anymore.

All my focus is on the sensation inside my ass.

He spanks more—even harder. My thighs tighten but I find he's right—I almost welcome the pain now. It's like scratching the itch. It satisfies the burning need that's growing hotter with every moment.

There's a pause and I catch my breath.

And then I gasp when Master R brings the vibrating tip of a dildo to my pussy.

"Oh!" I cry in surprise.

Yes.

It feels. So. Good.

He screws it inside me and leaves it there, then spanks me some more.

Now it's too much. Not the pain—the sensation. Everything at once. The plug in my ass jostling as he spanks me. The constant vibration in my core. The sting of pain with each slap.

I need completion.

Desperately.

To make it even worse, he starts fucking my ass with the plug, still slapping me with the other hand.

I'm embarrassed by the sounds that come from my throat.

Wanton.

Needy.

Crazed.

"Please," I beg, although I don't even know what I'm begging for. More? Less? Something else?

All I know is I need to find it, whatever it is.

"Please Master, may I come," he guides me.

Seriously? Fine.

"Please Master, may I come?"

"*Da*. Come now, *kotyonok*. But show me your face."

I can't focus on what he said beyond *come now*. My core tightens, pussy clenching around the vibrator.

He grabs a fistful of my hair and uses it to turn my face in his direction, still fucking my ass the entire time with the plug.

I open my mouth in a soundless cry and my gaze tangles in his. His eyes are dark and I see heat in his normally cool expression. I clench around both phalluses, humping his lap and wondering what it would be like to be filled by him.

Will I find out?

His cock presses hard against my hip. I want to suck it again. Want to return this incredible pleasure that's still coursing through me in what must be the longest orgasm on record.

Ripple after ripple of pleasure flow through me. Every time I think it's done, the slightest movement jostles the plugs and I come all over again.

"That's it, my lucky lady. Keep coming," he coaxes, slowing the speed of the plug-fucking, but still continuing. "Now you see the benefit of delaying your pleasure."

"Oh God, yes," I admit. I may be prideful, but I'm certainly willing to admit when I was wrong.

Especially when I'm so filled with gratitude. And warm, delicious pleasure.

∼

Ravil

I'M ENCHANTED.

I don't know what it is about this woman I find so fascinating but seeing her come undone undoes me.

I want to get her number. Date her. Make her fall in love.

And I don't do any of those things. Especially not with women I play with in a sex club.

I won't. I can't. I don't even live in this city.

But it disturbs me how much I want to.

Her flawless face is flushed with color, her hair fans around her in a wild mess.

But what moves me most is the way her eyes locked on mine. The startled ecstasy that showed in them as I wrung orgasm after orgasm from her.

The new softness to her now.

What changes might overcome this powerful, sexy woman if I made her come like that every night? Who might she become?

Because sexuality is power. And women who own their sexuality own the world.

I slide the vibrator from her and turn it off. Then stroke her back to get her to relax enough to get the plug out. I quickly clean the devices again and return them to the bag they came in.

"Come here." I help her sit up on my lap, then spin her legs in the opposite direction so she can lay back in my arms. "Just enjoy for a moment." I brush the hair back from her face, then stroke my fingertips down her arm. "You feel good, no?"

71

Everything about her face has changed. The tightness in her jaw is gone, the tension in her neck. "So good," she agrees. "Thank you."

I reach down and slide her dress up enough to stroke between her legs. Not to bring her to another orgasm, just to relax her.

A shiver runs through her, but she makes a contented sound—a light humming.

"What do you do for a living, kitten? Will you tell?"

Some of her wariness returns, and I instantly regret prying. I don't know why I am, anyway. I won't see this woman again. It hardly matters. She could be whatever I imagine her to be.

She shakes her head.

"I shouldn't have asked," I concede. "Your mystery is part of the appeal, anyway."

She blinks up at me. "Do you find me appealing?"

I nod. "Very."

"I don't even know what I'm doing."

I smile indulgently. "It's part of the charm." I slide my hand inside her dress and cup one of her breasts. "Are you thirsty? Do you need water? Or another drink?"

She sits up and my body protests the distance between us. I could've kept her lounging in my arms all night without complaint. "I would like a water, please." She smiles sheepishly. "Thirsty work, orgasming."

"It is." I lift her to stand and follow her up, then lead her back to the bar and order a bottle of water for both of us.

"I enjoyed watching you," the man on Lady Luck's other side says.

My lips curl back in a snarl, but I keep it in.

He leans forward and catches my eye. "I would've fucked that ass hard if I were you, though."

I'm normally completely in control. I show no emotion, nothing gets me ruffled. But white-hot anger flares. And swift retribution has always been a part of my world.

My hand snaps out and catches the guy by the throat. "Disrespect her again, and I'll tear out your tongue," I warn. Then I let go, as quickly as I started.

Hardly anyone around us saw. Maybe only my beautiful submissive.

The man chokes and coughs, looking around for support while I pin him with a death glare.

A loud bang from somewhere nearby makes me and everyone at the bar jump and turn. A sign fell over on the other side of the bar. Ever aware, I note Lady Luck's movement before I even turn back.

Then I see her striding quickly away, hips swaying, hair tossed back with a snap of her head. Gone is the softness of a moment ago.

Now, she's all business, taking long strides in those heels like she was born in them with her back stiff and straight as a rod.

Blyad.

I take off after her.

I don't want to make a scene. Black Light has dungeon monitors everywhere, and everyone here considers us to be part of the entertainment. There's no such thing as privacy at Black Light on a night like this.

I hustle to catch up with Lady Luck, without calling her name.

She's near the exit. "Hang on." I catch her elbow, then immediately release it when she shakes off my touch. "Don't run."

When she whirls, she has fire in her eyes. "Red."

Fuck. I cover her mouth and back her up against the wall. "Shh. Don't. Please don't. I'm sorry you saw that. I know you're upset. Will you stay and talk to me?"

I release her mouth. Covering it was a direct violation of Black Light rules. You can't muffle a safe word. I'm definitely crossing a line here, but I'm not willing to accept this ending.

Not for us.

Not yet.

She stares back at me. "I know what you are."

Her words hit me square in the chest. Harder than a punch from Boris, my top enforcer. Harder than a gunshot through a kevlar vest. Or the bone-crushing blow of a prison guard's billy club.

I've known shame. I've lived with the shame of what I've done. It's a violent world I grew up in. Most of my crimes I can live with. A few I can't.

But the shame that lances through me now is fresh and potent and curls through every pore like a cancer.

"What do you know?" I barely croak it out.

Her gaze is steady. She may have been nervous before, but I see now it was fueled by sexual tension, by uncertainty about her role. Now, she knows herself. Knows what she'll allow and what she won't.

And she's cutting me out.

"You're Bratva. Russian *mafiya*." Her eyes drop to my exposed forearms, where the black ink marks my prison time, my crimes. "I know what those symbols mean." She swallows. Now I see a hint of fear. "You're a killer."

A single tear drips down her face. I didn't even see it coming. No other part of her face looks like she's crying.

It could be sub drop from the scene we just had. Or her regret at tangling with a man like me. At her attraction to me—because even now her body responds. She's softened against me where I'm crowding her. Like it feels right.

I wipe the tear with my thumb. Lean my forehead against hers. "Yes," I admit.

I feared my admission would frighten her further, but instead, it seems to settle her. Like she just needed the truth.

So, I give her more. I never share secrets. Keep my cards very close to my chest, even with my own cell. But I spill it all now. "I came to D.C. to grease a wheel." I tip my head in the direction of Valdemar, who is flogging his submissive on the St. Andrew's cross. "The wheel wanted me to come here with him tonight, so I did."

She doesn't move. Just absorbs my words like she's holding her breath.

Is there something I can say that would change her decision to walk out before we finish? Something I can do?

The tear is gone but I continue to lightly brush her cheek with the pad of my thumb. The fact that she allows it encourages me to go on. "I never imagined I would meet... Well, you're something special," I admit. "Different. I've enjoyed our time together very much. I think you did, too."

Her lashes flicker and I know I have her agreement on that, at least.

"I'm sorry I let the streets of Leningrad show through. I've known violence. But I never meant to scare you. Or offend you. I just didn't like hearing you dishonored like that."

I sense a tremble start up in her body. A vibration, a tremor. Is it from indecision? Is that what makes my beautiful Lady Luck tremble? Or is it desire?

"Please don't let my mistake end our night together."

She has lovely brown eyes. Big and slightly turned down at the edges.

"Please. You have one more spin of the wheel. It would please me to show you more pleasure than you've ever had."

"You already have." It's just a whisper. Like she doesn't want to admit it or for anyone but me to hear.

Emboldened, I stroke my palm down her side. "There's so much more, kitten. One more spin. Please stay. I won't cut anyone's tongues out. Or threaten to. I promise."

This wrings a smile from her and the weight on my chest lifts slightly.

"Will you stay?"

Her lashes drop. Her face tilts up. To my shock, her lips connect with mine.

I don't kiss women. Especially not at a place like this. I'm the fuck them hard and walk away type. But the moment I feel her tentative kiss, I'm all over her. I press her up against the wall and claim that beautiful mouth of hers. One leg insinuating between her thighs, I mold my body over hers, slant my lips and drink from her.

Her body goes soft, lips become eager. I find her hands on my arms, urging me closer. I grind my erection in the notch between her legs, trail my open mouth down her neck to nip her shoulder.

She bites me back.

I slam my hips against hers, suddenly desperate to consume her. In fact, I'm about ready to find a condom, roll it on and claim her right there against the wall, but she gasps, "Yes, Okay. One more spin."

Right.

One more spin.

The Roulette game.

I smile and lace my fingers through hers, adjusting my straining cock with the other hand. I walk beside her back to the stage.

I get one more scene with her. I'm going to make it good.

CHAPTER 4

LUCY

*I*t's hard to ignore the pulse of heat between my legs. The taste of the Russian on my tongue.

I wouldn't have thought him capable of passion—he's been so cool and manicured, but he showed me a bit of himself.

And that's the only reason I'm returning with him.

His show of weakness quieted the nagging voice in my head that's been wondering what in the hell I'm doing here.

I shouldn't have more confidence in the mobster now, but I do.

Hearing him threaten that other man—seeing how quickly he turns to violence was a wake-up call. It frightened me. Reminded me of exactly who this man is.

But he humbled himself with me. He begged.

It took some of my fears away. Returned my power.

And he wasn't violent with me. He's been only gentle. His threat was in my defense.

And while I don't approve, it's not so different from the ferocious way my dad used the legal system to protect and defend his family any time he sensed a threat.

They just come from different walks of life.

I glance down at the way our fingers are interlaced. There's a gentleness to the gesture. It's more of a union versus the dominant way he held my elbow earlier. That touch was appropriate then. This one is more appropriate now.

And it's that more than anything that eases my reservations.

The man beside me is completely sane. He's aware. He knows what the situation requires. What I require.

Hell, that's more than I ever got from Jeffrey, as nice as he was.

We step on the stage and the DJ greets us by name. "Lady Luck and Master R have returned for their final toss of the ball. Go ahead, Lady Luck." He hands the ball to me and I toss it in the spinning wheel.

Funny how I almost don't care what it lands on now.

I trust the man behind me. Even if I land on something that completely terrifies me, I have a feeling he would make it work for me.

But I don't.

The ball bounces and lands on the most ordinary act of all—you can't even call it a kink: *vaginal intercourse.*

I actually laugh a little.

The Russian smiles, but there's scheming in those blue eyes of his. Somehow, I doubt the sex will be straight vanilla. He's going to make it kinky after all.

The shiver that runs through me is all excitement.

Master R leads me off the stage and down the steps.

"I'm going to run to the restroom," I tell him.

"Meet me near the bar, I need to grab a few things."

"No condoms?" I ask in surprise. Because what else could he possibly need?

He smirks. "I have condoms. And it's a surprise. Meet me in five."

"Yes, Master." I say it with a smile. It's a bit mocking, but maybe also flirty.

The look he gives me makes my heart beat faster. It's the same inscrutable expression, with the air of indulgence. Very dominant. Very sexy.

I disappear to the restroom and when I return, I find him waiting for me in front of the bar.

He scans the open area of the club. Most of the benches and tables are in use.

He stops and looks at me thoughtfully. "Exhibitionism is not high on your kink list, true?"

I shake my head. "Not high, no."

"Come." He takes my elbow and leads me to an area Gretchen had mentioned with semi-private curtained rooms.

It might have scared me to be alone with him earlier, but now I'm only eager.

He pushes aside a curtain and leads me in. The moment we step inside, he tosses his bag of toys on the sofa and puts his hands all over me. Like we've been on a hot date and we just got back to my place.

He kisses me, backing me up against a wall as his palms coast over my ass, trail up my spine. My dress falls to the floor with a few quick tugs.

I welcome his hands on my skin. The hard steel of his body pressed up against mine. I tug his t-shirt up and he pulls it over his head.

He's covered in tattoos. Across his chest, over his shoulders, down his arms. Some are primitive. Some have a more artistic flow.

He's a dangerous beast, this man. A killer.

And in this moment, that only adds to the sex appeal.

I stroke my palms over the bulging muscles on his chest. It's covered in golden hair, soft and curling under my fingers. When I bite one of his pecs, he pins my wrists beside my head and thrusts hard between my legs.

"Have you been fucked up against a wall, *kotyonok*?" Another hard thrust. I feel his straining cock below his jeans.

I shake my head no.

"We'll start there, then." He pulls a condom out of his back pocket and unbuttons his jeans. We both watch as he rolls the rubber over his straining length. He pulls one of my knees up and rubs over my wet slit.

I moan when he sinks into me. I nip his ear.

"*Da*. Give me the claws, kitten. I knew you were fierce."

I've never considered myself fierce in the bedroom. In the court-room, sure. But my sexual history involved way too much anxiety for losing myself to passion.

His encouragement spurs me on. I wend my arms around his neck and score him with my nails.

"Wrap those long legs around my waist now."

I lift my other foot from the floor. The Russian palms my ass, fingers digging into my flesh as he drives into me. My back presses against the wall, holding up some of my weight as he manages the rest of it.

"Squeeze my dick tight," he tells me.

It's not an instruction I've ever been given before, but I contract my muscles around him, practicing my kegels as he snarls in pleasure.

"That's right, kitten. So tight."

I'm dizzy with pleasure, and shocked at the animalistic way we're going at it. How quickly we got from point A to point B. How far from my norm this whole night has been.

"Do you think I'll let you come like this?" he growls against my ear.

My breath stops for a moment as those words wash through me. Right. There's this whole thing of asking permission to orgasm. A dominant owns your pleasure.

Does he want me to beg?

"Please?" I ask, far more willing to beg than I would've been two hours ago.

He smiles—a genuine smile that makes him appear ten years younger. "*Nyet.*"

I gasp, driving my nails into his shoulders. "What do you mean, *nyet?*"

"It means no."

"Yes, I gathered that but—"

"Not yet, kitten. I have you for forty more minutes. You think I'm going to let you come in our first position?"

First... *position?*

Oh lord. This man is sex on a stick.

Knowing there will be more—much more—I relax into it. Of course, that makes me harder to hold up.

He lifts me away from the wall and drops me to my feet. As soon as I land, he spins me around and pushes me over the arm of the loveseat in the room. "Spread your legs."

I wait, expecting him to enter me again from behind, but instead I feel the sharp sting of the flogger, swung like a whip this time.

I gasp, my pussy clenching on air. "Ouch!"

He whips me again.

And again.

After six smacks, my skin gets used to the contact of the flogger. My ass gets warm and stingy. My core grows molten.

This.

This is why submissives crave pain. I understand now, because I only want more. Each slap of the flogger sends lust kicking through my body. Winds the coil of desire tighter.

He changes the way he uses the flogger, swinging it in circles— or maybe it's a figure eight. The tips glance off the globes of my ass like the strands of an automatic car wash mop moving around the car.

It's... divine.

Barely a sting. So much heat and pleasure.

He moves to my thighs, then my shoulders. I love every bit of it.

When he flicks the flogger between my open legs, though, I squeal.

"Keep them open." The command is guttural. His accent thicker.

I love knowing I'm having an effect on him.

I slide the stilettos wider. I've never felt so sexy in my life. Every part of me is alive. Activated. Singing.

He flicks the flogger between my legs again.

I catch my breath at the sting, then moan.

"Stand up."

It takes my brain a moment to process the order, and I find myself mildly disappointed at the change. Every time I'm starting to sink into something, he shifts it. I suppose that's part of the strategy.

"Face me. Hands interlaced on top of your head."

My brows shoot up, but I comply. He's earned my trust now. Besides, I left my pride behind somewhere between the first and second spin of the wheel.

The position lifts and spreads my breasts, presenting them to him.

He nudges my foot. "Spread your legs wider."

Oh God. I widen my stance. Now I'm really presented to him.

Buck naked, nothing but my heels. Standing before him like I'm under arrest. Or I'm a slave up for auction.

And that thought shouldn't get me so wet.

He begins to spin the flogger again. Yes—it's a figure eight motion —and this time spins the tips of the flogger across my breasts. My nipples harden and stand up under the abuse, the pink darkening along with the rest of my skin.

Again, it's wonderful. Everything I thought a flogger would be, and more.

He smiles. "You like it."

"Yes." I whisper it.

He flicks down my belly and across the front of my hips. "I like it when you whisper *yes* like that. Next time say it in Russian."

"*Da*," I tell him.

His smile grows wider, cock bobbing in the cradle of his unzipped jeans.

"You are as smart as you are beautiful, *kotyonok*. I'm glad I came here tonight. Glad I got to play with you."

"I'm glad, too," I murmur.

He reaches for the bag and produces a small jewelry box. I watch as he reveals a pair of—oh shit—nipple clamps. I'm not sure I like this idea.

My nipples are warm and tingly from the flogging. He opens one clamp. I flinch when he brings it over my nipple.

"Inhale, kitten."

I obey.

He closes the clamp. I gasp at the pain. My clit throbs in response. He repeats the action with the second clamp.

I let out a long, slow whimper.

He takes my hand off the top of my head and winds his fingers through mine, drawing me over to the couch. He sits down and pulls me across his lap and smacks my ass.

He's recapping where we've been, I realize. First the flogging, now the spanking. And I appreciate the reminder. Because it's so very different the second time. I was reluctant before.

Now I'm primed.

Ready.

Hungry for it, even.

He tosses one of the sofa cushions down onto his feet. I don't understand it until he lifts one of my legs to straddle him.

I yelp as he spins me face down over his legs, my ass spread over his lap with my knees bent and feet in the air. I brace my hands on the floor. The position is entirely ignominious. My pussy and ass are spread and open to his view. Presented to him. While I'm facing the floor.

Or rather, the pillow. I arrange it under my face and chest and hang on as he spanks my ass, first right cheek, then left. He rubs out the sting, tracing his thumb along my slit. The vibrator makes a reappearance, this time against my clit.

I moan and bite the pillow and wriggle as I grow more and more desperate.

"Please," I start to moan.

"Please what?"

"Please… may I come?"

"*Nyet.*"

He turns up the vibration on the toy and I moan plaintively.

Just when I think it's way too much, he adds the butt plug.

I'm a little sore from last time, but it goes in easier. I know to relax and breathe.

And like everything we've tried, the pleasure is greater the second time.

But so is the need. My inner thighs start trembling.

I hump his lap, rubbing my clit over the vibrator as he pumps the plug in my ass.

I start to lose control. I'm chanting things—begging, I guess. Maybe babbling—I don't even know.

"I know what you need," he's telling me, soothing me with long strokes of his palm down my back.

He throws another cushion to the floor. "On your knees for me, kitten."

He helps me swing my legs down from the couch to kneel on the cushion. When I stand on my hands and knees, he pushes between my shoulder blades until I drop my torso to the pillow.

He likes the humiliating poses.

Apparently, so do I, because I'm still moaning and begging. Through the thick haze of lust, I watch him roll a new condom on before he pushes into me.

And then it's pure ecstasy.

I never knew vaginal intercourse could be so satisfying. It never has been before.

But every thrust, every glide in and out is discovery. I'm finding me here. Finding pleasure, finding new heights I never knew existed.

My ass is stretched wide with the plug, making his every thrust twenty times more potent. And the angle? It's. Just. Perfect.

"Please, please," I babble, because I need it so badly now.

I need that orgasm more than my next breath.

He grips my hips and thrusts hard. Harder.

I whine for it, mewl. Beg some more.

But he's a stallion.

The man keeps it up until I'm light-headed. Trembling from head to toe. Completely lost.

He reaches around and releases the clamps on my nipples. The pain of the blood rushing back into them makes me gasp.

And then he says it.

"Come, kitten."

Pleasure explodes through me. Before he even thrusts deep and pushes me to my belly. Before he roars something in Russian so loud my ears ring.

I go hoarse with my own scream and when the room stops spinning I find myself on my belly, his large body draped over the top of mine. His lips at my nape.

I don't want to ever move. Nor do I want him to move.

I'm in a happy place I've never known.

Euphoria.

He nibbles my ear lobe. Murmurs something in Russian. I only catch the word *kotyonok.*

I hum, slowly waggling my ass beneath him. My version of purring.

He kisses the side of my neck. "*Spasibo.*"

"What does that mean?" My voice is rusty.

"It means *thank you.*" He kisses my jaw this time. "You were such an unexpected pleasure."

He eases out of me and I moan in disappointment, but then the air between us changes.

He pulls in a ragged breath and curses in Russian. The hair at my nape stands on end and a chill skitters down my skin chasing away the heat of the moment.

I look over my shoulder.

"I'm sorry, kitten, the condom broke." He holds it up, his expression slightly stricken.

I swallow. "It's okay." I push up to my knees and he helps me stand. "I'll take a morning after pill. It will be all right. I'm clean. Are you?"

"*Da.* Absolutely. I'm clean, yes."

"Good." My head floats around on my neck, like it can't quite decide if I'm nodding or shaking my head.

Master R disposes of the condom and brings my dress to me, helping me back into it. He strokes up and down both my arms, like he's warming me up. "Are you all right?"

"Yes, I'm good. Really good."

"Can I see you again?" I swear he almost looks surprised that he's asking the question.

I shake my head. I came here for an experience, not a partner. I'd decided that before I came. Even if I hadn't, I don't think I could enter into any kind of ongoing relationship with a member of the Russian *mafiya*.

It's just not something a smart woman does.

And that's one thing I've always prided myself on being.

"No, you're right. It's better this way, yes." And just like that, we're through. Two polite strangers thanking each other. "Come." He takes my elbow. "Let's get you a drink."

CHAPTER 5

LUCY

I'm a different person. Utterly changed. The cab ride back to Gretchen's place is a bookend on the beginning of the night and it highlights my transformation.

My life may forever be BBL and ABL: Before Black Light and After Black Light.

I just had all my walls torn down and the person I found beneath them is beautiful. And I never knew her. I just kept her locked up for fear she'd do something imperfect or wrong.

Gratitude buzzes in my chest for Gretchen, for Black Light. For my partner.

Gretchen looks over at me and smirks. "You had a great time."

I nod. "Yes."

"He was good? What was his name? I haven't seen him there before."

"Master R. I don't think he's a member, he is here visiting the other Russian—some diplomat."

"Valdemar, right. That man is an oaf. But how was his friend?"

I can't stop the warmth running through my body. My attraction to him still sings in every cell. I swim in the memory of his hands, his voice, his body. "He was good."

Understatement of the year.

"Just good? What did you land on? I only heard the *wax play* one."

"*Anal play* and *vaginal intercourse* with condom. Only the condom broke."

"Oh shit. You're getting a morning after pill first thing tomorrow." Gretchen gives me a severe look.

"Yes, of course," I say automatically.

Except I already know I won't take it.

All I ever wanted was to have children.

I'm thirty-five years old. I delayed the start of a family because I wanted to finish law school and establish my career first. Find the safe boyfriend, the one I thought for sure would be ready to settle down soon and be a dad.

But all that blew up in my face. I'm getting past my prime now, with no man in sight.

Maybe this was a happy accident.

A chance to have that baby without dealing with a father.

I will never see Master R again. We don't even know each other's real names. He wouldn't need to know.

I have the ability to raise a child on my own. I have a power job. I make good money as a defense attorney in my father's practice. I'll make a damn good mom.

And the chance of a thirty-five-year-old woman getting pregnant the one time a condom breaks are slim.

But then again, I'm Lady Luck.

Tonight I was picked by the perfect dom. I landed on the perfect kinks.

And the condom broke.

Maybe for once, I can trust the Universe to deliver something I desperately want.

A baby.

THE END... *for now.*

ABOUT THE AUTHOR

USA Today **Bestselling Author Renee Rose** loves a dominant, dirty-talking alpha hero! She's sold over a half million copies of steamy romance with varying levels of kink. Her books have been featured in USA Today's Happily Ever After and Popsugar. Named Eroticon USA's Next Top Erotic Author in 2013, she has also won Spunky and Sassy's Favorite Sci-Fi and Anthology author, The Romance Reviews Best Historical Romance, and Spanking Romance Reviews' Best Sci-fi, Paranormal, Historical, Erotic, Ageplay and favorite couple and author. She's hit the USA Today list five times with various anthologies.

Grab six free books for FREE here.

Please also follow Renee on:
BookBub | Facebook | Amazon | Instagram | Twitter | Goodreads

BREATHLESS

A BLACK LIGHT: ROULETTE WAR NOVELLA

By

Eris Adderly

CHAPTER 1

ANSON

*A*nson Morrow didn't believe in luck, and yet here he was, about to gamble with his mental health.

Get on the waiting list, Matthew had said. *It'll be good for you*, he'd said.

He glanced down at his phone on his way to the elevator. The new message stuck out in his notifications like a sore thumb because it was from an email account he'd created for one purpose, and one purpose only.

To apply for Black Light's Roulette event.

And here was the first email he'd received in that account, aside from the initial 'thank you for your application.'

Matthew had been pressuring him for at least two months. Because that's what friends did, apparently. Harass a body until they caved or developed a nervous tic.

You need to get out of your comfort zone, man. Take risks.

All of this he'd heard, over and over again, especially on nights they both visited the club. His only friend gesturing with a tumbler of liquor, yelling encouragement at him over the music. But charismatic Matthew—congressman from Maryland—inevitably would accept or make offers to play with one of his favorites, and he'd leave Anson to brood at one of the tables and watch the action by himself.

No matter how many times he'd explained it, Matthew refused to believe Anson liked it that way.

The soles of his shoes made a muted *ka-tak* on the marble ground floor of the Internal Revenue Service building. At the elevator doors, he twisted to press the button with an elbow. The car *pinged* open without pause, already on the same floor, and Anson stepped inside. He turned to face the closing doors but didn't go so far as to lean against the back wall.

Once the silent car began moving, he thumbed open the new email. His eyes skimmed, fast as light, to the relevant lines of text.

"Fuck."

Anson didn't engage in frequent profanity but this, he could warrant.

They'd accepted him.

He blinked at the tiny, bright screen.

Why, though? He was no showman. No big contributor; just paid his membership and came and watched for the last nine months. Matthew had to have greased some palms, no? For what other reason out of the whole list of applicants they'd made a big deal of, would the club owners have chosen... him?

The elevator bobbed to a halt and *pinged* again for the doors to open, and Anson leaned to step out onto the third floor.

Except it wasn't the third floor. It was the second. A woman stepped in with a small stack of manila envelopes under one arm and her own phone in hand. She gave him a stiff little smile, and then turned to face the doors. There were no moves to punch in another floor after she glanced and saw 'three' was already lit up.

He gripped his phone tighter as the car rose again.

The woman's clothing told him she did not work in this building. Blue jeans—fashionably torn in places—an uncollared blouse, light tennis shoes. She scrolled through something on her phone—a social media site, his discreet glances told him—and shifted her weight from one hip to the other. A mess of sun-bleached blonde hair fell past her waist, under no semblance of control whatsoever.

She didn't look his way again when the doors parted on the third floor but strode off down the corridor in the opposite direction from his office. His best guess was document courier. Probably got herself a useless art degree and then realized she couldn't eat the paintings.

Hippies.

Anson shook his head and made for his office. His need to catalog people was something he'd learned at a young age not to do out loud, but it kept him feeling like he had a handle on his surroundings. Like everything was in control.

His space was as he'd left it. Desk clear of papers. Blinds on the window half raised. Computer asleep.

He would *not* be logging onto a government computer to look at this BDSM club email some more. His chair swiveled under him as he took his seat and woke up his phone screen again before punching in his six-digit passcode.

There was an attachment. A waiver.

Smart.

He opened the PDF and began poring through the tiny text. He'd need to look at this again at home, but he nodded to himself at what he saw so far, lower lip jutting in reserved approval.

Nothing I wouldn't put in there. Nice and tight. Almost no loopholes.

His phone started buzzing and a contact lit up the screen, taking over from the waiver PDF. 'Matthew Stringer', it read.

For the love of—does he already know?

"Morrow." He answered the same way he always did, regardless of who was calling.

"Well?" Matthew didn't bother with greetings. Those were for constituents. "Did they tell you yet?"

Anson made a face into his empty office. "You tell *me.*"

"What's that supposed to mean?"

"*You* pressured me into this thing," Anson said, "and now here you are, calling me up five minutes after I get the email."

"*Well?*" None of his shaming ever deterred Matthew. Not in college, and not twenty years later.

Anson sighed. "They approved me."

"Fuck yeah, they did." There was some bang of noise from the other end of the call. Probably a palm slapping some innocent nearby furniture. The representative from Maryland was about as subtle as a fireworks display.

"You better not have had anything to do with this," said Anson.

"What do *I* need to have to do with it?" Matthew asked. "You're a Senior Revenue Agent. They don't want to piss off the IRS."

"First of all," Anson said, turning in his chair to poke a finger into the soil of the juniper bonsai on the windowsill, "I'm not *'the'* IRS. And second, there are plenty of other members holding influential positions, *Congressman.*"

"Whatever, man. You're going to draw a name and find someone to play with for a change, and it's going to be great. Stop sitting in the corner sipping your lemon water and staring at the rest of us like a fucking sociopath."

Anson let out a measured breath through his nose. "Remind me again how you ever got into politics?"

"Because I'm a crowd pleaser." The charming grin nearly blared through the phone. "Speaking of which, I have an interview in about ten minutes. I'll call you back."

"Enjoy."

The two men ended the call, and Anson woke up his computer. Logged in. While he waited for everything to load, he reached into one of his lower desk drawers and retrieved a bottle of water. With a careful hand, he trickled a small measure around the roots of the juniper and assessed the arrangement of tiny branches. Nothing needed pruning today. He put away the rest of the water in its spot next to the copy of *How to Stop Worrying and Start Living*—yet another 'gift' from the eternally optimistic Matthew—and shut the desk drawer.

Bonsai were the opposite of the chaos that was people. He allowed himself this one in his office, but he had another dozen or so at home. All different species of tree. A big ficus. A delicate Japanese maple. They accepted his guidance and care. They grew in a slow, quiet beauty that never ran wild or piqued his anxiety like so much of the rest of the world.

Like this coming Valentine's Day was about to do.

As he opened the software for his work email, the yellow sticky note hanging from the lower left edge of his monitor caught his eye.

'Do one thing every day that scares you,' it read.

Just because it was probably right didn't mean he had to like it. And this Roulette night ought to count for several days' worth of things that scared him. Or a month.

It was still over a week away. Plenty of time to talk himself out of it.

CHAPTER 2

ANSON

*T*here were luxury chain stores on 31st, but none of them would have been candidates for agreeing to host a back door into a sex club. That honor fell to an occult bookstore next to an alley.

Neon in the front windows touted the availability of psychic readings—Past! Present! Future!—and the crowded display cases and shelves bristled with all manner of superstitious paraphernalia. A soundtrack of some quiet mountain stream mixed with soft piano notes came piping into the over-scented space from hidden speakers, and it was about the only thing Anson found tolerable as he made his way to the curtain in the back.

People loved relying on little totems. Little charms to bring them 'luck.' When unpleasantness happened, they could blame it on 'energies' they should have 'cleansed', or the stars, when the reality was, they had no idea what the causal factor was, and this made them feel out of control. And the idea of luck could help them relinquish some of that desire for control without having to manage uncomfortable feelings about it.

Anson Morrow did not believe in luck. That wasn't how probability worked. If a coin toss didn't go your way nine times, it wasn't any more likely to do so on the tenth, no matter what special crystals a body wore or candles they burned.

And so, what's the probability you'll get paired with someone who won't safe word after just talking to you for five minutes?

He already had his card out to show the big man named Luís, who checked memberships just behind the curtain. Had anyone ever tried to get past him? Would anyone dare? Anson kept fit enough, but he was nowhere near the size of this guy.

The man shined a small UV light over his card and nodded as he handed it back. "Mr. Morrow."

Anson nodded back and tucked the black plastic rectangle into a pants pocket as Luís pulled open the door to let him pass through to the stairs. The smell of patchouli left him behind, and Anson breathed deep.

The tunnel running under the alley and back toward Black Light was a concrete chute propelling him from the sterile world of corporate tax returns and trading activities audits toward all the sticky strobing and grinding of raw human desire of which Anson sat on the periphery.

He thought he knew what he wanted but had too much anxiety to go hunting for it. Not in any real sort of way. It was always too much risk. Too likely it would end the same way it had the last time he'd dared to play, and that had been six years and four months ago.

She'd left in tears. In the weeks that had followed, Anson had started snapping at his only friend more than usual. Matthew had gotten him drunk—one of only two times in his life, both of which, his friend had been responsible—and dragged the more pertinent details out of him. Tried to assure him it hadn't been his fault. 'She just wasn't ready. You did everything right; there's no point in going into a shell over it.'

It hadn't mattered. For someone who refused to buy into superstitions, he'd also done a great job of refusing logic.

Just because you had a problem with one partner, doesn't mean you're going to have a problem with every partner.

He tried not to let Matthew's words make him sour as he approached the second door that led to the locker room. The man was right. Anson just didn't like that the whole thing was trying to make him have emotions, which were rarely useful. Emotions were always a mess. Numbers he could put in columns and understand.

The only way he'd get through tonight would be to keep the things he *could* control at the forefront of his mind. He could control himself, including his reactions to people and events. And to some degree, unless the wheel paired him with a real brat, he could control his sub for the night.

You know you can't control other people, Anson.

He pulled open the door and stepped into the dim lighting of the locker room. Even through the walls, he could already hear music thumping from inside Black Light proper. If this didn't count as doing 'the one thing that scared him' today, he didn't know what would.

"Mr. Morrow." The security guard, Daniel, was already greeting him, even as Anson shrugged his way out of his coat. It did not fail to impress Anson that the man was able to remember so many different members' names.

"I see you're on the Roulette list tonight." The guard's tone as he looked down to consult some reference atop his podium was far warmer than the more serious Luís back at the first door.

"So it would seem," said Anson, handing over his membership card for a second time, along with his driver's license.

Daniel verified both and handed them back for Anson to slip into his wallet for the night. "Locker forty-six, and there's a two-drink max for Roulette participants this evening."

Forty-six. Not great. Not terrible. Prime, if you divide in half.

"Noted." Anson cracked a dry smile as he folded his coat down to where it would fit in the locker. The security guard might remember his face from this room, but he clearly hadn't watched Anson *inside* the club: he drank water and that was it, no matter what Matthew tried to push on him.

His phone went next into the locker. The club took extensive measures to ensure member privacy, but it made Anson shake his head every time he left his phone out here. He had no interest in taking pictures of anyone or anything inside, no. The disparity just always struck him at the level of worry people reserved for the possibility anyone would discover their kinks, when what should really terrify them was other people discovering the wild bullshit listed on their tax returns.

But Anson Morrow did not have the same sorts of worries as other people.

He shut the locker.

"Good luck in there tonight!" said Daniel, unfazed as always by Anson's spartan responses.

"Thank you." It was the proper thing to say. People didn't appreciate him being a pedant about things like 'luck.'

A wall of music hit him in the face when he opened the final door to the club. Or at least, more music that he was used to, which was none. There wasn't a live DJ yet—Anson was half an hour early—but the sound system throbbed and skittered a suggestive trance over the glass and neon of Black Light, all the same.

Bodies packed the space already; far more than an average night. He scanned the high-top tables, seats at the bar, even the chairs in front of the stage—every place to sit was occupied. People stood clustered around groups of dungeon furniture, drinks in hand, laughing, talking. Sizing each other up. There were subs who already knelt, Doms already trailing fingers in their hair. Up on the stage, the roulette wheels gleamed in place, a conspicuous pair of new additions for the evening.

"Excuse us."

Anson snapped out of his cataloging of the space at the sound of a male voice behind his shoulder. A couple had come through the door from the locker room, and he hadn't made it more than five steps into the club.

"Sorry." He moved to one side and let them pass, still unsure in this crowd where he was going to find a place to—

Someone was waving at him from a high-top. Making familiar eye contact.

That someone was Matthew.

And he's here early? Sign of the apocalypse.

Anson made his way over to the congressman, his mouth firming up into a line as he had to squeeze and sidle past shifting bodies.

There was enough room at the small table for him to stand, but if there had been additional stools, someone had nicked them already.

"You can't seriously be here to watch me," Anson said over the music.

Matthew tilted a tumbler that was now mostly ice at him and grinned. "I'm here to watch you *show up*, son. Make sure you don't panic and back out." He downed the last of the liquid just as a server materialized, tableside.

"Another, sir?"

"Absolutely." Matthew flashed her his politician's smile with a keen edge of flirtation and slid the glass toward her on its little black napkin. She retrieved it and turned to Anson.

"And for you, sir?"

"Water," he said, before his friend could try to jump in and liquor him up. "With lemon, if possible."

"I'll bring those right back for you." She let her eyes twinkle on Matthew again before bustling off.

"Well, I didn't back out." Anson stated the obvious. "I'm here. And if this isn't the stupidest thing you've ever talked me into doing..." He slipped his right hand into his pants pocket to touch the comfort of nitrile gloves, there if he needed them.

And if the night continued as intended, he would. He'd been wise to bring more than one pair.

Matthew shot him a derisive puff of air. "I talked you into *way* stupider stuff in college. This isn't even"—his eyes turned up to scan his own memories—"top five."

"Yes. Well. We were both in our early twenties."

"Listen. You keep playing the same games, you're gonna keep winning the same prizes, man." The representative from Maryland leaned forward, elbows on the table. "Tonight is perfect. You're going to get paired with someone who—at a bare *minimum*—is motivated to play, *with a stranger*, and only has a handful of hard limits. The world is your oyster."

Anson *humphed*, watching the crowd. "And you're going to irritate a pearl out of me before the end of the night."

"That's my jolly tax man!" Matthew slapped his arm, jostling him, just as the server returned with their drinks. His friend offered a bill between two fingers to the woman, only to pluck it back with a wolfish grin when she reached. She snagged it on the second try with a musical laugh, and Anson imagined from the way she switched her hips on the walk away, she'd be topless in the congressman's limo before tomorrow morning.

"Do me a favor," Anson said. "Just don't come stare at me during my scenes, will you? Find somewhere else to be."

"Don't worry, I'm trying." Matthew's eyes still followed the server around the room.

"You know," said Anson, taking a sip of his water, "there are plenty of people to play with here who aren't employees."

"You worry about you, my friend. That young lady wants to get spanked by a congressman, and who am I to get in the way of her dreams?"

Anson made a face. "You need help."

"*You* need help." The other man took a draw from his second drink and set it back down. "That's why you're getting on that stage tonight. Come on. What did you put down for hard limits?"

If Matthew thought to jar him, he was off track. Why should Anson's preferences embarrass him? They were mere facts. "*Water sports*," he said. "*Blood play.*"

"*Pff.* Obvious."

Anson shrugged. Those two *would* be obvious to anyone who'd known him more than a day. He finished the list: "*Role play.*" The club had allowed up to four, but those had been the only choices to make his teeth grind.

"*Role play.*" Matthew's brows popped up. "Really."

A seed had descended from the lemon wedge to the bottom of his glass. Anson swished it around and contemplated fishing it out. His lip curled without his permission. "I don't need to be someone else," he told his friend. "It's enough of a struggle just to be *me* in a scene. I can only keep so many plates spinning."

"Maybe you'll get lucky and your sub'll have a thing for socially aloof sadists who are anal enough to have white carpet in their house."

"Remind me why we're still friends."

"Because you'd never do a damn fun thing without my bad influence," said Matthew.

One of the dungeon monitors turned sideways to slide past their table—a huge man, for whom Anson had overheard the apt nickname 'Muscles' during previous visits—his hand only just touching a petite woman's shoulder as he pointed toward the roulette setup on stage. She nodded, a waterfall of hair rippling down her back, lit purple and pink from the neon. The tasseled ends led his eye to the short hem of a dark skirt, out from under which hung a long foxtail. Anson had no doubts as to the means of its anchor.

He took another sip of his water.

"There's the problem," he said to Matthew. "I think your idea of 'fun' things and mine are on different planets."

His friend gave a smug chuckle. "Whatever you say, fox hunter."

Anson snapped his gaze away from the woman still asking the monitor questions.

A younger man had stepped up onstage and was making precise adjustments to the sound equipment. He scooped half a pair of bulky headphones up to an ear while his other hand danced between a laptop and some other interface Anson couldn't see from his vantage.

It was almost time.

Others had seen the DJ turned MC and were congregating around the stage. Anson's tongue stuck dry to the roof of his mouth, and he polished off his water in an icy gulp.

Matthew grinned. "It's about to get real, Morrow. You ready?"

"No."

Anson slid his glass to the center of the table, eyes on the impending unknown disaster across the club. He let out a breath.

He's right. It's all set up for you. All you have to do is play.

When he rounded the table's edge, Matthew opened his mouth for some last word, but Anson knew the look and cut him off. "If you say 'good luck' to me, I *will* tell your ex-wife about at *least* one of your offshore accounts."

The man put his hands up and curled a guilty smile. "Have *fun*, then," he said. "At least try, for fuck's sake."

"Right."

Anson left his friend behind without a backward glance. They'd known each other too long to stand on ceremony, and he had more pressing things to worry about just then. Like the group of women gathering near the steps that led to the stage.

Submissives, every one.

And among them, someone whose name he would roll.

A subset of a sub set, if you will.

With thoughts like that, was it any wonder he hadn't found a play partner in years?

There was a change in the lighting as Anson approached the side of the stage to join the conspicuous cluster of Doms. A man with salt-and-pepper hair gave him a nod of camaraderie on his approach, and Anson nodded back, but kept his hands in his pockets. He wasn't about to use his entire travel-size bottle of hand sanitizer on some stranger who wanted a shake.

How was he even going to do this? He'd been through it in his head time after time, but to be here now, in the reality of it all, made the blood rush at his temples. Real people played and got messy. Real people were constantly generating fluids. Who knew *what* kink the wheel would spin out for him and his as-yet-unknown partner? He'd put down the worst offenders for his hard limits, but what if they rolled 'oral?' Or some other equally moist activity he couldn't think of just now?

"Welcome to Black Light!"

Cheers rose up from around the club and all eyes and ears went to the night's MC, who had taken the mic.

"I know we're all anxious to get this show on the road," the younger man said, "and—trust me—I can't wait either. This is the fourth annual Valentine Roulette here at Black Light, and it's going to be dirtier, naughtier, and sexier than ever!"

Anson groaned inside. Hoots and applause burst from the crowd. The DJ was introducing someone. Possibly the club owner. There were too many stimuli, and Anson's focus refracted in ten different directions.

This was going to be terrible. He wasn't a people person like Matthew. He didn't make women smile. He made them panic. He'd be too much for the sub they paired him with tonight. Too intense. Too odd. Too severe. Too cold.

'Too Morrow,' as his classmates had taunted him over twenty years ago.

"Thank you all for coming, and let's hear it for DJ Elixxir!" The club owner, Jaxson, had finished his speech and was handing back the mic.

Elixxir began explaining the rules Anson had already seen in the email. Spinning roulette wheels to demonstrate. The Doms would draw numbers for order of spin, they'd each spin for the name of their scene partner, and then their partner would spin for their first kink.

There were prizes for couples who could make it through the whole event, but that was of least importance to Anson. While the membership dues were nothing to sneeze at, he stood alongside this stage to gain something more intangible than a sum of money he could always recoup.

He was out for understanding.

Of himself.

Was this life for him, or was he delusional? Could he master his grab-bag of neuroses for long enough to be the kind of Dom at least *someone* would be interested in playing with? More than once?

*Every*one's safe word tonight would be 'red', Elixxir was saying. How quick would Anson's partner use it? He almost hoped she would. He could go home. Have a free pass from anxiety. At least anxiety about *this*.

As if it wouldn't be enough to have people watching him. Tonight, there'd be even *more* voyeurism—people would be watching so they could vote on scenes. Just what he needed. An attentive audience.

You've been watching people play for months.

But, so what? Just because someone liked to watch, didn't mean they owed it to the world to be an exhibitionist.

Well you're going to be, tonight.

"Alright, everyone, who's ready to get this party started?"

More shouts and applause from all around. The participating Doms for the night began to head up the steps and file onto the stage, and Anson found himself among them as though he were a passenger in a vehicle being driven by someone else. All the lights and colors in the club blared brighter with every step.

The men were lining up to face the crowd, and Elixxir had scooped up a handful of something from a cup. When Anson saw the man held popsicle sticks, he could feel it in his teeth, and the muscles in his chest and upper arms bunched.

No. Absolutely not.

He was going to safe word if they made him touch one of those.

The DJ made his way to the far end of the line and began offering the handful of vile little sticks to each Dom. This had to be the drawing of numbers mentioned in the email. Why? Why did they have to do it this way? Xylophobia was not that uncommon. Just the thought of it. That texture. Anson repressed a shudder. He can't have been the only Dom in four years to have a problem with this.

Closer. Closer the fistful of Nope was coming, and Anson squeezed his right thumb in his left fist as he watched the other men each daring to touch one of the things like it was nothing.

And then Elixxir was in front of him, holding up the remaining four numbered sticks with a charming smile on his face. Anson's eyes darted and his lips went tight.

"This is going to be your number," said the DJ. "Here." He lifted his handful to get Anson to draw a stick.

Now. Figure it out.

"I, uh"—he cleared his throat—"I can't touch that," he said to the poor man who was just trying to do his job. Anson jerked a nod and pointed to the stick fanned out on the far right. "Just—that one. I'll remember my number."

Something twitched amid the man's black brows and he opened his mouth to say something, but then appeared to switch gears. "Okaaay…" He plucked out the stick Anson had pointed to and gave it a look. "Seven," he said, and switched the number marker to his other hand.

"Seven," repeated Anson. "Got it. Thanks."

Prime. Perfect.

Elixxir gave him a confused little nod and moved to the next Dom in line, who of course also had an odd look for Anson before selecting his own number with no issues. The revenue agent let his shoulders drop with his breath. Of all things, they'd had to start with fucking popsicle sticks.

He let his eyes scan out over the top of the crowd now and when he passed by Matthew, the congressman raised his glass. No doubt his friend was rolling in amusement at Anson's expense. He couldn't bring himself to let his focus settle on the group of waiting submissives.

Six men would roll for partners before him, and eight after. The DJ was already calling for the Dom who held 'number one.'

The wheel spun. The marble rolled. A woman peeled away from the group and joined her partner for the night onstage. The marble rolled again, and Elixxir announced the kink. The first couple stepped down to stand just alongside the stage.

Two. Three. Four.

Anson wished he'd brought his water up here.

Five couples, paired.

The cluster of subs was shrinking, along with the line of Doms.

Six.

One thing that scares you.

"Aaand number seven!"

White noise hushed in his ears. A man beside him coughed, and Anson forced that tiny switch inside himself up and on. The emergency switch that let some other part of him work on autopilot when anxiety had the rest of him glitching in place like a worn-out VHS tape.

He arrived beside the wheel on feet that carried him without his own guidance.

"Mister M!"

Elixxir called out his compromise on a nickname for the night as Anson approached. Just like he wasn't able to manage role play, it had felt too odd to invent some moniker for the form he'd filled out. An initial was the most he was willing to work out, for anonymity's sake.

The wheel was already spinning. Elixxir was holding out the marble with raised brows, probably wondering if Anson was going to give him any more trouble like the popsicle sticks. He didn't. His social autopilot took the marble, driving right over his internal hand-wringing by insisting that they were absolutely *not* going to be putting gloves on while standing under a spotlight with a forest of eyes on him.

Before he could think, his hand was releasing the marble into its little track to chase in the opposite direction of moving numbers. He could just hear the hollow circling sound over the music.

The marble lost momentum and skittered among slotted black and red pockets. Bounced. Settled.

He snapped his focus up to the group of women without even looking at the name on the wheel. Without thinking about rubbing his hands with the sanitizer in his pocket after handling that marble so many others had touched.

"Miss Pain!"

Anson blinked. A woman shouldered through from the back of the huddle and watched the placement of her high heels on the steps. She joined him onstage, a fox tail hanging from beneath her short, black dress. From back among the high-tops, Anson heard a familiar whoop.

He made eye contact, reality clamoring in around him, and the woman gave him a nervous smile. Shifted a mess of long hair over a shoulder.

Then her eyes widened.

"I... I just saw you," she said, and her head tilted a degree to one side. "The other day."

A jangle of pieces slapped into place. Ripped jeans. Wild hair. Cell phone.

"You were in the elevator," the woman said, looking even more untamed here, with legs on display and neckline plunging.

Anson's mouth was dry, but there was no point in denying it.

"I was."

"Miss Pain?" Elixxir was waiting with the marble. "Would you like to roll?"

"Um... yes." She spared another glance for Anson before taking the tiny white ball and casting it into the wheel with a loose wrist, in complete contrast to his own stiff tension. The woman stood with her weight on one leg, the lines of her spine, hips, thighs flowing in a beautiful asymmetry. Orchestrated and improvised at once, like one of his trees.

The marble clattered to a stop, and the man with the mic leaned over to see the result.

"And Miss Pain has rolled *latex!*"

She turned back to face him, teeth pulling on her lower lip, and came to his side amid some cheers from the crowd. The kink clearly wasn't among her limits.

"After you," he said, nodding to the stairs. They couldn't stand in the way while eight more couples needed pairing.

Anson followed her offstage to stand near the growing cluster of Roulette partners. Some were already touching and flirting. Others stood with more tension. Fidgeting hands. Dom number eight was at the wheel.

'Miss Pain.' He wouldn't have guessed that from the looks of the woman with whom he'd shared an elevator.

"Don't you think that's a rather on-the-nose nickname for a sub?" he asked as she had zero qualms about standing close enough for her shoulder to nestle nearly under his arm.

His sub for the night grew half a smile that knew more than it let on. "It really is," she said, eyes on the proceedings.

If the woman was on edge, even in the slightest, none of it showed on her face or in her stance. It was as if, from the second Elixxir had called her name, she'd simply integrated the idea of 'Mister M' as her partner into her existence. It was fact, now, for all she was concerned.

At least as far as Anson could tell.

Her hair shifted against the sleeve of his sportcoat, and some scent rolled up to greet him. Citrus. And perhaps a tea of some sort. Anson inhaled.

This was real. This woman was real, and she was just standing there. Expecting to play with him.

In latex.

He hadn't even stopped to consider the kink she'd rolled. Here at Black Light, he'd seen plenty of latex play. Never participated himself, but he'd gleaned at least a working knowledge of the logistics. But the acts his mind already began to pair with it?

You watch too much porn, Morrow.

Those images had the Dom in him twitching to life, but the last time… The last time he'd opened that door and truly stepped inside, apologies had not been enough.

So be a gentleman. Give her an out.

"You can safe word," he said to the top of her head.

She turned light-colored eyes up to him—blue or maybe grey, he couldn't tell under the colored neon—and gave him an unsure look. Hippie as he'd assessed her back in the elevator or no, she had a look of exquisite recklessness about her, somehow fragile and hot-burning, at once.

"You don't have to do this," said Anson. "If you don't want to."

Now her brows knit to full skepticism, though she'd hadn't moved out of contact. Instead, she turned her body to face him. To search his face—a blunt assessment that made his skin feel electric. She squeezed the fingers of her one hand in the other.

"Do *you* want to do this?" she asked.

Anson swallowed.

"Number eleven!" the DJ called out from onstage. The applause sounded faraway.

The first of any sort of worry made a fine line between her brows, and he saw the thing that had him backpedaling. *Does he not want me? Am I not good enough?* The voices of fear began to spread on her features like an infection. He was standing there making her feel the exact thing he'd been dreading all night.

And rather than remove herself from the source of anxiety, like Anson might have, Miss Pain went toward it, chasing after what she wanted, even with insecurity hot on her heels. Her eyes shifted downward, deliberate, and she angled her face with them. Off to one side, baring her neck, pouring it on.

Submissive.

"Sir," she said, "I want what you have."

He could barely hear her over the music and crowd, but the soft voice wrapped around his spine and spun downward to wake up his cock.

Here. In person. Real.

What the fuck are you afraid of, Morrow?

Autopilot Anson had had enough of his anxious bullshit. In what was for him an outrageous move with a stranger, he lifted a bare hand to splay just above her breasts. Her ribs rose and fell when he slid his touch up over her collarbone and let his thumb play in the hollow of her throat. She kept her eyes on the floor.

"You don't know *what* I have, Miss Pain."

Maybe some part of him was still trying to scare her off, but she only arched her neck into his caress.

"Yes, I do," she said. "You have control. Sir."

And if her last word didn't have certain machinery grinding to life inside him...

Anson leaned close, just to be in her space. He let his fingers circle into a grip at the base of her throat. "And you want control, little sub?"

Her shoulders melted forward and he felt her exhale.

"No, Sir. I want *you* to have it."

Her words made a shadow come billowing in over Anson's psyche. A long-awaited eclipse, and he could do whatever he wanted here in the dark. *Be* whoever he wanted. No—be who he *was*.

"Lucky number thirteen. Master R if you'll come spin?"

Anson slipped his hold down to her shoulder and scooped the woman in a rough move, so her back was to his chest. She didn't even flinch, just curved her spine back against him.

Anson Morrow was a Dom. And tonight, Miss Pain was going to submit.

They stood there like that, watching the remaining couples pair off. His thumb was back to drawing circles on her throat while the wheels spun out names and kinks. Glossy black images pulsed in his head, the scent and snap of latex a growing promise. When his dick filled out in response, Anson made sure to shift it against her ass. Whatever this well of confidence was, he was going to drink deep from it before it ran dry.

She pressed back and he felt a hum under his palm at her neck.

Both her hands came up into a gentle hold on his wrist. Not to pull his touch away, but to cling. Oddly intimate for two people who didn't know each other. Chance meetings in elevators notwithstanding.

The stage had emptied out.

"Everyone's paired up," Elixxir announced into the mic, "and you know what that means! It's time to start Valentine Roulette!"

She could safe word if she wanted out.

Anson was ready to play.

CHAPTER 3

VIOLET

*O*ne of the other subs had actually warned her. About this exact guy, right here. And now Violet Payne was standing, ass nestled against his growing hard-on. Man, did she know how to pick 'em.

But you didn't pick him. The wheel picked you.

The sub, Kierra, who'd sort of taken Violet under her mother hen wing over the last few months had looked over a shoulder at the Dom Violet now knew as 'Mister M.'

"And if you get paired with that *one?" She shifted eyes rimmed in smoky shadow back to the straight-postured man standing at one of the high-tops. "And he does anything super weird or creepy? You safe word right out, bitch, and the DMs will have your back."*

"What's wrong with that guy?" she asked, making sure not to look again.

"He just sits there and watches. Every time he comes in. Never buys a drink, just gets water."

Violet snorted. "So it's weird now not to be an alcoholic?"

Kierra made a face. "Just seems like a fuckin' serial killer, to be honest. Too quiet."

She didn't know about any of that, but what Violet *could* tell was that Mister M was definitely not a politician. Or anyone in sales, like her ex. He didn't have that 'shaking hands and kissing babies' field of charisma around him that tried to lure people in. This man had more of a... hmm, not barbed wire... a hi-tech security system of an energy. Warnings for people to stay out unless they had a right to be there. She'd watched him war with accepting her credentials.

Not a serial killer, no. And not a politician. Maybe corporate lawyer.

She smiled into the jungle of neon and clubgoers. The man probably thought Elixxir had called her name out as 'Miss Pain.' It would be fine, for now. He could just go on thinking she'd chosen a ridiculous nickname.

If she were to judge by the firm hold of his forearm across her chest, the play of his thumb at her throat in a way that was already building a hum between her thighs, Mister M was probably not thinking about nicknames.

There were no more couples onstage. Elixxir made a sweeping gesture at the crowd. "Everyone's paired up," he said, voice resonating through the sound system to carry over the din, "and you know what that means! It's time to start Valentine Roulette! It's time to get this party started!"

More applause and cheers, and the music thudded back to a more motivating volume. Not normal dance club loud, but more than it had been during the roulette spins.

Mister M had been Dom Number Seven. Seven was her lucky number.

See? A good sign.

People began to disperse. Roulette Doms and subs moved off to hunt for furniture and gear. Spectators went back to the bar to refresh drinks.

"I see latex isn't among your hard limits," a smooth voice said above her right ear.

Violet turned her body again so she could look up at him. Her Dom for the night was paler than she was, like he didn't get outside much. His hair was either black or the darkest seal brown, and perfectly combed, like a news anchor's. Or a dentist. There were never dentists with crazy hair. His eyes... might be light green? They'd have to move into better lighting for her to be sure. They looked poised to dissect her.

"I've... never tried *latex* before, Sir, but... I don't think it'll be a problem."

If the man had an opinion about this one way or the other, his face didn't show it. Unlike a few minutes ago, when she'd been certain he was looking for ways to bail. God, she couldn't deal with that again. At least not tonight.

She'd put herself entirely up on the block. 'I'll do anything except these four things. Anything you want. Just take me someplace new and not horrible,' was the statement she'd been making by putting her name on that wheel. Black Light vetted these people. There were dungeon monitors everywhere. How bad could it be?

Her new Dom's eye ticked back and forth across her face in some silent assessment. Did the man smile, ever?

Bad. It could be bad.

Whatever he saw, it brought him to some decision. He switched focus to somewhere over her shoulder. Then that same hand that had hypnotized at her throat slid around to the back of her neck. Mister M moved forward, and Violet had to go with him.

"Let's find out," he said, and guided her away from the stage.

Rather than any furniture or play space, he led them to a person. Garreth, one of the monitors, who was already watching them approach.

"We've rolled *latex*," said Mister M as they approached. "Is there somewhere we should go to pick out gear?"

Garreth smiled at her and bobbed a nod to her Dom. "We have some things already set out," he said, "if you'd like to have a look. We have the latex items over here instead of in the costume room."

"We would," said Mister M. "Miss Payne?"

They followed Garreth a short way to a compact metal clothing rack wedged in by the end of the stage near a St. Andrew's cross. Several hangers dripped with glossy latex pieces, most in black, but she could see a flash of purple and red peeking out.

"We have a few different things here," said Garreth, sliding some of the hangers apart while his eyes kept a scan of the club behind them. "Two or three catsuits. Couple hoods. Stockings. Cinchers."

Violet felt herself breathing through her mouth. She'd be *in* some of this gear. Soon.

"You have powder?" her Dom asked.

That was right. She *had* heard you couldn't just pull latex onto bare skin.

Garreth pointed a flat hand away from the stage. "Powders and lubes are on that small table against the back wall. If you need other gear, we have an area set up out in front of the gift area for Roulette participants. It's on the other side of the bar."

She followed the line of his arm and found the table. Jars and bottles of all sizes stood on top in a cluster, along with other low, open containers, full of what, she couldn't see from here. It was a lot. A lot to take in. A lot about to happen with this man she didn't know.

And yet the warmth of his hand at the top of her spine was somehow draining off tension. Making her want to stand up straight.

"Anything else you two need help with so far?" The dungeon monitor made eye contact with her, and Violet shook her head. "Miss Payne."

He wanted verbal. This one was a stickler. "No, Sir. I don't need anything else."

Garreth grunted and pushed away from the clothing rack.

"Are there ballet heels available?" said Mister M.

Violet took a breath at the kind of spectacle he wanted to make of her, but the monitor shook his head. "We'd have to keep too many sizes."

"I thought that might be the case. Thank you, though."

This Dom of hers was polite, if a bit stiff here and there.

"Miss Payne. Mister M," said Garreth. "I'll be nearby if you have any more questions. Need any help."

What kind of help would they need?

'Fuckin' serial killer.'

So dramatic. He can't be that *bad.*

"Thank you again," said Mister M to Garreth, who was already turning to another couple who'd approached looking like they had questions.

"Miss Payne?" Her Dom guided her to the rack, palm gentle. "Would you please find a catsuit that will fit you? If there's more than one, choose one with zipper access. And a cincher. If you would be so kind."

A nervous giggle bubbled out of her throat. She couldn't help it—he sounded so formal.

"Is something funny?"

"No. Sir." Violet bit her lip to make herself stop.

"And yet you're laughing."

She cleared her throat. Her eyes watered. "You're... you're very polite, Sir. Asking me 'would you please' and 'if you'd be so kind.' You know I'm your sub, right?" That last she regretted in an instant. Who *knew* how much sass he would put up with?

His body closed in at her back again, and Violet felt the man's breath on her ear. "I'm quite frequently kind and polite when I ask for things, Miss Payne." That soft hold turned firm, then hard, on the back of her neck. *"The first time."*

Hairs stood up on her arms, and his next words came just above a whisper.

"You're welcome to test what my manners look like when I have to ask a second time," he said.

Nooo thank you. Violet was a lot of things, but a brat wasn't one of them. And the monitors had unnerved her enough about this guy.

"I won't try to make you ask twice, Sir."

"Then pick out your things," he said and let go his hold. "I'm going to go find the rest of what we need, and then I'll meet you right back here. Do not change out of your dress yet, please."

And then the heat of him was gone. Violet turned to see the man slipping away across the club. Her thighs squeezed together.

Fuck me.

She'd applied for Roulette in a burst of desperation. A last-ditch effort to stop wallowing in misery and rip the proverbial bandage off. To pair up with someone wholly new and drown the echoes of mistakes out of her head.

Well, now she was going to drown them in latex. The first of the suits she pushed to the side—it looked cut for a man. Another had legs that looked way too short. This stuff stretched, but not that much. Nerves had her that she wouldn't find what he'd asked for, but a simple black number with a high neck and back zip looked promising. And then there were cinchers and corsets, clipped sideways to hangers. She lifted one upright and turned it over with a critical eye.

Why be nervous? You're getting just what you asked for.

And she was. This Mister M was new as fuck. Nothing like her ex, nothing like anyone she'd played with, so far.

Violet pulled a cincher to go with her catsuit. It had buckles, a few D-rings, and was black like the suit. She'd seen latex scenes, but never up close. The scent of the material wasn't quite overpowering, but she couldn't deny the dirty doctor vibes it sent crawling over her skin. Thank god she didn't have a latex allergy.

Just as she turned from the rack, her Dom was moving back into view. Something dark dangled from his left hand. In his right, he brought a low, wooden stool. Instead of heading straight for her, he stepped up onto the raised area of the floor that highlighted a cluster of dungeon furniture and set the stool down. Next to a pillory.

Her jaw went slack.

Mister M laid his handful down atop the stool and, at the very least among the pile, she could make out the tails of a flogger dangling. He straightened and found her. Headed in her direction.

Violet's night was about to go from zero to sixty real quick.

"You've found something that will work, Miss Payne?" he asked on approach.

God, this was happening. A cocktail of fear and excitement had her feeling her pulse in strange places: her fingertips. Her lower lip. "I think so, Sir," she said, the catsuit feeling heavy draped over her arm. "We'll see when I try to put it on."

He grunted. "Good." And moved past her to the rack again. Began sliding hangers.

Didn't I just...

When he turned back to face her, it was with a shiny black hood in hand. Some feeling of compression circled her ribs. This guy was going to shrink-wrap her like a... like a piece of meat. She'd never really given latex a second thought; it hadn't been on her ex's agenda, and before that? Nothing she'd tried had been so involved.

But there it was. That awareness between her thighs.

Interest.

Her body agreeing, saying, *Let's see what happens. If he takes you there.*

The hood went on the stool with the rest of his gear, and then an intense amount of focus centered back on her. Violet's feet moved without thought, bringing her to stand in front of the man like he was some goddamn sorcerer.

No. *Dom.* He wasn't loud or verbose, but he didn't need to be. Not like fucking *Brian.* This one had her pulled in like a magnet with no more than an expectant look.

"I would like you to set your shoes aside, Miss Payne."

She pushed them off with her feet, eyes on his, and nudged the patent heels aside.

"Neatly." His tone dipped into a key of warning, and Violet dropped, knees together, to find and straighten her shoes. She placed them upright, as if on display for sale, at one of the wooden legs of the pillory, before standing again.

"Does your dress come off over your shoulders?"

Happening.

"Yes, Sir."

"Then take it off that way, please."

Her heart thumped. A few people milling slowed to watch as she reached with one hand to take down the opposite shoulder of her dress. She'd normally pull it from the bottom over her head, but the fine knit stretched, and this way woul—

"Eyes up here."

This way would take more time.

His entire pale green focus was on the reveal. She watched him, as he'd said, instead of the distracting crowd. Saw his eyes flit back and forth while she shrugged out of the tiny sleeves. Violet could all but feel his gaze tracing the lines of black against her skin where her bra cupped and strapped its way around.

And no panties. They wouldn't have worked with her fox tail, so as soon as she hooked her thumbs in at both sides of her waist and shifted first one hip, then the other, past the bunched fabric, Mister M —and everyone else—was going to see everything.

You've been naked here before. Big deal.

She bent to step out of the dress. Stood to take it over where her shoes sat.

"Stop."

Violet blinked at him; dress gathered in a fist.

Her Dom stepped forward with a critical eye, and she followed his gaze to her tattoo. A cherry tree bonsai in full bloom wrapped around her right side, from hip to just under her breast, petals, ink on skin, trailing off in imaginary breeze along her ribs and belly.

He lifted a hand. Traced out a line along the artwork of trunk and branches with the barest tip of a finger. She watched his lips move, as though he said something to himself, but no sound came out, and something in the whisper of a touch had her close to shivering.

Not her ass, not her pussy. This was what the man had chosen to focus on the minute she got naked. The hand touching her was pale. Neatly-manicured. He definitely worked in an office.

He definitely was stepping around behind her.

Violet's arms pebbled in gooseflesh when fingers brushed the mass of her hair off her neck. He shifted it over her left shoulder, and then small tugs began at the back of her bra.

It went neat and quick. One second there was tension under her breasts, the next: none. He slid the straps down her shoulders, and she could feel the occasional brush of his clothing, a breath-quickening contrast to her own nudity.

Mister M circled her again, and his eyes added everything new he saw to whatever catalog he appeared to be making in his head. Violet's nipples tightened down to points, the stainless hoop she had in the right one gleaming in the brighter light above the dungeon furniture. He handed over her bra.

"On the stool, please."

He meant the clothes, not her, and Violet went, folding her dress in a tidy square with his admonishment about the shoes fresh in mind. She hadn't been kidding about not trying to make him ask twice.

In putting her dress and bra aside, she saw the rest of what he'd laid out on the stool. Violet swallowed. Had he wanted her to see?

When she stood and turned back, the man was already folding his jacket. Draping it over one of the rungs of the stool, now that they'd covered the seat in gear. He unbuttoned his cuffs in that mesmerizing way and folded his sleeves back—the most meticulous she'd ever seen —to his elbows. Mister M had a fit look to him; the shift of his charcoal shirt over shoulders and chest had her biting her lip. Wishing he'd untuck it. Let her work apart those buttons.

Okay, this is working for me. Yeah.

He was tugging something black out of a pants pocket. Moving close to her again.

"Why the plug?"

Gloves. He'd brought gloves out of his pocket, and was stretching them over his hands, one at a time, the thin, rubbery noises going straight to her pussy for no good reason. Violet inhaled.

Who is this guy?

"Miss Payne?"

The plug. Right. She could feel the furry tail brushing the backs of her thighs.

"I thought"—she cleared her throat and stood straighter—"I thought it would help me tonight. Sir."

"Oh? And how's that?" He snapped the second glove in place at his wrist, but the whole thing felt medical rather than sinister. His question curious instead of mocking.

"It's... it feels like a costume, Sir. Or a mask." He was stepping around her again, and her explanations felt inadequate. "It's like when I wear it... my head is in a different place. Like I get to be who I want to be. I calm down. I'm more confident. I needed that tonight."

She trailed off with a nervous laugh and felt the fox tail move. He was lifting it back there. Not pulling, but subtle movements like he was looking it over. It was still enough to nudge the stainless little bulb she had sucked up between her cheeks. Her thighs shifted, slick now where they met. He dropped the tail, and she had no sense of his reaction to what she'd told him.

"Did you want me to take it out, Sir?"

Gloved fingers traced her spine at her lower back before he came around from behind her. His face was a series of coldly handsome angles, but none of them screamed disapproval.

"For now," he said. "Clean it off and give it to me. There are wipes over there on the table." He nodded to the back wall, where the DM had pointed out lubes and powders. And then he stood there, fingers warm under nitrile to take hold of her chin and watch her face twitch while she pulled the plug past her body's tight seal.

With the first hint of a smile, at the very corner of his mouth, her Dom let her go to do as he'd said. She did and returned, and he took the tail from her and stuck the stainless end in a pocket. The tail hung out of his slacks like some weird, smuggled hunting trophy.

And now she was really naked.

No more superhero cape. No more fox tail to make her feel like, *Yeah, that's right. I'm a kinky bitch. I can take anything you can dish out, Mister.*

Now she was just Violet, and this stranger, with his gloves, looked like he was seeing through to her every worry and flaw. He was going to turn them each over with his careful fingers and want more information for his records.

They hadn't even gotten to the latex, yet.

"Why did you sign up for this, Miss Payne?"

Her eyes snapped to his. He wanted explanations?

Violet tried not to squirm. "I was… looking to play with someone new, Sir."

"Miss Payne." God, his eyes were a trap. "You did not need to offer yourself up on that roulette wheel to play with someone new." There was no avoiding anything under that stare; it was like a fishbowl. No walls to hide behind and no corners.

"Sir?" Her voice came out much higher than she would have liked.

"You are a well-behaved sub—so far—and you're almost too beautiful to be here." Heat crept onto her face, but he continued as if ticking items off a list. "Any available Dom you asked would play with you. So why the need to sign up."

It wasn't even a question, because answering wasn't an option. Not in response to *that* voice. Her ribs tried to squeeze in and compress her lungs.

"Because I can't trust myself," she said. "To choose anymore. To choose a partner."

The man grew a considering look. The slightest tilt of his head. He moved close to slip a hand up under her breast. To test and squeeze the small mound there. To pinch a nipple—but careful, experimental, not cruel—and watch her reaction.

"Why can't you trust yourself?"

His exploratory touch moved to her arm. He picked up her hand, wildly intimate, and turned it over, looking at what, she didn't know. He didn't seem like the sort of guy who was into palm reading.

"I thought I could in the past, Sir," Violet said, as he brought a knuckle to tip her chin up. "And it turned out I was wrong."

Those eyes weighed every part of her answer. Fingers tilted her face to one side and then the other. A gloved thumb pulled at her lower lip, and Violet had never felt so under a microscope. And yet it wasn't terrible, but the reasons why were only still trying to coalesce into something she could make sense of.

"What did you put down for limits tonight?"

The question spun her. "Um ..." How was he chasing every last thought from her brain? "Needles?" Why did it come out like that? Was she no longer sure?

"Mm?" He prompted her, brows up, while making the choice to examine her piercing. The metal tugged at her nipple and, with his gloved fingers moving the jewelry, it sent her back to the piercing parlor when she'd had it done.

Violet chewed the inside of her lip to summon her other limits. "Age play, Sir." The man grunted along with a single nod, as though he approved. "Fisting. Humiliation."

"I see pain isn't on the list." He brought the ring away from her breast until the nipple stretched with it. Until she inhaled through her nose. He let go and she wanted to scream. Not at any hurt—he'd

124

barely started pulling—but at not knowing how to handle a Dom like this.

Brian would have had her on her knees already, crawling. Making a big scene. How was she supposed to just stand here, unmoving, and deal with this quiet, concentrated force of a man?

"Why not humiliation?"

It was getting a little scary how he seemed to zero in on the heart of her issues with every new question. Her features tightened. "My last Dom… liked it."

"And?" He was circling again. Probably enjoyed the way it put her on edge. She fussed with her fingers at her sides.

"He liked to degrade me," she said. "That was his thing. In front of others. Have them take part." Some of it had happened right here in this club. "It was more about his ego than us having fun. Together. Sir."

The man gave a short *humph* at her back. "Sloppy," he said, and Violet felt some thrill to hear even the one-word judgment of her ex.

He was pushing her hair over her shoulder again to bare her back. Asking his questions in a low voice. It was clearer by the minute this man didn't give one shit about the night's competition. He wasn't making their conversation loud, so an audience could hear. His tone was personal, his entire focus on her, as though there were no other people in the noisy, crowded space.

Gloved fingertips traced out the angles of her shoulder blades, both at once in symmetrical precision. She felt like he was marking her up for a surgery.

"And where is this unobservant Dom of yours now?" he asked.

"Unobservant? Sir?"

"If he'd been paying even half the attention he should have been to your reactions," he said, voice coming from right above her ear, "he would have seen right away you're not here to be part of a show. So." Thumbs pressed in above her tailbone. "Where is he?"

She'd been all night wanting to forget, but with that voice melting her now, saying every unnerving true thing, Violet wanted to curl back against his chest. She didn't, because he hadn't told her to do any such thing but, plied this way, she had no problem throwing Brian under the fucking bus.

"I found out he was married," she said. "And his wife didn't know about me. That was the end of it. I was done."

"Hmm. So you didn't want to be humiliated. And you didn't want to be shared. But neither of those things caused you to end it."

Who are you, my fucking therapist?

"That's why I can't trust myself, Sir."

Another considering hum, but then his warmth left her back. Mister M had stepped away to the table of lubes.

She'd tried talking to Brian about not wanting to be shared. Not wanting to hear the cruel words from him or anyone else. But the cocky pharmaceutical rep had brushed her complaints off as just another stiff place she needed to stretch. Her boundaries had been easy to smudge, and she'd wanted approval so bad she'd never mustered the courage to safe word when she should have. Finding out about his wife had just been a convenient excuse.

And now he'd gone somewhere else to play, but the entire year's membership he'd bought her in advance still had several months on it. Every time she showed up, Violet half expected someone on staff to tell her the membership had been cancelled, but it never happened. Probably covering his own ass: trying not to rock the boat with someone who could rat him out to his wife. Destroy his career.

Violet didn't care about his career. She just wanted to start over. And she had zero problem using what was left of that asshole's membership money to do it.

Mister M returned with a small container in hand and stood in front of her. "We can't play these games without honesty, can we, Miss Payne."

This man was relentless.

"No, Sir."

"That's right," he said, "which is why I need you to be honest tonight. With me. With yourself."

Violet swallowed. There might have been no one else in the club, the way he spoke to her.

"Don't wait," he went on. "If you need to safe word. I've heard latex makes some people claustrophobic." He raised brows as though she might pipe up about the fear, but that wasn't one of her problems. When she said nothing, Mister M continued.

"Don't keep going because you're trying to impress me or anyone else watching," he said. "Or because you're trying to win the month of membership. You want a free month—I'll pay for it. I just need you to be clear if I take you too far. Understood?"

Holy hell, he'd thrown a lot at her. But it all boiled down to her one trouble area: recognizing her limits. And honesty.

Well you're here to start over, so...

"I understand, Sir."

Now don't fuck it up.

"Very good, Miss Payne." He nodded and offered her the container he had in his hand. "Now cover yourself in powder, or we'll never get you into this suit."

He was right. If they took any longer, a DM would probably come and disqualify them from the event. She took the powder from him and began squeezing it out in little puffs into her palm. Smoothing it over calves, shins, thighs. Higher, she worked, getting her stomach, her breasts, her butt. Mister M stood there holding the catsuit while she finished her arms and shoulders. The upper part of her back probably didn't matter—the suit had a zipper up to the high neck, and she wouldn't have to force herself into that part like she would a sleeve or leg.

Her Dom handed over the oil-slick in clothing form, zipper already undone to the lower back, and Violet leaned a palm on the pillory for balance. Then she realized her mistake—there was no way she was going to stand on one leg, even leaning on the wood, and wrangle herself into latex without falling on her ass.

Mister M saw it, too, because he was transferring equipment from the top of the stool to the floor.

"Thank you, Sir," she said as she sat and tried again.

The latex was stiffer than she'd imagined. It took effort to pull past a foot, and then she had to spend time smoothing out creases, shimmying it back down, pulling up and smoothing again. With one leg in place to the knee, she started work on the second. This suit didn't have gloves or feet to it like some others she'd seen, which probably gave it just a little more wiggle room for people of different heights. Not much, but some.

For whatever reason, getting the top part of the legs up her thighs wasn't nearly as time-consuming, though the benefits of the powder were already making themselves clear. She had to stand and wriggle the whole thing past her asscheeks after that and, once it was in place to the waist, the first half of the suit felt like a really aggressive pair of tights. If tights were made out of a thick party balloon.

The crotch of it was already snug up against her bare lips, and Violet didn't miss the way the back zip travelled all the way under to end above her mound in front. In fact, there was a second pull for opening the suit just there.

The arms were the last part she could take care of herself, and they went quicker than the legs. At the end, she scooped her hair off her back, and her Dom was stepping in without her having to ask to slide the zipper up to the top of the high neck. As it sealed closed, Violet stood up straight.

She couldn't help it. Everything now felt like a bra. Hoisting. Compressing. Even her tits stood up on their own; modest half-rounds, suspended in black gloss. She could make out the contour of her nipple ring on the one side, where the material smoothed out everything but the metal.

Mister M moved back to the stool and dipped down to grab something. He turned back, spreading open the cincher, and Violet let the prickles of arousal radiate from just under that zipper between her legs. The man didn't wait but came around behind to wrap the thing in place and start tightening down buckles.

"This suit fits you well, Miss Payne," he said while fitting the cincher down with small jerks.

"Thank you, Sir." Her words were almost inaudible over the music and crowd. After a few more tugs, he made some satisfied grunt, and then he was pulling her hair into his hands.

Violet braced for him to get a fistful. For him to yank her head back or pull her off her center of gravity and into some dominant, growled question or promise, but instead there were intricate motions at the back of her neck. Nitrile gloves brushing her nape.

The man was braiding her hair.

There were little tugs at the bottom of her scalp as he went, and it made her not know what to do with herself. Like she had as a child, she had to just stand there, useless, and wait for it to be done. Where had he even learned how?

"Do you know why I'm doing this?" he asked.

She blinked. "No, Sir?"

An amused *huff* of air hit the back of her neck. "Because you have way too much hair, Miss Payne. It'll never fit inside the hood. But I don't want it all over the place."

Violet couldn't help a smile at this. She *did* have a ton of hair, and it *always* got into everything. And she was never cutting it off, either. She could just get old and look like a witch.

"Hold this." He handed her the end of the braid when he finished and returned to reach for something under the stool. She'd already had a glimpse of what he came back with, and it had made her shiver the first time: a clothespin. There had been several. He folded the loose end of her braid in a loop and clamped it down with the little wood peg, which was good enough, because she hadn't brought a hair tie.

It was when he brought over the hood that her breaths began to deepen, and the cincher exaggerated the feeling.

"I'll help you zip," he said, and handed her latex.

As she got the halves of it spread apart, Violet knew at least some relief. It wasn't any of those hardcore styles that had a respirator built in, or the creepy condom-like mouth insert. This one was just a simple head-covering with wide eye and mouth holes, though she did take note of the attached blindfold dangling by one of its undone buckles.

Well. Here we go.

She brought the thing up and over the crown of her head. There was some molding to the structure of it, and it took a few tugs to position the nose—which also had two breathing holes, thank goodness—where it belonged, but that seemed to align everything else. Her eyes and mouth were free, but damn if the rest of her face didn't feel like she'd stretched a rubber glove over it.

"Um, it's on, Sir."

At the back of her head, Mister M began tucking the open sides of the hood together. Shoving strands of her hair underneath. Then the careful draw of tiny teeth down the back of her head, and the whole thing tightened like a second skin. He did some final straightening work where the neck of the thing overlapped the catsuit, and then Violet stood there, encased from top to bottom in latex.

It was almost as good as the fox tail, as far as costumes went. She wasn't used to it, but it did make her feel like someone else. Someone who was up for this tonight.

"If you'll put your shoes back on please," he directed.

The heels stood at the base of a pillory leg where she'd left them, and Violet slipped the pair back on. She was a few inches taller in an instant, but not quite as tall as her Dom.

The man paced a slow path around her, inspecting. He stuffed a finger between the top of the cincher and her ribs, to check the fit. To trace the zippers down the back of her skull and along her spine, stopping for the first time to palm a handful of her ass, fingertips hooking way into the cleft to smash the latex between her lips. And then his hand left to come back in a swift smack to her cheek. Violet sucked in a breath.

When he came to face her again, the Dom took the time to smooth out some creases at her shoulders. To trace the hood's opening around her mouth with a fingertip. His eyes flicked from one area to another, meticulous. There was something about the combination of boldness and unfamiliarity: as though he wanted something but wasn't entirely sure how to go about getting it.

"I can see the appeal of this," he said, almost to himself. "One last thing."

So can I.

But it wasn't necessarily the latex. It was more his attention. She was the entire focus, and that focus was intense.

Mister M moved over to the pillory and began unscrewing some hardware where the restraint plank met one of the legs. She wasn't sure what he was doing until one entire end of the crosspiece shifted down over a foot. He made a similar adjustment on the opposite side, and Violet couldn't help the widening of her eyes.

He was undoing a latch on the left side of the plank. Parting it like a huge jaw on a hinge at the other end to open the neck and wrist holes. Where she'd thought he might be restraining her in the thing in a more-or-less standing position, now she saw he'd have her bent over at the waist, torso nearly parallel to the floor. It would take way more effort to keep her feet under her.

"Miss Payne?"

The Dom turned in her direction and made a sweeping gesture with an arm, as though he were unveiling a prize on a game show. Who the winner was remained to be seen. There was nothing to do but go where he wanted, the rope of her new braid and its clothespin tapping her on the ass as she went.

'Inviting' was the wrong word for the open restraint plank, but she did see now that someone had engineered in some leather-covered padding on the inner circumferences of the holes. At least the edges of the wood wouldn't be bruising visible lines into her body. She had to go to work on Monday.

Violet exhaled and set her wrists into the cutouts. Leaned—*allll* the way down— and placed her neck in the center.

"Will you be able to keep your footing at this level, Miss Payne?"

"I think so, Sir." Maybe. Hell, she'd try.

"Perfect." He moved around to the side of the pillory where her head stuck out, and she heard metal hardware clink. And then wood clacked on wood, dull but definite, and the opposite halves of the leather pads closed around her wrists and neck.

Your safe word is 'red', tonight. Not the usual.

Which was fine, because this probably wasn't a guy she could tell her normal safe word was 'Pisces.'

The latches snapped into place off to her left, and then Mister M was squatting on his heels in front of her face. She lifted her head as much as she could to look at him.

"Are you afraid of the dark, Miss Payne?"

They were in a room full of neon. "No, Sir?"

His hand came up to catch hold of something near her face. She'd forgotten about the fucking blindfold.

"A shame." Latex swung over her face.

Lights out.

"Still," he said, working the buckle at her right temple, "I want you to tune this room out. Focus on what you feel."

What she felt was knuckles sliding over her latex-covered jaw. The blood rushing in her ears when she couldn't see *anything* anymore, not even a hint of light, because latex-on-latex made a perfect seal.

And now she stood there—leaned there?—trying to keep her forward weight on her wrists and not her throat, her feet planted at least shoulder-width apart, because straight legs together seemed like an unsteady choice. The barrier of the hood over her ears muffled the din of the club somewhat, but not so much that she couldn't hear sounds nearby. And the smell of it: medical and a little creepy, just like those gloves he'd put on.

Yeah, but who knew you'd like it?

She *did* feel everything now, the first thing being one of those same gloved hands trailing down her spine. God, what did she look like back there? Glossy and propped up for use. His touch dipped under her ribs to smooth over the suspended package of her breasts; to knead and circle a thumb around a tightening areola. Her body's reaction spread, and it was as if he knew it, because his palms began to migrate.

The attention returned to her ass, both hands palming and massaging cheeks now. She could feel the vibrations of his steps on the raised platform telling her he'd stepped directly behind her. All she could do was maintain the posture, presenting herself like a cat in heat while he cupped and squeezed, separated the globes of her buttocks with thumbs until the zipper sank way down into her crack. While his splayed fingers slipped down the backs of her thighs and her skin prickled all over at the unexpected warmth of him through the material.

An actual moan came out of her when the man bent over her back to reach around and claim handfuls of both tits—sure, the attention to her latex-coated breasts was novel and exciting, but it was more the obvious press of trousered erection he wanted her to feel lining up along the cleft of her body.

There was a fucking condom on that stool. You saw it.

And all these people were watching.

No. Don't do that. That's not what he said.

Violet screwed her nagging thoughts down tight and tried to focus on what she was feeling, like her Dom had told her to do.

There were fingers sliding over her mound. The latex was warming to her skin, and he massaged in slow circles until she felt the rubbery material go smearing against her pussy, her own arousal lubricating the movements.

And then she felt him tug at the zipper pull.

Cool air painted a widening line between her legs as he revealed humid flesh. She'd already been stark naked for the man, but not while bent over. Not splayed like a damn doctor visit. He unzipped the suit all the way to the crack of her ass, and somehow it made her feel more exposed than just standing around with her clothes completely off. All the focus was *right there*, a spotlight on her humming cunt, saying, 'Everyone look. *Look at this dirty girl right here. Look how wet she is for this stranger.*'

At the barest touch of gloved fingers to her exposed flesh, a shudder of breath left her throat.

Forked digits traced the swell of her lips, and Violet tried to keep her knees locked. It was the lightest touch, like the guy made watches in his free time, or repaired the wings on bumblebees, or something. By the time he brought a single fingertip to pet the peaking ruffle of her inner lips, her guts had tensed to the point that a begging whine squeezed out through her teeth.

The fingers burrowed, one-two, her wet center swallowing him up at the barest push.

"Sir!"

It wasn't a complaint. Violet tried to keep her knees locked, and some clubgoer off to her left called out a low, masculine, "Yeeaah."

Watching. They're watching.

He began to explore. To twist the fingers in and out, nitrile gliding smooth along her walls, as though he were prepping her. Stretching her. The medical exam feel of it was off the charts, but as her wrists jerked, involuntary, against the restraint plank, Violet wallowed in what it really was.

This man had her locked into place. He could stuff whatever he wanted into her pussy right now, unless she decided to scream out 'red.' His fingers felt way too good for that, though. Violet bit her lower lip and let her spine bow, tilting her hips up, shameless.

He pulled out to rub circles around her clit, and the fucking pillory wouldn't let her back up onto his hand any further! Even in heels, she stood on tiptoe so she could please—please!—get more of it, but her Dom for the night only gave her just enough to make her strain backwards.

When he lifted his touch away, Violet was panting. The cincher made her feel every breath, and her head turned at the sound of his steps traveling. His footfalls made a complete circle around her, with a slight pause where she remembered the stool standing, off to her left.

Something smooth brushed over her pussy that was not his fingertips. A light touch. Not a heavy object. It gave against her body, rather than the other way around, like a heavy fabric.

Like leather.

There had been a flogger on the stool. The wide falls caressed her bare flesh now, almost as gentle as the first touch of his hand. Violet's thighs flexed.

Her Dom introduced the leather to first one of her upturned cheeks, and then the other, a casual *fwap* against muscle, nothing serious yet. Still, her breath came through her mouth.

And then, the first real kiss of the instrument.

He didn't start with anything vicious. Almost a lazy-feeling stroke to her right cheek. The impact told her this flogger was more 'thud' than 'sting', though with the latex intervening, her judgment of that second one might be clouded. A matching stroke landed on the opposite side and, from the placement, Violet guessed he had to be standing square behind her.

She exhaled. He kept the falls coming, alternating sides in such a symmetrical way it made her wish she was also in the audience so she could watch his technique. He wasn't ramping up the intensity yet, but with the steady rhythm, her backside was already warming, even inside the catsuit.

A stroke right up the middle had her sucking in air. It wasn't real pain, yet, she'd just been falling into the pattern. Relaxing into what he gave her, when—*swap!*—the falls met her exposed lips.

Now he was warming her there. The slaps kept coming, not too heavy, but one immediately following the last, until her pussy was humming, and her hands balled into fists on the other side of the plank.

Violet somehow both jerked in her restraints and melted at the same time when the leather ceased, and his fingers returned. They dipped and she felt puffy around him. Heated.

"Wet," he said, and slipped two gloved fingers inside. He explored her with a different kind of stroke, and Violet could feel a thumb and pinky splayed on either side of her ass. She pushed herself against him as much as the pillory allowed, but he took his fingers back anyway.

That slick touch found her clit, instead.

"Nnnh! Sir!"

God they would see a slut, straining backward. Aching for the way he was smearing his fingertips in circles, enflaming her nerves. An eyeless thing; a glossy, woman-shaped sex toy that made so many noises.

Easy. Easy. Doesn't matter what they see.

The sticky dessert of his touch went away too soon, though. The flogger came back, and it was time to take her medicine again. Mister M was being more serious, now. She didn't get a sense of a spray of individual falls meeting her ass, anymore—the strokes had become solid, singular impacts, back to back to back, and they were starting to make her skin smart.

And during a normal flogging? With a bare ass in the air? The cheeks could rest and cool between impact. Not under latex. Oh, no. The material clung and shifted over heating skin, a constant reminder of the way he was lighting her up like a Christmas tree.

Except the one part of her that *wasn't* under latex, just now.

One of the new, firmer strokes snapped straight over her mound, and Violet *yipped* in surprise. Another one came, and another, and she found she could absolutely stand on her toes, even in spike heels. Just when she started to squirm under the blows, his fingers took over again.

Her breath could not keep up with what he was doing. Fingertips curved toward the floor and began to plunge in and out, a thumb to circle with no mercy at her clit. Another hand palmed one of her buzzing cheeks to keep her spread, and the back of Violet's head rocked from side to side, blind against the restraint plank while he worked her.

A stranger's voice hooted from off to the left, and her Dom wouldn't be able to know her whimper was both for what he was doing, and for the bitter *zing* of fear wiggling down her back.

It felt so good. So *good*, but oh God, these *people*. They were all around. Fucking watching. Sneering, probably, at how pathetic she was. Just whoring herself for some strange man while h—

"Fuck!"

Falls replaced fingers, the strongest blow yet, right across her singing cunt. It was enough, for a moment, to snap her out of her bullshit. All that was Brian in her head, and he wasn't here. It was Mister M laying the leather down on her ass, now. Mister M making her grind her teeth, because he'd stopped playing and started making her jump.

Now, she was letting out an audible grunt with every stroke. He was not *even* fucking kidding, and Violet's fingers alternated splaying and making fists. Her knees worked at staying locked while the rhythm slowed, and each pass of the flogger became more intense. By the time he switched to fingers again, a ragged cry left her throat.

He said something back there, but it was too low with the noise from the club and the latex to understand more than a murmur. How many now? Two? Three fingers worked her, and Violet's moan was for too many things.

His knuckles ground against swollen lips, and her entire ass was humming from the flogger, but there were voices—not his— approaching the stage. He crooked those fingers inside her, and Violet wanted to stamp a foot.

Male laughter—not his—bubbling up from nearby.

Watching you. No. No!

Her Dom's palm on her tailbone, holding her in place, while his other hand made her toes curl.

"Sir! Please!"

Footsteps—not his—mounting the stage. A new pair of voices bouncing above her.

Violet whipped her head back and forth, blind and scrambling.

No.

Where were they? Coming up here?

He filled her pussy with fingers, and it felt like another restraint.

Another trap.

Footsteps. Voices.

Not again! No!

"Yellow, Sir."

It came out such a pitiful, low whine.

"Mm?" Fingers churned between her legs.

"Yellow, *fucking* YELLOW!"

CHAPTER 4

VIOLET

She was panting when the words burst out of her, full volume, in a panic at not being heard. Her body clamped down, ready to buck off his touch, but now there was nothing there.

"Is everything alright, Miss Payne?" His voice was near her head, now, as though he bent down.

"I said I didn't want to be fucking shared!"

Violet yanked her wrists against the plank, tears welling hot against the back of the blindfold.

Just safe word. You're a mess. You can't handle this.

She bit into her lower lip, regret for the scene she was making instant.

Metal clattered in a growing bubble of quiet, and there was nothing pressing into the back of her skull, either. A hand was holding hers, lifting. Guiding her to stand. Fingers moved quick at her temple, picking apart a buckle, peeling back latex.

Violet cringed and blinked into the bright lights above the pillory, unsteady on her feet as Mister M came into view.

"Have a seat, Miss Payne."

She scanned the jumble of people and lights, her world nearly upside down as he guided her to sit on the stool. Her entire outfit creaked on the way down, and the man came down with her to take a knee. Just to the side of the platform, Garreth hovered, eyes hard on her and her Dom.

The fuck is happening?

Her knees came together, ankles wide apart, arms crossing over her chest to hug herself. She turned the heat of her face from the watching club members. Mister M touched fingertips to the top of her foot, just where the latex ended and skin peeked out.

"Miss Payne, why do you believe I intended to share you?" His voice was oh-so-calm and rational. Violet wanted to kick him.

"I heard footsteps." She frowned, hating the way her eyes stung. "On the stage. They were right on top of us."

His brow furrowed, assimilating information. "Do you see that couple over there?" The Dom angled his head rather than point, and Violet followed his line of sight. There was a man and a collared woman in close conversation near the stage, her eyes down and his fingers tracing out a line on her collarbone.

Violet nodded, blinking wetness she didn't want to swipe away with a hand and get mascara everywhere. She inhaled, working to slow her heart, just sitting on the dumb stool with her pussy weirdly out while she tried not to melt down in front of her Dom.

"They stepped up past us," he said, way too reasonable, "to get something from the lube table, and then they left."

God, I'm so stupid.

She was going to start crying all over again. *Fuck.*

"Do you think I would ask anyone to share you," he went on, trying to duck his head to meet her lowered eyes, "when you just got done telling me you didn't like that?"

Violet floundered. Yes. Yes, she *had* thought that. Brian would have fucking done it. He'd pulled a blindfold off her one time only for her to find a cock—not his—in a jacking fist inches from her face, and seconds later a stranger's cum was splattering her shocked open mouth.

It had been their biggest blowout, and he'd acted like she was being so dramatic to have reacted in any way other than arousal.

And this was why she couldn't trust herself. She hadn't chosen wisely with Brian; who was to say she'd be more perceptive with her next choice? Everyone had the potential to be a self-centered douchebag.

She sniffled and wished there were tissues nearby. Mister M knelt there, green eyes sincere and waiting.

He's not like Brian. Not at all.

The man reached up to tug her wrist out of her armpit. He took her hand, gloved thumb pressed gently just above her bare knuckles, fingertips nested in her palm. It was too much. Over the top. Kierra had acted like this guy was a psycho, but so far he was the only one behaving like he gave a shit. Like he wanted to examine every single part of her with the utmost care and make sure each was polished to a shine and working in fluid motion with all the others, zero friction if he could help it.

"Do you want to stop?" he asked. "Altogether?"

His voice was quiet, but it parted the noise of the club like a blade through damp sand. His focus separated her from everything that tried to crowd. To oppress. Her shoulders fell as just the hold of his hand and his patient eyes sheared away tension.

"No, Sir."

A squeeze of thumb and fingers came with a small nod. "Okay," he said. "And how were you with the flogger? Was that a yellow, as well?"

Violet's cheeks flushed. He'd had her so close until those people had walked by and her paranoia had exploded.

"That was... that was bright green. Sir."

Her Dom rewarded her with his first full smile, and she felt her knees begin to fall apart. "I've never flogged anyone in latex before," he said, stroking his other hand up the back of her calf. "I have no idea how red your ass is getting."

The laugh he pulled out of her was weak, but recovering. Her backside definitely *felt* pink.

"Would you like to get back in this pillory and bend over for me again?"

Heat flared where the catsuit gaped open between her thighs. This was the same voice in which he'd declared her 'wet.' Asked her if she was afraid of the dark. His Dom voice was smooth and dark as limo glass. Her response fluttered like her pulse.

"Yes, Sir."

His hold on her hand tightened. "Good." The man lifted her wrist like he might kiss it, but stopped just short of contact to inhale, a long drag as though she were perfume, and then rose to his feet. She stood with him and, from the corner of her eye, saw Garreth backing off.

Again, Mister M guided her into the restraint of the wood. Latched it back in place. Again, an eye of latex framed her naked pussy for an audience, but this time the worry about it didn't hang from her like a weight.

He wasn't going to do that to her. It was just them, dancing this dance under a little spotlight. All the others were so many swirling leaves, like the parts of her tattoo that swept down her belly. They were present, but no longer a part of what was important.

Her Dom came to stand near her face. "No blindfold this time," he said, running a knuckle down the latex bridge of her nose.

"I'm okay, Sir," she said to his belt buckle. "I just panicked that first time."

"Well I'm going to be the judge of what you can handle right now," he said, "and I'd rather not risk it. We're going to do something else."

Why did words as vague as 'something else' make her nipples tighten?

He stepped to the left for a few seconds, and then his black slacks came back into view. Leather and metal dangled from one hand.

"Have you worn a gag before, Miss Payne?"

Could the people watching see her getting wet? Violet swallowed. "Yes, but ..."

"But?"

"Only a ball gag, Sir."

"Is there a problem with a ring, Miss Payne?" He ran the bit through his fingers. She knew what ring gags were for, and it made her want to press her thighs together.

"No, Sir."

"Good," he said. "Open."

Violet obeyed, and he stepped close to pry her jaw wide and to fit the circle of stainless steel behind her teeth. She could feel the heat of him, standing near as he worked the buckle at the nape of her neck.

The latex squeaked in little creases where he snugged the strap of leather down.

"Do you know why I've chosen a ring and not a ball?" he asked.

Was this a trick question? She shook her head and made an 'uh-uh' noise like she was at the fucking dentist's now. Her Dom squatted on his heels again to lift her chin with his touch and take hold of her eyes.

"Because I'm not trying to prevent you from making noise, Miss Payne." Holy hell, she was ready to let him do whatever the fuck he wanted. *Look at those eyes. So goddamn serious.*

"You can make any noise you need," he went on. "What I'm trying to prevent"—he took a firm hold of her chin—"is you having any control over what goes into and out of your mouth." His grip shifted and two fingers pushed back with nothing to stop them over her lower lip, and then to flatten her tongue. "That's for me."

His fingers slipped all the way back, and she felt saliva pool down behind her lower teeth. Was it too soon to beg for his dick?

But now there was nothing in her wide-open mouth, and the man was bringing something into her line of sight with his other hand. "Do you know what this is?"

Violet got an eyeful of the palm-sized red foam ball. She nodded.

He stuffed it into her left hand and closed her fingers around it. "Hang onto it," he said. "Tight. If you get to 'red' *or* 'yellow'—*or yellow*, do you hear me?—let go. I'll be right here to ungag you, and you tell me what's going on. Yes?"

He hovered there, waiting.

Violet nodded, her 'yes' a weird drunken sound with the gag in place.

Mister M leaned close and traced the side of her hooded face with a thumb.

"Good girl."

Had she been sitting on that stool, she would've slid right off.

Her Dom stood, and she heard his steps move back around. There was a long pause where he said nothing. Nothing touched her, and the entire surface of her skin tingled, electric with the unknown.

Then the leather hit.

Violet shouted though the gag, eyes popping wide as her head came up.

There was no warm-up this time. It was clear her Dom for the night considered her 'already warmed up.' Now he descended back into the scene like a hawk diving for prey. A second stroke came right after the first, just as sharp, and then a third, a fourth, each side of her ass blaring back to instant heat. There were several more—he had her too off-kilter to try counting, now—before he centered a stroke along her cunt.

She cried out, instinct to hunch away, but her knees had to stay locked or she'd collapse. And who knew what Mister M was like about punishments? There was nothing to do but present her pussy for flogging, and the man went at it until she was jerking every time against the plank. And just when it felt like a million tiny insects had stung her, cool, gloved fingers probed into her helpless snatch, hooking down and assaulting that place inside her that made Violet feel like she was going to come or pee or both.

Her eyes focused on nothing and she warbled around the gag. Saliva collected below her lip and trickled down her chin. As soon as she began to surge and buck her hips, the man took her pleasure away and painted her ass with fire.

Oh God. Oh God, why? Yes!

There was nothing but a wall to look at. The very far end of the bar. Each blow came vicious and beautiful, and Violet let herself go wild against the restraints. She made ugly noises into the gag to match the screaming of her backside. Another rapid round of strokes blazed along her swollen lips, and then her shriek became something ragged when his fingers replaced leather for the kill.

She couldn't stop him. Couldn't scuttle away while he murdered her g-spot. Her eyes went crossed. Her noises were unglamorous. Fingers from his other hand found and scrubbed her clit, and Violet burst into a latex-covered mess.

She came on his hand, crying out in abandon. Blood rushed in her ears and the way for his squelching fingers went puddle-slick. Somewhere in the fuzzy background, hoots and a smatter of applause rose and fell like a flock of starlings. The all-round pressure of the catsuit was the only thing holding Violet together.

When her insides quit clutching at him, and he took his fingers away, she was sure everything she knew was going to come dribbling out on the platform. All she could do was exist there, belly trying to heave with her breath while the cincher denied it, the red ball a damp wad in her left hand.

The next thing she thought she'd hear was the metal of the latch coming apart, but instead she heard his shoes. They moved around and paused before Mister M stepped into view. He lowered himself to eye level, and Violet knew she was a sight: lips stretched in an obscene ring, no doubt strings of drool roping down from her chin. Watery eyes, but she hoped he saw there the utter release he'd let her have.

"Are you still green, Miss Payne?"

More?

She nodded, panting and wet.

He brought an object up close to her face and she had to cross her eyes. Another of the clothespins. He tapped her on the nose with it and smiled.

Oh God, more.

Her Dom stood again and returned to the scene of the crime. The first pinch of fingers on her swollen labia was warm and friendly; a handshake. The springy bite of wood that replaced it was not.

Oh, *oh!* It didn't let go! And she was plump and buzzing against its tight pinch. This one was high up, near her entrance, and even while she was whining against the first clamp, he had a second one secured into place on the opposite side.

Violet wiggled and squealed against the pins, and they waved around flapping against her protests. A palm landed on her already-sore ass.

"Good girls hold still."

She breathed and whined, but fuck, this man made her want to be a Good Girl. Violet flexed her thighs and tried to calm down.

A third clothespin and a fourth latched into place lower down, alongside the frill of her inner lips. It was like someone shifted a spotlight to everywhere she could already feel her pulse. When those gloved fingertips began to spread sensitive flesh and isolate her clit, Violet's heart really began to race.

A sound rose out of her like a desperate question when the last pin clamped into place. There was no getting away from it. Her poor little clit stood out raw from orgasm, and now the little jaw held it there, pinched away from her body and trilling with every movement.

Mister M took the time to tap each one of the clothespins with a finger and set it swaying. Violet still mewled from that as he brought a thumb up to trace around her pouting hole. She had to look like a damn pincushion back there, all splayed and bristling and pink.

His touch left, but the pins held. More footsteps, what *could* he be up to, now?

A palm splayed over one side of her ass, and the bridge of her nose wrinkled against the sting. There was no way to grimace with a ring in her mouth. He squeezed, pulled her cheeks apart with a thumb, grinding the torment home.

Then something cold as a fucking iceberg kissed up against her asshole.

The gasp of air she took in ended in a high-pitched thread of sound she couldn't have described.

What the f—!

Her entire puckered ring tried to suck itself back inside her body, but the Dom followed it with whatever freezing cold thing while her toes curled inside her high heels and the clothespins grabbed on with glee.

No. Not 'whatever cold thing.' Violet knew this shape. It was the stainless bulb of her foxtail plug. This motherfucker—that's what 'Mister *M*' stood for, didn't it?—had to have had it sitting in ice-water or something. It was the kind of cold that made her want to climb up the wall. To leap away from waves on the shore in fucking February, but there was nowhere left for her to go.

He came with the plug, fingers keeping her cheeks wide, until her shoulders pressed hard against the plank and her head whipped back and forth in denial. The thing was slippery, too, most definitely lubed and, despite the involuntary tightening of her hole, was dilating her in a stretch that would have made her teeth grind. If she could bring her teeth together.

Violet whined as he ushered it home, but did the sadist let her breathe when her body swallowed it up, at last? No, he did not. This perfect bastard, this 'Mister M', took hold of its base and drew it out again. Then he stood there, teasing the frigid stainless past her angry little ring, over and over, fucking her hole with it while the clothespins captured the throb and desperation of her pussy.

Somehow he managed to stop before she hyperventilated, but the plug stayed in place. Her Dom, however, did not.

She heard wood clunk on wood, and he pulled the stool to where she could see. He sat and laced his gloved fingers between wide knees. Everything behind her was abuzz with sensation. Every inch of her skin, snug in the latex.

"Do you know how beautiful you are right now, Miss Payne?"

Violet let her eyes travel up to his. *Beautiful like a trainwreck*, she would have said if she could have made words. But there was nothing mocking on his face.

"Your cunt is red from the flogger," he said, and now her face probably was, too. "Your lips are puffing around the clothespins, and everything pink up the middle is wet. Glossy under the lights. And the way your asshole looked when it was swallowing down that steel for me?" He clucked his tongue, as though he had to squirm through the memory, himself. And each thing he described called Violet's attention to it all over again.

"And this gag?" Fingers came up to trace the metal behind her lower teeth. "I can see your pretty tongue moving inside. And look at this." The hand disappeared below her chin, only to lift back up with a web of drool spread between black, nitrile fingers so she could see. Violet whimpered. "You can't hold it back, can you? When I flog you and finger you and pin you." He smeared the spit along the jaw of the latex hood, and Violet's pussy hummed. She made and unmade fists against the plank.

"Do you know how backwards this all is?" he asked. "To have you all sealed up and sterile, but then to have the filthiest parts of you exposed for me to play with?"

146

The man was standing again, and Violet squirmed. Her body nursed at the plug and she could feel the length of her braid swinging like a pendulum off one side of her neck. Mister M was fishing in a trouser pocket. Unzipping.

His dick was out. The black of his glove stroking along the shaft far hotter a sight than she would have guessed. Violet shifted her weight from leg to leg and put every tone of begging she was able into the wordless sounds she made.

So wet, oh God, he needs to fuck me already.

Now there was a condom, and he was tearing the wrapper. Rolling it down the blush of his length, and it was one of those fetish black ones. When he got it to the base, slacks only unzipped but belt intact, he looked glossy and threatening, like some intimidating new dildo she'd buy and then have second thoughts about. He matched her now, ink black and covered in latex.

She was ready for him to walk behind her, but instead he stepped close.

With a condom?

But no. That was smart. They didn't know each other. And it fit the scene.

"This cock is going in your mouth, Miss Payne."

And it did.

No further preamble. He came so near his shape blurred, and then warm, latex-sheathed man made contact with her tongue.

There was no warning with the gag in place. Nothing sliding past her lips or teeth. The cavity of her mouth was empty and then it was full. It was like his fingers, with the gloves. A crude medical exam, but more wrong.

Mister M dragged himself out, and then moved back in with a slowness, as if to impress upon her the complete lack of say she had about the situation. Well. That wasn't true. There was always the red ball, but this was the kind of say she wanted not to have.

He pressed her skull back against the wood with his hips, balls flush to her wet chin, and filled her to the throat. There was nothing to see for a moment but fabric, and Violet felt him leaning over the plank. Leaning, *leaning*, and she coughed. Her hands splayed. And then the pressure was off, but her eyes went wide.

The plug shifted in her ass. A small tug—he had a hold of the long fox tail. The clothespins kept her in the present.

Her Dom began to fuck in and out past the gag, a slow, circular motion, and if Violet thought she'd been streaming saliva before, it was nothing compared to the glut he plumbed out of her now. Twitches from his hand to the fox tail made the bulb of the plug talk to sensitive nerves. She couldn't help but grind her hips in the air, and that set off the pins. Her eyes rolled and low noises moved up from the throat he was packing full.

"You like this, don't you?" He palmed the back of her skull, the latex making sticky noises under his hand.

Violet made incoherent affirmative sounds around him and the gag,

And then he wasn't in her mouth. He was doing something to the back of her neck. A tight feeling released. Fingers were picking metal out from between her teeth, and Violet smacked her lips. Swallowed. She heard the gag hit the platform.

"Show me how much," he said, holding his prick at the base. "Show me how much you like it."

Violet showed him.

With lips and eager tongue, and suction. It was all she had, without hands to help, or play in her neck. She hummed and slurped, and he fed it to her, weirdly obscene with that condom slicking him past her tongue.

The first restrained grunts began to fall overhead, and she felt him get leverage from somewhere—probably a grip on the pillory—and begin to truly seat himself home. To fuck her face. Strokes that shunted deep and held for a pause, each a fan on the flames where she tried to breathe against the throatful. Against the hug of the cincher. Against the *tug-tug-tug* of the foxtail and the one-two throb of her pinned clit when the rush of blood had nowhere to go, and Violet...

Was coming.

Again.

Again! Oh fuck oh fuck oh fuck!

She wailed and her hips jerked. One of the clothespins on her lips popped off and her squeal yipped higher, but nothing dampened that rhythmic grip between her legs.

The dick in her mouth went rock hard, and Mister M growled. She felt him kick against her palate and closed in around him to suck. He'd be filling the latex with semen; every pulse came hot behind that barrier, and Violet opened to the wild notion that maybe they were in the same place together, just then. Both coming, both restricted by latex. Some kind of bizarre simultaneous punishment and reward for each of them.

It felt like she'd never take in enough air, and then he was out of her mouth and she was panting. Humming, swallowing spit, trying to get her jaw to work. Her fingertips had gone tingly, and Violet tried to flex the feeling away while her Dom moved off to do who-knew-what.

She groaned when 'who-knew-what' became the first clothespin to come off. Second, if she counted the one she'd knocked loose. He pinched two more away, and then the one at her clit, and she didn't know whether to cry out or moan when his gloved hand plastered over her entire pussy to massage away the bite of little wooden jaws.

He was lifting her out of the pillory just when she thought her knees would give and began to walk her around to the waiting stool. Violet tried not to stumble.

"Sit down here, and I'll bring you a bottle of water," he said. He already had his slacks done up, and she had no clue what he'd done with the condom.

"You don't need to leave," said another voice, and Violet could see Garreth reaching an arm into the platform spotlight. "Here." He held out a bottled water to Mister M, who took it with a brief 'thanks' and twisted the lid off. Handed it to her.

She drank without ever bothering with the stool. Just stood there, still in full latex and gulped at least a third of it straight down. Her Dom chuckled and hooked her around the waist with an arm, pulling her back to let her lean on his chest while he set his spine against the pillory.

There was an ease to his gestures. A familiarity to his hold that hadn't been there at the beginning of their scene. Violet let her weight go against him while his arms circled around her middle to peel off his gloves. When he had those draped over the top of the pillory, he moved to unzip the hood. Her face was damp and cool when air hit it, as latex peeled away from her skin. The hood went hanging alongside the gloves. Then his arms were back, but this time in a loose hold.

"You can probably let go of the ball, now," he said near her ear.

It was her turn to laugh. Violet released the grip she'd been holding for what felt like ever, and the red ball bounced lightly to the platform. She took another sip of the water, this time less urgent.

"Did you enjoy the *latex?*" One of his hands traveled down her left side, evaluating the material.

She cocked her head and could feel wisps of her hair, limp with perspiration at her temples. The catsuit still wrapped her limbs and buttocks and breasts in a perverse hug, and only served to amplify the planes and angles of the man pressed at her back.

"Yes, Sir, I did," she said. "It feels like being squeezed all over. And it focuses my attention on the skin that's expos—"

"It's not alcohol!" A woman was yelling, and Violet's eyes snapped toward the bar. "Give it back!"

The woman teetered on heels, a hand reaching for what looked like a water bottle Garreth had in his hand. One of the Doms Violet had seen on stage earlier hovered behind the woman's shoulder, scowling. Mister M's arm around her circled tighter, protective, as though the drama might tumble their way.

Interesting.

Garreth had the cap off the water bottle and jammed his little finger inside. Pulled it out and stuck it in his mouth. Unlike the woman, he wasn't yelling, but even from where she stood, Violet thought she could hear him saying it was vodka.

She could feel her Dom's head shake behind her. "Two drink max for participants," he said under his breath. "If you can't follow the rules, don't be here." The scorn in his voice could have stripped paint, and Violet decided she never wanted it aimed her way.

The tipsy woman's Dom was ushering her over to the bar. Gesturing at the bartender, probably to get his sub some water.

Well, they're probably disqualified.

"Would you do it again, Miss Payne?"

Violet shook herself away from the distraction. "Do what, Sir?"

"The *latex*." He shifted his weight, and her ass moved over the front of his slacks.

She tugged on her lip with her teeth. "With you, I would, Sir."

"You'd be the fucking first," he muttered, and Violet got the sense he might not have intended to voice the frustration outside his head. And that swearing wasn't normal behavior for the man.

But she *would* do it again, that was the thing. He might be odd at times, but Mister M seemed to know how to find new buttons to push. Buttons she was scared to use on her own or thought they didn't work anymore.

And he knows how to treat me with some fucking respect. How's that for a change?

She turned in his hold, letting the neck of the water bottle dangle between her fingers near their thighs. When she found his face with her freshly-fucked smile, the man looked like he was trying to push his features back into a mask of control. A wall of calculations went on behind pale green eyes, but he left his arm in place to hold her close. His lips separated the smallest fraction of an inch, as though he were going to say something, but he only watched her.

Violet found herself wanting to kiss him then, but that would be way, *way* over the line in a situation like this.

What happened to him?

The intimacy became weird, and she dropped her gaze to his chin. "I should probably hand this catsuit over," she said. "They won't let us roll *latex* twice." She finished with a little smirk, letting him see her satisfaction again.

"You're right," he said, "But leave your plug in and your dress off." Her eyes snapped to his again, and her insides fluttered. "I want to watch your tail wag while you go roll our next scene."

He'd recovered into a knee-weakening half-smile, and Violet wanted a lot of things that were not appropriate right then. She settled for accepting his help out of the cincher, and then stripped the rest of the latex off her body, only to stand again, and frown out over the platform.

"I think we should just hang it over the pillory," Mister M said of the catsuit draped over her arm. "They'll want to have everything cleaned. And put your shoes back on," he said, as she moved to lay aside the gear. "This isn't the kind of place you want to walk around barefoot."

Between that and those gloves... was he worried about her wellbeing, or just a germophobe in general? Maybe both?

The wheel had chosen better than she could, that was for sure. *Her* choices had led her to fucking *Brian*, who'd made her into a damn accessory. The wheel had given her to Mister M, and he'd made her feel like she was the only person in the club who mattered. Sure, they'd played in front of others—and parts of that had clearly, sharply yanked on all her fears—but none of the exhibitionism had figured into her Dom's gratification that she could tell. It felt like the only thing he wanted to watch was her responses.

Violet stood nude in her heels, fox tail brushing the backs of her thighs, and took a deep breath. The stage was right there, just steps away, and the roulette wheels gleamed under Black Light's neon. Another sub was just finishing up her second spin. The woman's hair was soaked; maybe water bondage? A shower scene?

She turned her face back to Mister M, grinned, nervous again but for new reasons this time, and then walked her naked ass toward the stage. He followed behind, carrying her clothes and his jacket, and let her hear his hum of appreciation for the display, but didn't climb the stairs—he just stood offstage, waiting.

The DJ transferred his attention to Violet as the other woman moved off with her Dom, and she gave him a sheepish smile.

No need to be embarrassed—there's naked women all over the place in here.

"Hi," she said. "I guess I'm rolling another one, now?"

"Alright," Elixxir said, sounding congratulatory, "here you go!" He passed her the tiny marble and spun the wheel into motion.

She let the ball go, and it popped into place without a skitter or bounce.

"*Blood play*," Elixxir read aloud, his voice dramatic even when he was off the mic.

God.

Violet twisted to raise her brows at Mister M.

He shook his head. "Hard limit," he said, making his voice project so the DJ could hear.

Elixxir leaned over to check some paper on the podium and nodded. "Yup. Hard limit for Mister M. Roll again." He handed her back the marble and made the wheel spin.

Come on, roulette. It's my lucky night. Let's go.

The ball left her fingers and rasped around the track, momentum carrying it longer this time. It kissed the side of a pocket, bounced bounced bounced, and then settled. Violet's eyes widened.

"*Breath play!*" said the DJ.

This time when she turned to her Dom for confirmation, the man had a look on his face. A glint to his eyes and a subtle curve to one side of his mouth, like he'd just showed up at someone's house for dinner only to discover they were serving his favorite thing.

Violet's skin prickled under that look. Her nipples tightened to points.

Down near his hip, the man twitched a pair of fingers at her—*come here*—and she had to breathe through her mouth.

She made her way down the stage stairs with extreme care, so she didn't fall and break an ankle or something. Her fucking knees were weak.

They were about to jump off the damn deep end, weren't they? Exercises in trust, hell!

But he heard you, before. He listened.

When she came to stand in front of him again, his arm circled her shoulders so he could grip the base of her braid and tilt her head back.

"Tell me, Miss Payne." A keen glint in green eyes. "How much do you enjoy breathing?"

CHAPTER 5

ANSON

*H*is sub stared back up at him, lips parted, eyes searching his face. "I... um..." A slip of pink tongue came out to wet her hips. "I don't..."

It was not his usual style to tease, but the unfolding of the night had Anson in rare form. "You don't like to breathe?" He let mock concern pinch his brows together while he still had a handful of the hair he'd braided himself. The woman's body didn't squirm, but her face did.

"I've never... done *breath play* before."

Anson had.

Ohh, *had* he.

"But it wasn't among your hard limits."

"N-no..." She shifted her weight, features smudging to one side as though she wished she could go revise those limits right this minute.

He could've stood there for an indefinite amount of time and enjoyed the play of her, naked and nervous against his clothed body, the silver of that nipple ring glinting as her breath made it rise and fall under the neon. But *he* had to gather *himself* just as much as Miss Pain appeared to need the same, before they dove headlong into another scene.

This scene.

"Do you know what bondage tape is?" he asked.

Her throat bobbed. "Yes, Sir."

"Then head over to where they have supplies"—he dipped his head to indicate the direction he'd gone for the flogger—"and bring back a roll. White, if there's a choice. And meet me at the massage tables." He let go her braid, and she blinked up at him.

"Naked? Sir?"

Anson glanced at the short black dress and bra he still had in hand. He smiled, an act he was allowing himself more and more around this woman, and said, "Yes. Naked."

She held his eyes for a beat and then let her focus travel down to his waist and back up, as though she'd memorize his appearance. Then his submissive slipped around him, off to find the supply station.

Anson turned to watch her go, that long fox tail swinging across her thighs. He was far from the only set of eyes in the club with attention for the accent to her heart-shaped little ass.

Didn't really think that was my kink.

Maybe it was, and maybe it wasn't. Either way, the plug had served to bring her to the edge and help push her over back there at the pillory, so credit where credit was due.

What *was* his kink was fucking breath play. The odds had been slim for her second roulette spin to turn up his one Achilles heel, and Anson had needed to pack his shock away with impressive speed. It was never a good idea to have a Dom's nerves bleeding over onto his sub, at least not for how *he* felt comfortable playing.

A breath scene was what had sent him scuttling to the voyeur fringes of the community the last time. *That* had happened in private, not at a club. She hadn't understood her own limits. He'd been too wrapped up in the thrill of watching her struggles to be paying the kind of attention he needed. By the time it was all over, she'd had a full panic attack.

They'd never spoken to or seen each other again.

It had taken the structure in place, the pressure to act surrounding the roulette event tonight for Anson to venture out again. He didn't know what it said about him that the disaster with his former sub hadn't put him off the idea of breath play. No, that was still at the tip-top of his list of kinks. Where it had made him unsteady was his confidence at reading people.

But Miss Pain was shoring him back up, tonight. He could somehow gauge the language of her limbs, her face. And he was watching every last twitch. That was why he'd stopped damn near everything, even when she'd only called 'yellow.' There could be no assumptions. No half-measures.

She wouldn't trust him if she thought he wasn't listening.

But that was why the breath play scene was going to succeed this time. He knew himself better. And he trusted her to speak on her own behalf. She already had.

Anson squinted around the outer walls of the club, deciding where exactly to hunt for the thing he wanted. He hadn't seen one when he'd selected the flogger and gag, and there hadn't been one with the latex gear because, well, they were usually leather. As a last resort, he settled on the costume room. If there wasn't one in there, he'd have to rethink his whole approach to how he'd manage Miss Pain's breath.

He wove his way across the floor to where he remembered the costumes being, trying to avoid touching or bumping anyone as he went. Members clustered in small audiences right and left to watch other Roulette pairs deep in their respective scenes, just as a small circle had gathered to watch him play with Miss Pain.

The latex had been another thing altogether, when experienced in person. No video could ever do justice to the feel of it under his gloves. The stretch and crease of it as it moved with her curves, right in front of his face. The catsuit and hood had kept her entire body sealed off, and he'd been able to focus only on the most sensitive places.

He wished he could have done a better job of helping *her* focus. The blindfold, he'd hoped, could have been a way to block out the sight of the audience for her. Maybe to help with the concerns she'd expressed about humiliation. But he hadn't counted on the sounds around them, like footsteps, also being a trigger. Nor had he under-stood from their conversation the depths to which the hooks of her problems with her previous Dom had sunk into this woman's psyche.

Had he changed course enough? When she'd been almost ready to tap out?

Because that might have been the more terrifying factor. Anson Morrow didn't just want to control and manipulate this woman's experience—motives he could admit made his dick hard.

No, with every sharp little breath she took, as he asked her to experience this or that, the lonely Senior Revenue Agent had come to understand he wanted her to enjoy it. To enjoy *him*.

Because that's what you are. Lonely.

If Matthew could hear his internal monologue right then, the congressman would be having a field day.

Anson found a velvet rope fencing off the door to the costume room once he made his way there, but no one on Black Light staff manning it. He leaned forward, as though he'd get a peek into the room, but another man spoke from his right.

"She's in the back," he said, "hunting me down a schoolgirl outfit." One of the other Roulette Doms gave Anson an amiable shrug, hands tucked in his trouser pockets while he waited at the rope.

"Ah." Anson stuffed his own hands in his pockets, that universal male posture of waiting, and felt the second pair of nitrile gloves folded on the left side. His need to carry a pair or two everywhere he went had already saved him in more ways than one, tonight. Least of all, his inspiration to bring those clothespins into play. The damn things were close enough to popsicle sticks to make his skin start to itch.

And you liked the opportunity to push your fingers into all your sub's wet places, didn't you?

A young woman came out of the costume room with something pleated and plaid on a hanger. She handed it off to the other waiting Dom, and then turned to Anson. Her nametag read 'Jayla.'

"Mister M, what can I help you find?" Her smile was bright, fingers laced at her waist. She'd clearly been paying attention to names during the announcing of Roulette pairs.

"Do you have any posture collars back there?" he asked.

Jayla cocked her head, and her eyes narrowed in that search for information that lived elsewhere. "I *think* so. Let me go check."

"Thank you."

Anson let his eyes wander around the club for what was probably less than a minute, before the woman returned with something black in her hand.

"Found one!"

He took it from her and turned it end over end, and then made a face. It was a plain circlet of stiff leather. "Do you happen to have one with a chin support?" he asked. "It'll look something like the neck of a pitcher?"

The woman's face broke into a grin, and her eyes glittered. "Feisty," she said in approving tones, and took the black collar back from him. "You know, I think we have a small collection of asylum-themed gear —I'll go see if there's anything in there." She turned on a heel and left him at the rope again.

This was taking long enough that Miss Pain was probably already at the massage tables, looking around for him. Waiting. Naked, save the fox tail.

God, he'd wanted to fuck her.

Just watching her shake back there, when his fingers had chased her to a climax. The jerk of her backside at each lick of the flogger. But it would have been too intimate. Too soon. Somehow oral was less personal, but it had done nothing to slow him down. The moment Anson had imagined her bare mouth on his cock, no condom to spare him every visceral stroke, he'd come with a rage that nearly had him bending fingernails backward as he'd gripped the top of the pillory.

And that had thrown him, as well. On any other night, the idea of that sort of contact with bodily fluids would have sent him recoiling in a panic. Not emptying a nut under a spotlight. Hell.

But there had been no way he wasn't going to indulge after watching Miss Pain lose herself that way, especially after her turn-around from the panic. A second condom sat in his pocket, alongside the gloves, in case Anson reached that level of need again.

"So, how you like that tattoo?"

Anson nearly leapt out of his thoughts at the sound of Matthew's voice. His friend stepped around from behind him, grinning, drink in hand.

"Tattoo?" Anson said.

Matthew gave him a look. "The bonsai? Come *on*, what are the odds?"

Anson's mouth went into a line. "I'm sure there are trends in tattoo design for women in certain age demographics that at least make it somewhat likely th—"

"Oh shut up, Morrow, she's fucking *made* for you. You either like the tattoo, or you don't."

The coincidence *had* been fairly staggering, especially paired with their roll of breath play. But Anson didn't like how much the narrowest odds working in his favor smacked of the 'L' word.

I do like the tattoo, though.

"I thought you weren't going to watch my scenes," Anson said.

"Look at *this* guy, trying to change the subject." Matthew sipped his drink. "I didn't stand around and ogle you, but it's hard not to stare at a naked woman on the way by."

"Will this work?" Jayla emerged from the costume room to hand Anson something new: a white and tan leather padded collar with the chin support he'd requested. The colors gave it an institutional feel.

"Perfect," he said. "Thank you."

"You're welcome!" She turned to greet a petite brunette, and Anson stepped sideways, out of the way.

"Well," he said to Matthew, "my sub is probably *still* naked right now. I need to be getting back. Breath play." He raised the collar to make his point.

"Oh shit!" His friend's eyebrows shot up. He was the only other person who knew about what happened with Anson's former sub.

"I know."

"Well good lu—"

"I *will* make it look like an accident, Matthew." Anson made a firm gesture with the collar before turning to head back into the crowd.

People and their precious 'luck.' Let it go.

Miss Pain stood beside a vacant massage table when he found her, arms folded behind her back, but head up, since she had to pick him out of the crowd. The colored neon overhead painted out highlight and shadow on her curves, and she smiled when she saw him. Anson found himself smiling back.

Yet another thing bolstered his spirits for the night: Miss Pain's air of ready obedience. She wasn't a brat—at least not so far—and that went a long way with Anson. Those kinds of obedience games were tedious; he preferred getting straight to the business of curating his partner's sensual experience.

On the table at her side sat the roll of bondage tape, white like he'd asked, and inside the roll was another of the red foam balls. The woman had realized this sort of scene would probably leave her without her voice again, at times, and brought the alternate safe word option.

"Smart," he said, setting the collar down on the table and tapping the foam ball with a finger. Miss Pain's eyes met his after getting a glimpse of the collar. She wet her lips with her tongue, and every line on her face smacked of nerves. "Do you need a minute?" he asked.

"Can, um…" One of her ankles tilted to the side in a patent heel. "Can we just talk a little before we get going?"

She'd never played this way. His sub wasn't saying 'no,' but the obvious stalling was both understandable and—he could admit —endearing.

"We'll work up to it," he said, and patted the leather of the massage table. "Sit up here, please." Anson pushed their gear to the foot of the table with his forearm, before folding her dress, bra, and his coat to hang over the support rung between the table's legs.

She did as he said, hoisting her backside up on the table with a small hop and the thrust of her arms.

"Lie back, Miss Pain."

Nervous or no, the woman went, flat on her back before Anson instructed her to bend her knees toward the ceiling. The limbs leaned together to form a small pyramid, and her fox tail and braid trailed out from under her body. Anson reached for the tape.

"May I ask you a question, Sir?" she said to the lights overhead.

He was pulling at the edge of the tape. "Kind of late to ask permission, don't you think?" Anson turned up half a smile at his own stuffy humor and lifted her left ankle from the table, so her leg bent back at the hip and her calf was touching the back of her thigh. He removed her shoe and set it on the floor beneath the table before anchoring the end of the tape with one hand and beginning the loop around ankle and upper thigh. "Ask."

"I've been trying to guess all night," she said. "What do you do? For a living?"

Anson smirked. "Is *that* what you've been thinking about the whole time?"

The woman made a flustered face, and he let her sit in it for a moment, just to enjoy her emotional squirming. He stretched the bondage tape, spiraling it around her doubled leg. The stuff had a texture like window cling film, and only stuck to itself. It was a clean, efficient alternative to ropes, which, whether natural or synthetic, had way too many tiny crevices and porous surfaces for Anson's comfort. Bacteria were everywhere, and no joke. Plus, the tape was disposable.

"I work for the IRS," he told her at last, when he tore off the tape and pressed down the end to seal off the first leg.

A laugh sputtered out of his sub, and Anson raised a brow as he took the tape roll and moved around the table to her other side. He took off the next shoe. "Is something funny, Miss Pain?"

She made a gesture to include him and the table. "Breath," she said, giggling. "Breath and Taxes."

And *his* jokes were bad. Anson shook his head and gathered up her second ankle. "I don't know if I should punish you for that, or not." He tried to play the stern Dom but couldn't keep the corner of his mouth from twitching. "Would you like to share your line of work? Aside from smiling at strange men in elevators?" Glossy white tape began binding her other leg.

"I'm a document courier," she said. "Mostly stuff around The Hill. Some real estate things, here and there. And I volunteer at a women's shelter. Not that that part's 'a living,' but…"

Anson snorted as he wrapped tape. "Would you believe I guessed that?" he said. "In the elevator? The document courier part at least. My other guess was that you had an art degree."

She lifted her head off the table to look at him with suspicious eyes. "That is an oddly-specific guess," she said, "and I *do* also have an art degree." His sub cocked her head with a frown that looked like it wanted to add an *Are you fucking with me?*

He shook his head and sealed off the second leg. Now both sides shone with tape, from knee to ankle, the limbs doubled as though she were kneeling. "It's a thing I do," he said, setting the roll aside. "Years of classifying people. I can't say it makes me popular. Can you sit up, Miss Pain?"

The woman shoved her torso upright with her arms, her bound legs butterflying out at the hip when she leaned on her palms. Anson pulled out his second pair of gloves for the night and began to wiggle his fingers into the first one.

"It's not part of the kink is it?" she asked, and then added, "Sir."

"What's that?"

"The gloves."

Ah. Yes. Now that they weren't in the latex scene, there was no passing it off as fetish. Well, he wasn't going to start lying, now. "People wear condoms," Anson said, tugging on the next glove, "but we run around touching far dirtier surfaces all the time with our bare hands." To his ears, the logic sounded obvious, but he knew plenty of people found his standards neurotic. "Do the gloves bother you?"

"I was just curious, Sir." Her eyes were on his every move. "It's... actually kinda hot."

Some combination of relief and heat flooded his veins. She wasn't just tolerating his quirks.

Anson moved alongside her and found the release tab that let him angle up the table's backrest as high as it would go. In a concert of limbs, he brought himself to sit behind his sub on the padded surface. His knees splayed wide, feet dangling as though he rode a horse, and he lifted her braid over her shoulder so he wouldn't trap and yank it when he pulled her by the hips to wedge between his thighs.

"The collar please, Miss Pain," he said. "And the ball."

Her spine curved as she leaned forward to retrieve the gear, and Anson took the posture collar once she sat up straight.

"Chin up."

She obeyed, and he pulled the leather circle open to fit around her neck from behind, again moving her hair so it wouldn't get caught in the buckles. He fastened both of the leather-and-metal closures, and the need for further commands to keep her chin up disappeared. She would not be able to duck her head, and that would form the cornerstone of his methods for the scene. Much easier than a rebreather hood for an immediate halt, if she safe worded.

Plus, he could watch her lovely face.

And so could everyone else, apparently. Several clubgoers had collected at a respectable distance to sip drinks and watch. One Domme had her sub kneeling at her feet, a bit gag in his mouth while she stood behind him with a hand on his bare shoulder. Anson was beyond caring what any of them saw.

He let his spine go against the backrest. "If you'll lean on me, Miss Pain."

His sub put her shoulders on his chest, her head falling to the right side of his chin. The buckles of the collar dented in just above Anson's ribs. He circled his right arm around her waist, pulling her close.

"Knees apart, please."

She obeyed without question, and he knew a zing of thrill when her legs folded out to display her pussy. The view from over her shoulders was a tableau of pert breasts, the firm rise of her mound below the dip of her navel, the enticing half-girdle of bonsai branches, and a tuft of fox tail peeking from between her bound legs.

That last part added its own special contribution to the surge in blood flow below his belt. She was already plugged. Her body would be fighting sensation the second they started.

"Are you comfortable, Miss Pain?"

"Yes, Sir." She tried to roll her eyes up to see his face, and her words came compressed because of the collar's chin support. He indulged himself in smoothing his palm up her ribs to cup her breast.

"Then I would like you to put a hand between your legs and touch yourself," he said. "And I am going to decide when you're allowed to breathe." Her ribs expanded at this, and his cock twitched in response. "I would like you to remember not to come, please. Not without permission. You'll drop your ball if you're at 'yellow' or 'red.' Do you understand?"

"Yes?" Her voice was a squeak. "Sir?"

"Very good," he said. "Begin."

Whatever fears she had, his sub did not balk. Her left hand had a grip on the red ball, but her right rose to smooth, palm down, over her belly. Fingers split off to trace the shape of her labia. To make a first, feather-light pass at exploring each little hill and valley. The dip of her entrance, the rise of her clit. It was enough to get her started.

"Deep breath," he said.

Miss Pain inhaled. Anson brought a hand up over her mouth.

The heel of his palm pressed into the rim of the collar's chin support while his thumb and forefinger closed together over the tip of her nose. Between his grip and the stiff leather restraint, her mouth would only open again at his mercy.

A ten count was all he gave her that first time. When Anson fanned his fingers away from her face, the woman puffed out air in a rush before sucking down a new lungful. "Oh, *Sir.*"

Oh *yes.* That was the sound of sudden comprehension. Miss Pain had discovered what she was up against in this scene, and he let her breath even out while she drew slow circles over the sensitive nub between her bound legs.

"Again," he said. "Deep breath."

She filled her lungs. He clamped her airways shut.

This time a count of fifteen, but she toyed with her pussy like he'd asked, the whole time. Near the end, her abs began to bunch, her body readying a response to buck and expel the air. He let her, and the breath shuddered out. Her taped legs fell wide atop the table.

Anson drew them into a cycle.

His warnings of 'deep breath' became simplified to a mere 'now.' She would fill her lungs with air. He would cover her mouth and nose. Her fingers would play in the valley between her thighs until those small grunts of protest strained at the back of her throat. Then her head would thrash back and forth—as much as it could in the collar—fighting the sensation, even as her left hand clutched tight to the ball.

And then he would let her go.

Her gasps each time had a musical rasping quality, like some hard object being drawn in a swift line over a taut stretch of canvas. The sound of them, every time, the pure, instinctual desperation of a body to keep a grip on that tether to survival, made his erection thump at the small of her back. The way she jerked in his grip, begging with her whole body for him to stop, all while holding back her safe word meant that somewhere within her struggles was a core of trust.

She *trusted* him. And the obscene swell of power this allowed Anson to feel was both addictive and terrifying. He wanted to fall on his knees and press his face to her hands and thank her for it. But he could do all that later.

Right now, he was making an entire mess of his sub.

Miss Pain sucked down air once again, this time like each before it requiring more wide-eyed gasps than the last, and her fingers slowed to haphazard swipes while she tried to gain function elsewhere. She'd be getting lightheaded. Heart rate erratic. He knew exactly where he was taking her and failed to regret it one bit.

"Do better than that," he said over her shoulder. "You know how to touch yourself. Do it."

His voice had gone gruff, and she let out a whine. Pulled her bound knees back to spread herself further. The movements of her hand tightened up to something that looked practiced, coordinated. She panted while he let her build up steam.

"*Sir.*" The word came out of her a moan, and the woman bit her lip. "Now."

She inhaled, quick, as he yanked her back into the cycle with a start. His hand clamped her mouth and nose, but Anson knew where she was, now. Too close. That's where she was.

Her fingers worked, tight specific patterns over her clit. Her eyes squeezed closed. Head began to toss. Hips to buck.

Anson held her, his cock hard as stone against her frantic efforts.

When the sounds in her throat merged into a single, constricted scream, he let her go.

She gasped, a loud, upsetting caw and, as the new surge of oxygen hit her system... she came.

The heaving sub between his knees let out raw, feral sounds as her abs crunched and her fingers strummed pink flesh, shameless in front of the watching crowd. Someone off to Anson's left let loose a knowing chuckle, but he let her ride it out. Let her breathe and quiver and melt back against him.

They'd both gotten what they'd wanted, in a way.

Anson moved a gloved palm down over her chest, past her navel to slip under her own slackening hand. He smeared a wet circle over her pussy with the flat of his fingers and earned himself a hum of satisfaction.

"Ohh, Miss Pain." He brought the fingers up and pushed two of them into her mouth. Her tongue lapped at him, gloves and all, and her eyes rolled back. "I asked you *so* politely not to come."

Pale eyes snapped open.

"Didn't I."

He savored the long seconds in which all she could do was catch her breath and stare at him, upside down. Her brows tilted up in the center, a little prayer against the implications of what she'd done.

"Y-yes? Sir?"

"Yes Sir, what?"

She swallowed. "You told me... not to come, Sir."

Anson was enjoying her nerves too much. "Yes, I did," he said. "Now put your hands behind your back."

His sub chewed her lip but did it.

"I'd like to say I won't enjoy punishing you"—his hand splayed back over her belly and lower, to cover her mound—"but we both know that's not true."

She cried out when his palm made its first, crisp contact with her pussy.

"Sir!"

A second spank, and then a third landed, and they'd be all needly sting, unlike the duller hits of the flogger.

"*Yyynnh!*"

"Hold still," he said, firming his left arm up around her wiggling middle. "You will be still and accept what you've earned."

Miss Pain grimaced but kept her knees wide, and Anson brought smack after smack down upon her swollen, sensitive flesh. Between them, he could feel one of her hands clutch at the front of his shirt, but he didn't count his strokes. The threshold meter for Anson as a

Dom was not some predefined number. The punishment could end when her face and body showed him actual regret.

It turned out to be quite a volley of impacts before she got there.

Somewhere in the relentless rhythm, her left knee whipped to center. She was all instinct now, broken outside of all reason other than pain avoidance.

"Sir. *Sir*! Please!" Her face was red above the white leather of the collar, and she sniffled between ragged pleas.

Anson turned his palm to her thigh and pushed it wide again, black nitrile sinister over white glossy tape. His fingers returned to cup and smear between her legs, where she had to be on fire.

"You think I should stop, Miss Pain?"

"No! Sir! *Please*, I need..." She'd slid down during her exertions and was now looking at the ceiling more than in his same direction. Her eyes shone wet and unfocused, however, pupils wide under the club's neon.

But she hasn't safe worded.

He jolted her with another smack. "*What*, Miss Pain. What do you need."

Muscles in her body jerked, and his sub found his eyes. "I need your cock, Sir." Her ribs heaved. "I can't take it."

Anson blinked at her, and his spine straightened.

This is no time to lose control.

"Only good girls get cock," he said to the woman between his knees. The woman who hadn't pulled her arms from behind her back.

"Sir!" The word was pure, tear-stained dismay. She rolled her hips under the cup of his palm, straining, and he took his touch away.

Anson wasn't about to lie and say her distress didn't have him about to burst through his slacks. But was it him she wanted, or just a relief from punishment?

"Explain to me why you deserve it," he said, "after you came without permission."

You're going to be a sucker, aren't you?

"I *don't* deserve it, Sir." The words flooded out of her at the slim opening he allowed. "But I only want to be a good girl for *you*, and I'm *sorry* I came. It came out of nowhere!"

Probably. Probably going to be a sucker. He let his hand drift back, and began to massage in wide, slow circles. "Hmm, and you'd probably come again 'out of nowhere,' if I kept doing this," he said. "Wouldn't you, Miss Pain."

Her face made some small movements, as though she tried to nod, but the collar was there. The line of her mouth curved into a miserable frown, even as she spread her knees wider for his touch.

"*Why* did you come?"

Her voice was quieter, now, and Anson made an effort to hear her over the music. "I never had anyone control my breath before, Sir," she said. "It was too much."

A skeptical brow rose on his face. His hand stilled. "You came from me holding your breath for you?"

"And... and from imagining you, Sir."

His erection was raging. The rest of him didn't want to move. "Imagining me?"

"Inside me." She let her eyes come open to find his again. "Fucking me." That second one hit him like a punch in the gut, but she continued, "And your cock was against my back and I couldn't stop thinking about it." Her tongue dipped out to wet her lips. "I need it."

The naked honesty had his internal landscape shifting.

"Go on."

Miss Pain hesitated, and her shoulders shifted between his arms. "I... I think you need it, too. Sir." She made a face as if to flinch, but when he didn't contradict, she said, "I think I was the one restrained, but I think *you* might be more restrained *all the time*." Those wide eyes cradled his, upside down, and her last words were her quietest, yet. "I think you need to fuck something until it screams."

And *he'd* been observing *her*.

"Is that what you think?" Anson tried to play it cool, even dangerous, but the woman had his number.

"I'll scream for you, Sir."

It wasn't even a challenge, the way she said it. The way she waited, half-bound and half holding herself where he'd asked. It was the most patient of offers. Compassion, where others had shown exasperation. It was no one act or organ his sub wanted to fill herself with.

It was him.

"Yes, you will," he said.

His sub shuddered a groan, but Anson was already extracting himself from behind her. Helping her to lie back while the table's legs creaked under the shift in weight. The woman looked like a sacrifice and, when he came to stand at the end of the table, her bound legs fell open to him.

She gasped when he jerked her close by the thighs, and the fox tail dangled toward the floor from between the curve of her buttocks. The condom that had been in his pocket was in his hands.

Zipper down, cock out, latex snapping.

When he slid the length along her pussy, Miss Pain whined and splayed a palm low over her belly. Her other hand still held the red ball.

Anson leaned on a locked arm over his collared sub and fit himself at her entrance. At the place where he'd made her cry out in pain and release, and yet from which he'd somehow succeeded in keeping himself separate.

He needed to be part of it. That was the point. It was the separation that was breaking him down. Year over year. Moment after moment.

"Miss Pain," he said. "This is a breath play scene. Take a deep one."

Her eyes shimmered in that beautiful panic, ribs expanded. Anson cut off her air and impaled her on cock.

His fingers covered her mouth, pinched her nose as before, but now he could stare directly into the surging tide of surrender on her face. Now he was *inside* her, the grip hot like her mouth, but closer. Her face pinkened to red as he began to fuck.

Anson moved his hand and she gasped. Kept gasping while his hips kept moving between her glossy, bound thighs. The length of her braid trailed off the edge of the massage table and, through the thin places past which he worked his prick, he could feel the hard bulb of the plug in her ass, jostling with the motion.

She made so many sounds as he overloaded her senses, and there were some raised words of encouragement from onlookers, but Anson could hardly hear them, now. Miss Pain was a beautiful, inexplicable mess spread out underneath him; he who preferred everything so tidy and accounted for.

He took her breath again. Felt muscles squeeze down inside her. Saw her belly flex when he dared a look down to watch his latex-coated cock disappearing into her body.

Her hips jerked, along with her face as best it could above the collar. He gave her air. Fucked her while she panted. Threw up the wall again.

Miss Pain watched him, blue eyes tearing, chest reddening, her entire existence belonging to him just then. She let a hand drift up, not to pry his fingers from over her nose or to claw while she struggled long into a single held breath. No, only to brush knuckles alongside his face. Down the forearm with which he held himself upright.

Absolutely a sucker.

The woman shrieked out air as soon as his hand went elsewhere.

One-handed was not the easiest way to unbuckle her collar, but Anson hilted himself while he fumbled at it. There was too much, and he tried not to look any of it right in the eye. Not the drawing of a prime number, not the tattoo, not even drawing breath play of all the fuck-damned things.

There was no way he was going to even *think* the word.

If he did, it might go away.

He had the collar off and tossed it above his sub's head on the table. She followed his every movement, throat bobbing, face flushed. Her lips parted, pink and wet.

Bad idea, Anson.

But he was feeling ... *something* tonight.

He leaned lower, elbow on the table.

"Deep breath, Miss Pain."

There were so many reactions on her face. The Dom exhaled while his sub filled her lungs.

He covered her mouth with his.

His hips snapped to life again, and her groan came deep from beneath her ribs, even as she didn't try to let go her air into him yet. He still had to hold her nose, which he learned he hated from this position because it meant he had to cover too much of her face, but the way she jerked her pussy against him at the edge of the table … The way she did claw now at his sleeves and at the back of his shirt in what seemed only an effort to drag him closer …

But Anson needed air this way, too. It almost made him forget the knuckle-tightening co-mingling of fluids he'd brought upon himself. As he pumped into her, the woman lost control and released her held breath the only place it could go: into him. And a body couldn't last on recycled air—not for long.

When he lifted his face and dragged his hand away, Miss Pain rasped in breath only to cry out.

"*Sir!*"

Far, *far* too much. He plowed into her, heedless of what he might look like. Wet tracks streaked from the outer corners of her eyes down to the leather of the table. Between them, she clutched tight to the ball.

"Now."

Out. In. What was the stuff of life without another to share?

He took her lips. Sealed off her nose. Drove himself up into where she was hot and tight without mercy until she'd handed over her breath, her squeals, her perfect trust.

Anson only backed off for a second. Miss Pain screamed for air, but then he was kissing her. Beyond all reason, for him to be doing such a thing, but she could just breathe through her nose.

He could just keep fucking her on this table in front of all these people while her little feet bobbed in the air on both sides of him, and he could keep trying not to short-circuit at the feeling of her tongue sliding over his in a way he hadn't allowed in an appalling number of years.

The woman was trying to eat him alive from below; his cock and mouth at once! She was grinding her cunt at his base, her kisses, still a novelty, growing sloppy. Her little grunts became pained.

"Sir, can I—*nnh!*" She hissed and their teeth clacked. "Sir, *please!*"

Anson was delirious.

"Come."

He'd barely smeared the word over her open mouth when Miss Pain let out a wild noise. His hips worked to give her what she wanted, but even that didn't slow her from trying to gyrate from below and consume every available scrap.

And, just like in the pillory, there was no way he could watch this woman orgasm. Not while he was inside her. Not while her eyes rolled back and she lost herself.

It tore out of him, and he barely bit off a yell. Semen thundered into the condom. Her body gripped him from all sides even while his flesh kicked and his fingers made dents in the side of the table.

Long, heaving seconds passed before the neon of the club filtered back into his vision. Before he saw the limp woman beneath him twitching an exhausted smile.

"H-happy Valentine's Day?" she said.

Whatever look was on Anson's face made her smile grow and her body shake with weak laughter. The clutch of her had him grunting in a final jolt of sensation.

"I, um…" It wasn't like him to stumble over words. "I don't think we'll have time for a third scene tonight."

"No." She shook her head, features warm and relaxed. "I don't think we will."

"I'll uh"—he cleared his throat—"I'll deal with the tape. One moment."

Anson pushed himself up on his arms. Stepped back while Miss Pain lay there on display. What else could she do, with her legs bound like that? Someone gave a low hoot of approval from behind him, but he didn't look. And tried not to smirk, as well. It wasn't a noise he would have made, himself, but he could admit it mirrored his current mood.

As he was sliding off the condom, Anson saw some stealthy person had, at some point, slid a medical wastebasket below the head of the massage table. Probably one of the DMs, but they had to have been in an out like a ninja. It didn't matter—it meant he didn't have to go far.

And while large parts of his psyche cringed for a wet wipe, if not a full-on shower, other parts—the ones that had overruled all caution and decided trading saliva was an acceptable risk—had him tucking himself away for now, sticky skin be damned.

Miss Pain lolled on the table. He moved to an ankle and felt around for the end of the tape. It came away easy when he peeled, and he had the first leg free in under a minute. She hummed when he made a slow show of unbending her knee to drape it over the padded edge. With the second leg undone, he stuffed the used tape into the wastebasket. In theory it could be used again, but that was for private settings.

Anson kept moving and took up a dangling calf. He began to knead at the muscle, gloves still on out of habit, and the woman groaned. There was a thigh to work, as well, and an ankle. A foot. And then the other side.

When he slowed and gave the back of her knee a light squeeze, the woman pushed herself up on her arms. She gave him a lopsided grin and held a hand out. He took the red ball.

They'd made it.

"Are you able to dress yourself, Miss Pain?"

The sub watched him, features dreamy in a way that might have irritated him before. It didn't, now.

"I think so," she said.

He leaned down to pull her dress and bra from the crossbar of the table and hand them over. The clubgoers who'd been circling around to watch their scene were already drifting elsewhere to find more excitement. She was tugging the black fabric down past her hips when she turned to look at him over a shoulder.

"I get the feeling you don't kiss a lot," she said. It wasn't snide. More... hopeful?

Anson peeled the gloves off, at last. "I don't."

What did you do? *You don't even know this woman!*

"My real name's Violet," she said, turning to face him. "Payne."

She looked so tiny, one hand clasping the other in front of where panties would be if she'd worn any. Above a canyon of thumping music and strangers, offering him this.

"So, the nickname..." His brows rose, but he stepped closer to hear.

"Yeah," she said, "P-a-y-n-e. Payne."

He cracked half a smile and reached a hand to bring her braid over the front of her shoulder. There were *two* people not interested in silly nicknames, he'd just taken all night to catch up. But tonight felt like the right kind of night for taking risks.

He just wasn't going to put a name on it.

"I'm Anson. Morrow."

Her smile was genuine. *Violet's* smile was genuine. "Mister *M.*" Mischief glittered in blue eyes and she shifted weight onto a hip.

"'Mister Morrow' is fine," he said, closing to loom over her in a way they both wanted. "Or 'Sir.'" Her lips parted while he fished in a pocket. "You can earn 'Anson' some other night. If that interests you."

A white rectangle appeared between them, and the woman blinked.

"Did you just hand me an actual business card?" She looked at him like he was a time traveler.

"Our phones are out in the lockers."

She pulled the card from between his first two fingers. He wanted to hear his phone ring already. Her bare knees would press Zen-like little valleys into the white carpet of his living room.

"Mr. Morrow." She let her hand fall to her side. "Can I kiss you again?"

It was his turn to try breathing.

Just let her. You've done it once and you're not dead.

And he wanted it. The rest was just fear talking.

"Yes."

Her eyes closed and they tilted in, but she only pressed him with soft lips. No tongue, no nipping teeth. Violet saw *his* boundaries, too.

His shoulders eased. Patience. Respect. Maybe they could get there.

She tapped a button on the front of his shirt once she stood back. "You know, seven is my lucky number," said Violet.

Anson controlled his face because that was his job as her Dom.

She put up with your *nonsense, didn't she?*

"I don't know much about luck," he said, "But I'd like to know about you. Something to drink?" He would still only get water, but he didn't think Violet would care.

She slid her fingers into his bare hand and smiled.

"Yes, Sir."

THE END

ABOUT THE AUTHOR

Eris writes dark, escape-from-reality romance full of criminals and outcasts. Her stories are the stomping grounds for bada** heroines, untameable alphas, a spectrum of sexuality, and a serious disregard for convention. Expect the decadent and filthy, the crude and sublime, sometimes all at once. Pick a safeword and grab a towel before reading. She is a complete nerd and possible crazy cat lady. She will annoy you with puns.

Sign up for my email (http://eepurl.com/beYqU1) to be notified about upcoming releases

Find Eris Online:

- Website: http://erisadderly.com/
- Amazon: http://www.amazon.com/Eris-Adderly/e/B00PV5I0PG
- Goodreads: https://www.goodreads.com/eris_adderly
- Bookbub: https://www.bookbub.com/profile/eris-adderly
- Facebook: https://www.facebook.com/ErisAdderly
- Instagram: https://www.instagram.com/golden_apple_grenade
- Twitter: https://twitter.com/erisadderly

BURN

A Black Light: Roulette War Novella

By

Kay Elle Parker

CHAPTER 1

FINN

*C*ity life would never appeal to him.

Tapping his fingers on a broad thigh encased in black jeans, Finnegan McLeod watched Washington D.C. stream past outside the tinted window of his hired car and dreamed of home.

Grass, mountains, and the sight of his herd on his own land.

All eighty-thousand acres.

Finn had left the comfort of home to attend several necessary business meetings, but anticipation of tonight's event had made the trip somewhat more bearable. In his world, connections were everything, and he'd lucked out with an old friend who remembered Finn's... proclivities, from years gone by. Joshua had extended an invitation before Christmas which Finn curiously accepted, taking time out of his busy schedule to fly to D.C. to check out what Joshua referred to as the best goddamn kink club going.

Apparently, Valentine's Day in Washington D.C. meant one thing: Valentine Roulette at Black Light, *the* most exclusive BDSM club on the east coast, and one Finn considered himself lucky to be able to attend for the evening.

One intriguing visit in December and Finn found himself not only with a membership but applying for Roulette as soon as sign-ups opened in January and—God help him—looking forward to it.

Finn smiled to himself in the warmth of the car as it cruised toward his destination. He recognized the street they were on, estimated another five minutes before arrival. The balls started spinning at seven-fifteen and he had no intention of arriving late.

It had been six months since he'd held the softness of a woman in his hands. Far too fucking long for his sanity. He had a craving to bring blood rushing to smooth skin, mark firm flesh with the tools at his disposal, and make a pretty little subbie sing.

At forty-two, he was in his prime. Physically, he'd never been fitter —ranching was a 24/7 job—and Finn didn't shirk his duties when he was home. The people he employed, the animals under his care, deserved the best he could give them, and that meant not sitting on his ass while his staff did the grafting.

Finn was aware he made an imposing figure—three inches over six feet, one-hundred-and-ninety pounds of muscle, and shoulders that earned him the nickname, 'Bull.' He might use that to his advantage a time or two, but it wasn't his physical strength that kept an errant subbie in line.

Voice and eyes; the best weapons in his arsenal.

The car pulled up smoothly around the corner from his destination, engine idling as the driver called out, "Are you sure this is where you need to be, Mr. McLeod?"

"It sure is," he drawled, shifting to the edge of his seat. "If I don't text you beforehand, James, I'll be ready around eleven-thirty. Here, if you don't mind."

"I'll be here, Sir. You have a good evening."

He sure as hell would, Finn decided. No matter the spin of the wheel or the submissive caught up in the whirl, he was going to enjoy every moment of his three hours. God only knew when he'd get another chance to play like this.

He stepped out of the limo, watching it pull away into the city traffic a second after he closed the door. Give him a strong-minded quarter horse any damn day; he'd go crazy dealing with the cacophony of cars and pedestrians surrounding him from one journey to the next.

Thinking of a currently nameless, faceless woman he could ride hard and put away wet, Finn strolled along with his hands in the pockets of his long coat, shielding them against the chill. He thought he detected a hint of snow in the air, prayed fervently it would hold off until he was safely on his way home in the morning.

Humming under his breath, stepping lightly for such a big man, he rounded the corner toward the Psychic shop. A thrum of excitement bubbled in his blood when he saw the light in the window; some of the weight resting on his broad shoulders started to fall away.

When a man strapped down his dominant side for weeks, months at a time, he could create a monster. Sometimes even exhausting himself couldn't contain the demands of the Dom and he had to listen to that part of himself lecture him on the merits of taking a permanent submissive under their wing. One of their very own. To keep and treasure, train and fuck.

The answer was simple—No. Few women were capable of handling the sheer exclusion of living in the middle of a vast wilderness with a handful of cattle workers and several thousand cows for company. It would take a special kind of submissive to take her place at his feet with those conditions placed on her.

The bell jingled above the door as Finn pushed into the shop, his gut twisting. With a nod to the woman manning the counter, he walked past her toward the curtain in the corner.

Never had he found a sub he'd even contemplated asking to live with him; he had a feeling the few women he'd been tempted to invite would have laughed at him.

He'd rather live the rest of his life working his ranch by day and listening to his dominant side bitch by night than have his affection thrown back in his face. Isolation he could deal with. Humiliation was a hard, no-fucking-go limit.

Nudging the curtain to one side, he acknowledged the security guard stationed behind it. Big, burly, Hispanic, even Finn might've thought twice about tackling him in a fight. He wondered if that was where the man had gotten the scar marring one cheek. "Luís, right?"

"Yes, sir." The smallest glimmer of a smile accompanied the reply. "Membership card or invite?"

Finn pulled his wallet from his coat, flipped it open and flashed the glossy black membership card worth a small fortune. He put his wallet away but kept the card in his hand; he'd need it soon enough.

"Thank you. Hope you enjoy your evening." Luís stepped aside to give him access to a set of steps leading to Black Light.

"You too." Hearing voices enter the shop behind him, Finn jogged down the steps and marched along the neon-lit concrete tunnel. He quite enjoyed the secrecy surrounding the club, not to mention the quality of discretion. More steps greeted him at the end of the tunnel, and a security door.

It was what waited behind it that had his cock paying attention.

He walked into the dimly lit room that posed as both the security and locker room after the locks buzzed clear. He remembered the man sitting behind the desk, inclined his head. "Been a while, Danny."

He got a grin in return. "Master Finnegan. You picked a good night to come back to Black Light."

Finn produced his card again. His own grin flashed wickedly. "Thought I'd better make an appearance. Wouldn't want to leave one of those lovely subs you've signed up standing on that stage all on her lonesome now, would we?"

Danny laughed. "Definitely not. We've got a sub for every taste tonight." He tapped quickly on his tablet and a locker popped open. "All valuables and electronics in your assigned locker please."

Finn stripped his coat off, folding it neatly and setting it inside along with his phone. Knowing the drill, the only valuables he'd brought were his phone and wallet. He closed the door, straightened the hem of his vest. He'd gone for simple—black western boots, black jeans, white long-sleeved shirt and charcoal suit vest. He couldn't abide ties so had left the collar of the shirt open two buttons.

"My bag?" he queried as he turned. Before Danny could answer, Finn's attention latched onto the beautifully formed, scantily clad submissive standing by the door to the club, his bag in her hand. "Can't fault the service, Danny."

Another chuckle. "I should hope not. Spin a winner, Master Finnegan."

Finn took his play bag from the pretty sub with a quiet nod and escaped into the club as a woman's soft laughter broke into the locker room. He stopped for a moment, drawing in a deep breath and taking in the sight before him. As he exhaled, he felt the dominant side of him stretch and flex.

Oh, tonight was going to be so much damn fun.

His gaze skimmed over the room. Classy was the first word that came to mind. He appreciated class as much as he did quality, and Black Light had both in spades. He recognized several politicians—this was D.C. after all—and thought he spotted a renowned model lurking across the room, chatting with a mixed group of patrons including actors, singers, and oddly enough, a woman who resembled a recently retired pornstar.

By the stage where two huge roulette wheels waited, a couple of apprehensive subs were already in line. A little early, he mused, but he'd take that over tardiness any day. Eagerness and nerves made such a delightful combination to play with.

He noted the handful of bags already tucked away on one side of the stage, weighed his own in his hand. Shipping his toys to the club for the night had sent his blood into a frenzy at the time; now it was simmering in his veins along with the excitement of acquainting himself with some of his newer purchases.

Finn slipped around the edge of the hustle and bustle of Roulette night, eyes tracking over people and play stations. The scent of leather and money was strong, but more than that, sex and anticipation smothered the air with every second counting down to the opening ceremonies.

Dungeon Master Spencer Cook, a formidable man Finn had met on his previous visit, cut through the center of the attendees with a face harder than the Big Horns. The low lights glinted off his silver hair, cast shadows over his face. Whoever had tripped the guy's switch was in for one hell of a dressing down.

Checking his watch, Finn kept moving toward the stage. With every step, he shed his casual, easy-going persona and let the Dominant show himself. Shoulders and back straightening a fraction, opening himself to the balance of power and responsibility that came with holding someone else in his hands.

By the time he set his bag beside the others, Finn was gone.

Master Finnegan stood in his place, surveying the club with an assessing gaze. Arms crossed over his chest, he leaned back against the stage and just *watched*.

More people were coming through the doors, more flesh becoming exposed as they did exactly what he'd just done; discarded the front they used for the purpose of societal boundaries and embraced who they were at the core.

Such a fascinating process.

Daddies and littles, Masters and slaves, Owners and pets. The lifestyle offered an abundance of choices, a wide variety of kinks, and no one batted an eye. Whatever the kink, there were others to share it with and learn from.

Finn recognized the beauty of it. Breathed it in.

He caught the curious attention of several Dungeon Monitors and made mental notes of which ones he had already met and who required the pleasure of an introduction. With any luck, he wouldn't need them tonight, but it was always good to know where to look for assistance.

Impatience gnawed at him.

Twenty minutes to go.

CHAPTER 2

AVA

*Y*ou'll never amount to anything.
Should have drowned you at birth.
No one will ever want you—what is there to want?
Gripping the edge of the tiny bathroom sink, Ava banged her head against the mirror and tried to banish the voices plaguing her. They were with her every day, her constant companion, dragging her down to the depths of despair.

Failure.
Useless.
Stupid.
They'd picked a doozy of a time to hit her tonight.

It had taken weeks of lectures from her roommate, days of deliberation and fingernail biting, and one visit to the ER to get her to put her name forward for Valentine Roulette at Rosanna's new favorite playground, an exclusive BDSM club with the alluring name, Black Light.

Rosie claimed it was the best club around, and Ava didn't doubt her best friend in the slightest; she just wasn't sure it was the right place for her. She didn't fit in with people, no matter where she went, and the idea of being partnered with a man she didn't know from Adam, letting him do *things* to her she had no control over, when he probably felt no attraction to her whatsoever, seemed like a cruel punishment.

For them both.

It was a contest after all, with a coveted prize of one month's membership—what if she cost this nameless, faceless Dominant his chance at winning?

She rested her forehead against the cool glass, abhorring the woman staring back at her in the reflection. Misery was never a pretty picture.

Her eyes slid down to the drawer just inches from her hand. Her private drawer, one she knew Rosie rifled through daily to check for sharps. For each one she found, Ava had another stashed in a different place.

Pressure piled onto her chest, sitting between her bare breasts like a car. Soundlessly, mouth agape in deference to the shock of it, Ava rapped her fist against the swell of panic.

Foolish girl, did you actually think you had the balls to go through with this? Can't hold a job down because your head's so screwed up, can't handle a relationship because you're too goddamn weak. Where are your dreams now, huh? Soon you'll have no one left to hold your hand when you're bleeding out on the floor...

She shoved away from the counter, staggering back and hitting the bathroom door as she clamped her hands over her ears and bit back the scream threatening to tear her apart.

"Ava? Ava!"

As though she hovered in mid-air, Ava saw the vision of herself slumped on the floor, eyes glassy with blood loss and remnants of the high of the burn, while Rosie wrapped a towel around her limp, stained wrist.

One cut too far, too deep.

The door humped at her back, sucking her from the past into the future. Dazed, she stepped away and caught her friend as she pushed into the bathroom. "I'm okay, Rosie."

The crimson-haired bullet crashed into her, nearly sent them both to the floor in an insane game of human Twister. Dark chocolate eyes searched hers intently before they scanned the room. Obviously finding nothing out of place, Rosie met her eyes again. "I can see it, Ava. You're not okay, and you're damn sure not pulling out of Roulette."

"I wasn't—"

"This is exactly why I wanted you to give this a shot," Rosie interrupted sharply. "Tonight will give you a safe place to explore the side of you that needs the pain, without me worrying I'll be coming home to a corpse."

Oh, ouch. Ava sucked in a breath.

"I did it once, I can't deal with it a second time. So, seeing as we're running late, get that ass into the clothes I laid out on your bed and let's get moving." Softening her tone, her friend pressed warm palms to Ava's cheeks. "I know you, babe. Drowning yourself in the voices won't give you what you need. Cutting isn't the answer. There are other ways."

When Rosie clamped a hand over hers, Ava realized she was tracing lines over her wrist. She flushed, tried to yank her hand free, but Rosie wasn't to be deterred. She flipped Ava's wrist over so the bathroom light illuminated the extent of the scars scribed into the flesh.

"This right here is a diary of your life." She angled the other so both wounded limbs were spotlighted. "Emotional pain caused by that fucker you call a father. The voices in your head are all him, and it needs to stop. Before he puts you in the ground, Ava."

Ava swallowed hard, blinked back the weakness of tears. No one understood how much the burn helped her silence the muttering in her head. It didn't matter how carefully she tried to explain it, nobody grasped how a blade cutting through her skin doused the fuse leading to a powder keg of years of repressed memories and psychological torment. "I'm sorry."

"Don't be sorry. Just promise me you'll give tonight your best shot. Open yourself to pain other than this," Rosie urged, stroking her fingers over marks still red and sore.

"Okay." What else could she say?

Tell her the truth, foolish girl. Tell her how inept you are, how stupid. You'll never be normal. No one's ever going to love you. She's the only one left in your pitiful life trying to fight for you. But that will end. She'll give up, cast you aside the next time she finds you with a knife in your hand.

"Hair looks fabulous, make-up could be better but it's not like you need a lot." Oblivious to the internal struggle warring inside Ava, Rosie released her and clapped her hands together. "Any Dom worth his salt is gonna be drooling over you, babe. Now, time to get you into the dress and then I think we're ready."

Ava lifted a brow at what her friend wore, and the amount of skin she showed. The black dress hit Rosie's shapely thighs a handspan away from her crotch, emphasizing the length of her legs along with the admittedly sexy matching heels. Her shoulders and arms were bare, and the material barely contained the bounty of her impressive breasts. "Please tell me we're not doing the twin thing."

Rosie's laugh was devious. "Absolutely not. You're going on stage, babe; that calls for something a bit more enticing."

"Shit."

~

AN HOUR LATER, Ava rued letting someone else have control of her life.

Standing in a line with fourteen other women—all of whom were prettier and obviously more suited to the submissive atmosphere—she felt ungainly and completely out of place. The underlying hum of anticipation running up and down the selection of submissives piqued her curiosity but Ava tamped it down by pulling her cloak of aloofness tighter around her.

The journey between getting dressed and being shoved into position by a weirdly excited Rosie blurred in Ava's mind. The urge to run, the desire to cut, combined with frazzled nerves had turned her into a malleable form for Rosie to steer where she wanted.

Not to mention dolling her up like a... a slut.

Glowering down at herself, Ava plucked at the slinky material covering her from breasts to ankles. The dress attached to her like a leech, showing every curve. Perhaps the color was pleasing enough to the eye—the rich plum made her white-blonde hair pop—but for someone used to jeans and hoodies on a daily basis, Ava felt ridiculous.

Beside her, a woman pulled a water bottle from her bag, sipped nervously, repeatedly, before capping it and returning it to her cat-sized purse.

Ava shifted in Rosie's borrowed high heels, feeling her balance wobble and the long slit running down the dress from ankle to hip parted to expose more pale leg than she liked.

"Hey, I love your gloves," the woman to her left murmured. Curious green eyes smiled warmly at Ava when she turned her head. "Seriously classy, very lady of the ball."

She managed to offer a small smile, tried not to pull at the elbow-length fingerless gloves she'd found in Rosie's drawer. They covered her scars, hid her shame, but couldn't distract her from the need to find something sharp and burn away the anxiety roiling in her gut.

Slut. Whore. Coward.

You should be at home, drowning in tears and blood.

"Th-Thank you. I-I borrowed them from a f-friend." Crap, her cloak was slipping. Her eyes drifted over to the gathering of strong, stoic Doms at the other side of the stage and wondered which one would be furious with her for failing him by the end of the night.

"First timer, right?" Her new friend nudged her with a gentle elbow. "It's okay to be nervous. I know a few of the Doms playing tonight and they're all good guys. A couple don't look familiar, like the jolly brooding giant at the back there, but Black Light has an extensive screening process and they're big on safe words."

Ava pressed her hand to her stomach, breathed.

"I'm Tanya, by the way." She reached down and clasped Ava's frozen fingers in the warmth of hers. "Whoa, ice cube alert! Are you sure you're up to this? I can get Garreth."

The lights dimmed and flashed, then a single spotlight illuminated the night's MC in a wash of light. Heavy bass started booming in time with Ava's heart and the excitement of the evening exploded in a tide of people drawing closer to the stage as the MC—young, black, and pretty damned attractive—lifted his shirt to show off a perfectly defined set of abs.

As the women in the audience let loose with screams and catcalls, Ava shut out the noise, her own insecurities, and did what she always did when she was overwhelmed—she brought in her wall of steel and stood behind it like a queen. Distanced herself from everyone around her, using the impenetrable wall as her main defense.

Applause deafened her, and she watched a tall, impossibly graceful man walk across the stage to meet the MC, lifting his arm to wave at the sea of admiring kinksters who obviously adored him.

She knew him, she realized. Recognized him from the media and the illustrious career both he and his husband were famous for even before they'd openly come out as a threesome with the pretty young woman they loved.

Jaxson Cartwright-Davidson.

Ex-model. Dominant. Father of… twins, she thought.

Lucky man.

Her vision blurred unexpectedly, and she quickly shored up the hole in her wall. She wasn't here to find love—love would never be in her cards for this life—and she needed to remember that.

Tonight was about finding a new way to silence the voices, nothing else. She just needed to be strong, banish her weaknesses, and try her damnedest not to make whichever Dominant was unlucky enough to spin her name hate her by the time the clock struck eleven.

She listened to the MC—Excalibur? No, no… Elixxir, that was his name—run through the rules of the contest. Dungeon monitors, the club safe word—*red*—at least thirty minutes for each activity spun on the wheel, and time for clean-up and aftercare.

It made her feel just a little nauseous.

Tanya squeezed her hand as the Dominants filed up the stage steps to draw numbered wooden sticks from MC Elixxir. "Here we go. Three hours of submission, sex, and sinful debauchery."

The crowd seemed to be a living entity as the wheel started spinning for the first time that night. It moved as one, reacted as one, even as her eyes dissected individuals from the throng. When the ball dropped into the slot, the reaction of the voyeurs in waiting astounded her.

One by one, the wheel paired up Dominants with their submissive partner for the evening, then their initial activity. The buzz intensi-fied, electrifying the air. As per the rules of Valentine Roulette, no couple could start play until everyone was matched.

The jolly brooding giant, as Tanya dubbed him, was the sixth Dom to be drawn. Pewter eyes scanned the remaining submissives intently.

"Master Finnegan, the wheel has paired you with..." Elixxir almost crooned the word as the wheel tick-tick-ticked to a halt on stage. "A very lucky lady indeed. Could Ava make her way up here?"

The mention of her name jerked her attention away from people watching. She blinked once, stumbled as Tanya gave her a little push and a thumbs-up along with an encouraging smile. More than a little on edge, Ava met the DM waiting patiently at the bottom of the steps, hand extended for hers.

When she wobbled, he cupped her elbow. "Steady there. You okay?"

Ava nodded. "Yes, thank you."

They navigated the steps together. "You're new. Nice to see a fresh face among the regulars. I'm Owen. You need me, or any of the other guys, you just shout."

"Thanks," she murmured as he left her at the top of the steps. She winced as the lights caught her eyes, then felt her stomach twist, back-flip, and wither when she saw up close who the wheel had chosen for her. "Oh hell."

The voice in her head laughed maniacally.

"Come here, little sub," the giant in devastatingly sexy clothing ordered. Well, *drawled*. Wherever he'd sprung from, it wasn't D.C. His voice was warm, rumbling, and stirred her pussy into weeping grateful tears.

Ava cursed Rosie for not letting her wear so much as a thong.

Blowing out a breath, she straightened her shoulders, drew herself to her full height, and met his eyes—beautiful dark-gray eyes—with a resolve not to make an absolute ass out of herself. Her gait was easy for two steps... until the third sounded like she'd shot herself and she toppled helplessly toward the side of the stage.

She flailed, knowing just how much hitting the floor was going to hurt, then squeaked in surprise when she was yanked flush against a rock-solid body. The mountain moved fast, she thought as her hands curled around biceps bigger than her slim thighs.

Applause rang out when Master Finnegan simply lifted her and carried her to the wheel. Baffled, she stood trying to keep her balance as he bent on one knee and skimmed rough-palmed hands over her ankles, to the straps of the cursed shoes.

"Step out," he said firmly, and tossed the shoe with the broken heel to one side before repeating the move with the undamaged one. "Better."

Speechless, Ava gaped at the top of his head. Dense black hair covered his skull, and she had an irresistible urge to run her fingers through it to see if it was as soft as it looked. "Thank you."

Master Finnegan pushed to his feet, looming over her as he grasped her chin in his hand tightly. Gray eyes glowered at her. "Thank you what?"

Her wall was toast. It hadn't imploded with a scatter of bricks and mortar; no, the big lummox had walked up to it and simply pushed it over. "T-Thank you, Sir?"

One finger stroked beneath her chin as reward as he drew his hand away. "That's your first and only warning, little dove. Respect at all times, understand?"

"I-I... yes, Sir."

"Good girl." Moving like a ginormous panther, he circled behind her and, with only the fingertips of his hand spanning her lower back, nudged her toward a grinning Elixxir and the gleaming white ball in his dark hand. "Spin."

"Looks like you two have hit things off already." Elixxir winked and passed Ava the dreaded activity ball. "Now, you both have humiliation down as a hard limit, but let's see what the wheel has in store for your first scene." He sent it whirring, around and around until the slots became one vicious blur. "Anytime, Ava."

She dropped the ball like a hot coal, watched it bounce... and bounce... and bounce. Her heart thundered in her chest as the wheel slowed and the ball rocked to a stop.

"*Impact play!*"

194

CHAPTER 3

FINN

*W*ell now, this one was different.

Finn navigated his prize away to the side as Elixxir moved onto the next Dominant in line. She was rigid beneath his hand, yet there were moments when it felt as though she might relax. A submissive fighting her own submission, what fun.

Pretty little filly, he thought in admiration. Skittish too.

He set them apart from the other couples waiting for the games to begin, turning her to face him. She had the prettiest eyes, he mused as he studied her face. Blue with little gold flecks. Full of apprehension as she let him look his fill.

Her face was lean, almost gaunt, and her hair was so white it gave her skin a nearly unnatural pale cast. Either that or she was scared bloodless. Never mind. By the time their first scene was over, she'd be a healthier shade of pink... all over.

God knew he couldn't wait to get his hands on the long, lean length of her once that provocative tease of a dress was puddled around her feet. She'd look good with a pair of cuffs around her wrists, those dainty feet spread, and her body stretched from the rigging he had his eye on.

"Are you scared?" he asked bluntly, pushing several stray locks of hair away from her face.

"No. No, Sir," she corrected quickly before he could amend it for her.

"Good." He meant it. A scared sub could bolt, could safe word. His size alone was enough to deter a few timid women, but he had a feeling this one wouldn't. She was here for a reason and she didn't seem like the type to back down from a challenge.

Slowly, he paced around her, taking stock of her from all angles. Held herself well, although there was some trembling starting to take hold. He pulled the limit cards from his pocket, scanned over hers as he traced a line down her spine from nape to crack.

Humiliation, blood play, needle play, and ABDL.

Not the strangest limits he'd ever encountered.

Elixxir was wrapping up the last few Doms quickly, much to the audience's pleasure. Finn cast his gaze over them, saw on the waiting faces what was at a boiling point inside him.

"My name is Master Finnegan," he told her as her feet shifted restlessly on the stage. "You will address me as such, or as Sir. I like a sub who knows her manners. Obedience will give both of us satisfaction; disobedience will make your ass, and your ass only, incredibly unhappy. Are we clear on that?"

"Yes, Sir."

Finn frowned. She was definitely beginning to shake, even if she denied being afraid. He sighed and tucked the cards back into his pocket, deciding he didn't need to be quite so much of a hardass at the start of their new dynamic. Safe wording at this point of the evening would gain neither of them anything worthwhile.

"Have you ever taken part in a scene before?" he wanted to know. "Ever been exposed in front of an audience?"

The audible click of her swallow told him everything.

Stepping up behind her, he collared her with his hand, squeezing lightly. Her reactive peep of surprise made his cock stand to attention in the confines of his pants. "When I ask a question, it will be answered. Quickly and honestly. Hesitate, lie to me, and this ass will be mine in more ways than you can imagine."

Fuck, her whine vibrated against his hand and turned his erection to pure steel. "Could you… would you… expand on that, please… Sir?"

His chuckle was dark, and loud enough several Doms looked at him with smirks. Ignoring them, he let his free hand slide over her side, following the contour of her body, then down and around to cup the curve of one firm cheek. "I wouldn't be so eager for punishment, little dove. I find making naughty girls' bottoms ripple under the cane before I fuck their tiny hole is the best form of penance. I'm a big guy," he added in a sultry murmur as her breath hitched, "in *all* respects."

Ava moaned softly, her thighs and buttocks clenching tight. He held her like that for a moment more, fingers caressing her throat, her ass, before she went rigid in his arms. He didn't relinquish his grip until she relaxed, then simply turned her into him.

Finn was a big believer in eyes being the window to a person's soul, that looking hard enough through the window showed everything beyond the glossy surface. A submissive's eyes were extraordinarily easy to read in the right light, and his new sub was no different.

His little dove had secrets, and there was nothing he liked better than ferreting them out. Time ticked past as he used his fingertips to map her face, all the while watching those eyes mirror her every thought.

"Everyone's paired up, and you know what that means! It's time to start Valentine Roulette!"

Elixxir's proclamation broke Finn's study and he grinned at her with all the devilishness he could muster. "Ready to play with a Master, little dove?"

It fascinated him how she tugged on her protective shield, becoming the woman she'd been in those few seconds on stage before her heel snapped and sent her tumbling. Outwardly strong and independent while the heart of her quivered. She hid her vulnerabilities well, but she was in a room full of wolves now and going head-to-head with the Alpha.

"I am, Sir, if you are."

"Excellent answer." He bent and tucked his shoulder into her midriff, lifting her effortlessly. She was too skinny, he decided, and weighed well under what she should. That just made it easier for him to clamp his hand around her tense thighs as he stalked toward the edge of the stage, cutting through the pairings heading for the steps and their stations.

Gauging the drop, he didn't slow his stride. He heard murmurs as he reached the end of the stage, gasps and long *ooooohs* switching to awed applause as he simply stepped off the edge of the world.

Ava gripped the waistband of his pants, her cry swift and sweetly fearful.

His boots hit carpet with a heavy thud and his sub never moved from her tenuous position. His hand patted her thigh as a reward as he turned to grab his bag from the stage.

"Showing off, Master Finnegan?" Owen commented, walking toward them. The burly DM lifted an eyebrow when Finn gave him a wolfish grin. "We have health and safety regulations to follow, you know. I'm not sure that stunt complies with the club's concept of safety."

Finn nodded, unsure whether the stoic dungeon monitor was yanking his leg or not. "Ava is in perfectly safe hands, I assure you. A little frivolity never fails to set uneasy nerves to rest in my experience, and this little one... well, I've dealt with flighty fillies before but Ava here is something different."

Owen's dark eyes narrowed for a second as if evaluating, then his expression cleared into wicked appreciation.. "Yes, I can see that. I might have to come and watch you tame her."

His grin sharpened. "Watch all you want. Taming's the best part." He patted Ava's upturned ass and gave the smirking DM a nod as they went their separate ways through the crowd.

Bag in hand, and sub subdued over his shoulder, Finn cut through the dispersing crowd and multitude of tables toward the rigging. Ava was quietly maintaining her dignity for the moment; that wouldn't last much longer.

Finn swung her to her feet beneath the rig closest to one of the spanking benches, allowing her to slide down the front of him slowly. Letting her cling to him until the blood rushed out of her head back to where it belonged, he pushed his fingers through her hair and tilted her face back. "I'm strict, Ava, but I'm not cruel. If there's something you don't understand, ask me. I'll strive to push your limits, but I won't fucking break them."

Those damned eyes of hers were going to be his undoing.

"If I ask what color you are, you'll give me one of three answers—green for full-steam ahead, yellow for hit the brakes, and red for *get me the fuck off this train*. Although that will end our fun for the night, so I hope we don't get there." He cocked his head in question. "Are you ready to take this step with me?"

Ava nodded slowly, carefully. "Yes, Sir. I'm ready."

"That's a good girl." With one last assessing look over her, Finn squared his shoulders and dropped his tone an octave. "I want you to strip. Fold your dress and set it to one side with anything—everything—else you're wearing."

Releasing her as she blanched, he took a firm step back and crossed his arms over his chest, fingers drumming lightly on his biceps as he watched the war battle over her face. New submissives were adorable.

It took ten seconds for her to blow out a heavy breath and bend to grasp the hem of the dress. She gathered fabric in her hands until it bunched at the top of her thighs. She had the most graceful limbs, he noted, itching to run his hands up them from ankles to pussy.

She hesitated at her waist, then simply wrenched the clingy garment up and over her head. For the first time, a dusky shade of pink worked over her skin as she hugged the dress to her chest.

"Clever girl. What else did I ask you to do?"

The blush deepened; Ava shook the material out and folded it, giving Finn his best view of the night so far. She was perfection. Small breasts his hands would have no problem cupping fully, tight and already tipped with budded nipples matching the color of her embarrassment.

She was definitely too lean, he decided. He liked his women with a bit more flesh to squeeze, but her figure was flawless. If she was his, he'd make sure he fed her often to banish the subtle jut of her ribcage and hips. He wondered if the stress of her secrets had anything to do with her trim shape.

As well as foregoing a bra, she'd declined to wear panties. Not even the slim covering of a thong protected her shaven pussy from his hungry gaze. She played a dangerous game; he was incredibly grateful he was the one capable of claiming such a prize.

All he could think when she angled herself away from him and bent over to place the dress on the floor was *Jesus fucking wept*. His flogger would make that stunning ass sing. And if he didn't fuck that precious pink pussy peeking at him between slender thighs before the night was over… his cock might just stage a revolt.

Eyes downcast now, she faced him again, worrying her fingers together anxiously.

"Gloves," he told her calmly.

Her shoulders sagged. Hands shaking, she peeled off the right glove first.

Anger surged through him as the track lights cast their glow over the marks in her flesh. He kept his tongue still as she rolled down the other glove and tossed both toward her dress.

Shame radiated from her as clearly as the scent of her arousal. It touched a sensitive part of him he didn't usually allow to show when his Dominant came out to play, but the simple act of removing her physical defenses had come close to breaking her.

Reining in his considerable temper, Finn stepped up to her, took her wrists in a firm grip and studied the scars. Most were old, already silvered and fading into her skin, but there were some more recent, still pink and healing. One in particular caught his attention—thicker, longer than the rest, and surrounded by a boundary of small white dots.

Stitches.

"Look at me, little dove," he commanded, expecting to see tears to go along with the shame. But when she finally met his eyes, there was a painful defiance in them. "This is why you're here tonight."

Her head jerked, her hair cascading around her face like a shield.

"No, you don't hide this. You can't hide it from yourself or from me." His thumb ran along her forearm, touching each scar. "Is this what you need tonight? Something to take the pain away? Or someone to give you the pain?"

After a few seconds, she asked simply, "How did you know?"

CHAPTER 4

AVA

*M*aster Finnegan's hands inspected her scars, work-roughened callouses scraping lightly over each one and sending her skin into rapture. Wherever he touched, she grew warm beneath his caress, and moisture slicked between her thighs.

He'd been angry.

For the first time in her miserable existence, someone with no knowledge of her circumstances had felt something on her behalf. He was the first man to *see* her, what she was, without her saying a word. She'd seen hot emotion flash in his eyes when she risked peeking at him and it stained his words, but he hadn't lifted a hand to her. Instead there was the shadow of concern, an understanding he didn't state but that she felt vibrate between them.

Master Finnegan *knew* her at her core level, maybe better than she knew herself.

Releasing her arms, he stalked to his bag and crouched, black denim stretching taut over tree-trunk thighs and one of the most divine asses gifted to mankind. It was kind of a drool-worthy moment.

Even if the evening veered off course, even if she messed up, she would always have the vision of that ass to remind her she had the guts to stand up in front of an audience of experienced kinksters and attempt to expand her horizons with the spin of a ball on a kink wheel.

You think he *wants* you? *Keep dreaming, Ava. He's here for one thing and one thing only. Beat you, fuck you, and kick your ass to the curb when the night's over. Men like him need a queen, not the serving maid.*

Her hands dug into her thighs, nails scoring flesh. That small flush of pain rushed through her blood like a drug, soothing jagged nerves.

When her Master pushed to his feet in one easy move and turned to her with a pair of leather cuffs dangling from his fingers, his eyes dropped to her hands, darkened with a tempest of emotions she couldn't easily decipher.

"How do I know you need pain?" he queried, crooking a finger and summoning her to stand before him. "It's my responsibility to know what you need, Ava. To give it to you in a safe, sane, and consensual manner." He scowled down at her when she padded hesitantly toward him. "Do you know the difference between hurting someone and harming them?"

Ava blinked slowly. "Um... no, Sir?"

"Intent." Carefully, he fastened a fur-lined cuff around her wrist, slipping his finger between her skin and the soft fluff. Obviously satisfied, he repeated the motion with her other limb so her hands were linked by a short silver chain. "I intend to hurt you, little dove. By the time I'm done with you, you'll have cried your heart out, your muscles will feel like water, and this tight little cunt will be begging me to fuck it until you come screaming on my cock." Lips curved, he reached between her legs and dragged those damned rough fingertips along her slit. "Bad girls take my dick like a champ. How much of a bad girl are you?"

She recoiled slightly. "I-I'm not a bad girl."

"No?" His wet fingertips tapped against her lips. "Suck."

Storm-dark eyes bored into hers as she obeyed, leaning forward to close her mouth around two thick digits. His moan betrayed him when her tongue cleaned her juices off his skin along with the salty tang that was all him. "Good girl. Do you know what good girls get, Ava?"

He withdrew his fingers from her lips with a quiet *pop* of sound as he broke the suction formed by her eager service. "Cuddles and a lollipop, Sir?"

Finnegan laughed. "Not quite. They get a promise, little dove. These marks on your body? They were caused by intent. Intent to harm. I won't tolerate it. So, I'm promising you now, I'll give you exactly what you're searching for. I'll give you the pain, but I will not harm you. Trust me?"

To her horror, her bottom lip quivered. From sexual threats to solemn promises, she wasn't prepared for the ride his words sent her on. His voice went to battle with her father's, the two clashing together in a head-on collision. But it was Finnegan's eyes on hers, his hands gripping her shoulders now, and her father was a thousand miles away. "I…" *Fuck it. If this was just for one night, she was taking it.* "I trust you, Master Finnegan."

The smile curving his lips warmed his eyes, lightened them. "Excellent. Now, arms up. You have your safe word," he continued as he reached up for a length of chain attached to a section of rigging. He dragged it down, attached a silver clip to the end of the chain. "This is a panic hook. Quick release. All I have to do is pull this bit here"—he demonstrated, and the clip snapped apart—"and you're free. You tell me if you have any issues with numbness or tingling in your hands. I will be checking."

Ava rocked slightly as the clip hooked onto the chain of her cuffs and she felt the world sway with her. She set her feet apart to keep her balance, growing warm as she suddenly realized just how many people were gathering around the rigging area to watch her submit to one of the tallest men in the room.

"Color?" Finnegan demanded.

"Green, Sir."

"Good girl. Prompt answer." The heat of him pressed against her back as his arms came around her. One of his big mitts pressed between her breasts as his erection poked against her spine. "Now breathe with me, little dove. Deep breath in… in… hold." His chin rested on her shoulder, his own breath stroking the shell of her ear. "Release slowly."

Her eyes closed, shutting out the eager faces watching her. Already there were subs on their knees, mouths occupied with their Dominant's cock or being fondled. They were distractions, pulling her attention away from Finnegan's scent wrapping around her and the steady rise and fall of his chest against her bare back.

Time drifted past as they breathed as one. Ava found herself relaxing, leaning into her restraints as she lost herself in Finnegan's quiet breathing, in the rhythm of her own. She murmured a protest when he stepped away, his hands running across her shoulders, down the length of her back, over her ass and thighs. She felt his fingers pulling her hair into a long tail, the magic of them weaving it into a plait he placed over her shoulder.

She shivered when he muttered, "Fucking perfect."

Moments later, something light with many strands dragged softly over her shoulders, following the path his hands had taken. Back and forth, back and forth, working down her body in sweeping motions that set her skin humming.

Her head fell forward, rocking with the swing of the flogger.

It reached her thighs, making her shudder as the fronds caressed sensitive flesh, then returned to her shoulders. A little harder but maintaining the same soothing rhythm. Back and forth, back and forth.

Over and over, he teased her with the motion from shoulders to thighs, each volley growing in strength. Her skin began to sing, warmth turning to heat. Good, healing heat that wormed inside her to the bad places.

"Color?"

"G-green, Sir?"

"That's my girl. Stepping it up now," Finnegan told her quietly.

She lurched forward as the snap of the flogger grew harder, striking high across her back. These weren't soft strands lashing her now; she was beaten deliciously with heavy fronds that thudded the ache deep into muscle. An ache mirrored in her pussy, her womb.

Master Finnegan crisscrossed her back with the new implement, moving down, down, down until the flogger snapped hard across her ass. Left, right, left, right. Snap, snap, *snap*.

Riding the burn—so much better than she'd ever achieved with a blade against her skin—Ava offered her bottom instinctively, moaning pitifully. She was close enough to orgasm she could see it floating in front of her like a hot, bright sun.

"If you come without my permission, your ass will know about it," Finnegan warned ominously. He didn't even sound out of breath, yet she was a limp, sweaty, burning mess perilously tempted to forfeit her ass's safety in favor of coming... and coming... and coming... "Color, little dove."

White, she thought. Everything seemed so white and pure.

"Green," she slurred softly, smiling as the word slipped through her lips like a whispered dream. She liked it here—the voices were gone, pain was her beautiful, wonderful master, and her body was alive in ways she'd never experienced.

She arched into the next blow then squealed as the backswing hit. It didn't thud over her skin, it seared. Her cry of surprise morphed into a moan of pain as the sting spread over her flesh. Before she could catch her breath, pain pounded over her shoulders followed swiftly by the lash.

Oblivious to everything but the beauty of the strike, she came.

Finn

SNEAKY LITTLE MINX slipped that one through, Finn mused as he upped his rhythm and watched her legs tremble through her orgasm. Most submissives he'd had opportunity to play with would have given in and called *yellow* by now, but Ava was shuddering through her orgasm and sagging in her bonds like a queen.

She'd pay for the orgasm, of course, but she was a fighter.

His eyes met Owen's in the glow of the dim lighting, the DM lurking in the shadows among the spectators. Owen nodded once in approval and drifted back from whence he came.

When Ava's feet slipped out from beneath her, Finn dropped the floggers and looped an arm around her waist, taking her weight off the restraints as she sagged. Her skin was the most impressive shade of pink, scored with heavier red marks from the knotted flogger, and thin, glowing welts from his new rubber one.

"Oh... my... God," Ava purred reverently as his hand skimmed over her shoulders. She stayed limp in his grasp as he lifted her a little, unclipping her cuffs one-handed. "I didn't think anything could make me feel better than cutting."

Finn bared his teeth and, before he could stop himself, cracked his open palm on the smooth curve of her butt. She yelped, hips jerking forward, and gripped his arm as he carried her to the spanking bench, pressing her face to the cool leather by her nape. "Do you know how mad it makes me to think of you desecrating this beautiful body with a blade?" he demanded. "Don't make me add to your punishment; you've earned one already for coming without permission."

With her ass already warmed up nicely from the flogging, Finn had no qualms about going to town on her with his hand. His world narrowed down to the snap of flesh on flesh, Ava's grunted *ah* of pain with each spank, and the incessant throbbing of his cock trapped in his stupid jeans.

"M-Master Finnegan, p-p-please!"

Damn it all, how was he supposed to punish her when her ass lifted into every harsh slap? He tightened his fingers on her neck, heard her mewl. "Stay right here, little dove. Move an inch and what I give you next will be twice as bad. Understand me?"

"Y-Yes, Sir!" she panted, gripping the edge of the bench desperately.

His cock protested as he stepped away to retrieve his bag, rummaging through for the toys sealed in clear plastic baggies. He studied a couple, chose his weapon, and with baggie and lube in hand, returned to his sub. From the copious drops of arousal gathered along her slit, lube wasn't strictly necessary—she was providing him with more than enough of her own. "Pain isn't just your escape method, is it, Ava? It's your drug, your high. I could fuck your ass without lube and you'd scream, you'd cry, but I bet you'd fucking beg me for more."

A strangled groan matched the one rippling around the spectator circle. More than one couple were engaged in service—he spotted three subs on their knees, hair fisted in their Dominant's hands as they were throat-fucked almost in sync with each other. It was poetic. Another sub, a middle-aged woman with her breasts wrapped in Shibari bondage, bent over toward the scene while her tank of a Dom fucked her enthusiastically from behind.

Finn set the items down and twisted Ava's braid around his wrist, pulling her head upright from the pool of saliva gathering beneath her cheek. Carefully, he manipulated her movement so she could see everything happening around them without damaging her neck. "See all these nice people, Ava? They're here to see you in all your glory. They want to see perfection submit to dominance."

Her eyes fluttered as she smiled up at him.

"Are you submitting to me, little dove?"

"I... yes, Sir."

"Sure about that? Because good girls don't come when their Master tells them not to. They don't push their asses out for the flogger." He reached down between her spread legs and shoved his thumb into her pussy, biting back his own groan as muscles sucked at him frantically. "They certainly don't get this wet at the thought of punishment."

"I'm not. It's you. It's all you, Sir," she whimpered.

"All this is for me?" he murmured in her ear, bending down to keep the moment between them. "All this slick juice is just for me, hmm? That must mean this cunt is mine," he added, fucking the tightest pussy he'd ever had the pleasure of touching with his thumb. "And this ass must belong to me, too—how fucking lucky am I?"

Her stunning eyes rounded into moons when he removed his digit from velvet wetness and pressed it against resisting muscle. She squeaked out a breath, stiffening as he pushed firmly until the breadth of his thumb pierced her.

"Oh fuck. Oh fuck me."

"Are you gonna make me feel like a king, little dove, and tell me I'm the first to be in this perfect hole? Because it sure as fuck feels like it." Finn grinned down at her when her mouth dropped open. He might be the first, but she liked it. "Say it, Ava. Say the words that'll make me real happy."

She whined. "You're the first in my ass, Master Finnegan. Jesus, I need more. Please, I-I need…"

"I know what you need." He withdrew his thumb with a pop, felt her shudder. Unwrapping her hair from his wrist, he eased her head back onto the table, reaching for the baggie and removing the butt plug. Longer as opposed to thicker, it was a beginner's plug and perfect to keep her occupied for the remainder of their scene.

Across the room, one of the Roulette Doms stalked up to a DM with his submissive in tow. The woman seemed unsteady on her feet, and the Dom was clearly not happy. Attention caught by the drama, Finn absently slipped the plug between her labia, thrusting the cold metal into heat as arms began to wave and the submissive fought with the DM over her bag.

Ava's filthy moan of approval brought him back to his own sub. While he appreciated drama—he didn't need it right now. His cock was providing more than enough entertainment trying to force its way through his zipper.

"Deep breath, Ava. Push out." He dragged the blunt tip of the plug up to her anus, notching it, inserting it slowly as Ava's hips danced against the edge of the bench. He gave her ass a slap and returned to his bag. "Now that you're all warmed up, I think we can finish the scene with a bang."

Her ass clenched.

"A-a bang?" she asked tremulously.

Finn slipped a long blue velvet sheath from his bag, untied the strings at the top, and slid the toy onto his palm. Sixteen custom-made inches of rock maple formed into a honey dipper—a damned big one. He ran it through his hands, making sure the wood was as smooth as it looked. It could double as a dildo in a heartbeat, but he intended to use it for its original purpose.

"What is *that?*" she whispered nervously. "You could knock a Rottweiler out with that thing!"

His smile was slow and ominous yet didn't stop her pretty pussy from clenching. His little dove loved to fly, and she wasn't afraid of taking the hard ride home. He spun it around in his fingers like a baton, testing the weight, then set it beside her head and felt the blood surge through his veins when she slowly licked her lips.

CHAPTER 5

AVA

*H*e was going to beat her to death with Winnie the Pooh's spoon.

Master Finnegan stared down at her as he flicked open the button on his shirt cuff and rolled the material up a muscular arm bearing a deep tan, with scars of his own, and dark hairs. The tendons in his forearm flexed and released, much to her delight.

His was the kind of forearm she could gnaw happily on, licking the salt from his skin. Hell, she'd go to bed cuddling the damn thing. But if his arms were this hot... what about the rest of him?

When the material bunched above his elbow, he repeated the action with his other arm, deft fingers working quickly. Deft, firm fingers that curled around the smooth end of the stick capably and slapped it down hard on his palm with a meaty connection.

Ava bit her lip.

Jesus, that was a raw sound. She flinched when his hand stroked down her body in one long glide, cursed herself for showing the weakness. Gathering herself behind her wall, she waited for her Master to unleash hell on her presented buttocks, but he just caressed her tight muscles with his calloused touch until some of the tension eased.

"Better," he told her decisively, giving her tender butt a quick pat, jostling the plug. "When you're wound tight, it'll hurt more. I'm not aiming to give you a panic attack, Ava. I want you to open yourself to the pain, breathe it, live it, *become* it. You've become used to letting it control you, dictating to you when and how you need it."

She sighed, nodding her agreement with her cheek slicked with cool saliva. Somehow, a stranger could see right through her darkest, most painful and shameful secret. He had every right to turn away from her, to discard her back to the reject heap and spend the night drinking at the very impressive bar behind them, but he'd buckled down, taken her straight into submission, and earned her trust.

She could count on the fingers of one hand the number of people she trusted.

She was used to being stared at, ridiculed, lambasted for who she was and what she was driven to do. People stared at her scars as though she were a freak, and even if she had them covered up, her paranoia screamed at her to say they could see through the clothes to her weakness.

Master Finnegan watched her like she was a diamond glinting in the sun.

Precious. Rare. Beautiful.

"When you're with me, little dove, *I'm* the one in control. *I'll* be the one dictating to you how and when you take *me* in whatever hole I please, whenever I fucking want." His fingernails bit lightly into the nape of her neck, dragged down her spine over sensitive skin and raised welts to the bump of her raised buttocks, eliciting a sharp squeal from her lips. "I'll ask you outright, Ava, before we wrap up this lovely little scene: do you trust me?"

"Yes, Sir." There was a vehemence in her tone that hadn't been in it before. A surety. Ava nodded again as her confidence swelled, in him, and in herself.

"Will you trust me to take care of you even as I hurt you?" He dragged the rounded tip of the implement in his hand down the shallow valley of her spine.

She closed her eyes, blew out a long slow breath. She knew what came next. "I think you're the only one I do," she murmured. Her cuffed hands gripped the head of the bench. "Maybe the only one I can."

His response was the backs of his fingers brushing over her cheek before he moved away. "We're going for ten, little dove. Move and I'll tie you down. Remember to breathe."

The only warning she got was a quick double-tap of wood against flesh. The initial strike was gentle compared to the harder smack of the second but combined... *oh boy*. It took everything she had not to rear up and howl as the sting stabbed into her ass.

Opening her eyes and glancing over her shoulder, she saw Master Finnegan flip the toy in his hand, catching it easily and laying another double-tap swiftly beneath his last target.

Tap, smack, thud.

Tap, smack, sting.

Tap, smack, thud.

The rhythm caught her up, tossed her into the serenity she usually found when she huddled in the corner of the bathroom, blood trickling down her wrists. The faster he struck, the harder wood met flesh, the deeper she sank into peace until the murmur of the audience faded away into the rush of blood pulsing through her ears.

Tap, smack, thud.

The plug in her ass detonated like a bomb, sending waves of vibrations spiraling up her spine, forcing her pussy to spasm greedily around nothing. A keening cry erupted from her throat, strangling her, as her body arched and bucked.

Heavy weight covered her, an arm banded around her chest over the tops of her breasts while another slipped between her hips and the edge of the bench as she banged against it. "Ride it out, Ava. There's a good girl. I've got you."

Splinters of pleasure and pain intertwined, urging nonsensical babble to spill from her lips. Her fingers scrabbled against the bench top, needing to hold on to something before she spun away and became lost in the chaos.

"Steady, Ava." Finnegan's rumbling voice purred against her ear. "Listen to me now. Open yourself to it, little dove. I've got you safe."

The heat of him scorched her back and she was burning up from the inside out.

She dropped her head to the bench, breathing hard and shuddering as pleasure continued to thrum through her body like she was a maze of wires and the orgasm was a jolt of electricity. A moan hummed in her throat. She arched against the body at her back, her skin quivering with the contact. Mindlessly caught in the spin and swirl of the chaos he wreaked upon her, she listened to Finn's patient, nurturing murmurs as her system started to settle.

There was a God after all, and he smelled like the earth. Clean, fresh, with an oaky undertone.

Ava wanted to giggle, but found it quickly tightened her throat and brought tears to her eyes. Her emotions rocketed from top of the world to lowest of the low, and she wondered what he thought of her. She wasn't clean or fresh; she'd been dragged through hell by her hair and it had stained her.

"Color, little dove." Finn's mouth brushed against her ear.

She tried to croak out green, but it came out strangled. Clearing her throat, swallowing down tears, she gave it another attempt and managed to form the word without betraying herself. "Green, Sir."

"Are you sure? You flew pretty high there."

"Don't worry about me, Sir, please. I'm not worth it."

Her Dom snarled furiously, and she shrank into herself beneath him and waited for hell to rain down on her head. He slipped his arms free, deepening her fear, then grasped her by the shoulders, straightening her carefully from her bent position and turning her into him. When he wrapped her up in his embrace,

She buried her face against Finn's shoulder and trembled.

"Remind me to spank your ass later for that comment," Finn rumbled. "Don't ever put yourself down that way again."

Her mumbled, "Yes, Sir," was barely audible.

"Everything okay here?" A stern voice joined the fray, and Ava cringed. Her current position shielded her bare pussy but she was positive the metal end of the butt plug was the focal point for several pairs of eyes. "Master Finnegan?"

"No problem, Spencer." Finn's voice was easy. "Ava's just telling me how I shouldn't be worrying over how hard she just came apart. Would you do me a favor and pass me that blanket?"

Something warm draped over her back and she burrowed deeper into Finn when he lifted her effortlessly, bracing her on his hip like a child. She just wanted to go to sleep exactly where she was and forget about the mortification of this scenario. Even with the blanket covering her, she was sure the plug in her ass was screaming for attention..

"As long as you're both enjoying yourselves, I'll leave you in peace. I have enough shit on my plate dealing with the Dom unlucky enough to spin a fucking sub smashed out of her head on contraband vodka." There was a pause, then, "Master Finnegan, don't forget the private rooms if you need some downtime. I'll have a server fetch you some water and whatever else you require. Enjoy the rest of your evening."

"Thanks, I think we'll take you up on that." Finn kissed the crown of her head as she continued to tremble. "Just the water will be fine."

"No problem."

"Come on, little dove, you can stop hiding now."

They were moving away from their play area, and she sighed as his long strides ate up ground. She sensed the presence of people around them, heard murmurs, and then it seemed like the world opened itself to her ears and let the full force of Black Light wash over her.

The smack of implements meeting flesh, the resultant moans and cries. Someone somewhere was screaming, the sound so euphoric it sang in her blood along with the darker thrum of jealousy. Her ears burned when the hard, fast tempo of sex reached into her pussy and sent a fresh flood of arousal coursing through her. Nearby, the indelicate coughs and gasps of a woman choking were harsh enough to have her lifting her head weakly.

Finn's hand cupped her cheek, urging her to rest again. "She's okay, I promise. Her Dom is taking a great deal of pleasure from fucking her throat, that's all. Everything's fine."

Ava wet her lips at the thought of servicing Finn that way. She'd never been very good at blowjobs, had always gotten criticism, so she'd abandoned any further pursuit of the act. She turned her head so she could scan the room with heavy eyes until she found the couple in question.

Holy shit, that wasn't a blowjob.

A short, squat man stood ten feet away with his legs spread and pants open just enough for his cock to spring out. His hands fisted in the dark brown locks of a woman on her knees, her hands at the small of her back, with an intricate weave pattern of ropes binding her from wrists to elbows.

Her only point of balance was her Dominant's grip on her head, and he was using it to his advantage, feeding his cock through her rounded lips before slamming his hips forward and making her take the full length of his shaft down her throat.

Ava turned her head away from the abundant strings of drool dripping down the woman's heaving breasts. She wasn't sure she was confident enough to let someone else have control over her breathing like that... and she sure as hell didn't have faith in her gag reflex.

"Not your thing?" Finn whispered into her hair.

She shook her head, her hand gripping his vest. Closing her eyes, she could still hear the woman going strong, only now she was joined by grunted jibes from her Dom. She was relieved when Finn carried her away and the noise of the main room dimmed considerably.

"We'll stay here for a little while," he told her as his body folded and he settled her firmly on his lap. She squeaked and jumped as her new position pushed her metal friend deeper inside her back passage. Finn just chuckled and let her squirm. "Get your bearings, little dove, and then you can decide if you want to spin again."

She thought of going back up on that stage beneath the lights, the smoothness of the ball in her hand, and the way her stomach did nervous little flips as the ball hopped around. She wanted to do it all again, this time without worrying over what kind of Dom she was playing with. "Will they let us spin again?"

"They have no reason not to. Everything was safe, sane, and consensual, and you didn't safe word. If I haven't scared you off, the only person who can stop us from rolling again is you." He shifted, changing his hold on her so he could tuck the blanket more firmly around her. "The choice is entirely yours, little dove."

"Thank you," she murmured. "I… I liked that scene."

"Yeah? It worked for you, huh?" Finn pressed a kiss to the top of her head. "Even that last part?"

She bit her lower lip. "You mean where my butt exploded?"

A long rolling laugh filled the little room. "I'm quite sure your butt didn't explode, but yes, that part. It was incredibly arousing to watch you shatter, Ava. I think I'll enjoy it considerably more when it's my cock being strangled by that tight hole, but I'll take it as a victory for now."

"What did you do, play whack-a-mole with the plug?"

"Direct hit." Finn rocked her, his hands giving her support she hadn't known she needed. "How are you feeling? You're definitely brighter."

She tilted her head to look at him. "I was dull?"

"No, Ava. I mean your eyes are clearer, your voice is stronger. You're coming off the high. I thought you'd hit subspace but I think we were just shy of the mark this time."

Subspace? "Um…"

"Master Finnegan, may I enter?"

Ava's head jerked up and she gaped at the stupendously tall, stunningly slender server standing at the threshold with a tray balanced neatly on the fingertips of her right hand. Long blonde hair, several shades more golden than Ava's own shock of white, cascaded down to her navel, twin streams of gold running over each shoulder and covering her otherwise bare breasts. Wearing only thigh-high boots with impossible heels and what was essentially a G-string made out of wire, she kept her eyes lowered.

"Sure," Finn drawled.

"Thank you, Sir." She reached them in three strides, sinking gracefully to her knees without so much as wobbling the tray. "Dungeon Master Cook asked me to bring your supplies, with his compliments. I have your water, and some brownies one of the littles brought in for the crowd. I believe your station is being cleared, and your bag will be brought to you shortly. Can I do anything else for you, Sir?"

Finn reached out and took the bottle off the unwavering tray, along with a small plate of brownies oozing with chocolatey goodness that made Ava drool. "This is perfect, thank you."

Like a marionette, the server shifted seamlessly back onto her feet, almost perfectly reversing the moves she'd used to adopt her position.

"Is that normal?" Ava asked a little loudly. She offered the woman a smile when the blonde head turned, blushed when she was given a wink in return.

"Some people are born to serve others; it gives them gratification. Clubs like this are where they thrive—there's no judgement, no derision, just an understanding. Where people thrive, they become almost iridescent with the pleasure they derive from being what they see as their true self." Selecting a brownie, making it seem like a crumb in his big hand, Finn brought it to her mouth. "Open up. You're too lean, little dove. Someone needs to fatten you up."

She scoffed. Stress and an appetite the size of a walnut didn't make for a fuller figure. "If my ass gets any fatter, there'll be no whack-a-mole. You'd be hard pressed to find the plug, never mind nail it with a giant stick." Her mouth popped open when his hand smacked down on her still-sore ass, then she was choking on chocolate.

"I'll spank this ass every time you put yourself down, Ava. If your ass is so big, why can I feel the hilt of your punishment digging into my thigh while you soak my pants with that delightfully wet response?" Grinning deviously, Finn jiggled his leg beneath her ass, bouncing her on the broad span of his thigh until the scent of her arousal renewed and deepened. "My cock isn't used to being jealous of a finger of metal. Maybe I should replace one with the other."

Holy shit. *Holy shit.* Holy... *oh.* Ava's nails bit into the hard muscles of his arm as the plug jostled, touching naughty, sensitive places and ripping a pleading moan from between clenched teeth.

"Here, little dove, have a drink. Your voice cracked at the end there," Finn told her, chuckling as the rim of the bottle touched her lips. "Drink as much as you can. If we spin again, I don't want you passing out from dehydration. When you get home later, you drink more, okay? Stay hydrated."

"Yes, Daddy," she mocked under her breath, then stilled when something dark and virulent flashed in his eyes. They searched hers, narrowing in speculation, before clearing.

His fingers kneaded her ass firmly, and like a whisper of breath into a tiny ember in the depths of a fire, set her alight again. He nudged the blanket off her shoulders, ran his nose along the slender line and up the side of her throat.

She damn near came when his teeth nipped her earlobe at the same time his fingers stroked over her small breast and pinched her nipple. Twin shocks of pain speared straight between her legs, triggering her limbs into springing open to give him access.

"My little pain slut," he murmured, rolling her nipple harshly between thumb and forefinger. When she stiffened, the beautiful fire dying as though doused by a bucket of water, he didn't stop fondling or nuzzling. "Not big on being called names, Ava?"

She shook her head adamantly. If name-calling could be on a limits list, it would be carved in stone and bronzed. Her father liked to call her horrible things—slut, whore, cunt, twat, and his absolute favorite, cum dumpster—because he loved to watch her self-esteem die an inch at a time, day by day.

Her voice was hoarse when she whispered, "I'd use my safe word."

Finn's temple rested against hers as he pulled her close. "Which one?"

"Red." A tear slipped down her cheek. She wouldn't blame him for getting up and walking away from her now—she'd heard the language used in the club, had heard Doms using the terms on their subs, and she couldn't judge them for it. It wasn't her right to do so. It was part of their scenes, part of building sexual tension and maybe even staking territory, but what did she know about it?

The damage her father had done to her emotionally, mentally, couldn't be undone. He'd branded her as those things, rewired her brain to see only the negativity in them, and taken great delight in making her bow to his demands by using them to break her.

Ava wept when Finn's arms tightened around her, cocooned her against him, and he said simply, "Good girl. Don't ever be afraid to say no."

They stayed that way for a few minutes as the tears came and went in waves. He was so attentive, the warmth and scent of him a blanket all its own. When she finally calmed, he reached into the pocket at his side and pulled an honest-to-God handkerchief free, wiping her face before telling her to blow her nose.

Feeling stupid, she obeyed.

He made her eat another brownie, though her stomach protested, and she finished the bottle of water under his eagle eye. Then he just studied her critically for several long seconds before asking, "Would you like to take another spin of the wheel with me, little dove?"

Because she didn't want him to leave, she answered with, "Please, Sir."

CHAPTER 6

FINN

Finn stalked toward the stage with Ava hurrying along beside him. She was adorable, trying to shield herself using his body, but he was lusting after that long, pale form and didn't see a reason why anyone else should be denied the privilege of lusting after it too. Touching, however, was another matter entirely.

If he was more of a sadist, he'd have his branding iron searing his mark into the pristine flesh of her ass cheek before he claimed her thoroughly—mouth, pussy, ass, and every delicious inch between—and often.

From the way she responded to pain, he imagined she'd ride that high better than a bull rider in the goddamn PBR.

Subtly, he adjusted his cock in his pants as they reached the three steps leading back to the wheel. Taking her hand in his, he urged her ahead of him so the brighter light illuminating the stage spotlighted every last lash and welt. That rubber whip had done a fucking amazing job, he mused. And the honey dipper... well, from this angle, she was definitely going to be tender once the excitement of the night faded completely.

Elixxir greeted them with a grin as he bobbed his head to the music thrumming low on stage. It was barely audible, but the man seemed to be able to discern the beat easily enough. "Ah, Master

Finnegan and Ava, right? Great to see you back up here tonight. You enjoying yourselves so far?"

Finn answered his grin as his hand curled around his shy sub's neck. "Couldn't have asked for a better spin of the wheel."

"Fantastic. That's what we like to hear. So, you're aware of the rules. Thirty minutes minimum in whatever scene you draw, safe words apply, you know the drill." Elixxir's head hadn't yet stopped grooving with the tune. "Ready to spin?"

Ava's hand trembled as she reached for the little white ball the MC offered; Finn's squeezed reassuringly on her nape, his thumb stroking soft skin as Elixxir sent the wheel whirring. He felt her take a breath before she dropped the ball.

They watched it bounce and roll erratically, and Finn eased her closer as she shivered. He pressed his other hand against her belly, as much to capture her physical reaction as to offer comfort.

"And your next scene is..." Elixxir called out loudly.

The ball rocked to a stop.

"Fisting!"

Finn blinked. In a heartbeat, Ava's stomach sucked in so quickly he lost contact with her skin. Beneath the warm light, her skin turned chilly, and both she and Elixxir dropped their eyes to the hand at her midriff. From the floor, a barrage of cheers erupted.

The MC lifted his eyes to Ava's face, then Finn's as he cleared his throat. "If I remember correctly, ah, fisting wasn't on either of your, ah... limits lists. Are you both okay with this, Master Finnegan?"

The use of his club name snapped Finn out of his shocked stupor. It was rare for something to take him by surprise and this really took the prize. But he was the Dominant in this dynamic, and he had a responsibility to his submissive to make sure she was...

His train of thought stuttered and died when her shaking fingers gripped his hand, lightly stroking over his fingers, the back of his hand. He turned it over, captured her cold hand in his. "Safe word, Ava. There's no shame in it."

Her throat clicked when she swallowed. "No, Sir."

Damn it, she was stubborn. "Fine, then I will." He pinned Elixxir with a glower. "R—"

A tiny hand slipped over his mouth as Ava whirled and silenced him. Her wide eyes conveyed she understood just what she'd done, but she shook her head fiercely. "No, Master, please don't. Not unless you believe I can't do this." Her shoulders sagged as she let her hand slide away. It dropped limply to her side. "For once, I wish someone would see I'm not weak."

He bared his teeth. *Weak?* She was the last person he'd ever consider weak. Torn, he offered her the truth and hoped she'd take the right way out, while knowing she wouldn't. "I'll hurt you, little dove. Maybe I'll mean to, maybe I won't, but you're going to scream either way when that tight cunt stretches around my hand."

She turned a little green but held her ground. Held her ground and threw his words from earlier in the night back in his face. "You told me you'd give me the pain and promised not to harm me. Does that not still stand?"

Fuck. Crafty little minx. "I don't break my promises, Ava."

Elixxir watched the exchange with intrigued eyes. "I, ah, the medical play area is currently available," he interjected politely. "But it might not be for long."

Finn glared at him a second before Ava flattened him with three little words.

"I trust you."

The barrage of swearing he released could have put him in the history books as a sailor. Unwilling to lose control, he ground his teeth and willed himself to calm. There was consent, she was willing, and he had total control over the scene from start to finish. "You promise me, Ava, you fucking *promise* me the moment you need to, you safe word out."

When she hesitated, he let his Dom have full rein. Stepping into her, crowding her, he gripped her by the throat firmly enough her eyes lost that nervous edge and rapidly dilated into pools of black liquid.

Christ, she was intoxicating.

"Promise me," he growled threateningly. "Or I drag you to the locker room and borrow something for you to wear out of here, right here, right fucking *now*."

"I promise, Master," she breathed.

He was on her in an instant, his free hand yanking her head back by her disheveled braid while he flexed his fingers around her throat. Her eyes remained on his, transfixed by whatever she saw in them. "Louder, sub."

"I promise, Master!" she said again, her voice stronger this time.

"And if you break that promise, little dove, what am I going to do to you?" Finn leaned down and nipped at her jaw, at the pulse bounding below his fingers. "Tell our curious Master of Ceremonies over here just how I'll make you pay for breaking your word."

He'd lay his hand on a Bible and swear she orgasmed in that moment. Her eyes fluttered, her teeth sank into her lower lip. A rich red flush spread over her pale cheeks like spilled red wine over a pristine snow-white carpet.

Rapid flutters of breath washed over her lips as her tongue darted out to wet them. "You'll fuck my ass, Sir."

"Hell yes, I will." His mouth took hers savagely in a kiss hotter than a Montana drought. The kiss might have been blisteringly hot, but damn if she wasn't a drink of cold water in the heat. Innocent and refreshing, tentative in the face of his aggression before her own sexual drive kicked in and she came back at him with just as much passion.

Drawing away from her cost him, but he managed to ease back before they got ahead of themselves and gave the Black Light attendees a different show than the activity they'd spun.

Finn swore he heard Elixxir mutter a prayer of thanks as he grasped Ava's hand and tugged her off the stage. Aware of the small gathering following on their heels as he beelined for the medical play station, he realized their next scene would pull in enough attention to make her uncomfortable.

A male server stopped him as they reached the station, barefoot and nude aside from the cock cage strapped in place. "Master Finnegan, I'm sorry. You were already on stage by the time I gathered your things." He held out Finn's bag.

Taking it, Finn nodded. "Thank you."

When the server sashayed off, Finn stepped forward but Ava did not. He looked at her; she was worrying her lip as she studied their next play area. "Just say your safe word, Ava. We can pack it in, get dressed, go for a coffee." Though it galled him to offer it knowing she'd be playing with another Dom, he added, "I'll cover your month's fees for Black Light. You'll win either way, little dove."

Her fingers twitched in his. "No, I won't, Sir. Not in the way that matters."

She would, eventually. Finn was certain of it. This was more advanced than she was ready for, but if she felt it necessary to test her limits, at least he could provide a safety net for her to fall into when she needed it.

"The only thing that matters is you," he murmured, and finally her eyes came to him. "When we go in there, I want you to get on the table, lay back, and put your feet in the stirrups."

"You've done this before, right?"

Finn ignored the smattering of laughter as he towed her into the doctor's office. He really didn't think she'd appreciate knowing his experience with this activity came from long, miserable hours of freezing to death with his arm in a cow's vagina up to the shoulder. Cows were roomy, unless the calf was stuck.

Ava wasn't a cow and she definitely wasn't in calf.

He gave her a smack on the ass as he urged her toward the padded exam table and watched her quibble over her choices for a minute. Her face was so expressive, she'd be the first one naked in a game of strip poker. "Relax and let me worry about what experience I do and don't have."

He tucked his bag beneath the counter, leaned back against it as he unfastened his watch and set it to one side with one eye on her. Her thigh muscles were trembling as she ran her hand over the equipment. His fingers worked down the buttons on his vest, his shirt, before he unrolled his sleeves. Shrugging out of the clothes, he heard someone —a distinctively female person—purr loudly in approval.

Ignoring it, he inspected the fingernails on his right hand, running the pads of his fingers over each one to check for sharp edges. Clean, short-cut, they wouldn't pose a risk to her delicate inner flesh. Causing her injury was not going to happen.

Someone called out in encouragement as Ava awkwardly boosted herself onto the table, and despite his own misgivings over the scene, Finn found himself brimming with pride.

"Good girl," he praised, and grinned when she flushed bright pink. He did like her with color in her cheeks.

Curious to see how far she'd push herself, he busied himself with little things that built into the collective *big moment*—gathering gloves and lube, scrubbing his hands meticulously before checking his nails again, debating standing versus sitting. He set a fat tube of lube and the gloves on a tray, then grabbed a towel. The club might have an excellent cleaning crew, but this much lube would be a bitch to mop up.

When he turned, tray in hand, his heart twisted and flopped.

Perfectly still save for the tremors rippling through her muscles, Ava was exactly as he'd ordered. Her eyes were trained on the ceiling, hands clutching the sides of the table, and she breathed deeply through her nose, exhaling slowly through barely parted lips. Those lithe legs were spread, not far enough, not yet, but he caught a glimpse of the pretty pink pussy he was about to make scream. Her plug nestled cozily between her cheeks.

If she was determined to try, he needed to change his tune.

He set the tray on the handy stand beside her, ran his hand along her thigh. She jolted, her breathing hitched, and she continued to stare at the light above her. Well, that was easily rectified now, wasn't it?

More voices joined the hum of curiosity from intrigued voyeurs watching the scene. The light was bright enough above the table and dim enough outside the station that she couldn't see just how many people wanted to watch this kink in action. Hear them, yes, but it was one thing to hear a rabble and another entirely to be able to count each one as they observed.

He took her wrist, stroked down her arm, and attached the restraint before she could object. They were loose enough that if she reacted violently, her hands would pop free with enough force. Tight enough to let her believe she was captured.

"I didn't think you'd be tying me down, Sir."

"This is unlike anything you've done before, little dove. Safety precautions, that's all." He skirted around the head of the table and affixed the second cuff. "Plus, it has the added benefit of you look really fucking hot."

When he strapped her feet into the stirrups, she started to look a little more concerned, her legs moving restlessly. He'd gone on the side of caution with her feet—dainty though they were, he'd taken a kick or two off riled females before—and made sure they were secure.

Her breath whistled as he drew the padded strap over her hips. "What—"

"Shush, Ava. Trust me. Just close your eyes and give me control. I'm not going to let anything happen to you, okay?" His tone dropped an octave, adding power to his statement. "Relax and breathe."

When she obeyed, pride swelled.

Time to begin.

∽

Ava

She was so fucking stupid.

Tied down, all of her body on display for the people she could hear murmuring quietly, with Finn standing over her... arousal went head to head with terror.

For the first time since they spun the wheel, she wanted to cut.

Why couldn't they have spun something mundane, like tickling or age play? She'd seen those on the wheel and they seemed innocuous compared to the granddaddy of kinks they were stuck with. Why didn't they have limits on the size of someone's hands for this? Had they not *seen* Finn's hands before he came to play?

Her hips arched of their own volition, yanking her from her thoughts, when coarse hands rested on her knees, cruising leisurely down her thighs, back up. She desperately licked her lips when they cupped the inside of the joints and pushed, spreading her obscenely wide.

Cool air wafted over her.

She heard the stirrups lock into position. Sounds of sex echoed in her head as someone tittered. Paranoid, she tried to close her legs, only for Finn to pat her foot gently.

Fingers circled the metal bulb in her ass, tugged it firmly. "Think we need to remove this now, don't you?" he asked pleasantly. "You've been so good, holding it for this long."

She wanted to be good, she wanted to be strong.

She also wanted to wiggle when the plug stretched the rim of her ass. The burn was what she needed, and she mewled when Finn removed it completely.

Warm fingertips traced her labia, parted them. Stroked along the slick seam carefully. "Not nearly as wet as you need to be, little dove. I'm gonna help you with that."

His voice had thickened with a slow drawl and, combined with what she thought of as his Dom voice, wrecked her in an instant. Slow, deep, and dark obviously pressed all her buttons.

Her eyes popped open when a warm tongue followed the path of his fingers. Gripping her thighs from beneath, Finn's dark head was the only visible part of him as he crouched in the vee of her legs and tripped the switch to the floodgate inside her, magic tongue exploring every nook and cranny he could find.

He used his fingers to keep her open, pushing that damned tongue inside her while his thumb strummed her clit like a guitar pick on a string.

Ava almost screamed in frustration, unable to lift her hips enough to hump his face. And by God, she wanted to. There was no room for fears or doubts or those shitty little insecurities in this moment—there was only Finn.

Then the bastard took her to the ledge, balanced her on her tiptoes above the crevice… and left her there.

"No!" she howled the word out of sheer desperation.

"Patience, little dove," was his reply as he surged to his feet.

Damn near frothing at the mouth, she cursed him silently even as she watched him pull on a clear latex glove with precision. Those doubts crawled back inside her as he slathered viscous gel over his index and middle fingers.

"Color, Ava."

"Green!"

He arched a brow at her. "Green what?"

"Green, Sir. Please… I just want to come, Sir. Please let me come."

She flinched as cold gel met heated flesh, then simply moaned in delight. Two thick fingers pushed slowly inside her, stretching her snug channel until she hissed with the ache. They scissored and twisted, intensifying the sensations. So many sensations.

The slick slide of lubricated latex over her clit sent electricity snaking down her spine, hotwiring it directly to her brain and cutting out the body between. Her hands fisted, straining against the cuffs.

"Are you ready to come, little dove?"

"*Yes!*" Jesus, did he not understand he held her sanity in his hands?

"We had such lovely manners earlier in the evening," Finn admonished sternly, slapping the inside of her thigh sharply and thrusting his fingers deep. They crooked up, sparking the fuse. "Say please, little dove. Say please, real nice."

Her legs tried to jerk straight; her hips rose an inch off the padding of their own volition. Her body, goddamn it, was no longer hers. It was his, every inch, and he fucking knew it. She didn't say please *real nice*.

She screamed it.

Her brain imploded from stimulation. Her vision frayed at the edges, shattered into glorious fragments where she was reduced to nothing but a heartbeat floating in empty space.

Bumping back to earth wasn't as thrilling. Calmer, a little bit strung out and perspiring freely, Ava's eyes rolled around the station. They landed on the giant still looming between her legs, his serious mouth curved at the corners, his hand still working her pussy.

"Did we win?" she slurred.

His unoccupied hand hit the table beside her head and he leaned over her to study her eyes. Broad, *broad* shoulders blocked out the light from above. And still he pushed deeper, stretched her further with just two digits. She felt more connected to him in that moment than if it had been his cock forging inside her.

"Not quite, Ava. Ready for me to stir things up again?"

Looking into his eyes, she wished her hands were free. The urge to slide her fingers into his hair and tug him down to replicate that scorching kiss was ridiculously strong. She'd never been kissed like that, like she was the central star in a man's universe. "It's going to hurt, right?"

Gray eyes were sympathetic before they switched to devious. Finn twisted his hand, did something that brought a strangled cry from her lips. "Fisting probably wasn't the most ideal spin for this tight pussy," he crooned, twisting his hand again and almost catapulting her through the ceiling. "But you like the pain, don't you? Your eyes don't lie, Ava, so don't let your mouth betray you."

Fuck, he was hot when he was like this. She'd never imagined finding a dominant man attractive, sure as hell hadn't thought she'd be spurred on by words that could quite easily have been callous. "Yes, Sir. You know I do."

"Yes. Yes, I do." Still, he watched her face for a few more seconds before he eased back, slipped his fingers from her with a wet sucking noise that, absurdly, mortified her. He reached for the black towel on the tray, the one that probably cost more than her life was worth considering it was emblazoned with the club's initials, and shook it out, folded it in half, then slid it under her tender ass.

Her breath shuddered out as he slicked more lube over his hand, liberally coating all four fingers until it dripped from the blunt tips. Big hands, solid fingers. Working man's hands. "W-What do you do for a living?"

CHAPTER 7

FINN

"You're choosing now to ask me that?" Finn asked, amusement evident in his tone. His cock wasn't quite as entertained—it was halfway to busting out of his pants and diverting the scene to a more satisfactory ending. "I run about twenty-thousand head of cattle over eighty-thousand acres of prime Montana real estate, darlin'."

"Cattle… cows?"

He chuckled, screwing two fingers back into her opening as he talked. She grasped him greedily, driving him insane, and on the next thrust of his hand, he added a third finger. *Christ, she was tighter than a maiden heifer.* "That's right. Open up for me, Ava. Just relax."

She whimpered, blue eyes glazing over.

"Watch, Ava. I want you to watch my hand and feel me inside you."

Feet away, the gathering of spectators grew. Finn could feel them, the press of them around the area as lust ebbed and flowed from person to person.

He swiveled his wrist from side to side, adding a little more pressure this time to work his hand against the resistance of her snug hole. He had doubts he'd get the pronounced heel of his thumb or the wide bridge of his knuckles past her narrow entrance. He swore to

God his little sub was either a virgin or she hadn't been treated the way she deserved.

A woman like Ava wanted fucking relentlessly, that nervous body sated with orgasms and the pain she needed, then being tended to like a queen. If she didn't have a life here, a home here in D.C., he'd be thoroughly tempted to offer her a seat on the plane home in the morning and take care of her the way she deserved.

Finn cursed under his breath and grabbed the lube again, pouring it over his hand and engaging an almost piston-like motion. She'd done as he ordered, and her eyes were locked on where they joined, watching his fingers plunge in and out. Lube and her own juices combined into a thick, slick mess that squished wetly, dripping down the crack of her ass to pool on the towel.

When she started to whimper in her throat and the constriction surrounding his hand eased, he knew he was making progress. Her labia bloomed around his fingers, bright red now rather than blushing pink, and her clit resembled a ripe berry.

Finn closed his eyes, concentrated. He thanked God he'd had the foresight to strap her hips down; he wasn't sure whether her undulations would have hindered or helped. They weren't helping him quell the urge to shove his pants down and mount her as though he was one of his prize bulls.

Focusing on the warmth and wetness around his fingers, the squeeze of her muscles, he changed the angle of insertion and gained a smooth inch. There was something primal, carnal, in the way her flesh submitted.

He was a man who relished the feel of a woman squirming beneath him as his cock spread her open, pushed deep. Watching apprehension dawn in their eyes was probably a sadistic pleasure, but he loved to see fear turn into knowledge, knowledge spiral into ecstasy.

Ecstasy devolve into sheet-clawing, toe-curling hunger.

But this... Ava's trust and willingness to surrender was something else.

She grunted hard, her whimpers coming a little faster, almost guttural.

Finn opened his eyes, assessing her carefully. He eased his fingers out carefully, muttering under his breath as her pussy tried to clamp around them. "Color, little dove."

Her laugh was slightly desperate. "I don't know."

"Think and think hard." He straightened and stretched the tension out of his shoulders, taking a few moments to revel in the raw beauty of her. Crouching, he inspected her gently, pleased to see no bleeding or bruising. "Made your mind up yet?"

"Maybe..." she swallowed nervously and, adorably, her toes curled into the stirrups. "A yellow shade of green? Like more yellow than blue?"

Finn rose and pulled her thigh against his side, wrapped his arm around her calf, then bent to press his lips to her raised knee. "Are you sore?"

"A little. I think I'll be more so when you're..." Another swallow, tighter this time. "What if..."

Ignoring the collective hum of impatience from outside the station, Finn watched her face as she trailed off. Something was worrying her, eating away at the arousal and undermining her pleasure. She wouldn't meet his eyes, just tucked her chin into her shoulder away from the voyeurs. "You can tell me, Ava. Don't be embarrassed if you have concerns."

Those slim shoulders shrugged listlessly; Finn slapped her thigh. "Shrugging is not an answer, little dove. Give me the words and, while you're at it, let me have those eyes."

They slid back to him, beautifully blue and looking strangely reminiscent of a puppy that had been kicked. "What if you get stuck?"

Someone laughed, a Dom from the sound of it, and someone who should have known better. Ava turned beet red and tears shimmered under the lights. She yanked at her wrist restraints. "Fuck this. This was a bad idea. Let me go."

"No, you don't, little dove." Finn pressed his hand between her breasts, pinned her down, then seared the crowd with a look. Scanned the faces he could see with an intent to cause grievous bodily damage. He raised his voice to make sure all and fucking sundry could hear him. "Anyone who laughs at a sub's concerns shouldn't be a fucking Dominant. You listen when she raises a valid point, and you address it with the respect she deserves." He ripped the glove off, tossed it aside when her breath caught in all the wrong ways, then leaned over her and gripped her face in both hands so she had no choice but to look at him. "You think after all the time and patience I'm putting into breaking into the art gallery for this divine piece of art, I'd damage it on the way out?"

Her response was part-sob, part-chuckle.

"It's a vagina," she said weakly. "Not the Smithsonian."

"Correction: it's *your* vagina, and I'm feeling rather attached to it." He kissed her, softly, sweetly, breaking out of the scene and not giving a damn. "There's a medic on standby, Ava. I can see him lurking. None of us here are going to let anything bad happen to you."

His thumbs wiped under her eyes as wetness glimmered beneath them.

"Is this how yellow works?" she asked in a whisper.

"Yeah, little dove. With me, this is how yellow works." Another kiss, another thirty seconds of fucking heaven, then he levered himself away from her and gave her a salacious wink. "Now, are we ready to finish this journey together?"

Her eyes darted to the waiting audience.

"Ava. Give me a color."

"Green, Sir." She wiggled a bit in her restraints, but to his relief, she looked more settled. "Master Finnegan... I'm sorry."

Busy pulling on a fresh glove, he glanced at her in surprise. "For what?"

"I know I'm not the best submissive you could have drawn from the pool tonight, and I-I have issues, and... I think you're more hard-core than you've let yourself be with me tonight, so I'm sorry for screwing things up for you."

Nodding slowly, he drenched his hand in lube as he considered her words. Perhaps she was right in one sense; he had been easier on her than he might with another, more experienced player. His kinks walked a fine line but Ava had proved herself capable of handling them well enough so far. In his mind, his evening might not have been so enjoyable without her company.

"You think you screwed things up for me, little dove?" He set his free hand on her stomach, just below her breasts, and dug his nails lightly into her skin. Lips pursed, he dragged them down her torso slowly as he mused. "No, I don't think you have. I'm having the time of my life actually; how about you?"

She squirmed, high-pitched giggles escaping her as she sucked her stomach in. The giggles died as his nails reached the cradle of her pelvis, scraped over her mound. He stopped above her clit, grinned wickedly at her.

"I've got the best sub I need tied down in front of me," he told her quietly, using just the nail of his index finger to score a line over her clit. Infinitesimally slowly. "She's so easy to torment."

"Please! Please, please!"

Thrusting his gloved fingers back inside her, he gripped the swollen bud of her clit hard, using enough pressure to still her frantic movements. If she'd been his to keep, he'd train her, just like this, to come with a word.

With his gaze on wide, blue eyes, Finn formed a cone with his fingers, tucking his thumb into the center, and pressed forward. Her eyes turned into saucers, a quick flare of pain and panic in the depths before they started to glaze with the rush of endorphins. Her eyelids fluttered.

Soft little grunts filled the space, her breathing hard and quick. Leather squeaked as the cuffs did their job and held her still. The heave of those small breasts was appealingly erotic. The perfect handful for a man with hands his size, peaked nipples made for his mouth.

He wasn't against kidnapping her and taking her back to Montana.

Strong muscles fluttered wildly around his questing fingers as he delved gently deeper. There was a tight ring of resistance around his hand now, sitting just in front of his knuckles. She was doing better than he'd imagined she would—her trust in him was immense, more than he could have dreamed for.

"Still with me, little dove?" he made his voice low and easy, exhibiting none of the exertion it took to pump and twist against her, the muscles in his forearm, biceps, and shoulder working to keep pressure centered against her clutching sex. Persuading that reluctant gate to heaven to part for him just a fraction more. "Relax this shy little hole for me, darling," he coaxed when her eyes drifted lazily to his. "That's it, Ava. A little more."

The muscles in her thighs quivered, and his cock surged when soft grunts became sexy little mewling whimpers. "Hurts. Fuck, hurts."

He should have pulled her up for swearing, but hell, she could have cursed him out in that breathy voice and he'd want to hear more. "Want me to stop?"

"No, Sir." Blue eyes blinked at him. "Please, please can I come now?"

～

Ava

APPARENTLY DIRTY TALK, a big hand in an unusual place, and the mother of all torture on her poor clit was the catalyst for orgasmic Armageddon. She was actually dreading the moment he released her clit more than she feared his hand gaining entrance to her body—she knew both combined might be more than she could take.

"You'll come when I say you come," Finn admonished, killing any hopes of climax she had. His eyes were slightly narrowed in concentration, his brow furrowed, but they gleamed with lust bright enough to lighten the dark gray irises.

Maybe it was just the club lights, but she didn't think so. It was getting pretty damn hard to think of anything but the ache of her pussy and the answering echo in her womb.

"Deep breath," he commanded. *Commanded* in that strict as fuck Dom voice she'd heard once or twice during the night. The one that gave her no room for debate but simply compelled her to obey. "Exhale, push out and relax, Ava."

Again she obeyed, and the world simply shattered.

She shuddered on the table, back arching as the broadest part of his hand squeezed through her opening and finally, *finally* he filled her. Her hips pushed against the strap desperately and the strangest keening sound reached her own ears, the most sexually wanton noise she'd ever heard.

Finn's answering groan was twice as deep, just as long.

This was a different kind of pain—a non-pain. Sensitive flesh stretched and burned with discomfort, but without the raging forest fire of agony she'd expected. She just felt absurdly full, pushed to her limits, yet was so finely balanced on the line of destruction even a whisper would have pushed her over the edge.

Slowly, carefully, Finn pumped his fist inside her, igniting every nerve ending he touched, and he touched *everywhere*. "Come now, Ava. Take it."

The brutal pinch on her clit disappeared abruptly, giving her a split second of relief before angels screamed broken hymns from above and the fires of hell opened beneath her jerking body and swallowed her whole.

Ava gasped, nonsensical babble bubbling free. There wasn't an orgasm on earth capable of destroying a woman this completely—he was overriding every preservation instinct and rewiring her body to his specifications.

Through the grip of pleasure, she felt his hand on hers, giving her an anchor, a grounding point to center herself on. The fur was beginning to chafe her wrists, the softness unable to compete with the force she exerted on her delicate limbs. It only added to the furnace building inside her with the twist and slow roll of Finn's hand.

"P-please... the straps!" She wanted to move of her own volition, let her hips and pelvis drive the fullness to higher climbs. "My wrists."

Finn's eyes snapped up from her pussy, alarmed, and all internal movement stopped immediately. "Are they hurting you, Ava?"

"Nooooo," she moaned, more in protest of him stopping than in answer to his question. "Don't stop, don't stop, don't stop. Don't—oh!"

His fingers curled into a fist, the rounded points of his knuckles doing crazy things to her channel. But the kill shot came as they unfurled again, stretched wide and deep so she believed with everything she was that he possessed her entirely. From cervix to labia, he *owned* her.

She simply gave him the rest without question.

"Come, Ava," he ordered, and she tumbled into the abyss again.

Screaming, thrashing, decimated into nothing but ash, she plummeted into ecstasy. Her own keening cries mingled with Finn's words of encouragement, then comfort. Almost blind with shock, limp with sated exhilaration, she grimaced when he eased his hand free of her clutching sex, then felt empty and dejected.

Latex snapped, then hands were on her face, stroking away sweat and... shit, were those tears? "Don't ever let anyone tell you you're weak again, little dove," Finn murmured against her ear as he bent close, his mouth nuzzling the shell. "By far, you're the strongest woman I know."

Pressure built in her chest; sobs hiccupped in her throat.

The cuffs were off in an instant, rough palms rubbing the sensitive skin gently as the fur-lined restraints fell away. The strap around her hips released its biting grip. Then she was gathered into strong arms, her face held against the heat of his bare chest as she cried for all she was worth.

"What do you need?" Owen's voice was low, respectful.

Finn stiffened for an instant, then relaxed again. Every muscle in his body had a purpose, was honed for one, yet he used them to do nothing but keep her safe and warm. "I need to get her cleaned up enough to get her into a semi-private area. Can you get her out of the stirrups?"

She clung to Finn as hands cupped her ankle, quickly and efficiently releasing the straps holding her foot hostage. A moment later, her other foot was free, and she managed to hook her limp legs around the back of Finn's powerful thighs, grabbing onto him like a monkey.

"Let me check you over and clean some of this mess up," he said quietly, kissing her hair. "I'm not letting you go, Ava, but I just need you to lie back for a few minutes so I can take care of you, okay?"

She resisted when he laid her down again, whining when he stepped back to take a bowl and cloth from the Dungeon Monitor studying her with approval in his eyes.

"Shout if you need anything else—there's a blanket just there." Owen jerked his head toward the counter. "Master Finnegan... you should be fucking proud of what she's given you tonight. Maybe you'll tame her yet."

"Oh, I am, and maybe I will. Might be she's taming me," Finn replied easily, dipping the cloth into the bowl and squeezing it out. His eyes were on her when he paused an inch from her pussy. "This might sting, Ava. Just breathe."

She hissed between her teeth, then let her head thunk back in defeat as he painstakingly cleaned her tender parts. Everything felt raw—not just her pussy—and she was more vulnerable in that moment than she'd ever been. Her emotions, her body, her heart... she knew it was stupid, fruitless, but they simply opened for him and left her defenseless.

"No blood. A little bruising perhaps, and you'll be sore for a few days." Tossing the cloth aside, Finn ran his hands over her from the neck down, checking her wrists carefully, and finishing with her feet. He snugged a clean blanket around her, wrapping her up and carrying her to a chair in the corner. "Stay here for two minutes while I tidy the station for the next players."

Ava huddled into the softness, dozing quietly. The viewing window was almost clear of faces and the hum of voices had died so the noise of Valentine Roulette in full swing could be heard. She listened to the crack and snap of whips, laughter and screams and moans, and she swore in the haze of exhaustion she heard the crackle of electricity.

Why had she never tried this before? Well, obviously, Black Light was well out of her monetary means. She barely made enough to contribute to the rent and still afford groceries, let alone pay an astronomical membership fee to a kink club. Losing jobs so often through her mental problems meant her paychecks were few and far between.

But knowing she could find a deeper, more lasting burn to sear the voices from her head without carving lines into her flesh and sobbing with despair? Tonight had been priceless, in more way than one. The only problem was, she didn't think she could experience that burn, that relief, with anyone but the man currently whistling as he tackled the mess they'd left behind.

Her thighs clenched, twinging uncomfortably from being spread apart for so long. Her clit still throbbed and she pondered the possibility she was ruined for sex now. There wasn't a penis in existence that could come close to replicating the fullness, the movement, the orgasms Finn had given her.

She weighed him up through bleary eyes. Big hands. Big feet. Big everything. Surely *everything* included a cock to match the rest of him?

Wondering, Ava fell asleep.

CHAPTER 8

FINN

*H*e was in over his head.

On a loveseat in a quiet corner of Black Light, Finn's mind was elsewhere. The contest timer was ticking down to eleven, but he didn't care. Only just under an hour of play remained before Roulette was over, but he was content to sit here, his prize curled on his lap like a little girl.

Maybe those Daddy Doms had a good thing going.

Ava snuffled softly into his chest, her cheek using his pec as a pillow and her hand tucked under her chin. She was on the verge of waking and he was in no rush to hasten her. He'd given her one hell of a working over and she deserved to take what time she needed.

Owen had told him he should be proud of what she'd given him.

Pride was only a fraction of what he was feeling toward her right now. There was a riot of emotion in him, a tangle he needed to unravel and assess because, as he sat here, his biggest desire was to claim her as his permanently.

His hand ran up and down her back beneath the blanket, smoothing over the blemishes left by his floggers, playing his fingertips down the overstated bumps of her spine. Compared to him, she was a delicate little sprite, something he could snap in two without thought, yet she'd offered him absolute control over her body, her orgasms.

"Finn?" she mumbled.

He preferred Master Finnegan during a scene; it helped separate the man he was to the outside world from the one who laid dormant too much of the time. But hearing his name in that breathy, uncertain voice did things to him. It blurred the line between reality and actuality of who he was.

"I've got you, little dove. Go back to sleep if you want."

She blinked sleepily, cogs whirring to life as her eyes ticked around the club. A frown marred her forehead. "Everyone's still playing? Why aren't we?"

His eyebrow winged up. "You flew pretty damn high, Ava. I wasn't sure you'd feel like spinning again." His lips twitched when she rubbed her cheek against his chest gently. "And I think you're a little blissed out, darlin'."

"I'm not, I promise. I just feel really, really good." She smiled and sighed, eyes half closed. "I'd like to spin again if there's enough time, Sir."

"Haven't I tortured you enough, Ava?" Resigned to leading her across the stage again, he chucked her under the chin. "Okay then, let's go see what's in store for you next."

She shivered delightfully, moaning when he just scooped her into his arms, blanket and all, and bulled his way through the people in his way. There was barely a stitch of clothing left on a single submissive, and most were engaged in private scenes with their Dominants. Handjobs, blowjobs, several interesting scenes of full intercourse were scattered everywhere he looked, but he counted more than a few head of folk gathered around the other official Roulette scenes still ongoing.

There was a small but evidently loyal gaggle of spectators on Finn's heels; they waited eagerly at the base of the stage as he carried Ava back to the dancing MC and set her on her feet. He tugged the blanket away, folded it over his arm, then let her lean back against him when she swayed a little. "Still sure you want to spin again?"

"Yes, please, Sir." Her hand linked with his, squeezing nervously as

Elixxir greeted them with a big smile. "Just... pray for something nice... like cuddling."

"Cuddling probably isn't on the kink wheel tonight," he said with a laugh. "And you don't need to spin if that's what you want. I'm happy to spend the remaining time cuddling you, darlin'. Just ask."

A considering hum brightened his night further. She was definitely keen on expanding her experiences tonight. Tilting her head back, she gave him a coy smile, almost little-like. "If we spin again, do we get to cuddle after?"

The things he could do to her, with her. "Why not?"

Ava bounced, actually bounced on the balls of her feet.

"We ready to throw?" Elixxir asked politely. Aside from blatant curiosity in his eyes, he was acting incredibly professional considering he knew their previous spin. He gave Ava the ball and spun the wheel into motion. "Whenever you like."

She gave Finn's hand another squeeze and dropped the ball. It amused him how her head moved with the circular rhythm of the wheel.

"For your next adventure, you've spun..." Elixxir paused and then cried out, "*Biting!*"

Ava jerked and Finn became the recipient of that head tilt again. She tugged her hand free of his and turned to face him with a quizzical look on her face. "*Biting* as in..." She bared her teeth and used her index fingers to mimic fangs.

"I believe that is what the wheel has dictated. There won't be blood," he assured her, remembering she'd listed blood play as one of her four limits for the night. "But you can be damn sure you're going to be marked for everyone to see." He swept his gaze over the club and felt his mouth curve into a salacious smile as he spotted the perfect apparatus.

As though she was nothing but a bale of hay, he hefted his little sub over his shoulder—much to her vocal delight—and headed for the sleek curves of a padded sex chair bathed in soft shadows. He could definitely work with those curves.

He stalked back across the room with his admirers in pursuit and dropped Ava onto the oddly S-shaped piece of furniture, grinning down at her as she sprawled and gave him a world-class view of a swollen and glistening pussy. She squeaked, flushed, then muttered to herself when he lifted a finger to stop her protests. "Stay here. Do not move. Do not cover yourself."

Without pausing to check her obedience, Finn turned on his heel and retraced his steps to the loveseat to snag their belongings and slipped a condom from the bowl on the side table into his pocket. When he returned to Ava, she was precisely as he'd left her, but scrutiny from other members had taken the edge off her excitement.

He set their gear at the head of the chair then moved to stand at the foot of it. Impatient fingers tapped slowly on his silver belt buckle "Spread those lips with your fingers, Ava. I want to see that pussy begging for me."

Her eyes dropped to his crotch, widened. "Are we..."

"If I have your consent to fuck you, I'd like to, very much," he told her quietly. He didn't want her to think she had to submit to sex, especially if she was sore. Damaging her was not part of the game. "Don't feel you're under any obligation to, Ava."

"I... I'm not." Her hips lifted a fraction off the chair as she licked her lips. Her hand moved slowly over her hip, her belly, to the wanton spread of her legs, then hesitated for a moment before she did as he directed and parted herself. "I'd like you to fuck me, Sir. Very much."

His boots were toed off and kicked aside in seconds. The hiss of his belt through the loops at his waist ignited a fire in her eyes he relished. The buckle thudded to the carpet followed swiftly by his jeans—after he rescued the condom.

The fire in Ava's eyes became an inferno when he gripped his cock in his fist and stroked himself from root to tip in one long move. "Stand up."

Scrambling to get off the unusually shaped chair, Ava nearly fell off it in her rush. But she stood beside it eagerly, hands clasped in front of her.

"Hands behind your back, grip your wrists," he ordered as he settled himself into the dip of the chair and rested against the rising curve behind him. "Good girl. That's better. Now, come around in front of me." He waited until she stood where he had a moment before. "Such a beautiful little dove. All mine." He set the condom near his navel, just above the crown of his cock. "Get to work, Ava. The faster the condom goes on, the quicker I can fuck that pussy."

She shuddered from head to toe in what might have been a full-body orgasm before she—quite elegantly—draped herself over the smaller hump of the chair leading from the dip. She reached for his cock, stopped herself, and then questioning blue eyes met his. "Please may I... touch you, Sir?"

For a woman so unacquainted with BDSM and its rules, she really was a damned quick study. Finn granted her a sharp nod and braced. His cock was primed for her touch, throbbing with impatience. "Free rein, Ava."

He almost snarled when she brushed her fingertips over his shaft, following the veins pulsing for her. Her skin was warm, smooth as she drew circles around the tip with a single digit, then clutched him tight in her fist and stroked down in one firm draw. "Fuck!"

Her mouth closed over the head, suckling gently, tongue fluttering.

It took him every ounce of willpower not to grip her hair and force that wet, warm mouth over each inch of his cock until she choked. Small hands worked his length with just the right amount of pressure to set his balls tingling as her tongue coaxed curse words from his own.

"Enough." He did grip her hair now, yanking her mouth off him before he did the unthinkable. "You little minx."

The smile she gave him was completely innocent—*completely*. There wasn't a fraction of coyness or mischief on her face. She didn't have a goddamn clue she'd brought him to his fucking knees in seconds—she was just happy making *him* happy.

Finn ripped open the condom, rolled it on himself, not trusting he wouldn't ejaculate immediately with her hands on him again. Instead he patted his thighs and thought of his projected losses of cows and calves for the coming calving season. That took the edge right off his need to come. "Pony up, minx."

She slipped backwards, onto her knees at the front of the chair, then rose and hurried around to his side. He held his hand out to steady her as she swung her leg over him, pretty face contorting with a wince, and straddled his thighs. Then she looked nervous. "Pony might be right, Sir."

He chuckled. "Are you saying I've got a donkey dick, Ava?"

Humor flashed in her eyes as she blushed. "I, ah, no, Sir?"

"Good girl, didn't think so. Get that sweet cunt settled on me, Ava. I've got things planned for you." Finn drew in a breath as her fingers closed around him, held his erection upright, then groaned when she used her weight to sink onto him that first blessed inch. Big hands clamped around her hips, urging her down to the tune of guttural moans and pained squeaks.

She fit him like a hand-tooled glove, taking him to the balls.

"Oh. My. God." Spoken like a prayer, she let her head fall back.

Grinning, Finn savored the feel of her clamping down on him. She was swollen after the fisting, muscles twitching and flinching in reflex, but there was that fire in her eyes devouring each and every flicker of pain.

Finn eased her forward, enjoying the snaps of pleasure sparking in her eyes when his cock rubbed and pressed inside her. He kissed her, slow and sweet at first, then harder as her hips started to grind into him. She yelped when he bit her lip gently, teeth sinking into that plump lower lip.

"Tonight has been better than I could have imagined," he murmured, trailing his lips down to her jaw, nipping at her skin. He moved up toward her ear, nibbling as he went. "Playing with you, *finding* someone as special as you, is my wet dream come to life." His teeth found her lobe, left indents in the soft flesh. "The things I could do to this body with you in my bed, Ava."

She moaned, long and deep, eyes closing.

He continued to roam, nipping and biting down the graceful line of her neck until he reached the slope between neck and shoulder. He ran his tongue over the flesh, felt her clench. "In my bed, in the forest, in the fields. Hell, I'd take you outside and lash you to the hitching post in the yard, fuck you in front of the ranch hands so each and every one of them knew just whose cock you need to make the world go away."

Ava shivered and pressed herself closer, breasts against his chest. Her head angled to the side to give him better access.

"My dirty little minx likes that, does she?" Finn paused, wondering if his use of *minx* would give her cause to call out her safe word. Relief flooded him when she whimpered and rocked on him, trying to take him deeper. "My little minx wants everyone to watch this perfect pussy get fucked, wants everyone to hear her scream... now whose name might that be?"

"Finn," she whispered.

He lifted her as high as he could, yanking her down as his hips jerked up. Her eyes popped open; her jaw dropped. "I don't believe they heard you, minx. Try again. With the correct honorific."

"Master Finnegan!" she cried out.

He struck, biting deep but stopping on the verge of breaking skin between his teeth. He felt her convulse, body cruising at full speed toward orgasm, and cracked both his palms down on her bare ass. "Don't you dare fucking come, minx!"

Her mewl of protest nearly undid him. "Sir..."

He ignored her, nipping at her arms, licking at the skin, until he lifted the first of her scarred wrists. Gripping her limb hard, he picked out the worst scar. "I know you, Ava. I understand *this*, but it doesn't happen again. I'll take your ass to the bank with a bullwhip if I ever find a fresh scar. Understand me?"

Panting, she nodded.

"Let's make sure you do." He sank his teeth into the scar, holding on as she bucked and writhed on his cock. They didn't have much longer left before his restraint would snap. "You give me your pain, Ava, and I'll only offer back what you can handle."

He marked her other wrist in exactly the same way, choosing the newest, pinkest scar to replace with the imprint of his teeth. "I could give you every filthy fantasy you dream of and worship the ground beneath your feet." He slipped his finger between her cheeks, found her hole, and pressed. "Fuck this tiny ass until you cry, come inside you and watch it all trickle out... then treat you like a queen. *My* fucking queen. Everything is about balance."

"Please, Sir, let me... let me..."

"Let you come? No, I don't think so. Dirty little minxes want to be fucked hard, don't they, Ava? They want to be punished, they want to burn alive with the absolutely exquisite pain"—he leaned her back and bit her nipple sharply, making her squeal—"that only their Master can give them. Who's your Master, Ava?"

"You are, Sir!"

"Try again, Ava." He suckled on her other breast, sucking hard on the peaked point to make it harder, more sensitive, while his fingers rolled and pinched the one he'd already bitten. This time when his teeth snapped down, her hips bounced.

"Master Finnegan!" she wailed, sobbing now.

Finn eased back, studied her torso. Wherever he could reach, she was marked. Small red nips raising like miniature welts, bigger bites already swollen and bruising, but not a trace of blood. Her breasts were a tapestry of crimson dots, her nipples hard and ruby red.

He ran his hand along her thigh, grasping her hip as she mindlessly tried to ride him, urging her into a fast, smooth rhythm. Dirty talk and biting, he thought, definitely spurred his flighty little filly on.

Her hands grasped his head, his neck, fingers clawing through his hair. The abject hunger on her face was impossible to deny any longer; she needed sating and she was going to get *exactly* what she needed.

Finn smacked his palms down on her ass again just to hear the strike of flesh on flesh and her feverish moan. Then he gripped her cheeks, making sure his fingertips found uncomfortable welts to clamp onto, surging effortlessly to his feet with her clinging to him like moss on a tree.

"Do you know what I'll do to this ass when you're mine, Ava?" Stepping over the sex chair, he raised her up so his length slipped from her until only the thick crown remained. "Look at me, filthy minx. I want to see those goddamn stunning eyes watch me take you."

They locked onto his. Sweat ran like tears from her hairline, followed the contours of her face as she nodded frantically. "I see you. I see you."

Finn dropped her, grunting as she enveloped him again in delicious heat, then fucked her hard. Pounded into her as her arms slipped around his neck and his mouth found the pulse point in hers. "I'll tie you facedown, little minx, and mark this ass with my brand. My initials seared into this backside," he panted heavily, orgasm rising quickly at the thought. "Mine forever, just like I'll be yours."

Ava stiffened and keened, the muscles in her cunt spasming around him, barely hanging on. *"Please!"*

"Come, Ava. Milk my cock like the dirty minx you are."

She shattered apart in his arms like glass under a bullet. Her body bucked, riding him better than any dream cowgirl. Her head fell back on a wailing cry of, "Master Finnegan!"

Fuck, he was done. His name in that sweet, blissful voice was the extra nudge over the edge. He roared, slamming her down to take every last inch of him as pleasure speared up his spine and crippled him. As semen filled the condom in painful spurts, his knees gave out.

They hit the chair with an ominous creak of wood.

CHAPTER 9

AVA

*M*aster Finnegan had broken her.

Destroyed her flawed body, stripped it down, sanded it, left her ruined.

Ava slumped over the slab of pure beefcake beneath her and couldn't care less that she was half the woman she'd been before the night started—if she'd had words, she would have thanked him. She might have been akin to dead weight on top of him, but inside, she felt so much lighter.

Tomorrow, she'd ache like a bitch. But she didn't want to think of tomorrow, of a day without Finn's voice in her ear, his hand brushing hers. In a matter of hours, he'd changed her, altered her perception on pain, and made her long for something... more.

Made her need him.

Her head lolled on his chest as it rose and fell beneath her cheek, their breathing almost in sync. Body temperature cooling, her heart rate calming, she almost purred as a big hand caressed her back from nape to butt lazily, gliding over sweat-slicked skin.

"You doing okay there, darlin'?"

For a man with such strength packed into hard muscle, he was surprisingly comfortable. Her fingertips explored his skin, tracing the rim of a scar she found on his ribs. Drifting on a high, she frowned at him. "You got kicked by a horse?"

Finn peered at her with one eye. "You haven't answered my question, but no, not a horse. That one's from one of my best cows, a bitch of a thing. Hell of a temper on her but throws nice calves." He closed his eye, brought his hand to her nape and squeezed firmly in warning. "That scene finished more roughly than I planned, Ava. You need to tell me if you're okay, or whether I need to summon the medic to check you out."

That was him being rough? Ava snuffle-snorted a laugh and pressed her nose to his nipple, punch-drunk on orgasms and pain. She'd take that kind of rough twice before breakfast and more besides on a daily basis. "Were you holding back on me, Master Finnegan?"

"Don't make me spank an answer out of you, little minx."

Rubbing her nose on his manly nipple, she sighed. "I'm fabulous, Sir."

"Any pain I should know about?"

She frowned. Even if there was, she wasn't letting a stranger—DM or no DM—poke around. She'd had enough of that tonight, thank you, and she wouldn't let the memory of Finn's touch be eradicated by someone else's. Tonight's memories were all going in her mental lockbox on the special keepsakes shelf. "No, just a bit sore, I think."

"Okay, good girl. Looks like the night's wrapping up, little dove. I think we have time for a quick shower if you feel up to it?" Finn stretched lusciously, lifting her with his massive chest and flexing his cock inside her disastrously sensitive pussy. "Have you got plans for the rest of the night?"

She bit her lip. "Not that I can think of, Sir. You?"

"Well, I don't have to be out of my hotel room until eight but my flight is at eight-thirty. I'd like to get to know you better, Ava. I meant what I said," he told her earnestly, cupping her face in his huge hands and maintaining intense eye contact. "My whole life is ranching, and ranching is a minefield of possibilities and asking nature for mercy. Praying for rain for the crops, wishing for an easy winter to make calving time go smoother. So many variables that go wrong, and I gamble with it all every time I open my eyes in the morning and make a decision that could cost more than just money.

"Tonight, with you? Absolutely the biggest gamble I've ever made in my life and undeniably the best. I can see myself with you—five, ten, twenty years down the line." He kissed her, gently, sweetly. "The question I need you to ask yourself is, do you feel the same way?"

Yes. Ava nodded, throat closing with tears.

Finn grinned at her, a triumphant expression resembling a predator cornering delicious prey. "Okay, so my proposal is this: we take a shower, maybe go for a coffee. Back to my hotel if you're comfortable with that. You're still a little dazed so I'm not holding you to anything you say until your mind's clear enough to make rational decisions."

She hummed as his fingers removed the tie from her hair and began to carefully unbraid the strands, untangling it from its unruly state and probably making it worse. She'd end up looking like a ripe dandelion, no doubt, but the look in his eyes wiped every concern from her head.

"We're going to talk, long and hard, about what you want. What you need. What we want to accomplish together."

"What about what you want?" she asked.

"If I have you, little dove, I'll have everything I want."

Her bottom lip trembled; his thumb stroked over it, stilled it with a touch. He had the power to do that, to incite shivers and trembles or stop them dead in their tracks.

Someone cleared their throat; Ava's eyes slid to the right and up, up, up. She flushed furiously under the scrutiny of Black Light's owner, Jaxson, then buried her face into Finn's chest when her lover chuckled and greeted the ex-model with a friendly hello.

How embarrassing.

She became keenly aware she was naked, thoroughly claimed, and still locked tight to Finn. She flinched as warmth draped over her back, huddled into the blanket Jaxson placed over her before he drew up a chair and perched on the edge.

"My apologies for intruding," he began, addressing Finn directly. "I trust you've had an... entertaining evening, Master Finnegan?"

Finn's purr of satisfaction reverberated through Ava's body, awakening tiny fires. "Couldn't have chosen a more perfect sub myself, or more interesting kinks."

"Excellent. Well, you've seen the evening through, congratulations. I'm afraid I'm going to need to hurry you along; the cleaning crews are eager to get to work. And there's a rather anxious submissive and her Dom waiting for Ava in the locker room."

Ava's head shot up. *Rosie!* Shit, she'd forgotten her friend existed tonight. Her thoughts turned to the activities she and Finn had spun, all the ways he'd had his hands on her, in her—oh fuck, *in* her—and the blood drained from her face. Had Rosie watched?

"Someone you know, little dove?" Concern marred Finn's brow when she bolted upright, urging his semi-hard cock deeper into her sore center. His hands grabbed her hips before she could wrench herself off him. "Easy, Ava. Calm down."

"She's my roommate," she blurted in a wheezing voice. Mortification soured every happy, pleasant memory from the last few hours. Tainted them with judgement and a sudden, overwhelming fear of how she'd be seen in her friend's eyes.

Slut. Whore. Impostor.

Jaxson's eyebrow lifted. "I'll inform the relevant parties you'll take care of her?" he asked Finn as strong arms snaked around her, restraining her from bolting.

"Please." Finn's tone was grim. He rattled off a hotel and room number. "For safety purposes, that's where she'll be. We'll get dressed and let your crew get to work."

Shaking, Ava fought against his embrace until she was too tired to struggle anymore. After the evening's excitement, it didn't take long. But he cuddled her, really cuddled her, rocking her until the panic attack eased.

When she stopped shaking and sagged into the comfort he offered, he lifted her effortlessly with an arm around her waist, disengaging them without too much mess or fuss, and disposed of the condom. "Come on, little dove. I think any decisions made tonight are going to be null and void. You're exhausted."

A server hurried past, stopped and backtracked. "Would you like me to take your gear to the co-ed shower room, Sir?"

"Dedicated down to the last clients," Finn murmured, then addressed the little brunette directly. "That would be appreciated, thank you. We'll be there in just a moment."

She almost curtsied, then quickly gathered his straps and the rest of their stuff. "I believe a pair of shoes, one with a broken heel, has been handed in to Danny in the locker room if you're missing a pair." She offered him a winning smile before whisking away.

Ava wanted to hate her for it but didn't have the energy.

"Arms and legs around me, Ava."

Like a child, she obeyed. Her head rested on his shoulder as he stood, completely naked, and carried her through the club, now drastically empty. There were people tidying up, servers at work cleaning alongside staff in plain black clothing. A tall, leggy blonde moved behind the bar more elegantly than a stunningly ethereal ghost.

A beautiful, cathartic night. Three amazing, testing kinks. A new outlook on life. A skilled, caring, handsome Dominant who wanted *her* of all people.

All of it tainted by her fear of what someone else thought.

Finn wound through empty tables and stations, beelining for the showers. They were deserted save for the DM still prowling on duty, who tapped his wrist with a wink when they walked through the door. "Always a tardy one or two," he said with a wide grin.

"We won't hold you up much longer," Finn assured him and swept her inside. He set her on her feet beside his bag, steadied her as her knees buckled. "Take a seat, Ava. Close your eyes, just rest."

She sighed and dropped her head in her hands. "Am I a bad person?"

Finn laughed and the sound was a little stunned. "What the hell makes you say that? Unless you're a murderess in disguise, I'd say you're probably the sweetest, most appealing young woman I've had the pleasure of meeting."

She glanced up miserably, then lifted her arms when he gestured for her to do so. Her words were muffled by her dress sliding over her head, but she knew he caught her drift by the way his eyes hardened. "Am I a bad person for liking what we did tonight?"

"Are you asking this for you or because you're worried about your roommate?"

"Both?"

He sank to his haunches, resting his hands on her knees. "If we were judged solely on our kinks, little dove, the world would be a fucked-up place. You're sweet and kind, you want to please. A bad person wouldn't worry about their roommate; they wouldn't give a shit about anyone but themselves. Accepting who you are and what you like is part of this journey."

She let him kiss her, moaned when he drew away and rose, watching him cover up that incredible body one piece of clothing at a time. By the time he was dressed immaculately once again, she was ready to take his hand and start the next chapter of her life with him, no questions asked.

She walked barefoot through the club beside him, finally finding pride in coming out at the end of the night with experience under her belt and hope in her hands. A milestone in her life she'd never even considered, let alone dreamed of achieving.

"Hotel," Finn decreed, pushing into the locker room and ushering her through. "Hot bath, food, and sleep."

"Ava?"

Her head snapped around, meeting Rosie's shocked face. Her friend waited with her Dominant as Jaxson said.. "Rosie? What are you still doing here? Jaxson said he would let you know I was going back to Finn's hotel room for the night."

"He let us know, all right. Did you think I'd be okay with just walking out of here without checking to see you were okay first?" Disapproval simmered lightly in her friend's voice as she gave Ava a swift but thorough appraisal. "My best friend isn't wandering off into the night with a strange guy if he hasn't got the official BFF stamp."

Ava's stomach plummeted. "This is what you wanted for me, Rosie."

"It is. Of course, it is. You look happy, Ava. Or you would if you didn't look nauseous." Rosie touched her arm, rubbing lightly. "You're not sick, are you? I can take you home if you're not well. I'm sure Master Finnegan would understand."

Ava's laugh was soft, edged with relief. "Finn has taken care of me all evening. He's done things to me I can't even describe, and he's *helped* me. I want to spend a few more hours with him before he goes home." *So many miles away.*

"You're sure you can trust him outside the club? No offense, Master Finnegan," Rosie said, addressing him formally and with a respect Ava hadn't heard from her friend before, "but playing in here is one thing. Ava's my best friend and I don't want to see her hurt."

"No offense taken. It's a valid point. I swear to you, Ava's precious to me. Whatever happens when we walk out those doors to the outside world, I'll protect her." Finn's voice resonated with what Ava thought of as his Dominant tone. Inarguable and strong enough to bend steel. "I want what's best for her, Rosie. If she wants to go home, I won't stop her."

"Finn?" Ava pleaded, looking up at him.

Tears welled as he took the coat Rosie held out, bundling Ava into it. He slipped a card into her pocket. "If you decide to go home, anytime you need me, you call me. Night or day, Ava. I'll wait for you to call and tell me you're ready to be mine."

Rosie took the broken pair of shoes from a watchful Danny, handing them to Ava. They made her lopsided when she put them on, but that didn't stop her from standing tall and leaning into her Dom. Heat from his big body enveloped her and those arms she loved curled around her.

Finn kissed her, then rubbed his cheek over her hair. "It's always your choice, Ava. Don't ever be afraid to say no."

Ava met her friend's eyes and smiled. Three hours with Finn wasn't enough. Three days, three months, three years might never quench the thirst he roused inside her, but surely she was entitled to at least a night to explore this new and slightly terrifying direction in her life.

Rosie's lips twitched and acknowledgement flared in her eyes. "You're sure you're happy with doing this, babe?" At Ava's eager nod, Rosie raised her formidable gaze above Ava's head. "Okay then. I'd like this on record, Master Finnegan: you may be some bigshot millionaire rancher, but if you hurt Ava, I'll castrate you myself. D.C. style." With that as a warning, she linked her fingers into her waiting Dominant's and stepped forward to kiss Ava's cheek. "Be careful and have fun. Like your Dom said, don't be afraid to say no."

Watching her best friend leave with her man of the night, Ava gripped Finn's arms and sighed contentedly as he kissed the side of her neck. "Why would I say no when all I want to do is say yes?"

THE END

ABOUT THE AUTHOR

Kay Elle Parker is a British author living in the wilds of Yorkshire. She has an eclectic taste in music, reads anything when she has the time, and loves Fell ponies and Border Collies. Her sense of humor is wicked and often misunderstood, downright dirty and infectious.

Writing romance is the dream, and Kay has books in dark, BDSM, and paranormal romance. Just recently, she released her first contemporary romance, Speechless.

She loves writing all things vampire and shifter. She loves to chat to readers!

- Website - https://kayelleparker.com/
- Facebook - https://www.facebook.com/kayelleparker/
- Twitter - https://twitter.com/kayelleparker

INFLAMED

A BLACK LIGHT: ROULETTE WAR NOVELLA

By

Golden Angel

PROLOGUE

ELLIOTT

Ding dong.

Dammit. He'd just managed to sit down. Sighing, Elliott stood up, stretching his arms up before he turned to go answer his front door. Who the hell was there anyway? This was supposed to be an afternoon to himself. He'd needed it after last night when he'd realized he needed to break up with his current girlfriend. Now he just had to figure out how to do it.

Not that she was officially his girlfriend. They'd only been dating for a couple of months, but it was long enough that he didn't feel right ending the relationship without talking to her. Not something he was looking forward to. Peggy was gorgeous, quick-witted, and incredibly interested in BDSM, but the more Elliott had gotten to know her, the more he realized she wasn't as submissive as she'd first presented herself to be. *Manipulative* was the better descriptor.

Maybe they could have still made that work, but last night he'd taken her and her best friend, Melody, to Black Light with him and, well... he'd seen an uglier side of her. A jealous, mean-girl side that he hadn't liked at all.

Peggy's quick wit could be cutting, and Melody had always laughed it off in the past, making Elliott think it was just him that was bothered by it, but last night Peggy had just been cruel. Even if it didn't bother Melody, it bothered him. He'd scened with Peggy, feeling responsible for bringing her there and getting her expectations up, but they hadn't had sex and his heart hadn't been in the scene. He'd just been going through the motions.

The doorbell rang again, increasing his annoyance. It had only been a couple of seconds. What was so important that—

Yanking the door open, he groaned internally.

Speak of the devil and she shall appear.

Not that he thought Peggy was the devil, but she was definitely an unwelcome sight right now. Especially because she was standing with her hip cocked out, a flirty smile on her lips, and twirling the belt of the trench coat she was wearing in front of her. Gorgeous? Yes. She'd done her hair up to expose her neck and her makeup was flawless, enhancing every one of her features in the most flattering way possible... The coat she was wearing covered everything but immediately made him wonder what she had on underneath it.

His dick lifted in interest.

His dick was also really stupid sometimes. *We're not going there, so don't bother getting excited.*

"Peggy," he said, keeping his expression blank. "I didn't expect to see you today."

Her expression faltered slightly as she realized she wasn't getting the reaction she'd anticipated, but she rallied after just a moment, tossing her head and putting both hands on her coat's belt. "I wanted to surprise you."

"I don't really like surprises, remember?" It was something he'd told her before. Either she'd forgotten or she had decided she didn't care, and he was betting on the latter from the frustration that flashed in her eyes when he didn't respond how she wanted.

"Well, I didn't think you'd mind *this* kind of surprise." There was an edge to her voice, one that Elliott had heard before. The last few times, he'd ending up spanking her when she'd gotten bratty about getting what she wanted... but this time he wasn't inclined to.

This wasn't how he wanted to break up with her, but he was also having trouble seeing how he was going to get out of this without doing so. He could try at least.

"I'm sorry, but I'm really not up for company right now," he said carefully, leaning his shoulder against the door frame to make it clear she was unwelcome in the house. Her lips pursed together, eyes narrowing.

"Is someone else in there?" she accused, her voice going high and shrill. Elliott almost winced at the sound. Peggy put her hands on her hips, no longer playing the seductress. "Are you *cheating* on me?!"

He straightened up. "Hell no. I'm completely alone. Which is how I wanted it this afternoon, which is what I told you."

Surprisingly, she seemed to take him at his word, immediately turning apologetic. There was a glint in her eye though as she stepped toward him, putting her hand on his chest, and Elliott realized that she hadn't really thought he was cheating on her. She was just manipulating the situation. Manipulating *him*.

"I'm sorry, Elliott," she murmured, rubbing his chest with her hand and looking up at him. But this time he saw through the contrite expression on her face; he saw calculation in her eyes rather than true emotion. And it left him cold.

Reaching up he plucked her hand away from his chest. "I appreciate the apology, Peggy. I think it's time for you to go now."

His resistance shocked her, but that shock quickly gave way to fury and she jerked her hand away from his.

"You can't send me away!" She jerked open the belt of her coat and spread it wide so that he could see the lacy bodysuit she was wearing underneath. It covered everything and concealed nothing, and his dick was not immune, unfortunately. "I dressed up for you and everything!"

Closing his eyes, Elliott reached for patience. While he was still physically attracted to her, all it took was remembering her manipulative behavior from moments earlier for his arousal to wilt. When he opened them again, she was smiling expectantly.

"I don't think this is working out between us, Peggy," he said, keeping his voice calm and level. Her mouth dropped open and he took advantage of her shocked silence to keep going. While he hadn't wanted to break up with her like this, he was just at the end of his rope. "I can't be with someone who doesn't respect my boundaries.

And I don't think we're looking for the same thing in a relationship. Knowing that, it's better to end this sooner rather than later."

"Are you fucking kidding me?" she exploded, dropping the sides of the jacket and pointing an accusing finger at his chest. "I let you tie me up, I let you spank me, and do all sorts of perverted things to me—" Ah fuck, Elliott really hoped his neighbors weren't home. His gaze skittered around the street, trying to see whose cars were in their driveways. "And you're just going to dump me?! Because we aren't looking for the same things? What the hell else are you looking for?"

Someone who actually wanted to submit. Someone who would *enjoy* submitting to him, not just say she 'let him' do it. Someone who loved the pain and the pleasure and giving up control to him.

And that someone wasn't Peggy.

"I'm sorry, Peggy, but this is over," he said, and stepped back, closing the door almost in her face.

It wasn't the suavest move, and it wasn't the kindest move, but he honestly didn't know what else to do. Calling her out on using sex to manipulate him seemed crass. Especially because he doubted she'd admit to it. He didn't want to get into an endless argument with her on his doorstep, but he hadn't wanted to let her in either.

Something told him that if he'd let her inside, he would have had an even harder time getting her to leave.

As it was, she kicked his door several times, screamed a bunch of curse words, and then finally stomped off just before he started thinking that maybe he should go back out there and try to reason with her. This was exactly why he'd wanted this afternoon to try and figure out how to handle the breakup.

When she finally drove away, he sank back onto his couch, dropping his face into his hands and leaning on his elbows. "That could have gone better."

He wasn't broken-hearted exactly, but he felt a bit... bruised. In the beginning, he'd really liked Peggy. Enough to introduce her to kink. To bring her to Black Light. And he'd honestly thought she was into it at first. Now...

He just didn't know.

No more vanilla girls, he decided. No more dating women outside of the club. No more women who were just playing around at being a submissive. It never ended well for him.

Lisa

"HE'S HERE!" Lisa half-squealed the words, grabbing onto her friend Melody's arm.

The hottest Dom in the club—in Lisa's opinion at least. And not just because he did fire play, although she absolutely appreciated the pun. Lisa had been long-distance crushing on Master Elliott from the first time she'd visited Black Light with Melody and Melody's Daddy, Kawan.

Daddy Dom, that was. Not her actual dad. Lisa didn't totally understand the dynamic, but what she did understand was that Melody was deliriously happy with Kawan, and that was good enough for her. Lisa was a little envious of their relationship actually, but she was also really happy for Melody. They'd both been juggling their grad programs and real life, but somehow Melody had made it work for her. Lisa had been the one to eschew a social life.

Now that Lisa was post-doc, she had just enough time to squeeze in a weekly visit to Black Light with Melody and Kawan, and she was having a blast exploring everything the club had to offer. If a Dom offered a new experience, she wanted to scene with him.

Master Elliott and fire play were on her Black Light Bucket List.

"Are you going to ask him?" Melody asked, giving Lisa's hand a squeeze. She sounded a little worried.

Melody knew Master Elliott because he was her ex-best friend's ex. He and the ex did not have a good breakup and Melody hadn't done more than say hello to him at Black Light since then. From what Lisa had seen, he didn't seem to have a problem with Melody, but he did make her nervous even though the woman in question was now an ex to both of them. A crazy ex. Lisa had met Peggy back when she was still Melody's best friend, and she was a real piece of work.

But she didn't judge someone just because he'd once dated a twat waffle.

Next to Melody, Master Kawan sighed. At first, he'd tried to keep Lisa from approaching the Doms, telling her that it was customary to wait for a Dom to come to the submissive he was interested in, but he'd given up on that weeks ago. To his surprise, most of the dominants she asked to scene with her were willing. Some were even flattered.

"Yup. Doing it now." Before she lost her courage. Because unlike a lot of the Doms Lisa had scened with, she actually had a crush on Master Elliott. He was sexy, confident, kind to the submissives he scened with, and paid attention to detail. Lisa wanted to scene with him, yes, but she also wanted to get to know him better. Which was why she hadn't tried to talk to him before.

She'd needed some time to work up the nerve.

"Good luck!" Melody whisper yelled as Lisa walked away.

Shoulders back, Lisa moved toward the sexy Dom. He was setting up his station, totally focused on what he was doing. Lisa really liked the idea of having all of that focus on her. Swaying her hips, she sauntered up to him. When she was close enough, he looked up and his dark eyes nearly made her steps falter. He was more intimidating up close than when she was lusting after him from afar.

But Lisa had never been one to back down from a challenge. "Hi." She smiled leaning her hip against the table, somewhat amused when his brow furrowed in confusion. He wouldn't be the first Dom to wonder what the hell she was doing, walking up to him. Tilting her head flirtatiously, she leaned toward him. "I hear you're *the* master of fire play for Black Light."

Master Elliott blinked. "I'm one of the masters allowed to do fire play here, yes."

Oooookay. Maybe flattery didn't work on him. Most of the other Doms she'd approached had puffed up a little, pleased by her acknowledgement of their reputation.

"Are you doing a fire demo tonight? I've always wanted to be set on fire." She winked.

The blank expression on his face didn't give away any emotion, but the way he was staring at her did make her feel incredibly uncomfortable. Like she was doing something wrong. It was kind of similar to the way Kawan had looked when he'd told her to wait for the Doms to come to her, but with a lot more judgment in it.

Then he did the last thing she would have expected. Instead of answering her, he just turned away and went back to unpacking his toy bag.

Lisa froze. For several long seconds, she stood there, unsure of what to do. "Um… so is that a no?"

"I don't play with little wannabe submissives. Especially ones who don't know proper etiquette." The lack of emotion in his voice for some reason just made his words even more hurtful.

Spinning on her heel, Lisa stomped off, an ugly, unhappy feeling rising in her chest. What a dickweed! *Wannabe submissive.* Just because she wanted to try a bunch of different things didn't make her a *wannabe.* Neither did looking for what she wanted. Kawan's advice rose in the back of her mind, reminding her that he'd warned her not all the Doms would be amused by her pushiness.

But how was she supposed to get everything she wanted if she just waited for them to come to her? Although, it didn't look like she'd be playing with fire any time soon. There were other Doms who did fire play but… she'd wanted *him* dammit. Trying with someone else would feel slightly tainted.

Out of the corner of her eye she saw Master Owen leaving the bar and she quickly changed course. Shibari was *also* on her Black Light Bucket List. If she wasn't going to get to play with fire tonight, then she was damn well going to check off a different item instead!

CHAPTER 1

ELLIOTT

*O*h no... *please tell me* she *didn't sign up for Roulette.*

The blonde head bobbing her way through Black Light, heading for the side of the stage where the Roulette participants were gathering was all too familiar to him. Sometimes he felt like he couldn't move through the club anymore without tripping over Lisa. Usually looking stunning and sceneing with another Dom.

The club was packed tonight, fuller than he'd ever seen it before, so he wasn't surprised to see her there, but if he'd thought about her and Black Light's annual Roulette game, he'd assumed she would be an audience member. Not a participant. The wheel was for *real* submissives and dominants.

People didn't just sign up on a whim. Well. Maybe *she* would. His lips pressed together. For someone so smart, she was incredibly impulsive sometimes. That had been his first impression of her actually, since their very first interaction had been when she'd interrupted his prep time, trying to flirt with him so that he'd do a fire demo with her. Her pushy demeanor, her rude interruption, his physical attraction to her, and her flirting with him to get what she wanted all reminded him starkly of Peggy.

Elliott had just stared at her and then turned away. He didn't engage with little wannabe subs who didn't know proper etiquette, which was exactly what he'd told her when she'd chased after him instead of leaving him alone like she should have. The hurt expression on her face after he'd turned her down still rose up in his mind at inopportune moments. In that moment, she hadn't reminded him of any of his exes, but the moment had been over quickly.

She'd turned up her nose at him and stomped off to find someone else to entertain her for the evening. The next time he'd seen her, she'd been asking a million questions about shibari while having a rope dress tied around her body. If someone had gagged her, he would have enjoyed watching.

He was attracted to her. He just didn't want to be. It was Peggy all over again.

Unfortunately, his dick made poor choices all the time, as witnessed by the last few women he'd dated. And every time he saw Lisa, his dick voted to make another bad choice. But that was why Elliott didn't listen to his dick anymore.

Elliott wanted a real submissive, a real *relationship*. It hadn't escaped his notice that a surprising number of couples came out of Roulette night, which was why he'd signed up. He'd been lucky he was picked this year. One of the dungeon monitors had privately told him it had been because Spencer was determined to 'show' someone in California that the government workers here at Black Light weren't stuffy. He was just a clerk for the D.C. Court of Appeals, but apparently that counted.

He didn't really care how he'd been chosen, as long as he was.

What he didn't want was to be paired with someone who just played at being submissive, who flitted from dom to dom like a butterfly visiting flowers, and who probably wouldn't be able to handle any real pain. She didn't come to Black Light that often, but when she did, all of her scenes were on the lighter side. Elliot was a sadist—*none* of the scenes he'd seen her do would satisfy that side of him. Although she hadn't safe worded the one time a dom had used a cane on her, she hadn't taken more than three strokes either.

Not that he'd been watching that closely.

Liar.

Whatever. The point was, she was exactly what he *wasn't* looking for, in any way. The chances of them actually being paired together tonight were pretty low anyway. Although, if it did happen, he could have some fun showing her what it was actually like to submit.

Unlike the other doms she played with, who kept things light because they were just doing one scene together, Elliott would be happy to push her limits. And he'd have the excuse of Roulette to do it, because that's what tonight was all about. He wondered what four hard limits she'd chosen.

Stop it. Don't borrow trouble.

And she was trouble. That was one thing Elliott was sure of.

Lisa

I AM A DUMBASS.

It wasn't really true. She even had the PhD to prove it. In addition to common sense, which she acknowledged that some truly intelligent people didn't have, but she wasn't one of them. What *she* lacked was emotional intelligence. Was that a thing? Because it felt like a thing.

Her brain was smart, her heart was dumb.

Ah ha. There he is.

The cause of her emotional malfunction, the man who got her panties wet even when he was ignoring her.

"Are you sure about this?" Melody asked, following Lisa through the crowd toward the stage. Melody was the reason Lisa had come to Black Light in the first place, when Lisa had confessed her kinky fantasies. So far, unlike Melody, she hadn't really found a dom that suited her, but she loved sceneing in the club.

"Kind of late to back out now, isn't it?" Lisa responded, shrugging with a nonchalance she didn't feel. She'd be a fool not to be a little nervous. Only four hard limits and a roulette wheel full of scary possibilities. Scary, exciting possibilities.

Melody's Daddy Dom, Kawan, gave her a look. "It's not. If you want to back out, I'll make sure it happens. There's a wait list to be involved."

"No, I don't want to back out," Lisa said immediately, before Melody could speak up again. She loved her friend, but Melody could be kind of anxious and sometimes those anxieties rubbed off on her. Lisa looked over at Master Elliott, who was across the room talking to another dom. "I'm going to make it through the whole night and I'm going to get my free month. Gotta risk it to get the biscuit!"

Because she could really use that free month to save up enough money to get another month's membership.

And she was going to spend that first month metaphorically rubbing it in Master Elliott's face that she'd faced the Roulette wheel and made it through the night.

'Not a real submissive'. I'll show you, Sir Butthead.

The lights dimmed and then flashed, lighting up DJ Elixxir onstage. Lisa grinned as anticipation and just a little bit of fear surged through her and she moved closer to the stage. She'd seen the DJ at Runway before. He was damn hot, and she cheered when he lifted up his shirt, showing off some very nice abs.

"Welcome to Black Light! I know we're all anxious to get this show on the road, and—trust me—I can't wait either. This is the fourth annual Valentine Roulette here at Black Light, and it's going to be dirtier, naughtier, and sexier than ever!"

Lisa cheered again, excitement pumping through her. She was so ready for this. Dirtier, naughtier, and sexier than ever sounded perfect for showing Master Elliott that she was a real submissive. When Jaxson, the club owner, stepped up to speak for a minute, she accidentally tuned him out as she imagined Master Elliott coming up and apologizing for casting aspersions on her and asking her to scene.

But would she tell him yes or no?

Whoops, she'd gotten so busy daydreaming she'd completely missed everything Jaxson said. Shaking off her fantasies—she had to get through tonight to even have a chance of anything like that happening—she refocused on what DJ Elixxir was saying about the rules. Not like she hadn't practically memorized them already, but still. Hearing him say them aloud, talking about the subs finding out who their dom was going to be and then spinning the wheel...

For some reason it almost hadn't felt real up until now.

272

Her eyes drifted over to the men lined up on the other side of the stage. One of them was going to be able to play with her tonight. Do whatever the wheel spun... Her eyes landed on Master Elliott.

He was looking back at her.

Lisa almost ducked down to try and hide but instead she made herself stare back at him. Insolently. The disapproval in his expression grew. What would he do if she stuck out her tongue at him? The thought made her smile and he glared back at her.

The world suddenly got brighter, and she jumped, her attention jerking back to DJ Elixxir who had just hopped down a couple steps to gesture to the ballot box that she was standing near.

"Whenever you've decided you've seen the hottest scene of the night, the dirtiest act, the best Dom and sub in the game, just fill out your ballot and drop it in the box here to the right of the center stairs!" DJ Elixxir turned around and sauntered back up the stairs, giving Lisa the opportunity to check out his very fine ass. Much better scenery than Elliott's glower. "The couple who receives the most votes will each win an additional free month of Black Light membership. That's right, *two* free months! I know I'd appreciate that in my pocket!"

Lisa applauded along with everyone else, licking her lips. Two free months of Black Light *and* bragging rights that her scene was the dirtiest, the best... that would show Master Elliott. She just hoped whatever Dom drew her name was up to the challenge, because she was in it to win it.

She bit her lip nervously as DJ Elixxir handed out the labeled sticks to the doms before moving back to the center of the stage. Holy crap. This was actually happening. She was actually doing this. It didn't escape her notice that Master Elliott grinned at the stick he was holding. Obviously, he liked his number.

DJ Elixxir clapped his now empty hands. "Alright everyone, who's ready to get this party started?"

Me!

CHAPTER 2

ELLIOTT

*N*umber one. He'd be the first dom to go. Which meant that his chances of spinning any one sub were very low. And if there was a little bit of disappointment tinging his relief, that was just his dick talking.

"Dominant number one, please step forward."

Every eye in the room swiveled to look at the line of doms. Although he'd grinned when he'd seen his number, Elliott kept his expression serious now, stepping forward. He didn't want any of the submissives waiting to get the idea that he was a pushover. Although he recognized quite a few of them, he didn't know all of them, so it was likely they didn't know him either.

His gaze skipped over to Lisa. Lips pressed together, she looked nervous as hell, but her chin lifted defiantly when their gazes met.

If I spin her name, then I get to play with her and it's not even my fault.

Well, that was one way to look at it.

Elixxir handed him a marble and spun the wheel. Taking just a moment to watch it spin, Elliott mentally crossed his fingers before setting the marble on the wheel. It circled the wheel several times before popping into the slot marked 'Lovely Lisa.'

Of course, it did.

His lips twitched as he suppressed a groan. His dick cheered. To say he was conflicted was a bit of an understatement.

"Lovely Lisa!" Elixxir announced, turning around.

Not my fault. Not my choice. It's pure chance. Maybe this is fate's way of letting me get over my attraction to her. We'll play, she'll do her usual, it'll be disappointing as hell and then I won't be tempted anymore.

Elliott gave himself a quick second to compose himself before turning as well, crossing his arms over his chest as he did so.

Looking frozen, Lisa stared back at him. He raised his eyebrows at her with just a hint of exasperation. Was she seriously going to back out this early?

Apparently, his reaction was the only prod she needed. That chin went right back up again and she practically sprinted up the steps to join him and Elixxir onstage. No smile for Elliott, but she beamed at Elixxir, holding out her hand for the marble.

"Are you sure you want to do this?" Elliott couldn't help asking in a low voice as the marble dropped into her hand. "I'm not going to go easy on you."

Her eyes narrowed at him, fingers closing around the marble. "I'm not asking you to."

∽

Lisa

BACK OUT NOW? Condescending dickweed. She'd show him. Doing all three scenes for Roulette and being able to rub it in Master Elliott's face would have been satisfying with *any* dom, but when *he* was the dom? Yeah, a million more times satisfying. She'd be able to show him firsthand that she could take anything he was going to dish out.

Then maybe he'd stop sending her those little judge-y looks every time they were both at Black Light.

"Oooo… I'm sensing some tension. Be careful with this one," DJ Elixxir teased, tilting his head at Master Elliott. "He doesn't have any hard limits listed on his card."

Lisa's mouth dropped open in shock and a little ripple went

through the watching crowd. Seriously? Not a single one? She'd put down blood play, ABDL, anal intercourse, and water sports.

She'd spent *hours* deciding, because she'd definitely wanted to list more than four. In the end, she'd ended up making a list of *all* the ones she wished she could put down and rolling dice to decide. BDSM with a side of D&D. They both had Dungeon Masters, right? It had made sense at the time, even if her hard limits had come out a little wonky. She'd almost switched out the anal intercourse and rolled for something else, but that would have been cheating.

Besides, the whole reason she'd added anal intercourse to the options for her hard limits had been because she felt like it was too intimate to do with just anyone. Plus, she figured most of the doms wouldn't list it as a hard limit, so that would give her a better chance of her dom having a limit that she wanted but hadn't chosen.

But no hard limits?

Master Elliott smirked at her.

Anything you can do; I can do better.

She drew herself up. "I want to remove mine also."

"I—uh..." DJ Elixxir looked down at her card and then back up at her. "I'm sorry, what?"

"I don't need any either." Liar, liar pants on fire. She didn't even know why she was being this dumb. Oh, yes, she did. Because it was Master Elliott and she had something to prove. "I only put them because I thought we had to."

DJ Elixxir blinked at her and then glanced off stage at Master Jaxson. The entire room fell silent. Master Jaxson nodded his approval and DJ Elixxir turned back to her, his expression serious and maybe just a touch concerned. "Alright. That's... up to you, of course."

Across from her, Master Elliott shook his head disapprovingly, looking unamused, but he didn't protest either. The sadistic gleam in his eye was both scary and exciting. Lisa knew he was a sadist. That was half the reason she'd been attracted to him. A lot of the scenes she'd tried at the club hadn't done enough for her. She'd wanted more, more, more... but she'd specifically wanted it with him.

Well, at least, she'd wanted it with him until he shot her down just for asking for a scene. Now she just wanted to prove that he'd been wrong to do so.

Pretending a lot more confidence than she actually felt, she spun the roulette wheel.

And almost laughed out loud when the marble landed.

Gleefully, she looked up at Master Elliott, almost tauntingly. "Looks like you're going to have to set me on fire after all, *Sir.*"

~

Elliott

FIRE PLAY. Of course.

Somehow the fates had aligned, and the little brat was going to get exactly what she'd asked for—a fire play scene with him. He didn't respond to her taunt though, just moved forward, taking her by the back of the neck and using his hold on her to turn her around and direct her back off the stage.

Behind him, DJ Elixxir was already calling up the next Dom, while Elliott's mind whirled with possibilities.

He was definitely going to need to address her brattiness.

Moving off to the side, he was surprised when she was actually quiet as the rest of the participants were paired off, although he could feel her begin to quiver with tension as each dom was paired with a sub and then spun the wheel. But as long as she was quiet and behaving, he didn't say anything, he was just going to enjoy it for as long as it lasted.

The last pair walked off the stage and DJ Elixxir grinned.

"Everyone's paired up and you know what that means! It's time to start Valentine Roulette!"

Immediately, Elliott began moving to the Saint Andrew's cross he'd already mentally picked out on the other side of the room, his fingers still gripping Lisa's neck to point her in the direction he wanted.

"Where are we going?" She tried to dig in her heels and turn toward the table, where he usually operated.

Rather than answering, he reached down and slapped Lisa's ass. The short PVC skirt she was wearing was barely any protection and she yelped, making him smile.

"Get moving. I can still spank the hell out of you, if you give me a good reason to, before I set you on fire." He deliberately phrased it that way even though he wouldn't actually be setting her on fire.

With a little squeak, she picked up the pace and they were the first to reach the cross, claiming it for their first scene.

"Strip," he ordered her. "Everything off."

CHAPTER 3

LISA

*W*ow, so much for foreplay. Although, the bossy thing was admittedly pretty hot on its own, she'd thought there'd be a little bit more to the beginning of the scene. She scowled, but before she could even open her mouth, he was striding away toward the Dungeon Monitor standing off to the side.

Strip.

Simple, one-word order.

She blushed a little when she realized there were expectant eyes on her already, but the audience was just part of Roulette night. Melody wasn't part of the audience around her, but Lisa had no doubt she'd be over soon. They were both really fascinated by fire play and had watched Master Elliott do more than one demonstration scene.

Which was also why she was so confused right now.

Unlacing the front of the black leather bodice she was wearing, Lisa frowned at the Saint Andrew's cross. She'd never seen Master Elliott do a fire play scene where the submissive wasn't lying down. Maybe he thought the cross would make a better display... but how was he going to put the alcohol on her?

The last time she'd watched him, she'd been mesmerized by his movements. Alcohol swabbed over the submissive's skin, the lighter flaring and then the flickering flame dancing, and then his hand with a cloth moving to dampen it only seconds later. It was a beautiful and dangerous dance and Lisa had been dying to try it.

Now all she could think about was the alcohol dripping down her front to her pussy... she wasn't completely bare on her mound and fire seemed like a really bad way to remove the hair.

"You're moving too slowly." Master Elliott's voice made her jump and she quickly tugged off her skirt, taking the pink thong she was wearing underneath with it.

"Sorry, um, Sir," she said, straightening back up. She'd gotten so lost in her thoughts that she'd been just standing there, doing nothing. So much for showing him what a good submissive she could be. Keeping her hands by her side, she ducked her head a little before looking up at him. Her nipples tightened under his gaze.

A little furrow appeared between his brows and then cleared; his dark eyes thoughtful.

"Here, drink this," he said, handing her a bottle of water, his eyes skimming over her body and making her want to preen.

"Why?"

"Just drink it," he said, barking out the words as an order. Lisa opened the bottle and put it to her mouth without even thinking twice. She had a tendency to always want to know the 'why' of every-thing, but Master Elliott's bossy tones had her jumping to obey.

Again, the expression on his face as he watched her was hard to determine, but she thought he looked maybe a little confused. Hm. Wondering at her sudden willingness to obey?

Hey, it wasn't like she *couldn't* submit. She just hadn't really found anyone who made her want to. Lisa *played* when she came to Black Light and she knew it. So far, she hadn't found someone who made her feel the way Melody did with Kawan, and she didn't want to settle for anything less.

"How much have you had to drink today?" he asked as she lowered the bottle, already a quarter empty.

"Seven of my eight-ounce glasses," she said, smirking at the way his lip curled in amusement before he controlled his reaction. She was being serious though. Hydration was very important, and she had a massive water bottle as long as her forearm to ensure she got her full serving every day.

Nodding his head, he took her at her word, which made her like him a little bit more. "Have you ever been burned before?"

"Uh, no." She blinked. "Are you planning on burning me, Sir?"

Any amusement that had been in his expression was gone now, and the flat look he leveled at her made her want to shrink away a little. "It's fire play. Anything is possible."

She might have thought he was kidding but motion behind him caught her eye. The Dungeon Monitor he'd been talking to had returned to his spot—with a fire extinguisher and a friend who was holding both a bucket and a blanket.

Um. Had she ever noticed that being necessary before? Lisa had to admit, she never really paid attention to the prep. Just the spectacle.

"You're an expert in this though, right? Sir?" There. Nice, calm question, no shakiness to her voice at all. Totally not starting to quake with anxiety.

The serious expression on his face didn't budge an inch. "Anyone will tell you, if you play with fire, eventually you get burned."

Lisa waited for his expression to crack, staring at him desperately as she waited for some sign that he was joking. He just stared back at her, completely sincere.

Fuck me sideways.

Elliott

NORMALLY, he was more into reassuring a submissive who did a fire scene with him, but he was more worried about Lisa's enthusiasm and impulsiveness. And a little bit of fear never hurt anyone. Especially because the mind fuck was half the fun of a fire scene. His cock was already hardening, partly because she was a beautiful, naked woman standing right in front of him and partly from watching her anxiety rise.

Biting her lower lip, she looked like she was trying to come up with another question.

"Finish your water," he said sternly. He believed her about the seven glasses she'd already had today—she might be snarky but that was too specific to be anything but honest. The better hydrated she was, the better her skin would handle the contact. Dryness, post scene, was a very real problem, especially with a submissive who was dehydrated. "As soon as you're done with it, I'm going to put you on the cross. The cuffs will be quick release."

Pulling the empty water bottle away from her lips, she opened her mouth to say something, but he kept going.

"The club safe word to pause is 'yellow.' You will use it if you feel burning that lasts for more than a couple of seconds and you will use it *immediately*." He pointed at Garreth, who was holding the bucket of water and blanket that Elliott had requested. "Master Garreth is an EMT. He'll be on hand in case anything goes wrong."

Her face paled as her gaze moved over to the Dungeon Monitor. "Seriously, Sir?"

"That was supposed to be reassuring." When she kept looking at Garreth, Elliott reached out and pinched her nipple, making her jump and squeal. Her eyes were wide as she looked up at him. There was the healthy dose of fear he'd been looking for. His cock jerked in his pants.

Yeah, he was an asshole for getting off on that.

The truth was, he was fairly confident in his abilities—mostly because he worked to never become *over*confident. He was always prepared, always aware of the dangers, and took every precaution he could. Some people would think that the blanket, water, *and* fire extinguisher were overdoing it, but Elliott didn't want to take chances.

Especially since they were indoors in a packed club.

That was also why he'd chosen this cross, which had the largest hardwood space around it. All of the wood flooring in Black Light's play spaces had been specially treated to be fire resistant, but he still preferred to use the largest space, because the carpet was still flammable.

Gentling his hold on Lisa's nipple now that he had her attention, Elliott caressed her more gently, soothingly, and leaned forward, lowering his voice.

"I'm going to take very good care of you," he promised, the air heavy with tension between them. Her breath was coming in soft, short pants, her nipple stiff between his fingers, and the mix of fear, arousal, and excitement in her eyes was perfect. "That's what all the precautions are for."

His lips hovered over hers and for a moment he almost leaned down to kiss her, but then he remembered who she was, and he pulled back.

They were paired together for Roulette. Kissing wasn't necessary.

Although the disappointed look on her face almost made him change his mind.

~

Lisa

EVEN WITHOUT FIRE PLAY, that was some serious heat coming off of Master Elliott. Lisa could almost swear he'd been about to kiss her. But then he'd gone back to being all business and that...

Well, that was disappointing. Until she remembered that he was a big jerk who didn't think she was a real submissive and she was supposed to be proving him wrong, not working her way back into a crush on him. So, it was better that he hadn't kissed her.

And now she was pressed up against the hard wood of the Saint Andrew's Cross, totally naked and Master Elliott was drizzling water over her hair.

"Is this really necessary?" she complained, not because she actually objected, but because she was getting so nervous that she literally couldn't keep quiet. Oops, she'd almost forgotten— "Sir?"

Rather than answering her verbally, she felt her hair shift, and then a hard hand swatted her ass, making her jump. Her breasts moved against the wood, stimulating her nipples and her pussy clenched. Even though he'd scared her a little with all the precautions he had taken before the scene, the bondage and his bossiness and her antici-pation meant her arousal was stronger than ever.

The little sting of pain from the slap just added to her excitement.

Her now wet hair was twisted up high off of her neck and clipped into place. Master Elliott's fingers brushed over her shoulders, checking for any stray hairs that may have escaped his notice, and Lisa's fear and arousal climbed even higher. She pressed her thighs together, squirming at the soft caress of his fingers over her skin. Even though she knew he was performing a kind of safety check, it was surprisingly sensual.

Or maybe he was doing that on purpose. That wouldn't surprise her either. *And* he'd made it so she couldn't see.

His fingers stilled. "What is the sigh for?"

Oops. She hadn't even realized she'd sighed—and not in a 'I love your touch' kind of way. That had definitely been a disappointed sigh.

"I wanted to watch you set me on fire, Sir," she admitted, turning her head so she could try to see him, but she was too tightly bound in place. The cuffs might be quick release, but they were still strong enough to hold her easily, and he'd spread her arms wide enough that she didn't have much room to maneuver. "All the other subs you played with got to watch the fire."

She expected him to say that naughty girls didn't get what they wanted. Or maybe tell her that she'd just have to learn how to submit. Something patronizingly bossy that would make her want to kick him. What she didn't expect was to hear a low laugh, to feel his breath on the back of her neck, making her break out in a rash of goosebumps.

"That's because I'm not setting you on fire, Lovely Lisa." His fingers stroked up the center of her back and then down to cup her ass, squeezing it with suddenly rough fingers and making her pant. "I'm going to flog you with it."

CHAPTER 4

ELLIOTT

*A*s soon as he finally admitted his plan to Lisa, he could hear the hitch in her breath, feel her quiver under his fingers. He leaned in closer, less than an inch away from her body, so that she would feel how small she was next to him.

"Now hold very, very still," he murmured in her ear. Water slid down the side of her neck, curving over her collarbone and down between her breasts. She shivered, and he wasn't sure if it was because of him or the water dripping from her hair. "I would hate to miss a stroke."

She froze, like a deer in headlights, and Elliott grinned as he slid away. From the way she'd been squirming, he knew she was aroused, and now her nerves would heighten and amplify the whole scene.

Garreth was holding the Kevlar flogger for him, soaked and ready to be lit now that Lisa was in position. The lights above their play station dimmed, so that it would be easier for him to see the movement of the flogger.

Out of deference to the number of people in Black Light tonight, Elliott had decided to use just one flogger. The air was warm enough already, and one flogger was easier to control and safer.

A murmur went through the audience when he lit the flogger, the front of his pants tightening even more against his cock. He wasn't a firebug, but there was something primal about playing with fire... about a submissive trusting him enough to use fire to play with her body.

Lisa was now trying to look over her shoulder at him, making him shake his head.

"Eyes forward, Lovely Lisa," he ordered harshly, bracing himself in place behind her, keeping one eye on the flogger. "*Don't move.*"

At the order, her head moved back into place and she let out a long shuddering breath. Adrenaline coursed through Elliott's veins. Because, if he were being honest, deep down, he'd wanted to play with her since the moment she'd asked him to set her on fire.

Lifting the flogger, he swung, and the flames streaked through the air.

∿

Lisa

HEAT WASHED OVER HER BACK.

I'm burning!

She almost screamed, but the heat was gone almost as soon as she'd felt it and there was a whoosh of cool air in its place. That's when she realized the flogger hadn't even touched her and Lisa had to bite her lip against shrieking or cursing.

Bastard! He did that on purpose!

Panting for breath, Lisa leaned against the support of the cross, thankful now for the position that Master Elliott had put her in. She'd wanted to watch, but now she closed her eyes, thankful that she couldn't see the flogger. Holding still was harder than she'd thought it would be, even when she couldn't see it coming.

More heat, air moving over her skin, but no impact. Her breath caught in her throat anyway. Any second now and she'd feel the real flame. A tiny whimper fell from her lips, her body tightening in anticipation.

The murmurs of the crowd pricked at her senses, the admiration, the wonder. Lisa almost wished she were one of them, watching this happen to someone else. Not being able to see was messing with her. Every time she felt the heat rush past her skin, she tensed, sure that she was about to be burned. Master Elliott's serious expression kept flashing in her mind, his careful consideration of all the dangers made them feel all too real.

Despite that, she could feel her arousal growing anyway, almost in defiance of her nerves. She pressed her thighs together, waiting, waiting… if he didn't hit her soon…

Then the flogger slapped against her skin, hotter and stingier than she'd ever experienced and she cried out. Her entire body tensed, expecting pain—*real* pain—but it was already gone again. Almost too fast to even register it. She sucked in a breath, shuddering as cooler air rushed over her skin in the wake of the flogger, making her feel extra sensitive.

More heat, the flogger passing near her skin but not touching it, and then it hit again. The sting was intense, but it felt good too, and she almost wanted to laugh out loud with glee—she was being flogged with fire and she liked it!

A slightly ragged sob of relief lodged in her throat and she slumped slightly, letting the cross and her restraints hold her up as her muscles all turned to liquid. When the flogger hit her ass, instead of her upper back, she jumped, but then relaxed again as the new pattern continued. It had completely messed with her head waiting for the flogger to land.

The fire caressed her skin, leaving hot arousal in its wake, her fear subsiding. The danger wasn't gone, but she trusted Master Elliott to take care of her. To keep her safe. Her heart might still race, and she tensed every time she heard someone else gasp, but she also relaxed into it. Left back, right back, left ass cheek, right ass cheek… the pace was almost hypnotic. Her arousal and tension swirled.

Master Elliott was flogging her with fire.

But she wasn't burning. She was flying.

Elliott

287

COCK HARD AS A ROCK, Elliott carefully adjusted his pattern, ensuring that he wouldn't land the flogger in the exact same spot too many times. The flames created a beautiful tapestry, woven through the air, but the murmurs of awe from the audience were distant. All of his focus was on his swing and the beautiful woman he had bound for his pleasure.

Fire streaked through the air, the flogger moving so quickly that in the dim light it was easy to see the trail as it passed through the air. The beautiful figure eights danced over her form, pinking her skin every time the fire landed a blow, the flames licking across her skin. Elliott kept a sharp eye out to make sure that it never touched her skin for more than a second or two, and that no flame remained behind afterward. All it would take was one stray hair laying against her skin and she could easily be burned. Not terribly, but Elliott didn't want a single blister on her.

Thankfully, Lisa was almost perfectly still except for the occasional little squirming wiggle when she pressed her legs together. She was enjoying this as much as he was. Maybe more.

And he had to admit, he was impressed at how quickly she'd submitted to the flame and flogger. That she hadn't panicked when she'd first felt the heat. Or when the flogger had first landed. He'd been prepared for both. After all, they hadn't ever played together before and he'd never observed her being particularly good at submitting.

But she'd submitted beautifully for this.

For him.

Examining the 'why' would have to come later though, when he had the concentration for it. The flame on the flogger was beginning to fade and Elliott let out a long, low breath, bringing the swing to a natural end. Garreth immediately stepped up with the bucket of water so they could douse it.

One of the perks of doing a fire scene at Black Light was that he could trust the Dungeon Monitors to take care of his implements for him, while *he* took care of his sub. Leaving them to it, he moved swiftly to Lisa to check her skin.

Pink. The surface was warm to his touch and she shuddered as he ran his fingers over the splotches on her back, her low whimper going straight to his cock. No actual burns and she was so blissed out, her eyes were unfocused and hazy when she opened them.

"Please," she whispered, her body trembling under his touch.

If it was any other night, if she were the sub he'd chosen, he'd take out his cock and fuck her from behind right there... but she was going to need aftercare, they had two more spins of the wheel to do, and it was *her*. Elliott didn't even know if she'd *want* him to fuck her.

But he couldn't ignore that sweet, soft plea either. Sliding his hand between her body and the cross, he pressed his fingers over the little strip of hair adorning her mound and into the wet heat of her pussy.

She was soaked. Gritting his teeth against the punch of arousal that hit him, he swirled his fingers, stroking her clit. Immediately she cried out, her hips moving, pressing forward for more, body shuddering in response to the stimulation. Elliott pressed against her, helping to hold her up so that all of her weight wasn't on her wrists while she cried out in glorious orgasm.

His cock ached in envious response.

Fuck.

Lisa

SOMETHING COOL SPREAD across her back and ass, soothing the heat that had found its way under her skin. Not that the heat had felt bad. But the cool felt nice.

Then warmth. A hard lap. Arms holding her securely, comfortingly. It was like being in a cozy little nest. Her pussy still throbbed with the aftermath of her orgasm, although it hadn't entirely assuaged the need kindling inside of her. But enough for now. Especially because she was enjoying the snuggling.

Mmm. Nice.

The deep rumble of a voice.

Wait a second.

She knew that voice.

Master Elliott. Jerk face.

'Not a real submissive.'

Lisa shot upright. Or, well, almost. She tried to, but the muscular arms around her tightened almost as soon as she moved, holding her in place as easily as if she were a kitten. Which would be really sexy if those arms belonged to someone else.

Okay, that was a lie. It was still really sexy even though they were Master Elliott's arms... just, frustrating too. Bad enough she was attracted to him, did he have to snuggle her too? What was he thinking while he was doing so? Was he judging her for not being able to handle the fire play?

How long had he been cuddling her? Was she going to lose her chance to spin the wheel twice more and prove to both of them that she was not only a submissive, but an *awesome* submissive? Why hadn't he gotten her moving once they were done with the scene?

"Would you hold still?" His growling voice sank into her bones and she froze, although she didn't sink back into his hold the way she wanted to. "What is wrong with you?"

"We have to spin again," she said automatically, because that was at the forefront of her mind.

The exasperated sigh she heard in return was much more in line with how he usually treated her than all this cuddling was.

"Can't you just sit still and enjoy the moment? Aftercare is expected."

"I don't need aftercare," she said automatically, despite the immediate urge to snuggle back into his arms and forget the rest of the world. That was the best reason to *not* indulge, as far as she was concerned.

Hmph. *Expected.* Yeah, it was his duty as a dom to provide her with aftercare if she needed it. She never had before. Although, if she was being honest with herself, she knew that she'd never done such an intense scene before either.

Part of her wanted to sink back into his arms and just enjoy the moment, but she knew that was a dangerous idea. The only thing Master Elliott felt for her was disdain. Well, and going by the hard cock against her hip, he maybe felt something else for her too, but she was pretty sure that wasn't personal.

Besides, it was too late.

"Fine," he snapped out the word, sounding angry and a little hurt. "Next scene. Let's go spin the wheel."

From the tone of his voice, she almost expected to be dumped to the ground when he stood up, but he held her firmly, keeping his hold on her arm until she was settled on her feet. The loss of his arms around her made her want to cry out and she bit her lip against the sound. Dammit.

Providing her aftercare didn't mean he thought she was weak or anything. She didn't even know why her mind had gone there. Maybe just because she really did have something to prove to him. But he wouldn't have thought any less of her if she'd indulged in some cuddling… she shouldn't have snapped at him. Even if she was trying to protect herself.

His hand settled around the back of her neck again, like it belonged there, and it was disconcerting how reassuring it felt. She almost wanted to apologize for rejecting his aftercare, maybe even take it back and climb back onto his lap, but he slapped her ass.

The sting was greater than she anticipated, probably because her skin was sensitive after being flogged with *fire*.

"Move, girl."

Ugh. She resented how much that order turned her on.

CHAPTER 5

ELLIOTT

en minutes, Elliott fumed. She'd given him just *ten minutes* of aftercare, and the moment she'd come to her senses she'd pushed him away.

Elliott *liked* aftercare, dammit. It was like letting out a long, deep sigh after holding his breath. Calming. Centering. And he could have really used more time to reflect on how different sceneing with Lisa was than he'd expected.

At least, it *had* been different. Until she'd come to her senses and immediately started shooting off from her mouth. Not for the first time, he yearned for a gag to use on her. Although she was suspiciously quiet now that he was steering her back to the stage through the crowd.

He was curious about some of the other scenes going on, but there were enough people that he couldn't really see much of what was happening elsewhere. They were already drawing some new eyes, aside from the spectators they'd had for their first scene, as the eager audience realized they were headed for a new spin.

Glancing down at Lisa, Elliott couldn't see enough of her expression to even take a guess as to what she was thinking.

Which might be for the best.

They stepped back up onto the stage and Elixxir grinned at them. "That scene was *hot!*"

Lisa giggled and Elliott had to tamp down an unexpected flare of jealousy. But really? That was a terrible pun.

"It was pretty good," Lisa said, smiling widely at Elixxir.

Oh. Hell no.

She was going to pay for that little remark. Elixxir's eyes widened as he cut his gaze to Elliott to see his reaction, before turning back to Lisa and shaking his head.

"You are trouble, aren't you?" he asked her, moving aside so she could spin the wheel. Lisa smirked at him. She ignored Elliott entirely, as far as he could tell. Yep. She was definitely asking for some punishment.

The choices flew by.

Something with spanking... whipping... so that I can smack some respect into her sweet ass...

The wheel rocked to a stop. Elliott's heart lurched and a slow smile began to spread across his face.

"CNC! That's uh..." Elixxir glanced down at his notes. "That's *Consenting Non-Con*."

Elliott released his hold on Lisa's neck and looked down at her. Wide, startled doe eyes stared back up at him, wary and unsure. He leaned toward her until his face was only a couple inches away from hers, his voice low and threatening.

"Run."

~

Lisa

OH FUCK... *oh fuck, oh fuck, oh fuck...*

CNC had been on her list of choices for hard limits. She hadn't rolled it, but it had been there. She'd been so caught up with feeling guilty about how harsh she'd been to Master Elliott right after the scene and feeling dumb for thinking that he'd think less of her for indulging in some aftercare and even dumber because she *could* have still been cuddling with the hot man, she'd blanked when DJ Elixxir had first announced it.

Honest-to-goodness hadn't been able to remember what *CNC* was until he explained it.

It had been on her list because it had sounded scary.

But it hadn't sounded half as scary as Master Elliott had been when he'd leaned in, a sadistic smile on his face, and whispered, soft and low and creepy. *Run.*

The worst part about running was that she *knew* he was going to catch her.

She'd bolted off the stage, not caring about all of her jiggly parts wobbling for everyone to see. Some of the audience moved out of her way, others made her go around them, all of them watching with varying degrees of amusement and glee as she darted through them, trying to escape the Dom that was now hunting her.

The Dom that had no reason to go easy on her.

The Dom that basically now had permission to do *whatever he wanted with her* when he caught up with her.

The skin on her back and ass felt tighter than ever, leftovers from having been *flogged* with *fire*. Which had been utterly amazing, no matter what she'd told DJ Elixxir. She'd just wanted to see Master Elliott's face when she said it. And, in that moment, it had seemed worth it to see how pissed he'd gotten.

Now though...

Would it have killed me to be just a little *more respectful?* She thought mournfully. But that was her. Impulsive to a fault. And it was a fault, in this case.

Looking over her shoulder, she squeaked in dismay. Master Elliott was tall enough he was easily seen through the crowd, coming for her with eyes blazing and a sadistic smile of anticipation on his lips. Sexy and terrifying all at once.

I'm so fucked.

Probably also in the good way... eventually... She couldn't deny that she was getting turned on even as she ran from him. That was the consenting part, right? But who knew what he'd do to her when he caught her? Literally, whatever he wanted.

And, considering how she'd been behaving, she doubted he'd be nice about it. Especially since he was a sadist.

Ducking down, hoping that she might be at least a little bit harder to see that way, Lisa darted to the right. There was a sudden open space in front of her, between her and the people at the bar. Everyone else was behind her, watching the scenes.

Room to maneuver, but not to hide. Her brain froze.

Which way?!

Too late.

An iron band wrapped around her middle and lifted her as she shrieked in surprise and shock. Eyes whipped around from the bar, everyone who was ordering drinks turned to see who was screaming so close to them. Not that any of them were going to be any help.

Lisa tried to kick back, tried to stomp on Master Elliott's instep... but the damn man was still wearing his boots while she was totally naked and barefoot. A fair fight it was not.

~

Elliott

BENDING LISA OVER A TABLE, Elliott shook his head. The woman needed to take a self-defense class. She was flailing more than she was fighting, although it did make it easier for him to grab her wrists and cuff them behind her back.

"No!" she shrieked, trying to pull her hands away.

Chuckling, Elliott pulled her by her cuffed hands so that she was pulled backward off the table, guiding her to her knees. She looked good there, arms behind her back, breasts thrust out, lips slightly open, and his cock jerked in anticipation.

Grabbing a handful of her wet hair, he pulled her forward by her head as he freed his cock with his other hand. It bobbed in front of her face and her eyes widened, a hot blush spreading across her cheeks.

"No biting, Lovely Lisa," he said silkily, his voice heavy with threat, before he pushed the head of his dick between her sultry lips. Whatever her response would have been was muffled by his cock and he groaned with pleasure, thrusting into the wet heat of her mouth.

He'd dreamed of stopping her smart mouth, and the reality was so much better than the fantasy.

Although, she tried to pull her head away, struggling against his grip, she didn't bite down. Smart girl. Elliott ignored her struggles, tightening his fingers in her hair and reaching down to fondle her breast with the other hand. He pinched her nipple hard enough that she squealed, and the vibrations of her protest traveled over the length of his cock.

Fuck that felt fantastic.

Staring down at her, he watched as his cock vanished between her lips. There was a little wrinkle in the center of her brow, like she was concentrating really hard, and he groaned as he felt her tongue curling against the underside of his cock.

For a few long, slow, languid pumps, he just enjoyed her efforts and watching the shiny length of his dick sliding in and out of her mouth. Part of him wished he could take a picture—Lovely Lisa, silent because her mouth was too full of his cock to talk. As it was, he knew he'd be jerking off to this image a lot in the future.

But for now, he wanted to see some tears.

CHAPTER 6

LISA

Sucking Master Elliott's cock while he pinched her nipple—harshly but not so roughly that she couldn't handle it—was easier than she'd thought it would be. It didn't immediately occur to her that he was deliberately being easy on her. She'd just started to get into the rhythm of sucking and using her tongue when his fingers tightened again and suddenly his cock was thrusting much deeper than it had been before.

He'd been *letting* her suck his cock.

Now he was fucking her mouth.

The difference was acute. Drool slid from the corners of her mouth, tears stinging her eyes as he thrust so deep that she gagged—but she couldn't pull away because he was controlling everything. She couldn't even attempt to fight him with her hands bound behind her back.

Helpless. Choking. Sucking in air through her nose when he pulled back, and yet it wasn't enough to stop the slow burn building in her chest. Her nipple throbbed in his grip and she tried to scream around his cock, to cry out, but he just kept using her mouth for his own pleasure, his eyes alight as he watched her.

His cock rammed deep into her throat and Lisa's jaw tightened reflexively, her teeth nipping at his cock.

Immediately, his expression changed, darkened, and he pulled his cock out, leaving her gasping. Tears slid down her cheeks as she gasped, dizzy with the sudden influx of oxygen. Her lips felt swollen, her throat used, and she was uncomfortably aware of the way her pussy was pulsing between her thighs despite—or maybe because of—his rough treatment.

"What did I tell you about biting me?" He growled the question, pulling her to her feet by her hair and spinning her around.

A bar table hit her right at waist height, and he forced her upper body down over it. Her breasts were pressed flat against the cool surface and she could hear some chuckles coming from the audience around them.

"I didn't mean to! I was choking, you asshole!"

SMACK!

The hard slap to her backside hurt way more than it should have and Lisa screamed, high and shrill, barely registering the laughter of their audience. The stinging burn flared hot; the feeling of her skin being too tightly stretched over her body increasing the pain. She couldn't even enjoy the laughter around them, since she wasn't sure if it was at his or her expense.

Fingers probed her pussy and she moaned, in both humiliation and denial—she was soaked.

"At least one part of you liked it." The mocking amusement in his voice ticked her off even more.

Hands tied behind her back, bent over a table, she finally managed to kick him... and immediately wished she hadn't.

SMACK! SMACK! SMACK!

Elliott

"Nooooo, I'm sorry, I'm sorry, stop, please!"

Shifting out of the way of her flailing feet, Elliott pinned Lisa's bound wrists in the middle of her lower back, peppering her ass with short, crisp swats. Her bright pink ass jiggled with every slap, her cries ragged and pleading, and her pussy glistening wet with invitation.

In other words—fucking perfection.

Because he'd been carefully watching, he'd known she'd been near her limit with the rough oral, and he'd been about to pull out to give her a break when he'd felt her teeth. That had just given him an opportunity to spank her the way he'd always wanted.

His cock jerked every time his hand landed, and he decided he'd been patient enough. This wasn't supposed to be a spanking scene, after all.

Letting his hand fall one last time, he rubbed the hot flesh of her ass, enjoying the way she slumped against the table when she realized her spanking was over. She wasn't crying very hard, but there was a definite hitch in her breath. Elliott dug his fingers into the soft, hot flesh of her buttocks, deliberately rough.

"Ow! Stop it!" She writhed, trying to squirm away, but there was nowhere for her to go. He pinned her down on the table, pressing his hand on her lower back to keep her in place, while his free hand dug into his pocket to retrieve the condom waiting there. Ripping the packet open with his teeth, he pulled out the rubber and sheathed his cock.

His pants sagged slightly down his thighs, he positioned himself behind her and then thrust forward, hard and fast, impaling her on his cock. She screamed, struggling even more, although her increased efforts were just as useless as her previous ones.

Despite her cries and protests, she was so wet that it only took him two thrusts to fully embed himself in her sweet pussy. Her muscles gripped him tightly, squeezing and contracting around him as he held himself very still inside of her.

"Noooo..." Her voice was a low moan, a mere whisper, and he paused, waiting to see if she was going to safe word... but she just squirmed again, and Elliott grinned. This was a *CNC* scene, hearing 'no' just made it hotter for both of them. Her pussy quivered.

Gripping her wrists, he pulled out and thrust back in hard and fast. Lisa cried out again as his body slapped against her hot ass, his cock splitting her open again and again, ravaging her while she was pinned helplessly against the table. The appreciative audience around the bar turned him on even more.

Then he felt her slump against his thrusts, no longer struggling or fighting, but submitting to his ravishment. Hmm. That wouldn't do.

Elliott shifted one hand.

∾

Lisa

Was this what hate-fucking was like? Because it kinda felt like what she'd always imagined hate-fucking would feel like.

Raw. A little terrifying. Incredibly hot.

Her throat was sore, her ass was on fire, and her pussy was throbbing with need. Tears were still sliding down her cheeks onto the table beneath her. People were staring at her. Watching her being fucked, seeing her helplessness, witnessing her inability to make Master Elliott stop.

Sure, she could have used her safe word but... she didn't actually want him to stop. She just wished she'd put up a better fight. Except fighting now might mean that he'd stop fucking her. And she *really* liked him fucking her.

Then his hand moved, and something pressed against her anus.

Lisa squeaked in surprise, trying to wriggle away from the insistent pressure. "No!"

He just laughed at her and her adrenaline shot up. "That's right, fight me sweetheart. You're making this too easy."

"Asshole!" The second the insult dropped from her lips, laughter rang out around them and she wished that she'd chosen any other name to call him.

"And a very nice one it is, too," Master Elliott said loudly, to more laughter, just as his thumb popped through the tight ring of muscle.

Writhing, Lisa tried to lurch forward, tried to kick back at him, neither of which did anything. His thumb burrowed deeper inside of her, making her feel twice as full, while his cock rammed into her pussy again and again. Twisting, she managed to catch his shin with her heel, but it was like kicking a cinder block.

"That's right, sweetheart, fight me." The mocking drawl dug under her skin and Lisa tried to buck. Her holes clamped down around him, drawing another groan of pleasure from his lips.

Panting, she slumped against the table again, already out of breath, muscles quivering. Master Elliott made a soft chiding noise and then something tugged on her wrists, and the next thing Lisa knew, her hands were free.

It's a trap!

But the Admiral Akbar style voice screeching in her head didn't stop her from immediately trying to take advantage of her newly freed hands. She yanked them forward, so Master Elliott couldn't grab them again and immediately tried to push off from the table.

His thumb popped out of her ass, making her squeal, as he grabbed her by both hips, holding her lower body in place, still fucking her. Pushing herself up, her back pressed against his front and she tried to shove the table away from her... but it was heavier than she'd anticipated, and it barely moved an inch.

Almost immediately, she was bent forward over the table again, this time with Master Elliott's hands pinning hers down to the hard wood, his cock surging inside of her. Now his weight was fully atop her, somehow making her feel even smaller and more vulnerable than when her hands had been bound behind her back. He was holding her down with his own strength, which was so much greater than hers.

"Come on, Lovely Lisa," he said in her ear, his voice mocking and dark. *"Fight me."*

CHAPTER 7

ELLIOTT

The slick heat of Lisa's pussy tightened around him before she tried to buck again, holding him inside of her even as she tried to fight against him. She shifted underneath him, trying to get a leg up to kick, but the position didn't allow her to get any leverage. Her foot brushed past his shin, barely making contact.

Elliott moved his hips, pulling back and thrusting in.

Not hard.

Not fast.

No, he used a long, measured stroke, ensuring that Lisa could feel every centimeter of his cock as he languidly filled her pussy. There was nothing hurried about his movement; he was deliberately taking his time, showing her with his body that there was nothing she could do to stop him. That he didn't need to rush.

"No!" She choked out the word, bucking again, which pushed her back onto his cock faster than she would have been otherwise. "No, no, no, no, no..."

She was chanting the word as she started struggling more and Elliott flexed his muscles. Straightening his arms, he left some space between their upper bodies, taking more of his weight on his hands to help pin her wrists, but also give her room to try and maneuver.

The operative word being *try*.

As he'd expected, she immediately pushed upward into the space, twisting her upper body to no avail. No matter what move she made, none of the long, slow strokes in and out of her pussy even faltered. She whimpered, clenching around him, every time she found another boundary that he'd set down, her helplessness stoked her arousal.

Fucking and fighting at the same time. His self-control was waning with every slow, measured stroke, which was part of why he was taking his time. He didn't want it to be over too soon.

When she jerked her head back—he wasn't sure if she was actually trying to slam the back of her head into his face, but she almost managed it—Elliott dodged and then bent his head forward to sink his teeth into the soft muscle between the base of her neck and her shoulder. Lisa screamed, clenching hard around him as she nearly came, her elbows buckling.

~

Lisa

CAGED in by Master Elliott's larger body, Lisa didn't think she'd ever felt so small, so vulnerable before. He was all around her, inside of her, filling every one of her senses. The ease with which he'd over-powered her was almost humiliating.

And for some reason, having her *no* ignored was turning her on even more. But that was the whole point of CNC, right? To fight, to say no, and to be fucked anyway. It was hotter than she'd imag-ined it could be. To feel this helpless. This overwhelmed. This out of control.

I'm a filthy pervert.

At least she was in good company.

The more she'd struggled, the more turned on she'd gotten, until she'd gotten so into it that she'd actually tried to head butt him. Which was when he bit her. The pain flashed through her body, nearly making her orgasm just from the new sensation as her pussy spasmed around him. It felt like he was using his teeth to hold her in place, like an alpha wolf forcing his mate to submit.

"*FUCK!*" She screamed the word, jerking underneath him, pussy shuddering as her orgasm hovered just out of reach.

Master Elliott held her pinned in place for one long moment, his punishing grip keeping her immobile. She whimpered, almost ready to start begging. The teeth digging into her shoulder retreated, leaving behind a burning circle, as if he'd marked her. Had he marked her?

Part of her hoped that he had.

Suddenly her hands were free, but she didn't have time to try and do anything about it before he'd grabbed ahold of her hair, pulling it from the messy bun. Water dripped onto her shoulders as his fingers squeezed the mass and she cried out as cold water slid over her hot skin.

Pulling her head up, Master Elliott used her hair like reins, his thrusts coming faster and harder. The sudden change sent her body reeling with sensual shock. With her hands free, she should have been able to fight back now, but all she could do was brace herself against his punishing thrusts. Her pussy burned from the sudden increase in friction, her neck aching as he pulled her head back, forcing her body into an arc.

Her breasts bounced, nipples brushing against the hard wood of the table and adding another point of stimulation. Lisa cried out, her pussy clenching and releasing, trying to hold him in place, trying to slow him while she struggled to adjust to the overwhelming mix of sensations.

"Please," she begged, her voice higher than usual. "Please, Master Elliott, slower!"

Just as he'd ignored her 'no,' he ignored this request too. He pumped, harder and faster, slamming into her, making her entire body jerk with the power of each thrust and Lisa felt tears rolling down her cheeks. Her scalp tingled from the tightness of his grip, each tug of her hair sending a new surge of pleasure to her core.

The building need inside of her was too much to bear. The potent mix of pleasure and pain, humiliation and desire. His cock stroked her g-spot with every powerful thrust, sending her soaring.

She screamed when her orgasm hit, her body pulsing with the intense overload of sensation.

The grip on her hair released and she fell forward, still shuddering with orgasm. Master Elliott's hands gripped her hips, holding them tightly in place as he actually began to fuck her harder, faster, his pleasured grunts punctuating every deep thrust. Lisa sobbed beneath him as the hypersensitivity of her post-orgasmic pussy began to turn her pleasure into a kind of torturous rapture.

Too much of a good thing. Far too much. Her body couldn't handle it.

"Stop," she begged, crying out as Master Elliott thrust home again, right on the heels of her plea. "Oh God… I can't take anymore, please, stop!"

∼

Elliott

RATHER THAN RESPOND VERBALLY to Lisa's begging, Elliott lifted his hand and smacked her ass, making her shriek and tighten around him. He could hear the ragged edge in her voice, feel the way her pussy throbbed around him. Already she was building up to a second, more intense climax… but for some women, such a thing could be more painful than pleasurable.

It sounded like Lisa might be one of those women and Elliott wanted nothing more than to force her to a second, agonizing orgasm.

"Please no, please no, please no," she chanted, but 'no' was not her safe word and Elliott kept thrusting. The table clattered beneath her as he rammed into her, letting loose the reins of his self-control. He groaned as he fucked her hard, the slick channel of her pussy clenching around him, massaging his cock.

She was no longer trying to fight back, she was just holding onto the table beneath her, crying out and pleading with him to slow down, to stop, even as her body begged for more.

The pink skin of her ass rippled with every thrust, his body slapping against hers, cock shiny with her juices. Lifting his thumb to his mouth, Elliott sucked on it to lubricate the small digit and then lowered his hand back down to her ass. She cried out, jerking again, as he pushed his thumb into the tight ring of her anus, her body shuddering in reaction.

Her pussy gripped him in a vise so tight it was almost painful, and he knew she was coming again. Riding her hard, he felt his own orgasm swelling, his balls tightening as they slapped against her wet flesh. Lisa sobbed out again as his rigid length impaled her, his erection throbbing inside her as he finally started to come.

Pulling his thumb from the tight grip of her ass so that he could lean forward again, he thrust hard and filled her completely, the soft flesh of her ass flattened by the weight of his body. The walls of her pussy sucked at his cock, pulling the cum from him in throbbing spurts that left him breathless and shuddering above her.

Bending his head, he panted, jerking slightly as her pussy contracted around him, drawing another spurt of cum from his sated cock, filling the condom. He rested his damp forehead between her shoulder blades, running his hands over her sides as they both came down from the incredible high.

When he heard their audience applauding, he could only shake his head and laugh.

CHAPTER 8

LISA

*W*hen Master Elliott bundled her into a blanket and set her on his lap for aftercare, Lisa didn't protest. Even if it was dangerous because of her crush on him, which she'd thought she'd gotten over, but she definitely hadn't. But her body needed the time to recuperate.

The man had a big cock and he had *not* been gentle.

And she'd loved every second of it.

"Drink." A water glass appeared at her lips in time with the order and she immediately obeyed. She was thirstier than she'd realized and quickly drank almost the entire glass before pulling away. Coolness spread through her chest and she slumped back into Master Elliott's arms.

"Ow." She murmured the word, wincing slightly when she moved, a sore muscle next to her hip twinging. Being bent over a table was definitely hot, but some of the lingering effects were not very comfortable. Something padded would have been better...

But this had probably been more fun.

Unfortunately, her small 'ow' was enough to put Master Elliott into uber protective Dom mode.

"Ow? What hurts?" It was more of a demand than a question, although concern laced his tone.

"I'm fine," she said, slapping his hands away when he tried to pull the blanket open to look at her, feeling annoyed. Before he'd been mad when she hadn't wanted to cuddle, now he was trying to end their cuddle session in favor of checking her over. "I can handle anything *you* dish out."

She'd meant it as a joke, but there was more of an edge to her voice than she'd intended, some of the feelings she'd had going into Roulette night making themselves known in that one simple statement.

Master Elliott stilled. "What do you mean by that?"

"Nothing, I'm just teasing," she said quickly, but the damage had already been done.

Strong fingers caught her jaw, forcing her to turn her head and meet his gaze. The expression on his face was guarded, but she could see the tension in his shoulders, the way his eyes blazed.

"Are you trying to prove something to me?" Master Elliott asked. His eyes flashed with intense emotion. "Would you even have said your safe word if you needed to?"

"Yes!" *Probably.* But she didn't like the way he was looking at her. Like he couldn't trust her. Lisa smacked him on the chest, palm flat against the broad muscles. "I didn't need to say it, okay? Three orgasms, and you really feel the need to question me?"

His eyes narrowed, his fingers not relaxing their grip one bit, so she couldn't turn away from him. "Sweetheart, if I want you to come for me, I'm going to make sure you come for me."

She huffed, trying not to squirm too much because, hey, that was hot. But her pussy really was sore.

～

Elliott

THE SQUIRMING subbie on his lap was nothing like he'd expected her to be. But now he wasn't sure if he'd accidentally taken advantage of her desire to 'handle whatever he dished out.' When they'd started the evening, he'd wanted to prove to her that she *couldn't* handle actual submission.

So far, *she'd* proven him wrong.

Had she wanted to safe word at any point, but *not* because of what he'd said to her before? If that had happened... Elliott could already feel the guilt and self-recrimination welling inside of him. Maybe the real problem in his life was that he wasn't a good dom.

After all, shouldn't he have noticed that his previous girlfriends weren't actually submissive? That they were just placating him or, worse, play-acting to manipulate him? Shouldn't he have realized that Lisa had come into tonight with something to prove? Shouldn't he have been keeping an eye out to make sure she didn't bite off more than she could chew?

"Hey!" She smacked his chest again and he blinked, and then scowled, letting go of her chin to place his hand over hers so she couldn't do it again. The tiny sting didn't hurt, but it wasn't exactly respectful.

"Stop doing that," he ordered.

"Then stop thinking whatever you're thinking," she sniped back, scowling right back at him. "You haven't done anything wrong. I haven't done anything wrong. *I* thought we were having a good time, up until now."

"We were—are—I just..." How did he explain that he was worried she was lying to him without it sounding insulting? Easy answer—he couldn't.

BDSM was about trust. They had to trust each other. Something which he knew he struggled with, because his trust had been broken before. Knowing that she felt she had something to prove to him, having never seen her involved in a scene as intense as the two they'd already had tonight, how could he trust her to know her limits?

Lisa pressed her lips together, looking annoyed. "I'll use my safe word if I need to, okay? I honest-to-goodness have not felt like I needed it. I'll admit, I got *close*. Close, but not actually there. Okay?"

"Okay," he said, despite still feeling uncomfortable. Rewinding the evening so far in his mind, he couldn't help but wonder when she'd gotten close. There were several points that might have been.

When she leaned into him, her hand still pressed to his chest, resting her head on his shoulder, he relaxed a little. Unlike after the first scene, she wasn't acting out of sorts with him. If anything, he felt like maybe they'd turned some kind of corner. Elliott no longer wanted to prove that she didn't belong at Black Light. He didn't even think it was possible.

Instead, he was starting to wonder if maybe—in this case—his dick wasn't so stupid after all.

~

Lisa

WHEN SHE THOUGHT of Master Elliott, snuggly was not one of the adjectives that immediately leapt to her mind. She'd never really paid attention to whether or not he did aftercare with other submissives. Aftercare had never been high on her priorities.

But with him?

Maybe she needed to reorganize her priorities. Because she could seriously cuddle with him all night. She didn't even know how long she sat on his lap, just enjoying the feel of being in his arms, before he finally spoke up.

"As much as I'm enjoying what we're currently doing, we do have a third spin to do and time is ticking," Master Elliott murmured into her ear. "Unless you want to give up having a third chance at winning hottest scene?"

Give up? Hell no. Those words were not in Lisa's vocabulary. Even if part of her thought that more snuggling with Master Elliott might also feel like winning. But he was right, one more scene was one more chance to win. And she wanted that third scene with him. Wanted everything she could get. There'd be time for more cuddling afterward.

"After our first two scenes?" Lisa shook her head. "I feel like we have a chance at winning *two* months free here. I'm not going to give up a chance at one month, much less two."

Master Elliott chuckled. "I have a feeling we probably have some pretty stiff competition tonight, but you might be right."

"You need to work on your confidence," Lisa scolded, and then frowned. "Or your optimism. Maybe both."

He had to laugh, shaking his head, and she grinned, shrugging her shoulders. Sometimes her mouth ran away from her, but she was mostly okay with it.

"Maybe you're right," he said, helping her stand up from his lap. Lisa immediately missed how comfortable she'd been. "Maybe we do have a chance at winning tonight."

Even though she really hoped that was true, Lisa felt her heart squeeze a little and she realized it's because she wanted their scenes to mean more to him than just a way to win a contest. Because, deep down, she already knew they meant something to her. There was no way she was going to be able to get him out of her head after tonight.

So much for keeping her old crush under control.

CHAPTER 9

ELLIOTT

*A*s they approached the roulette wheel for the third time, Lisa seemed oddly pensive. He couldn't exactly pinpoint the difference between this silence and her quiet before, but it was there. Like she was thinking very hard about something.

Funny. Earlier this evening, he'd been thinking that all he wanted was for her to be quiet so that he could get through the night. Now he was wondering how to get her to talk to him.

He'd been wrong about her.

Considering how strong Lisa had come on to him initially, he gave himself some leeway on that, but he'd still been wrong. She might need some lessons on proper club etiquette, and she was one hundred percent a brat, but she was definitely submissive. Elliott had just judged her too harshly at first, based on one encounter.

Elixxir grinned at them as they walked up to him for the third time. "Just under an hour left for your final scene... Roll a good one!"

Those nearby watching to see what they got next all chuckled. Elliott smiled. It really didn't matter to him what they got. He was already feeling good and relaxed after their first two scenes, and no matter what came next he knew he'd enjoy it. Lisa looked nervous again, as she should.

The only scene he hoped they wouldn't get was Dom's choice.

312

Since they'd already done fire play, he really didn't have a clue what he'd choose to do instead. Sure, he could come up with something, but for once he'd rather go with the flow.

Once the wheel started to spin, Elliott reached out and tucked Lisa under his arm. The fuzzy blanket wrapped around her tickled his side as she leaned into him, watching the wheel turn with wide, nervous eyes. He could feel the air whoosh out of her when it finally came to a stop.

Anal sex.

Sounded good to him.

To his surprise, rather than announcing it, Elixxir stepped in closer to them, looking a little concerned. "Lisa, are you sure you want to rescind your hard limits?"

Ah, shit.

$\sim$

Lisa

Butt stuff. Of course, her final spin was butt stuff. The one option she'd included in her list of possible hard limits, not because she didn't like it, but because of how intimate it was. Because she hadn't wanted to go there with a Dom.

However, Master Elliott wasn't just a random dom and right now... well, she didn't mind going there with him.

"Yes," she said, nodding decisively.

"No," Master Elliott said, at the exact same time.

Turning her head, she glared up at him. "You don't get to decide what my hard limits are."

"And I'm not going to have you doing something you don't actually want to do just to prove something," he countered, glaring back down at her. "If something is a hard limit for you, it should be respected."

Lisa made a frustrated noise and felt a blush rising in her cheeks. "It's not... I didn't. Ugh." She looked at DJ Elixxir. "Can we have a minute?"

DJ Elixxir gestured with an open hand, nodding his head, and she grabbed Master Elliott by the arm, pulling him over to the side of the stage. She didn't want everyone being able to hear how she'd chosen her hard limits. Yeah, she was pretty comfortable letting her nerd flag fly most days, but that didn't stop some people from being jerks... and if Master Elliott was going to laugh at her, she'd prefer that not everyone know why.

Crossing his arms over his chest, Master Elliott looked down at her and raised his eyebrows. Feeling more vulnerable than she had all night, Lisa's fingers tightened their grip on the aftercare blanket, holding it together in front of her chest. It wasn't like having a blanket around her instead of being butt naked was that much better, but it did make her feel a little less exposed.

"I had more than four things I wanted to put as a hard limit," she said, doing her best to keep her voice loud enough for Master Elliott to hear but too quiet for anyone else to overhear. "So, I made a list of every single thing I didn't want to do and then I rolled dice to choose which four made my actual hard limits list."

Master Elliott blinked. "You rolled *dice?*"

She scowled at him. "I'm a D&D nerd, okay? It made sense to me at the time."

"Okay," he said slowly, but at least he didn't sound judgmental.

"And the *only* reason I put butt—um, anal sex on the list was because to me it's a very intimate thing and I didn't want to do it with just anyone and I didn't know who I'd be paired with."

He just blinked again. Damned if she could tell what he was thinking.

"I almost re-rolled after I rolled it, because there were so many other things that seemed way worse that I wanted to put as a hard limit. Then I decided that it was really unlikely that a Dom would put it as a hard limit, whereas it was much more likely that they'd choose one of the other things I didn't want to do. So, I decided to leave it. Plus, it felt like cheating to re-roll. I didn't realize I'd end up with a Dom with *no* hard limits."

Cocking his head to the side, Master Elliott's lips pressed together in a thin line for just a moment. "So, you find anal sex really intimate and didn't want to risk having it with someone you didn't feel anything for?"

Now it was Lisa's turn to blink. There was something odd about his phrasing... but, she couldn't quite figure it out. "Right."

"But you're okay having anal sex with me?"

Heat bloomed in her cheeks and he grinned as the hot blush spread across her face. Which didn't help, because when he smiled at her like that, all wicked and looking at her with sexy intent in his eyes, it just made her blush even harder.

"Yes."

"Okay then."

This time it was Master Elliott's turn to grab her arm and pull her back to the front of the stage where DJ Elixxir was waiting for them. Glancing between her and Master Elliott, DJ Elixxir's gaze finally settled on her. "Are you going to re-spin?"

"No, thank you," she said politely. Master Elliott chuckled, sounding extremely pleased and her blush brightened.

"Remember, the club safe word is 'yellow' or 'red,'" DJ Elixxir reminded her. Not that she needed the reminder, but he was obviously concerned, and she appreciated it.

"She won't need it," Master Elliott said reassuringly, before his big hand wrapped around the back of her neck, guiding her off the stage again. Her butt cheeks automatically clenched as nervous anticipation surged up inside of her.

Elliott

SPANKING BENCH? Medical play table? Cross?

No... He grinned when the perfect piece of furniture caught his eye. Not only would it ensure he could keep an eye on all of Lisa's reactions—he was mostly reassured she had told the truth about this particular limit—but, considering her reason for putting anal sex as a hard limit, it would also increase her discomfort. His sadistic side nearly cackled with glee.

Because he was watching her from the corner of his eye, he saw her surprise when she realized where he was headed.

The people standing near the black leather chaise parted for them as they drew closer. Elliott released his hold on Lisa's neck and grabbed the blanket she had wrapped around her, yanking it off from behind. Blankets weren't club wear, but they were such easy access. He had to admit, he was a fan. She gave a startled little shriek as the blanket was pulled away but didn't try to cover herself.

"Up on the chaise," he ordered, gesturing.

The black leather gleamed under the lights. Leather straps hung from its sides, promising an abundance of ways a subbie could be secured to it. There were also cuffs hanging from a chain at the top of the chaise, which could be lengthened or shortened as desired.

It was perfect for what Elliott had in mind. He grinned, watching Lisa get up onto the chaise on her knees, placing her hands on the backrest. She was going to be in for a surprise in a moment.

But there were a couple things he needed first.

CHAPTER 10

LISA

*P*eeking over her shoulder, Lisa saw one of the DMs handing Master Elliott a small tube of lube and a plastic wrapped butt plug. At least, she assumed it was lube in the tube. Black Light was prepared for all the scenes, and anal sex pretty much required lube. If it wasn't lube, then she really *was* going to have to safe word...

Master Elliott leaned toward the DM, clearly making another request. Probably for something to torture her with.

Her pussy quivered. Lisa almost wanted to groan, thinking about how she'd wanted a break for her sore vagina. Maybe she should have been a little clearer about that wish, because the universe had a perverse sense of humor.

Not that she wanted to change her mind now... she was just nervous.

And the waiting wasn't helping.

A sudden bang made her jump, yelping in surprise. She popped up from her position, stretching as high as she could while kneeling on the chaise to see what had made that noise. People around the bar swirled and she realized one of the standing banners propped up there must have fallen.

Catching her eye, Master Elliott gave her a sharp look and pointed his finger, indicating that she needed to get back in position. Then he turned back to the DM. Jerk. He was obviously getting off on making her wait. As evidenced by the slow way he sauntered toward her. Lisa's fingers dug into the soft leather of the chaise and she pressed her lips together to keep herself from blurting out something insulting.

For her, the hardest part about being a submissive was keeping quiet, even when she knew that what she wanted to say was probably going to get her in trouble.

"Bend forward," Master Elliott ordered. "I want that pretty ass up in the air."

From the way he eyed her curves as she positioned herself, he wasn't lying about thinking her ass was pretty. Most of the Doms she'd met liked her butt, but she still liked to hear it.

In this position, her breasts hung down underneath her and she had to spread her legs to balance herself with her knees apart on the seat of the chaise. She felt the leather padding shift slightly when Master Elliott moved behind her and then she gasped in surprise when he actually kissed her buttock, only inches away from her pussy. Her elbows pressed against the back of the chaise as she leaned forward, instinctively jerking away from him.

'Kissed' might not be the right word. His lips pressed against her flesh but then he bit down, his teeth scraping over her skin. Was she still sore from the fire flogging? Because she definitely felt a little more tender there than usual. His tongue flicked out, licking her, and she squirmed, trying to get him closer to her pussy.

Instead, he moved to her other ass cheek, kissing her there too, teasing her with his mouth. She growled a little under her breath but stilled the moment she felt one wet fingertip pressing against the entrance of her asshole. Anticipation, arousal, and trepidation washed over her in equal measure.

Rather than immediately plunging in, his finger circled the tight hole, teasing the sensitive nerve endings there and Lisa whimpered. Her hips rocked, pushing back against him. Only then did his finger slide inside of her and she gasped, clenching down around him.

While it might have been a while since she'd had actual anal sex, she used toys regularly enough that the stretch felt more pleasant than uncomfortable, and her pussy spasmed in response.

It *was* breathtakingly intimate. Perversely erotic. Wonderfully filthy. Not something she wanted to do with just anyone. Not something she had expected to want to do with Master Elliott. If it had been her first spin, she might have reclaimed her hard limits.

His finger moved inside of her, slick and hot and probing. She was so glad it had been her third spin instead.

～

Elliott

HEAD HANGING DOWN, Lisa was panting for breath as Elliott stretched out the tight ring of her sphincter. Pulling far enough out that just the tip of his finger was inside of her, he added a second and she shuddered at the increased stretch. On his lap, his right hand finished opening up the plug. It was about as long as his fingers, but thicker around – not as thick or as long as his cock, which meant she'd still have to stretch even more to take him.

Moaning, she moved her hips with his fingers, shuddering. She adjusted very quickly though, her ass easily taking both digits. Which meant she was no stranger to anal play. Elliott's cock, already hard, practically throbbed with interest. He'd be able to be a little rougher than he'd anticipated. He'd thought that her reluctance must have at least something to do with inexperience or maybe a slight aversion...

On the contrary, she was loving every second of his fingers and obviously craving more.

When he pulled his fingers out, she actually mewled in disappointment, her ass moving with him, trying to find them again. Elliott gave her ass a little smack.

"Hold still, Lovely Lisa, the plug is a little bigger than my fingers."

Her head lifted and she turned to look at him over her shoulder, winking at him, eyes filled with lust. "Good."

Elliott grinned. Well if it was like that... He quickly lubed the plug and pressed the tip to her ass, pushing it in fast enough that he felt a little resistance as it sank into her. The crinkled hole stretched, and she gasped, moving forward slightly... and then moaning and pushing her hips back again.

He fucked her with the plug, pushing it to the widest section and then pulling it back out again to the tip. Lisa moaned as her hips moved along with the motion of the plug and Elliott pressed his hand against his cock as he watched. The tiny hole was shiny with lube, easily opening for the plug.

So he pressed it all the way inside of her and she threw her head back when the widest part pushed past the tight ring of muscle guarding her entrance and settled against it from the inside.

"Fuck!"

Chuckling at her sexual frustration, Elliott stood and quickly slapped the cuffs at the top of the chaise's back around her wrists. That done, he grabbed her by the hips and flipped her over so that she was in a sitting position, leaning her upper body against the backrest, arms secured above her head. Her eyes were slightly glazed, cheeks flushed, breasts thrust toward him with hard nipples begging to be attended to.

Which was when the Dungeon Monitor swung by with the clamps and chain Elliott had requested. Perfect timing.

"Thank you," he said, holding out his hand. Terry dropped them in, nodding before moving away to keep an eye on the rest of the proceedings.

Lisa blinked. "What are those for?"

Holding up two of the clamps, chains hanging from them until they connected to a single chain which hung even lower, a clamp dangling from its end, Elliott raised his eyebrows. "Do you want to take a guess?"

Lisa

No, she didn't want to guess. She was pretty sure she already knew where they were going, she just wasn't sure she liked the idea. This was supposed to be butt stuff, not nipple and clit torture. But Doms were also given a lot of leeway with what they did within a scene, and if she was being honest… she was kind of curious what the combination of sensations would feel like.

Her nipples pulsed, as if saying they were ready. The base of the plug in her ass was pressed against the seat, making her feel like the plug was burrowing deeper inside of her, and her muscles clenched around it. It all made her want to squirm and press her thighs together to relieve the ache on her pussy.

"Let me show you," Master Elliott said silkily, when she didn't answer right away. His hand cupped her breast, caressing and gentle and completely at odds with what she'd expected. When his fingers tightened a moment later, she gasped at the sudden rough handling, her pussy spasming in response.

The clamp pinched her nipple and she cried out, back arching as the pain stabbed through her. Holy crap that was tight! She gasped for breath, hands jerking at her cuffs, all too aware of Master Elliott's intense scrutiny. Tears pricked at the back of her eyes before her breathing slowly adjusted. Her nipple throbbed in the tight confines of the clamp, but it was bearable.

"Good girl," he murmured, and that accolade somehow made the pain even more tolerable. Right up until he moved his hand to her other breast and clamped that nipple too.

Fuck!

This time, tears did spring to her eyes as she gasped and writhed for him, her breasts heaving as her nipples protested the torture. The expression on his face was almost serene as he watched her, taking pleasure in her pain… Being able to see his reactions was fascinating, infuriating, and arousing all at the same time.

Tiny needles stabbed her nipples when she finally relaxed, her breasts aching from the constriction of blood flow. The chain was cool against her stomach and she moaned when he picked up the last clamp.

"Please, please, no," she begged.

The jerkface just chuckled. "*CNC* was last scene, sweetheart. But don't worry, you can take this."

Lisa bit her lip to keep from crying out prematurely as his fingers spread her labia open, revealing her swollen clit. Because it was swollen. Swollen and sensitive and an all-too-accurate barometer of her arousal. When the clamp closed down around it, she almost screamed... and then realized it didn't hurt that much. It stung, it pinched, but it wasn't the sharp, piercing pain that the clamps on her nipples had initially caused.

Instead, she let out a sigh of relief that was half laugh. Watching her expression, Master Elliott smiled cruelly and then she felt the clamp tug at her clit, and it tightened.

"Ow!" Her arms jerked forward, immediately stopped by the cuffs.

Her sadistic lover's lips quirked. "A little tighter I think."

"No, please—ow! Ow, please, that's enough!" To her relief, he stopped, although not before her clit was throbbing with pain, a kind of ecstatic agony that made her entire body feel tightly wound.

She stared up at him, wondering what was going to come next.

CHAPTER 11

ELLIOTT

The rubber-tipped clamps gripping all of Lisa's most sensitive buds were on the easier end, as clamps went, letting him know that she didn't have a lot of experience with them. But she didn't need it. He liked that it was so easy to make her squirm and cry out, liked watching her breathe in and absorb the pain, to take it for him.

She was nowhere near using her safe word, but she wasn't sitting comfortably—and not just because of the plug in her ass. Elliott was very much looking forward to seeing how she would react to the clamps being on her while he fucked her. Quickly, he pulled his second condom from his pocket before shucking off his pants and getting back into position on the chaise.

Pulling her legs over his forearms so he could spread her wide, Elliott grasped her by the waist, canting her hips forward so that her lower body was no longer resting on the chaise, but was draped over his thighs with her legs spread wide. Lisa gasped, and he initially thought it was because the clamps must have pulled at the movement, but then she started to buck and try to wiggle away. Not that she had any hope of doing so.

"What are you doing?" The tone of her question was almost outraged, and Elliott cocked his head at her, his hand sliding around the outside of her hip so he could reach underneath her to grip the base of the plug.

"I'm getting ready to fuck your ass, sweetheart," he said. His fingers touched rubber and he gripped it, twisting the plug in her ass and making her shudder at the sensation. Her lips parted again on a gasp, eyelashes fluttering, before she managed to compose herself.

"Like... like this?" Her voice squeaked.

Realizing what her problem was—since it was exactly why he'd chosen this position, although he hadn't expected her to actually protest—Elliott let his lips curve in a sadistic smile as he tugged the plug free and let it fall by the wayside.

"Just like this," he said, the tip of his cock pressing against her slightly gaping entrance. Her body pressed down, since she couldn't hold herself up in this position, stretching her open. She gasped, pupils dilating, as he pressed in. Elliott leaned forward, his voice lowering so just she could hear him. "So I can watch every expression that crosses your face while I fill this sweet ass."

And his hand roughly gripped her buttock as he surged forward, the head of his cock popping into the tight, hot space. They both gasped at the same time as her body spasmed around him, her eyes flying wide open at the intrusion. The condom was lubricated, and there was extra lube from his fingers and the plug, allowing him to slide deeper while she twisted slightly against his grip, panting through the discomfort of her narrowest space being stretched open by his cock.

Watching her expressions, the slight flashes of pain, the way her eyes met his and then flitted away in embarrassment as a blush rose in her cheeks... fuck he loved it. Loved seeing the struggle, the discomfort, and the determination to bear it, to please him.

Elliott let gravity do its work, slowly impaling her on his cock while he watched every single little reaction.

Lisa

NEVER TELL a sadist why you don't want to do something...

Yeah, that would have been good advice, if only she'd thought of it earlier. She should have made up a reason why she didn't want to do butt stuff. Because if she'd thought anal was intimate before, that was nothing compared to how incredibly intimate Master Elliott had chosen to make it.

The twinging pain and discomfort of the stretch barely registered compared to her emotional discomfort as Master Elliott's gaze bore into her. She couldn't hide her reactions from him, try as she might.

She hadn't ever had anal sex in any position other than bent over. Hadn't even considered it was a possibility. Had been sure, right up until he'd positioned himself underneath her, that he was going to turn her back around once he was ready. And when she closed her eyes, he tugged on the clamps, sending pain spiraling through her pleasure.

Lisa cried out, arching as the clamps pulled at her tender bits, her eyes flying wide open.

"Eyes on me, Lisa," Master Elliott ordered, his voice implacable.

She moaned as her ass settled against his lap, her gaze flitting up to his and then away again. She wanted to obey his order, but she couldn't quite bring herself to meet his eyes for more than a moment or two while he was buried in her ass. His hips flexed, rocking her on his lap and Lisa shuddered, the stretch burning through her muscles and filling her with pleasure.

Pain... pleasure... it was two sides of the same coin.

And he felt so good inside of her. Toys were fine in a pinch, but they were harder, less yielding, and there was no substitute for the throbbing and jerking of a hard cock responding to her muscles' clenching.

Master Elliott's arms moved, sliding further up her legs, forcing them further apart so that he could grip her waist... and then he started to fuck her. His cock receded, pulling at her insides, rasping against the sensitive nerves around her anus. Then he surged upward, letting gravity take her so that she slid down his shaft as he thrust into her, making her clench and spasm and whimper as she was filled, too quickly. The clamps and chain bounced, pulling at her, adding to the influx of sensations.

"What's your color, Lisa?" The question was more of a demand.

Color? Oh, right, color.

"Green, so green," she whispered throatily, looking up at him.

Their gazes met. Clashed. Her breath caught in her throat. The dark desire in his eyes made her entire body tingle.

"Good girl." His hands gripped her hips more tightly and he began to move, staring directly into her eyes the entire time.

Lisa wanted to look away, wanted to squirm free, but it was like she was pinned by his gaze, her insides twisting as he began to ride her with long, sure strokes. Every thrust had his cock rubbing against a spot inside of her that sent a surge of pleasure through her entire body, counteracting the sharp pinches from the clamps as they were bounced by his movements.

The tugging on her clit was driving her wild, but the more her clit swelled, the more the clamp bit in and the more it hurt. She was moaning, shuddering, crying out, and wildly out of control... and she couldn't look away from Master Elliott's gaze. It felt like he was seeing inside of her to every perverse desire she'd ever had, every filthy fantasy, and stripping her bare.

Rapture burst inside of her, unlike any orgasm she'd ever experienced, and she screamed his name. Her pussy spasmed emptily, the fullness of her ass making her writhe in ecstasy. Her clit screamed in agony as the clamp was pulled from it, and Lisa screamed with it, starbursts of pain and pleasure ricocheting through her.

Elliott

Lisa's eyes rolled up into the back of her head and Elliott quickly reached up and released the clamps on her nipples, freeing him to fuck her clenching ass as hard and fast as he wanted. She was lost in a storm of exquisite agony, crying out his name in climax, and it seemed she barely registered the pain of the clamps being removed.

Her nipples were like ripe berries on her chest, much darker red. Looking down, he could see the slick folds of her pussy, her swollen clit red and angry, peeking out at the apex. Leaning forward, he rubbed his groin against her clit, pulling another shout from her lips.

Riding her hard, he fucked her into the chaise, their bodies pressed so closely together he could scarcely tell where he left off and she began. Her muscles squeezed his cock hard as she sobbed out, another wave of pleasure overtaking her. The base of Elliott's spine tingled, and he cried out with her, shoving deep inside of her.

His cock throbbed, forcing cum past the gripping ring of her muscle, squeezing the base of his dick, and into her bowels. They rocked together and he emptied himself inside of the condom, panting as he felt her slump against him, completely wrung out. A shudder wracked him as the last spurt of cum was milked from his cock by her clenching muscles, and he leaned against her, covering her completely with his body.

He didn't know how long they stayed there. Long enough that when he looked up, most of their audience had dissipated. Squinting at the clock, he smiled. Just under the time marker.

Although, surprisingly, he didn't care as much about that as he had before. Sure, a free month of membership was always good… but he was now realizing that he wasn't going to be interested in playing with just anyone when he visited Black Light. He wanted to play more with Lisa.

'Play' might be the wrong word.

Date was a better one. And play, at Black Light.

If she was amenable.

First things first though. Elliott got both of them up and cleaned up, before wrapping Lisa back up in an aftercare blanket and reclaiming the chaise. Someone came by with a bottle of water for each of them and Elliott just leaned back against the chaise, holding her securely and comfortably in his arms. At one point, Melody walked by with Master Kawan and gave him a discreet thumbs up, making him smile and shake his head.

Considering that his most recent ex had also been Melody's friend, her endorsement might be a little suspect, but in this case, he thought she was probably right.

~

Lisa

SHE WAS AFRAID TO MOVE.

Because she was afraid that if she moved, Master Elliott might take that as a signal that aftercare was done, and then the night would be over. Even when Melody walked by and gave her a thumbs up, Lisa didn't even return the gesture. Just in case.

Head resting on Master Elliott's broad chest, tucked under his chin, she could hear the slow, steady beat of his heart. Feel his arms wrapped around her, holding her securely on his lap. And feel all her well-used, completely sated lady parts. She was pretty sure she was still going to be feeling the aftereffects tomorrow.

Which was going to be bittersweet if Master Elliott still wanted to have nothing to do with her after tonight.

Probably shouldn't have agreed to do the butt stuff with him.

Not that butt stuff was a declaration of anything. It wasn't like she expected him to take her out to dinner just because they'd had butt sex. It would be nice though.

"Lisa?" His voice was soft, almost gentle.

Crap. Time was up. She felt tears prick the back of her eyes. *Suck it up, buttercup. It's time to go back to the real world.*

"Yeah?" she asked, doing her best to keep her voice casual. She would not cry if he just said 'see ya later' and left.

Master Elliott cleared his throat, an odd sound, almost like he was embarrassed. She peered up at him, intrigued.

"Some of my friends and I are starting a new campaign in two weeks. Our cleric moved away a couple months ago, and we haven't found anyone to replace him, so we were just going to play without one but if you'd be interested…"

She blinked. Sat up and stared at him almost accusingly. "You play Dungeons and Dragons?"

A slow smile spread across his fast. "Sweetheart, I'm the Dungeon *Master*."

As a pun, it was terrible and she smacked his chest, trying to stifle her laugh. Grabbing her wrist with one hand, Elliott wound his hand around the back of her neck and pulled her in for a deep, claiming kiss.

When he pulled away, his eyes were sparkling. "I take it that's a yes?"

"Definitely." She paused. "Um... you're going to take me out on a real date too, right?"

He shook his head at her brazen question, but his eyes were sparkling with amusement. "A real date and claim all your scenes at Black Light for the foreseeable future."

Lisa threw her arms around him for another kiss. She didn't even care if they won for hottest scene. She already had everything she wanted.

THE END

ABOUT THE AUTHOR

Angel is a self-described bibliophile with a "kinky" bent who loves to write stories for the characters in her head. If she didn't get them out, she's pretty sure she'd go just a little crazy.

She is happily married, old enough to know better but still too young to care, and a big fan of happily-ever-afters, strong heroes and heroines, and sizzling chemistry.

She believes the world is a better place when there's a little magic in it.

Find Angel Online!

- Amazon → http://amzn.to/2DplX3X
- BookBub → http://bit.ly/2G68e3O
- Facebook → http://bit.ly/2Ds7c0e
- Goodreads → http://bit.ly/2rt4rdL
- Instagram → http://bit.ly/2CkqiqZ
- Website → http://www.goldenangelromance.com

MEANWHILE AT BLACK LIGHT WEST...

MADISON

Black Light West
February 14ᵗʰ, 7:18pm

SHE'D SPENT weeks helping to get the Valentine's events organized and ready to go for both Runway and Black Light, but the massive crowd crammed into the theater seemed even larger than they'd estimated. People seemed to be in every bit of available space, and the heat was intense.

Of course, that could be the leather outfit she'd worn — because it was now tradition — or the spotlights aimed at the stage.

Either way, the party was going to kick off soon and it was her job to keep it going, even if she suffered heat exhaustion in the process.

"Most of all, we just want you all to have fun and enjoy yourselves. Roulette is my family's favorite event at Black Light each year, and we're glad you've all joined us tonight. Now, I'll hand things back to your lovely MC for the night, Madison!" Chase turned toward her, his bright smile making her laugh as he clapped, and the audience joined in. The man had become a good friend, along with his husband and wife, and the trio made working at the two clubs a total adventure.

Giving Chase a quick hug, she heard him whisper, "Knock'em dead!" before he moved out of the spotlight.

"Thank you, Chase Cartwright-Davidson!" Madison clapped as well, waiting for the audience to quiet down before she started reviewing the rules for the night.

She'd practiced her speech in front of the mirror enough times that she didn't even need to glance at her cheat cards as she spoke. Explaining their guidelines for both audience and participants, as well as the new voting element for this year's Roulette. *That* was all due to the pissing contest between Elijah and Spencer, which she thought was pretty ridiculous, but Madison had no plans on losing. There was extra vacation on the line, and she and Trevor could definitely use it. There were islands in the Caribbean calling to her.

"Dominants, if you'll join me on the stage," she called out, gesturing to the stairs as the group of men, and two very tall women, gathered in the spotlights. Taking the popsicle sticks down the row, she tried to match faces with the profile sheets she'd memorized as she went. It wasn't easy, but by the time she'd handed out the last number she was confident she knew who was who.

A buzz of excitement rolled through the crowd as she returned to the roulette wheels and picked up the little white marble that would decide the fate of so many throughout the night.

"We have three matches to start the night that were pre-determined based on preferences. First up, Mistress Agonee, and her sub for the night — Corey! Come spin your first kink, Corey!" Madison welcomed them on stage, pairing off the male sub and his domme with their kink. They were followed by two women, and then two men. The last male sub getting a swat on the ass as his dom led him off the stage.

"All right, now we're back to what Roulette is known for. The game of chance where dominants spin to discover who they'll spend the evening with. First up is Master Adam!"

The couples paired off quickly, efficiently, and Madison felt like all of her preparation and planning were at least partly to thank for it. She was still riding the high of the last couple's entertaining *classroom role play* spin when she turned to look for the man who had drawn number five — and her stomach dropped.

Shit, what is his name.

He was a Daddy... a Daddy with a weird letter starting his name. The silence felt deafening in her ears as she started to panic, all of her overconfident comments to Trevor before they'd arrived coming back to haunt her. *Zane? Zurich? Xavier!*

"Our next dom up to the wheel is Daddy Xavier. Come on over and roll for your submissive!" she called out, sweeping her arm at the roulette wheels as she smiled broadly to cover the momentary lapse of memory. Fortunately, it seemed no one noticed the lengthy pause, and the handsome man approaching the wheel was plenty distracting for the subs waiting their turn. "Here you go," she said, handing the man the little marble as she set the wheel to spin.

Daddy Xavier dropped it without hesitation, and a moment later it found its mark.

"Dolly!" she announced, looking to the group of submissives, waiting. No one moved.

Shit.

"Dolly?" she called again, taking a few steps toward the stairs. "Is Dolly here?"

Finally, a tall, dark-haired woman broke away from the group and started toward the stairs where Daddy Xavier met her like a real gentleman. The two seemed to be struck with each other, moving closer together, and Madison felt the ticking of the clock inching toward the start time.

"There will be plenty of time for staring adoringly into one another's eyes later," she said, interrupting their intense gazes. "Come on over and spin for your first activity, Dolly."

A few laughs filtered through the audience as they joined her at the wheel and Dolly took the marble, dropping it in almost as soon as Madison set the wheel spinning.

"Pet play!" she announced when it stopped, smiling at the woman. "Oh, how fun! You'll make the cutest kitten or puppy, Dolly." Giving her a wink, she watched as Daddy Xavier led the woman off stage.

Scanning the group of men, she found the one who had drawn

number six. He was definitely attractive, but she got the feeling he wasn't very friendly. The rest of the dominants had talked with each other, but Pierce Montgomery hadn't even looked at them. He'd barely even looked at *her* when he drew his number.

Summoning a broad smile, Madison looked over at him. "Next up is Pierce! Are you ready to find out who you'll spend Valentine's with?" she asked, but he didn't even try to respond. His eyes were skimming the group of submissives, trying to see through the bright lights as she offered him the ball. "Looking for someone specific?" she asked away from the mic and he finally looked at her.

"It's all random chance, isn't it?" he replied, a smirk teasing his lips as he took the ball from her hand.

"True," she acknowledged and spun the wheel. He dropped the marble in without hesitation, and it clattered until it came to rest next to one of the other littles. "Baby!" she called, immediately wondering how this odd mix would turn out.

When the woman didn't move, Madison almost groaned aloud. Taking two steps toward the edge of the stage, she repeated the summons, "Join us up here on stage, Baby, so you can spin your first kink!"

Unlike Daddy Xavier, Pierce didn't move to meet the girl wearing a cute schoolgirl outfit. And it seemed like Baby wasn't excited about her pairing, because she stopped several feet away from him at the edge of her wheel.

Offering an encouraging smile, Madison handed her the ball and whispered, "You got this."

The wheel spun, and Pierce moved behind the little sub, whispering something against her ear that made the girl's eyes go wide before she dropped the ball into the wheel. It bounced high, rattling around before it finally began to whir around, bouncing until it landed.

"Humiliation!" she announced, unable to hide her grin as Pierce led the stunned babygirl toward the stairs.

That will be an interesting pair.

Several couples matched up relatively quickly, including a nervous girl in a red dress that managed to drop the marble for the roulette wheel. Her dom had chased it down with good-natured laughter, and whatever he'd whispered in her ear had seemed to calm her down, because she was smiling by the time they spun *wax play*. Madison had a warm, fuzzy feeling in her stomach as she watched them walk away, and she turned her attention back to the last dominants.

"Tanner47 you're up!"

The dom stepped forward, looking relaxed, carefree, and his smile lit up his whole face as he met her at the wheel, dimples giving him a boy-next-door charm. "Put me in, coach," he said softly and she couldn't help but laugh a little.

"Well, let's get right to it!" she cheered, returning his smile as he took the marble. "Spin the wheel and drop the ball for your play partner for the night."

The room was abuzz with activity already with almost all of the couples paired off, many of them getting to know each other near the steps to the stage, and the dom and subs steadily dwindling.

And one more sub was about to be off the docket. "Quinn!" she announced as the marble chose his play partner for the evening.

Tanner47 seemed to be familiar with the woman, welcoming her with a wide grin. The woman, Quinn, seemed less excited than him, but she took the ball when Madison offered it.

Spinning the wheel, she waited for the woman to drop it, but the sub was distracted, which she couldn't blame her for. The man was handsome. "Just drop the ball once the wheel is spinning, and we'll find out your kink for at least the first thirty minutes," she reminded Quinn, and the submissive finally let the marble go.

Oh, this will be good.

"*Diaper play!*" she called out excitedly, a little louder than necessary, because that was sure to earn them a few points in the war with Black Light East.

"Is that on your hard list?" Tanner47 asked, and Madison looked at Quinn's irritated expression. For a moment she thought the sub might lose her temper, but the woman's eyes just closed as she took a breath.

"No," Quinn answered.

"Mine either," her dom replied with a chuckle.

"Great. Looks like you're set then!" Madison smiled, waiting for them to clear the stage so she could knock out the last few pairs.

A well-liked shibarist got matched with a masochist, spinning *watersports* which neither had placed on their limits list. Then another dom was paired to a curvy redhead that she knew enjoyed pain, and as they spun for their kink Chase stepped up behind her.

"There's a small problem, we may have to use an alternate for the last dom," he whispered, and Madison kept her cheerful expression plastered on her face as butterflies took off in her stomach. Chase gave her an encouraging pat on the back and continued, "Karly Starr still isn't here, but her Uber is supposedly close. I need you to stall until I figure out what we're doing."

The pornstar?

Unfortunately, Madison couldn't draw attention to Chase by asking him any of the questions whirring through her head, so she just gave him a quick nod before announcing the couple's kink, "*Flogging!*"

Glancing over at the final dom, Master Wilde, she could see Chase speaking with him, but he wasn't giving her any kind of signal. So, she stalled.

"Before we get to our final couple and get Roulette started, I'd like to remind all of our attendees that just like last year we have an amazing silent auction happening in the bar area tonight. Proceeds from your bids will go to support some great, sex-positive charity organizations here in Los Angeles, and I took a peek earlier so I can tell you that you will *definitely* want to check it out." Madison checked on Chase and Master Wilde again, seeing Chase on his cellphone, but he caught her eye and rotated his finger in the air. *Keep stalling. Okay.* "For those of you looking for something for your playroom at home, we have some gorgeous handmade BDSM furniture from our very own dungeon monitors, Tyler and Dave Darden! There's also some beautiful toys and tools from our local BDSM community, some getaway packages, and some spa days if you feel like treating your sub to something special after an intense session."

Chase moved close, but he didn't stop her, so she continued to ramble. Reminding participants about their responsibility to cast their vote for their favorite scene or couple of the night, as well as the available snacks and drinks. The crowd was starting to get antsy when she finally saw one of their security staff leading Karly Starr, a well-known pornstar, through the crowd. Her blonde hair was pulled into a high ponytail, but Madison was surprised to see her in a rather subdued business suit instead of a revealing outfit.

That's a surprise.

"Go ahead and introduce them," Chase whispered.

"Okay, we're ready for our last couple to meet each other and to see what they are going to roll on the wheel," Madison called out, spreading her arms toward each of them. "Let's welcome our last submissive, Karly Starr, to the stage to join her Dom, Master Wilde."

As soon as the two met at center stage, their height difference was apparent. Master Wilde towered over the actress, and Madison noticed that part of the reason for the difference was that Karly Starr was... barefoot.

Don't ask.

Handing Karly the marble, she spun the wheel and waited for her to drop it as Master Wilde stepped behind his sub for the night, whispering something to her. Karly dropped it in, and Madison felt as anxious as everyone else to get the event started.

Click. Click. Click.

"*Pony play!*" Madison announced, but the pair in front of her were busy whispering to each other. Fortunately, Master Wilde looked over as the wheel stopped moving and caught sight of their first kink, a chuckle rolling out of him.

The couple wasn't moving, but they were already several minutes past the start time, so Madison stepped around the table to face the crowd. Putting all of her positive energy into her voice, she smiled and kicked off Roulette with an energetic, "I can tell our couples are excited to get started, so everyone have fun and play safe!"

Everyone started to pour out of the overheated theater, and Madison knew that the fun was just beginning. They'd spun a fun collection of first kinks, and their members were always adventurous — she just had to hope they outperformed the East Coast.

Because after tonight, she'd *definitely* need her Caribbean vacation.

WICKED

A Black Light: Roulette War Novella

By

Jennifer Bene

CHAPTER 1

PIERCE

*N*ot having his phone inside Black Light was one of his least favorite things about the club, the other was the obnoxious members. They were a bunch of fake L.A. shells, and he was the asshole with a trust fund and no interest in dealing with them. Even with his reputation people seemed to think he wanted to listen to their bullshit stories or answer meaningless conversational filler questions. But they were as deep and interesting as a puddle of piss on Sunset Boulevard.

At least if he had his phone he could scroll an article, or watch porn — anything to strategically avoid the desperate looks of the random subs in attendance for Roulette. Watching or participating.

Fuck.

Speaking of desperate, from across the room he saw a silver mini-dress flittering in the lights heading directly toward him. The woman's name was Anna, or Sarah, or… something that rhymed with *blow-out-my-fucking-brains-uh*, and he'd made the unfortunate decision to fuck her three weeks before. And despite avoiding her, his money meant she wasn't giving up her pursuit so easily.

If she's on the wheel for roulette, I'm walking out right now.

"Pierce!" she screeched, holding her arms wide as she approached as if she actually thought he'd hug her. When he only raised an eyebrow at her, she dropped them to her sides to giggle. "Oh my God, I've been looking for you, you dirty boy! Where have you been hiding?"

"What do you want, Sarah?" he asked, not even looking at her as she tittered again.

"It's Neva, silly! Neva Hawthorn. And, *duh*, I'm here to watch Roulette and you should come sit with me."

Pierce didn't even try to hide his complete lack of interest in being anywhere near *Neva Hawthorn* as he brought his unimpressed gaze back to her. "No."

"What?" Neva's voice was a screech that reached a pitch only small, yappy dogs could hear, and Pierce gritted his teeth at the sound. "Um, do you not remember that we had an awesome time together?"

"You made sure the entire club knew that *you* had a good time, that's for sure." The comment was half under his breath, but she managed to hear him even over the din of conversation and the low music.

"And what does *that* mean?" she snapped, scoffing.

"It means that you screaming like a b-rated pornstar isn't even remotely attractive, and no amount of plastic surgery is going to gift you a decent personality, *Neva*." It was almost worth tolerating her presence just to see the look of surprise on her face as her artificially plumped lips parted in shock.

"Are you kidding me? You want me to apologize for coming loudly? Whatever, Pierce! You liked it! *You* got off!" Neva was raising her voice, and people were looking. The vapid rabble hungry for a little bit of gossip, and he was done.

"I have a dick, Neva. It's not complicated. A lot like you."

"You're an asshole," she accused, and he laughed.

"That's one of the only honest things I've heard out of your mouth," he replied, but he stopped himself from saying the other shit on his mind. He saw through her like he did the rest of them. Her blatantly obvious need for outside approval, her obsession with her image, the bottomless pit of self-esteem issues that was the deepest thing about Neva Hawthorn. Pierce shook his head and tried to remind himself that he'd signed up for Roulette to toy with someone *new*, not get kicked out by the DMs for causing a scene.

"You're going to come crawling back to me when you want some in a few weeks and I—"

"You'll *what?*" he challenged, letting a smirk spread across his face as he finally met her eyes. They both knew, if he just snapped his fingers, she'd ride his cock for the off chance he'd take her out. Hang out on her arm. Bankroll the lifestyle she wanted. When she just stood there, Pierce pushed himself off the wall, standing to his full height of 6' 2" to tower over the little idiot. Her neck craned back as he looked her up and down and shook his head. "It's not happening again. Go entertain yourself somewhere else. Now."

Instead of scaring her off, Neva's pupils dilated, a flush darkening her chest and cheeks as she stared up at him without moving. "I like it when you talk like that."

"I don't care."

"Look, the nonchalant dom thing is hot, but I just want you to come sit with us. My friend and I reserved a table in the bar area when we didn't get into Roulette this year. We can catch up, watch the fun, and then maybe later all three of us could—"

Chuckling, Pierce rolled his eyes and leaned against the wall again. "Not interested."

"WHY!" Neva shouted, a furious pout on her lips, but he just laughed under his breath.

"Because I *am* playing in Roulette this year." He shrugged a shoulder and shoved off the wall, scooping up his bag from the floor. "And I'm not playing with you again. Ever."

Without wasting another molecule of oxygen on the girl, he marched toward the theater where he saw members already filing in. It was an excuse to get away from Neva's desperation, and allow him a few more minutes to examine the potential toys for the evening. At least Roulette had defined edges and whichever sub he spun on the wheel would understand that this was a one-night thing. A head fuck, a real fuck, and then a little aftercare to put her back together again and keep himself in good standing with the club before he moved on.

It would be *his* entertainment for the night.

Entertainment that hopefully wouldn't follow him around Black Light in the coming weeks trying to snag him for Instagram fodder like Neva fucking Hawthorn.

Pierce weaved through the gathered attendees and dropped his bag near the base of the stairs, scanning the women who had lined up on the submissive side of the stage. They were all so easy to read. One of them was clearly uncomfortable in the short dress she wore. Bright red and barely covering her ass, it was like a neon sign that screamed 'insecurity' in bright letters. Her eyes were flitting around the room like a trapped bird, and he knew he'd have her in tears before the first kink was half-over. Of course, the woman to her right wasn't any better. Textbook L.A. Probably a D-list actress from a daytime soap opera with declining ratings who thought she'd be the next big name. She'd have the haughty attitude to match and not a true submissive bone in her body. Hell, *he* would call red before he'd put up with that shit for three hours.

It's not like he needed the free month.

And, really, he didn't know what the fuck he needed.

Need was too complex to contemplate, but Pierce knew what he *wanted*. A sub that he could put on her knees, push her face to the floor while whispering in her ear what a dirty little slut she was. A woman who would crawl for him, drool for him, let him use her like furniture. Like an object. And when he had her so spaced out she didn't hesitate to obey, to come to whatever filthy name he called her — then he'd make her come until she cried. Fuck her until there was nothing else in the world but his voice in her ear, owning every single inch of her body.

Then… then it would be nice if he could actually talk to her. To not be *bored.*

But years of this bullshit had confirmed for him that a woman like that either didn't exist or was already with someone else.

The only women he seemed to find were the ones that liked the way he looked, but not the way he played, or the ones that found out about his family money and were willing to do anything if they could take a selfie on his sailboat to post online. *#trustfund #golddigger #fuckoff*

He hated it. He hated these people. Black Light was supposed to make all of that shit a non-issue, but it seemed there was always another rung on the social ladder and women like Neva Hawthorn were more than happy to use him to reach the next one.

Maybe after this he would take his friend Devon's advice and head back to the East Coast for a while. Close to the original Black Light location so that he had a better chance of finding someone with reasonable conversational skills. Someone interesting that he could tolerate for more than a few hours. Someone who enjoyed his games, who bent to his will, but wouldn't break.

Like that will ever fucking happen.

Just when Pierce was about to turn around to people-watch the kinksters in the audience, he saw a new sub join the ranks beside the stage. She caught his eye because she was broadcasting alluring innocence. A *little*. A pretty little babygirl in a schoolgirl button-down and an impressively short, frilly skirt. Complete with lacy layers and ribbons. Her white, knee-high stockings, black mary janes, and the twin pigtails resting on her shoulders — with more ribbons — finished off the look that was nothing more than a costume hiding whoever she was underneath.

He would be her absolute fucking nightmare.

And... he liked that.

Pierce felt his lip curl into a smirk as he studied the little brunette waiting for a Daddy to sweep her off her feet, but all he could imagine was her make-up smeared from fucking her face until she sobbed before he made her lick her drool off the floor.

Crossing his arms, he kept his eyes on her until the weight of his stare brought her attention to him. Wide brown eyes stretched even wider, but he didn't give her anything. Not a smile, not a wink, and he didn't return the awkward little wave she offered.

The little sub shifted uncomfortably, trying to look away, to pretend she wasn't curious, but she had no self-control. It wasn't even a full thirty seconds before she snuck a peek at him again and he had to clench his jaw to keep from grinning.

If I get you, little princess, I'm going to enjoy taking you apart piece by piece before I watch you come undone. I'll leave you a dirty, wet mess with no more pretty lace to hide behind.

I'll show you what you're really made of.

CHAPTER 2

TORI

The blond dom near the other side of the stage was definitely staring at her. In fact, she wasn't sure if he was even blinking. Every time her eyes wandered back to him, she found his piercing stare on her. Intense and *not* friendly, which was disappointing because he was definitely hot with that serious expression and his sharp, clean-shaven jawline catching the lights.

She didn't know him, but he seemed familiar all the same. She was sure she'd seen him at Black Light before... she just couldn't remember a specific scene.

Could he be a Daddy?

Her nose wrinkled a little as she watched him out of the corner of her eye. *No.* Nothing about him looked like a Daddy Dom. He was wearing a tailored suit, but he had an empty expression on his handsome face. He was missing the softness in the eyes, the care and concern she looked for when finding a play partner. No, Mr. Stares-a-lot definitely wasn't a Daddy, but something about him still had her thighs pressing together. There was a tingle that made the hair on the back of her neck raise a bit, and that buzz stroked slowly down her spine with every repeated moment of eye contact.

He wasn't just staring, he was... evaluating. As if he'd zeroed in on her like a predator on prey, and something inside her was responding to it. A small tremor in her stomach that spoke of danger and risk — but that wasn't what Tori did.

Tori didn't go for the sadists or the flashy performance doms. She dated Daddies. Men who treated her like a naughty little girl, who spanked or paddled her when she misbehaved, and then took care of her. Tucked her in, cuddled her. She was always one-hundred percent safe with them, and this guy with his blond hair that looked windswept even though they were inside did *not* say safe.

Maybe he was one of the owners' model friends? It wouldn't surprise her to find out he was a model because he was... very nice to look at.

But not for her.

Forcing her gaze to look past him, she searched the other dominants gathering by the stairs. There were a few men that fit the profile of a possible Daddy. Older than her, dressed well, with a face that spoke of both compassion and stern lectures that always led to a very warm bottom. Yes, any of them would work.

Maybe she could even find a new Daddy tonight. Someone that would be *right*.

The lights dimmed and Madison, the same MC from last year's Celebrity Roulette, arrived on stage with a spotlight and a roar from the crowd to begin the event. Butterflies immediately took over Tori's stomach. She'd been a member of Black Light last year when Roulette had gone on, and it had been incredible to watch. There had been so many amazing scenes, and all she'd wanted was to be a part of it. To find a dom like so many of the subs had that night, and the moment she'd found out that sign-ups this year weren't just restricted to celebrities she'd probably been one of the first applications in because she wanted that. She wanted—

Stop.

Taking a slow breath, Tori tried to push down the excitement and shove away her dreams of the perfect Daddy. The one that would understand her, would see what she needed and scratch all of her itches.

Please, please, please...

Chase Cartwright-Davidson was on stage now, his charming smile and boisterous energy a welcome distraction as Tori added her voice to the cheers and applause. Then Madison returned in her sexy, black leather outfit, reviewing the rules that Tori already knew by heart. *This* wasn't what had her stomach twirling into knots, it was what came next.

Her eyes drifted over to the gathered dominants again and there was Mr. Stares-a-lot. Still watching her, only now he had a smirk on his face like he was laughing at her. Part of her bristled, but another part urged her to stand up straight to hide the sinking feeling his strange look had summoned inside her. It was a relief when Madison eventually summoned the doms to the stage to choose their spin order, because the man couldn't continue staring at her through the bright lights cast on the stage at the front of the theater.

Handsome or not, she didn't like the guy. He looked cruel, and she didn't like *that* at all.

The spins started and Tori was distracted by a girl in a bright red dress next to her who leaned close to ask, "Are you as nervous as I am?"

Tori reached over to squeeze her hand, offering an encouraging smile. "Totally, but it was a pretty amazing event last year, so I've got my fingers crossed tonight is going to be magical."

"I wasn't here last year," the woman confessed on a whisper, and Tori could see the anxiety in her face and feel it in the death grip she returned.

"Just give it a chance. Whatever you spin, the DMs are here to keep you safe, and it's a chance to try something new, right?" Tori smiled, but the other woman couldn't quite manage it as another couple paired off on stage.

"I guess so," she answered.

"You'll do great," Tori encouraged her, trying to bolster her own confidence at the same time as couple after couple were matched by the luck of a spin. So many possibilities, so many kinks, and Tori's head was spinning with what she would end up with — *who* she would end up with.

"Our next dom up to the roulette wheel is Daddy Xavier. Come on over and roll for your submissive," Madison called out and Tori's eyes lifted instantly.

Daddy?

The large man on stage was definitely handsome. Absolutely sexy, and a little rugged in his black jeans and dark gray shirt, the sleeves already rolled up like he was ready to dive in to Roulette with both feet. Tori bit down on her lip, crossing the fingers on both hands as she pleaded with the universe to guide the little marble to her name as he dropped it.

Come on...

"Dolly!" The name felt like a blow to her chest as she started to look around at the other subs. A moment later a tall, beautiful woman with short, dark hair separated from the group. Daddy Xavier moved to meet her at the steps, and Tori blew out a breath as the two connected instantly.

It was impossible not to feel a ghost of disappointment as she watched the gentle care that the man had for his new sub for the evening, but there were still a lot of dominants left to spin and two of them looked like they might like the same things she did.

It's okay, you'll still have fun. This is a chance to try something new.

"Next up is Pierce! Are you ready to find out who you'll spend Valentine's with?" Madison asked, smiling at the line of doms as Mr. Stares-a-lot stepped forward without returning Madison's peppy energy. He didn't hesitate at all to drop the marble as the wheel started spinning.

The woman in the red dress touched her arm, moving closer to whisper, "I heard that guy being an asshole to this girl earlier. He was—"

"Baby!" Madison called, and the world halted. Something on her face must have alerted the girl in front of her that *she* was Baby and was now paired with the man who had apparently already been an asshole tonight on top of staring at her like a creep.

Great.

Madison moved forward a little, beckoning her once more. "Join us up here on stage, Baby, so you can spin your first kink!"

Red dress girl gave her an apologetic look as Tori started toward the steps, keeping her eyes on the floor and *not* on the man who had spent the last thirty minutes boring holes into her with his stupid smirking face.

Pierce didn't move to meet her like Daddy Xavier had for his sub. He stood at the set of roulette wheels with his hands tucked in his pockets and an empty expression, but his blue-green eyes were focused completely on her with the same intensity as before. Just like a predator, only now she really was his prey. For three whole hours.

Avoiding him, Tori stopped beside the second wheel and struggled to return Madison's encouraging smile as Pierce took a couple of sauntering steps forward to close the gap between them. His presence was just as electric as it had been when they'd both been waiting in front of the stage, something magnetic that urged her to look at him, but she didn't. She refused.

"You got this," Madison said, and Tori took the offered marble as the MC set the wheel to spinning.

Just when Tori was about to drop it in, Pierce leaned close, his warm breath brushing her cheek as he whispered, "I'm curious, do you normally have trouble paying attention? Or just when you're pretending to be a *baby*?"

Heat flushed up her face and the marble slipped off her hand, bouncing high, almost out of the wheel before it settled into a spin and the whirring kinks blurred into an unreadable stream of colors.

"I'm not—"

"Don't be a brat, *Baby*." He was mocking her with the name she'd chosen. It didn't sound sweet or endearing when he said it, no, it sounded like a curse. His hand landed at the small of her back, inching up slowly until his fingers found the nape of her neck and squeezed firmly. "You should know that I expect subs to pay attention and I do *not* tolerate brats. At all. Being a brat will only make your evening miserable, so, decide right now — are you going to be a good girl and answer me when I ask a question or not?"

"Yes, sir," she whispered, trying to show him that she wasn't a brat as the marble clattered and the wheel began to slow.

"We'll see," the asshole replied with a low chuckle as the marble settled into a slot that made her eyes go wide.

"*Humiliation!*" Madison called out, still smiling, but Tori's smile was nowhere to be found as Pierce leaned close enough for his lips to brush her ear.

"Time for you to learn your place, little whore."

Oh, God.

Her nose wrinkled at his harsh words, but that same tingle returned with a mix of fear and nervous energy, concentrating low in her belly and only amplified when his grip on her neck tightened as he led her off the other side of the stage. People made way for them at the bottom of the stairs, clearing space where several other paired couples were standing together.

"On the floor, slut," he commanded, applying pressure to the back of her neck until she slid to her knees beside him obediently, trying to be a good girl. Then Pierce simply released her, continuing to watch the pairings on stage as she shifted and tried to get comfortable — but that was impossible.

Her cheeks were burning, and she could feel both embarrassment and anger warring inside her chest because no one else had put their sub on the floor. Others were talking softly, getting to know each other, while she was surrounded by a forest of legs on one side, unable to see the stage, and more than a few audience members were staring at her from their comfortable chairs while Pierce ignored her completely.

'*He's doing this because I spun Humiliation,*' she thought, but even as the words passed through her mind, she knew they were a lie. This had nothing to do with the kink the wheel had chosen, this was her dom for the night. The asshole who was absolutely, unequivocally, and completely *not* a Daddy.

He probably would have treated her like this no matter what she'd spun.

Risking a glance up at him, she saw the strong line of his jaw, the blue-green of his sharp eyes focused intently on the couple on the stage — and then he caught her staring. Smirking, he looked down at her, pinning her with his intense gaze.

"See something you like?" he asked, and she dropped her eyes back to the floor, his low chuckle floating through the air above her.

Tightening her hands into fists, she pressed them into her thighs, refusing to give him the satisfaction of knowing that she did find him attractive, but half a second later she felt a sharp tug at one of her pigtails. Reaching for the painful burn on her scalp, Pierce caught her wrist, trapping it as he bent down slightly, keeping his other hand firmly in her hair. A whimper escaped her lips as he pulled harder and forced her head to the side.

"Look at that... you're being a naughty brat already," he whispered. "What are you supposed to do when I ask you a question?"

"You said to answer," she whined as quietly as possible, adding "Sir" out of desperation as the sting in her scalp spread.

"Correct. So, tell me, do you see something you like?" His voice was hushed, taunting, and she clenched her hands into fists to stop reacting. He wasn't a Daddy, not nice, but he *was* gorgeous. Dangerously so, like how the most poisonous plants were beautiful.

"Yes, sir," she whispered, feeling completely naked under his stare as his gaze drilled into hers. And, for some reason, as she drowned under the overwhelming weight of his focus, her mouth kept going. "But I think you're well aware of how attractive you are."

Pierce's eyebrows lifted a fraction and Tori felt like the floor shifted beneath her knees.

Oh shit.

CHAPTER 3

PIERCE

For once in his life, Pierce found himself speechless as the pretty little princess at his feet called *him* out. He'd expected her to lie, or play the brat, but she'd admitted it. Admitted that she found him attractive, and then turned it around on him.

Interesting.

He hadn't expected this babygirl to have a spine, but it was in there somewhere. Under the ribbons and lace. Those wide brown eyes stared up at him, a hint of fear and panic brewing there as he released her wrist and twisted her pigtail around his fingers to angle her head backward. Baring her throat, making her vulnerable before he finally answered her.

"You're right," he acknowledged calmly, and it was true. He knew he was attractive. Sure, part of it was genetics, but he worked hard to stay that way and he was proud of it. Leaning down further to invade her personal space, he brought his mouth dangerously close to hers, and he felt her desperate little intake of breath. "But looks can be deceiving."

Another hitch in her breathing, a swallow that rolled down her throat and made him think of shoving his cock past those soft pink lips that were perfectly devoid of artificial fillers. She blinked doll-like lashes, her tongue teasing her bottom lip before she whispered almost too quietly to hear, "Like oleander."

Oleander? What the fuck?

This girl had stunned him twice in less than a minute, and this time he was more confused than anything. A huff of a laugh escaped him before he regained control of his expression. "What did you just say to me?"

"Um..." Her fingers were worrying the hem of her skirt, gripping and releasing, telegraphing her nerves just as well as her expressive eyes. "It's like oleander. Pretty on the outside, but poisonous. Deceiving."

He was speechless again, and Pierce didn't like it at all. He needed time to think. Shifting his touch to the back of her neck, he bent her forward, pressing her forehead to the floor as he commanded, "Stay. Silently."

Baby did what he asked when he released her and stood upright. She didn't move an inch, didn't make a peep, and he crossed his arms as he tried to focus back on the stage, but he soon found himself looking at her again. Bent over her knees, that skirt was showing off her ass to everyone behind her, and he didn't even know if she had underwear on or not, but people were definitely looking. Not that he cared if they did, she was his for the night and now he was even more intrigued by what the little princess was hiding behind her outfit.

And he wasn't talking about her body.

As the last dominants found their submissives, Pierce's mind was turning over everything he'd learned so far about the little girl at his feet and he knew exactly how he was going to begin their first scene. *Humiliation* could mean so many things, could be done in so many ways, and while *Baby* was definitely hiding behind all the trappings of DDlg, she was very easy to read. He would use that to his advantage, and he'd get what he wanted.

"I can tell our couples are excited to get started, so everyone have fun and play safe!" Madison announced over the mic, releasing them, and he didn't hesitate to lean down and rip his sub off the floor by a pigtail. The mewl of pain went straight to his cock, and although her hands came up instinctively toward his, she stopped herself. Little fists forming at her sides as her arms went rigid with self-control.

That's right, little princess, show me what you're capable of so I can push you further.

Dragging her back to the stairs, Pierce scooped up his bag and then led her out of the theater with the slow-moving crowd. A few of the audience members had already chosen his little slut as a focus for their attention, but he ignored them as they followed at a somewhat respectful distance. As soon as he passed through the curtain to the play area, he scanned it for the perfect space to play out this show.

A platform. *That one.* But it needed some tweaks.

He still had her pigtail wrapped in his fist, using it like a leash, but she was silent as he pulled her toward it. Submissive or scared? Time would tell.

"Down," he commanded, applying pressure with his grip on her hair, but it wasn't necessary. She did it, and he let go to test her some more. "Nose on the floor."

There was a flicker of hesitation, but then she bent over her legs again, knees spreading so she could get her nose all the way to the floor.

Strangely, he felt frustrated by her silence, her complete obedience, and he crouched down to grip the back of her neck, pushing her more firmly to the floor. "How are you supposed to respond to a command, little whore?"

With his hand on her neck, he felt the wave of tension, the reaction to the name, and his smile spread out of her line of sight as she replied, "Yes, sir."

"That's right. Maybe you should spend the next few minutes focusing on paying attention while I get our space ready." He let go of her and stood, leaving her there to grab the first Dungeon Monitor he could see. Santiago was passing nearby, and he signaled to him with a hand as he approached.

"What'cha need?" the DM asked, glancing past him toward the girl on the floor with an appreciative smile.

"I want to use this platform, but I need the stocks taken off. Can you replace it with a chair to one side, a nice chair. Leave as much floorspace as you can." An idea came to mind, and he couldn't suppress the sadistic grin that spread across his face. "And I need clear plastic on the floor. Do you have that?"

"Of course," Santiago answered with a chuckle. "You spun *humiliation*, right?"

"Yes." Pierce nodded and the DM gave him a knowing look, offering a quick salute.

"We'll get it done."

With the DMs on top of what he needed, he took a slow, leisurely walk around *Baby*. He'd been right that her skirt revealed her entire ass in this position, but the white underwear concealed her cunt from view.

She hadn't moved from where he'd put her, and if this was how most littles acted, he *might* have been able to see the appeal — but too many of them were brats. And he didn't do the Daddy bullshit. He liked to see them cry, to make them obey even beyond what they thought they would do. Pushing limits was his favorite pastime.

Limits. Dammit.

Rolling his eyes, Pierce moved in front of her and snapped his fingers. "Sit up."

A muffled, "Yes, sir," came from her as she lifted onto her knees, and he was rewarded with the bright pink of her blush on her cheeks, accented by the reddened skin of her forehead and the tip of her nose. The fact that she'd obeyed well enough to mark her own skin had his dick twitching in his pants and the sadist inside him whispering too many dark ideas.

Patience. Information first.

"Obviously *humiliation* wasn't on your list of limits, but what did you choose, little whore?"

"I..." Her voice trailed off as her eyes flicked up to his for a moment before dropping back to the floor, a nervous swallow moving the ivory column of her throat again. "I chose *blood play, needle play, watersports,* and, um... *sensory deprivation.*"

"You sure about that last one?" he asked, raising an eyebrow a little. "You don't sound very confident."

She nodded hard, her pigtails dancing on her shoulders with the movement. "I am, sir."

"Okay. So, you're scared of the dark?" he asked, shifting closer and planting one of his shoes between her spread knees. Using the toe of his shoe, he flicked the hem of her skirt. "Or is that just part of this baby girl routine?"

"I just don't like not being able to see and hear what's going on around me. Sir."

"Sure," he replied, letting the single word drip with his doubt. She was probably lying. So many of the subs here lied, pretended, faked shit to get what they wanted. Snapping his fingers again, he stepped back from her. "Get up and strip all this shit off. I hate costumes."

~

Tori

HER STOMACH DROPPED at his words. It wasn't that he told her to get naked, she'd been prepared for that, it was his complete derision for *what* she wore.

"You really won't like it if I have to make you strip, slut," he growled, and she looked up at him. Intense eyes were focused completely on her and she had no doubt he'd follow through with the vague threat.

"Yes, sir," she muttered. Standing up, she undressed without any teases or demure glances at him. He wanted her naked, he thought her clothes were *shit*, and so… fuck him. She wasn't ashamed of her body, her curves, or the slightly softer belly she had now than a few years before. Leaning down, she unbuckled her shoes and dumped them next to the pile of cloth, adding her stockings to the top without folding a single piece.

A Daddy wouldn't have tolerated that. He would have called her naughty, would have made her fix it before he spanked her.

Pierce didn't even spare a glance at the clothes as he moved close, forcing her to tilt her head back to continue looking into his face as a smirk teased the edge of his mouth. "You *almost* did what I asked."

Her head spun with confusion, looking down at her nudity, but a hard grip on her chin yanked her face back up before he let go to run his fingers through each of her pigtails.

"I said *all* of it," he clarified, grabbing hold of the little hair ties near her scalp and yanking them down along with the ribbons she'd added. The sting of hair pulling free was a momentary distraction, but it was over fast. Still, it felt wrong to feel her hair pooling around her shoulders at Black Light. She always wore the pigtails — they were part of her personality here. The little girl she got to be when she played with a Daddy who made sure she didn't have to make any decisions, who coddled her and took care of her.

But it was clear that Pierce had no plans on doing any of that… so… maybe the pigtails didn't matter. She just wished the sudden tightness in her stomach agreed.

"Why are you into this babygirl shit anyway?" Pierce asked, still way too close to her as that evaluating gaze traced her face.

Tori pulled her lower lip between her teeth, chewing on it as she tried to figure out how to answer, but he caught her chin in his grip and plucked it free with his thumb.

"Answer."

"It makes me feel safe," she whispered, chin still caught in his fingers, and she watched as his eyes narrowed. Judging her. "I know what's expected of me, I never have to think about it. It's… easy to be a good girl."

"I don't do easy." Pierce slid his hand down to her throat, just under her jaw, angling her head back even further as his fingers tightened just enough to make her pulse race. "I don't do the babygirl shit, and I'm not calling you *Baby* tonight. What's your name?"

Even in the vulnerable position, she felt her back stiffen. He didn't have the right to ask for her real name. Her scene name *was* her name inside Black Light. She didn't have to be Tori Brewer inside these walls. She paid a fuckton of money to *not* be Tori Brewer while she was here. Clenching her teeth, she forced a slow breath through her nose to build up the confidence to say, "I don't have to tell you that. Sir."

He chuckled, a dark smile lingering on his lips as he brought his face down to hers. "True. But you spun *humiliation*, little slut, so I can spend the next three hours watching you lick the shower floor clean with your tongue and we won't be disqualified. Or, you can tell me your name and I can show you how *I* like to play."

Fuck.

Something about the way he said that made heat bloom between her thighs, and her breath shuddered as temptation danced before her. It was an offer. A dark promise. Something completely new, and wasn't that what she'd told the woman in the red dress they were both here for tonight?

Screw it.

"Tori," she answered, feeling the blush in her cheeks burning even as she squeezed her thighs together to suppress the tingling his grin summoned.

"Tori," he repeated, his voice a satisfying rumble. "Let me guess… you came here hoping to find your fairy tale prince who was going to sweep you off your feet and keep you as his pretty pretty princess forever. Am I right?"

"N—" Before she even had the chance to finish the single syllable of denial, Pierce's fingers tightened on her throat, cutting it off and making her cough as her breaths became uncomfortably thin.

"I'm relatively sure you haven't lied to me yet, so let's not start now or Black Light is going to have a *very* clean shower floor."

The pressure on her throat eased and she pulled in a desperate breath, digging her nails into her palms as she squeezed her eyes closed.

"Look at me, whore," he growled, and her eyes popped open again, his handsome face filling her vision. "Last chance."

"Maybe," she whispered, and he chuckled, shaking his head slowly.

"Maybe, what?"

"Maybe I… maybe I wanted to find someone tonight to sweep me off my feet. A Daddy that would know what I needed," she mumbled, hating that he was making her look into his eyes for this confession. Her cheeks were on fire, her muscles trembling, and she wasn't even sure if he'd *started* with the kink yet, or if this was just how he tormented subs all the time.

"And what do you need?"

Tori's lips parted to answer, but her tongue didn't move to shape any words because... there were no words. That was why she'd ended things with Max, and John before him, and every other Daddy before that. She'd needed something *more* but whenever they'd talked about it, she'd never had the answer, and she didn't have it now. Wetting her lips, she stared into his eyes as she whispered, "I don't know."

Pierce's lips curved into a sinister smile, a predator about to tear out the throat he held in his grip. "I believe you. But here's the thing, Tori... I'm not a prince, and if this *was* a fairytale, I'd be the wicked man who shows up to drag the pretty little princess into the dirt."

Fire washed up her body, licking across her skin at the same time a chill raced down her spine because his words touched something inside her she didn't know was there. That was the *opposite* of what a Daddy would say. It was threatening instead of comforting, dangerous instead of safe. But fuck if she wasn't wet at the idea of Pierce dragging her into the proverbial dirt.

Wicked is right.

"Your station is ready, sir." One of the DMs spoke from beside them, but Pierce didn't break eye contact with her. His gaze held her as firmly as the fingers he still had wrapped around her throat.

"Thank you, Santiago," her dom answered, and then she watched as his menacing smile widened, revealing perfect, white teeth. "Time to see what makes you tick, Tori."

CHAPTER 4

PIERCE

*I*t was the fucking wide-eyed innocence thing she had going for her that was messing with his head, but he'd never been into that shit. At least he *thought* he wasn't, but his dick seemed interested because it had twitched behind his zipper when she'd knelt at his feet without a single complaint. No eyerolls, no muttered comments under her breath — just submission.

But he wasn't a *Daddy*. He didn't play with *littles*, and, more importantly, he didn't believe it.

The schoolgirl shit had just been a costume, a shell, a shield to hide who she really was... and he wasn't falling for it. Tori wasn't innocent, no one was, and so he didn't hesitate to shift his fingers into the loose hair at the back of her head and bend her over so he couldn't stare into those warm brown pools anymore.

"Move," he commanded, pushing her ahead of him as he grabbed his bag on the way up the steps.

He kept her uncomfortably bent with his grip in her hair, but she made it up the stairs without him having to catch her, and he felt the sudden jerk of her muscles when her foot landed on the crinkling plastic covering the platform. She tried to stand upright, but he forced her down, enjoying the way her knees buckled to the floor and her hands slapped the plastic to catch her.

"Stay on all fours."

"Yes, sir." Her voice floated out of the curtain of hair shielding her face, and for a moment he regretted ripping the pigtails free, but they were part of her costume and he wanted to find the *real* Tori. Audience members drifted closer now that her body was on display on the platform, and he was sure that the plastic had them just as curious as Tori.

Without hesitating, he unzipped his bag and dug around, setting a few items aside on the clean plastic before he picked up the one he wanted to start with.

Santiago had done well, bringing in one of the high-backed leather chairs from the bar area. It was exactly the kind of differential he'd wanted, and he quickly removed his suit jacket, draping it over the back. As he sank into the plush leather, he became keenly aware that he had the start of a hard-on... and she hadn't even cried yet. *Weird.*

"Crawl to me."

Tori's head turned, lifting slightly before her hands and knees made the plastic crinkle loudly. Anyone nearby would hear the sound, even over the music and the striking sound of a paddle hitting skin, and he could tell she hated it. The plastic stuck to her hands for a second each time she lifted them, and it was causing each of her crawling steps to be exaggerated. Limbs lifted higher, moving slower, but it gave him one hell of a view as her breasts swayed and she chewed on her lip again, those brown eyes seeking his whenever she was brave enough to look up at him.

She stopped with her hands in front of his shoes, and a couple of men positioned themselves directly behind her around the platform, staring right between her thighs. He felt a strange urge to tell them to fuck off, but this was what they'd paid for. He couldn't tell them what to look at or not look at. Still, he told her to "Kneel."

Tori sat back on her heels, looking up at him with that blush still present, and he couldn't suppress a grin because she was broadcasting her nerves at top volume.

"Why did you choose the name *Baby?*" he asked, hiding the item beside his thigh as he started to roll up his sleeves.

There was a flash of defiance in her eyes before they dropped to the floor in front of her knees. Her breath shuddered before she spoke up. "I like it."

"You like to be called *Baby*?"

"Yes, sir."

"Are you into that diaper stuff? Being treated like a baby? Given a bottle, a pacifier?" He sounded more irritated than he actually was, but it definitely wasn't his kink, or anything he was interested in trying. Even for *humiliation*.

"No, sir," she replied, and he almost called her a liar, but then it hit him. The only other reason someone would choose the scene name of *Baby*.

"Ohh… I get it. You like it because it's a term of endearment. You like being called *Baby* because it makes whoever you play with feel more familiar, makes the whole scene — whatever it is — feel more intimate." He knew he was right when Tori's shoulders curved in, a subtle shift in body language that showed how much she was trying to defend against his words, but he wasn't letting her have that. "Look at me."

Tori raised her head, and he saw the hint of pain in her eyes, so he knew just where to push the first button as he picked up the hidden tool he needed.

"Stand up and put your hands behind your back."

"Yes, sir," she muttered, taking the position he'd requested without hesitation, but her arms twitched when he revealed the marker in his hand.

"Be still." Leaning forward, he grabbed her hip and tugged her a step closer so he wouldn't have to reach so far. Right across her belly, he wrote 'BABY' in large letters, moving the marker slowly so she felt every line as he continued to speak. "You realize that intimacy is fake, don't you? It's a lie. They're not calling you 'baby' because they like you, or love you, or whatever, it's because you told them to. It's just a name, a word, and in a scene it doesn't mean anything at all because *you* chose it."

As he drew the bottom half of the 'Y,' Pierce looked up at her and saw the shine of tears in her eyes and his cock kicked to attention against his zipper. Rock hard in an instant.

Fuck, she's pretty.

He'd acknowledged her curves before, but with all the babygirl shit he hadn't been able to really see her... and now he did. There wasn't a single fake thing about Tori's face. No plastic surgery, no ridiculously oversized lips, and even her makeup was subdued — and she was absolutely beautiful with those tears in her warm brown eyes. *Damn.*

"Say it," he pressed. "Say that *Baby* doesn't mean anything."

Tori's lip quivered and he hated himself a little for just how much the sight made his balls pull tight.

Reaching over the side of the chair, he picked up the little silver bullet vibe and held it up between two fingers. "Honest girls are good girls, and good girls get a reward."

"Ba—" Tori bit down on the name she'd chosen, the first of her lies to herself, and he reveled in the way the muscle of her jaw twitched before her lips parted again. Her eyes were on the little vibe, and not his, but he let it go just to hear her say, "*Baby* doesn't mean anything."

"Why?" he asked, pushing her harder as he twisted the little bullet on and let it buzz in his fingers.

"Because I told them to use it," she whispered, eyes drifting closed for a second, and he waited for tears to spill, but they didn't come.

Disappointing.

"Eyes," he reminded her, and those brown orbs were back on his, burning into him with unshed tears. "You know what I think?"

"No, sir," she answered, shaking her head slightly as her gaze drifted to the little silver bullet that promised her escape from the discomfort of reality.

"I think you chose to be a *little* because it was easier. Because it didn't push your boundaries or test your limits." Reaching forward, Pierce traced his empty hand over her hip, gliding it down as a little shiver ran through her muscles. "I think you—"

"Didn't I earn a reward, sir?" Tori interrupted him, and he couldn't help but chuckle as he used his hold on her hip to spin her, leaving the little bullet vibe buzzing against his thigh to deliver a hard spank to her ass. She let out a sweet cry, her grip on her wrist releasing, but he admired the shape of his handprint as it bloomed on her skin before turning her back to face him.

"Hands behind your back again, and do *not* be disrespectful."

"Yes, sir," she whispered, her breaths coming a little faster, and his eyes drifted over the hardening peaks of her nipples.

She likes the punishment, that's real.

"Are you a dirty girl, Tori?" he asked, squeezing her hip in a firm grip. "Have you ever been treated like a filthy little slut, or have you only let people call you *Baby*?"

Her brows pulled together, a flicker of something on her face that he actually couldn't figure out when she replied with, "I've only let people call me *Baby*, sir."

Hmm...

Lifting the marker, he carefully wrote the words 'DIRTY GIRL' on her right thigh. "Do you know what dirty girls get, Tori?"

"No, sir," she replied, her eyes glued to the stark contrast of the black marker on her pale skin.

"Exactly what they deserve." Sliding his hand up the inside of her thigh brought him the response he wanted, Tori shifted her legs farther apart, giving him room to trace a finger through the warm flesh between her thighs. *Not quite wet yet.* Still, she gasped, her shoulders pulling back, and he let the tip of his finger brush her clit, which brought the sweetest tremor through her muscles. When he slid another finger through her folds, purposefully avoiding her clit, she tilted her hips, trying to grind against them, but he wouldn't give her the pressure.

Not yet.

"Everyone here can see what a dirty girl you are, Tori."

"Sir..." she whined, eyes closed, face aimed at the ceiling as he brushed the lightest touch across her clit.

"Do you like that? Having everyone know what a dirty girl you are? A filthy little slut, hungry for someone to touch her?" Pierce felt his breath catch, waiting for her to give him *that look*. The one that so many women like Neva Hawthorn had. The one that said, *'I'm only tolerating this because you're attractive and rich.'* But Tori didn't even look at him, instead she let out the softest sound toward the ceiling, so close to a moan that he felt it like a buzz over his balls.

And the next stroke through her folds was slick.

No way.

"Are you a filthy little whore, Tori?" he asked, giving her just enough pressure so that she could grind against his hand, and she did. Hips working as he pressed against her clit, spreading her juices over his fingers. "Do you want someone to use you like the slut you are?"

"Oh God," she breathed, the words almost lost if he hadn't been so utterly focused on every shift of her body, every sinful grind of her soaked cunt against his palm.

"Turn around," he snapped, pulling his hand away as she obeyed. Reaching across his lap, he grabbed the still buzzing vibe with his left hand and then, before he could second-guess himself, he slid one of his wet fingers between his lips. She tasted so damn good, feminine, tangy and sweet, but she'd have to earn his mouth between her thighs.

Her hips swayed from side to side, her feet planted wide enough apart that he could see the puffy lips between her thighs, her cunt desperate for attention.

"Tell me what you really are," he growled, low and soft as he brought the buzzing vibe between her thighs, barely brushing her with it as she whined. "Tell me."

CHAPTER 5

TORI

uck, fuck, fuck.

Every nerve ending in her body was tingling, and the teasing buzz of the vibe so precariously close to her clit was scrambling her brain. What did he want from her? What did she have to do for him to stop torturing her with things she didn't want to think about?

"Please, sir," she begged the ceiling above her, holding onto her wrist hard to keep her hands behind her back. One of his fingers teased past the vibrator, tracing around her clit as she fought the urge to bend her knees just for a stronger brush of the silver vibe. But if she caved, if she did that, she knew he'd take it away.

"You're not a *Baby*, are you, Tori?" he asked, and her body went taut as he slipped the silver bullet between her lips, directly on her clit, and everything went tense with brilliant pleasure until he pulled it back again and she whimpered. "You're not a little girl, a babygirl, or a sweet little princess… are you?"

Goddammit.

With anyone else she would have defended it, would have begged to have her pigtails back — but with Pierce she didn't feel like that girl. She'd said tonight was about something new, and this was new and scary and somehow an incredible fucking turn-on.

370

"Answer me, Tori," he commanded, a fierce spank on the other side of her ass forcing her hips forward for a moment as the burn of it turned into a humming sting that joined the buzz of need between her thighs.

Words wouldn't work, her mouth wouldn't move. She'd been *Baby* since she'd met her first Daddy Dom. So many men who had called her *Baby,* so many she'd called *Daddy,* who had coddled her and comforted her, but none of it had felt remotely like this. That was a cool, placid pond, and Pierce was a stormy sea. He wasn't here to please her, to be sweet. He'd let her drown in her lust, he'd keep her from coming for eternity, and she knew it. There would be no pouting her way into what she wanted, and she realized she didn't even *want* to beg him to let her come, she wanted to earn it.

"Last chance, Tori. Are you a *Baby*? Are you some Daddy's darling babygirl?" His finger dipped through her wet heat, teasing her clit with a feather-light touch, and she shook her head.

Not just a little. Her hair whipped from side to side as she dug her nails into her opposite wrist, holding her hands behind her back like he'd asked.

"That's right," he purred, and the vibe slid against her clit, almost buckling her knees as she whined past clenched teeth. Panting as his palm overlaid the little bullet, keeping it in place as the marker traced across her back. "Only a slut humps someone's hand like this in front of an audience."

She was pretty sure she had just felt the sweeping curve of a 'U' on her back as he wrote the word on her back that from any other man's lips would have sounded like an insult. A disgusting catcall. But Pierce said it with reverence, overlaid with unspoken promises of ecstasy, and as the crippling pleasure built between her thighs, she couldn't help the moans, the desperate pants as she rocked from heel to toe, craving more.

"Say it for me, Tori," he growled, pressing the little vibe against her more firmly and she licked her lips as the edge called out to her.

"I am," she whined.

"You're what?"

"I'm a sl-slut. A dirty, dirty girl," she said softly, and just behind the buzzing vibe, two fingers slid deep inside, and her knees shook as he started to move them in measured thrusts. *Too much, too much.*

"Louder, Tori. You've got an audience that wants to know what you are." A hard thrust of his fingers, a third finger joining the others just before he curved them toward her g-spot and she cried out, dissolving into whimpers when he backed off again, taking the vibe away. "Now, Tori."

People are watching. Listening.

Her face was on fire, her stomach in knots, but somehow she felt like Pierce was there for her. Or *would* be there if things went wrong. *Hopefully.*

"Now!" he commanded.

"I'm a dirty slut!" she shouted, desperate for more, for release, for whatever lay beyond this agonizing edging, and she kept her eyes shut tight so she didn't have to see the faces around the platform. The people watching her body shudder, held taut on the edge with Pierce's fingers buried inside her.

"Again."

Biting down on her lip, she tried to ignore the buzz of voices, the sound of someone chuckling outside the platform. This time it wasn't Pierce laughing, and when she whimpered, he brought the vibe back to her clit. It was fuel on the fire, spiraling the heat up her spine in a tight coil as his last command floated on the surface of her awareness. *Again.* "I'm a slut! I'm your dirty little slut! I want this, please! Sir!"

"You can come." Pierce granted permission she hadn't even been aware she was waiting for, but with those words the world flipped, light stroked down her spine and shattered in a bomb of ecstasy as she cried out.

∾

Pierce

IT WAS pure instinct when he caught her.

He hadn't planned on it, hadn't even been prepared, but as Tori came, her legs buckled, and he'd pulled the vibe away to catch her.

Wrapping his arm around the front of her hips, bracing her against his shoulder. Her cunt squeezed the fingers he still had buried inside her, pulsing in spasms, her body trembling against his, and his dick was so hard it hurt.

She'd called herself *his* dirty little slut.

Jesus Christ.

Nothing about the little schoolgirl outfit had prepared him for this. He'd thought she'd start crying, that he'd break her down and then make her come until she forgot to complain about his head games — but Tori hadn't broken at all. The truth had hurt, as it always did, but his penchant for name calling, for degradation... *that* had turned her on. She'd been wet before he'd even really touched her, before he'd rubbed her clit or used the vibe.

The tremors were starting to subside, and he felt her leaning into him, trusting him to hold her up, not to let her fall, and he took the responsibility on without question. Slowly, she slid down, his fingers slipping from her, but he never moved his arm from her front. Keeping her safe as he shifted back far enough in the chair that she was able to sit on the small bit of cushion between his thighs.

Tori, the babygirl who should have been terrified of him, was leaning back on his chest, her breathing still rushed, with her soft ass nestled directly against his rock-hard cock.

Fuck.

Looking down the front of her, he ran his hand across the swell of one breast, around the hardened peak of one nipple, moving to trace the marker on her stomach, and then he slid his fingers back between her thighs. She gasped, brown eyes open as she turned to look up at him from where her head rested on his shoulder, and then her gaze dropped to where he traced her slick cunt. The puffy lips, swollen from her arousal, and when he shoved two fingers inside, she arched against him with the sweetest little sound.

"Knees apart," he whispered, meeting the gazes of several audience members who were watching, practically eye-level with her pussy as he touched her.

"Sir," she whimpered, and his cock twitched against her ass, wanting her, but it was too early in the evening for that.

He was teasing her, listening to the sounds she made with each brush over her clit, watching the rise and fall of her breasts as he flicked off the vibe and set it aside to capture her nipple in his fingers. Tori gasped and — the lights went out.

The fuck?

Pierce tightened his arm around her waist, listening to the drone of voices rising around him, and he felt her lean into him as dull emergency lights kicked on around the club.

In the half-light, he felt Tori wrap her hand over his forearm, the one he'd used to catch her, the one that had instinctively pulled her closer when the dark hit, and for some reason feeling her cling to him didn't bother him like he thought it would.

"I got you," he whispered, and immediately clenched his teeth tight.

Where the fuck did that come from?

That wasn't him. He wasn't the kind of dom that comforted his submissive — at least, not until *after* he was finished torturing them, and he was just getting started with her.

As quickly as the lights had turned off, they came back on, and he almost forced her to the floor in front of him. His cock liked the idea, and visions of her soft, pink lips wrapped around his shaft made him groan internally, but... he couldn't make himself do it. Tori was still tucked against his chest, her small hand squeezing his forearm lightly where he still had it banded around her waist.

She was holding onto him like a life raft, which he wasn't, *at all*, but he wasn't letting go of her either.

Fuck, fuck, fuck.

"That was weird," she said softly, and it broke him out of the haze of whirling thoughts in his head.

"Yeah," he agreed, clearing his throat quietly as he pried his arm away from her waist. He shouldn't be holding her like some lover, like a *Daddy* comforting his little, but he couldn't bring himself to stop touching her completely.

Tori was still breathing fast, likely a combination of the orgasm and the dark, and it did wonderful things to her body. Her breasts rose and fell, she shifted constantly, occasional shivers rushing through her muscles as he traced a hand over her curves. The other cupped her breast, pinching her nipple lightly, and the sweet sigh that escaped her lips as she dropped her head back on his shoulder was pure sin.

He couldn't resist dipping the fingers of his other hand between her thighs. Soaking wet, slick and warm, and each movement pulled more delicious sounds from her.

Pierce wanted to fuck her throat, *needed* to feel her wrapped around his cock somehow, and sooner rather than later — but not yet. No. He wanted to peel a few more layers of his sub away before he let her taste him.

What to do?

Orgasm torture wasn't out of the question, and he still had the little vibe to put to good use. Her hips were lifting to every lazy stroke of his fingers between her soaked thighs, soft, breathy sighs humming out of her chest, but he was just keeping her focus on his touch while the audience got an eyeful. And she had quite the gathering at the edge of the platform.

More than he'd expected, actually.

Some unfamiliar part of his brain wanted to move, to go to one of the fantasy rooms where they'd have more privacy, where she'd be exposed for him and only him... but now wasn't the time to discover some previously undiscovered possessive tendencies. The audience would be voting on their favorite couple and exposing her was drawing a decent crowd. It didn't matter what strange thoughts were running through his head, this was meant to be *humiliation*, wasn't it?

Snap out of it, Pierce. She's not your type. You're not hers.

She's only putting up with this because of Roulette.

Get your head in the game.

"Open your eyes, slut," he whispered directly into her ear, nipping the round of it through her hair, and he felt the jerk of her muscles when she saw the audience. Her knees twitched inward, but he pulled his fingers free to jerk one leg wide again, draping it over his. "Don't make me hold you open, dirty girl."

"But, sir..." Her voice trailed into silence as he glided his fingers back up her inner thigh, and this time he gave her three fingers, listening to the throaty moan buzzing in her chest as she took them in.

"You like that, don't you?" he asked, but it was mostly rhetorical. Her hips were rolling, seeking, hungry for more and he wondered what it would feel like to bury his dick between those thighs, to say the words he wanted to right against her ear and feel her come underneath him.

Not yet. Maybe she'll be able to handle it later, but not yet.

"Oh, fuck," Tori whined, pressing back against his chest, completely exposed to the audience, and he pushed back his own urges so he could dig the marker out of the cushion beside him while he let her fuck his fingers.

"You're so wet," he growled against her neck, nudging her hair out of the way with his nose so he could bite down on her shoulder as he drove his fingers deeper.

She let out the prettiest whine, an unspoken plea for more or less, he didn't really care — he knew what she needed.

He pulled his fingers free and teased her entrance with the buzzing bullet vibe for a minute, waiting for her sounds to turn desperate before he pressed it inside, catching her hip when she arched hard, moaning through gritted teeth.

"Spell wet for me, little whore."

Planting the marker just above her cunt, he stroked her clit gently, waiting until she whimpered out a breathy, "W."

He drew it, poorly, upside-down, but it was clear enough. The kiss he pressed to her shoulder wasn't planned, it was an accident, a weird instinctual thing that he turned into a nip as he urged her to continue. "What's next?"

"Sir, pleaaaase!" Tori was trying to grind against his hand, but he wasn't giving her any of the friction she wanted. A second later, she let out a frustrated little scream. "Jesus, it's E!"

"That's right," he purred, fighting the urge to laugh at her desperation as he wrote the next letter and his balls ached with the urge to take her. "One more, slut. Tell me that last letter and I'll let you come again."

"Fuck! It's T! Please!"

"Good girl," he growled, drawing the T with a pair of fucked-up, shaky lines as he circled her clit hard and fast.

"Oh, God!" Tori cried, arching away from him as she whined and then came with a shout. Without thinking, he grabbed her hips to pull her back against him, torturing himself with every wiggling squirm on his cock as the orgasm rocked her, but she was too perfect for the audience to be the only ones who got to watch her fall apart.

Damn. She was beautiful as he leaned back with her in the chair, her bottom lip caught between her teeth, brows pulled together and eyes squeezed tight as the shivers rolled through her muscles. Her legs were clamped tight together now, but he didn't care. Every roll of her hips was a tease, a promise of what it would feel like to be inside her when she came like that.

As her shivers slowed, she pulled air in on a gasp, breathing hard as he worked his hand between her thighs again. Palming her, he applied the slightest pressure and grinned when she let out a soft, keening whine. "Sir…"

"What's wrong, little whore? Sensitive?" He chuckled when she just groaned, her hips shifting in a cruel, unconscious tease against his hard shaft. *Naughty girl.* Pierce lifted his hand and brought it down in a sharp smack against her soaked pussy and her eyes flew open. "Answer me."

CHAPTER 6

TORI

The stinging swat between her thighs resonated across her nerves, meeting the little aftershocks from the bone-melting orgasm he'd just wrenched from her — but it only amplified the lingering pleasure, the wicked thrum burning through her bloodstream.

Fuck, this is insane.

"Answer me." His command had her turning her head to meet his gaze as she leaned against his shoulder. He was so close, lips inches from hers, eyes burning. Tori was barely on the chair, at the very edge of it, but his iron grip on her hip meant she wasn't going to fall, which was good because her muscles were jelly. Except now he wanted her to speak, when her mind was still a chaotic whirlwind of electrical signals.

What did he ask?

Sensitive. Right.

The word brought a breathy laugh past her lips as she finally nodded. "Yes, sir. Very sensitive."

"Good," he purred, sending a thrill down her spine as he pulled her legs wide again, draping them over his knees, exposing her to the people gathered around them. Then she felt him shift her on his lap, angling her slightly so he could keep his gaze on hers. "Now, I want you to come again like the wet little slut you are."

"I can't," she answered instantly, an edge of panic to her voice as his fingers found her clit again and her whole body tensed as they swirled.

"Look at me."

"Sir, please…" Groaning, she obeyed, but it was hard. Almost impossible to keep her eyes open as he rubbed the over-sensitive button. It wasn't pain, not really, but it was damn close — and didn't everyone in the community always say how close pleasure and pain were?

Well, she hadn't tested *those* waters very much, but she felt pretty confident they were right.

This was torture. Her thighs jerking as he toyed with her, making her shudder and whimper, and of course, the incessant buzz of the little vibe inside her wasn't going anywhere either… and then there was *him*.

Pierce. The asshole dom with the gorgeous eyes that seemed to see into her very soul. The one who'd played her body with impossible expertise while saying things to her that *no one* had dared to say to her.

"Come on, whore. Give us another show." He tilted his head at their audience, but he never looked away, wouldn't release her from his captivating stare for even a moment. His fingers slipped inside her, finding the little bullet and pressing it directly on her g-spot.

"God!" she cried out, clenching her teeth as pleasure teased her for a moment and then became overwhelming a breath later.

"That's it," he encouraged, finding every sensitive place, grinding his hand against her clit, but all she could do was shake her head and whine.

"I can't, sir." The words were barely a whisper, but she knew he'd heard her because a wicked smile spread across his face.

"You don't know what you're capable of, Tori." Pierce leaned in, so close that she felt his warm breath across her lips, imagining what it would feel like if he kissed her as he added, "But I'm going to show you."

Oh hell.

She expected him to pull back, to sit up straight again, but as he tugged the little vibe from her and pressed it against that overworked bundle of nerves, he didn't move an inch. It was too much, the best kind of torment, because that razor's edge of pleasure and pain was a brilliant, blinding place and Pierce was forcing her to stay there. Not letting her squirm away as he tightened his hold on her hip and kept the torturous buzz exactly where she needed just a moment of respite. A moment to breathe, to pull herself back together. But he wasn't going to give her that, and the way his breaths shortened, growing rough, was utterly mesmerizing. Hypnotic. He was just as caught up in the chaos as she was, stealing each little sound she made with every inhale, and the world fell away outside of his gaze.

There was no more audience, no club, she couldn't hear anything except his breaths.

This was more intense than anything she'd ever experienced, a terrifying wave rising inside her, promising destruction, devastation when it finally crested and crashed.

"Let go, Tori," he whispered. Not a command, but an urging, a gentle nudge as he rubbed the vibe back and forth, adding friction to the torment, and all she could do was hold on. One hand on his arm, above the iron grip on her hip, the other scrambling for purchase on his leg, fingers fisting the fabric of his pants as the insane swell of sensation inside her became something new. Something otherworldly.

And then it blinded her, a brilliant explosion of ecstasy that singed her nerves and ripped the air from her lungs — or maybe that last part was because his lips had crashed into hers just as she'd tried to cry out. She was on fire, the orgasm rocking her, dragging her back and forth across that line between pleasure and pain until it was impossible to tell them apart, and as he plunged his fingers inside her she fell apart again. Her moan nothing more than a buzz between their lips and tongues, echoed by the growl she could feel coming from his chest as he ground his hard cock against her ass.

After what felt like an eternity, he broke the kiss, his fingers still buried inside her, but he wasn't tormenting her anymore. He held her there, her core squeezing around the invasion, spasming with each new aftershock as they just stared at each other. Panting, his eyes wild as his tongue traced across his lower lip, raw lust painting his expression.

He kissed me.

She was still buzzing from the fierceness of it, her lips tingling while the rest of her body shivered with another sinful echo of bliss. Part of her wanted him to kiss her again, her fingers untwining from the fabric of his slacks to seek his shirt, to pull him down, but then he turned away. His gaze burned over her skin, a quiet gasp escaping when he slid his fingers free and dragged her wetness up her stomach.

Wordlessly, he brought them to her mouth and when his eyes found hers again, she opened, tasting herself as he pushed them in. Stroking her tongue, the sweet tang flooded her, and a low groan rumbled in his chest when she started to suck.

"You know what?" he asked softly, breaking the silence with a rough edge to his voice that hadn't been there before. "I don't think you're a pretty little princess at all. I think you're a dirty, filthy little fuckdoll, and you want to be used like one, don't you?"

With his fingers buried between her lips, she could only nod, lost in the bottomless ocean of his eyes. Pierce wasn't safe, he wasn't like anything she'd ever experienced, but if this was what it was like to play with him… she'd gladly drown in his dangerous waters.

"On your knees," he growled, pulling his fingers free as he nudged her forward and she slipped to the floor, quickly turning around on her knees to face him. Pierce jerked his chin up as he stood. "Move back."

Shuffling back in the kneel, she felt her mouth watering as she watched him work his belt, the button and fly of his slacks open a moment later, and then his cock was in his hand. She wanted to taste him more than anything, needed to return a fraction of what he'd given her, but when she reached for him, he snapped his fingers to stop her, shaking his head slowly.

"Oh no, little whore, hands behind your back. I told you I was going to use you, and that's exactly what I plan to do."

"Yes, sir," she whispered, slowly moving them behind her back to take hold of her opposite wrist. A smirk tilted his lips as he stroked his shaft slowly, a devilish look that slid down her body like a promise.

"If you move them, I'll tie them in place. Understand, slut?" Pierce moved closer, slipping his fingers into her hair with the glistening head of his cock tantalizingly close.

She nodded as much as she could as his fist tightened, summoning skittering sparks across her scalp. "Yes, sir."

"Good girl," he purred. "Open."

It wasn't like he needed to say it, she wanted to taste him, and she immediately stuck out her tongue and opened her mouth for him, not caring the least what she looked like. *A slut. A dirty, filthy little fuckdoll.*

His fuckdoll.

A hushed moan rolled out of her as the velvet texture of him stroked over her tongue, moving deeper, teasingly slow.

"You're going to take it for me, aren't you, whore? You're going to take every inch and trust that I'm going to let you breathe as I fuck your throat." The words had her squirming, wet thighs squeezing together as she raised her gaze to look at him above her. He was watching her, that wicked smirk spreading across his face as she gave a muffled *'yes'* around his thick girth. "Good girl. Raise your hand if you want to call yellow but do *not* push me away."

A sharp jerk to the grip on her hair was the only warning she got before he thrust in, pushing past her gag reflex in an instant. Her body jerked back, or at least tried to, but his hold on her was absolute as he started to move, punishing her throat with hard, bruising thrusts that had her choking, drool spilling past her lips as she tried to keep her lips over her teeth. It was too much, too fast. She gagged, her stomach twisting, but Pierce didn't stop, didn't seem to even care as she swallowed down the urge to throw up. Tears filled her eyes, spilling past to wet her eyelashes as he used her. Hard. Just like he'd said he would.

Then he pushed deep again and held. Nose pressed to the skin of his stomach, for a moment she could only focus on the ache in her throat and the relief his pause offered... but it didn't last. The urge to breathe was instinctual, demanding, and she tried to pull back, but his other hand wrapped around the back of her head, trapping her. Panic stormed in swiftly, burning her lungs and spreading adrenaline through her veins until she jerked, convulsed, desperate for just a small sip of air.

He said he'd let you breathe.

Another torturous second and she felt the panic rising, her body's need overriding everything else as she dug her nails into her arm and tried to beg past his cock buried in her throat. Whatever small sound buzzed in her chest wasn't enough, and before she knew what was happening she was pushing at his thighs and he let her go. Tori buckled to the floor, catching herself on her hands as she choked, gasping air past a raw throat as drool spilled to the plastic.

At the edge of her vision she could see his shoes, shining in the lights above them, and as the oxygen flooded her and the panic ebbed it was slowly replaced by a creeping feeling of embarrassment. Failure.

Do not push me away.

Fuck.

Sniffling, Tori sat back on her heels, scrubbing the tears from her cheeks before she looked up at him. His expression was patient, expectant, and she swallowed again, feeling the ache roll down it as she met his gaze. "I'm sorry, sir."

"What did I tell you your non-verbal safe word was, little whore?"

"Raise my hand," she replied quietly, her eyes dropping, but he didn't stand for that. Stepping close, he yanked her head back up with a fistful of her hair. She hissed air between her teeth, but bit down on the sound because she deserved this. He'd given her one rule, and she'd broken it. Pierce leaned down close, his intense gaze searching her face for a long moment.

"If you remember it, then why didn't you use it?"

A blush burned her cheeks, more tears welling up, but it had nothing to do with the lingering soreness in her throat or the fierce hold he still had on her hair — no, this was guilt. For failing him. Pulling in a shaky breath, she whispered, "I panicked. I'm sorry, sir. I-I won't do it again."

Pierce tilted his head, eyes narrowing for a moment. "Won't do *what* again?"

"Touch you. I'll keep my hands behind my back. I promise, sir."

"You want to continue?" he asked, but it was so quiet that it was barely a whisper. Not meant for the audience, just her. Something in his tone was different, not exactly gentle — nothing about Pierce seemed gentle — but it was the only word that came to mind as she nodded.

"Yes, sir."

"Do you remember what I told you I'd do if you moved your hands, my little fuckdoll?" This was louder, the cocky tone returning with the devious smirk on his lips, and she remembered his words with a sinking feeling.

"You said you'd tie my hands, sir." Tori heard her voice wobble, a tease of panic returning as his grin spread.

"That's right. So, tell me again, you sure?" *Do you want to continue?* He was asking the same question again, as if he really thought she'd want out, but she'd just panicked. That's it. No Daddy had ever used her like this, fucked her face so roughly, but underneath the need to breathe had been a low thrum of arousal. A buzz between her thighs that reminded her of the incredible orgasms he'd given her, and she wanted to give him that. She wanted to please him. Wanted to taste him when he came, and that left only one answer.

Straightening her back, Tori moved her arms behind her back again, looking up at him with more confidence than she'd ever felt in a scene before. "Yes, sir. I'm sure. I want you to use me."

CHAPTER 7

PIERCE

She wasn't lying.

Tori met his eyes, posture perfect, and with her shiny, reddened lips she'd said she *wanted* him to use her — and meant it. His balls ached, wanting him to shove his cock back into her tight little throat and make her swallow every single drop he spilled. Just the memory of her desperate sounds, the choking, the impossible squeeze around his shaft, the sight of her tears spilling down her cheeks and the shine of drool on her chin had him squeezing the base of his cock and thinking about that time he'd seen the old bastard next door sunbathing in the nude just so he could stave off the urge to come.

One slightly traumatizing memory later and he felt like he could breathe, the pressure easing back enough for him to trust that he wouldn't come all over her face and tits if he moved. She was beautiful, vulnerable, and waiting for him to use her. A fucking wet dream come true.

But what if she's only doing this because of Roulette?

Doubt prodded him like a pitchfork from the devil on his shoulder. That side of his conscience probably should have been an angel, but no one had ever accused him of being overly emotional. No, if anything, he had a pair of devils, it's just this one was criticizing him. Challenging him.

Was he pushing her too far? Abusing the situation?

He let go of her hair after taking one more look at her warm brown eyes. So open, so honest — *maybe*. Turning away, he popped his boxers into place and walked quickly to his bag, grabbing the pre-tied rope cuffs out of their bag and a bright red ball. Looking back at her was torture of the highest order, an absolute test of his self-control. Pretty little Tori was holding position, the drool that had spilled over her breasts catching the light from above them, and he had to summon that horrifying memory again just to stay on task.

"I need a volunteer," he said, loud enough to catch the attention of the audience still gathered around the platform. Several hands shot up, way too eager, probably hoping to get to participate. *Not a fucking chance.* One Dom brushed his hand over the head of a blonde woman kneeling beside him before stepping forward.

"I'll watch the ball for you," he said in a serious voice that gave Pierce the confidence he needed. The man would take the job seriously. Wouldn't wander off for some other scene. He looked between the man and the woman slightly behind him. She was wearing a collar, nipples pierced and propped up by the corset. They were an older couple, probably married and in the lifestyle for a long time. Trustworthy, for this anyway.

"Thank you," Pierce said, nodding to the man. "My name is Pierce, get my attention however you need to if she drops it. Understand?"

The man just nodded back, stepping back beside his submissive where his fingers wove back into her hair like it was muscle memory created from years of the same movement. She looked up at him, their eye contact lingering before her eyes drifted closed, her forehead leaning against his thigh, and all Pierce saw was perfect trust. No bullshit, no ulterior motives.

It was fucking refreshing.

Making a mental note to buy the man a drink sometime, he let his eyes drift back to Tori who was watching him expectantly. For a second he thought he saw the same kind of trust in her gaze that he'd caught in the man's sub, but that was impossible. He'd just choked her with his cock long enough to make her freak out, almost ruined the whole goddamn night because she felt so fucking good.

She's always been someone's baby, their little princess.

She'd never want someone like you.

Not without Roulette.

The devil on his shoulder was prodding him again, spawning doubt in his stomach as he squeezed the red ball in his fist, pouring all the tension from his body into that tight, white-knuckled grip.

Shifting to one knee beside her, Pierce slid the rope cuffs over her wrists, pulling the piece that let him tighten them before he tied it off. *Be sure.* "Did you hear what I said about the ball?"

"Drop it if I need to call yellow. Someone is watching for you." Tori twisted to look at him, surprising him with how calm she seemed after her panic. "Thank you, sir."

"For what?" he asked as he tested the cuffs, running his fingers along the inside of each so he knew they weren't too tight.

"For keeping me safe," she whispered, and he felt the doubt burning in his belly.

Shit.

Catching the back of her neck, he held her firmly as he leaned in close to whisper against her ear, "Do you need me to back off?"

"No, sir," she said just as quietly, but it wasn't enough. The goddamn doubt wasn't going anywhere.

Fuck. Fucking fuck.

"Listen to me, Tori." He paused, touching his head to hers as he tried to sound as sincere as he was. "I promise I would never let you get hurt. Not really. I know it's impossible to trust someone you just met, but I need you to *believe* that at the very least."

Tori pulled away from him, and as he dropped his hand from her, for a split second, he felt true, raw, stomach-dropping fear that he really had pushed her too far. Crossed a line. Ruined whatever this was. But then he saw her. The look on her face wasn't panicked or angry — well, she looked a little annoyed with the way her brows pulled together and her mouth thinned, but it was... cute. Then she shook her head a little, voice serious. "That's not true."

"What isn't?"

"I do trust you, sir." She shifted her shoulders back, straightening up again as she met his gaze without a single waver. "I want you to use me like a... filthy fuckdoll." Her cheeks burned bright with the word, and he couldn't deny the way his cock returned to an almost painful hardness as she braved on. "I do. I want you to fuck my face again. I want to take it like a good girl, or a slut, or *whatever*. I just want to taste you. I promise. I believe you, I trust you, and I know you wouldn't hurt me." A little smile quirked up one side of her mouth and she tilted her head a bit with her cheeks still perfectly pink. "Well, not like *that* anyway. Not in a bad way."

Pierce was stunned into silence again. *Goddamn.* The girl had a weird habit of doing that to him, and his brain fumbled to catch up, trying to process everything she'd just laid at his feet like a gift. After everything he'd already said, already done, he couldn't see a single sign of deception in her. She meant every word. She trusted him.

"Thank you." That was all he could get past his lips before he reached up, pushing her hair behind her ear to catch her by the back of the neck and pull her into a fierce kiss.

He shouldn't have kissed her the first time, caught up in the heat of the moment, in the heady power of feeling her come in his arms even when she'd thought she couldn't. It had felt amazing, she'd tasted as sweet and innocent as her outfit had pretended to be — but it had felt wrong the moment it was over. Kissing her like *that* just after he'd criticized her for pretending intimacy with her scene name. It was impulsive, hypocritical.

This kiss, though... it tasted like fire.

A blistering heat that poured down his throat with the first desperate little moan he stole from her, keeping it just for himself. This wasn't for the audience, it wasn't for Roulette, this was because of *her*. Tori. Her sweet submission, her strength, her bravery to continue playing with him... and most of all her trust. That was what stoked the fire inside him into an inferno, burned the doubt away, leaving behind the absolute *rightness* of this. The feel of her as he slid his arm across her back to pull her further into him. It was perfect, singeing his lips and tongue even though her chin was still wet with saliva. She was a beautiful mess, kissing him back just as fiercely, nipping him back as their tongues danced. Tori was bound and at his mercy, willingly handing herself over to him and trusting him to keep her safe, to make every twisted moment worth it in the end.

And, *oh*, the things he wanted to do to her now that all the lights were green.

Nipping her lip one last time he pulled back just enough to lean his forehead against hers, finding her brilliantly bright eyes focused on his, wide and hungry. "Tell me how bad you want it, little slut."

"I want it. Please, please use me," she begged, breathy and panting and the sound went straight to his balls as he groaned.

"What are you, Tori?"

"I'm your filthy little fuckdoll, sir. Please fuck my throat. I promise I'll be good." Her wicked tongue danced across her bottom lip and he felt a growl in his chest as a hundred ideas whirled through his head. A thousand things he wanted to do to her, a million times he wanted to see those warm brown eyes looking up at him just like this.

Pressing the red ball into her palm, he wrapped her fingers over it and squeezed them closed. "If you drop this, I stop, and we don't continue again. We'll spin something else, something—"

"I can handle it," she interrupted, a fierceness in her voice that made him grin as she tacked on, "Sir."

"Brave little slut, aren't you?" he taunted, pushing himself up from the floor, and her eyes followed him up before dropping to the bulge of his hard-on. All she did was nod, opening her mouth as she moved back into position, and he chuckled. "Forget something?"

"Sorry, sir. Yes, sir, I'm... I'm a brave little slut."

"That's right," he said, circling her to trace his fingers across the large, black letters that spelled out 'SLUT' across her back. A shiver went through her muscles, but it wasn't fear or even humiliation anymore. Tori was squeezing her thighs together, her hips shifting slightly, and he knew she would be soaked if he checked, but he had a better idea. Snagging the marker off the chair, he quickly tilted her chin back with a light grip on her throat and wrote 'FUCKDOLL' across her chest. Tossing the marker back onto the chair, he squeezed his grip on her neck just enough to feel the heady beat of her pulse under his fingers and tapped the dark letters he'd drawn with his other hand. "What else are you, Tori?"

"Your fuckdoll," she answered, and he groaned.

Mine.

"That's right. *My* fuckdoll." Releasing her, he pulled out his cock again and tempted fate with a single stroke down his shaft, but it was worth it just to see the way her eyes followed his hand. "Open."

"Yes, sir." Her lips parted, still red from how rough he'd been before, but he had no plans of being gentle now. She wanted to be a brave little slut, wanted to be used like a filthy little fuckdoll, and he was going to give it to her.

Sliding into her mouth again was pure sin, her lips sealed around him, her tongue moving as she moved her head back and forth, sucking him. It was tempting to let her continue, but he took the control back, winding both hands into her hair to grip hard. "Don't forget about the ball. Drop it if you have to, because otherwise I'm going to use you exactly how I want to."

There was a hum of sound around his shaft that made him growl as she strained to pull him deeper, and he gave it to her. Thrusting past the back of her throat, into the tight heat that felt like a stroke of lightning up his spine when she struggled to swallow.

"Fuck," he grunted, pulling back so he wouldn't come already. Risking one glance at the audience, he made sure the dom was still there, watching for the ball in Tori's hand to move, and when he met the man's gaze, he nodded and looked down at Tori.

Not smart.

She was looking up at him, her lips stretched around his shaft, tongue teasing the underside of his cock, and he knew he didn't have long. He watched her take the next thrust, the way her eyes flickered shut as he forced it deep and held. It was pure willpower that kept him from coming as she choked, throat squeezing the head of his cock, but she lasted longer this time. Let him pulse his hips in shallow thrusts that kept her air sealed away, at his mercy, but he felt when her body jerked and he pulled back. A flood of drool followed the path of his shaft, air hissing desperately through her nose along with the sweetest little sounds, and then all that drool spilled over his balls when he drove deep again. Then he picked up the rhythm he needed, fucking her throat exactly how he wanted to

— hard, fast, only pausing to feel her body plead for air for a moment or two.

He wanted it to last forever, but it wasn't possible, not when he saw her tear-streaked face and felt the buzz of her moan along his shaft. Letting her steal another breath, he pushed as deep as he could go, and felt his balls draw tight, electric bliss rushing through his bones as he came with a shout, spilling into her throat. The world blinked out of existence for a long, perfect flash of white where there was nothing but mind-numbing ecstasy, compounded by the continuous ripple of her muscles around his cock as she swallowed every drop. It was glorious, heady, overwhelming as the rush faded. Then, everything wobbled, his heart racing as he opened his eyes to watch her squirming at his feet. Hips wiggling, arms working at the rope, but he held on. Waited until he felt her try to jerk back, a low buzz running over his sensitive nerves as she likely pled for air. A glance at the man in the audience confirmed she hadn't let go of the ball… because his fierce little fuckdoll was so much more than she appeared.

When another desperate squeeze of her throat became too much, he finally pulled back and released her, simply staring as she immediately dropped forward. Gasping and coughing, drool spilling past her lips to the plastic in front of her knees as little whines turned the noises into music.

She was beautiful. Better than he'd imagined as he stumbled a step back, tucking himself into his boxers before he dropped into the oversized chair to watch her. When she eventually looked up at him, still breathing hard, he actually felt his cock twitch even though there was no way he was fucking her yet — but he wanted to, *God* did he want to fuck her.

Later.

Shaking out his wrist, Pierce checked his watch and was shocked to see that it was already past nine-thirty. *Holy shit.* Three hours had seemed so long before. Before he knew who he had, before it was Tori. Now it didn't seem like enough.

Still, he wasn't ready to go back to the stage to spin. Not quite. He wanted to memorize everything about this moment. The way her makeup was smudged around her eyes from the tears, the flush in her cheeks, the wet redness of her mouth. And she was *so* wet. Her chin was shiny, her breasts sparkling with trails of saliva, and he knew exactly how wet her pussy got. He'd written the word right above her sweet cunt as a reminder.

As his eyes landed on the floor in front of her knees, he knew exactly how he wanted to round out their first spin.

"Tsk, tsk. Look at the mess you made, fuckdoll," he said, reading the word off her chest. A grin spread across his lips as her wide eyes dropped to the plastic under her knees.

"I'm sorry, sir."

"I think it's only polite if you clean it up like a good little slut." Pierce watched her shoulders shift, likely tugging at the rope still tied around her wrists, but Tori wasn't stupid. It only took a second or two before she looked back up at him, understanding dawning on her face, and he snapped his fingers before pointing at the spots of drool. "Now."

The audience shifted to watch her as she shuffled back enough to bend forward, spreading her legs to improve her balance before she started lapping at the wet places on the plastic. It crinkled with every movement, and a few chuckles and appreciative sounds fluttered around the platform as a few of the couples clapped before drifting away toward the next scene.

Only the older couple stayed behind long enough to smile at him, the dom nodding his head before he guided his sub away. It shouldn't have felt like approval — shouldn't have mattered at all — but for some reason Pierce felt a swell of pride from the acknowledgement.

He'd kept her safe like he'd promised to, made sure she could stop it if she needed to, which had let him push her further than any other sub he'd tried to facefuck.

And Tori had surprised him once again, although it was quickly becoming normal for the babygirl turned fuckdoll to stun him. He'd wanted someone interesting, and luck had clearly been on his side tonight.

He just had to hope their luck would hold out for the next spin, because he wasn't done with her yet.

CHAPTER 8

TORI

*T*ori was relieved when the crowd had dissipated before she'd finished licking her drool off the plastic, but it hadn't been as bad as she thought it would be. It was demeaning, *humiliating*, but when she looked at Pierce and saw the way he watched her, the hunger, the lust, she'd made sure there wasn't a single drop left behind. Of course, *humiliation* was what they'd spun, and he had delivered on it — and then some.

She could still feel the buzz between her thighs from the repeated orgasms, the hyper-awareness of her clit with every step they took toward the stage. He hadn't let her dress, hadn't even removed the rope from her wrists while he'd thrown their things in his bag. People stared at them as they walked through the bar area and back toward the theater, and she knew what they saw on her skin.

FUCKDOLL. BABY. DIRTY GIRL. WET. SLUT.

The burn in her cheeks was out of her control, a reaction to so many faces turning to follow her naked body across the room, but with Pierce's hand on the back of her neck she kept her chin high. She wasn't just anyone's fuckdoll, she'd never been someone's fuckdoll before at all, but she was *his* and that thought was rolling through her mind like a thunderstorm. Flashes of lightning illuminating parts of herself she'd never seen, never thought to seek out, but Pierce had seen them inside her. He'd seen past *Baby*, pulled all of the things away that made her feel like Baby, and shown her someone completely new.

A version of herself she would have never imagined in a million years... but she liked it.

She liked being *his* fuckdoll. *His* slut. *His* soaking wet dirty girl.

Of all the things written on her skin, the only one she didn't feel like right now was the name she'd walked in with. Those thoughts kept spinning, rearranging parts of herself as Pierce guided her up the stairs with a hand on her arm. When they got to the wheel, Madison's eyes went a little wide as she looked her over.

"You two seem like you've had fun," she said, smiling like they shared an inside joke.

"We're not done yet," Pierce replied, positioning himself behind her to shield her from the few people still sitting in the theater. "*Baby* needs to spin."

Tori's nose wrinkled when she heard that name from his lips, and the instantaneous reaction only added more confusion to the hurricane in her head. Madison's bright laugh pulled her back to reality. "Well, can you give her a hand?"

A second later she felt the rope loosening around one wrist, but Pierce didn't remove it completely.

"She only needs one, right?" Pierce said, his voice a sinful purr over her shoulder.

"Perfectly fine." Madison shrugged in acknowledgement and handed Tori the ball as she spun the wheel.

So many things.

There were so many things the marble could land on. Taking a deep breath, Tori let go and watched it bounce and then spin, the wheel clicking as it began to slow. Pierce's hand was on the back of her neck again, squeezing, and it made her feel a little better as the marble finally rocked into a slot.

"The *violet wand!*" Madison called, and Tori felt a chill rush over her skin as Pierce chuckled, low and dark.

"Come on, my little fuckdoll," he whispered into her ear, leading her off the stage and back into the play area. On the way back, Tori didn't pay attention to any of the stares, she was too distracted imagining the *violet wand*. She'd seen one before, and it looked like it fell out of a sci-fi movie and somehow found its way into a BDSM dungeon. The device crackled and popped, and the sounds the sub had made were anything but pleasure.

Suddenly, she was jerked to a stop by Pierce's fingers catching her hair. He stared down at her, eyes once more back to evaluating, judging, peeling away all her layers, but he only said one word. "Talk."

"What do you want me to say, sir?" she asked, and he lifted his brows, letting the silence stretch until it made her more uncomfortable than the subtle sting skittering over her scalp. "I've never played with the *violet wand* before."

"And?" he prompted, not giving her anything more, which left her once more with his silent, appraising stare. There was nowhere else to look as close as he was to her front, his shirt brushing her nipples.

"I'm not a masochist," she whispered, feeling guilty over it, her brain already reminding her of how disappointing that was to most doms... and someone like Pierce? He probably had a whip collection, or a wall of canes, and— "Fuck!"

The spank had caught her completely off guard, and it had *not* been a mild warning. It fucking hurt, and her ass burned where she was sure his handprint glowed in a perfect transfer, but before she could even finish reacting to that his thumb brushed over her nipple. Circling the hard, little bud in teasing strokes that had her leaning into his hand. "Your reaction to the spanking calls you a liar, little whore, and you know I don't like liars."

"But that— SIR!" Tori whined as his thumb and forefinger suddenly clamped down on her nipple, pain spiraling out like a wave from the singular point. When he pulled, she lifted onto her toes, trying desperately to ease the ache.

"Just wait," he commanded, his voice calm but serious. After another agonizing second, he let go, and she gasped as the pain receded. "Now, how do you feel?"

"I—"

"Don't just answer, fuckdoll. Think about it first. Evaluate yourself." He still had an iron grip on her hair, and so all she could do was close her eyes to get the mental space to do what he asked. The pain was gone, like someone had turned off a rushing faucet, but where there had been pain on her ass and her breast, now… it tingled. Like a strange, heady rush running through her skin.

"Kind of… fuzzy?" she tried, attempting to answer him to the best of her ability, and his slow grin confirmed she'd guessed correctly. He pulled her in closer, leaning down to nuzzle through her hair until his lips were on her throat, dragging heart-racing nips and kisses up her neck until he caught her earlobe in his teeth and nipped it sharply. Her breath caught with the flash of pain, but then his fingers were between her thighs, finding her clit in an instant, and there was no way to keep up with the mix of sensations as she spread her legs for him.

"That fuzzy feeling can grow," he purred against her ear, licking his way back down the column of her throat as his touch summoned magic below. She was still so sensitive, but it felt good again, a slow rising warmth washing up her belly. Promising more. Pierce's teeth grazed her shoulder, sending goose bumps over her skin, and then he flicked his tongue out at the same spot. "The more pain, the bigger the rush after. Endorphins. People describe it as euphoric."

"I've never done anything like that before." It came out as a breathy whisper, laced with the earliest beginnings of a moan as they hovered in the middle of the dungeon, so close together that she could only smell him. The spice of his cologne, the clean laundry scent of his shirt, and the warm heat of his skin underneath. She wished she could run her tongue over *his* skin. Taste him everywhere, because she already knew what he tasted like when he came, and she liked it.

"Do you still trust me, little slut?" he asked, low and rough, and she whimpered as he amped up the pressure on her clit below.

"Yes, sir." The words were barely out when his teeth clamped down on the place where her neck met her shoulder, blinding pain tensing every muscle in her body as she cried out. She grabbed onto his shirt with both hands, pulling at it, desperate for him to stop, babbling pleas as the agony swelled and built until he mercifully released her.

For a moment there was only the lingering ache, growing dull as it faded, and then she felt something new surge in to fill the space the pain left behind. It was like her nerves were… fizzing. A buzzing flood pouring through her that almost had her dizzy for a second, which only amplified as he thrust his fingers inside her.

"Someone's cunt is very wet again," he whispered directly into her ear, pumping them in and out in a sinful rhythm, and she could only stand there. Up on her toes, clinging to his shirt like it could somehow anchor her in the wildly new sensations bombarding her. "Sure you're not a teensy bit masochistic, my filthy little fuckdoll?"

"I don't know," she breathed, biting back a moan as he tapped at her g-spot, and her hips worked mindlessly, seeking more, but then his touch was gone. Tori swayed on her feet, supported only by her grip on his shirt, and the fist still buried in her hair. The look on her face must have shown her desperation because Pierce chuckled softly. Tapping her mouth with his fingers, he bit down on his lip when she took them in without a word, cleaning her wetness from them while he watched. A low groan was her reward, and she felt a bubbly excitement inside at having an effect on him.

"You want to come again, fuckdoll?"

"Yes, sir. Very much, sir." Nodding as much as she could within his grasp, she met his gaze and absolutely knew he wasn't going to let her come yet. The wicked glint in his eyes promised a lot more lessons in pain and pleasure before she earned *that*.

"Good to know," he quipped, grinning at her before stepping away, forcing her to release his shirt. Pierce pointed at the floor, leaving her with a quick, "Stay right there."

As he wandered away, she couldn't deny the way her veins were buzzing. *Endorphins. Euphoric.* Both of those things were very tempting, and she'd heard similar things before from the masochists at the club — but she wasn't one. She'd never been one.

You weren't a fuckdoll before tonight either.

You were 'Baby.' A little.

Her mouth felt dry, and her head was anything but quiet. She'd been Baby for years. She'd sought out Daddy Doms and dated so many at the various clubs in the area that she'd jumped at the chance to join Black Light, hoping she'd finally find the Daddy that would feel right. There had been a few in the last year that she'd tried to date instead of just play with. Max had lasted three months, but she'd ended things before December came. He had money and she knew he had something elaborate in the works for Christmas, and her conscience wouldn't let her keep pretending she was happy.

Not that she was *unhappy*.

Max had been a wonderful Daddy. Caring and stern, he'd loved to watch her color while he caught up on emails in the evening, and she never had to think about anything when she was with him. Utterly free, taken care of, safe.

But you never came like that with Max. Or John.

If she were being honest with herself, she was pretty sure she'd never come that hard in her life. Nothing about Pierce was slow and sensual, he wasn't gentle, he didn't call her sweet things, and when he'd called her Baby on the stage, she'd... hated it.

Movement caught her eye and she looked up to see Pierce walking toward her carrying an armful of things with a case at his side, and, most importantly, completely fucking shirtless.

Holy goddamn miracle abs.

Pierce was tanned, a warm tone to his skin that told her how often he was outside and accented just how fit he was. His arms were defined, his broad chest even better than she'd imagined from how it felt through his shirt — but it was his abs leading down to his belt that had her mouth hanging open. He needed to be preserved in marble, a carved statue in the tradition of the Greeks. Hell, she'd keep it in her fucking apartment just to remember the night when she was his fuckdoll.

The wicked smirk on his lips told her she was caught, but he didn't say anything as Tyler, one of the main Dungeon Monitors, set down a wooden pony in the empty space Pierce had claimed for themselves.

"Thanks, man," Pierce said, giving Tyler a wave as the DM looked her over with a quiet laugh.

"You guys need anything?"

"We're good—"

"Actually—" Tori froze as she realized she'd talked over Pierce, but he just looked at her, waiting. "Water?" she asked, and Pierce groaned.

"Fuck, that's on me. She's been a very wet little slut tonight, so if we could get a few bottles of water that would be great."

"I got you," Tyler said, giving a quick salute before he walked off toward the bar.

Pierce watched the man leave for a moment and then he caught her arm and spun her, delivering a resounding spank that felt like it instantly blistered her skin.

"OW!" she cried out, stunned, and then Pierce spun her back to face him, moving in close.

"If you're thirsty, you speak up, slut. Do you understand me?" His voice was so intense that she was sure he was angry, but then he caught her chin in his fingers, his thumb rolling across her bottom lip as he tilted her face up. "I'm a dom, and I'm pretty damn good at reading people, but I'm not psychic. If you need something and I'm not providing it, it is *your* job to tell me. Fail to do it again and I'll do a lot more than spank your ass, fuckdoll. Got it?"

"Yes, sir," she whispered, still reeling from the spank he'd delivered without hesitation. Tori stayed in his grip, watching his face as he seemed to almost say something else, but then stopped. She wanted to ask what it was, wanted to make *him* talk, but all she could do was try to wet her lips as she replayed his words. He'd somehow made her feel cared for, protected, *and* called her fuckdoll in the same breath. From anyone else on the planet, that would be too big of a contradiction to process, but from Pierce it rang true.

It felt *right*.

"Whoa," Tyler said, laughing as he approached. A warm, big sound that seemed to break the tense silence between them. "Looks like someone was a bad girl. That's an impressive handprint."

Pierce didn't answer for a moment, finishing whatever thought was passing through his mind as his gaze kept her pinned in place, and then he turned away with a light pinch to her chin. "Thanks, Tyler. And, yes, my little slut was learning the importance of speaking up about things like hydration."

"Water is very important," Tyler replied, chuckling as he passed off the trio of water bottles to Pierce. "If you need anything else, flag us down. Whatever you've got planned looks quite fun."

"Oh, it will be," Pierce answered, but it sounded much more like a threat to her ears. But, instead of fear, she felt butterflies filling her stomach with anxious anticipation. There were a lot of different things on the floor next to the wooden pony, and she wasn't quite sure about any of it... but she trusted Pierce. She really did, even if it sounded crazy or stupid in her own mind. They'd scened together, he'd taken care of her, and whatever his plan was — she'd be safe.

"Come here, little whore." He moved to the pony, tapping the side of it as he handed her a bottle of water. "Stand here, drink this, and spread your legs a few feet apart."

She obeyed, taking the first incredible sip of the cold water. It rushed into her stomach, chilling her from the inside out and slaking her thirst in the best of ways. By the time she pulled it away, the bottle was already half empty, and Pierce was on one knee, nudging her feet a little farther apart before he started to adjust the height of pony. The space between her legs could already remember the ache of the wood. It had been one of John's favorite time-out punishments when she broke a rule, but she was sure using it with Pierce would be completely different.

"Time to mount up," he said, standing up to offer her his arm as she swung her leg over the top and quickly realized that he'd left it higher than her ex ever had. Her heels couldn't touch the floor unless she wanted to put almost all of her weight on the rounded wood that slid easily between her folds to apply painful pressure to her pubic bone. Lifting onto the balls of her feet eased it, but Pierce just grinned. "How long do you think you'll be able to keep that up, fuckdoll?"

"As long as I can, sir," she answered, and she felt an answering smile spreading over her lips, a small laugh slipping out as his gaze turned dark and hungry. "What?"

"You're just..." Pierce didn't finish the words, instead he caught her by the back of the neck and kissed her. His tongue teased hers, a delirious rush that had her grinding gently against the wood as her fingers skimmed his side, brushing over the ridges of his abs. He was so *warm*, like all that sunlight he'd soaked up was stored in his skin, turning him into a heater as he claimed her mouth as his own. When he nipped her lip between his teeth, immediately soothing it with another bone-melting kiss, she would have given him anything. Said anything. Done anything.

400

She wanted him.

Really wanted him.

Not just tonight, not for however long they had left.

She didn't want this to end, didn't want him to stop kissing her, touching her. Years of wrong decisions made the choice brilliantly clear in her mind, clearing away the chaos that had been stirred up since he first told her to take off the outfit. Her costume. The one that let her stay where she was comfortable, where things were easy, where nothing was ever *bad*... but nothing was ever amazing either.

Pierce was completely different. The opposite of what she would have looked for on her own, but as soon as she made the decision, she knew in her bones it was right. *Finally right.*

A low, rumbling growl escaped their kiss as he pressed his lips to hers one more time and then leaned back. "Rope."

"What?" she asked and he pulled away completely, running a hand through his hair as his eyes skimmed the ground around him.

"I'm going to show you the *violet wand*, fuckdoll. And then I'm going to make you come until you beg me to stop." Pierce said it so casually that she almost laughed again, but she stayed quiet as she watched him crouch down next to her, marking the floor inside her foot with a bright strip of neon green tape. When he looked up at her, he growled again, standing up to capture her mouth in another fierce kiss, powerful enough to leave her breathless before he pulled himself back with a groan. "Don't do that."

"Do *what?*" she asked, the laugh bubbling out of her as his intense gaze seared her, and then his hands came up to hold the sides of her head, his thumbs brushing her cheeks lightly.

"Smile," he whispered, looking at her like something new. "Christ, I thought you looked beautiful when you fell apart in my lap, and then when you were a beautiful mess, after you trusted me enough to let me fuck your face until you choked and cried, I thought *that* was it." One of his thumbs brushed higher, like he was tracing the tears he remembered, or her ruined makeup, but all she could focus on was the word he'd used. *Beautiful.* Her heart raced; breaths too short to do anything but wait for him to continue. "But, fuck, your smile is... distracting. It's so *real.*"

There were no words. What was she supposed to say to something like that? Everything flitting through her head seemed too small, too flippant, and Pierce was neither of those things.

"If you get the urge to smile, fuckdoll, I need you to bite your lip or you're going to get us disqualified because I'm going to end up doing a lot of things to you, but using a *violet wand* isn't going to be one of them."

"Yes, sir." Tori wasn't sure how she managed to say the words because her mouth was dry. A fucking desert had taken up residence on her tongue, but as he tore his gaze from her to walk around and mark the floor beside her other foot, she couldn't quite remember how to get the water to her mouth.

Could he feel the same way?

It felt impossible, beyond her luck, but hope teased at her and threatened to make her smile, so she bit down on her lip like he'd commanded. Then she managed to drink the rest of the water, screwing the cap back on, and he took it from her, tossing it onto his bag. A second later, he was forcing a new bottle into her hand and she had to bite down on her lip to not laugh. "I'm not thirsty anymore, sir."

"You really want to argue with me when I'm about to have a violet wand in my hand, slut?" The tone was still edgy, dirty, but she heard the playfulness in it.

"No, sir," she answered, unscrewing the top to take a sip. He was working at the case, setting up the violet wand, and too soon he looked up at her with a smirk. The black handle in his hand started emitting a buzz, and then he brought the glass tube at the end near his arm and the quick *pop* made her jump, which resulted in her jarring her body against the pony and all she could do was groan as the ache spread.

"Oh, my little whore, this is going to be fun." The buzzing stopped and he set it down. "You need to be sure you're done with that water, because I'm about to tie your hands back up."

Fuck.

"Yes, sir." Just to be safe, she took one more sip, and he moved in front of the pony, watching her. His eyes skated over her curves, and she felt that flutter of excitement again. Nervous energy, anticipation, with a dash of fear. It was a surprisingly nice cocktail.

"Come on, fuckdoll. Hand it over so I can make you cry again." Pierce held his hand out, a devilish smirk teasing the edge of his mouth, and she was about to hand it over when she looked down her body.

'FUCKDOLL' was written just above her breasts, all caps, and below that, even larger, was 'BABY.' It was wrong. She didn't want it on her skin anymore, and even though she knew it risked a punishment of some kind, she unscrewed the cap to the water bottle and quickly poured some into her hand, using it to scrub at the large letters on her stomach before he could stop her.

CHAPTER 9

PIERCE

*W*hat the fuck?

He started to reach for the water, but his hand froze in midair as he realized what she was doing. The markers were washable, he wasn't *that* much of an asshole, but as she scrubbed at the large letters for 'BABY' on her stomach, they weren't fading very well.

More importantly than whether or not she succeeded was that she was actually trying to take it off.

"What do you think you're doing, slut?" he asked, keeping his voice neutral, and she froze, those wide brown eyes lifting to look at him. She wore her guilt like a neon sign. If she were his, he'd never have to wonder if she broke a rule. Tori would probably cave and tell him before he could even bring it up — not that it would matter after tonight.

"I was trying to... rub it off," she mumbled, a pink burn in her cheeks as she avoided his eyes.

"Do you have *permission* to remove something I've added to your skin?" Grabbing the water bottle out of her hand, he pried the cap from her fingers as well, screwing it closed before he tossed it to the side. She still had her hand covering the faded letters, and he snapped his fingers. "Arms down, whore."

She didn't say anything, didn't argue, but he could see the way her shoulders drooped as she obeyed him. It wasn't necessary to be good at reading people to see that she was unhappy about him stopping her. But that wasn't the most important thing for the moment.

"Why were you doing that?"

"I-I didn't want to have that name on me for this scene. Sir." Too quiet. Avoiding his gaze.

"Look at me when you answer me, slut." It came out harder than he meant it to, but it worked. Tori's eyes met his again, and he watched her take a deep breath.

"I didn't want 'BABY' on my skin for our last scene, sir."

"Why?" he repeated, trying to keep his own thoughts locked down. No jumping to conclusions, no—

"Because... I don't think I'm that girl anymore. I... I don't think it was ever right for me." Her brows pulled together for a moment, jaw clenching, and he thought she might continue, but she stayed silent.

"And what do you think is right for you?"

"This." She laid her hand on her chest, above her breasts, and then slid it down, skirting the word she wanted erased to brush over the word 'WET' and then stopped again where he'd written 'DIRTY GIRL.' "And this."

"And?" he pressed, unable to think of anything else as she braced her hands on the pony in front of her, likely seeking relief as she groaned. He was about to offer to help her off for the conversation when she let out a frustrated little cry and leaned up again, her hands moving to either side of her head, fingers tangled in her hair.

"And all of this! YOU!" she practically shouted, spreading her arms a bit before dropping them to her sides. "Fuck. Fuck, fuck, fuck." Tori buried her face in her hands, groaning. "So stupid, so fucking stupid."

Me? No way. Not possible.

Grabbing her wrists, Pierce yanked them away from her face, putting enough pressure into his grip to ensure he had her undivided attention. "First of all, slut, *I* am the only one that gets to call you names. Second, you don't get to decide what is or isn't on your skin. Who do you belong to right now?"

"You, sir," she answered softly, and he dropped one of her wrists so he could capture her chin in a firm grip.

"If you really believe that, then you already know what's going to happen for being disrespectful." The sadness that had been lurking behind her eyes flickered, shifting slowly into something else. Something more animated, more excited. Giving her chin a small shake, he leaned closer so that she had to maintain eye contact. "Tell me what it is, whore."

"Punishment."

"Exactly." He had to fight the urge to grin at her, because she looked fucking *thrilled* by the idea of being punished. Of course, that had the added effect of summoning his hard-on, because she didn't even know what it could be — and she wanted it. "Part one, you'll wear 'BABY' on your skin until Roulette is over, understand?"

"Yes, sir," she whispered, nodding her head slightly in his grip even though he could tell she hated the idea.

Well, that's what makes it a punishment, my little fuckdoll.

"Part two"—this time he couldn't suppress the grin—"you don't get off the pony until you get yourself off like the little slut you are." He could tell she didn't quite understand the stakes, but she'd figure it out soon enough. "You're going to get our wooden friend here nice and wet, aren't you?"

"Yes, sir." When she acknowledged the rules, he let go of her. Digging in his bag, past the clothes, he found the thick leather collar and an extra length of rope.

"I was going to have both of your hands behind your back so you couldn't lift yourself off the pony that way, but I think one is enough. Your other hand is going to be way too busy to help you anyway." Slipping the collar around her neck sent an electric pulse of need straight to his balls because Tori looked him right in the eyes while he did it. Eye contact had always been a turn on for him. He wanted to see the truth in his sub's gaze, to know how she really felt, and in that moment, he knew he'd been right earlier in the night.

It was trust. Real fucking trust.

Pulling his gaze away before he lost his focus again, he threaded the rope through a D-ring on the back of the collar, and then tied it off to the empty side of the wrist cuffs, keeping her arm firmly secured behind her.

With a deep breath, Pierce went and picked up the violet wand. He'd already tested it, on his own skin, because he needed to know what it was like. Tyler had told him to take his shirt off so he'd feel it like she would, and then the DM had taken some sick fucking pleasure in showing him the various settings.

Only one of them had left a red mark that lingered, and he'd stopped the man before he cranked it all the way up. He had no plans to use it on Tori like that, and no *interest* in letting Tyler get his rocks off using the devious little torture device on him.

Flicking it on, he liked the powerful hum of it, and even more he liked the way her eyes went wide at the sight of it. "Go on, slut. Show me how you're going to touch yourself for me, and if your feet move past that tape you get an extra zap."

"Yes, sir," she answered, reaching down to seek her clit, but then the realization settled over her and he let his grin spread. Tori had to angle herself backward to really reach her pleasure button, which made her slightly off balance, with no way to balance except rocking forward or using her stomach muscles. Even more challenging, the tape at her feet kept them far enough apart to limit how high she could lift herself from the wood, and he knew her current solution of lifting onto her toes would only last as long as her calf muscles held out.

And, best of all, she'd spun the *violet wand*, and he knew exactly how distracting the pops of electricity were.

"Having trouble, fuckdoll?" he taunted, watching as she tried to get a rhythm going over her clit, only to have to adjust her position somehow. The flash of raw defiance when she looked up at him had the asshole side of him grinning. "Trust me... you want to answer me right now."

Waving the violet wand back and forth had a much more respectful expression on her face in an instant, but her determination didn't waver. "I'm fine, sir."

"Great. Then we'll get started before Tyler comes by to ask why I haven't zapped your sweet ass yet." Starting a slow walk around her, he brought the glass of the violet wand close to his pant leg, and the subsequent *pop* made her jump, but it barely stung at all through his clothes. "I didn't even touch you with that one, dirty girl. Tell me, is your cunt wet for me yet?"

"Yes, sir," she answered, a slight whine to her voice as she concentrated on her clit. She'd found a position that worked for now, and he let her enjoy it for a moment, watching as her breathing started to pick up — and then he brought the wand to her ass. "Fuck!"

The little arc of electricity was pretty, but her reaction was much better. She'd lost her balance, whining as the pressure between her thighs drove the wooden pony into her most sensitive places.

She makes the best noises.

Except he wasn't the only one who noticed. They were attracting an audience again.

Pierce continued walking around, smirking at her as she found her position again, but he could already see her calves trembling. It wouldn't last. "Good girl," he encouraged her. "I want that pussy nice and wet, and if it's sore from the pony too… that's just more fun for me."

"Sir…" she whimpered, and he zapped her thigh. It was still on a low setting, but it was more than enough to make her drop again. A muttered curse escaped under her breath, followed by a desperate little whine when he shocked her other leg. "Sir, please!"

"What do you want, slut?" Tilting the wand back and forth through the air, he pretended innocence. "I told you exactly what you need to do to get off the pony and end our fun with the wand."

"This is impossible," she snapped, twisting on the wood while she struggled to find something that worked. As he watched her, he agreed it *might* be impossible, but it was way too soon to judge that, so he used the wand on her hip. "Shit!"

"You have such a dirty mouth, whore." Pierce grinned when she shot him a look that was full of feisty desperation. "Too bad I can't get my cock back in your throat with you up there. *That* might help you watch your tongue."

Tori just groaned, but her tongue snuck past her lips, wetting them in an unconscious tease that he felt like a stroke down his shaft.

Moving closer to her, he put his lips right against her ear. "You like that idea, don't you, my filthy little fuckdoll? You liked me using you, fucking your throat until I came and made you swallow every drop."

"God, yes," she moaned, and he glanced down to see she'd found her rhythm again.

"You liked it... but it hurt a little." Using his free hand, he cupped her breast, rolling his thumb over her nipple until it peaked. Then he pinched it between his fingers, and she rewarded him with a sweet little whine. "Just like this. It's pleasure and pain, right?"

"Like when you made me come again and again," she added, a breathy edge to her voice that told him she was much too close. So, he trailed the wand down her side, letting it scatter little shocks until she flailed, a frustrated scream captured behind her teeth. "Sir!"

"Stop fighting it," he urged, leaning in close again to keep his voice hushed as the audience invaded his space. "Think of the rush after the pain, the endorphins, the pending euphoria. Ride the pain so you get to the pleasure and use *that* to come."

"I can't," she whined, and he chuckled, brushing her hair aside to nip her ear.

"Then we're going to be here all night, little whore, and you know what that means?"

"No, sir." Tori tried to turn to look at him, but he caught her jaw, holding her there so he could speak directly into her ear.

"Then I can't fuck you like the dirty, filthy fuckdoll you are."

Tori

OH GOD.

His words haunted her as she tried to come, desperate to drop over the edge into oblivion, to escape this hell he'd created for her — but just as she got close, the zap of the damn wand would send that crushing promise of pleasure somewhere else. Hidden. Lost until she managed to get back on the path, trying to focus only on the trembling thrums from her clit. Not the ache between her thighs from the pony, or the way her muscles were shaking, or the people watching her, and definitely not the pending *pop* of the goddamn violet wand.

She had to come, she needed it more than air, more than anything, because she wasn't sure how much time was left, but it was counting down and she knew the consequences if she failed.

Then I can't fuck you like the dirty, filthy fuckdoll you are.

Pleading with every deity she could think of Tori begged, prayed that tonight wouldn't end before she got to feel Pierce against her, inside her. It would be too cruel. Even worse than the fact that he hadn't said a single word about her confession that *he* was right for her.

"Giving up so soon, little whore?" he mocked, and she knew he was enjoying her struggle, but it felt like it had gone on forever.

"No, sir." Ignoring the torture of the wood between her thighs, she found the path to freedom again. Pleasure teased her, nowhere near the overwhelming bliss she needed, but she narrowed her awareness until the strokes of her fingers became everything. She remembered how it had felt when he had her in his lap, the way he'd held her firmly as he'd brought her to orgasm again and again. Her breath caught, heart pounding — *zap!*

The initial shock short-circuited her again, but Pierce didn't pull it away this time. He left the glass tube hovering over her thigh, gliding it down slowly as it crackled and snapped. Vibrant arcs flashing with each new sting of pain, and she whined as tears burned her eyes.

"Please, sir," she begged. "Please, please, I can't. I promise I'm trying. I'm trying so hard!" The tears spilled and the violet wand lifted away as he moved behind her. She expected him to tease her again, or bring the evil electrified glass to her ass, but then she felt his skin against her bound arm, her back, and his arm slid around her waist to pull her tight against him.

"Lean into me," he whispered, and she obeyed, feeling the instant relief as her weight no longer rested on the wood. Every inch of tender flesh between her thighs, from clit to ass, throbbed with a dull ache.

Sniffling, she could only focus on stopping the frustrated tears, her fingers unmoving between her thighs, but he didn't say anything about it.

"I'm going to run the wand along your other thigh, and I want you to take a deep breath first, and then hold it while it passes. Just like you did when I bit you." He kissed the place on her shoulder before he brought the wand into view. "Ready?"

"Not really," she snarked and she could feel his chest shift as he chuckled silently.

"Want to try that again, slut?" Pierce nipped her shoulder and she sighed.

"Yes, sir. I'm ready."

"Deep breath," he warned, and she took it in and held. This time she was ready, watching as the first arc of electricity snapped against her skin, feeling the stinging burn of it, but each subsequent *pop* was easier to take. She knew what it felt like, and she tried to do what he'd suggested.

Ride the pain so you get to the pleasure.

As soon as he lifted the wand, she let out her breath in a rush and that first inhale made her dizzy as the lingering sting hummed along her thigh. Not quite euphoric, but it definitely wasn't as bad as before.

"Touch yourself for me. Get your cunt nice and wet so you're ready." His words buzzed along her skin, more effective than any supposed endorphins, and she leaned into him as she obeyed. Circling her clit exactly how she did at home, but he was the only one she was thinking about.

"Will you talk to me, sir? Please?" she begged, not even trying to pretend she wasn't, and she heard him groan low against her ear as he pulled her tighter to him, his hard cock pressed against her back.

"What do you want me to say, my little fuckdoll?" His voice was a sinful purr, a rumble that pushed her higher. "Do you want me to tell you about how much I want to taste your sweet cunt? That I want to make you come over and over on my tongue until you soak my bed?"

"God, yes," she moaned, circling her clit faster as pleasure spiraled, building slowly. *Wait, did he say 'his' bed?*

"Such a dirty girl." Pierce bit down on her shoulder, not as hard as before, but she groaned as the ache grew slowly, twining with the buzz of her touching herself for him. When he let go, the rush made her head swim for a moment, and oblivion was close. "What if I told you that I've been thinking about fucking you, but I can't decide if I want to bend you over that massage table over there or if I want to pin you to the floor so I can watch you come around my cock?"

"Please!" She was so close, so fucking close, and she didn't care where he fucked her, or how, she just needed it. She needed him. Now.

"I'm going to use you *exactly* how I want to, slut. I'm going to make you take every inch like the good little fuckdoll you are… and I'm tired of waiting." He released her, and she caught herself on the pony, shifting forward to regain her balance as his heat disappeared from her back.

"Sir?" she asked, twisting her head to try and find him, but his hands caught her by the hips first, yanking her backward, the wood sliding through her folds until she slid off the end. A sharp spank to her ass made her yelp, but she heard his quiet *tsk tsk* just before he bent her forward on the pony.

"You didn't make yourself come, slut, so it looks like I'm going to have to help you out." Palming her ass, he squeezed her flesh in a hard grip, pulling her cheeks apart with a low groan. "But you did make yourself nice and wet for me."

"Yes, sir," she answered, her words dissolving into a moan as he slid two fingers deep inside, followed quickly by three, and she arched, pushing up from the pony as pleasure spread.

"Down," he growled, pressing her back to the wood with a firm hand. "I told you that you weren't getting off this pony until *you* got off, my little whore, and I meant it."

"Oh God."

"Sir works fine, slut, but I'm glad you think so highly of me." There was a dark chuckle in his voice as he pumped his fingers inside her until she was squirming, panting, desperate to come. The ache of the pony digging into her ribs and chest didn't matter, the buzz of voices around them was unimportant — nothing else mattered but his touch.

"Please," she begged, whimpering as his other hand found her clit.

"You still sensitive, my little fuckdoll? Is this cunt nice and sore from the pony?"

"Yes, sir!" she cried out, so close to the edge when his fingers suddenly abandoned her, a whine pushing past clenched teeth... and then she felt him. His slick cock pressing against her entrance as his hand wrapped around her hip.

"Beg," he demanded, his voice a low growl of need behind her that echoed her own desperate sounds.

"Please fuck me! Use me. I need you, sir. I'm yours to—" Her words cut off with a gasp as he thrust deep in one sinful drive, stretching her, a sweet ache buzzing along with the hum inside her. Pierce wasn't waiting for her to adjust though, he pulled back and slammed deep again, and again, and again until she couldn't think straight. Babbling pleas and moans as she held onto the wood, feeling the rising heat as he fucked her mercilessly, driving her to new heights.

"Christ," he growled, his fingers digging into her hips. "Just like that, slut. Fucking take it. Take every inch and come for me."

She'd edged for too long, the devious pony and the fucking wand keeping her from oblivion, building her higher and higher until the precipitous drop into bliss was almost too intense. Everything went tight, heat rushing over her skin like a wildfire in her veins, and then the tension snapped. Pure delirium flooded her, and she was pretty sure she screamed out his name in the searing crash as pleasure finally won.

"Fuck, yes. Come on my cock like a good little fuckdoll. *Yesss*, squeeze me just like that." Pierce groaned, his fingers likely leaving bruises as he yanked her ass back to meet his next punishing thrust. He was still fucking her, even harder than before, his hips slapping against her skin, and it was overwhelming. Before she'd even caught her breath, before all of those trembling muscles could calm, she could feel another vibrant pulse rising from the place where his cock filled her so perfectly.

"Sir!" she cried, biting down on a moan as the ecstasy blinded her, threatening to send her over into breathless bliss once more. But she would do it. She'd do anything for him. Take anything for him. Bent over the pony, one arm trapped behind her back as he used her, she felt completely and utterly owned — and nothing had ever felt so right.

CHAPTER 10

PIERCE

*E*very wicked pulse of her cunt around his shaft was incredible, the best kind of torture that had him holding back just to feel it again on the next stroke. She was perfect, every cry that slipped past her lips only urging him on, making him yank her back onto his cock just a little bit harder so he could hear another. The slap of their skin coming together a sharp punctuation to every drive, only interrupted by the loud splashing of some couple in the pool, but he blocked them out.

He didn't give a fuck about the other participants, or the votes of the audience, or any of it — hell, he wouldn't move if the goddamn building caught fire. No, the only person that mattered was bent over in front of him, her cunt gripping his dick like a vise with every tremor that rushed through her muscles.

I need to see her.

Burying himself in her slick heat, he leaned forward to wrap his hand around her throat, over the collar. "Up," he growled, pulling her up until she was pressed against his chest, every shift of her hips like a stroke of lightning down his shaft, making his balls tighten dangerously.

Christ.

Before he could fuck up, he slid out of her, tugging the release on the rope cuffs so her arm wouldn't be in the way as he pushed her to her knees and then onto her back. Tori stayed propped up on her elbows for a moment, her face flushed, lips red as she stared up at him with those wide, innocent eyes.

"Spread your legs. Now." He couldn't hold back anymore, not a shred of patience left in him as she obeyed him, planting her feet wide so he could move between them. Catching her behind one knee, he held her open and lined up, thrusting back into her tight heat. The feeling was merciless perfection, but it was the way she gasped, pretty lips parting to make sweet sounds, that made him grab her other leg, bending her knees toward her shoulders so he could drive just a little deeper.

"Fuck!" Tori hissed air between her teeth, brows pulled together with a look of pain and pleasure as she squeezed his cock inside her.

"Look at me, slut," he growled, slamming deep, hard strokes that rocked her against the floor. When those warm brown eyes met his, he knew he wasn't going to last. He couldn't with her looking up at him like *that*. Not with her moaning with need and arching off the floor under him. His heart was pounding in his chest, breaths just as rushed as hers as the world narrowed down to just her. "I want to watch you come."

"Sir," she whined, chewing on her lip as her eyes closed for a moment before popping open to obey again. He knew it had to be intense now. Orgasm torture always did that, but there was always one more waiting on the other side of the sensitivity and he was absolutely going to watch her come, whether she wanted to or not.

Folding her legs further, he braced himself above her, shifting the angle of his cock until he pulled a new cry from her. *Fuck, fuck, fuck.* She squeezed his shaft, her back arching as her breaths became uneven, little murmuring pleas escaping — then her eyes widened and he knew he had her. "Be a good little fuckdoll and come for me. Come for me like the wet little whore you are, come all over my cock."

"PIERCE!" she shouted, eyes rolling before she closed them tight, her body straining against his arms as her cunt became a pulsing vise that he couldn't resist. Fire shot down his spine as his balls pulled tight, and then there was white. Impossible ecstasy crashed through his veins, rolling outward at lightning speed as he came, her pussy squeezing him in waves, milking him for every last drop that he wished was filling her. He wanted to watch his seed leak out of her, wanted to feel the slick heat without the barrier of a condom between them.

Later, he promised himself, trying to remember how to breathe as he released her legs to cover her. Skin to skin. They were both sticky with sweat, too hot with the heat the club was pumping in to keep out the evening chill, but he needed this. Needed to feel her breasts pressed to his chest, needed to taste the salt on her skin as he dragged his tongue up her throat before he claimed her mouth. She moaned, the delirious buzz of it humming between them, and he felt her legs wrap around his hips, pulling him as deep as he could go.

Pierce didn't want to move, didn't want to get up from the floor, but he knew the clock was ticking. They'd call for the end of Roulette any minute, and he growled into the kiss at the idea of Tori walking away from him.

Fuck that.

He hadn't planned on any of this, hadn't expected the little minx in a schoolgirl outfit to be anything beyond a vapid little girl, but she wasn't. Every time he'd thought he had her pegged, she'd surprised him. Shown him something beyond the costume that made him want more. Tori was one of a kind and something about her set his blood on fire. Summoned a hunger he'd never felt before, a craving from deep within that demanded he claim her tonight before they ended Roulette, because their games were far from over if he had anything to say about it. He wasn't sure exactly what he was feeling, unsure if there was even a word for it yet, but he knew one thing for sure — Tori was *his.*

Squirming under him, she squeezed him tight and he felt the groan rumbling in his chest as his cock twitched, slowly slipping from her no matter how much he wanted to stay buried in her heat. "You're such a good little fuckdoll," he hummed against her lips, stealing another kiss as her hands trailed down his back, trying to keep him there.

She said she wanted you. She said you were right for her.

Breaking the kiss, he pushed up from the floor, away from Tori so that he could gamble one last time before the night ended. "I have an idea, my little whore."

"What?" she asked, propping herself on her elbows as he moved from between her thighs, twisting to grab his bag and drag it closer.

"Be still." Uncapping the marker in his hand, he carefully wrote the letters on her stomach, noting the quick intake of breath as she realized what it said.

MINE.

Tossing the marker back on his bag, he rid himself of the condom and pulled his boxers into place so he could lean over her. She leaned back, letting him invade her space until she had no choice but to stare into his eyes. No way to hide her reaction as he sought the right words, trying to put thoughts he'd never had before into something coherent.

"You said this felt right," he said, brushing a hand over the word on her chest without breaking eye contact. Trailing it down, he squeezed the word on her thigh. "And this."

"Yes, sir," she whispered, her breath shaky, and he saw the vulnerability in her eyes, the hope that he had to admit he felt too.

"You liked being treated like my filthy little fuckdoll? You liked me using you?" Pierce could hear the lingering doubt in his voice, but it was unavoidable. He needed to know. Needed her to say it when she was this raw, this open, when there was no way to lie about it.

Tori's tongue slipped across her lower lip, and then he felt her hand on his arm, moving up from where he had it planted beside her until her warm palm found his cheek. "I liked— I *like* being your filthy little fuckdoll. I like it when *you* use me. I like it when you make me feel dirty, when you make it hurt just before it feels... incredible. I don't just like this, I like it from *you*, sir."

His heart was pounding, beating at the inside of his ribs as he watched for any hint of deceit, any sign that she could be lying, could be pretending — but he'd felt it. He'd felt her come over and over while he talked dirty to her, he'd watched as she'd tried to scrub the word 'BABY' from her body, listened as she'd begged him to use her.

It didn't feel real, didn't feel possible, but she was.

Unable to hold back, he pulled her up with him, dragging her onto his lap until she was straddling him, soaking his pants, but he didn't give a fuck. He needed her in his arms, needed to kiss her again and taste her skin.

Pierce kissed and licked and nipped his way across her chest, capturing her nipple in his mouth just so he could steal another soft cry from her.

"Sir, please," she whined, her fingers wrapping around his arms, squeezing when he only pulled her closer. "Pierce."

His name from her lips, not shouted in the chaos of an orgasm, made him lift his head to look at her. She was smiling, that brilliant fucking smile that punched twin dimples into her flushed cheeks and made it impossible to think straight. "What is it, little whore?"

"You didn't say anything back. Again." Her smile flickered for a second as her eyes dipped away from him. "I don't know what you're thinking, I can't read you like that, but"—she took a deep breath—"I want you to know I really enjoyed this and… if you ever wanted to do it again I—"

"Stop." He cut her off, feeling a wicked grin spread across his lips. "I guess I haven't made myself clear, fuckdoll, but when I put this on you…" Pierce ran his hand over the *MINE* scrawled across her stomach. "That was my way of saying that you're not walking away from me. Not tonight. Unless you can give me a damn good reason why not, I plan on taking you back to my place and tasting this sweet, sore little pussy for myself. I'm not going to let you sleep until my sheets are soaked, until you're crying and begging me to stop making you come. Then I'm going to fuck you again."

The flush in her cheeks brightened, her lips parted in what he hoped would soon be a 'yes.'

"Any arguments, whore?" Pierce brought his palm down on her ass, jolting her hips against him, and he loved the flash of desire in her gaze.

"None at all, sir. I think a plan like that warrants calling in to work tomorrow." Her smile widened, and there was only real excitement behind it.

"I can't wait to hear all about your job while you're squirming in my bed." Stealing a kiss, he nipped his way down her throat. "You're going to tell me everything. Spill all your dirty little secrets."

"Do I get to know anything about you?" she asked, a breathy laugh sneaking past her lips. "Like your last name?"

"Montgomery," he answered, grinning against her shoulder before he bit down, reveling in the way she ground her cunt against him as she whined.

"Mine is Brewer. Tori Brewer."

"I like that so much more than Baby."

She groaned, fingers tightening on his biceps. "I hate that name when you say it."

"That will be the last time. Trust me." He grinned as he captured her nipple in his mouth again, teasing the bud until she moaned softly. "I like you as my little fuckdoll."

"Me too," she whispered.

"Good girl." Wrapping his hands over her ass, he pulled her cheeks apart and trailed his fingers from cunt to the tight little pucker that made her tense. "I think I'm going to like prying your secrets out, slut."

"Yes, sir."

"In case you missed it, time's up," Tyler said from above them, and when he looked up the man was grinning and offering him a towel along with two bottles of water.

"Thanks," Pierce replied, reluctantly removing his arms from Tori to take the items. "We'll be out of here soon."

"No rush, you're not the only ones lingering. But don't push it." Another laugh as he wandered off to do whatever the DMs did after the chaos of Roulette.

HE'D GATHERED their things while she got dressed again, hiding all of the pretty words on her skin, but he knew he'd have her naked again soon.

The whole night felt like a dream. A fantasy come to life, and part of him was still worried it would evaporate like one. That she'd be different outside of Roulette, outside of the club... but that was just years of bullshit in his head.

Tori wasn't like that.

She was beautiful, honest, and dangerously stubborn. Every other sub he'd ever played with would have quit the scene he'd created with the pony. Most of them before he'd even brought the violet wand within five feet of them, but all of them would have given up *eventually*. Called out 'yellow' or even 'red' just to escape the diabolical scene he'd worked up.

He'd wanted it to be challenging, meant for it to push her, but it had been *impossible*.

Pierce had realized it ten minutes in, and yet... Tori had refused to give up. Twenty-four minutes was how long it took before she finally cracked. The tears in her eyes had been a relief, because even though she hadn't used the word, that was her 'yellow' and it was all he'd needed to move in. To touch her the way he'd needed to so he could make her his. Still, he needed to remember that for the next time he pushed her pain limits. He had every intention of coaxing out her masochistic side, the one that got wet when he spanked her, when he nipped her skin, but he'd never risk pushing too far.

There was no way he'd risk losing this at all.

Still new, still so raw, but it felt *right*. Tori felt right.

"So, do you need to call into work too? Send an email or something?" she asked, smiling up at him as he tossed his play bag over his shoulder with a chuckle.

"I don't work, little whore."

A frown pinched her face, her brows coming together, and he couldn't help but grin at her confusion. She had no idea who he was, who his family was, and she'd still wanted him and all his twisted kinks. If there had been any lingering doubt in his mind, that obliterated them, and he yanked her against him to kiss her hard. Owning her mouth, claiming the back of her neck with one hand so that he could control it completely.

"You're amazing, you know that?" he whispered against her mouth, feeling the rapid puffs of her breath as she stared up at him.

"Sir?"

"I don't need to work. Money isn't an issue for me, or my family, but that's not what I want you thinking about right now." He grinned, keeping one arm around her waist as he led them toward the exit. "While I'm driving us home, I want you to think about how many times I can make you come before you pass out like a good little fuck-doll. Well-used, soaking wet, and covered in come."

"Oh God," she whispered on a moan, and he glanced down at her messy schoolgirl costume, the bottom part of 'DIRTY GIRL' peeking out from beneath the short skirt.

"That's right, slut. And that's just tonight... I have so many things I want to do to you."

The list was infinite, and it would take him an eternity to cross them all off. He wanted to own Tori Brewer in every way possible, wanted his dirty little fuckdoll to soak his bed every night, and wherever that led him would be just fine.

Even if that meant one day he put a ring on her finger at the same time he locked a collar around her throat.

THE END

ABOUT THE AUTHOR

Jennifer Bene is a *USA Today* bestselling author of dangerously sexy and deviously dark romance. From BDSM, to Suspense, Dark Romance, and Thrillers — she writes it all. Always delivering a twisty, spine-tingling journey with the promise of a happily-ever-after.

Don't miss a release! Sign up for the newsletter to get new book alerts (and a free welcome book) at: http://jenniferbene.com/newsletter

Connect with Jennifer:
   • Website: https://jenniferbene.com/
   • Facebook: https://facebook.com/jbeneauthor
   • Author FB Page: https://facebook.com/jenniferbeneauthor
   • Twitter: https://twitter.com/jbeneauthor
   • Instagram: https://www.instagram.com/jbeneauthor
   • BookBub: http://www.bookbub.com/authors/jennifer-bene
   • Goodreads: https://www.goodreads.com/jbeneauthor

TRAINED

A BLACK LIGHT: ROULETTE WAR NOVELLA

By

Sue Lyndon

CHAPTER 1

XAVIER

*X*avier stood on the upper balcony of the Ross Wellness Retreat, silently counting the number of clients returning from the morning hike. Once he was satisfied that Corey, his newest hire, hadn't left anyone behind, he allowed himself a long, appreciative look at the Santa Monica Mountains. The sun was just rising, bathing the horizon in rays of orange and pink. It was a beautiful sight, and he almost lifted an arm to wrap it around Sherry, but she wasn't there.

She was never coming back. Still, his arms kept aching to wrap around her, to hold her while they watched the sun rise over the mountains, as had been their morning ritual during the five years of their marriage.

Would the phantom ache ever go away?

Fuck. He ran a hand through his hair and turned just as a knock sounded on his office door. He exited the balcony and walked inside.

"Come in!"

Whoever it was, he was thankful for the distraction. The only thing that had kept him sane in the three years since Sherry's untimely passing was throwing himself into work, keeping the wellness retreat that he'd founded with his late wife running strong.

Corey entered his office, his trademark mischievous smile in place.

The young man always looked as if he were about to say something offensive, though he'd come with a glowing resume and he happened to be the son of one of Xavier's best clients, a wealthy movie producer, so Xavier had given the young man a chance.

"How'd the hike go?" Xavier asked. "You guys returned a bit early."

"We spotted a mountain lion," Corey said with a shrug. "Big fellow, too. But as soon as he saw me walking around a curve in the trail with several hikers close behind me, he took off. Needless to say, we turned the fuck around and came back early."

"Shit. Where exactly did this happen?"

"Around mile four on the Blue Canyon Trail. He ran over the rocky cliffs in the area." Corey smirked, crossed his arms over his chest, and leaned against Xavier's desk. Clearly, the sighting hadn't left him unnerved, but it was still concerning. The safety of Xavier's clients at the wellness retreat was his number one concern.

"All right. We'll avoid the Blue Canyon Trail for the next week and make sure hikers always stay in pairs during our longer hikes, even when they need to use the bathroom. Also, I'll personally accompany you on the evening hike and tomorrow's hikes as well." Xavier usually accompanied his clients on at least one hike a day anyway and he had already been planning to join this evening's hiking excursion into the mountains.

"Got it, boss. Anything else?"

"That should cover it. Thanks, Corey."

Xavier expected the young man to leave his office, but he lingered, his arms still casually crossed over his chest as he leaned against the desk. The mischievous glint in his dark eyes brightened and he displayed a quirky smile.

"Is there something else you wanted to talk to me about, Corey?"

"Yep, boss. There is, in fact. Did you know I'm a member of Black Light West?" Corey leaned forward and winked in a conspiratorial manner.

"I wasn't aware." Xavier wondered where he was going with this. Members weren't supposed to talk about the club to non-members, but as a member of Black Light West himself, Xavier had never run into Corey at the exclusive BDSM club. Though, in all fairness, Xavier didn't frequent the establishment on a regular basis. Only when he became so fucking lonely that he found himself driving into the city on a Friday or Saturday night, eager to find a willing submissive to play with for the evening. But *only* for the evening. He wasn't ready to settle down or attempt a serious relationship with a submissive yet, and he was careful to never play with the same sub more than once.

"Yep, I joined about two months ago. I saw you there one night, but that was before we officially met and I started working for you. But I'm sure it was you. Just saw you sitting at the bar, didn't witness you playing with anyone though."

Xavier lifted an eyebrow at his employee, still wondering where Corey was going with this. "And?"

"And I think you should sign up for this year's Valentine shindig, Roulette, as a participant."

"And I think you should go back to the Blue Canyon Trail and try to ride a mountain lion."

"Come on, boss. It'll be fun. I heard they're having trouble signing up enough players. *I'm* going to be a participant. I would hate to see it canceled just because they can't get enough players."

"Corey," Xavier said in a warning tone, seriously doubting that the club was having difficulty finding enough participants for the event. Corey had to be exaggerating. "I'm not interested. Also, how the fuck do you afford the monthly dues at that place? I sure as hell don't pay you that much. Been skimming money from me?"

Corey grinned. "Trust fund. Better treat me real nice, boss, or I could quit on you at any moment."

"Fuck you."

"No thanks. I like women. Beautiful, tall, strict dommes, to be precise."

"Well, shit, now you're tempting me," Xavier said in a mocking voice. "Now I want to sign up just for the chance to watch you get your ass beat."

Corey rolled his eyes. "Just think about it, bossman. I think it'd do you some good. You're always brooding. Don't think I've seen you smile once in the five weeks I've been working here. You need to let loose and have some fun. Get your freak on."

Get my freak on? Xavier thought with amusement. The young man had good intentions, but he didn't know Xavier's history. He probably had no idea Xavier was a widower of three years or that he was currently struggling with the idea of getting back in the dating scene. He might play now and then, but only when the loneliness became unbearable.

Of course, signing up for Roulette might not be so bad. When he did visit Black Light West, he kept to the usual daddy dom/baby girl role play scenes he enjoyed. But maybe he needed to branch out and try some new kinks. Mix things up a little. If he joined the Roulette event, he would have the opportunity to do just that. In any case, it would beat the fuck out of spending Valentine's Day alone again. Last year, he'd spent the evening feeling sorry for himself and drinking himself into oblivion.

As if reading his mind, Corey said, "Look, you shouldn't be alone on Valentine's Day, boss. Believe it or not, I worry about you sometimes." Maybe Corey did know Xavier was a widower. One of the other employees could've easily told him.

The young man's expression turned compassionate, catching Xavier off-guard. He sure as fuck wasn't about to discuss his feelings with this young, cocky, trust fund kid. But he couldn't help being touched by Corey's invitation and his concern.

"Fine. I'll think about it," Xavier grumbled.

Corey's face brightened. "Excellent. The information and sign-up forms are on the website. Take a look ASAP, boss."

"Like I said, I'll think about it."

FUCK THAT PIECE of shit trust fund kid and his ideas. Xavier growled as he read over the rules for Valentine Roulette. Staring at this particular section of the Black Light website, the temptation to sign up for the event kept growing.

Maybe it *would* really do him some good. Trying out some new kinks with a randomly paired sub wasn't a bad idea, especially on Valentine's Day. It would be the ultimate distraction, and it sure as hell beat the alternative—wallowing in despair all night by himself, pounding a bottle of scotch, and falling into an alcohol-induced coma.

With a deep sigh, he started filling out the application. When he got to the hard limits section, he only checked off *blood play*, *needle play*, and *breath play*. He also listed himself as a dom interested in an M/f pairing. For his play name, he entered Daddy Xavier, as that was the name he went by in the BDSM scene.

He read over the application one last time, just to make sure he'd filled the entire thing out and agreed with all the rules, then pressed the 'submit' button.

There. It was done.

An unexpected sense of excitement filled him as he pushed back from his desk. Usually, when he spent an evening at Black Light West, it was a spur of the moment decision. His loneliness would become so all-consuming that he would find himself driving into Beverly Hills, headed for the exclusive BDSM club, desperate to fill the aching void inside him. He would find a sub willing to be the baby girl to his daddy dom, and they would spend the evening playing, and just for a little while, the emptiness inside him wasn't quite so overwhelming. For a few hours, he could experience a sense of normalcy.

But making plans to play two weeks in advance, and knowing that he would likely try out something new—based upon which kinks he spun during the Roulette event—gave him something to look forward to.

He walked to his bedroom window to gaze at the night sky. This far away from the city, the stars shone brilliantly in the pitch-black sky, the half-moon casting a beam of white light over the pool below. After Sherry's death, he hadn't been able to bring himself to keep sleeping in their bedroom, so he'd remodeled the upstairs of the retreat and turned their old bedroom into another dormitory for the more budget-minded guests. He had then turned one of the VIP guest bedrooms into his new bedroom. Sometimes, he regretted the hasty remodel.

He had spent the years since Sherry's passing trying to push his grief away, rather than allow himself to actually go through it. There were times he still felt in denial, as if Sherry wasn't really gone. As if he might find her curled up beside him when he awoke in the morning. Other times, the guilt pressed in from all directions, leaving him suffocating and unable to catch his breath.

An accident. Logically, he knew the tragedy that had claimed Sherry's life was an accident, but he still couldn't help the immense guilt he felt over her passing.

It should've been me. Not her.

And I should've stayed closer to her...

Having met Sherry at a ski resort in the Swiss Alps, they had decided to celebrate their five-year anniversary with a trip to the same resort where they'd met. But on the second day of their trip, as he watched Sherry ski down the slope ahead of him, he'd heard a strange noise, a deep *whumph* followed by the rapid shifting of snow. Both of them, along with a dozen other skiers, had been buried in the avalanche, but the rescuers hadn't been able to reach Sherry in time.

In addition to grieving her loss, he also suffered from what a well-meaning counselor friend once gently told him was survivor's guilt. As her husband and daddy dom, it had been Xavier's job to protect Sherry, even with his life. Not only had he failed, but the universe had seen fit to allow him to survive. He would've given anything to take Sherry's place.

His smart watch buzzed and he looked down to see an email from Black Light West. The email thanked him for signing up as a participant and included instructions for the night—arrival time and another run down of the rules. He exhaled a long breath and returned his gaze to the night sky.

He knew Sherry would've wanted him to move on and find happiness, and if he had been the one to pass away, he would've wanted her to do the same.

Move on and find happiness.

Five little words that sounded simple yet were anything but.

Busy as the wellness retreat kept him, he didn't have a lot of time for dating. Of course, he was starting to realize he was using the retreat as an excuse for his failure to move on. His infrequent trips to Black Light West didn't help him in the long-term. They were short, quick fixes to help hold the loneliness at bay, to keep the darkness from swallowing him whole.

He needed a companion.

He needed a real relationship.

For a moment, he considered backing out of the event. It would just be another quick fix. He needed to start dating soon, to throw himself out there. He had looked at a few BDSM dating sites recently, though he hadn't worked up the courage to create a profile on any of them.

Lonely as Fuck Daddy Dom Widower Seeks Sweet Baby Girl for Long-Lasting Relationship. Yeah, he needed to think of a better tagline for his dating profile.

One more quick fix, he decided, as he continued staring at the night sky, *and then I'm going to get serious about this whole dating thing. After Valentine's Day and Roulette, I'm going to finally start looking for my baby girl.*

CHAPTER 2

RACHEL

*R*achel Murray entered Black Light West, her heels clicking on the floor with each rapid step. She'd arrived precisely thirty-five minutes before the start of Roulette, just as she'd hoped. She needed a little time to herself before the event started, just to calm her nerves. Navigating through the crowd of people, she made a beeline for the bar, where she asked for a glass of rosé.

People-watching always helped her settle before she played at a BDSM club, so as she sat at the bar, that's exactly what she did. She watched a domme leading a cute young blond man around by a leash, the couple heading toward the movie theater located off the main play area, where Roulette would get started. The sub wore a crop top and a thong, revealing his recently punished ass cheeks. He had a nice butt, too, and she didn't look away until they disappeared in the crowd near the movie theater.

Anticipation spiraled through her and she checked the time on her watch, but only a minute had passed. She took a sip of her drink and started to relax further, continually watching people pass by the bar area.

After a few minutes, a handsome dark-haired man with piercing blue eyes approached the bar and ordered a drink. The bartender soon handed him a tumbler of scotch. Rachel couldn't help but stare.

The man drinking the scotch was breathtakingly gorgeous, but in a woodsy, mountain man sort of way. He was wearing black jeans and a dark gray shirt with the sleeves rolled up to reveal his massive forearms. Her heart fluttered at the sight.

He looked like the kind of man who could chop down trees and turn them into a cabin, all by himself, with nothing but an ax and sheer determination. He looked both smart and capable. And he looked dominant to the bone. An aura of power and confidence radiated off his huge, muscular form.

Her pussy spasmed and she couldn't resist squirming in her seat as she continued watching Mr. Mountain Man. She had never seen him at the club before and wondered if he was a new member. He leaned against the bar with his gaze on the crowd as he drank his scotch, appearing to savor each sip. She sucked in a shaky breath every time he swallowed. Even his throat was sexy and masculine.

Though his hair was mostly dark, it was white streaked in a few places, particularly around his temples, and he had a well-trimmed salt and pepper beard to match. She judged him to be in his late thirties or early forties.

Every so often, Mr. Mountain Man's gaze softened and he appeared sad, perhaps lost in thought. She had the sudden urge to sidle over to him and keep him company, if only to see the sad, lonely look leave his blue gaze. Though he was a complete stranger and she didn't even know his name, for a reason she couldn't fathom, she wanted to see him smile, to see his eyes brighten with joy.

Before she worked up the courage to approach him, he finished his drink and walked away. Rachel mourned the loss of his company, even if he had been standing on the other side of the bar and hadn't looked in her direction once. She couldn't help but wonder if he was here tonight as an observer or as a participant in Roulette. God, she could only hope it was the latter.

But even if he was a participant in the event, her chances of getting paired with him weren't good. After all, fifteen couples would be matched for the evening. One in fifteen weren't the best odds. She watched as he walked toward the movie theater, a heated flush overtaking her.

She finished her rosé but didn't order another one. As a participant in Roulette, she was permitted up to two alcoholic beverages before tonight's festivities got started, but she was kind of a lightweight and wanted to keep her wits about her.

She remained at the bar though, not yet ready to head to the movie theater. *Blood play*, *watersports*, *needle play*, and *fisting*. Those were the four hard limits she'd selected on the website sign-up form. But that still meant a lot of other possible activities remained, many with which she didn't have much experience, and though she had been active in the BDSM scene for years, she suddenly felt like a newbie. She had no control over what activities she would spin on the roulette wheel tonight *and* no idea with whom she would be playing. The uncertainty added some extra excitement, but it also left her a bit nervous.

But she was in it to win it. She had signed up because, despite the anxieties currently running though her, she craved the challenge of the unknown. Participating in an event like Roulette was something the old, timid, *scared of her own shadow* Rachel would've never done. But she wasn't that girl anymore, or at least that was what she kept telling herself.

I'm brave. I can do this.

Finally, she left the bar and made her way to the movie theater. Her pulse raced as she navigated through the crowd and took her place near the stage where the other subs were gathering. Her heart leapt when she spotted Mr. Mountain Man standing on the stage with the participating dominants and dommes. Holy crap.

He's really up there and maybe, just maybe, I'll be lucky enough to spin his name.

She quickly pushed this secret wish aside. She didn't want to get her hopes up and then be disappointed by the dom with whom she was matched. She allowed her gaze to wander over the other doms on stage and found them all attractive. Of course, none caught her eye the way Mr. Mountain Man did.

Crap. Why couldn't she stop looking at him?

He turned his head and his blue gaze suddenly locked with hers. Her stomach flipped and heat pulsed between her thighs. She tried to glance away, but she couldn't manage to tear her eyes from his. It was as if he was keeping her captive, demanding her obedience and ordering her to hold his gaze. A thrill ran through her, goosebumps rising all over her arms. A pleasurable shudder shot down her spine and her breath kept catching in her throat.

Mr. Mountain Man held her gaze until another dom approached him and started talking to him. After he turned away, she found herself gulping in air. She was standing perfectly still, yet she felt as if she'd just jogged here from the bar.

"Are you all right?" the tall, beautiful blonde standing next to her asked.

"Oh, I'm fine," Rachel said with a wave of her hand. "It's just kind of hot in here, don't you think?"

"Yeah, all these bodies in here," the woman replied with a wave of her hand. "I'm Alice, by the way. It's only my third time here. I recently joined Black Light West."

"It's nice to meet you, Alice. I'm Dolly," Rachel replied, using her play name, a name she'd chosen at random the first time she visited a BDSM club. But the name had stuck and she rather liked it. She liked being Dolly, the girl who never felt shame over her submissive desires, the girl who had found both acceptance and freedom outside of her backward hometown and repressive upbringing.

"Nice to meet you, Dolly." Alice shot her a nervous smile. "I've never seen you here. Are you a newbie, too?"

"I've been a member of Black Light West since December, though I've been going to BDSM clubs for years. But, even though I'm not a newbie, I will confess that I'm feeling a bit anxious right now. Signing up seemed like a good idea at the time, you know, a fun and exciting challenge, but to be randomly paired with a dom and three activities? Well, I guess you could say I'm feeling a bit out of my element right now." Rachel watched as the last of the reclining seats filled in the movie theater, leaving only standing room. Just a few minutes until start time, she realized, as her stomach did a somersault.

"Have any pointers for a newbie?" Alice asked with a chuckle.

Rachel looked at the gorgeous blonde. "If you're worried about a scene or feeling unsure about something, politely ask your dom to pause and walk you through it. A good dom will be patient with you and won't be upset by your questions."

Alice's face lit up. "Oh, that's great advice. Thank you."

"No problem."

"So, are you from California?" Alice asked. "I'm from L.A. Born and raised."

"I'm from Kentucky, but I moved to L.A. when I was eighteen," Rachel replied, as dark memories rushed back. She'd fled her hometown of Graceville, KY in the middle of the night, desperate to escape her tyrannical father. Desperate for a life outside the ultra-conservative community in which she'd been raised.

"Oh? Are you an actress?"

"Nope. I'm Kimmie Walters' personal assistant."

"Get out of town! Really?" Alice's eyes widened.

"Yep, for the last six years. She came into a boutique where I was working and I helped her try on some dresses and the next thing I knew, she was offering me a job."

"I love her talk show. She's amazing. You're so lucky."

"Yes," Rachel agreed. "I am very lucky. She's so sweet and authentic. She helped me turn my life around." When the boutique had knocked her down to part-time status, Rachel had been struggling to make ends meet and worried she wouldn't be able to pay her rent the following month. The chance run-in with self-help guru Kimmie Walters had saved her from becoming homeless, or perhaps turning tricks just to pay her bills.

Suddenly, the lights in the theater dimmed and the stage became illuminated with spotlights. The murmuring of the crowd quieted and a collective sense of anticipation swept through the movie theater.

"Oh, looks like things are about to get started," Alice said, and Rachel focused her attention to the stage, where Black Light West co-owner Chase stood holding a mic as he peered over the crowd.

Chase welcomed everyone to the club and soon passed the mic to the emcee for the evening, a young, petite blonde named Madison who was dressed in a sexy black leather outfit. Rachel quickly realized she had seen the blonde at Runway West, the dance club located directly above the Black Light West BDSM club. She'd gone there a few times with Kimmie.

Rachel tried to listen carefully as Madison went over the rules for tonight's event, but her mind kept wandering. Her recent conversation with Alice had dredged up dark memories, memories she wished she could permanently erase from her mind. For eighteen years, she had lived in constant fear, all the while dreaming of the day she would turn eighteen so she could leave home for good.

She had run away twice before her eighteenth birthday and both times the police had found her and taken her back home. A shudder ran through her when she recalled the lonely hours she'd spent locked in a cold, dark closet afterward, enduring her father's preferred method of punishment. Now twenty-five years old, Rachel still hated the dark and she slept with the lights on every night.

'You filthy little sinner. Do you want to burn in hell where monsters will claw out your eyes? Because if you leave Graceville, that is exactly what will happen. You'll fall in line with the fornicaters, the adulterers, the liars, the cheaters, and the sinners. You don't want that to happen, do you? Now, you stay in here until you've learned your lesson. Pray, Rachel. Pray for forgiveness.'

But she hadn't prayed for forgiveness. Instead, she had prayed for freedom, prayed that she would one day succeed in escaping.

She took a deep breath and tried to will the memories away. Her father's voice was a deep, painful echo in her mind. She wished she could forget his face, forget the way his voice sounded. Rachel took another deep breath and tried to focus. Madison was getting ready to start the non-M/f pairings, and the M/f pairings would follow next.

Breathe in. Hold five seconds. Exhale slowly.

She coached herself through the deep-breathing exercises Kimmie had taught her, a method that worked well for preventing panic attacks. Rachel hadn't had one in over a year and she wasn't about to have one in the middle of Roulette. She'd been anticipating this event for weeks. No way would she allow ghosts from her past to ruin her evening.

She stood next to Alice as they watched the non-M/f pairings get matched. Her heart skipped a beat when she noticed Mr. Mountain

Man staring at her again. To her shock, he appeared concerned. Had he noticed her panicking? Oh hell, had it been that obvious? When he gave her a soft smile and a nod of encouragement, she realized he must've witnessed her nervousness. Warmth panged in her chest and she envied the sub who matched with him tonight, whomever it would be.

Only three non-M/f couples needed to be paired up for the evening, so Madison soon started matching up the M/f couples. Rachel waited for her name to be called, trying to be patient as she focused on breathing in and out, slowly and carefully.

Every time she glanced at Mr. Mountain Man, he was still looking at her, staring at her with an intensity that stole her breath.

"Our next dom up to the wheel is Daddy Xavier. Come on over and roll for your submissive," Madison said in a cheerful voice, her blonde ponytail bouncing as she made a sweeping gesture toward the roulette wheel. Rachel watched with her heart in her throat as Mr. Mountain Man himself emerged from the group of doms to take his turn rolling for a submissive.

She held her breath and waited for Madison to announce the winning submissive. Time seemed to stand still and a loud buzzing noise filled Rachel's ears. It took Alice nudging her to break her out of her anxious trance.

"Hey," Alice whispered. "That's you, right? The emcee just called your name."

"Dolly?" Madison said, walking closer to the gathered submissives, her heels clicking on the stage floor. "Is Dolly here?"

Rachel stepped forward and started walking toward the stage, feeling as though she were in a dream. She couldn't believe it. She was going to belong to Mr. Mountain Man for the next three hours.

Daddy Xavier. Her heart beat faster. He was a daddy dom.

The dom who'd been staring at her helped her step onto the stage, his large warm hand clasping hers with a firmness that sent pleasurable shivers down her spine. He gave her a brief smile, his eyes warm. "Good evening, Dolly."

"Uh-hi. Hi, Mr. Mount—I mean, hello, Daddy Xavier." Her face flamed over the mistake she'd almost made. *Daddy Xavier, Daddy*

Xavier, Daddy Xavier... She repeated his play name in her mind over and over in hopes that she wouldn't slip up. How embarrassing would it be to accidentally call him Mr. Mountain Man? She would never be able to meet his dreamy blue eyes again.

He squeezed her hand and drew her closer. As he stared down at her, the noise of the crowd faded into the background. She heard the distinct thump of each heartbeat in her ears and swallowed hard as heat pulsed through her.

What would it be like to submit to Daddy Xavier? Would he be a soft cuddly daddy who liked to dote upon his submissive, or would he be extremely strict? She exhaled a shaky breath. Oh, she hoped he was a mix of the two. Gentle and caring sometimes, and stern and demanding at other times.

"There will be plenty of time for staring adoringly into one another's eyes later," Madison said, her voice cutting through Rachel's dazed reverie. "Come on over and spin for your first activity, Dolly."

A few people in the crowd laughed and Rachel's face flamed hotter. She didn't blush often, as she wasn't easily embarrassed, but in Daddy Xavier's presence she felt unsettled and vulnerable. That sexy blue gaze of his seemed to pierce straight to her very soul and left her feeling stripped of all her defenses. She got the sense that he wasn't the kind of dom from whom she could hide anything.

Rachel finally extracted her hand from Daddy Xavier's and accepted the offered marble from Madison. She spun the activity wheel and tossed in the marble.

"*Pet play!*" Madison announced a few seconds later. "Oh, how fun! You'll make the cutest kitten or puppy, Dolly." The emcee winked at her before moving on to the next pairing.

Pet play. Her palms broke into a sweat as Daddy Xavier guided her to stand near the other paired couples. How was she supposed to act like a kitten or a puppy or some other kind of pet? She gulped hard and fought the urge to fan herself.

Daddy Xavier grasped her hand and smiled down at her, his eyes once more filled with warmth. "Have you ever done *pet play* before, Dolly?" he asked.

Heat seared her cheeks. "Um, no, but it seems kinda hot." She certainly wasn't averse to trying it, though she couldn't help but worry she would screw up the scene and ruin the evening. *Please let him be patient and understanding.*

The warmth in his eyes increased, his eyes gleaming a brighter shade of blue. "Well, I'm glad you think so," he said, placing a finger beneath her chin. His touch sent a heated wave of awareness throughout her entire body. "I think you'll make the most adorable little kitten."

CHAPTER 3

XAVIER

*X*avier wrapped an arm around Dolly and pulled her closer, thankful that he'd been matched with her. When he'd first caught sight of her in the crowd, he'd been struck by her beauty. Then, when he'd glanced back at her a short while later, he had thought she looked upset, as if she were panicking and having trouble breathing. He had been ready to rush off the stage to help her when she'd glanced up and met his gaze, at which point she had started to appear calmer.

He couldn't help but wonder what had upset her. He peered down at her, admiring her short, dark locks. Normally, he preferred submissives with long hair that he could wrap his hands around, but the short haircut suited Dolly. She kept her gaze trained on Madison as the emcee directed the final couple to roll for their activity.

The fun was about to get started and Dolly would belong to him for the next three hours.

His cock hardened in his pants as he took in her curves and long legs. She was tall, though at six-foot-three he had a few inches on her. As he observed her every little move, the quick but rapid breaths she inhaled, the nervous manner in which she repeatedly clasped and unclasped her hands together, and the timid sidelong glances she occasionally shot him, his protective instincts rose to the surface.

He wanted to wrap this little sub in a blanket, set her upon his lap, and rock her gently until the last of her nervousness dissipated. Yet at the same time, he also wanted to push her limits and watch as she struggled to obey his commands.

She called up both his caring and his strict side.

He couldn't wait to get started.

Pet play.

Heated arousal coursed through him with such sharpness that his vision momentarily blurred. He tightened his hold on Dolly and reveled in the startled gasp that escaped her throat. She turned slightly in his arms to meet his gaze. He wasn't sure if seconds or hours passed, but the world ceased spinning as he leaned closer and cupped her face in one hand.

"I can tell our couples are excited to get started, so everyone have fun and play safe!" Madison's announcement jarred him out of his trance. It was a bit after eight o'clock and all the couples were now matched.

Still cupping Dolly's face, he rubbed his thumb along her cheek and leaned in to inhale the floral scent that clung to her. When he straightened and met her eyes again, he said, "I'm going to enjoy training you, little kitten."

XAVIER LED DOLLY through the crowd of spectators in the main play area. She was quiet, her face was flushed, and he sensed her growing excitement. Guiding her toward the wardrobe area, he kept her hand firmly in his. He liked the feel of her tiny hand in his large one. Again, that urge to protect her rose from deep within.

"Have you ever done *pet play* before?" Dolly asked as they arrived at the wardrobe.

The wardrobe assistant was already helping one of the other couples, so Xavier drew Dolly close while they waited their turn. "Yes, though it's been quite a while," he replied, holding her gaze, mesmerized by the golden flecks in her gorgeous blue eyes. "*Kitten play* is my favorite though, and it's probably also the easiest for a novice like you."

Her eyes narrowed. "I'm not a novice. I've been going to BDSM clubs for years and I've watched a few *pet play* scenes. I've just never actually participated in one myself," she said in a defensive tone.

"Why not?" he asked, reaching for a lock of her hair to brush it behind her ear.

Her face reddened. "I-I'm not sure. I guess, well, I enjoyed watching the scenes—they were hot—but the idea of behaving like an animal and even making animal noises..." Her voice trailed off and she looked away for a moment. "It seems embarrassing. I'm not sure I could actually do it."

He grasped her hand and peered at her intently. "I'll be with you the whole time, Dolly, making sure you're all right and that you're enjoying the scene. It's my intention for you to enjoy it, little kitten."

"Hi, can I help you?" the man behind the counter asked.

"Yes, we're doing a *kitten play* scene," Xavier explained. "Do you have a collar and leash, a tail, and maybe some cute ears?"

The man smiled. "Of course. I have a *kitten play* kit that comes with all that, sealed in a package. Do you want to use a changing room here or would you like to take the items with you?"

"We'll take it with us, thank you."

The wardrobe assistant disappeared into the back for a minute before emerging with a small black bag. "Here you go," he said. "Makes it easy to carry after you open everything. I included a bottle of lube, too."

Xavier accepted the bag and peered at the *kitten play* kit inside that was sealed in clear plastic wrapping. "This'll be perfect. Thank you."

He led a red-faced Dolly out of wardrobe and back into the main play area, where he scanned the room for a good location to conduct their first scene. The place was packed with spectators, but he finally spotted a platform along the wall that would work. Conveniently, it contained a spanking bench.

Dolly's eyes widened as they got closer to the platform. He helped her step up onto it and a few spectators instantly gathered around them. He noticed Dolly was trying very hard not to glance at the onlookers. Did being watched make her nervous?

He peered into the black bag and reached for the *kitten play* kit, tearing open the clear plastic wrapping before shoving it all back inside the black bag, getting everything ready for easy access. Then he turned and looked Dolly up and down. The outfit she was wearing, a tiny black dress with a plunging neckline, worked well for her kitty persona.

Cupping her face, he waited for her to meet his gaze. She gulped hard and stared at him, her face bright with excitement, her cheeks flushed and her chest heaving faster than before.

"You're my little kitten, Dolly," he said in a firm tone. "And every good little kitten needs a strict but caring owner to tend to her needs."

A half-moan, half-whimper escaped her, and in the next moment, he noticed her fidgeting in place, pressing her thighs tightly together as she stood before him.

"Some kittens call their owners *Master*, but you're a very new baby kitten, so you'll have a daddy instead, and you may call me *Daddy* throughout our scene, little kitten. Do you understand?"

"Yes, Da-Daddy." A fresh flush appeared upon her cheeks. He thought she looked radiant as she stood trembling with excitement and blushing bright red.

"Good kitty. Now, step out of your heels and get down on your hands and knees like a sweet little baby kitten."

CHAPTER 4

RACHEL

*R*achel's heart pounded in her ears as she stepped out of her heels. After losing her four-inch heels, she was struck by how exceedingly tall Daddy Xavier really was. She glanced up at him in awe before remembering his command. He wanted her on her hands and knees. *Like a sweet little baby kitten.*

The memory of his words, delivered in his deep, sexy voice, made her tremble with need.

She lowered herself to the floor, all the while conscious of the many eyes upon her. From her peripheral vision, she noticed the crowd of spectators growing. Being watched had always embarrassed her, though with that shame her arousal never failed to rise higher and higher, and as she settled upon the floor, her pussy throbbed harder.

Her dress was so short that she felt the fabric moving up to the curve of her bottom, leaving her barely covered. A quick glance at her bosom showed her cleavage had shifted forward. She wasn't wearing a bra and when she wasn't standing up straight, the dress didn't exactly support her.

On her hands and knees, she awaited further instruction from Daddy Xavier. Her pulse quickened when he stepped closer and his boots filled her vision.

I'm a kitten and he's my daddy.

She thought about the contents of the bag from costume and her tummy did a quick flip. Would he really make her wear a tail? Would he make her crawl around? Would he collar her and walk her with the leash while everyone watched?

He knelt beside her and reached for her hair. Gently, he stroked his hands through it, up and down, even working his hand down the back of her neck.

"That's a good little kitty," he said. "Daddy likes it when you obey."

Heated waves coursed through her, even as goosebumps rose on her arms. He continued petting her for another minute, petting her as if she were a real kitten who needed attention from her daddy. She leaned into his caresses with a soft sigh, anticipating each gentle stroke of his hand through her hair.

Still petting her with one hand, he moved to her side and pushed her dress up to her waist, revealing her thong-clad bottom. He made a stern *tsking* noise that sent flutters to her stomach.

"Little kitties don't wear thongs," he said in a matter-of-fact tone. "Little kitties wear tails. We're going to have to fix that. But first, Daddy needs to put a collar on you. Ears, too." Leaving her ass bared for all to see, he reached into the bag and withdrew the thin black collar. There was a tiny bell attached to the front that jingled as he brought it closer to her neck. "Hold still, little one. This collar will help remind you that you're my pet, my belonging. You belong to Daddy, don't you?"

"Yes, Daddy." She peered up at him as he deftly fastened the collar around her neck. Next, he reached for the kitten ears and placed them upon her head, taking his time to adjust them.

"Beautiful," he said, once more stroking her hair. "I can't wait to get you up on the spanking bench, my pet. It'll be easier to get your tail into place if you're up on the bench with your legs spread wide and your privates revealed to me."

Again, she leaned into his touch, enjoying his soft caresses so much that she couldn't keep herself from making little noises of enjoyment. She wasn't quite purring, but she could easily imagine herself getting there if he continued.

"Now, little kitten, Daddy wants you to stand up for a moment."

She rose on shaky legs, with his help, and hearing the bell on her collar jingling with her movements made her face flush, though she wasn't sure why. Maybe because it reminded her that she was a little kitten, completely dependent on her owner, her daddy. And she would have no choice but to lay upon the spanking bench with her legs spread wide while he inserted her tail.

Would he at least pet her again soon? God, she hoped so. Something about that simple action alone made her insides quiver and heat quake fervently between her thighs. The strip of fabric covering her pussy was probably soaked through by now.

He guided her to stand beside the spanking bench. Her dress was still bunched up around her waist, as it was rather snug and the tight fabric wouldn't move down over her hips unless she gave it a hard pull. Daddy Xavier's gaze landed upon her center and he reached between her thighs, lightly drawing two fingers overtop that scrap of fabric.

"Let's get this off you, hm?" He pushed the thong down her legs and helped her step out of it, then he balled the thong up and placed it in his pocket. Again, his gaze dropped to her center, to the part of her that was aching so intensely that it took all her strength not to beg him to touch her there.

If he turned around for a moment to do something, she hoped she possessed enough self-control not to reach between her legs in order to caress herself. She could feel each distinct pulse of her clit and felt a trickle of moisture on her inner thigh. Her face heated further. She couldn't recall ever having blushed so much during a scene before.

And they were just getting started.

She whimpered when he stepped closer and touched the outer folds of her sex. Eventually, he slipped a finger inside her aching core and circled through her gathering wetness. Then, to her great relief, he dragged his moistened digit directly atop her pulsing clit.

"Oh!" She closed her eyes and savored the moment, her hips jerking forward as she sought more of his touch. If only he would insert a finger fully inside her...

Too soon, he removed his hand from between her thighs. A glance into his eyes showed him looking rather stern.

"Little kitties don't say 'oh,' he said. "If you want Daddy to keep stroking your privates, you need to make little kitty noises."

Her cheeks flamed. She swallowed hard and tried to think. She doubted he wanted a literal, spoken 'meow' out of her, but maybe something a little more realistic.

Desperate to have his finger stroking over her clit again, she jerked her hips toward him and emitted a tiny, high-pitched *mmwoww* sound. Heat flared in his eyes, a look of pleasure overtaking his features.

"Very nice. Does Daddy's little kitten want more pets on her privates?"

Yes, please. She shuddered as his hand delved between her thighs, his finger spreading moisture in circles atop her throbbing nubbin. She repeatedly made the *mmwoww* noises, and he kept caressing her in all the right places, bringing her close to the precipice of a release as she stood up on the platform, dozens of people watching.

"Good kitty," he said. "Now your kitty privates will already be nice and wet and plump when you get up on the spanking bench. I can't wait to get you up there and spread your legs wide. Everyone is going to see what a wet kitty you are."

His words made the pulsing in her sex increase, and as he pulled his hand away from her pussy she gave a disgruntled *mmwoww* that made him chuckle. He grasped her hand and helped her up onto the spanking bench, arranging her so that her legs were on either side of it, and yes, he made certain she was spread very wide to his liking.

She expected him to insert the tail into her bottom immediately, but to her delight, he commenced petting her again. He started at her head and worked his way down, drawing his hand over every inch of her body that was exposed. Endorphins rushed her scalp and she felt deliriously lightheaded as he lavished her with attention.

"Such a sweet kitten," he said, running his hand over her bottom. "And just look at how wet you are between your thighs." He splayed her bottom cheeks apart without warning, causing her to gasp and stiffen on the bench. "Why, your privates are so slick it looks as though you've gone into heat."

Her bottom rested at the end of the bench that angled toward the main play area, where the crowd stood watching. All those eyes on her aching private parts. Though the knowledge of her vulnerable exposure embarrassed her, she couldn't help raising her hips once in an attempt to get Daddy Xavier to pet her pussy. Unfortunately, he moved away to search for something inside the bag.

She watched as he withdrew the tail and a bottle of lube.

"Time for your tail," he said, approaching her. He stroked her bottom and then pulled her cheeks wide apart, revealing her secret pucker. "But before the tail goes in, Daddy has to lube up your bottom hole. Be a good kitten and hold very still. Don't be naughty. Remember, naughty kitties get their butts spanked by their daddies."

CHAPTER 5

XAVIER

*F*ucking hell yes. Xavier was enjoying this scene.

Well, it wasn't just the scene. It was Dolly that he was enjoying. Her nervousness combined with her growing excitement, her huge blue eyes that kept looking up to him for guidance. His rock-hard cock pressed at the front of his pants and his balls kept drawing up tight.

He wanted to unzip his pants, free himself, and plunge home into her wet, plump folds. Maybe he would get lucky and they would roll *intercourse—oral, vaginal,* or *anal,* it was all good as far as he was concerned—for one of their next two activities.

He set the tail on the bench between her thighs and focused on keeping her spread wide for the application of the lube. He squirted a generous portion of lubrication atop her dark pink pucker and watched as it clenched and unclenched. He circled her rosette with one finger and then pressed inside, breaching her tight entrance.

Fuck, she was tight. She had claimed she'd been going to BDSM clubs for years, but he couldn't help but wonder how much anal experience she had.

"Little kitten?"

"Yes, Daddy?"

"Have you ever taken a cock in your ass before?"

"Yes, a few times, though not in a while."

"What about a plug?"

"Yes, Daddy. I've taken plugs. Small ones, though. I-I am especially tight back there. Doms always think I'm an anal virgin."

At the mention of other doms, a surge of red-hot jealousy swept through him. He glared into the watching crowd, as if expecting some random jerkoff to raise his hand and say, 'Yep, Dolly's ass was tight when I fucked her last week.' He was ready to inflict violence upon anyone who dared to make such a claim. However, no one in the crowd said a word, other than quiet murmurs during private conversations that he couldn't quite hear. He breathed out slowly in an effort to calm the raging jealousy that left him stunned.

He hadn't felt such possessiveness for a woman since...

No. He wouldn't allow himself to complete the thought. Dolly was a sweet girl and she didn't deserve to spend three hours sceneing with someone who was thinking about another woman the whole time, even if that other woman was no longer alive. After one more deep breath, he felt much calmer.

Returning his focus to Dolly and her tight bottom hole, he continued pushing his finger in and out as he prepared her for the tail. The plug attached to the black tail wasn't overly large, but he still wanted her to be comfortable. He finally reached for the tail and poured lube onto the plug, then he touched the plug to her bottom hole. He kept her cheeks splayed wide apart with one hand while he started working the plug inside her tightness.

"Relax, little kitten. The base is almost inside you. Just a bit more," he said in an encouraging tone. Turning and pushing the plug, he worked it inside her until the base was fully seated in her tight bottom hole. He swept the attached tail aside, drawing it to rest over one of her cheeks, allowing for an unhindered view of her pussy.

He stepped back to survey his handiwork and his cock jerked in his pants. Everything between her thighs gleamed pink. Her nether lips were entirely bare and he appreciated the recent wax job she must've had. With her legs spread wide, she was completely exposed. He could even glimpse her engorged clit peeking out from amidst her plump folds, as if it were begging for more of his touch.

"You look adorable wearing your tail, little kitten," he said, stroking down her back and over her tail, allowing it to finally settle in place to cover her privates. She arched her back and lifted her hips, making another cute *mmwoww* noise.

Suddenly, everything went dark and the background music died. A collective gasp went up in the crowd just as the emergency lights turned on, though none were near the platform. Still keeping a hand on Dolly, Xavier looked toward the main play area, though he couldn't see much, just a sea of dark bodies in the dim lighting. When he felt Dolly tensing beneath his hand, he leaned down to whisper in her ear.

"Just a power outage, little kitten," he said. "I'm sure the lights will come back on soon. Don't be afraid. Daddy's right here with you." He couldn't be certain she was afraid of the dark, but he got the sense that at the very least it made her uneasy and he wished the platform was closer to the nearest emergency lights. He petted her hair and down her back over and over, listening carefully for any sounds of distress from his sweet little kitty.

Just as suddenly as the lights went out, they came back on, along with the music. He doubted more than thirty seconds had passed. A few people in the crowd clapped and cheered. He looked down at Dolly, anxious to glimpse the expression on her face. He wanted to make sure she was all right.

Her eyes met his and she gave him a soft smile that made his heart clench.

"Thanks for staying with me in the darkness, Daddy," she said, and he sensed a deeper meaning, or perhaps a story, behind her gratitude. He couldn't explain how, but it felt as though an invisible force kept pulling him to Dolly, and in that force, he could sense her emotions, even without glimpsing her face and staring into her eyes.

"You're very welcome, little kitten," he said. "Would you like to pause for a moment, or do you feel ready to continue?"

She graced him with another sweet smile. "I-I'm ready to continue, Daddy."

He started petting her again, continuing until he drew another cute kitten noise from her. She was so responsive, so lovely.

"You look so cute wearing this tail, little kitten, that I think perhaps we'll leave it in all night. Unless, of course, we roll *anal intercourse* for one of our remaining activities."

A shudder ran through her and he spotted goosebumps rising on her arms.

"I can smell your arousal," he said, moving a hand between her thighs. She arched greedily into his touch. "Perhaps my little kitten would like some pets on her privates?"

Another desperate high-pitched *mmwoww* left her and she lifted her center to press it harder against his probing hand. As she moved, the bell on her collar jingled, and when she turned her head to the side, he noticed her face was still flushed.

He shifted her tail aside, once again exposing her pussy for all to see. She whimpered and shifted upon the bench, and when she took too long to stop moving he gave her right cheek a sharp swat.

"Be still, little kitten," he scolded. "Naughty kittens don't get pets on their privates."

"Yes, Daddy," she replied in a demure voice, as she finally ceased squirming.

"Good kitty." He began by dipping two fingers between her plump nether lips, seeking out her gathering wetness.

Caressing moisture atop her swollen clit, he forced her legs wider apart and bent down to get a better look at the sweetness between her thighs. The pleasing but musky scent of her arousal drove him wild, causing his blood to heat and his cock to stiffen to the point of painfulness.

She gasped and made kitten noises as he applied more pressure to her nubbin, stroking her expertly with two digits, occasionally dipping back into her core for more wetness to rub over her most sensitive spot. Her kitten noises turned to needy whimpers and her hips began to gyrate. He paused and gave each of her cheeks a firm swat.

"Naughty kitten," he said in a stern voice. "Daddy told you to remain still."

"I'm sorry, Daddy," she whispered. "It's just so difficult. It feels so good when you pet me there."

"Try to behave, kitten, or Daddy will have to punish you right here while everyone watches. Is that what you want? A public spanking?"

"No-no, Daddy, please. I-I'll be a good kitten. I promise." She stilled and from the looks of it, she was also holding her breath.

Deciding to be merciful, he increased the pace of his strokes upon her clit, all the while admiring the faint redness covering her bottom cheeks. He'd only slapped her ass three times, but God, he fucking loved the sight of his handprints on her ass. Perhaps later he would redden her ass further, make her squirm and beg while he gave her a good spanking.

He pressed harder upon her clit and circled faster. "You may come whenever you wish, little kitten, and you can move now if you would like. Show Daddy how good it feels when he pets you."

CHAPTER 6

RACHEL

*R*achel pressed her eyes shut as the waves of pleasure overcame her. She writhed her center against Daddy Xavier's hand, riding the sharp surges of ecstasy that stole her breath. When the last quaking wave receded, she trembled in the aftermath of the intense orgasm, feeling as though her arms and legs had turned to jelly.

The darkness. Warmth filled her as she recalled how Daddy Xavier had stayed with her during the brief power outage. He had stayed right next to her, petting her and whispering comforting phrases in her ear, as if he'd sensed her unease.

She drew in a deep breath as her energy began to return. She sighed with contentment as Daddy Xavier helped her off the spanking bench and gathered her close to his chest. He leaned against the bench while hugging her, running his hands through her hair as he held her tightly. Again, her heart panged with warmth.

"We've been at this scene for over thirty minutes, little kitten." His lips brushed along her ear, causing a shiver of excitement to rush through her. He pulled back to meet her gaze.

Her heartbeat quickened as she stared up at him, mesmerized by the caring gleam in his eyes. She'd always had a thing for daddy doms, though she'd never dated one. Of course, she kind of had herself to blame for that. She had a habit of pushing men away and none of her relationships ever lasted long. She craved intimacy, yet she also feared it.

But as she became lost in Daddy Xavier's intense gaze, she found herself daring to believe that a relationship with him would be different than any she'd entered before. There was a fierce possessiveness in his eyes that left her both frightened and hopeful. She doubted he was the kind of dom who would allow her to push him away, nor would he easily let her go.

"Um, should we go spin for our second activity, Daddy?"

"I think we should, but I would like you to keep your kitty outfit on for the rest of the night. Ears, collar, and tail. You look adorable." When he gathered her closer, she felt the hardness of his cock in his pants. She quivered with need, the aching between her thighs surging back with full force.

"That sounds good to me," she said, feeling her face heat. "I-I enjoyed playing a kitty." It wasn't simply that she enjoyed the *kitten play*, it was because Daddy Xavier was such a good owner, a good daddy. He was the perfect mix of caring and stern. His commands had made her heart flutter, and his gentleness had warmed her all over.

"Furthermore, I plan to keep calling you my *little kitten* for the remainder of the evening, and I would like you to keep calling me *Daddy*." He reached around and cupped her bottom, then ran a hand down her tail, reminding her that she still had the plug seated in her bottom hole. With each breath or movement, she felt its presence inside, the delicious fullness.

"Okay, Daddy." Excitement rushed through her that this fun scene didn't really have to end, even if they were going to spin for their second activity. Apparently, Daddy Xavier wanted to keep the *kitten play* going. Though the newness of it still made her a bit nervous, she couldn't help the heated anticipation that left her pressing her thighs together.

He placed a kiss on her forehead and she melted. She felt as if she were glowing, as if she were the luckiest submissive in the whole club, all because Daddy Xavier was hers for the night. And she was his.

Her heart raced. Would he want to see her again after tonight?

Oh God, she hoped so. As she stared up at him, lost in his gaze, she could easily imagine playing with him again and again. In fact, she could imagine seeing him outside of the club, too. She envisioned herself curled up in bed beside him, sleeping in his arms while he spooned her from behind.

He grasped her hand and stepped back to arrange her dress, pulling it down to her hips, though not quite low enough to cover her pussy. He released her hand and walked around her, running a hand over her tail in a casual manner, as if he were inspecting her appearance. He patted her bottom and then picked up the black bag.

She watched as he placed the bottle of lubrication in the bag. But when he pulled out a leash, her pulse skittered and she inhaled a shaky breath.

He set the bag aside on the spanking bench, met her eyes, and approached her, still holding the leash.

"Get on your knees, little kitten."

She dropped to her knees and lowered her head, a wave of submission rolling through her. He stepped closer and she saw his boots in her vision, black and gleaming, and she waited with bated breath for him to attach the leash.

He ran a hand around her neck in a sensual manner, readjusting the collar and causing the bell to jingle. She heard a faint clicking noise as he attached the leash, and when he gave a slight pull on it, causing her to lean forward, a spasm of warmth pulsed between her quivering thighs. Her owner, her daddy, had just put a leash on her, and now he was going to walk her back to the movie theater so they could roll for their next activity.

"Stand up, little kitten, and put your heels back on," he said, placing the shoes on the floor in front of her. "For now, you'll walk. It's too far for you to crawl."

She rose with his assistance and stepped into her heels, and as she glanced down she couldn't help but realize her pussy would be on display as they walked through the main play area. He hadn't pulled her dress down any further and she glimpsed the gleam of her arousal on her inner thighs.

As he guided her off the platform and through the crowd, he kept a firm hold on the leash, but he also kept an arm laced around her waist. Heat emanated from his huge, muscular body and she couldn't help but wonder what he would look like without his clothes. She really hoped their next activity would involve some serious nudity on his part.

He guided her into the movie theater and her heart raced as they headed for the stage.

CHAPTER 7

XAVIER

"*V*aginal intercourse!*" Madison called out. "Congrats! You both totally look like you need it." The emcee flashed a radiant smile and then winked at them, but her attention was soon taken by another couple who were approaching to roll for their second activity.

Vaguely, Xavier realized it was Corey and his domme walking up onto the stage. The young man appeared so enamored by the tall woman who was leading him by a leash that he didn't seem to notice Xavier standing nearby.

"Come on, little kitten," Xavier said, guiding Dolly down the steps. "We're going to find a bed." He leaned down to speak directly into her ear once they were exiting the movie theater. "I'm going to make you take it from behind like a good little kitty."

Her eyes widened and her lips parted on a tiny gasp, and he detected a tremor running through her as he tightened his hold on her. He wound them deeper into the club, going down the long hallway dubbed the 'Red Light District' of the club before turning right where several fantasy rooms were available. He was headed to the nursery, hoping to find it empty. It wasn't that they'd rolled age play, but he knew that room had a bed that he planned on putting to good use.

They were in luck. The room was not in use, but the observation window was open for spectators. Already, there was a small crowd following them, and he gave a gentle tug on the leash to guide Dolly inside.

A bowl of condoms rested on a table next to the bed. He still had the black bag with him, though it currently only contained the bottle of lubrication, and he set it down next to the condoms.

He dropped the leash and circled around Dolly, appreciating the rapid rise and fall of her bosom. Admiring the sight of the tail protruding from her bottom, he paused to stroke it. He leaned against her and felt her shudder. His cock hardened as erotic images danced through his mind. Soon, he would be pounding into the tightness between her legs, thrusting fast and deep.

"I'm trying to decide if I want you on your hands and knees, little kitten, or if I want you bent over the bed. Hm. Decisions, decisions." He circled around her and cupped the side of her face, forcing her gaze to his. She looked mildly startled, though he also saw the need flaring in the depths of her pretty blue eyes.

She peered up at him, her lips slightly parted, her cat ears still in place, and he had the sudden urge to kiss her.

So, he did.

He leaned down and pressed his lips to hers, softly at first, but he soon slipped his tongue inside to tangle with hers and increased the intensity of the kiss. He felt like fucking devouring her, this sweet little kitten who was all his. And fuck, he couldn't imagine just walking away from her tonight.

He imagined her standing at his large bedroom window that over-looked the mountains, wearing nothing but a bedsheet hastily wrapped around her body. In his vision, her short dark locks were askew and her lips were swollen from his kisses. Her pussy lips were also puffy and red from hours of brutal fucking.

He kissed her harder, wanting more than anything to make his imaginings come true. How would Dolly react if he asked her to come home with him tonight? And if she didn't wish to come home with him tonight, would she at least agree to see him again?

The little whimpers and moans that escaped her as she returned his kiss made his dick harden further. Christ, he would pass out from the sheer want of her if he didn't plunge his cock into her soon. Clutching her face, he deepened the kiss, drinking her in and savoring the sweet taste of her. *My little kitten.*

When he finally broke the kiss, she panted breathlessly in his arms, her face flushed and her eyes glazed over with desire.

"I've made my decision," he said, holding her stare. "I'm going to bend you over the bed. As hard as I plan to fuck you, little kitten, I think you would fall over if you were on your hands and knees."

"All-all right, Daddy," she whispered in a shaky voice. She gulped hard and eyed the bed.

"But first, I need to get my little kitty naked." He reached for the hem of her snug dress, which was still resting at her hips, and pulled it up over her head. She lifted her arms as he drew it off her body, leaving her standing in nothing but her kitten ears, tail, and heels.

His gaze dropped to her rounded breasts. He hadn't thought she was wearing a bra and seeing her gorgeous tits for the first time took his breath away.

He cupped her breasts and she gasped. Running his thumbs over her hardening nipples, he leaned in to run kisses up and down her neck, sometimes pausing to drag his teeth along her flesh, and other times pausing to lick her. Her responsiveness spurred his own passions to rise and he started urging her toward the bed.

"Bend over, little kitten, and spread your legs wide."

He watched as she obeyed, bending over the bed as she inched her feet apart, opening her thighs. Her tail hung between her legs, concealing her privates, but he loved knowing that if he moved her tail aside, he would see her pink, glistening folds. She looked so fucking sexy, bent over to his liking, while still wearing her heels.

"Good kitty," he said in a praising tone as he tossed her dress onto a chair. He trailed a hand over her bottom and gave each of her cheeks a firm squeeze. Then he backed up to undress. He shoved his shoes underneath the chair and placed his clothing atop her dress. His blood hummed with desire and his stiff cock jutted out as he returned to his kitten, hard and throbbing and ready to plunge inside her.

He swept her tail aside, revealing her swollen pink pussy. Her folds were gleaming just as brightly as he had expected, and he couldn't resist trailing his fingers through her gathering moisture. So warm, so slick. She trembled at his touch and arched her back, giving him better access to the part of her he would soon claim.

"Such a wet little kitty," he said. "And you're laying here so sweetly, so obediently, just waiting for your daddy to pound into you."

She whimpered and fisted the covers in her hands as he rubbed her moisture over her clit. He deliberately kept his ministrations slow and light. The next time she came, it would be when his cock was deep inside her.

With his free hand, he stroked her lower back and bottom, occasionally calling her a *sweet kitten* or his *good kitty*. He felt her melting under his praise, soft sighs of contentment leaving her along with faint *mmwowws* and other noises that sounded close to purrs. When desperate whimpers started escaping her, he removed his hand from her center and reached for a condom.

His dick throbbed unbearably, and his vision blurred as he tore the foil and rolled the latex onto his stiff length. Goddammit. He needed to be balls-deep inside her. Right fucking now.

"Daddy's going to pound into his little kitten's privates now, and you're going to be a good little submissive kitty and lay there and take it. Aren't you, Dolly?"

"Mm. Ye-yes, Daddy," she replied in a dreamy voice.

He settled himself between her spread thighs and grabbed her hips. Her tail rested over her right buttock, and the sight of the plug seated in her bottom made him delirious with the need to surge into her tightness. He released one of her hips in order to guide the head of his cock inside.

"Are you ready, little kitten?"

"Yes, Daddy."

He jerked his hips forward, driving his cock hard and deep, all the way to the hilt in one rapid thrust that left her moaning and writhing beneath him. Fuck, she was tight. If he didn't already know otherwise, he would've worried she was a virgin.

He paused for a moment, his fingers digging into her hips, as he allowed her to become accustomed to the sudden fullness of his cock.

A shuddering sigh left her when he withdrew partially from her center only to ram straight back into her, just as hard as the first time. Again and again, in and out, he fucked her with all the intensity of his passion that had been building since he'd first laid eyes upon her in the movie theater.

He heard a few gasps from the doorway, as well as murmurs from the window, though he didn't glance over to see how many spectators were gathered watching them. Instead, he focused solely on Dolly. On the sweet little kitten who needed her daddy's cock. Gripping her hips harder, he slammed into her over and over again.

Mine. My little kitten.

CHAPTER 8

RACHEL

*W*ith each drive into her aching pussy, Daddy Xavier's balls impacted heavily upon her clit. She gasped with each thrust and clutched at the covers, thankful he hadn't ordered her to get on her hands and knees. Hard as he was fucking her, she wouldn't have been able to maintain the position for long.

Bent over the bed and spread wide, she was completely at his mercy. From the corner of her eye, she noticed bodies in the doorway and window, but she didn't care how many people were watching. Despite knowing they had an audience, Daddy Xavier's complete focus on her made it seem like they were the only two people in the club.

With the plug filling her bottom, she felt the fullness of each plunge into her pussy. Pressure coiled low in her belly and her skin prickled with awareness. There were moments it seemed she was floating in a haze of hedonistic pleasure, lost in the rhythm of Daddy Xavier's hurried drives as waves of ecstasy soared toward her, as if in slow motion despite the rapidity of what was happening.

As her orgasm neared, she started clawing lightly at the covers in front of her, moaning as she kneaded the blankets quickly, like a kitten enjoying herself in play. He responded by growling and pulling

466

on her leash, just hard enough to remind her that she was still wearing it, that she was his kitten and he was her owner.

"You may come whenever you like, sweet kitty. Come while Daddy's filling you up with his cock."

His words propelled her into a shattering release. She gasped as her orgasm hit her, crashing over her in a violent wave of sensation. Panting for breath, she shuddered over and over, feeling the hugeness of his cock inside her while he continued ramming into her. Fucking her as if he were mad at her, as if he were punishing her. This thought made her insides clench with desire, heated pulses afflicting her already throbbing center. Dizziness assailed her.

He growled again and tensed behind her. Then she felt it—the intense pulsing of his huge cock as he came inside her. She almost mourned the fact that he was wearing a condom. How nice it would be to feel his seed spilling into her, filling her depths, then to stand up and feel the stickiness of his essence leaking down her inner thighs.

Maybe one day.

Her face heated at the thought and she chided herself for catching feelings. Fuck, what was wrong with her? What if this was only a one-time thing? She shouldn't allow herself to become so attached to Daddy Xavier. As much as she was starting to like him, she didn't know anything about him.

But just as she tried to erect a wall around her heart, he withdrew gently from her and kissed her on the cheek before moving away. A peek over her shoulder showed he was disposing of the condom in a trash can. Before she could draw in her next breath, he returned to her side, lifting her in his arms as if she weighed nothing. She marveled at his strength as he settled on the bed while holding her close, cradling her against his chest with his chin resting atop her head.

In this instant, all her intentions to push him away crumbled to the floor.

She found herself lacing her arms around his waist and hugging him tightly, soaking up the tenderness he was offering. Her pussy was sore, but she liked knowing it was his cock that had caused the hurt. For the next couple of days, every time she sat down or shifted in place, she would feel this delicious soreness, this reminder that Daddy Xavier had fucked her long and hard.

"Are you all right, little kitten?" he asked, his deep voice vibrating against her ear, causing her entire body to flush with tingling warmth.

Little kitten. She liked that he was still calling her that. It was a pet name no one had ever used on her before. A special name just for her and Daddy Xavier.

"Yes, Daddy, I'm good." She pulled back to stare up at him, needing to peer into his handsome gaze. Her stomach flipped at the affection she saw reflecting in his gorgeous blue eyes. God, if they hadn't just met, she would almost believe he cared about her.

He stroked her hair, petting her with long, firm caresses. She closed her eyes and leaned into his touch, reveling in the attention. A short while later, to her utter shock, she felt something hard beneath her bottom. She jerked her head back and peered straight into his eyes, only to find them darkened with lust. She couldn't believe his cock was getting hard again already. Talk about stamina. Daddy Xavier must eat his spinach.

"This time, I want you on your hands and knees, little kitten," he said, "but I promise to be gentle—mostly. Don't worry, I won't push you over."

Somehow, she found the strength to rise up onto her hands and knees upon the mattress, though her legs wobbled a bit at first.

She glimpsed his cock as he helped her into position, finally getting a good look at the appendage that had left her sore between her thighs. Indeed, it was as huge as she had suspected. She couldn't help but openly stare. Holy hell, Daddy Xavier wasn't just large, he was massive. Long and thick and perfectly formed, he could've been in porn.

"Naughty kitten," he said, settling behind her and giving her bottom a sharp slap. "Hasn't anyone told you it isn't polite to stare?"

"Sorry, Daddy," she said. What would it be like to suck on a cock so amazingly huge? Waves of heat seared her face and her pussy pulsed, knowing his hugeness would soon be back inside her.

She felt him playing with her tail, giving it slight tugs that reinvigorated the pressing fullness in her bottom hole. As she was reminded of this particular part of her body, her stomach did a major flip.

Oh God. What if they rolled *anal intercourse* for their next activity?

He would destroy her.

She gulped hard and sucked in a shaky breath, praying they rolled anything but *anal* when they returned to the movie theater. She doubted Madison would let her roll again even if she politely described the huge size of Daddy Xavier's cock. Rules were rules, after all, and she'd agreed to follow the rules of the game this evening.

She heard the tearing of foil and realized he must've grabbed another condom when she hadn't been looking. Eagerly, she leaned down, arching her back and jutting her bottom out, ready for the first plunge of his cock, even if she was already beyond sore. Despite the pain, she craved every fucking inch he would give her, hungered for it so intensely she would start begging if he made her wait much longer.

"You're so wet, little kitten," he said, dragging the tip of his cock through her folds. "Daddy likes it when his kitten's privates are swollen and wet and ready to be fucked. Daddy likes it when his kitten is in heat."

Jesus, the things he said. She'd never been that skilled at dirty talk herself, but Daddy Xavier seemed to have a fucking Ph.D. in it. She whimpered and lifted her hips higher, desperate for him to sink inside her. Luckily, he didn't make her wait long. In the next moment, he gripped her hips and slid into her, his movements as gentle as he'd promised.

He set a slow rhythm inside her at first, though his pace gradually built, until his balls were once again impacting upon her clit with each drive, the faint slaps just enough to bring her to the brink of another shattering release.

Just as her orgasm hit her, he tensed and growled and started fucking her faster. They came at the same time, and she reveled in the feel of her muscles contracting around his hugeness.

"Good kitty," he said, stroking her hair. He withdrew from her, disposed of the condom, and once more gathered her in his arms.

She liked it when Daddy Xavier held her.

CHAPTER 9

XAVIER

*X*avier watched as Dolly tossed the marble onto the spinning roulette wheel. When Madison called out, *"Oral sex!"* a few seconds later, he almost whooped in excitement.

He would fucking devour his little kitten's pussy.

After he got Dolly out of the movie theater, he escorted her back to the same room where he'd just fucked her. Though he'd come twice in a row, his cock was already rock hard again. It seemed when it came to his kitten, he couldn't get enough.

He guided her into the room, an arm around her waist even as he held the leash. A noticeable tremor raced through her when she glanced up at him, her cheeks flushed an adorable shade of pink.

She was once again wearing her tight black dress, though he hadn't allowed her to pull it all the way down, which left him with a tempting view of her pussy, as well as her tail. God, she made the perfect kitten. A little skittish, very sweet, and exceedingly responsive.

Her moans, whimpers, and kitten noises made all the blood in his body rush straight to his cock. He couldn't wait to hear her while she was in the throes of another release as he licked her pussy and sucked on her clit. Fuck, he couldn't wait to taste her, to make her writhe upon the bed as he forced yet another orgasm from her.

He removed the leash and set it aside, then helped her out of her dress. This time, he also ordered her to step out of her heels. Once she was naked to his liking, still wearing her tail, collar, and the kitten ears, he made quick work of removing his own shoes and clothing.

He gathered her close, basking in the feel of her bare skin against his. Everything about her was soft and sweet, and she seemed to melt into him as he embraced her. He put his lips to her ear, licking from the top all the way down her lobe, eliciting a deep shudder from her. Reaching between her thighs, he stroked through her vast wetness, dipping his fingers into her soaking core to spread the moisture all around her pussy. She arched into his touch with a needy whimper.

Withdrawing his hand, he brought his fingers to his lips and licked them as she watched. "Fucking delicious. Now, get on the bed, Dolly, and spread your legs wide. Daddy wants to feast upon his kitten's sweet little cunt."

"Yes, Daddy," she said, scrambling to obey. He watched as she settled upon the mattress, scooting back to make room for him as she parted her thighs wide, revealing her glistening, pink folds.

He joined her on the bed and advanced on her, forcing her legs further apart as he bent down to taste her. He licked up and down, delighting in her whimpers and moans, and tasted her with gentle licks over her engorged clit. He had never seen a woman with a clit so swollen and large before. His cock jerked at the sight of it, and he soon began circling the sensitive nubbin with his tongue as he gradually applied more pressure.

Taking his time, he continually brought her to the edge of a release, only to move away from her clit at the last moment, leaving her whining and clawing at the covers in frustration. After the sixth time he did this, she blew her breath out in exasperation and threw her hands up in a gesture of impatience. She shot him a frustrated look and opened her mouth to say something, but he was fast to interrupt.

"Naughty kitten," he said in a scolding tone. "That's not polite behavior and Daddy is going to have to punish you now."

Holding her down, he kept her legs spread as he smacked her wet pussy lips with the flat of his fingers.

"Oh!" She tried to lurch up, but he easily held her down. When she attempted to block the second slap with her hands, he *tsked* at her and shook his head back and forth.

"No," he said firmly. "Place your hands above your head and leave them there. If you try to shield your pussy again, I will ask a DM to bring restraints and I will tie you to the bed. If you force me to do that, little kitten, you'll receive extra smacks to your tender, pink folds."

Her eyes widened and she opened her mouth, looking as if she were about to argue, but she soon pressed her lips together and threw her hands above her head—a bit dramatically, though at least she obeyed.

"Good girl. You ought to know better than to display such disrespect while you're getting your pussy licked. You're supposed to be grateful for each swipe of my tongue upon your clit and your smooth folds, and you certainly don't get to control when you come, little kitten. If you take your punishment well, I'll allow you to have an orgasm—eventually."

A pained look crossed her face, though she didn't respond. Her chest rose and fell rapidly and tiny shudders wracked her curvy little body. She was so beautiful when she was frustrated and on edge. And fuck, her clit had grown even larger. Round and slightly distended, he couldn't wait to feel the pink nubbin pulsing against his tongue again. But first, he had to see to her punishment.

"Now, hold very still while Daddy spanks your privates."

He saw her visibly brace herself, and in the next moment he brought the flat of his fingers down upon her glistening folds, delivering a firm slap that caused her to gasp. He gave her five more smacks in quick succession before pausing to rub his fingers through her folds. Her moisture was growing. In fact, she was so wet, with arousal gleaming brightly from her inner thighs, that it almost looked as though she'd had an accident.

"Five more," he announced. "And then, my sweet pet, you're allowed to come whenever you like."

"Yes, Daddy." Again, she braced herself, closing her eyes and wincing as though he'd already resumed smacking her.

He centered the final five slaps on her clit, though he kept them light, and as soon as he finished delivering the last blow, he bent down to caress her punished parts with his tongue. After only three rapid swipes over her clit, she cried out and writhed beneath him, moaning as her mouth formed a perfect 'O' shape. As she came, her clit pulsed almost violently against his tongue as her entire body shuddered, and he didn't withdraw from her center until she'd finished convulsing and lay limp upon the bed.

"Good little kitten." He moved to a sitting position, though he remained between her spread legs, and reached down to cup her pussy. "This is mine," he said with a growl. "Do you understand?"

Her eyes went wide. "Yes, Daddy."

But it didn't feel like part of their scene. It felt real—his firm declaration that her pussy belonged to him, as well as her sweet agreement in the matter.

He squeezed harder, causing her to grimace. Fuck, what was wrong with him? He heard someone in the crowd gathered outside the bedroom comment that it was nearly eleven o'clock, and suddenly, he saw red.

No. The evening couldn't be ending already.

He needed her. He wanted her.

Holding her gaze, he said, "I'm serious, little kitten. This is mine." He squeezed her pussy again. "*You* are mine."

"Wha-what do you mean?" Her eyes became large, round pools of blue.

"I mean I want you to come home with me tonight." He couldn't believe what he was saying. He had never been one to rush into a relationship, but fuck if he would allow her to go home alone tonight. She belonged in his arms and in his bed. And not just as his latest quick fix. He had planned to start dating again after Valentine's Day, but fuck his dating profile idea. The perfect submissive was right in front of him, and he would be damned if he let her go.

"I-I don't even know you," she said, a troubled look crossing her face. "We just met and... I don't know your real name and you don't know mine. I-I don't know where you live or what you do for a living.

I don't know where you were born and raised or what your favorite color is. And I don't know—"

"My name is Xavier Ross, little kitten. I live about an hour away from here in the Santa Monica Mountains, at the Ross Wellness Retreat, which I own." What else had she wanted to know? Ah, yes... "I was born and raised in Florida and my favorite color used to be green, but now it's blue, the same blue as your eyes."

~

Rachel

WHAT THE HELL WAS HAPPENING?

Daddy Xavier aka Xavier Ross, who apparently owned the renowned ultra-posh Ross Wellness Retreat, wanted her to go home with him? She could scarcely believe his words, yet his dark eyes gleamed with sincerity. Warmth filled her to bursting and hope flared in her chest.

This was what she had wanted, wasn't it?

She took a deep breath to steady her nerves and met his gaze, summoning all her bravery. Accepting his offer would be taking a huge risk. And yet, she couldn't fathom going home tonight to her empty guesthouse on Kimmie Walters' Hollywood estate. She couldn't imagine sleeping alone.

"Yes, Daddy," she forced out before she lost her nerve. "Yes, I-I'll go home with you tonight."

An immense look of pleasure crossed his face. He drew her closer and wrapped his arms around her, holding her tight as he stroked her hair.

"I'm Rachel, by the way," she said in a low voice so only he could hear. "Rachel Murray."

"I'm pleased to meet you, Rachel," he replied in a whisper, pulling back to stare into her eyes.

"Likewise," she said, feeling her face heat.

Her heart raced and she became jittery with excitement. Daddy

Xavier wanted to take her home tonight. Could they possibly have a future together? Hope brimmed inside her at the prospect.

He cupped her face and pressed a soft kiss to her lips. When he pulled back, his gaze was heated with desire. His hard cock pressed against her bottom and she heard a spectator comment that Roulette was ending in just ten minutes.

To her surprise, Daddy Xavier kissed her forehead quickly and got off the bed. He stuck his head out the door and motioned for a DM to approach. She couldn't quite hear what he said to the burly man, but Daddy Xavier waited in the doorway, unashamedly buck naked with his hardened cock jutting out like the weapon it was, until the DM returned holding something round and shiny. Daddy Xavier accepted the item and turned to face Rachel.

Confusion spread through her when she realized he was holding a silver bowl.

"Get on the floor," he commanded, a dark gleam in his eyes. "On your knees."

She obeyed, crawling off the bed and sinking to the floor. He approached her and sat the bowl on the bed. Though she was curious about its purpose, she couldn't bring herself to ask. All she could think about was the fact that his massively huge cock rested but an inch or two from her mouth.

A whimper of relief left her when he guided her head forward and pressed his length to her lips.

"Open up and let Daddy in, little kitten."

She parted her lips and accepted him into her mouth. *Yes.* She loved the musky, maleness of him and took him deeper.

"Brace yourself," he said. "Daddy is about to be very, very rough with you, little kitten."

With a growl, he grasped her head in his hands and held her in place while he thrust in and out of her mouth, ramming the tip of his cock into the back of her throat. She struggled to breathe through her nose as he slammed into her again and again, fucking her mouth almost as hard as he'd pounded into her pussy earlier in the night.

Tears streamed down her face as he continued pummeling into her mouth, but just as she started to feel lightheaded, he abruptly withdrew. She watched, in utter surprise, as he gripped his cock and turned just in time to erupt into the bowl.

Before she could find her voice to ask what he was doing, he placed the bowl, filled with his essence, on the floor in front of her. His eyes were dark and intense as he rose to his feet and loomed over her.

"Be a good kitten and lap it all up."

Shock resounded within her. She stared at the bowl as her insides heated and everything between her thighs pulsed with an intensity that left her dizzy. Breathing deep, she placed her hands on the floor and slowly leaned down to the bowl.

"Go ahead," he said in a coaxing tone. "Show me how a good little kitten drinks her daddy's cum."

The desire to please him hummed through her. She had never lapped water or milk or anything out of a bowl before, though she had watched other submissives do it. Except this wasn't water or milk and she ought to be somewhat repulsed by his brazen command. And yet... she craved this taboo act and found herself hungering for the entire contents of the bowl.

"That's it," he said after she lapped up a small amount of his essence. "Be a good little kitten and lap it all up. Every last drop."

She continued licking his salty essence from the bowl, only pausing when she needed to swallow. By the time she had the bowl licked clean, per Daddy Xavier's orders, her clit was throbbing so hard it was all she could do to keep from reaching between her thighs and stroking herself.

"Good kitty." He placed a hand upon her head and began petting her.

She *mmwowwed* and leaned into his caresses, soaking up the attention as she became vaguely aware of someone announcing the end of the game.

It was eleven o'clock and she'd made it through the entire three hours of Roulette with Daddy Xavier. A deep sense of accomplishment filled her, but most of all, she was beaming with the knowledge that Daddy Xavier didn't want their time together to end just yet.

He helped her to her feet and sat on the bed, drawing her down to sit upon his sturdy, muscular thighs. All the while, he kept running his hands through her hair and down her back. "You'll keep the tail in until we reach my house, little kitten."

"Yes, Daddy."

He pressed his lips to hers and she melted.

THE END

ABOUT THE AUTHOR

USA TODAY bestselling author Sue Lyndon writes steamy D/s romance in a variety of genres, from contemporary to historical to fantasy. She's a #1 Amazon bestseller in multiple categories, including BDSM Erotica and Sci-Fi Erotica. She also writes non-bdsm sci-fi romance under the name Sue Mercury. When she's not busy working on her next book, you'll find her hanging out with her family, watching sci-fi movies, reading, or sneaking chocolate.

- Website: www.suelyndon.com
- Facebook: https://www.facebook.com/AuthorSueLyndon/
- Twitter: https://twitter.com/SueLyndon

UNEXPECTED

A Black Light: Roulette War Novella

By

Measha Stone

CHAPTER 1

JACK

*J*ack Wyatt grabbed a stool at the bar and sat down, startling the woman next to him. Her shoulders tensed, and she craned her neck to give him a good glare before turning back around, giving him the full of her back. He rolled his eyes, gave a shake of his head, and motioned for the bartender.

"Rum and Coke," he ordered and pulled out his wallet. Tossing a few bills on the bar top, enough to cover the drink and the tip, he waited for his drink. The day had been long, but it was finally over. One more day down, another case finished, and it was time to let the evening's events wash away the tension in his body.

His drink appeared before him, and already his muscles were beginning to ease.

"You playing tonight?" the bartender, a cute brunette in a black leather halter top, asked him.

He picked up the drink. "In the Roulette? Yeah, I'm playing tonight." He sipped the drink. Normally, he'd rather go for something with a little more spine to it than a mixed drink, but he didn't know who his partner would be for the evening. Going into the night with a crystal-clear head was warranted.

"You can put this on your monthly statement, you know," she reminded him waving the bills at him.

"I like paying as I go," he explained. The monthly membership fee was heavy enough without adding drinks to it. Using cash throughout the month kept his budget tidy.

"Okay then. And don't forget, two drinks max." She wiggled two fingers at him.

"I'm aware." He pushed the cash toward her. "I'm only having the one." Not that a second wouldn't be welcomed after dealing with Mrs. Towers that afternoon.

After leaving the ranks at the FBI, he'd gotten his private investigator credentials and embarked on helping those the law couldn't. Unfortunately, lately that meant helping spouses prove infidelity to override their ironclad prenups. Mrs. Towers already knew her husband was a cheating bastard but seeing the photographic evidence of his betrayal had thrown her into a spiral of anger that ended in a fit. He kept her in his office until he was sure she wasn't going anywhere but her attorney's office after leaving him. And he'd relieved her of her handgun as well.

No matter how long he lived in L.A., he still found himself surprised at the characters he came across daily.

Jack spun around on the stool, leaned his back against the bar, and watched the crowd. He had applied for his membership to Black Light as soon as their doors opened. The privacy of the club drew him in. Being able to shed his investigator hat at the door and not worry about who would see him and whom he would see relieved him. He could play to his heart's desire with no strings attached or morning-after regrets.

Best money ever spent.

Even if it meant he had to deal with the Mrs. Towers of the city in order to pay the monthly membership. But tonight gave him the chance to win one free month. He could get his fun on and eliminate the hefty bill for an entire month, so long as his partner didn't safe word out before the end of the night.

Glancing to his left, he noticed the woman's hand shake slightly when she picked up her glass of wine.

"I didn't mean to scare you." He leaned closer so she could hear him over the chatter of the other guests.

Again, she tensed.

Turning on his stool to face her, he tried again. "Sorry. I did it again, huh?" He tried to laugh it off, but her fiery eyes met his, shutting down his attempt.

"You didn't," she said after a long pause. "I just didn't expect anyone to sit down. I was... thinking." She took another sip of white wine.

He gave an exaggerated nod, not one to admit to being startled. Okay, he wasn't going to dig into it. It was his night off.

"Are you playing tonight?" he asked. They weren't going to start the festivities for another twenty minutes, and she didn't seem to have anyone with her.

She finished her wine before answering. "Yes." She slid her glass forward and waved for the bartender.

"This is your second."

"I know," the woman snapped. "I mean—thanks." Once the bartender walked away with the glass, she curled her lips into her mouth and heaved a heavy sigh. Regret for being a bitch toward the bartender?

"I know it sounds cheesy, but I haven't seen you around here before. Been a member long?" he tried again. The woman was obviously nervous. Maybe he could calm her down before an unlucky Dominant got ahold of her and they both had a miserable time.

She cast him a side glance before settling her gaze on her folded hands on top of the bar. "No. Just signed up right before they started taking applications for Roulette."

"So, you haven't been here before?" he asked, leaning forward.

"I was here once before." She turned a hard stare at him. "But it wasn't for long. Just to get the lay of the land."

Her wine appeared and, before she could reach for her bag, Jack had his wallet out.

"Wine's included in the event tonight," the bartender waved away his attempt to pay.

"I didn't need you to do that." Another quick shot with a sour tone, only to be counteracted when her shoulders slumped.

"Didn't think you did." He tucked his wallet back into his jeans.

Her jaw tensed. If he plucked her the wrong way, she'd break—she was wound so damn tight.

"Thank you, though," she added in a rush, as though her manners just caught up with her from outside.

"So, what do you think about the event tonight?"

She shrugged. "It's just a night for some fun. Whatever happens happens." Exhaustion underplayed her tone. Maybe this was more than nerves for the night. Maybe she was looking for the same relief he was and just wanted to get the party started.

"One month free membership for each person is a pretty good incentive, though, right?"

"Yeah. I suppose." She brought her wine to her full lips and drank down half before putting it back on the bar. "It would be nice to have at least one month free," she said with a small smile starting to form.

"Even better if your scene wins then you'd have two months free," Jack pointed out.

"Yeah, but I'm not counting on it. Having some fun is enough, why push my luck." Her smile faltered, and her lips pinched together. Resealing the vault, he supposed. Her gaze lowered and she gripped the stem of her wine glass harder.

"Still, it'd be sweet," he said, hoping she'd relax more. Tension rolled off of her, more than a single glass of wine would fix. This girl was stressed.

"Hey! Jack!" Brody wiggled out of the crowd and waved. "I forgot you said you'd be here tonight." Brody smacked his heavy hand on Jack's shoulder.

"Hi, man." Jack shook his hand. "Are you a spectator tonight?"

"Yes. I. Am." Brody grinned, showing off newly whitened teeth. His gaze swept over to the woman Jack had been talking with. "But my play card is wide open for tomorrow. Who's this lovely lady?" He raised an eyebrow.

Jack's stomach tensed. Having Brody's attention on her felt wrong. Not that Jack knew anything about her—not even her name—but she wouldn't fit into Brody's love'em and leave'em lifestyle. Where Jack was upfront about sceneing at the clubs and not taking any of it home with him, Brody used a much more hidden approach. He didn't want just one night—he wanted as many as he could get while he was interested then dropped them when it became boring. Which typically happened a few weeks in.

"This is..." Jack looked over at her, giving her a chance to fill in her name.

"Here, you can have my seat. I'm going to get closer to the stage anyway." She hopped off the barstool, giving Jack a full view of her. Sitting had hidden all of her curves. Dressed all in black, she almost blended into the room. Her blouse was buttoned up to her throat, but it didn't do a good enough job of hiding her breasts. And her pants hugged her hips, giving him a damn good idea how curvy she was beneath.

He dropped his hands to his lap. It may be dark in the room, but with the neon lighting, she might be able to make out his cock stiffening.

"Okay, well. Have fun." Brody waved her off, making a sarcastic face.

"Maybe I'll see you later," Jack said, but she'd already spun around and hurried into the crowd.

"Wasn't she sweet?" Brody hopped on the empty stool and called out for a beer.

Jack lost her and turned back to the bar, still nursing his rum and Coke.

"She's just nervous, I think."

"Pfft. Or she's just a raging bitch." Brody tossed his membership card on the bar and swiped up the bottle of beer the bartender brought him.

Jack gave him a hard glare. "I don't think so."

Brody raised a shoulder. "Doesn't matter. There's plenty of ass here tonight."

Jack raised his brow. "Yeah, I can see that."

Brody took a long pull of his beer, obviously oblivious to Jack's meaning.

"Looks like they're getting ready to start." Brody nudged his chin toward the main stage. "Fuck, is she one of the subs spinning tonight?"

Brody's voice dripped with hunger at the sight of Madison in her leather outfit.

"She's the MC." Jack put his drink on the bar and stood from the stool. Madison may be rocking the dominatrix look, but his gaze traveled over the crowd for someone else entirely.

"Still. Sign. Me. Up." Brody licked his lips.

"Dude." Jack smacked his shoulder. "Try to keep yourself in control."

Brody shrugged. "I'll do my best. Hey, where you going?"

"Getting ready to spin," Jack said. "See you later."

CHAPTER 2

QUINN

*Q*uinn tugged at the hem of her blouse while sliding farther off to the side of the crowd waiting for the next Dominant to be called on stage. She shouldn't have had the second wine. Or maybe she should have had a few before she'd embarked on her crazy idea of joining Black Light's Valentine Roulette.

It had made a lot more sense when she'd filled out the application than it did standing among the rich and famous waiting to see who spun her name. Having made the full move from Chicago to L.A. only a few weeks before didn't give her much time to get to know anyone. Not that she would have even if she'd been in town for months.

She did alone pretty damn well, and there was no reason to mess with what worked.

Buried in work and planning for the opening of her new office in L.A., she hadn't found a moment of relaxation. Finding Black Light had been a message from the gods. In Chicago, she had a small circle of Dominants who were more than happy to straighten her ass out when she found herself wound too tight. All of them good friends, and none of them looking for more than a good time. Now that she'd found Black Light, she hoped to find a similar setup—but for the immediate future, Roulette would have to do.

"Tanner47 you're up!" the woman in the delicious catsuit called.

Quinn's stomach lurched. Another Dominant, another spin, another chance to be called.

This was what she wanted, right? A scratch for her itch. But it had been so long since she had to put the effort into meeting someone new, she wasn't sure she was up for it. Hell, she'd had a three-second interaction with a devastatingly hot guy at the bar and fucked it up royally. No matter how much she tried to temper her bitchiness, when she was stressed or nervous it just flowed from every pore of her body. He probably thought her repulsive after the way she'd acted. Why couldn't she keep her tongue still and just stay quiet? It would be less abrasive than how she'd behaved.

Her breath lodged in her throat the moment her eyes landed on the Dominant stepping onto the stage. The man from the bar.

Another twist of her stomach.

"Well, let's get right to it. Spin the wheel and drop the ball for your play partner for the night." Madison handed him the little white ball as the wheel spun.

"Fuck, I hope I get him." A whisper came from behind her. Quinn stiffened.

"Quinn!" Madison called out.

The room froze.

Tanner47 looked up from the wheel and scanned the crowd. Quinn took a shaky step forward, raising her gaze from the wheel to the man staring straight at her.

Was he disappointed?

He couldn't ask for another spin, could he?

Several steps later, she made her way up to the stage.

"Quinn." His lips spread wide into a grin, showcasing a deep dimple on his left cheek.

"Uh. Hi." She refocused her attention to Madison and took the ball she was handed.

"Just drop the ball once the wheel is spinning, and we'll find out your kink for at least the first thirty minutes," Madison explained again.

The wheel spun before Quinn could get a good look at the kinks listed. There probably wasn't any way to swing the results her way, but she wanted to try. Impact play would be amazing. Now she would just have to trust her luck.

Not that it had ever done her any favors in the past.

She dropped the ball where Madison pointed and bit down on her lower lip as the wheel continued to spin around, around, around. The little ball started dancing as it slowed.

Clank.

Clank.

The kinks came into view.

Impact.

Fisting.

Vaginal Sex.

Clank.

She didn't take her eye off the ball as it bounced.

Edging.

Clank.

Slower and slower.

Knife play.

Clank.

And then it stopped.

Quinn's jaw fell open. All her blood rushed to her face.

"Diaper play!" Madison called out with entirely too much energy. Quinn raised her gaze to the woman, a searing comment burning her tongue.

"Is that on your hard list?" Tanner47 stepped up to her before her mouth could form the words.

She closed her eyes.

"No." She had seen it on the form and figured the chances were so slim of getting it, she used her hard limits for other activities.

"Mine either," he chuckled.

"Great. Looks like you're set then!" Madison smiled. If the woman bounced up and down, Quinn would lose her resolve to keep her bitchy self in check.

"Come on, let's get away from the stage so we can talk before we start." Tanner47 wrapped his hand around her wrist and pulled her away from the wheels.

Diaper play.

How the fuck do you even play with a diaper?

Quinn pulled back on him once they were a safe distance from the crowd and could hear each other easily.

"Tanner—"

"Jack." He cut her off. "My name is Jack."

"Oh." She wrinkled her brow. "Sorry. I assumed from your handle."

"Yeah." He rubbed the back of his neck. "I hate picking those things. I figured… ass tanner… Tanner…" His smile faded on the edges. "Cheesy as hell, right?"

"A little." She nodded. Small talk hurt. It was awkward and clunky, and she almost always stuck her foot so far into her mouth she would trigger her own gag reflex.

He laughed.

"So, from your reaction, I'm guessing diaper play isn't your thing." He motioned toward a high table for them to move to. Having something between them would make the negotiation part of this easier, even if it was just a small table.

"No. Not really." She admitted. They wouldn't be able to stray from what they spun, but maybe she could still get what she wanted. "But I guess we can make it work."

His head tilted to the side. "How so?"

"I mean, we probably just need to start with that, right? I mean put the damn thing on, then take it off for the real fun." Like a hard ass beating. Maybe then her nerves would settle enough she could carry on a conversation without wanting to bolt from the room.

"And what do you think the real fun is?" His chin lowered and his eyes narrowed—all signs she should tread lightly. But the nerves dancing in her stomach blocked her filter.

"You know, like flogging, paddling, spanking, whippings. Stuff like that. Fun." She smiled.

"Impact play." He nodded. "Have you ever scened with anything else?"

There hadn't been a need. She wanted a beating, she called up one of her Doms, and they delivered it. What would be the purpose of playing with anything else?

"Not really, no."

"And by not really you mean…" He rolled his hand.

"No," she snapped. "I guess not." Dammit, there was the bitch again. Couldn't she just bunk down for one night and let Quinn make somewhat of a decent first impression?

He dragged in a loud breath through his nose and gave a slow nod. "So, you're a pain slut?"

She shoved her hands into her pockets. "Something wrong with that?" She curled her toes tight until they hurt in her shoes. He could still walk away from her; he could demand another roll. She had to find a way to relax.

His left eyebrow arched to a point. "Didn't say there was. It was just a question."

"Okay, then." She nodded. Decision made. They'd start with the damn diaper but then move on to the impact stuff. Good.

"You like the pain because it relaxes you?" he asked.

She sighed. Good. He understood. "Yeah. It's better than any hot bath I've ever taken."

He nodded some more, glancing toward the stage. "They're on the last couple."

"Do you have a play bag you need to get?" she asked.

"Not yet." He slid around the table, closer to her. "You don't think any other type of play or submission can give you the same relaxing effect?"

Ugh! Were they still on this?

"We can do the diaper thing because we rolled it. That's fine." She tried to force some lightness into her tone, but she feared it came out just as snappish as before. "I mean, yeah. The diaper thing is fine." Was that the same or worse?

"Hmmm." Again, with the nodding.

"What?" she snapped when he didn't say anything else.

"Nothing." He shrugged. "But, before we start, you understand you're the sub here? You get that I'm the one calling the shots and, unless you call the safe word, you're mine for the next three hours?" He slid his hand up her arm to her throat then snaked it behind her head until he had a firm grip on her hair.

Pain shot down her neck, kicking every nerve ending in her body awake until it jolted her clit. Every muscle softened with a simple tug of her hair.

"I get that," she whispered, searching his eyes.

He moved closer to her, leaning forward so she couldn't see anything other than his face.

"I think you're someone who deflects emotions with bratty behavior and snarky comments. Someone who's shy and looks intimidating, but once those barriers are taken down, you're something entirely different."

She swallowed around the lump forming in her throat. They'd only had one brief conversation where she'd been damn close to rude to him. How could he know anything for certain at this point?

"I didn't mean to sound rude," she said, and she meant it. People threw her into the bitch category before getting to know her. She wouldn't blame any of them. First impressions weren't her strong suit.

His lips cracked into a smile, not a pleased and handsome one, but rather a grin that soaked her panties—a knowing grin filled with dark and sinister promises.

"I know you didn't." His fingers tightened, sending another jolt of fire through her scalp. "And I know you weren't trying to manipulate me into letting you top from the bottom."

She opened her mouth to agree with him, but the arching of his brow stilled her tongue. That was exactly what she'd been doing.

"I don't think we're supposed to start yet," she said instead.

His smile didn't fade as his other hand caressed her jaw.

"I can tell our couples are ready to get started, so everyone have fun and play safe!" Madison's voice boomed over the crowd.

"Now we are." He released her hair. "Let's go."

CHAPTER 3

JACK

*J*ack held fast to Quinn's hand as he led her to the costume room. He'd never played the Daddy Dom before, but after their short conversation he knew exactly what she needed. It wasn't the little girl she needed to find in herself to get that relaxation she wanted; it was getting out of her own head. And that he could work with. The diaper was just a prop.

"They might not have the right size," she said as they made their way down the darkened hallway to the costumes room.

Jack stopped and spun around to her. "What does that mean?" She had curves, maybe more than some men would like, but there wasn't an ounce of her that didn't speak straight to his cock. When he got her out of her blouse and pants, he'd get the real picture, and he couldn't wait for it.

"It means I'm not average size, and they might not have one that will work," she said straight to his face, not backing down in her attitude an inch. Her nerves must be riled pretty hard. The moment the words left her mouth, regret flashed in her eyes. How many people saw her kneejerk speech and assumed she was—like Brody did— a raging bitch? At first glance, he might have agreed, but there was something softer beneath her exterior. The attitude—that needed to be dealt with soon if he was going to have any fun with her— felt like more of a defense measure than the truth of her personality.

"We'll make it work."

"Or, we could just roll something else… you know… if they can't fit me," she tried with a lopsided grin. Again, working her way toward a spanking instead of what they'd rolled. She had no idea how much he wanted to oblige her—give her the hardest belting he'd given in ages, not only because he thought she could handle it, but because she really deserved it.

"Like I said, we'll make it work." He tugged her along to the room.

"How can I help you?" Annie, the assistant in costumes, asked him. He'd worked with her before, putting together costumes for some of the subs he'd played with. She'd never steered him wrong.

"Yeah. We're looking for diapers," he said, not bothering to lower his voice. If anyone heard him, it would only aid in his objective and, glancing over at Quinn, he could see he was on target. A sweet blush covered her cheeks, and her gaze lowered to the floor.

Annie grinned. "For you or her?"

"Oh God," Quinn mumbled behind him. He squeezed her hand.

"For her, please. And we should probably take a pacifier if you have it… oh, and a rattle."

"Fuck me," Quinn groaned quietly.

"We have a whole kit put together for tonight. Let me grab it." She leaned to the side to get another look at Quinn before walking off.

"We don't need a pacifier," Quinn said as soon as Annie walked away.

"I disagree." He lifted a shoulder. "You have trouble keeping your words in your mouth when they should stay there."

She bit down on the bottom corner of her lower lip. "I'm not using a pacifier." She raised her chin an inch and pulled her hand out of Jack's to fist on her hip.

He gave her an exaggerated appraisal and smiled. "I see."

"I don't think you do."

"Oh, I see perfectly fine, Quinn. If you weren't going to play by the rules, why bother signing up tonight?"

496

She dropped her hand from her hip. "It's not that I don't want to play by the rules."

"It's that you really want that ass whipping so you can get the relief you're looking for. Because you've never experienced anything other than impact play." He crossed his arms over his chest and fixed his gaze on her.

"Would I prefer impact play to diaper play? Yes, but I'm not trying to manipulate you into spanking me," she defended. "I mean—I don't mean to be doing that."

He believed her.

"I'm also guessing you've never actually submitted to a Dominant before. You had a few on speed dial, spanker friends who would scratch your itch when you called, but nothing outside of that."

If she'd only ever played with one form of submission, how could she know the relief that could come from all the other forms? There were more outlets for her stress than she knew, but he needed to get her mind set right before he could teach her.

She blinked several times before a forced laugh erupted. "No!"

He touched the tip of his nose. "I think you're being less honest with me than you should be considering I'm the one who decides if you'll get out of the diaper before or after you've used it."

All color dripped from her face. Her jaw slacked. If her eyes could leap out of her head, he had no doubt they'd be lying on the floor at his feet.

"I... I'm not... no way—"

He leaned toward her. "Then I really suggest you behave yourself." No matter how hard she pushed, he would not give in and give her the spanking she obviously craved. She'd drink as much water as needed to fill her bladder, and he'd bind her to a chair until she filled the diaper before he gave her one slap on her asscheek, if her attitude didn't start to change.

"Okay, here you are. There's a few diapers in here, a bib, a bottle, a pacifier, a rattle, and a blankie." Annie held the bag of items out for Jack.

He moved back a step, keeping his eyes on Quinn. "I need water for the bottle."

Quinn's lips pinched into a thin line, but she kept quiet.

"Sure thing. Want me to fill it up?"

"That would be great." Jack took the bag from her once she removed the bottle.

"You can't be serious," Quinn hissed once she was gone again.

"Oh, baby girl, you have no idea how serious I can get. Now, I don't know about you, but I wouldn't mind a free month, so I'd rather you not cry off. But if you don't think you can handle this… that's the only way out."

Her nostrils flared with her huff.

"Whatever." She rolled her eyes.

He laughed. "I think maybe the prospect of having all these little decisions taken away from you is appealing."

"I think you've known me for all of five minutes and are making a whole lot of assumptions," she snapped.

Jack opened the bag and fished out the pacifier. "I can see we'll be starting with this." He plunged it between her lips and held it in place. "Spit this out and you'll be sorry. I don't spank bad girls." In actuality, he did, but she wouldn't respond appropriately to a punishment spanking yet.

Her resistance to the object ceased.

"Good girl. Now keep it in, suck nice and hard on it—practice for when I replace it with my cock." He winked and released his hold on the pacifier. The little pink blush blossomed crimson, but her pupils expanded right before his eyes.

Ah, his little pain slut had a lot to learn. And he had the next thirty minutes to start her first lesson.

CHAPTER 4

QUINN

*Q*uinn stared at the pink blanket dangling from Jack's hand. She would argue with him further, except the pacifier was still lodged in her mouth. The walk from the costume room back to the main play area had lit a fire under every butterfly in her stomach. They were banging off the walls of inside her. She didn't bother trying to make eye contact with anyone as he marched her back into the main room.

She chewed on the pacifier bit as he laid out the blanket on the bench, smoothing out the wrinkles.

"Okay, up you go." He turned to her.

Dragging her gaze up from the blanket, she stared at him. How could she do that? Get up there and let him put a diaper on her? As much as she disliked the pacifier, at least it kept her from saying something so obnoxious he quit on her.

She blinked hard a few times, unable to get her body to move. She was frozen in place.

"Baby girl, you need to start obeying, or this isn't going to be as much fun for you as it will be for me." He laid the blanket back on the leather padded table.

It would have been easier to fly Brian or Ben out every other weekend to have some fun than to go through all of this. Why did she think she could actually go to a new club and play with someone new? She'd been so buried in work, pushing her company to new levels of success for so long, meeting anyone outside of a professional capacity no longer felt natural.

Jack seemed nice. He hadn't brushed her off yet, but the limit was coming. He'd realize what a socially awkward mess she was and hit the road. This was a bad idea. A horrible idea.

Once he had the blanket adjusted to his liking, he approached her.

"Just breathe, baby," he ordered in a soft tone, collecting her hands in his. She stared into his dark eyes. "Breathe with me," he said and inhaled deeply. "Let me help you, Quinn."

She could really mess up this scene if she let her panic take over completely. Every Dom she'd every scened with had played so nicely in the impact zone, no one tried to push her outside those boundaries. What if none of this worked out right? What if her nerves were more rattled, her anxiety soared too high for her to get what she loved so much out of these play scenes? If he didn't spank her, could she find the relief she wanted?

Jack seemed to understand how quickly her mind was reeling away from her.

"Breathe with me," he said again, putting her hand flat against his chest so she could feel him inhale. How the hell was she supposed to concentrate on his breathing when she could feel his hard pecs. "Do it, Quinn." He pressed his hand against her chest.

With her eyes locked on his, she dragged in a slow breath, letting her chest expand at the same rate his did until he instructed her to exhale. In and out, he conducted her breathing pattern until the butterflies were dancing gently instead of having a gangbang in her stomach.

"There. Better?" he asked.

She nodded. Much better, actually, but she couldn't articulate very well with the damn pacifier in place.

"Now, let's get you out of these clothes." He worked the buttons on her blouse while she continued to stare at his face. After he finished unbuttoning the blouse, his gaze lifted to hers, and the edges of his lips pulled up gently. He slid his hands inside the shirt and she felt their warmth as he caressed her stomach. "No, don't stiffen up on me now." He lowered his chin, kicking up the look of dominance in his expression.

His thumbs flicked the underside of her breasts. Even through the satin fabric of her bra his touch sent a current through her body.

Moving farther up, he rested his hands on her shoulders then shoved the blouse down her arms. He tossed it onto a nearby chair.

"Pants next, baby girl," he said and squatted down in front of her. Heat pumped through her veins with each heartbeat.

He opened the button on her pants then pulled the zipper down, casting a smile up at her briefly. She tried to step back, but he had a firm grip on her pants and shook his head. She bit down on the plastic of the pacifier. No one had undressed her before.

It had always been more efficient for her to strip and get ready for her Dominant. Letting him remove her clothes—that would have been intimate. Too intimate for a spank and run.

Her pants were pulled down to her ankles.

"Lift your leg, baby girl," he instructed, and she complied. He slipped her shoe off then pulled the pant leg free. He repeated the actions with her other leg, leaving her standing in her bra and panties and the fucking pacifier.

He grabbed hold of the waistline of her panties—a comfortable cotton brief—and yanked them down to her ankles without cere-mony. Instinctively, she sucked in her belly.

"Don't do that," he said without looking up at her. He folded her panties and tossed them onto the pile of clothes on the chair before standing up again, bringing his blazing gaze to hers. "Your bra." He twirled his finger in the air, telling her to turn around.

She tried to reach behind herself to undo the hooks, but he grabbed her hands and slapped them both hard.

"Turn around," he ordered. She shook her hands once he let her go. The fire was supposed to be on her ass, not her knuckles!

She spun around so fast she stumbled, and he had to catch her before she fell onto the table.

"See what your attitude gets you?" he whispered into her ear from behind her. "I'm going to give you what you need, Quinn. But you have to open your mind to it for me. You can't resist, or it's useless."

A shiver ran down her spine at his words. Did he know what he was asking her for? *Trust.* He wanted her to trust a perfect stranger to give her what she needed in a way completely foreign to her.

Without peeling his body away from her, he worked the hooks open and dragged the straps down her arms. Her heavy breasts fell free from the cups. She lifted her arms, folding them beneath her tits. She wasn't overly obsessed with her body—it was what it was at this point—but she didn't like her boobs hanging so fucking low.

"Nope." He tossed her bra then pulled her arms down to her sides. He wrapped his arms around her, playing with her nipples while his warm breath washed over the shell of her ear.

"You're not playing fair," she said around the pacifier. Garbled, but clear enough he probably understood.

"Oh, a nipple girl?" He chuckled and twisted each nipple hard, pulling downward.

She gasped at the jolt of pain, then everything went black. The room fell into complete darkness and abrupt silence when the thumping music stopped on a dime.

"What the fuck?" he muttered and released her nipples, pulling back from her but still holding her arms.

People all over the dungeon started asking what was happening. Emergency lights flickered to life.

"Don't move. Just stay here," he said, holding her firmly. Where was she going to go? Run off into the dark naked?

She moved the pacifier to the side of her mouth so she could speak a bit more clearly. "I'm not scared of the dark."

"That's because I'd slay the monsters for you," he said.

She laughed. "You really like to lay on the cheesy stuff, don't you?"

He squeezed her arms. "Just keep that pacifier in place until it's time for your bottle."

The lights flickered back to life, settling down the crowd. She squirmed her way free to face him. He couldn't be serious.

But he was.

His eyes were fixed on her, his jaw set firm. No, he didn't look like someone she could easily persuade to change his mind.

Not that she wouldn't try.

"Now. Up on the table." He slammed his hand on the leather.

Time to either submit to the game, to him, or safe word. She'd not only be giving up her free month but would be costing him one as well. A dungeon monitor walking the room paused near them. He was watching. Because she hesitated? Because if they didn't get started, they could be disqualified? Her skin felt too tight for her body; her heart didn't seem too worried about staying inside her chest either.

"You need to breathe, Quinn," Jack stated. "You keep holding your breath. Just let out the air and get on the table."

She released her breath. When had she started doing that? Had she always?

"I don't think I can actually use it," she whispered around the pacifier. No need for the DM to overhear everything.

"Then being a good girl is the best way to avoid having to." Jack patted the table again. He wasn't backing down, and she couldn't tell if he was just trying to push her buttons or if he meant it. Would he actually make her use the diaper, or was he just dangling the threat?

She pressed her ass to the edge of the table and pushed herself on top of the soft fabric of the blanket. He hadn't even touched her yet, but she could feel the blush all over her body.

Jack noticed the DM lingering nearby and called him over. "Sorry, man. I forgot to grab my play bag before we got started. Mind grabbing it for me or watching my girl here?" He pressed a hand to her shoulder, forcing her to lie on her back. "I don't want my baby to roll off the table."

Her face ignited. Actual flames could probably be seen, but she wasn't going to open her eyes to find out.

"I'll grab it. Where is it?" the deep voice responded. She clenched her fists at her sides while she forced her mind to block out their conversation.

"We need to wait for him before I can put the diaper on, but you should have your bottle while we wait. Sit up a little," he directed. Once she pushed herself to a sitting position again, he hopped up behind her, wrapping his legs around her waist. He pulled her closer to him and yanked the pacifier from her mouth.

"Jack—"

"Uh-uh, I don't think baby girls call their daddies by their first names." He tweaked her nipple again.

"I... oh *fuck*." She rolled her head back, leaning into his chest as he twisted and pulled, sending a delicate heat through her body.

"Go on. You were saying something."

She blinked. What had she been saying?

The nipple of the bottle appeared in front of her. "While you're thinking, let's get some water into you."

Before she could object, the nipple was between her teeth. "Be a good girl now. Drink it all up."

He maneuvered his body back until she was lying in his lap, looking up at him. A casual grin danced on his lips. He wasn't mocking her in anyway.

She started to reach for the bottle, but he shook his head. "Daddy holds it, baby girl." He winked. And just that little gesture was enough to make her clit twitch. What the fuck was he doing to her?

Suckling lightly, the water fell onto her tongue. Looking up at him, she lost herself in his gaze. Warm and caring, he locked gazes with her.

"I'm not going anywhere, baby girl," he said softly cradling her in one arm and brushing her hair away from her face with his free hand. "I'm right here."

Muscles that had been pulled tight with the stress of work and moving and all the pressure she put on herself to build a successful company began to ebb.

"Such a pretty girl," he smiled down at her. "Drink it all gone."

Suckling harder, she downed most of the bottle without focusing too hard on what she was doing. Too easily, she became lost in his eyes.

"Here it is." The DM had come back.

"On the chair is fine, thanks," Jack said without breaking his stare with Quinn. The bag made a thump sound, but Quinn remained locked on Jack until the last bit of the water had been drunk.

"That's a good girl," he crooned and removed the bottle from her mouth. She licked the edges of her mouth then tucked her bottom lip between her teeth. She shouldn't feel so relaxed.

Jack helped her sit up and hopped off the table. At least he didn't try to burp her.

"Relax a second," he said and pressed a kiss to her temple. A warm touch of his lips, brief but the tingle lingered as he walked over to the bag the DM had brought him.

She lay back on the table, keeping an eye on him as he dug through his bag.

"Okay, I think I have what I need." He turned around holding a vibrator and a condom. then grabbed the bag of baby stuff and brought it back to the table. "Let's get your diaper on so we can really have some fun."

A snappy retort sizzled on her tongue, but she kept it behind her closed lips. They couldn't change what they rolled and fighting him on it wasn't fair to him. He'd done everything so far in a way to help ease her tension, to strip away her apprehension. Maybe if she leaned into him, she'd find the release she sought at Black Light.

Laying the diaper on her belly, he tore open the condom wrapper. "I've cleaned it, but just to be sure," he explained as he rolled the condom over the portion of the vibrator that would be inserted into her. She'd seen the toy advertised but never used one. Shaped like a U, part of it would be inside, while the other would lie over her clit. Supposedly the sensations would bombard her from both sides and drive her straight to an intense orgasm.

Jack moved to the end of the table. "Open your legs for me," he ordered, tapping her knees.

She let her knees fall to the side.

She expected to feel the cold touch of the vibe against her cunt, but he surprised her with a warm kiss to the inside of her knee.

"Just relax and feel everything, baby girl," he commanded, biting down on her thigh as he made his way to her sex. Her aching sex. How come his voice and words affected her in a way so far only a whip had done?

"Daddy wants to taste your little pussy first." He shoved her legs open wider and plunged his tongue into her cunt.

"Oh!" She grabbed the edges of the table as his tongue danced on her clit, flicking it before he sucked it into his mouth.

"Hmmm." The vibration of his hum played hard against her clit. "So sweet," he mumbled against her pussy.

She arched her hips toward his mouth as he rose. He couldn't leave her with such need!

"No!" She slammed her ass back to the table when he stood up, leaving her cunt aching even more for him.

His sadistic grin electrified her lust.

"Baby girls don't argue with their daddies. Do you need your pacifier again, Quinn?" he asked with raised brows.

She swallowed the retort dancing on her tongue. As much as his gentle rocking had soothed her nerves, she wasn't taking that pacifier in her mouth again.

"No," she said softly.

He tilted his head to the side, seeming to will her to change her answer.

"No, Daddy," she corrected and closed her eyes, waiting for the shame to wash over her entire body. A warm current skated through her, softening tight muscles and easing away built tension in her temples, but shame danced far away from the sensations he evoked.

When she opened her eyes, she found a satisfied grin plastered on his lips.

"Someone didn't think she could relax without a proper spanking, but here you are, all wet and sweet for me." Jack slid his finger slid through her folds. "Ready for your toy?"

Yes. The vibrator. That would make things better.

"Yes, Daddy." She smiled up at him. Again, no shame, only warm tingling coursing down her spine with the words.

"Then, let's get it done."

CHAPTER 5

JACK

*J*ack looked down at his curvy beauty lying on the table, staring up at him with surprise. She must really think she needed pain to find her happy place but had no idea there were so many ways to achieve her goal. Her cheeks reddened when she called him Daddy, but he'd felt her body soften as he'd fed her the bottle.

She was finding her groove, even if her mind hadn't caught up to it.

With two fingers, he spread her pussy lips apart and lined the vibrator up with her hole. No sense in denying himself—he leaned over and bit down on her clit. Only when he felt her body go rigid did he thrust the vibrator into her cunt, pushing it forward until it was fully seated.

When he stood back up, smiling at her, she had her entire bottom lip between her teeth. He forced himself to finish positioning the toy so that her clit was covered by the vibrating end.

"Okay, then." He grabbed the diaper from where he'd left it on her belly. "Ass up." He opened the diaper and held it to the table below her bottom.

She didn't move.

"Quinn, lift your ass off the table so I can get this under you." He dragged his gaze up her body. Only once he had her locked in a heated stare did she finally flatten her feet to the table and lift up. He slid the diaper beneath her. "Okay, back down."

She huffed but obeyed.

He smiled over the lack of snarkiness she currently displayed. Either she realized it wouldn't get her anywhere she actually wanted to be, or she was relaxed enough that her defenses were crumbling.

Once he had the white diaper with pink bows printed along the waistline secured, he put his hands on his hips and looked down at her again, studying her expression. Her eyes went soft. Her bottom lip trembled slightly.

He grabbed hold of her hands and pulled her up to sit on the edge of the table.

"How's that?" he asked, slipping a finger between the elastic band and her belly. Not too tight as far as he could tell.

"Humiliating," she whispered and lowered her face.

He snaked his hand into her hair, fisting it hard, and yanked her head back until she had to look down the length of her nose to see him.

"And inside here? How's that feel?" He touched her chest.

She let out a shaky breath. "Calm."

"And here." He moved his hand between her legs, pressing though the diaper until he felt the hardness of the vibrator.

"Oh," she sighed with relief. "That feels good."

He chuckled. "Just wait." He dug into his back pocket and pulled out the remote. Clicking the first button to turn on the vibrations of the clit stimulator, he tilted her head forward again to get a better look into her eyes.

"Oh fuck!" She sucked in air as she spoke. Her eyes widened as he increased the vibrations a click. "Fuuuuuucck."

"Hmm. Like that, baby girl?"

She tried to nod, but he held firm.

"What do you say to Daddy?"

"Yes, Daddy. Thank you, Daddy," The words jumped from her lips.

Jack released his hold on her hair and stepped back, taking away all his touch. She frowned.

Grabbing the blanket from behind her on the table he put it on the floor, laid out flat for her. "Let's get you down." He helped her from the table.

"Why?" she asked.

"Because Daddy said so," was his only response. His cock was too hard, too distracting, to give him much else to say. "Sit on the blanket, Quinn."

She sank to the floor, crossing her legs beneath her. He clicked the remote again, turning on the internal vibrator as well. She cried out, slapping her hand over her mouth.

He grinned and grabbed the bag of baby stuff he'd been given. Taking out the bib he squatted in front of her and placed it around her neck.

"Oh God," she groaned, looking down at the bright pink material with a white teddy bear embroidered on it.

"You're going to need this, baby girl," he promised and stood in front of her. "Time for your next feeding."

Quinn widened her eyes as he grabbed hold of his belt buckle, and she licked her lips as he undid his zipper. Scrambling up to her knees she gripped his thighs. Greedy little thing. He pulled his cock free from his pants.

"Open wide for Daddy." He leaned forward, bringing his dick to her mouth. "Suck Daddy's cock, baby girl."

She didn't need any more coaxing. Wrapping her lips around his shaft, she slid her tongue beneath the head of his cock, taking him farther and farther into her mouth until he butted up against the back of her throat.

He threw his head back and groaned. *Fuck*. Nothing felt as good as having her mouth around his cock in that moment.

Slowly, she withdrew from him, only to swallow him down again.

"Fuck!" He grabbed hold of her hair again, fisting it and pulling to give her the tension she enjoyed, the bite of pain she needed.

She moaned, sending vibrations down his shaft as she throated him again and again.

"Such a good baby girl." He thrust his pelvis, fucking her mouth as much as she was sucking him. "Hold still, baby. I'm going to face fuck you hard. You can take it right? You can do that for Daddy?" He pulled her head back until she was staring up at him, her lips already swollen and wet. "Tell me you can do that for me."

"Face fuck me, Daddy," she said without hesitation. She'd taken what she felt was humiliation and embraced it. The soft glow of submission took centerstage in her features. There was arousal, too, but he could see it, the sign of a submissive finding her sweet spot. And his girl was finding it without a paddle or belt.

"Open wide," he ordered and held his cock in his left hand, inching toward her again. "Do not close your mouth, or Daddy will have to turn off your toy." He nudged his foot between her legs, pressing up on the vibrator.

"No, Daddy, please don't," she begged prettily.

"Then, be good and keep your mouth open."

Her jaw dropped open, and she slid her tongue out, waiting for her feeding. Fuck she was beautiful.

Without giving her a warning, he thrust forward all the way into her mouth, not stopping until his cock touched her throat. He pulled her toward his groin, holding her steady as he pumped short thrusts down her throat. She swallowed around his cock, tightening around him.

"Fuck!" he groaned and pulled back out to give her a breath.

He switched the clit stimulator off and stuck the remote in his back pocket. She ground her pussy into his shoe.

"That's right, baby girl, fuck yourself with your toy. Your diaper will catch all your pussy juices. Go on," he encouraged her, lifting his foot up, pressing harder against the vibe.

"Oh." She started to lean back from him, but he shoved her down on his cock again, fucking her mouth hard and fast while she gurgled and gasped around his dick.

"Fuck. Fuck. Fuck," he chanted as his balls tightened. "Ready for your feeding, baby?" he asked, yanking her off him again.

Her chest heaved with deep breaths, trying to catch up to what she'd lost with a face full of cock.

"Hands behind your back, baby girl."

She adjusted her positioning and folded her arms behind her, giving him a clear shot at her face and her chest.

"Deep breath," he warned a mere second before stuffing himself down her throat again. Her saliva escaped around the seal she created with her lips, dripping down her chin. His balls bounced off her wet face as he plunged into her throat. She gagged, but he wouldn't give her room to breathe yet. Small thrusts then harder longer ones, until the first wave of his release crashed into him.

He yanked free of her mouth and wrapped his hand around his shaft, pumping and jerking his dick until thick streams of cum burst from his cock and painted her chin and cheeks. While gasping for breath, she stuck her tongue out for him. He tightened his fist in her hair as the last pulsations of his orgasm spurted his cum across her tongue.

"Swallow it," he ordered with the little bit of breath he still possessed. The intensity of his orgasm surprised him. He hadn't even dipped his cock into her sweet pussy, but her submission to him, to opening up to a new playground had dragged him right over the cliff into oblivion.

She ran her tongue along her lips, taking in as much of the cum as she could before curling it into her mouth and swallowing.

"Show me." He let go of her hair and bent over.

She giggled and opened her mouth, sticking her tongue back out. "All gone," she said.

"That's my girl." He patted her cheek. "Still kinda messy, though." He took the bib off and wiped the rest from her chin and cheeks. "See, you needed this."

She sank back on her heels.

"Is your diaper wet?" he asked, tucking his dick back into his pants.

She lowered her gaze.

"Is it?" He squatted in front of her.

"I'm wet, but not like that."

"Ah." He checked the time on his watch. Cellphones weren't allowed in the club, but, being a private investigator, he liked to know the time—always. "Well, seems our half hour is up. We should go spin again."

Her lower lip sucked into her mouth.

"What's wrong?" He tugged on her chin until her lip came free.

"I'm…" She rolled her eyes. "I'm okay with this."

"You like this?" He snapped the diaper band at her waist.

"Not the diaper, exactly…"

"Ah," he smiled. "You like feeling this, a little powerless, a little embarrassed?"

She sucked in a breath and nodded. "Yeah."

"Your pussy gets wet with the humiliation of being made to do what you don't want to do," he continued even though she was already agreeing. A little more driving the point home wouldn't hurt.

"Do we need to roll again?" she asked and, in that question, with her soft tone, he saw her. The part of her she'd hidden behind the wall of bratty and bitchy behavior.

"If I say yes?" he asked, testing the waters.

"Then we'll roll again."

He cupped her chin in his hand and tilted her head back, hovering his mouth right over hers. "Lie back, baby girl. I'm not done with you yet."

CHAPTER 6

QUINN

*H*e didn't kiss her!

His lips were right there, his breath hot on her face, but just when they were about to touch, he tucked his hands beneath her armpits and hauled her to her feet, then hoisted her onto the table. She cringed when her ass hit the table and the diaper crinkled.

She scooted back a few inches, and the damn diaper announced every movement. Jack nudged her shoulder until she was lying down again, but when he reached for the tabs of the diaper, she jolted upward. She could handle it herself; she didn't need him to take it off. Hadn't she endured enough with the damn thing?

"Stay down." He pointed a finger at her.

She fisted her hands to keep them out of his way and tucked them at her sides. As much as she wanted to rip the thing off, she wouldn't. She'd laid herself in Jack's hands and so far he hadn't disappointed. Trusting her needs would be met without her direction was as new to her as diaper play.

Jack hadn't disappointed, but how much further could they go?

"Now, let's see what sort of mess you've made in here." He pulled the tabs off the diaper.

"Jack—"

"What?" His sharp question cut her off.

She rolled her eyes.

"I mean Daddy."

He tilted his head to the side and narrowed his eyes. "There are other ways to punish a brat besides spanking her, you know."

After the way he'd already made her feel, she wouldn't doubt his word now.

"I didn't mean anything," she said hoping she sounded contrite.

He raised his brow. "We'll see."

His tongue touched his top lip while he pulled back the diaper to expose her sex, still stuffed with the vibrating dildo. How could he look so hungry for her?

Tugging on the vibrator, he removed it from her pussy and switched it off before tossing it on top of the table.

"One sec." He patted her knee then disappeared below the table for a brief moment. He straightened, holding the costume bag, and rested it on the table, between her legs.

"Quinn, you said this was your second time at Black Light. Are you new to the area, or just the club?" he asked with his hand in the bag, looking through her open legs at her.

He wanted to have a discussion now?

"I just moved here," she answered, trying to see what he was holding inside the clear bag.

"From where?" He continued the questions.

"Chicago." She inched her feet closer together.

"So, what made you move here?" he asked, using his free hand to shove her feet apart again.

Did they have to have this conversation while she was lying on an open diaper?

But she answered. "I'm opening a new branch of my systems security company."

He stilled. "Systems security. Like computer systems?"

"Yeah. We handle corporate tech security mostly,"

"Hmmm. Beautiful and smart as hell." He pulled his hand out of the bag finally and showed her what he'd grabbed.

The fucking rattle.

"We're going to play a little game." He handed her the damn toy. "If I ask you a question, you shake this once for yes and twice for no."

"Can't I just say yes or no?"

He laughed. "How would that be a game? No, you'll use the rattle. If you want to come, you need to shake it a lot. And I mean really let me know you're close. Got it?"

"Sure." She grinned at him, gripping the handle of the yellow plastic toy. The round bubble at the top filled with beans had blue stars painted all over it. A bit retro for her taste.

"If you sneak an orgasm, you won't get off this table until you give me three more. And I promise you, forced orgasms aren't as fun as you may have heard."

Right, reaching heaven over and over again would just be the worst possible thing. She kept her eyeroll in check and gave a solemn nod.

The right corner of his lips twisted upward, like he knew what she was thinking.

"How do you do that?" she asked.

"Do what?"

"Seem to know what's in my head. You're very intuitive."

"Comes with the job, I guess." He lifted a shoulder. "I worked for the bureau for ten years, but now I'm a private investigator. Reading people is what I do for a living."

She rose onto her elbows. "You're a PI?"

He grimaced. "I hate the way that sounds, but yeah. I am."

"Why'd you leave the FBI?"

His eyes hardened; the tilt of his lips went flat. "We're getting a little off topic." He pressed his hands to her thighs until her legs spread wide open.

There was a story there, she figured, but let it drop. This wasn't more than a playdate. Pushing the issue could ruin the night, and so far, he'd given her everything she needed—even if it wasn't what she thought she wanted. She wasn't going to ruin it for him now.

"Stay right here." He pointed a finger at her then disappeared for a moment. When he returned he had a small stool. "No need for either of us to be uncomfortable." He winked then sat on the stool, bringing his height level with her pussy.

"We can probably take the diaper away now," she said, squirming on top of it.

His maniacal grin returned. "No way. No more talking. The only way you communicate is with your rattle, baby girl."

She narrowed her eyes but clamped her mouth shut.

"See. Such a good girl." He winked and brought his mouth to her pussy.

Her hips shot off the bench when he licked her clit. She hadn't been expecting such a heated touch yet. He pinned her hips down with both of his hands and continued to lick and lash at her pussy with his tongue.

"Fuck," she moaned.

He pulled up.

"No. You don't get to talk. Now I have to punish you," he chastised with too happy a smile on his face to give her the impression he was anywhere near disappointed.

His nails dug into her thighs, sending the sweetest burn she'd felt all night through her body. Dragging his fingers across her skin, he continued down her legs to her ass cheeks. Instinctively, she clenched them, but he wouldn't be denied. Prying her cheeks apart, he looked up the length of her.

"Big fan of anal?" he asked stoically.

She swallowed. Truth or lie? Which was the right answer. What did he really want?

"Quinn, a lie right now would end very badly for you." His tone dropped to sincere proportions. There would be no funishments with him.

"Not a huge fan, no." She decided on truth. Maybe he wouldn't go there if he knew she wasn't an anal girl. "Oh, crap! I'm sorry." Realizing she hadn't used the rattle, she gave it two hard shakes.

"Nice save," he laughed. He stuck his middle finger in his mouth, dragging it out from between his lips. "This is enough lubrication for my bad girl."

516

"What? No, wait." She started to sit up, but his fierce stare put her right back down. She wasn't supposed to be talking.

"Unless you're calling your safe word, use your rattle," he instructed, finger touching her asshole.

She clenched her teeth and her ass.

"Soft or hard, my finger's going in. How much it hurts is entirely up to you." He gave her a millisecond to decide how to play it before thrusting his finger fully inside her.

She cried out with the invasion. He twisted his finger and bent it at the knuckle, feeling her out, stretching her just before working a second finger inside.

"No." She shook the rattle hard, eliciting a chuckle from him.

"Baby girl doesn't like my fingers in her asshole?"

She snapped her teeth at him and shook the fucking toy with more fervor.

"Temper, temper," he chided and thrust his fingers inside her faster, harder. She raised her hips from the table, but he was one step ahead of her. Bringing his arm across her pelvis, he pinned her down while increasing the discomfort in her ass. He spread his fingers, sending a new heat through her body.

"Bet if I do this, you'll calm down." He lowered his mouth over her pussy again, slowly dragging his tongue up through her folds, and flicked her clit.

Her eyes widened with the new sensation. The sweet torture of his tongue mixed with the burning stretch in her bottom brought her right to the brink.

He sucked her clit between his teeth while working his fingers in and out of her tight hole.

If he kept this up, she wouldn't last, wouldn't be able to tell him when she was close.

The rattle.

She shook it.

"Please, Daddy!" she cried out, still trying to move her hips upward.

He shook his head, without leaving her pussy, running his tongue over and under and on top of her clit.

"Oh!" She moved her hand between her legs, shaking it right above his head.

"Not yet, Quinn," he ordered and pressed harder on her pelvis.

His tongue dipped inside her pussy, and she let go. Her entire body tensed and shook and rattled as an orgasm ripped through her. Hard and fast. She screamed with each new wave. There was no crawling back from it; she was fully inside the tsunami of sensations.

She dropped the rattle to the floor and leaned back, dragging in long breaths. He didn't break stride; his fingers continued to pump into her ass.

"Did you just come?" It was an accusation.

"I didn't mean to," she said between breaths. It was the truth. There had been no stopping it. His tongue had hit the switch, giving her no chance at controlling it.

"Well." He rose to his feet, pulling his fingers from her and releasing her hips. "Remember what I said?"

She thought a moment. *Oh, yeah.*

"I get more orgasms." She'd just won the lottery. Maybe she wouldn't get a spanking from him, but she'd go home completely sated from coming.

He chuckled. "You've really never been with a man who kept you under his control for longer than a spanking, have you?"

"What's that mean?"

"It means you think you're about to get a prize." He walked over to his play bag and dug out another vibrator. The damn thing looked industrial grade. The little vibrating dildo she had at home did the job just fine, but his looked ready to inflict some serious damage. Instead of a dildo shape, this thing had a wand appearance. She'd seen them in porn flicks. He wasn't messing around.

She leaned up on her elbows again. "I'm not?"

He stood at the foot of the table again, between her legs, grabbed hold of the diaper, and yanked it out from beneath her ass, dropping it to the floor with the discarded rattle.

"No, baby girl. You're not." He winked.

CHAPTER 7

JACK

*S*he had no idea what was coming her way, and Jack loved every second of it. Whatever men she'd been playing with had been catering to her wants and not diving an inch deeper to find out her needs.

He didn't play that game. After tonight she could play her dial-a-dom game if she wanted to scratch her spanking itch, but right now, while he had her beneath his power, he was going to drag out every moment. She would get everything she needed.

"Sit up." He tapped her shoulder and hopped up on the table sitting behind her. What he was about to put her through would probably make her want to jump off, and he couldn't have that. It might be easier to grab some binds and tie her down, but he liked the feel of her against him.

Had any of the men she played with had the pleasure of her true submission? Had they felt her tremble beneath their touch? Had they enjoyed the sounds she made when she fought against herself and lost? Had they witnessed the harshness of her gorgeous green eyes dissolve into a puddle of warm arousal?

"It's your fault, you know," she said once he was seated behind her with her back pressed against his chest.

"How so?" he asked, curious as to how she could turn the tables.

519

"I've never had… well… what you were doing done. I couldn't stop it. It just happened." She shrugged, looking up at him by tilting her head back all the way.

"What was I doing?" he asked.

"You know."

He laughed. "Yeah, I do, but I want you to say it. What was I doing that made you come so hard and so fast for me that you couldn't obey my order of waiting?"

Quinn groaned; the vibrations of the noise danced against his chest.

"You had your fingers in my ass. No one's ever done that before." She looked away and shrugged.

"Have you ever been forced to orgasm over and over again even after you've pleaded to stop?" He wrapped his arm around her stomach, the tip of the vibrator dangling near her cunt.

A slight hesitation before giving her answer. "No."

"Then, for your sake, let's hope new experiences help you come fast all the time. Because you're not getting off this table until you've given me three more orgasms."

"You want me to use my rattle again?"

Little brat. She really thought this was going to be easy.

"You dropped it on the floor. This punishment is for big girls anyway. Now… any last words?" He flipped the switch on the side of the vibrator, bringing it to life.

Her body shook with her laughter.

"Sure, make me come." She snapped her fingers.

"Your mouth gives you away. You're nervous," he whispered into her ear, inhaling the sweet lavender scent of her hair.

"Pfft!" She lowered her chin and stared straight ahead of them. Scenes continued to play out all around them. He'd blocked them all out until that moment. Several of the onlookers were focused on them.

Excellent.

"See all those people at the tables? The ones who don't get to play tonight? They're watching you, Quinn. They've watched you wearing a diaper, being facefucked with a bib around your neck. They've seen your asshole stretched and fucked with my fingers. They've heard you call me Daddy and seen you drink water from a baby bottle." He ran his tongue along the shell of her ear. "And now they are going to watch you come for me. Three times, baby. No begging will work, but I bet they'd love to hear it."

Her body tensed against him. She must have forgotten the audience as well.

"Showtime." He brought the vibrator to her pussy and his heart sang when she jolted at the first sensations.

"Not so bad," she said at first, but he wasn't done yet.

"Barely started." He pressed the vibrator harder to her clit and rubbed her with it. She gripped his knees. There was no escaping it, her body would chase after the pleasure, and all she would be able to do was try to stay on the ride.

"Oh. Fuck." She gasped when he turned the vibrations up one notch.

"Good girl. Come on, come for us. Come for all of us," he said, reminding her again of the onlookers.

Her head bumped his chin, and her body pressed harder back against him. The tension in her thighs increasing.

So close.

He leaned down, biting on her earlobe, giving her the little zing of pain she craved.

And fireworks happened.

Her body bowed outward, her feet curled, and she let loose a scream as her first orgasm hit, but he didn't relent, didn't slow down for her to enjoy the ride. He increased the vibrations, grinning when she cried out.

"No. Wait." She tried to twist away from him, but this wasn't his first rodeo. He swung his legs over hers and pinned her with her legs open. He tightened his arm around her torso.

"Two more," he said and went up on the power one more notch.

"Oh fuck!" She started to bend forward, but he held her tight. "I can't!" she whined, but it was bullshit. She could and she would.

She'd be close, teetering on the edge, fighting what her body wanted to do but he wouldn't let her stay there for long.

He bit down on the soft spot behind her ear and pumped the vibrator over her clit.

"Oh! Jack! Jack! Oh God!" she screamed while her entire body went rigid.

"One more, baby," he laughed in her ear.

"No. Please." She gasped for breath, but he wasn't done. Would he ever be done with her?

"Sorry, baby, I never go back on my word." He took the vibrator off her clit, giving her only a brief reprieve as he held it up to her face. "Only two more clicks until we're at full strength." He thumbed the dial so she could see how close she was to having the toy on high.

"Oh God. No. Please." She wiggled in his grasp. "I'm sorry I didn't listen. I'm sorry." She twisted enough for him to see her tear-filled eyes.

"But you wanted pain. I'm giving it to you." He ran his tongue along her cheekbone, snagging a fallen tear.

"Not like this." She kicked her legs out as though there was any chance she'd get free of his grasp. He didn't win the college state championship in his wrestling weight class three years in a row without being able to keep an adversary locked in position.

"Then, next time don't be naughty," he whispered into her ear, slamming his leg over hers to keep her still, and placed the vibrator directly on her clit.

She screamed and bowed her body, but he didn't relent. He twisted and rolled and ran it over her sex while she squirmed and cried from the intense pleasure being forced onto her.

"I can't!" she pleaded, but her thighs were trembling. "I can't. Please." Quinn grabbed at his arm, but she moaned.

"Almost," he whispered. "Come on, baby, give me one more. Be a good girl for me. You can do it. You can come for me, can't you? Imagine next time, with my tongue all over your pussy, eating you and licking you until you're at the very edge. Imagine my cock thrusting into you, fucking you so hard you have to hold onto something to keep from falling. Think about it."

"Oh fuck!" Her nails dug into his forearm.

So fucking close.

"Think about me flipping you onto your stomach, spanking your ass so hard you cry. Imagine the heat, the sting and then spreading your ass cheeks and riding you straight into an orgasm." Fuck. If he wasn't careful, he was going to lose himself in the images he created.

"Jack. Please," she begged. He cupped her breast in his free hand and rolled her nipple between his thumb and forefinger. Her body melted into him when he twisted hard.

"Imagine the bite of clamps on these pretty nipples. Or better... my teeth." He pinched hard, drawing out another cry from her. She made the sweetest sounds when she cried; he wouldn't mind hearing her every night.

"Come for me, Quinn." He flicked the strength up to the last notch. Again, her hips bolted upward. "Be my sweet girl." He kissed her temple. "Do it for me." He pulled her nipple downward, twisting it as he repositioned the vibrator head and pushed hard against her clit.

"Fuuuuuccck!" she screamed, bucking her hips upward and smacking her palm into his arm. She was unglued.

And gorgeous.

He slowed the vibrations click by click until they were at the lower level before turning off the vibrator. She collapsed against him; her legs hung off the sides of the table, as did her arms. She'd been reduced to a wet noodle.

Meanwhile, his cock was hard as hell again.

Jack tucked the vibrator behind him and wrapped both arms around Quinn, holding her tightly to his chest as he gently rocked her. Her head lay in the crook of his elbow as she took deep breaths.

He kissed the top of her head and squeezed her tight.

"You okay?" he asked while glaring toward the pool area. All the splashing and party going on out there poured into the play areas.

Quinn stirred in his arms and turned to her side, resting her head on his lap and curling her legs up to her chest.

"I just need a minute," she said with her eyes closed. He brushed her hair from her face and continued to stroke her hair while she settled down. Playing with humiliation and forced orgasms all night had taken its toll on her.

"Take all the time you need." He readjusted his position to take some pressure off his back and still support for her head.

Jack waved over a DM walking by. "Can I get a blanket?"

They'd sit there all night if necessary. Whatever she needed, he'd give to her.

A quick glance at his watch made his heart stammer in his chest. Their night was half over. How was he supposed to say goodbye to her after such an intense evening?

He'd been looking to let off a little steam, but Quinn had given him so much more. She'd given him a piece of herself, and he wasn't ready to give it back.

CHAPTER 8

QUINN

"I think I can get up now," Quinn pushed up from his lap and sat beside him on the table. She pushed the hair from her face and dragged in a long breath.

"You okay?" Jack asked, running his hand in circles on her back.

"Yeah. Just needed to catch my breath," she said. Four orgasms back to back could take a lot out of a girl. The most she'd ever achieved had been two up until Jack got his hands on her.

"We still have time. I think maybe we should spin something else." He hopped off the table and stood in front of her, his hands cupping her knees. A simple touch, but it seeped into her the way a warm blanket covering her shivering form could.

"I'm game." She wiggled off the table and started to search for her clothes.

"What are you looking for?" he asked.

"My clothes."

"Oh. Yeah, you don't need those." He swiped the pile from the floor and tossed it into his bag. Since she was bound to be naked for the next scene anyway, she didn't waste energy arguing with him.

While he packed up his toys, she wiped down the table and folded the blanket. Jack gave her a wink when he took it from her and placed it inside his bag.

"To the wheel." He pointed in the direction of the theater and waiting roulette wheel and picked up her hand. He led her through the room, weaving around scenes still unfolding, in silence.

"Ready to go again?" Madison held out the little white ball.

Quinn took another look at Jack and nodded. "Yeah. Let's go again." She took the ball and held it over the wheel while Madison gave it a spin.

"Make sure you aim right," Jack teased from behind her. His hand rested on her hip.

She couldn't make out any of the activities, so she simply let the ball loose and watched it bounce around the wheel before settling in the groove. Around and around it went until if finally slowed enough for the ball to find a home.

"*Breast Torture!*" Madison called out with glee. The woman really needed to tone down the cheerfulness, but Quinn just smiled in response.

"I think I can manage this fine, you?" Jack nudged Quinn's shoulder.

"I can handle it." She turned to face him.

"Perfect. Uh…" he thought back to the open play spaces then snapped his fingers. "I remember seeing a whipping post open. Let's go." He snagged her hand again, lacing his fingers with hers and tugged her from the stage.

"We need a post?" She asked half giggling. The heavy stress of the last months had been weighing her down to the point of suffocation when she'd shown up at the club that night, but as Jack led her back into the play areas she walked lighter.

"Oh, yeah, we do." He assured her as they approached the space. "One sec." He dropped her hand and squatted with his bag to dig around. He put her clothes next to the toy bag then continued searching, finally standing back up with a proud smile. He had two coils of hemp rope in his hands.

"The spin was breast torture," she reminded him, keeping her gaze locked on the rope.

"Have you ever been bound before?" he asked, letting out the end of one bundle and dropping loose rope to the ground.

"Ben says I wiggle too much, so he puts me in handcuffs if he's going to go hard on me," she said before filtering herself.

"Is Ben just a friend or something more?" Jack asked, stepping to the post and looking up at the metal ring.

Quinn folded her arms over her belly. "A friend," she assured him. Ben wouldn't be breaking down any doors in a fit of jealousy to find her. He had plenty of playmates back in Chicago to keep his flogger going for years.

Jack crooked a finger. "C'mere, Quinn."

The sadist grin he flashed her lit up her soul.

Once she was standing next to the pole he held up the rope. "Put your wrists and your elbows together for me," he instructed while mimicking the position he wanted.

She watched with interest as he wound the rope around her wrists, then through the middle and weaved the rope one way then the other.

"You must have been a great boyscout," she teased.

He laughed. "I was actually. But they didn't teach this sort of knot tying in my troop. Had to learn it on my own."

After she was secured, he backed her up against the pole and raised her arms over head. Her arms pressed into her ears as he looped the end of the rope through the metal ring. She tilted her head back to watch, but the angle wasn't comfortable.

Once he was finished with all his tying, he stepped back appraising his work. Her body heated the longer he stared at her. Completely naked and bound, she was exposed to him.

"You're gorgeous," he said, but he'd said it so softly she wasn't sure she'd heard him right—or that she was supposed to hear him at all.

"Is this all we're doing?" she asked when her heart started to race.

His eyebrow arched and he pointed a finger at her. "Back to smartmouthing?" He exaggerated a head shake then went back into his bag. When he stood back up he held a handful of wooden clothes pins.

"Give me your tongue, Quinn." He pinched the ends of one clothespin and held it to her mouth. Oh, fuck. She really needed to learn when to be sassy and when to shut the hell up.

Slowly she slipped her tongue out from between her lips, and as soon as he could, he snapped the pin in place on her tongue. She jolted from the immediate pressure of it.

"Two more." He put the other pins on her tongue, one to the left and one to the right of the first. She tried to pull her tongue back inside her mouth, but she couldn't close her mouth all the way.

"There. Perfect." He patted her cheek. "Now for these breasts."

CHAPTER 9

JACK

Quinn stomped her foot when none of her words were getting across properly. Jack only laughed and picked a clothespin from his hand.

"Now, once I have you all pretty for me, the real fun can start," he explained as he pinched her breast and placed a pin.

"I know you like your nipples pinched, so we'll save that for last." He continued to decorate her heavy breasts with the clothespins until all twenty of them were used. She made such sweet sounds as he moved closer and closer to her nipple.

"Okay, deep breath, baby." He locked gazes with her as he let the last pin close on her puckered nipple. She whimpered as it gripped her tender flesh. He flicked the end of the pin and watched it dance, listening to the melody her mewls played. "So sweet." He stood directly in front of her, fingers poised at both nipples. "Ready for me?" he asked.

Her eyes went wide as realization seeped in at his intentions. She shook her head.

"No not ready? Need me to put more on?" he asked, jerking his thumb toward his bag. He only had maybe two or three more loose at the bottom, but she didn't know that.

"No," she said as best she could with the pins hanging off her tongue.

"You sure?" He played with the ends of the pin on each nipple.

She hissed and twisted, but there was nowhere for her to go.

"When we first met tonight, you were awfully rude." He tilted his head. "You didn't think you could find any sort of real fun playing unless you were getting your ass tanned."

He flicked the pins and watched her wiggle.

"Do you still think that?" he asked, positioning his hands at two more pins.

She sucked in air while shaking her head.

"No? Are you sure?" He flicked the ends harder. She whimpered and nodded her head. "Really sure?" He slapped her right breast hard and she cried out.

"Yeth!" she called out, pulling down on her binds.

He slapped her left breast and she twisted in the ropes again, but he straightened her out and delivered three more smacks to her breast. When she settled he searched her eyes.

"You are my little pain slut, aren't you?" he asked, brushing a strand of hair from her cheek. He left her on the post and went back to his bag. She was going to need a signal for him.

"Here." He stuffed the rattle into her hand. "If you need me to slow down, just shake it. If you need me to stop, drop it." He cupped her chin and pulled her gaze to meet his. "Do you understand, Quinn?"

"Yeth, Thir." She nodded and shook the rattle.

He sighed. He could have given up on her right at the get go. He could have written her off as a snarky bitch and just walked away. But he'd had a sense about her, a feeling in his gut that there was more to her. And here it was. The sweet submission he knew was hiding behind all her layers of anxiety and fear.

Jack pulled out his riding crop and his favorite flogger. Hand-crafted with thick leather falls and a handle perfectly balanced, it had found its way right into his heart from the first time he'd picked it up.

"First, we're going to take off the clothespins." He waved the crop in her line of sight. "Then, I'm going to make these tits blush for me."

He tossed the flogger over his left shoulder, letting the falls trail down his back.

Her chest began to rise and fall faster; her pupils enlarged. She'd been waiting all night for this and he was finally going to give her the bite of pain she craved.

"Ready?" he asked her.

She sucked in her belly and stood straighter, turning her face the other direction. As though burying herself could change what was coming her way.

The crop came down fast on her left breast, knocking off two clips at once. He grunted. He'd wanted only one of them to come off. He'd have to aim better. Another flick of his wrists and another popped off to the floor.

Quinn yelped as the fourth came off, but he wasn't stopping. In rapid succession he flicked his wrist knocking off pins from both breasts until only two remained.

He fiddled with the ends of the clothespin on her right nipple. "Just two more," he said, kissing her cheek. Tears built in her eyes, but she wasn't crying. He kissed her other cheek and moved back a few steps.

She closed her eyes and lifted her chin.

"One," he counted. Her eyes squeezed tighter. "Two." He inched closer to her. "Three." He softly pinched the ends of the clips and eased them off her nipples.

Her eyes flew open in surprise, and he laughed. But it wasn't over.

She whined as the blood began to move again and her nipples reacted to the pinch being removed.

Jack stepped back and tossed the crop to the floor. He pulled the flogger off his shoulder and held it out for her. "More?" he asked.

Her nostrils flared as her breath quickened. She raised her chin and gave a curt nod.

"Good girl," he crooned.

Her breasts, already decorated with red splotches from the clips, bounced as he began to flog her. One easy lash, another easy lash, followed by a hard hit. She would learn to expect the unexpected with him.

He continued to work her breasts over with the flogger until their blush mirrored the marks from the clothespins. Watching her expression, he watched as the last bit of stress faded.

After a particularly hard hit, she sagged in the ropes. He dropped the flogger and hurried to her side, hoisting her until she was standing upright again. Her head rolled to the side.

This. This was the face of a sated girl. Her eyes glassed over softly, fixated on him and her lips curled into a sweet smile.

"I'm going to take you down now," he whispered so as not to drag her too fast from her happy place. After getting the knot out of the ropes, he wrapped one arm around her middle to hold her against him as he took the clothespins off her tongue and worked the ropes loose.

"Jack?" Her arms wove around his neck once he had her off the post. He held her tightly, letting the ropes fall to the floor.

"Yeah?" He kissed her temple.

"Thank you for not getting scared away tonight."

Jack helped her to the chairs at the station and sat her in one. He took the seat beside her and cradled her in his arms. "It's going to take a lot more than a little attitude to send me running."

She sighed and snuggled into his embrace.

CHAPTER 10

QUINN

Quinn pulled the blanket around her shoulders tighter. The soft pink blanket she'd hated at the beginning of the night turned out to be safety net. While Jack went about winding up his rope and cleaning the pole, she held the warm blanket around her feeling calmer than she had in months.

The blanket would be going home with her.

"Here." Jack held out a bottle of water to her.

"Thanks," she said as she took it from him.

"Drink it. Don't just hold it." He twisted the cap off and motioned to it.

"So, you're bossy in and out of a scene." She tilted the bottle back and took a long drink of crisp cold water. All her screaming had made her throat sore. She'd blame Jack, except he'd probably just see it as a congratulatory comment.

And if she was going to be even slightly honest—he should.

She'd never come so fucking hard or so many times in one session with a man. Hell, she rarely had an orgasm when she played with her Doms. It was mostly impact play, aftercare, maybe a drink at the bar then she'd head home to bed, relaxed and sated. If she wanted the happily ever after, she had her trusty vibrator stationed in the night-stand drawer, ready for service.

And he'd given her the perfect ending to the night with the flogger. To her surprise, it hadn't been the sweet pain of the pins, or the heavy thud of the flogger that sent her nerves at ease. It had been his steady control. She could lean on him, and he wouldn't falter.

A trait she hadn't expected to find. She'd only been looking for a night of fun. A quick spanking to straighten out her anxiety and she'd be done. But she'd gotten so much more. So much better.

Jack brushed her hair from her face and tucked it behind her ear. "I'm bossy everywhere I go."

She laughed, too tired to come up with a snarky response.

"Too worn out to talk back. I'll have to remember this." He moved to her side and hopped back up on the table then wrapped his arm around her shoulders again.

"It's been a long day." She sipped the water. "And tomorrow will be even longer."

"When does your new office open?"

"We've already opened, but I just made the final move here. I've been living out of a suitcase for the past six months while we got things ready to open."

"Starting up a business is difficult enough. Trying to go back and forth between two places only makes it harder, I bet." He squeezed her shoulder.

"I shouldn't have to travel for a little while at least. The office back in Chicago is under solid leadership. Maybe, in a few months, I'll have to make a quick trip out there." She paused a moment. "What about you? You're a private investigator. Do you have your own company or work for someone?"

He stiffened slightly but didn't pull away.

"I have my own office. It's just me."

"Are you working a case now? Not right now, but I mean... you know what I mean." Her cheeks flushed. Talking to him while they were knee deep in kink came easier to her than friendly chitchat.

He laughed. "I just wrapped up a very compelling case this afternoon." He slipped his arm from her shoulders and folded his hands in his lap.

He was still wearing all of his clothes. He'd seen every inch of her body, but she hadn't glimpsed more than his cock when he pulled it out from his jeans. Did he have scars littering his body from his time in the FBI? Was he apprehensive about her seeing them?

"Oh?"

"Yeah. Big divorce case. Infidelity." His lips thinned into a straight line.

"Seriously?"

He grimaced. "Afraid so. Not all my cases are great, but they all pay well. In this town, there's money flowing, and where that's happening, shit tends to go sideways."

"So, you follow people around with your camera, snapping away when you find them cheating?" She couldn't quite picture him sneaking around corners and hiding in bushes.

"Not exactly." He tilted his head. "Some surveillance is needed, but usually by the time I'm doing that I already have what I need to present a solid case."

"I'm glad I won't have to worry about stuff like that."

"Stuff like what?"

"Like being cheated on. I don't get serious enough with a guy to make it an issue." She handed him the empty bottle.

"You don't date? Don't want to get married?" he asked with a raised brow.

"Married?" She laughed and hopped off the table. "I have great relationships. Good friends and Doms who enjoy the play as much as I do—and don't want to take anything home afterward." She looked over her shoulder. "Will you excuse me a second? I really need to pee." Between the bottle he'd made her drink at the beginning of their time and what she'd just guzzled, she really needed to relieve herself.

"I guess I missed my chance to make you use the diaper." He waggled his eyebrows.

"Oh, hell yes. I don't think I could have anyway." She pointed to the locker rooms. "I'll be right back." Snagging her clothing on her way, she hustled through the crowds of people to the locker room.

Once alone in the stall, she pressed her forehead against the door. No matter how attractive he was, no matter how much his dominance settled her nerves, and no matter how much electricity shot through her body when he kissed her—she had to remember this was all over as soon as she got dressed. One night of fun. A stress reliever. That's all.

Nothing changed.

She wasn't looking for anything but fun. Even she didn't believe herself anymore.

CHAPTER 11

JACK

"*H*ey, man. Saw your little show there at the end. Fucking hot!" Brody smacked Jack's shoulder.

"Thanks." Jack nodded. He already knew how hot the scene had been. He'd be remembering it for nights to come.

"Where'd she go? She take off already?" Brody looked around.

"She's in the bathroom. Why?"

Brody shrugged. "Thought I'd see if she wanted to meet up for a play session this weekend. She looks like she could take a solid beating."

Jack's teeth snapped when he clenched his jaw. Brody was a responsible Dom, Jack wouldn't deny that, but he would just be another in a string of Doms to give Quinn the pain she wanted without the attention she needed.

And the part that burned him the most—it wasn't his fucking business.

They'd been paired up by a fucking spinning wheel. That's all. They'd played a game for the night. That's all this was going to be.

She'd made it clear she didn't go looking for anything serious. She wanted what Brody had to offer.

"I'm not really sure she's your type," Jack said, rubbing the back of his neck. He had no right to intervene, but it would be a cold fucking day in hell before he willingly stood by and let Brody put his hands on Quinn.

"Why, because of her curves? Man, I don't care—skinny, plump, whatever. So long as the girl can follow directions, suck a mean dick, and not cry off after two lashes of the flogger."

How had Jack ever thought Brody was worth splitting a few beers with? Suck a mean dick? Well, fuck yeah, she did, but, dammit, Brody's cock would not touch her.

"Hey." Quinn appeared all dressed in her black blouse and slacks again, though she'd left three buttons of the top undone, giving Jack a bird's eye view of what he may never get to touch again. Unfortunately, it also gave Brody something to wet his fucking whistle.

"Hi, sweetheart." Brody stepped closer to her. "I didn't get a chance to really meet you earlier at the bar. I'm Brody." He stuck his hand out toward her.

Hadn't he called her a bitch at the bar? Telling her that little tidbit would probably spoil Brody's plans, but it would give him a shiny new label of asshat as well.

"Oh. Yeah. I was a little nervous at the start of the night, sorry if I was stand offish. I'm Quinn." She grabbed Brody's hand and pumped it before letting him go. Her gaze trailed over Brody's shoulder to Jack. Did she want saving, or was she interested and wanted Jack to haul ass?

"Nice to meet you. I was just telling Jack here your scene was pretty amazing."

If he licked his lips, Jack was going to punch his throat.

Quinn's gaze flickered back to Brody with a polite smile. "Thanks." She shuffled her feet.

"Your shoes." Jack walked over to the chairs where he'd stashed her flats and brought them back to her.

"Thanks." She took them and dropped them to the floor then toed each foot into them. "So, how do you and Jack know each other? Work together?"

Brody's horrified expression passed quickly. Work? Brody? No, he had grander aspirations. Like landing a main character part in any show or movie that came his way. In the meantime, he'd keep living off his father's millions.

"Uh, no. I'm more of an artsy guy." He raked his hand through his hair. "Have an audition coming up."

Quinn's smile brightened. Great, she went for the Hollywood type. Jack might as well kiss her goodbye right there.

"Really? Have I seen you in anything so far?" She slid her hands into the pockets of her pants.

"No, not yet." Brody's confidence waned.

"Oh well. I'm sure it'll happen soon," she said with a tilt of her head. His girl played the small talk game well when she wasn't wound up in nerves, but Jack could hear the tinge of sarcasm touching her tone. Brody wasn't impressing her in the least.

"Yeah." Brody nodded. "Hey, I was thinking, maybe you'd like to hook up this weekend? Have our own play session?" He touched his belt. "I overheard some of your scene, and you mentioned you liked impact play. I fucking love giving a hard-ass beating."

Jack's spine went stiff.

Quinn's gaze flittered over to Jack then back to Brody.

Fuck.

She was going to accept.

Why hadn't he suggested they meet up again? Why had he let the opportunity get past him? Now, he was going to have watch Brody put his fucking hands on her. There wouldn't be a snowball's chance in hell he'd stay away from the club if Quinn was going to be there with Brody. He'd be there to watch it, to make sure she was taken care of, even if he would have to stay fifty feet away and be unable to talk to her.

"That sounds like fun," she started. "But I have plans this weekend."

Brody raised an eyebrow and nodded. "Cool. Maybe next week, then. How about I give you my digits, and you can let me know when you're ready to hook up?" He pulled a business card out of his back pocket. Classic move for Brody, to have a calling card ready to go.

Quinn took it with a smile. "Sure."

Having finished with his task, Brody turned to Jack. "I'll catch you later, man. I see someone I need to talk with." He flashed Quinn another grin then stalked off toward the lounge.

"Looking for a score, I assume." Quinn tilted her head and smiled at Jack.

"Yeah." He chuckled. "Brody's… well… Brody."

"He's into just playing, no strings?" she asked, her gaze following Brody across the room.

Jack stepped closer to her. "Yeah. That's his MO."

Quinn swung her gaze back to Jack, her expression softening beneath his stare.

"I don't really have plans this weekend," she blurted out.

The twist in Jack's chest unraveled. "Hmm… lying? I'm pretty sure that's a punishable offense."

She chuckled. "I don't think I can handle any more of your punishments tonight." A soft blush covered her face.

"Then maybe we should meet up… I don't know… on Friday night. Here. Say eight o'clock, so I can deliver the spanking you so obviously deserve?" He slipped his hand along her jawline and sank his hand into her hair. Fisting tightly, he dragged her head back until he saw the flicker of pleasure fill her eyes.

"That's probably a good idea," she said softly, eyes focused on his lips.

"And maybe we should plan to go out to dinner afterward. You know, to be sure you've learned your lesson. And then you could spend the night at my place. Just to be extra careful about you slipping back into your deceptive ways?"

She licked at her bottom lip.

"I don't usually do that," she whispered, bringing her gaze to meet his. "But I'm up for giving it a shot."

He crushed her mouth with his. There would be no mistaking his intentions. He was not going to be one of her dial-a-doms.

When he broke the kiss, her lips were swollen, her eyes large with submission.

"Yeah. I think we should definitely make those plans," he said, running his thumb over her bottom lip.

540

"Do I get breakfast if I'm a good girl?"

He released her hair and laughed. "Pancakes in bed. And I won't even make you drink the orange juice from a bottle."

She scrunched up her nose. "Thank fuck."

Throwing his bag over his shoulder, he laced his fingers with hers. "You know you liked it," he teased and led her to the exit.

"I won't admit anything." She squeezed his hand. "But I did have a fan-fucking-tastic night. Thank you." She paused at the coatroom.

"I haven't enjoyed myself so much in a long time, so I should thank you, too. Did you drive yourself?" he asked, jerking his thumb to the door.

She slid her purse over her shoulder and nodded. "Yeah. I came straight from the office."

"I'll walk you to your car, then."

"Bossy man." She laughed.

He squeezed her hand. "And you like that, too." He covered her mouth with his hand. "No, don't try to deny it, otherwise I'll have to punish you even more for lying." He grinned down at her. "As gorgeous as you are, I think a gag would really bring out your features. Yes. We'll try that on Friday." He dropped his hand.

"But I will get a spanking?" she teased.

"Oh, baby girl, you're going to get one hell of a spanking." And he was going to relish every single solitary swat and grunt.

She blew out a hard breath. "And I absolutely have to wait until Friday?"

"It wouldn't be much of a punishment if I gave you what you wanted right this second, would it?"

She pinched her lips together. "Fine."

He raised his eyebrows. "Attitude? That might cost you. You never know what I might come up with."

"With you, I think I'm going to learn to expect the unexpected and love it."

"I think you're absolutely right." He kissed her cheek and led her through the club and out to her car.

He hadn't expected to find anything other some fun for the night, but there she was. And if he played his cards right, if he did everything in his power to make it happen, there'd she stay.

And they would both learn to expect the unexpected.

Together.

THE END

ABOUT THE AUTHOR

Measha Stone is USA Today bestselling author of erotic romance. She's had #1 top-selling books in BDSM, and suspense. She lives in the western suburbs of Chicago with her husband and children, who are just as creative and crazy as her. Her vanilla writing has been published in numerous literary magazines, but she's found her passion in erotic romance.

Stay up to date on her latest releases, get a sneak peek at current projects, and exclusive glimpses at deleted scenes! Just sign up for her newsletter, and earn a free book, too! http://bit.ly/2B7buwt

- Twitter
- Facebook
- Instagram
- www.meashastone.com

FACADE

A Black Light: Roulette War Novella

By

Livia Grant

CHAPTER 1

SEAN

Six forty-five.

He'd waited long enough. Six-thirty had been too early. Seven would be too late.

Sean Wilde pushed to his feet, leaning down to pick up the leather duffel bag full of his favorite toys before grabbing the keycard from the desk and shoving it into the pocket of his jeans.

The door to his suite slammed closed with a thud as he took off down the hallway toward the elevator that would take him down two stories to his destination.

Black Light.

The BDSM club was an expensive vice. He'd told himself he didn't need to renew his membership since he only got to indulge in the club every other month or so. But then when the encrypted renewal message had arrived in his email box, he'd found his index finger twitching over the renew button multiple times. The day after his membership expired, he'd felt an odd fog of regret all day long.

Regret. That was an emotion he wasn't very familiar with, preferring to live life on the edge. So, when the ten percent renewal discount email offer had hit his inbox, along with the invitation to the annual Valentine Roulette event, his index finger moved into motion, charging the $22,500 annual renewal to his American Express Black Card in the blink of an eye.

He hadn't been nervous about his decision, at least not until the elevator doors opened and he encountered a crowded club.

So many damn people.

"Welcome back, Mr. Wilde. We've been expecting you. I know you're staying in one of our suites, but I just have to confirm, you left all electronics upstairs, correct?"

"Yep."

"Great. Participants are being asked to head into the theater by seven. You should have a few minutes to stop in at the bar if you'd like to grab a drink."

"Thanks," was the only reply he mustered for the dungeon monitor standing guard at the heavy velvet curtain separating the main club from the social bar area.

If he'd thought the club was full, the bar was jam-packed. His chances of getting to the bartender to order and receive a drink before seven were slim to none. Maybe he should have come down earlier after all.

Sean pressed through the crowd, making his way toward the theater entrance across the room. He didn't come often enough to know many other members, but he did stop to shake hands with a Dom he'd shared drinks with the last time he'd made it into town.

A scantily clad server carrying a tray full of champagne flutes crossed in front of him. It wasn't his first choice, but it would have to do.

Only after he'd swallowed the first swig of bubbly did he wish he'd settled for the bottle of water he had in his bag.

Damn French swill.

He didn't bother finishing the drink, choosing instead to set the half-full glass on the side table he passed as he weaved through the small groups of spectators.

Celebrities mingled with fans. Friends laughed together. Several couples were providing everyone with a preview of the night's entertainment—their sloppy blow jobs and spankings adding to the nicely building sexual tension.

Sean's own cock had been semi-hard all afternoon as he'd driven into the city from his winery southeast of L.A. He'd spent the three-hour ride on his Harley turning the list of kinks that would be on the wheel over in his mind, coming up with his plan for each spin. The only unknown was what hard limits would the sub he got paired with have on her no-no list.

Well, that, and of course her experience level.

"Shit, it's getting hot in here with this crowd."

Sean turned to find major league pitcher, Carlos Ferrara, pressed in next to him. Seemed like he would be a participant that night as well.

"Yeah, this room isn't really big enough for this event, is it?" he answered. Sean had never been in the theater before. He could watch porn at home.

"It was even worse last year. They've brought in better seating options to fit more spectators this year."

"You were here last year? I heard it was pretty intense."

The MLB player frowned. "Well, I was supposed to participate, but one of my crazy fans physically attacked my sub for the night. I spent the entire three hours the event was happening in the emergency room at Cedar-Sinai."

"Now that you mention it, I remember hearing something about that. That really blows."

"The Cartwright-Davidson's felt really bad. They ended up comping my next three month's membership fees and gave me the first right of refusal to take one of the slots this year."

"Nice. I've never talked to the owners, but I've heard they're pretty cool."

"They really are." The athlete reached out with his right hand. "Carlos Ferrara." The pitcher's grip was firm.

"Sean Wilde." The men stood awkwardly for a few seconds before he added, "Any subs over there you're hoping to end up with?"

Sean had been checking out the group of submissives gathering at the opposite side of the room.

Carlos changed his focus to take in the growing group as he

answered. "I honestly don't care as long as it isn't a rabid fan who wants to injure others."

Sean chuckled. "Yeah, at least I won't have that problem. One of the advantages of not being a celebrity."

"So, what do you do?"

He could tell the baseball player was just being polite as they tried to kill the time waiting for the event to officially begin. Still, he played along with the nicety game.

"My family and I own a winery and orchard out near Temecula."

"Interesting. What label do you sell under?"

The MLB pitcher may be talking to Sean, but he knew damn well he wasn't paying much attention to his answers. An adorable baby girl flirting with the men from across the room had the athlete's attention. To test his theory, Sean held off answering the hanging question long enough that Carlos totally forgot he'd asked it.

"If you'll excuse me, I think I have just enough time to head over to chat with someone I recognize across the room. Excuse me."

Instead of being butt-hurt about the slight, Sean was relieved to end his small-talk duties. He preferred to spend these last few minutes evaluating the growing pool of submissives across the room.

On the ride up to town, he'd told himself he was going to try his best to keep an open mind about being matched by the luck of a roulette wheel. But now that the sexy MC was taking the stage and preparing to begin, his open mind was closing quickly as he took stock of the growing group of subs across the room. Sure, there were some beautiful women to choose from, but there were also several *littles* who would be a disastrous match for someone with his appetite for edgier kinks.

The temperature in the room seemed to skyrocket as more people poured in, anxious for the matching to begin. He was pretty sure the club would get closed down if a fire marshal were to see how they'd packed so many people into the enclosed theater. He was grateful he'd gone casual for the night. The poor sap to his left was sweating like a pig in his business suit by the time the perky MC in the hot-as-fuck leather body suit welcomed everyone and got things started.

With each passing minute his nerves at signing up for the event grew. What the fuck had possessed him to voluntarily put himself through this stress?

The utter decimation of my sex life—that's what.

The MC calling the Dominants to the stage to pick their numbers for the spins dragged him out of the depressing memories of his ex-fiancée. One by one the Dominants drew what looked like popsicle sticks from Madison's hand. Despite being one of the first to pull a number, he glanced down to find he'd picked the highest number—fifteen. That meant he'd know who he'd be spending the night dominating not through his own spin of the roulette wheel, but instead through process of elimination.

He'd be paired with the last submissive standing alone.

He suspected he should be pissed about it, but as several of the subs dressed as *littles* in age play costumes and pigtails got paired up with other Doms, he could feel the tension in his chest loosening. That only lasted until they were down to just two couples left to be paired. The poor sap in the sweat-soaked business suit stepped forward to the wheel, leaving Sean alone in the Dom area of the stage.

His gaze scanned the area where the submissives had been gathered just minutes before, sure he'd catch a glimpse of his play partner, but found the area empty instead. The curvy redhead climbing the stairs was the last submissive. Was there someone hiding in the shadows? It was possible as there were several bright spotlights pointed in their direction.

What the fuck?

Funny how he'd been second guessing his decision to participate just minutes before, but now when it looked like he might not get to play that night after all, his disappointment was tangible. He waited for some explanation, but instead the MC started to go off on a tangent, talking to the audience about the silent auction and other bullshit announcements as if he were invisible.

"Mr. Wilde... I'm so sorry for the delay. The final submissive called and is running late. She assures us her car is pulling into our parking lot as we speak, but I can understand if you don't wish to wait for her. We do have an alternate ready to fill-in and can call her up to be your partner for the night if you'd prefer."

Sean had turned to face the man whispering to him about the missing submissive. He recognized him immediately as Chase Cartwright-Davidson, one of the owners of the club.

"Okay." He kept his voice low in turn as he could tell they were trying not to make a big scene about the missing submissive.

The event had already felt like a game of chance. Now it was morphing into a gameshow. Did he want to go with the submissive behind door number one or door number two?

"Which one is the alternate?" Sean asked the owner.

Without actually pointing, Chase nodded toward the petite young woman bouncing up and down with excitement in the middle of the front row. She was young, pert, and adorable... and that was the problem. She reminded him of his eleven-year-old niece, Lily.

No, thank you.

"I'll wait for the submissive who is late," he whispered back to Chase.

"Sounds good. I'll let Madison know she needs to keep filling for a few more minutes until your partner arrives. Sorry for the delay, but just think of the fun you could have punishing her for her tardy arrival."

Sean couldn't hold in the sly smile at the thought of using his worn belt to light up the ass of his mystery partner to teach her the value of punctuality.

CHAPTER 2

STEPHANIE

"*I* told you, my Uber just pulled through the front gates of the property. I'll be inside in two minutes. Please, just wait for me!" Stephanie shouted into the phone at the random employee she'd been talking to on her drive from LAX to Beverly Hills.

"It's almost eight o'clock. Mr. Cartwright-Davidson said it's no longer up to us. He's going to let the last Dom make the decision as to whether he wants to proceed with the alternate who is already in the club or if he would prefer to wait for your arrival. I'm afraid that's the best I can do."

"Grrr," Stephanie growled, hanging up the phone in frustration.

Nothing had gone as planned that entire day. If ever there had been a day when she needed a session at Black Light, today was that day.

God, I need to get laid.

She gathered up her sweater and other belongings, ready to jump out of the back of the Uber the second the car came to a stop in front of the massive front staircase that led to the Runway dance club. She normally entered Black Light through the back entrance reserved for members only, but she'd forgotten her membership card at home that she'd need if she wanted to get through the private gate.

Christ, I'm a hot mess.

Even as she thought it, she rejected the guilt. She wasn't a mess. She was over-committed—incredibly busy running her successful business. There was a difference.

Steph didn't have time to berate herself. There would be plenty of time for that later in the privacy of her own home. Right now, she needed to take the stone stairs two at a time, managing to break a heel as she rushed to the front of the short line waiting to be granted access to the mansion.

Hopping on one foot, Stephanie called out to the security guard, "Excuse me! I'm incredibly late. I need to get downstairs ASAP!"

A second guard standing nearby waved her to skirt around the Valentine's Day Runway partygoers and join him at the door.

"Ms. Starr. We've been expecting you. Come with me. I'll escort you to your destination." The guard glanced around the busy foyer, careful not to disclose to the vanilla Runway crowd that the premier BDSM club on the West Coast was just one floor beneath their feet.

Stephanie schlepped her carry-on suitcase and oversized Gucci laptop bag as they weaved through the Runway rooms packed with Valentine's revelers until they thankfully arrived at a locked door. The guard stepped forward to provide his retinal scan and the door's lock hummed, allowing them access.

Her suitcase banged loudly as they spiraled down the winding stairs into the bowels of the mansion, Steph getting more nervous as each second ticked by. She'd been so busy traveling to San Francisco for the emergency meeting with her suppliers that she'd had very limited time to think about the Black Light event. Considering how her pulse was racing, maybe that was for the best.

After so many twists and turns, she wasn't too sure where she was until the guard opened the locked door at the bottom of the stairs and she recognized they were at the end of the huge bar in the social area of the club.

"Let's leave your suitcase and briefcase behind the bar for now. The lockers in the women's locker room aren't big enough to hold those anyway and Susie and her team can help keep an eye on your stuff."

She let the guard wheel her things to safety, taking her high heels off and ditching them behind the bar as well to avoid hobbling in late with a broken shoe. She'd planned to get there in time to change into her sexy, skin-tight mini dress before the event—maybe even comb her hair and dab on a bit of make-up. Now, instead, she'd be arriving to meet her Dom for the night in her travel-wrinkled business suit... and barefoot.

I sure know how to make a great first impression.

The theater was jam packed. She had to hold onto the back of the security guard's shirt to keep from getting separated as they weaved through the standing-room-only spectators jamming the aisles of the theater. The guy was tall enough she couldn't see the stage until they were almost to the stairs leading to the elevated platform. The MC, Madison from Runway, was chatting away at the crowd with Chase Cartwright-Davidson standing nearby.

It wasn't until the guard stepped to the side and used his arm to usher her to take the three stairs up to the platform that she caught her first glimpse of him—the sexy-as-hell, angry looking guy in the perfectly worn jeans and button-down shirt that was just tight enough to hug his muscular body. But it was his dominant glare of disapproval that took her breath away.

He was pissed. Still, she was relieved the alternate wasn't already on the stage with him. Did that mean she'd get to play that night despite it being five after eight?

She got her answer when she heard her name being called by the MC on the stage.

"Okay, we're ready for our last couple to meet each other and to see what they are going to roll on the wheel. Let's welcome our last submissive, Karly Starr, to the stage to join her Dom, Master Wilde."

Stephanie both loved and hated the use of her stage name while at Black Light. It wasn't that she was ashamed of her seven years as the porn-industry's leading female star, because she wasn't. In fact, she was proud of the four AVN awards she had won. But it was just that she was so much more than the actress who'd made it big spreading her legs on camera.

Only when she stepped up close enough to him to catch a whiff of his yummy scent did she realize Master Wilde was seriously tall. He stood a full foot above her, making it easy for him to intimidate her when he encroached on her private space as he stepped up behind her to look over her shoulder as the MC handed her a small white marble and spun the wheel.

His voice was deep and gravely—seriously sexy—as he whispered against the shell of her left ear. "Roll us a good one, but know this… no matter what the wheel picks for us, you'll be starting your night with a punishment for being late."

The word *punishment* coincided with the release of the marble from her grip. It startled her enough that she used too much force, causing the ball to bounce and almost eject from the wheel completely. It seemed to take an eternity for the round glass to ricochet from slot to slot. The wheel was spinning too fast for her to read the kinks.

Just as the marble fell into its slot, the stress of the day and heat of the room combined with the dizzy feeling from watching the wheel spinning caught up to her. Stephanie wobbled on her feet enough that Master Wilde had to reach out and steady her with a tight grip on each of her hips. He crowded closer, molding his muscular chest against her back to help prop her up.

"Whoa, I've got you, baby."

Baby? Stephanie Kranowski was no one's baby. She sure hoped he wasn't one of those Daddy Doms she'd seen around the club. Her need for hard-core, edgy sex was pretty much the anthesis of wanting to be coddled by a Daddy, although she had to admit, if there were a massage in it, she'd make an exception.

"I'm not your baby," she whispered back, trying not to make a scene on the stage.

"Oh, baby. Tonight, you're gonna be whatever the hell I want you to be."

His ominous words flowed over her. Most women might be afraid of the edgy promise he'd whispered against her ear, but to Stephanie they were like a long-lost song she'd been waiting to hear again.

As the wheel finally came to a halt, her Dom for the night chuckled. "Hey, look at that. The perfect kink to marry up with the belting you're going to receive. I'll have to consider changing over to a nice crop instead of my belt."

Just great. I rolled Pony Play.

CHAPTER 3

SEAN

*K*arly Fucking Starr.

Rolling her as his roulette partner was kinda like choosing the door that had the expensive car hidden behind it. Thank God he hadn't elected to play with the Lily lookalike.

And rolling *Pony Play*? Maybe he should buy a lottery ticket later, because today was his fucking lucky day.

The lights were coming up in the dim theater and all of the couples had been dismissed to begin their night, yet Karly was still standing with her back to him, looking down at the roulette wheel as if the ball might miraculously jump to a different slot. It didn't take much to spin her until she was forced to face off with him.

"Now… let's get to know each other while we wait for the theater to empty out a little more." Sean pinned her with his best Dom glare before adding, "Let's start with you explaining to me why you were so late to such an important event."

Annoyance flashed in her eyes. "Who are you, my father?"

Feisty. Exactly how he liked his play partners.

"Careful. You're already in enough trouble for being late. I don't think you want to add strokes on for insubordination and sass, do you?"

"Listen, I had to make a last-minute business trip to San Francisco today and traffic from the airport was a bitch."

Tension was rolling off his little sub for the night. He knew just what she needed to relax. "Sounds like an excuse, but never fear. A nice belting will fix you right up," Sean promised. The look of fear in her eyes took him off-guard as he still held her close.

"Now might be a good time to tell you that... well... I didn't really join Black Light for the same reasons most people do. I'm not really into all of this game playing shit," she protested, trying to wiggle out of his grasp.

"Then it seems odd that you'd sign up to play a literal game called *Valentine Roulette*. If you don't like games, what exactly possessed you to sign up for tonight's event?"

He loved the defiant glare in her eyes as she proudly answered. "I just want to get laid, okay? Is that so hard?"

"Funny. I'm pretty sure people get laid all the time outside of Black Light. Why here? Why BDSM?" He genuinely wanted to know so he could try to figure out what made her tick.

"Don't we have to get started with our scene or something?" She tried to change the subject, glancing around as if looking for someone to come to her aid, forgetting that she belonged to him for the next three hours.

"Never fear, we'll have plenty of time for you to be my little filly in heat. For now, I need to understand why you're here if you don't like BDSM?"

Karly opened and closed her mouth a few times as if searching for an answer before replying. "There are a lot of celebrities that have joined Black Light for the anonymity it brings them. This is Beverly Hills, you know?"

"Don't lie to me. I met you five minutes ago and I can already see you like making grand entrances and have no problems using your celebrity name to make sure everyone recognizes you. Those are not the actions of a woman looking for anonymity."

"Shit... this was a bad idea," she whispered under her breath.

Sean would have kept grilling her for answers, but she swayed in his arms. "What have you eaten today?" he prodded her.

"Eaten? We aren't on a date. I can eat later. I really think we need to get started or we'll get disqualified."

Sean suspected she was more interested in ending his line of questioning than actually getting started with their scene. He pulled her closer. "I plan on pushing you hard tonight. That means you'll need energy. And while we're getting a few things straight, maybe now is a good time to remind you that you signed up to be my submissive for the next three hours, not the other way around. You might want to start getting in the right mindset or you're gonna find yourself pretty miserable."

Sean watched several emotions flit across her face before she settled on her next taunt.

"Yes, sir, *master*. Whatever you say, *master*." The grin on her face was like a waving a red flag in front of a bull to Sean. "Is that enough role playing for you?" she sassed.

He grinned back before adding, "You are digging yourself into a pretty deep hole. I'd stop if I were you."

He didn't give her a chance to reply. He could see the room had pretty much cleared out except for a few stragglers wanting to take advantage of the plush seats to have some of their own fun. Sean reached for Karly's hand and headed toward the stairs of the stage, stopping to grab his duffle bag of toys from where he'd left it.

As he dragged her into motion down the aisle, he noticed she was barefoot.

Sean pulled them to a stop. "Where are your shoes? Did you arrive barefoot?"

"My heel broke. I had to take them off."

Sean reached to pick her up and carry her, but Karly pushed him off. "I can walk on my own."

What in the world had possessed this woman to sign up for Roulette? At first, he wondered if she was purposefully bratting to convince him to punish her, but as he looked at her deeper, he suspected she wasn't acting. This was Karly Starr by day.

"I'm gonna thoroughly enjoy helping you shed your icy shell, Ms. Starr."

"The only thing I need to shed is this business suit. It's freaking hot in here," she said as she took off toward the exit.

You think the room is hot. Just wait until I light that ass of yours on fire with my belt.

Tonight was going to be so much fun.

Once in the bar area, Sean flagged down one of the servers with a tray of appetizers and piled a napkin high with all kinds of goodies for them to share. When he didn't see any of the beverage servers, he stopped at the bar and asked for a couple bottles of chilled water and then beelined it to a comfortable chair in the corner of the social area, out of the way of the major traffic. Some spectators had stopped to check out the silent auction table on the far wall.

Once seated, Sean motioned to Karly who was glancing around looking for another chair. "Kneel here in front of me. I want to talk more while you eat."

"Oh, for Christ's sake, I told you we don't need to waste time..."

"Sit... now," he barked. He liked a sub that would challenge him, but he was beginning to think Karly Starr didn't possess a single submissive bone in her body.

Sean waited for her to sink to her knees in front of him before lifting the crab-stuffed mushroom cap to her mouth.

"Open." When she didn't comply, he added, "Unless you have a food allergy, I suggest you open your mouth and eat now."

They were in a standoff and he knew if he couldn't convince her to eat a damn mushroom, the rest of the night would be a total waste of his time. He waited patiently for almost an entire minute before quietly informing the naughty sub at his feet, "I can keep this up all night, but know you already have at least a dozen strokes with my belt coming for arriving so late. And this is where I let you know you've reached the end of the line where my patience is concerned. I'll be adding a stroke with my Lexan paddle to your count for each one of these eight appetizers you don't eat in the next five minutes."

"But..." The first flash of fear registered on her face but was gone seconds later.

He held the mushroom to her lips again. "Open."

To his surprise, she did. Not once but again and again until all the appetizers were polished off. She ate in silence, which for them was an improvement. He used the quiet time to enjoy the view of the sexy pornstar on her knees, just inches away. Interesting—instead of skimpy fetish wear, she wore a stylish pantsuit—instead of layers of caked makeup, only a bit of eyeliner and mascara remained visible in the dim lighting. Her long, flowing, blonde hair was pulled back into a high ponytail, a few errant wisps curling to soften her face.

That ponytail will come in handy for our first scene.

He saw the annoyance in her eyes as he called her his "Good girl," when she'd finished, but at least she held her tongue.

"Now, before we head over to the costume room, why don't you tell me what your hard limits are tonight. I didn't get that info from Madison."

"I don't have any limits," she retorted proudly.

"Interesting, I didn't list any either. You missed most of the introduction material. We're using the stop-light system for safe words tonight. Got it?"

"I don't use safe words, either."

"Well that's bullshit. You'll…"

"Seriously. You do know who I am, right?" she asked defensively.

"What difference does that make? We're at Black Light. We play with safe words."

"Maybe you do, but I can assure you…"

It only took him two seconds to lean down and grab her long ponytail, yanking her face forward to within one inch of his. When Karly opened her mouth to finish her sassy retort, Sean clamped his free hand over her mouth, effectively shushing her.

"Now… I'm perfectly aware of who you are, Karly, and what you've done for a living, but I couldn't give a rat's ass about that. Tonight, you're my submissive and I'm your Dominant. That means I lead, you follow. If you'd like, I can ask Elijah, the Dungeon Master, to get us a dictionary and we can look up the definition of the word *submit* for you, because from where I'm sitting, you don't seem to understand the meaning."

Sean paused, enjoying the widening of her eyes as she internalized his words. Her spark of rebellion was still visible, but as seconds passed, he felt the tension leaving her body. He wasn't sure what had her so wound tight, but he looked forward to seeing if he could help her relax before the end of the night.

"Now, I'm gonna take my hand away, and you're going to answer me. And starting now and until you either safe word or it hits eleven o'clock, you'll address me as Sir or Master when you speak to me. Got it?" Sean slowly removed his hand from over her mouth, but he kept her close enough he could still smell her sexy perfume.

Her breaths were fast and shallow as she contemplated her options, finally turning her gaze toward the floor and answering with an almost contrite, "Yes, sir."

It was the first non-sassy thing she'd said to him. Progress.

"Good, girl. Now... let's try this again. What's your safe word tonight, Karly?"

"Yellow... or red, Sir, but..."

Sean saw the curve of her lips as she smiled mischievously.

"...I'm not going to use them." Several seconds passed before she hurried to tack on a quick, "Sir."

"We'll have to see about that now, won't we. Do you have any questions for me before we get started?"

Her eyes returned to his, her previous bravado slipping away before his very eyes when she asked him quietly, "Aren't you going to ask me if I'm clean?"

The question confused him. She may not have been dressed how most of the other submissives were, but she was certainly clean. Then it hit him what she was really asking.

"Why the fuck would I need to ask that?"

Karly's defensiveness was back. "Because every other guy I've hooked up with since I retired from filming has asked me, as if I'm a walking disease or something."

An irrational anger on her behalf took over. The look on his face must have scared her because Karly leaned away. He pulled her closer as he informed her, "I know we don't know each other yet, Karly. Unlike you, I came here to dominate my submissive—you—and I play hard. I can't promise that you won't end up regretting signing up for Roulette at the end of the night, but I can promise you one thing."

Sean paused, surprised that he was tempted to lean in and steal a kiss from her trembling lips. He resisted the kiss but delivered his promise.

"Not for one minute do I think you would be here offering up the gift of your body and submission to me if you weren't clean, and any asshole who would question you here at Black Light doesn't deserve you."

She must have liked his answer because the vulnerability in her eyes was gone in a flash, replaced with her previous sass.

I wouldn't have it any other way.

CHAPTER 4

STEPHANIE

The pounding music got exponentially louder as soon as they got on the other side of the thick velvet curtain that separated the social area from the heart of the club. She'd been a member of Black Light for over a year, but she'd never seen it as full as it was tonight. On a normal night, this crowd would annoy her, but she had to admit, knowing she was part of only fifteen couples officially playing, well, that felt a bit like being on set again.

And never... not once... in all seven years of her time in front of the camera, had she had a leading man as sexy as Master Wilde. She just hoped he was as impressive without his clothes on as he was dressed. She had always done pretty mainstream porn, if there was such a thing. She'd left the edgier kink work to others, which was why her pulse was racing at the thought of the promised belting for being late.

Surely, he'd been joking about that, right?

"Ouch! Shit!"

Some asshole in what felt like combat boots had trampled on her foot in the crowd. Without a word, Sean pulled her closer while leaning down to throw his right shoulder into her tummy, lifting her up and over like a sack of potatoes. If he thought she would object, he was going to be sadly mistaken. Not only did she appreciate the help cutting through the crowd, the view of his ass in his perfectly tight jeans was a nice distraction from the thought of what was awaiting her own butt.

Only once he'd put her back on her own two feet did she recognize where they were in the club. Another couple was already waiting in front of them at the door labeled *costumes*. It was an area of Black Light she'd never explored before.

Sean's arms encircled her as he hugged her from behind while they waited. The simple innocence of his embrace caught her off-guard. It took her a few seconds to realize why.

Men didn't normally bother with such frivolities as tender embraces when they were with an award-winning pornstar. The partners she'd been with since retiring had all subscribed to the idea that, like her movie directors before them, all they had to do was say 'Action!' and she'd be ready to perform.

"Have you ever done a *pony play* scene before?" His gravelly voice against her ear reminded her how different he was.

"No. I told you, I'm not really into all of the BDSM stuff." It wasn't often that she felt sexually inexperienced, yet admitting that she didn't have any experience with the kink they'd rolled made her feel just that. Almost like a newbie.

His grip around her tightened as he growled, "You forgot to add Sir or Master," he warned.

Her rushed, "Sir," was out before she could stop herself.

She was relieved he didn't make a big deal about the missed salutation until she heard his next question.

"You keep saying that. If you're not into BDSM, why Black Light?" he pressed her.

She'd been trying to figure out the answer to that very question. Her last few visits had been less than satisfying. In fact, she'd pretty much already decided that if tonight didn't go any better, it would most likely be her last time there.

"It's hard to explain... Sir."

"We're stuck in this line. I have the time for hard explanations."

Stephanie bit her tongue to keep from accusing him of lying to her. Why should he give a shit as long as he got a play partner with no hard limits for the night?

"I told you on the stage. I just come here to get laid. In case you haven't figured it out, I like sex." Several seconds went by before she remembered to throw in a quick, "Sir."

"Are you telling me Karly Starr needs to join a club just to find sex partners? Sorry, but I'm gonna cry bullshit on that one."

She sighed with frustration. "You don't get it. Guys fall into one of a few camps with me. They're either nice guys that are too damn vanilla and boring. Or they think they're going to be my white knight coming to rescue me from my old life of sin. But the worst are those that think because I was a sex worker that they can just treat me like shit because that's all I deserve.

"At least here at Black Light, where everyone is looking for edgy sex, the men are all looking for something more hard-core and the club's exorbitant fees keep out the real assholes."

"Yeah, but surely the Dom's eventually want to scene with you?" he asked, acting genuinely interested in what made her tick.

She couldn't hide her growing grin. "Oh they try, sure, but I like to remind them of how talented I am on my knees and they tend to forget about the BDSM games."

"So you manipulate them into just sex?" he countered in that gravelly voice of his.

"No, I…" Her breath caught, realizing she was giving away her tricks and needed to keep her mouth shut.

His arms tightened around her, making it hard to breathe. "Oh, Karly, you're in for a big surprise, my little pony. I am not so easily played. And for the record, I wouldn't count on getting laid tonight. Now that I know it's all you want from me, I'm gonna make you earn every orgasm with your screams and tears."

Holy shit, who was this guy? I think this might have been a mistake.

She was saved from coming up with a reply by the couple in front of them taking some age play gear from the costume guy and heading out to have fun.

"Well, look who we have here," the costume guy welcomed them, a spark of recognition in his eye. "I'm Dominick. How can I help you two tonight?"

Sean took charge. "Hey there. I'm hoping you're prepared for all of the kinks on the wheel. We rolled *pony play*."

The animated costume guy clapped his hands with excitement before answering, "How thrilling! I've been dying to have someone play with all of the awesome gear we have on hand for this kink. Hold your horses and I'll grab it from the back. Get it? *Horses?*"

Karly stifled her groan at the bad pun. She wasn't surprised when Sean didn't bother responding. His steely glare at the flamboyant costume guy must have conveyed his annoyance as the employee spun and took off down the small path between the tall racks and cabinets filled with all kinds of kink gear.

While they waited, a dungeon monitor stopped by to drop off a violet wand that some couple had already finished with.

"Wow, some couples are already done with their first spin?" she asked.

Her Dom seemed to have noticed as well. "Yeah, I'd better get us moving faster. I don't necessarily need the free month's membership prize, but the last thing I want to have happen is getting us disqualified for dragging our feet."

Before the DM left, Sean asked, "Hey, are there any platforms still open in the main room? My sub and I rolled *pony play* and I'd love to put her on display as I put her through her paces."

Karly giggled at his own lame pun which earned her a light pop on her ass.

The DM whose name she'd forgotten glanced back into the main room before adding, "Sure thing. There's the stage over closest to the swimming pool. I can set you up there. Any special gear you need?"

Sean seemed to know what he needed. "If you have a stock you could setup, it would be perfect."

"I'll see what I can do. I think we just moved one off of another platform. Meet you over near the pool in a few." And the guy was gone.

Dominick returned with his arms full, preventing her from asking further questions.

"I took a guess that the size six boots would be best for you. We only stock three sizes of those, but everything else is adjustable. Want me to run through it all with you?"

"Naw," Sean replied. "I have some experience with this particular kink. I'm good."

Karly's pulse spiked at that piece of news. She was in so much trouble.

CHAPTER 5

SEAN

*I*t only took a couple of minutes to wind them through the crowd to the only open platform. The DM from earlier had asked one of his co-workers for help in wrangling the heavy free-standing stockade up the three stairs of the raised platform. He wasn't sure if Karly realized she'd started pulling on his arm to slow them down, as if that might deter him from following through with his plan for their *pony play* scene.

"Strip." It was a simple command, yet it took several long moments for her to move into motion. He gave her a pass that she'd once again forgotten to acknowledge his command with even a simple *yes, sir*. He wasn't a strict enough Dom that it mattered much. All that was important to him was that he got inside his submissive's head and learned how to push her to the edge of her comfort zone. Well, that, and getting to fuck the living shit out of her before the end of the night.

But he wouldn't be disclosing that tidbit to Ms. Starr. At least not yet.

Karly was obviously comfortable in her own skin. Considering almost everyone in the club had probably seen her in one porn movie or another at some point, she stood proudly in her nudity. And damn if she shouldn't be proud. He had no idea how long ago she'd retired from filming, but her body was perfect. Curvy, yet toned. Natural breasts that were just heavy enough to droop slightly now that she was somewhere in her thirties. They called out to him, so he reached out to cup her flesh in his palms, lifting and squeezing until he drew a squeal from his submissive.

"Nice. Very nice."

"Thank you… Sir."

Sean shook his head to clear out the picture of spinning her and ramming his hardening cock deep in one thrust.

Patience. We have too much fun ahead before I can get my dick wet.

Sean had to release her tits in order to grab the bag Dominick had given them. After taking inventory of the top-quality toys in the bag, he decided to pull out the bit-gag with head harness first.

"What a nice pony you're going to make, although we have a lot of training to do before you'll be show-ready, don't we? And remember, only if you're a good girl will I actually go for a hard ride on you before we're finished."

Desire pooled in her deep blue eyes at his naughty innuendo, but it fled from her eyes quickly as soon as he held the six-inch-long, round wooden bit out to her and instructed her, "Now open wide and bite down like a good girl."

Karly opened her mouth slightly, but it was just enough for him to slide the two inch-round bit between her teeth. It was larger than he'd have picked on his own, but he had to admit he liked how wide it held her mouth open. She wouldn't be able to get too comfortable and she was sure to have drool spilling nicely onto those tits within minutes.

Since her hair was already pulled back in a high ponytail, it only took a couple of minutes to buckle the bridle and head harness into place and cinch it until it was snug around her head, holding the bit into place. He was satisfied it would stay there until he decided to remove it.

"So this is what I have to do to keep that smart mouth of yours from sassing me? Good to know."

His little spitfire for the night flashed him a defiant glare, reminding him of a feral horse running in the wild.

I'm going to have so much fun breaking her in.

Next came the leather reins, which snapped onto the harness on either side of her face. He was glad the owners of Black Light hadn't spent the money on the extra expensive horse-head full mask. Maybe *pony play* purists would see it as an oversight, but Sean preferred to enjoy seeing the emotions on his submissive's face as their scene played out. The full mask would have robbed him of watching her tears fall as they surely would be doing soon.

It took Sean a few seconds to place the next items he pulled out of the prop bag. Two leather pieces with snaps on them attached to the bridle. The blinders may not seem to add a lot to the outfit, but Sean knew they would limit Karly's vision enough that she wouldn't be able to distract herself from what he had planned for the other end of his horse.

Now that her line of sight was restricted, he could sense his submissive turning her head to silently track his movements as he went to the stockade to make some adjustments to the height. His pony wasn't overly short, but he wanted to make sure she had to bend over far enough that her posture would properly mimic a filly tied in her stall.

He watched her reaction carefully as he clucked his tongue while pulling on her reins, exactly as he would for one of the many mares in his stable back at the vineyard. Although, he was pretty sure they'd never given him the death-threat look Karly flashed at him as she was forced to step closer to the stockade.

He'd opened the wood gate, making room for her to fit her head through the hole in the middle of the heavy piece of furniture. "Front hooves into the slots for your wrists."

Sean stifled his smile at the gurgled curse, which sounded suspiciously like "Fuck you," that burst out around the large bit holding her mouth open nicely. When she didn't follow directions, he reached to grab her left wrist and wrangled it into its slot and quickly slammed the top into place, effectively trapping her into the wooden structure, her naked body bent over to present her ass up to him perfectly.

Karly tested the bonds, groaning when she discovered the openings were a perfect fit to hold her tight without any chance of her yanking free.

Once he had her halfway restrained, he went back to the bag to pull out the next items for her outfit—leather mittens that would fit over her hands to replicate front hooves. Getting the one on her restrained hand was easy. Capturing her free arm while she flung it around wildly in an attempt to avoid capture, not so much.

"Come on girl, we have to get you ready." He used the soothing voice he always did with nervous horses, which fit because he sensed her growing trepidation as she was forced to come to terms with the fact that she was, in fact, about to do a pony scene. Because there wasn't a snowball's chance in hell that he was going to get manipulated like the Doms before him.

Sean slid the leather over her hand and tightened the clasp at her wrist that would hold it on until he decided he wanted to take it off. Getting her right wrist locked into the stockade took a bit more effort, but a swift swat to her naked ass brought his filly in line.

"Pretty girl," he muttered. Sean stepped back to admire his submissive from the side, enjoying how her heavy breasts now swung as she wriggled to be free. It wasn't really a traditional part of *pony play*, but if time permitted, he wouldn't mind wrapping those breasts tight in rope.

Before he could finish getting her setup the way he wanted to for their scene, Sean knew he had one very important thing to do. He stepped around again to the front of the stockade, so he was directly in the line of sight of his pony. He suspected it made him an asshole that the long line of drool spilling out from around her bit had blood rushing to his already semi-hard cock.

Christ, she looks vulnerable.

The revelation reminded him of why he'd stepped up to talk with her in the first place.

"I know you said you don't use safe words, but I do. Since I have you properly gagged and your hands are not able to hold an object, I want you to use either of your feet as your safe word. All you need to do is lift and stomp a foot up and down a couple of times and I'll stop what I'm doing and come up here to check in with you. Do you understand?"

This time, he was sure that her curse was "Fuck you" as she continued to resist submission.

"I'll take that as a yes, Sir. I'll also be sure to correct your lack of submission with a few extra stripes to your hind quarters with my riding crop to help remind you of your place."

Just as he was about to return to his bag of goodies, he noticed Karly struggling to hold her head up enough to see anything except the floor. A quick investigation of the quality piece of furniture confirmed his suspicion—there was a padded chin rest that could be slid into place below his captive's chin.

As he locked her head in place, he taunted his sub. "There you go. I wouldn't want you to miss out on watching the crowd gathering around to watch me punish my filly for her rebellious ways."

Once locked into place, it held her head up so that she had no choice but to look out into the growing crowd gathering around their platform, there to watch none other than Karly Starr turn into a frisky filly. He may not know her well yet, but he was taking an educated guess that anyone who had made a living having sex on-screen had to have at least some exhibitionist blood running in her veins.

Now that he had the front half of his pony in place, it was time to pay attention to his favorite end—her hind quarters. Christ, she had the perfect ass—round, soft, and the palest white where her Southern California tan lines ended.

I'm going to love turning that white skin red.

First things first. He struggled to get her feet into the platform boots purposefully shaped like hooves. The heel was not only uncomfortably tall, but it pushed her ass high enough that her back was now perfectly horizontal to the floor—exactly like a real horse's back would be.

A quick glance at his watch confirmed his worst fears. They were over thirty minutes in and he was still setting up their scene. Knowing time was short, Sean bypassed buckling on the full body harness still in the bag Dominick had provided.

But no matter how short on time they were, nothing would prevent him from adorning his sub with the final piece of her pony costume. Stepping up behind her bottom, Sean took the top off the bottle of lube and started dribbling the slick wetness down into the crevice of her ass cheeks. Like the experienced partner she was, Karly didn't balk at all when his fingers probed the ring of her anus, massaging in the oil for a few seconds before lifting the bulbous butt plug with the long sorrel-colored horsehair tail attached to her tight ring.

"That's a good girl. Let me get your tail shoved in where it belongs so we can get your training started."

Karly's ass opened up easily, sucking the large metal plug inside until it was fully seated. He let the flowing tail fall toward the ground as he nudged at her ankles, forcing her to spread wider. The open stance might help stabilize her on her feet, but more importantly, he was sure it would make her feel more vulnerable—on display.

"Very nice," he admired just as an audience member whistled appreciatively.

Sean stepped back, taking just a few seconds to admire the beauty that was Karly Starr restrained into submission, adorned beautifully with the trappings of the *pony play* kink. His own cock seemed to scream for permission to come out and play, but he pushed down his growing need in lieu of the long-term satisfaction he'd get dominating Karly all night.

The music was still pretty loud so he went to stand in front of Karly again so he could be sure that she'd hear the snap of his leather belt as he pulled it from his jeans. The buckle clinked as he wrapped the end in his palm.

The fear in her eyes was tangible. It was his reminder that while she may be experienced in the sex department, she was closer to a newbie when it came to power exchange games. He found himself wishing he'd probed a bit more to find out what experience she had with impact play, but there was no way he was taking the time to unbuckle everything now to ask her more questions.

He'd just have to trust his Dom instincts to know when she'd had enough.

He lifted the tail up and over Karly's back, exposing her ass fully to him again and, rather than dragging things out further, pulled his arm back and lashed his tardy filly with her first leather stripe. Her surprised wail around the bit in her mouth fed the sadist inside him nicely. His second and third stroke came so fast she didn't have time to cry out her complaint until they were both over. Still, she was wiggling her ass from side to side so hard she was almost dancing in those high-hoof boots.

There was no way to make out the words she was mumbling around the bit, but he suspected she was trying to convince him to go easy on her, but what fun would that be? Her distressed gurgles turned to pained whines that went straight to his cock.

This scene, right here, ranked an eleven on his hot-as-fuck meter. He was only a few minutes into their first kink and he knew without a doubt this night was already making his annual membership fee worth every fucking penny.

CHAPTER 6

STEPHANIE

*H*is belt was surely on fire. It had to be because it was leaving stripes of heat across her ass so hot she was sure one of the DMs would need to step in with a fire extinguisher.

She was unprepared for the pain. She hadn't been lying when she'd told him she didn't really get into all of the BDSM games of the club. The Dominants she'd played with before had been easily manipulated into providing the hard sex she'd wanted without the hardcore power exchange games other subs wanted.

But Master Wilde was having none of it, and for the first time since joining Black Light, she found herself contemplating using a safe word to stop their scene. Only her own competitive nature stopped her from stomping her foot. She would hate being a quitter. If other submissives could handle a few belt stripes, so could she.

It was just before his tenth stroke that the world seemed to go completely dark. For a brief second, Stephanie worried she was fainting and blacking out, because not only had her vision gone black, but even the pounding music had stopped. One second later, the line of fire from Sean's belt proved to her that she was, in fact, very awake. Surely every member in the club had to hear her howl of pain around the damn bit in her mouth in the otherwise silence of the club.

Despite the burn across her ass, she was grateful that Sean was at her side in a flash, leaning against her, stroking her hair and back softly while he comforted her.

"Hang on, Karly. I don't know what the hell is going on, but I won't leave your side until they figure it out."

Through her tears, she could tell the emergency lighting had clicked on, lending a bit of light to the space and throwing shadows throughout the club as spectators and roulette participants could be heard wondering what was going on around her.

But the hubbub around her faded to a blur when she felt Sean's palm gently massaging the heat of her ass. The sharpness of the pain had subsided, leaving a new kind of fever behind in its wake. The fire that had hurt so bad had somehow ignited a need unlike any she'd ever felt before, deep at her core. Sean's fingers easily slipping through the slick of her bald pussy told her she had an abundance of wetness leaking from both ends of her body.

"I see my little filly is enjoying her punishment." The sexy gravel of his voice was close as he teased her. "Too bad we got interrupted by the black out."

His fingers were too light. She wiggled her ass, this time trying to make him come into contact with her clit, but he was too careful and before she could get the friction where she needed it, the lights and music came blaring back on and his fingers were gone.

"Please..." Stephanie growled her frustration around the bit in her mouth as her Dom stepped in front of her narrow line of sight, leaning down so that their faces were just a few inches apart from each other. His tenderness as he reached out to wipe away a few of her tears confused her.

"Are you learning your lesson, or do you need a few more reminder strokes to drive my message home about being on time for important events?"

For the first time, she was actually grateful for the damn wood in her mouth, preventing her from speaking because, God help her, she wasn't sure she wouldn't be asking for him to belt her more. She'd been searching for the kind of sex to fill the gnawing emptiness deep inside her. Maybe her Master Wilde was onto something. If pain was what it took to stoke her fire of sexual need, she'd gladly take more.

"Interesting. Don't look now, but I think you're enjoying the BDSM games you swore you didn't like when we met." Either her face was too expressive or Master Wilde could read minds. "Don't worry, baby. I'm more than happy to finish teaching you your lesson. The real question is if I can make you come from just a punishment alone or if I might need to mount you like the stallion I am."

Her Dom's hazel eyes had gone dark with his own desire. Despite being restrained and immobile, Stephanie felt powerful, finally understanding how much the scene was turning her Dom on as well. The boots were too high as she wobbled and almost fell. Then he was there, his left arm lifting her up at her waist while his right palm connected with the heat of her ass.

Over and over he spanked her, varying the speed and strength of his swats, keeping her off-balance. Just when it would almost hurt too much, he'd back-off, massaging her flesh and letting the pain morph to feed her need until the spanking resumed. Over and over he edged her higher until the music and sounds of sex surrounding her blurred into a haze. The only thing that remained was the pulsing need of her pussy to be filled.

"You're taking your training well, filly." His gravelly voice was sexy as hell.

She'd thought she needed to get laid before she'd arrived that night, but now… now she needed it like she needed her next breath. The sound of animalistic growling reached her ears through her sexual haze and, seconds later, she realized it was her making the sound around the bit-gag.

The crack of something really hard against her ass was like an explosion of fireworks, beautiful and dangerous at the same time. Soft kneading followed, massaging the warmth and helping her ride out the pain like a surfer rode out a wave to its end.

Crack.

Again. Pain. Heat. Massage.

Need.

Crack.

Harder this time. Deeper pain. Intense hunger.

God, she needed his cock inside her.

She tried to cry out, "Fuck me, please!" but knew it had come out in an unintelligible cry. He answered with more pain.

Crack. Crack. Crack.

It was too much, yet it wasn't even close to enough. She was losing her mind. Scratch that. Her mind was gone. The only thing left were primitive carnal cravings, and the sexy as fuck man who was playing her body unlike anyone else, including herself, ever had in her entire life.

She was so close. He hadn't touched her pussy again. Not so much as a brush against her clit or a finger inside her, yet here she was, ready to explode.

The sound of his deep voice talking against her ear called to her through her fog, especially when she heard the crude story he was weaving for her.

"You'd love it if I mounted you right now, wouldn't you, filly? Did you know that's how they breed thoroughbreds like you, Karly? The filly's owners wait until she is in heat—fertile— just like you are now. Then they tie her into a narrow stall, immobilize her with only her sex on display for when the stallion and his long cock get led in."

His voice was mesmerizing her as he told the naughty tale of how he'd like to breed her.

"I can smell you. You're dripping wet, preparing yourself to be mounted and bred, aren't you?"

Her mantra of "Yes, yes, yes…" was unintelligible thanks to the damn gag in her mouth, but she suspected Master Wilde knew exactly how bad she wanted him inside her. A tiny sliver of her sanity suspected she was going to be embarrassed at the end of the night when she recalled how out of control she was in that moment, but she was too far gone to give a shit about that right now.

Her heart pounded to the same pulsing beat she wished he'd fuck her with—hard and fast—as she listened to his raunchy story continue.

"But the really rare horses… they don't even get the brief joy of breeding naturally. They have to be artificially inseminated—the sperm stolen from the stallion and injected into the filly without any satisfaction at all for either of them. Maybe that's what should happen to you, Karly, since you were a naughty submissive and were late. Maybe your real punishment is having to go home without even one orgasm. Is that what you deserve?"

Despite his harsh words, she counted on the fact that his own haunting need would prevent him from ending the night without coming, but then it dawned on her that as her Dom, he could push her to her knees and face-fuck her to his own satisfaction while leaving her bereft.

Surely, he wouldn't do that to her on Valentine's Day. But then again, this wasn't exactly a romantic dinner date between lovers.

She tried to shake her head to tell him that no, she didn't want to be left on the edge, but the stocks held her too secure. She was at his mercy. Still, when he left to walk behind her, hope flared.

Please, for all things holy, fuck me until I pass out.

CHAPTER 7

SEAN

*I*t would be so easy. All he had to do was whip out his dick and slam it home. Karly was primed and ready and, with her experience, she could no doubt handle a nice, long ride on his prick.

So why did that idea just feel wrong? It sure as hell wasn't due to some noble act of chivalry on his part. On the contrary, the only thing keeping his dick in his pants was that he didn't want to give her the satisfaction—at least not yet—of getting the only thing she'd joined Roulette for in the first place.

Anyone can fuck her. I want to rock her whole world.

Sean enjoyed edging her immensely. He suspected he'd just delivered her first dose of impact play, and if he were a betting man, he'd put all his money that it wouldn't be her last. The wetness spilling from her pulsating snatch betrayed just how much Karly had relished her punishment. He loved how uninhibited she was and her unapologetic craving for sex. Three hours would never be enough to exhaust all of the dirty ideas for bringing her pleasure and pain he had running wild in his brain.

So, he'd better cram as much in as he could in the time they had left.

He pulled the final item out of the leather duffle the costume guy had given him for their scene, grateful his sub couldn't see what was coming. Sean lined the leather crop up with the center of her ample ass cheeks and delivered a forceful blow that painted a welt from left to right. Her gurgled scream escaped from around the bit in her mouth, once again tempting him to unzip his own pants.

Her scream of "No!" was easy to understand around the gag, but it didn't match how she wiggled her ass toward him, subconsciously asking for more.

Had this been a real punishment, the next strike would have already landed an inch lower on her butt. If she were an experienced submissive, hungry for the pain and knowing it was the price to be paid to hit subspace, he'd be setting a steady pace.

Sean smiled at the irony that the retired pornstar was actually closer to a BDSM newbie than the other participants in the game they were playing. It was that realization that had him standing close enough to brush against her left hip as he leaned down to massage her bottom. He couldn't help but smile at the physical heat he felt radiating from the small welt forming.

He waited until Karly's breathing slowed before stepping back and delivering a parallel line of fire under his first stripe.

Sexy cry. Rinse. Repeat.

Her low-level growl as she rocked the back half of her body was seductive as hell. He was mesmerized watching her climb higher and higher until the perfect finale for her pony play scene came to his mind. He glanced at his watch, knowing most couples probably were on their second or hell, third, kink by now. But why the hell should he take a chance at rolling again when he had his submissive exactly where he wanted her.

So, after a particularly hard stripe with the crop, Sean threw the implement to the stage floor and leaned in to massage her again. But this time would be different.

"Such a good little filly. It's time to do an exam. I've inspected you from head to hoof. The only thing left now is your internal inspection."

Sean unbuttoned his cuffs, rushing to fold the fabric up his forearms before stepping closer.

She no doubt was expecting his cock to do the probing, so her groan of disappointment when she felt three of his fingers stroking her instead made him smile. She was so fucking wet and smelled like sex as he tested her, adding a fourth finger—and then steepling his thumb in and piercing through the copious juice spilling out of her pussy to push until he buried his right hand inside her cunt. His filly cried out around her gag as he forged forward until he was buried up to his wrist.

Sean paused long enough to give her a chance to stomp her safe word. He suspected if any woman in the club could handle an impromptu fisting, it would be his little pornstar, but he also didn't want to make any assumptions. She was retired after all, and a BDSM novice.

As his right fist flexed inside her, his left palm connected with the punished skin of her ass. He didn't even try to hide his grin when Karly's animalistic growl returned, this time accompanied by the sexiest damn wiggle of her ass he'd ever seen. If he wasn't going to move his fist, she was determined to throw her body around in an attempt to find the friction she was so desperate for.

My little pony is ready to be ridden hard and put away wet.

To be gentle with her would be insulting. Karly Starr came to Black Light to get laid. More accurately, she was desperate to come.

As he toyed with her, flicking her clit with his free hand, he taunted her. "It's time you learned. Any asshole with a dick can fuck you, Karly. Hell, most of the Doms in the club are even up to the challenge of making you come. But that's not good enough. I'm going to make you lose control tonight." The words were the truth. He wouldn't be happy with their game of chance unless he made her take her first ever trip to subspace.

So he got to work, flexing his fingers inside her into a tight fist, then extending them, brushing the walls of her tight pussy, searching for that magical g-spot. He knew he struck gold when her knees suddenly buckled, her ass dropping fast enough his hand got yanked all the way back to her wet, dripping lips.

Sean hugged her waist from behind, lifting her back into position just as he shoved his fist back inside her, this time deeper until several inches of his forearm stretched her open wide. With the hard bit in her mouth, the only sounds Karly could make were appropriately animalistic growls as he flexed his fingers, probing every nook and cranny of her cunt, pulling his arm in and out, emulating how his cock would be fucking her later.

The first contractions of her pussy walls squeezed his fist just as he used his left hand to pull the thick tail plug out of her ass and shove it back into place. She took the double-penetration like the pro that she was, but he needed to push her harder... higher.

"That's it! Take it. Take more, Karly," he dared her.

His left palm moved to her ass cheek with a loud crack. His right hand flexed inside her, exploring until he found that special button again. He was playing her body like a musical instrument. Experimenting with different combinations until he found the perfect harmony to make her fly high.

Sean flicked the g-spot deep inside her like he was strumming the strings of a guitar just as he drummed a hard and fast beat across her punished ass with his other palm. Karly exploded with a scream as squirt after squirt of wetness shot from her pussy, drenching his jeans in her juices.

He'd made Karly fucking Starr squirt.

I wonder if they pass out trophies for special accomplishments like this.

But he wasn't done. His left fingers slid through her wetness, on a mission to find her clit. The second he found it, Sean pinched her button and resumed strumming her g-spot.

Karly's legs collapsed from under her again, but he was ready. He lifted her until her boots left the floor completely. He literally held her up from behind, one arm around her waist, hand on her clit while his right arm had her skewered so deep he was grateful he'd rolled his sleeves up.

A smattering of applause from the crowd of spectators gathered around their platform coincided with the subsiding of the contractions squeezing his fist. With regret, he pulled his arm out, careful to still hold her steady until she was able to stand on her own two feet again.

"Whoa, there. I've got you now," he reassured her.

It took nearly five minutes to strip his filly of her pony outfit. He sure as hell hoped Black Light had a good dry-cleaning service on retainer because the club's *pony play* gear was in desperate need of deep cleaning, and he couldn't be prouder.

Karly didn't even open her eyes when he took off the blinders and head harness. She flexed her jaw when he pulled the bit free, but that was the only movement she made. Had he not been propping her up when he lifted the stockade to free her from the restraints, she would have face-planted to the floor. Sean scooped Karly up into his arms where she laid limp like a well-fucked ragdoll.

"Well done, Master Wilde. That was seriously hot." One of the Black Light DMs had joined him on the platform.

Sean held Karly close as he said, "I know I have some serious clean-up to do after that scene, but I'd like to do a little aftercare with my sub first. I'll be back after she comes down from subspace."

"Hey, I've got this. On a normal night, we ask couples to clean up after their scenes, but we have extra DMs on duty tonight for Roulette. I'll make sure the pony gear makes it back to Dominick. He's gonna lose it when he sees how well-used it is."

Sean would seriously owe this guy a huge favor. "What's your name, man? I really appreciate your help."

"I'm Tyler, and no worries. You gave me some serious stroke material for after I get off tonight."

Knowing the DM was handling things allowed Sean to focus on the naked woman now humming as she snuggled against his chest. He climbed down the few stairs and headed to a lone chair in a relatively dark corner of the main club. The music was still loud. The sounds of sex and punishments surrounded them, but in his arms, Karly was oblivious to it all, and he wouldn't have it any other way.

He glanced at the digital clock on the far wall. Ten after ten already. They had less than an hour left. For the briefest of moments, he contemplated standing and heading to the small elevator that would take him up to the suite he'd be staying in later that night. He'd love to carry Karly into the oversized shower to clean her up. The splashing water would wake her up enough that he'd push her to her knees and shove his cock down her throat.

Such temptation.

In the end, he was too competitive to just quit the Roulette challenge. They had time for one more spin so that meant he needed to find a cold bottle of water to help quench his sub's thirst. Once she came out of subspace, he could turn his attention to satiating his own craving for her body.

CHAPTER 8

STEPHANIE

*W*hat the hell just happened? Disoriented, Stephanie first thought she was waking up after a really sexy dream, but as the arms holding her hugged her tighter, snippets of memories flashed.

God, I hope that was real and not just a hallucination.

"Here. Drink some water."

It took a few seconds to recognize that gravelly voice. It was seductive as hell and she suspected she could get used to hearing it. As the rest of her body parts checked in with her brain, she was certain she could get addicted to the things the sexy body behind that voice did to her lady bits.

Every part of her body thrummed with a kind of satisfaction she'd never known existed before. Even as she thought it, nuggets of need sparked to life again. She had no idea what time it was, but she prayed it wasn't nearing eleven yet. She needed more of the magic that Master Wilde seemed to possess.

"How are you feeling? Up to another roll or would you rather call it a night?" he asked so politely that she panicked.

Was I that bad that he wants to quit Roulette early?

"I'm not a quitter," she argued before tacking on a quick, "Sir."

His chuckle helped her relax a bit. "Okay then. Neither am I, but considering you've been out of it for over ten minutes now, I didn't know if you'd be able to give it another go."

She took a long swig from the water bottle he was holding to her lips before answering. "I just needed a bit of a rest. I'm not usually a napper."

The chest her head was resting on rumbled with a chuckle.

"You weren't napping, Karly. You were coming down from subspace."

Subspace. She'd always thought that was just a mumbo-jumbo codeword submissives used to stroke a man's ego. She now knew there was at least one man capable of producing the magical mental state, and now that she'd gotten her taste, she wanted more.

"I've never…" Steph let her voice trail off, oddly insecure at the thought of admitting the truth. "…well you know. I've never hit subspace before."

"Then I've done my job as your Dom for the night."

She snuggled into a tighter ball on his nap, grasping the front of his button-down shirt. Dare she?

"Actually, I was kinda hoping you could do your job *again* tonight, Sir."

Sean Wilde used his right index finger to force her chin up until their eyes met. The need in his own gaze was a promise—a promise she looked forward to cashing in.

"Oh, Karly, I can most definitely help you come again… and again. But, before we go spin the wheel again, don't you think it's time you tell me your real name?"

What? Who was this guy?

"Why? What difference does that make?" Only after her words were out did she realize how defensive they sounded.

"Call me old-fashioned, but I like to know the real name of a woman I'm about to fuck into next week." The grin that accompanied his naughty promise got the molten goo of her insides boiling again.

Damn, this guy was good.

She wasn't going to make things too easy on him, though. "Tell you what, you make me come like that again, and I'll tell you anything you want to know."

There was a playful mirth in the Dom's eyes. This guy was actually taking the time to flirt... with *her*. Didn't he know she was a sure thing?

"Anything? Hmmm... game on. By the way, I plan on asking you enough questions that you'll have to finish up answering over tomorrow morning's breakfast delivery."

Stephanie felt lighter than she had in years... *playful*.

"Pretty sure of yourself, there, Wilde, aren't you? Fair warning, I'm coming off a pretty long dry spell so don't get over-confident. The guy who drove my Uber tonight could have got me off."

"Yeah, but could he have made you squirt out a gallon of pussy juice? I'm pretty sure I'm gonna have to send my jeans through the laundry twice just to get the sexy smell of you out of them."

His words were raunchy enough that she felt an uncharacteristic blush across her cheeks.

She wasn't used to men flirting with her—holding her gently—looking at her like she might say something important.

"You know, I'm not some insecure submissive who you have to lie to just to get in my pants," Stephanie said as she wiggled to separate herself from him.

"Enough!" He hugged her tightly, stopping any notion of getting away.

The gentleness of his finger on her chin was gone, replaced with his full right palm squeezing her throat hard enough that she had to fight for her next breath. Stephanie forced down a panic, waiting for him to loosen his hold on her. When he let go of the grip on her neck, he also let a few choice words fly too.

"Let's get something straight. I'm not nearly as interested in getting inside here," he grabbed the skin right above her pussy, before adding, "as I am at getting inside here," he said tapping against her temple.

His lips crashed down on her mouth with the same velocity as the damn belt had when it had crashed into her ass. The kiss was unexpected. Personal. *Intimate*. It robbed her of her breath and the last shred of resistance. God help her, but this man made her want to submit.

The kiss ended, but Master Wilde held her close, their foreheads brushing.

"For the record, I can't think of one single submissive I'd rather be playing with tonight—you know why?" Thankfully, he didn't wait long enough for her to answer before continuing. "It's because you're the perfect dichotomy of experience and newness. I hate playing with coy subs who are too afraid to voice what they want sexually. I love that you embrace your sexuality, but I'm finding your newness to the BDSM lifestyle specifically a huge turn-on for me."

She saw the truth in his eyes. Sean Wilde wasn't lying.

As if he had read her mind, he grabbed her left wrist and yanked her forward until her hand came into contact with his jeans.

Soaking wet.

Steph could feel the heat rising higher, making her feel flushed. How long had it been since she'd actually felt embarrassed—shy even —when it came to sex? But then again, what they were doing wasn't just sex, was it? The *pony play* scene had been so much more. Humiliation... punishment... edging... restraint... role playing... fisting... Hell, he'd made her lose control of her body completely and he did it without even taking his cock out of his pants.

What the hell magic could he wield if he actually takes his pants off?

"Master Wilde? Sorry to interrupt sir, I know you are in aftercare mode, however Elijah asked me to remind you that you need to either keep playing with your original spin's kink or you'll need to spin again if you don't want to be eliminated."

Steph could feel Sean tensing under her. Afraid he might just tell the DM to fuck off and end their night early, she finally looked up, their eyes meeting.

"So... you think you can make me get your pants even wetter tonight?" she challenged.

Her Dom paused before grinning and answering. "Sorry, but you won't be able to get my pants any wetter tonight," he teased, "since I don't plan on wearing any pants for our next roll, whatever the hell it is."

She felt a bit like a prima donna being carried in his arms all the way from the main club room, back through the social area full of nearly drunk observers, and into the small theater. The lighting was dim, and the room was noticeably warmer than the rest of the club. Madison waited on the stage, talking to some huge biker-looking guy when she turned to welcome them."

"There you are! I had to ask if you two had quit. The night is already in our last hour and I'm just seeing you back at the wheel. You must have had a really great time with your *pony play* roll."

Master Wilde finally lowered her legs to the floor, but she was grateful that he stayed close enough to help steady her as she took the small white marble Madison held out.

"Roll a good one," Sean prodded as Madison gave the wheel a strong spin. Stephanie released the ball above the blur, letting it bounce around until finally falling into a slot that was still spinning too fast to read the writing flying by.

The wheel had to almost stop before she could read their next kink.

Shit.

Now that she knew her Dom for the night wouldn't be letting her get away with just having sex, Stephanie found herself wishing she'd put a few of those kinks down as hard limits after all. If she had, this kink just might have been on her short list of limits since she did, actually, enjoy being alive.

"Well done, sub. I can't wait to continue your submissive education. I suspect you'll be a fast learner. Either that or you might pass out again, this time from lack of oxygen."

Fucking great. She'd rolled *Breath Play.*

CHAPTER 9

SEAN

*S*ean's mind raced with the possibilities at his disposal. *Breath play* itself wasn't a huge turn-on for him, but he did love the intimacy it offered. Trusting someone with your very life had a way of bringing people closer together.

And he planned on being as close as possible to his sub before their time together ended.

He threw Karly up and over his shoulder like the last time they'd left the theater. This time, spectators got the joy of seeing her perfect, naked body striped with belt and crop marks instead of her business suit. With each step he took toward the main room of the club, his plan for their upcoming scene solidified.

As he had expected, the open shower area at the back wall of the lap pool was open. There were a few couples sitting around the pool, their legs splashing in the water, but there were no swimmers that night.

He'd be changing that soon.

His anticipation urged him to pull her off his shoulder roughly. He had to hold her up with his left arm while reaching to pull up on the chrome faucet on the back wall. Cold water immediately sputtered out of the three different shower heads above them.

"Stop! Too cold!"

Sean jumped back out of the water spray trying not to get completely drenched. When Karly attempted to follow him out of the downpour, he cautioned her.

"No! You're a very dirty pony. We need to get you cleaned up before we can start our next scene."

He loved the emotion playing across her beautiful face. Sexual excitement with a dash of embarrassment and a hint of fear—a perfect recipe for a submissive.

The water must have warmed as Karly didn't try to escape the spray again, instead reaching out to press a few squirts of body soap into her palm from the dispenser on the wall. As she started to lather her body, Sean got to work unbuttoning his shirt. He felt her gaze warming as she watched him do his own brand of a strip tease.

Karly's eyes widened as he'd expected when he took his shirt off, uncovering the dozens of colorful tattoos blanketing his chest and arms. To the outside world, Sean Wilde may be the respectable and hardworking winery owner, but those closest to him knew he had a wild streak running through him to match his last name. The tattoos were just a small appetizer of his darker side.

He'd left his belt back at the pony play stage so it didn't take long to have his jeans unbuttoned and off. He'd come commando and it was almost orgasmic to release his hardened dick from the tight confines of his pants.

He didn't take his eyes off Karly as he waited for her reaction. He wasn't disappointed… and clearly, neither was she.

"See something you like?" he teased as she turned pink. Karly Starr had just blushed like an untried virgin seeing her husband's cock for the first time on their wedding night. As the thought came to him, he chuckled. Where the hell had an image of a wedding night come from? Playing with a stranger for three hours at a sex club was pretty much the antithesis of marriage. Still, the newness of their dynamic held the same level of excitement for him. And that kiss had been most unexpected.

Time to have some fun. Let your wild run free, Wilde.

He rushed forward, not giving her even a second to anticipate the start of their newest kink play. Sean's right hand squeezed at her throat as he pushed her body until they both crashed into the tiled wall of the open shower with a thud. With the hardness at her back, Karly was suddenly trapped between him and the wall.

Sean watched her eyes closely for panic while he laid down a few new rules. "Once again, I don't plan on giving you much of a chance to speak during this scene, so your safe word is now three blinks of your eyes. Got it?"

Of course, he knew she couldn't answer him. She had just started to panic when he barked. "Blink now to confirm you understand, Karly."

Her eyes fluttered wildly, her attempt at silently begging for a breath. Sean obliged.

Karly gasped and sputtered as he released her, reaching for a palm-full of soap for himself. He didn't give her any time to recover before shoving her back against the wall again, but this time his hands were all over her body, lathering her arms, caressing her tummy, and moving lower to her legs. He took his time, inspecting his prize as he admired her curves, liking the few extra pounds she'd put on since she'd retired from in front of the camera.

"Spread your legs," he instructed before adding, "Wider," when she barely moved her feet.

Sean lathered his hands again before placing both hands on her inner thighs, massaging her as he inched his fingers closer to her pussy—the same bald pussy that he'd enjoyed making messy earlier. He cleaned his sub's slit, preparing it for their next scene. Karly hummed with desire as he stroked her hooded gem just long enough to edge her higher.

And then he took his hands away from her and she growled that sexy growl of hers—this time with frustration.

"Settle down, sub. Let me rinse off."

He moved his hands across her body gently, easing her down from the edge he'd taken her to minutes before. Only once the water ran clean and the last soap washed down the drain along with her fear did Sean pounce again. Determined to keep her off base, he scooped his sub up into his arms and took a few long strides to the edge of the lap pool and dropped her like a rock.

Karly flailed her arms just before she hit the water with a flat splat. Her loud scream as she splashed had to attract a lot of attention from spectators in the area of the pool.

Once he saw her head duck under the water, Sean stepped into the pool right next to her, reaching out to capture her and drag her back down with him as he went under.

Within seconds she was fighting him like a wildcat, scratching and hitting in an attempt to break free. The only reason he kicked them to the surface as soon as he did was that her back was to him and he couldn't see her eyes. Had he known her better, perhaps it wouldn't have been as important, but tonight—their first time playing together —he needed to prove to her that he would honor her safe word if she used it. As a newbie to the BDSM lifestyle, she needed to know that while most Doms might break a lot of rules along the way, they would always honor the use of a submissive's safe word. If they didn't, they weren't a Dom, they were just an asshole who liked rough sex.

He felt a bit like an asshole himself when he realized how much Karly's gasp of air turned him on. Her back was still to him as he wrapped his left arm around her neck, keeping her above water while still holding her tight enough that she had to fight for air while in the headlock.

Sean leaned forward to growl against the shell of her ear. "Now, I'll ask again. What's your real name?"

Several seconds ticked by with no answer, so he upped their game. Releasing her neck, he shoved her head face first into the water. Holding her under was too easy. Karly flailed, trying to knock his hand away from the back of her head.

When he knew she had to be low on oxygen, he yanked her head out of the water by the totally messed up high ponytail. It would prove a wonderful handle for this kink.

Karly's sputtering was different this time. Less angry... more panicked. He didn't underestimate the importance of fear and panic to a kink like *breath play*. By its definition, he was playing with life and death. Still, he knew he would rather cut off his own dick than actually hurt Karly, but she didn't know that.

As she gasped for air, he demanded. "I can't see your eyes when I have you underwater so your safe word is now snapping your fingers. And now... I'll ask again. By the next time you come up, I expect either the word yellow or your real first name to come out of that pouty mouth of yours, got it?"

He didn't bother waiting for her to answer, shoving her head underwater again instead.

Sean counted to ten, not overly high, and yanked her back up again.

Her scream of, "Fuck you!" didn't surprise him in the least. Karly Starr was nothing if not a spitfire.

He struggled to spin her flailing body around in his arms. He needed to see her eyes. This wasn't the kind of kink play where he could guess.

The heat of her gaze had to have the temperature of the water warming up around them. The rough game was turning his little submissive on, and that turned him on even more.

Sean clamped his hand over her mouth, but couldn't manage to pinch off her nose so he did what every good Dom would do—he released her body with his left hand to pinch her nose and then shove her head underwater, following behind her himself.

While he had never been a competitive swimmer, he'd certainly honed his water skills by swimming almost every day in the hot California summers as a kid. He had no problems forcing them deep enough that he was able to kick off the bottom of the pool when he was ready to surface.

His hands released her face just as they broke above the water. This time Karly added coughing to her sputtering. She smacked his hands away as he reached to comfort her. The only reason he was able to subdue her relatively easily was her labored breathing—a combo of him cutting off her air, but also from the exertion from trying to escape.

Sean had no desire to push her so hard that it was no longer fun for his sub. He waited longer, giving her a chance to catch her breath as he swished away the long, wet hair that had escaped her hair tie and matted to her face.

"Now, are you ready to tell me your real name yet, or should we go another round?"

Karly coughed a few times before answering, "Why do you care so much?"

Why did he care?

"I guess because what we're doing together tonight is very personal. Intimate. It feels wrong to not at least know your real name. You don't need to tell me your last name if you don't want."

She still hesitated, before answering quietly. "Stephanie, okay? My name is Steph."

"Stephanie." He tried it out, adding, "I like it."

"So happy to please you, *sir*." Her answer was complete sass, of course.

"Not that you asked, but I'm Sean."

"Sean..." The grin that spread across her face was captivating. So much so, he didn't see it coming—her knee with a direct hit to his balls.

"Fuck!" he cried out as he released her, lowering his hands to his injured manhood. The only thing that had saved him from total disaster was the resistance of the water had slowed her kick to more like a grazing. Still, his little Stephanie had just upped the ante in their little game.

I hope her ass can handle the punishment she's just earned.

CHAPTER 10

STEPHANIE

The distraction had done its job. Master Wilde had released her to nurse his balls and Karly kicked away from him, making it to the edge of the pool. She struggled to pull herself out of the water without the aid of a ladder.

She could sense him getting closer by the time she succeeded at crawling over the edge to her knees next to the pool. Sean got to her in time to grab her wrist, but she yanked free, pushing to her feet as she started jogging back toward the shower.

Stephanie had no idea why the hell she was playing so hard to get. More than anything she wanted her Dom to catch her and shove that impressive cock of his inside her. If she'd been attracted to him before he'd taken his clothes off, she was literally drooling for him now.

And it wasn't just his cock that she admired. Sean Wilde was a perfect specimen of virility. Muscular, but lean. The perfect amount of dark body hair to scream that he was all man, and impressive tattoos that hinted at some of the dangerous hobbies he seemed to enjoy. Motorcycles, rock climbing, sky diving... The guy was a walking daredevil and had been disguised behind that conservative button-down shirt.

She suspected her Dom was hiding a few things from the world, just like she was. The idea made her feel closer to him.

That was the last thought before he caught up to her, hugging her hard from behind before she could even get past the last post. The half-dozen circular pillars that ran from floor to ceiling on either side of the pool gave the space a definite Roman bath vibe. Steph wiggled to be free, not willing to make things too easy on him as he dragged her the few feet to the pillar.

She took solace in noticing how hard her Dom was breathing himself as they struggled. She didn't realize he was working her hands above her head until it was too late. She felt the padded restraint around her wrist just before hearing the lock engage. Within seconds he had her second wrist restrained and only then did he step away from her so he could bend over, hands on his knees.

"You really are a little hellfire, aren't you?" he said as he took deep cleansing breaths.

"So glad you noticed," she shouted as she kicked off the pillar, trying to get free, but exhausting herself instead.

Her shoulders hurt like hell because she could hardly touch the floor with her tippy toes. Even when she stopped flailing around, she could barely get any weight off her arms with her toes, but then her feet would hurt. Back and forth she shifted, hating her predicament. When the pain grew close to too much, Stephanie growled, still refusing to call out her safe word.

Through the strands of messy, wet hair that had fallen in front of her face, she kept her eyes on the man currently playing the cat to her mouse. She was caught in his trap. All that remained was figuring out when and how he would pounce next.

But instead of pouncing, Sean reached out his right hand to take the already hard cock hanging heavy between his muscular legs in his palm, stroking himself slowly as his eyes devoured her from a safe distance.

Despite being the one captured and tied up, Stephanie felt powerful in that moment. It was her body that was responsible for the feral look filling the eyes of the man in front of her. Minutes went by while she watched his sexy show, her shoulders hurting more each second that passed.

She was about to beg him to let her arms down when he walked a few feet away to a small table along the wall where several bowls of items she couldn't see were placed.

Steph may not know what all of the items were on the table, but when Sean turned she noticed he was rolling a condom down the length of his long cock. Her insides cramped, anxious to be filled by that perfect erection.

Sean picked up speed with each deliberate step toward her until he took the last few steps at a jog. He lunged forward, returning both of his hands around her neck, and squeezing hard enough that he lifted her toes completely off the floor.

Stephanie panicked. She'd forgotten their roll of the wheel had landed them on *breath play*. Within seconds she started to feel light-headed as her pulse raced.

"Christ, I love holding your life in my hands, Karly. I can feel your blood pounding through your carotid artery. You like being at my mercy, don't you?"

Despite having her immobilized, Sean loosened his grip enough that she wasn't having trouble breathing, showing that her trust in him to take care of her wasn't misplaced.

"Lift your legs. Wrap them around my waist," he barked.

That proved easier said than done. As she struggled, she realized just how exhausted she really was. As much as she would hate for their night to end soon, Steph was running out of steam. Regardless, as soon as she succeeded, Sean moved one hand up to help hold her legs, effectively relieving some of the pull against her shoulders, while still squeezing her neck with his other hand.

The relief was palpable.

"Now, I think you owe me an orgasm or two, don't you, my little pony?"

Steph couldn't agree more, so when he lined his shaft up with the opening of her cunt and plunged balls-deep inside her, she cried out with both relief and a twinge of pain. She suspected she'd be feeling the effects of the fisting for a few days.

He was so big... long... filling.

And shit did the man know how to use that tool of his. Sean lifted and shifted her body until he had her positioned exactly how he wanted her and then the real fucking started. Thrust after thrust slid through her wetness, hitting places deep inside her. As an adult entertainer, she'd literally fucked hundreds of men in her life. She'd thought she had done it all sexually.

Tonight she knew just how wrong she'd been.

Sean Wilde had introduced her to a whole new world. Before roulette, sex had turned into a simple itch that she needed to get scratched every so often. But tonight, the itch had exploded and she wasn't sure if she'd ever get enough of Sean's domination. He'd introduced her to a new layer of intimacy.

"Eyes." His command was simple.

Complying was hard.

She'd closed her eyes, letting the physicality of his domination of her body wash over her. When she did gaze into his eyes, she was rewarded with that feral hunger she'd noticed earlier. Sean's eyes were wild with desire as his fingers along her neck tightened again, cutting off more of her precious air supply.

Sean shifted the angle of his body, driving the tip of his cock even deeper as he pounded her again and again. The metal clasp of her wrist restraints was banging against the stone pillar to the same vulgar beat as her fucking. Hard, fast, and steady he thrust while her vision started to be invaded by tiny white stars. Somewhere in her brain, the word *blink* came to mind, but the pleasure was too intense to worry about something as silly as breathing.

Her orgasm exploded without warning when Sean released her neck and, hooking his arms under the back of her knees, folded her body in half. Stephanie's pussy was more exposed than ever and Sean took advantage of the new angle by plunging back inside her.

The scream that rang out was hers. He was too deep. It hurt, yet it was somehow perfect. This, right here, was exactly what she'd come to Black Light for. The best fuck she'd have maybe ever.

He was generous, giving her another orgasm before he roared his own release. As if they hadn't already attracted enough attention before, every single person in the club had to hear his roar of satisfaction as he shot ropes of cum into the condom.

"Shit, that was amazing, Stephanie," he growled against her ear before placing kisses down her neck, nipping at her bare shoulder.

His use of her real name caught her off-guard. She'd forgotten she'd told him. How long had it been since a man had even cared enough to ask for her name, let alone use it? In her experience, men preferred to only think about how they were boning a pornstar when they were with her. It somehow fed their ego or some bullshit like that.

Should it really surprise her that Sean Wilde was once again different than so many of the other men she'd been with in the past?

An unexpected sadness filled her as the club lights started to brighten just as the sexy music started to fade away.

Their night together was over.

This had to be what Cinderella felt like when the clock started to chime midnight. To Stephanie, it seemed like her fantasy night was about to disappear—poof—up in a cloud of smoke, leaving her to once again don her wrinkled business suit and broken pair of shoes to wander back out into the real world where she'd once again turn into the CEO of her prosperous sex toy business.

The next few minutes felt like a whir as spectators and contestants interacted, chatting about the highlights of the evening. Sean left her wrapped in a huge beach towel while he gathered up their clothes and talked to one of the DMs.

By the time he came back to the comfy chair he'd left her in, her eyes were drooping. She was so damn tired, but she needed to pull it together long enough to call an Uber to drive her home to Huntington Beach.

Sean pulled her to her feet, letting the towel fall to the floor and holding out a plush black robe. "Here, put this on. I don't want you to catch a chill."

"I can't wear a robe in my Uber. Where's my suit?" She tried to muster her strength.

"You aren't taking an Uber. At least not tonight. It's too late."

Tears pricked at her eyes as she realized how much she liked having someone give a shit about something as mundane as calling a car. She didn't dare tell him she didn't want the night to end yet, but reality was closing in. This hadn't been a date. It was one night. A game.

"I live over an hour away down in Huntington. You don't need to play prince charming all of a sudden."

"Stephanie..." he started, but she cut him off to continue.

"Listen, it's after eleven. The game is over. You aren't responsible for me anymore."

"The hell I'm not. I pushed you hard as hell tonight. You're gonna be in subdrop for a while yet. I need to get some food and water in you. Then you need a hot bath, followed by an even hotter fucking while bent over the end of my king-sized bed. Then I'm going to tuck you in and spoon you while we both fall asleep."

Is this guy for real?

He'd stunned her into silence. He had her wrapped in the black robe before she woke up enough to pull away. "I'm confused. I don't know what happened here tonight, but I know this. I'm not going home with you, Sean. At least not tonight."

His handsome face with the perfect trace of scruffy beard lit up in a panty-melting grin. "That's great, because I'm not going home tonight either."

He wasn't making any sense.

"I rented a suite upstairs above Runway. We are literally steps away from the elevator that'll take us to our room. I'll have you in that hot bathtub in ten minutes, and well-fucked and sleeping within the hour."

Shit, that offer tempted her. She shouldn't. They barely knew each other.

He shoved his fist up your pussy and made you squirt, Steph. You know each other enough.

"Well-fucked and sleeping within an hour?" she asked.

"I'll be the perfect gentleman tonight. I promise." He didn't wait for her answer, reaching out to wrap his arm around her waist and pull her into motion toward a small elevator she'd never noticed at Black Light before.

It was only after the doors closed and the lift was in motion that Sean added a sly promise. "Now, in the light of tomorrow morning,

Master Wilde is going to press you onto your knees and shove his cock down your throat. Your breakfast is going to be a few ropes of cum. It will go perfectly with the ass fucking you're gonna get in the shower."

She'd come just wanting to get laid. It looked like she got everything on her wish list… and so much more.

THE END

ABOUT THE AUTHOR

USA Today bestselling author Livia Grant lives in Chicago with her husband and her furry rescue dog named Max. She is blessed to have traveled extensively and as much as she loves to visit places around the globe, the Midwest and its changing seasons will always be home. Livia started writing when she felt like she finally had the life experience to write a riveting story that she hopes her readers won't be able to put down. Livia's fans appreciate her deep, character driven plots, often rooted in an ensemble cast where the friendships are as important as the romance... well, almost.

- Livia's Website: http://www.liviagrant.com/
- Facebook: http://www.facebook.com/lb.grant.9
- Facebook Author Page to Like: https://www.facebook.com/pages/Livia-Grant/877459968945358
- Twitter: http://www.twitter.com/LBGrantAuthor
- Goodreads: https://www.goodreads.com/author/show/8474605.Livia_Grant
- Instagram: https://www.instagram.com/liviagrantauthor/

AND THE WINNER IS...

By Jennifer Bene & Livia Grant

CONCLUSION

CHASE

enver, Colorado
February 15ᵗʰ, 5:09am

MOVING AS QUIETLY AS POSSIBLE, Chase snuck into the house, leaving his bag by the door so that he wouldn't wake anyone. Hell, *he* didn't want to be awake. He'd tried to sleep a little on the plane, but it had been restless, like it always was when Emma and Jaxson weren't in bed with him.

It was the whole reason he'd refused the offer to stay the night at Runway West — he wanted to be home with his husband and wife and their kids. Wanted to be in *their* bed when he woke up.

Yawning, he stopped outside the bedroom door and stripped in the hallway so he wouldn't have to make noise inside. He felt clumsy, drunk with exhaustion, but after a minute he managed to get everything off. Gathering his clothes and shoes, he carefully opened the door and immediately felt better. With the faint light from the windows, he could see Emma curled up on Jaxson's chest, asleep. He was out too, although it looked like he might have tried to stay awake for him because he was still half propped up on some pillows.

611

I told you not to wait up for me, Jax.

Smiling to himself at his dom's hidden sweet side, Chase set his clothes and shoes down and climbed carefully into bed. He sighed with satisfaction as he slid under the sheets to wrap himself behind Emma's perfect curves, gently resting his arm over her hip so he could reach Jaxson too.

He might be exhausted from Roulette, and the travel, but it was all worth it for *this*.

A quiet murmur made him hold his breath, trying to be as still as possible, but Emma turned toward him anyway. "Chase?" she asked sleepily.

"Hey baby," he whispered. "I just got in. Go back to sleep and we'll talk in the morning."

"Missed you," she mumbled, turning to face him in bed, and he didn't resist the urge to pull her close, planting a gentle kiss on her lips.

"I missed you too. Now, sleep." Their sub smiled up at him before she let her eyes close again, nuzzling into his chest.

Totally worth it.

Emma felt amazing against him, the scent of her shampoo and her skin something that made him feel at home as he took a deep breath and closed his eyes. He was worn out, and on the long drive from the airport he'd felt confident that he'd pass out as soon as his head hit the pillow — but in the darkness the incredibly hot scenes he'd seen during Roulette kept flashing through his mind.

Throughout the night he'd wished that Jaxson and Emma were with him. There were so many hidden places that they could have snuck away to, so many things they could have done together with Roulette playing out behind them. All of those cries of pleasure and pain, the intense scenes unfolding. Before Chase realized it, his cock responded to the naughty images in his head, growing hard and slowly pressing against Emma's thigh.

Dammit.

Shifting his hips back, he tried to ignore it until it went away, but then he felt Emma's fingers wrapping around his shaft and his hips thrust instinctively. The first stroke of her hand pulled a low groan from his throat. He wanted it, wanted her — wanted both of them — but they needed to rest more.

"We need to sleep," he whispered, gently grabbing her wrist, but Emma pouted up at him as she rolled her thumb over the head of his cock in a tease that sent shivers right up his spine.

"I *did* get to sleep, you haven't though, and I think I know what will help you." Emma slowly stroked him, up and down, and he didn't have the willpower to pull her hand away when pleasure buzzed along his nerves.

"Oh God," he muttered under his breath, pulling her to him so he could capture her mouth in a kiss.

"Starting without me?" Jaxson's low voice, rough and drowsy, had them both turning to look at their dom. Emma's hand stilled on his shaft, and he couldn't help but grin.

"Emma decided I needed help getting to bed," Chase answered, and she shrugged a shoulder as she squeezed his dick gently, stroking him again.

"You poked me with it," she explained.

"I can't control it, especially when you snuggle up to me like that."

Jaxson leaned against Emma's back as he pulled the covers off them, revealing her hand wrapped around Chase's shaft. "Go on," their dom told her, leaning in to nip her shoulder. "Welcome our husband home."

"Yes, sir," Emma said, her voice breathy as she started to move her hand again. Each stroke was bliss, capped off with the teasing swirl of her thumb over the sensitive head, and then he saw Jaxson moving his leg between Emma's. Opening her up so that he could stroke through her folds.

Chase knew the moment Jaxson found her clit because her grip tightened, her body jolting forward, but she wasn't going anywhere. Not between the two of them.

"Focus, Emma," Jaxson whispered against her ear. "Get him nice and hard, but don't make him come."

"Sir," Chase groaned, biting back the sound as Emma continued to stroke him.

"I guess you saw some fun scenes tonight?" Jaxson asked, his fingers working their girl until she was making soft sounds.

"Yes, sir." He nodded, his heart starting to pound as Emma picked up the pace.

"Good. I did too, but we'll talk about *that* in the morning." With a sexy grin, Jaxson looked between the two of them. "Right now, I want to handle this, because I got home a little wound up as well, but I wanted to wait until you could join us."

"Thank you, sir."

"I just didn't realize it would be after five," Jaxson added, a hint of chastisement in his voice, but Chase knew he wasn't in trouble. Not really. "Fortunately, it seems our girl here is getting very wet. Aren't you?"

"Yes, sir," Emma said, a soft moan slipping out as Jaxson thrust his fingers between her thighs, the wet sound of her making Chase want to lick every inch of her pussy, but their dom had other ideas.

"Get on top of Chase, baby," Jaxson commanded, taking his hands away from her as he got up on his knees on the bed. "We both need you."

Emma's needy moan captured how they were all feeling, and as she straddled him, Chase could only feel how lucky they all were to have each other. Her pussy teased the head of his cock, and Chase stroked up her thighs, cupping the round of her ass as he waited.

"Ride him, Emma," Jaxson urged. "We saw a lot of things tonight, and I plan to introduce the two of you to several of them, but right now Chase needs to feel your sweet pussy."

"I wish I'd been there with you. Both of you," Emma replied, her hips swiveling above him, her wetness dragging over the tip of his cock, but he didn't have the patience for it tonight. Digging his fingers into her lush hips, he pulled her down, groaning as her slick heat wrapped around him.

"We wanted you there too, trust me," he groaned, lifting his hips to thrust inside her. She felt incredible, her pussy squeezing him as she braced her hands on his shoulders and started to rock. "Does it feel good?"

"Yes, sir," she answered, getting into it as he took a bit of the control, lifting her up before pulling her down harder, reveling in the way her body gripped him each time. Seeking their dom, Chase turned to find that Jaxson wasn't wasting any time opening the bedside table to grab the lube. This wasn't going to be a long session, and he knew Jaxson had probably felt just as tortured during Roulette on the East Coast.

"Down." Jaxson moved behind Emma, pressing her down against Chase's chest, and he wrapped his arms over their sub, holding her in place. The click of the lube bottle had her squirming, but Chase swatted her ass, grinning.

"Be still for him," Chase admonished, and he saw Jaxson's playful smirk as their dom watched her hips move up and down a few more times.

"Please, sirs, I need you," she begged, her voice breathy, but then she stilled, a soft groan buzzing in her chest, and Chase knew Jaxson was warming her up. Spreading the lube inside their sub's ass so the trio could be together in the way they liked best.

"Good girl," Chase whispered into her ear, pumping his hips to tease them both as they waited for their dom to join them.

"We'll talk about Roulette in the morning, but I want to be clear," Jaxson started, and Chase tilted his head to meet his dom's eyes. "We are never doing this again. I won't go to Roulette without both of you with me, even if we have to switch coasts every other year, because I'm not dealing with the blue balls. I want you both there so that we can enjoy the event like everyone else. No one gets left out, no one gets left behind. Understand?"

"Yes, sir," they both answered, and then Emma's breath caught and Chase felt Jaxson's cock as he pushed past Emma's tight ring, sliding into her back channel where thin tissues let him feel every slow pulse of Jaxson's hips until he was buried inside her. The three of them groaned in unison, all of the tension of being apart, of watching Roulette without his husband and wife at his side, just melting away as they came home to each other.

"Ready, Emma?" Jaxson asked, and Chase squeezed her waist, feeling Jaxson's fingers overlay his as they prepared to take her.

"Yes, please!" Their sub rolled her hips, encouraging them, but Chase waited until Jaxson met his eyes and nodded.

Just as Jaxson pulled back, Chase lifted his hips to bury himself in her slick heat. It was muscle memory at this point, the perfect rhythm that had them alternating who filled their sub, but soon the tension started to build. Every thrust sending a delirious buzz echoing through him, the pressure of Jaxson's cock in her ass making the moments they were both buried inside her almost torturously intense.

Their pace picked up, and soon Emma was moaning, whining softly, and the squeeze of her pussy was going to send him over the edge sooner rather than later.

"Sir," Chase groaned, begging as he felt his balls tightening, that electric tension flooding his skin. "Please—"

"Please, please, please!" Emma begged, rocking as she chased her own bliss, and Jaxson just smiled.

"Come for me, both of you." Burying his dick inside Emma's ass, Jaxson added the extra pressure they both needed, and Chase only managed a few more hard thrusts before Emma came, her body gripping him in waves as she cried out and pulled him over the edge with her. Chase came with a shout, all of that electric tension turning into brilliant light as his cock kicked deep inside her, filling her in jerking jets as the world shrank down to the unbelievable pleasure of her body.

Emma trembled, grinding until he was buried as deep as he could go, both of their breathing erratic, and then they both moaned as Jaxson slid back and thrust hard again. They were both so sensitive, but Emma knew what their dom needed.

Pushing up, Emma braced herself on Chase's shoulders, her breasts swaying as she lifted onto her knees. Chase slid from her as she took position, but it was so Jaxson could pull her back onto his cock, and Chase got a front row seat to the beautiful expressions she made. Tense pleasure pulling her brows together, her breathy little cries like music to his ears.

"Are you going to come for him, Emma?" Chase encouraged, reaching between her legs to find her clit, rubbing in tight circles as she moaned louder. "Are you going to come like a good girl?"

"Yes, yes, yes," she babbled. "Sirs, please!"

"Not yet," Jaxson growled, his hips slapping against her ass as he pounded into her, and Chase loved to see his arms flexing as he pulled Emma back onto his cock. His tight stomach muscles rolling with each drive.

I'm so damn lucky.

"Almost," Jaxson warned, and Chase started to rub her faster, listening to Emma's soft little whines and mumbled pleas. "Now!"

Their dom gave permission and Emma cried out, her arms buckling as she collapsed on Chase's chest, her ass still in the air, held up by Jaxson's firm grip on her hips.

He was still thrusting, the pop of skin meeting skin filling the air until he drove deep and held, Jaxson's sexy groan telling him their dom had filled her too.

For a moment all they could do was catch their breath, and then Emma leaned forward to kiss him, her soft lips perfectly sweet.

"God, I needed that," Jaxson mumbled, smacking Emma's ass lightly before he dropped to the bed, leaving just enough room for their sub to be sandwiched between them.

"Me too," Chase replied as Emma moved to take her place.

"I was here all day with the twins, *I* needed that." Emma laughed a little, but Jaxson cut her giggle short with a kiss.

"I promise we won't be separated next year," Jaxson whispered, pressing another kiss to Emma's lips before he looked up at Chase. "Any of us."

"I'd like that a lot more, sir," Chase said, and Jaxson leaned over Emma to pull him into a kiss. His dom's tight grip on his hair had him groaning as their tongues danced, the rush of submission calming all of his anxious nerves, but it was over too soon.

"Next year, we pick one club. We leave the twins with one of your parents and make it a getaway for us." Jaxson looked between him and Emma, his gaze intense, and it was a promise Chase would definitely hold him to — for all their sakes.

"Yes, sir," Chase and Emma answered, and then Jaxson pulled the covers over them.

"Now, let's try and get a little more sleep before the twins wake up. We have to make a lot of decisions tomorrow."

Chase yawned as he snuggled up to Emma's back, reaching over to brush Jaxson's ribs. The three of them linked together like they were meant to be — and this time, sleep came easily.

Jaxson

THERE WASN'T enough coffee in the world for how tired he felt. Luckily, Sam and Jonah's nanny didn't mind watching the twins as well for the day, which meant he could look over the notes he'd taken the night before during Roulette without distraction. Comparing his notes to the votes was an interesting study in kink preferences, because the scenes he'd starred were only a handful of the overall votes.

The good news was that everyone in attendance had enjoyed the night. Tons of positive comments on the voting cards, which had been transcribed into columns for each of the participating couples by Maxine sometime in the middle of the night. The time stamp on the email was after three AM her time, and he felt a bit guilty about that as well.

Elijah and Spencer's stupid war had caused a ripple of unforeseen consequences, none of which the two Dungeon Masters seemed to be burdened with.

He'd had to leave at the crack of dawn to make it to the East Coast Roulette, and Chase hadn't made it home until almost dawn because of the West Coast. Now, his two managers were staying up the whole night to gather votes for some pissing contest.

Jaxson wanted to ring their necks, but instead he took a deep breath, drank more coffee, and continued reading.

Every comment made him remember something he'd seen, or heard the audience talking about excitedly. Whenever he'd seen a larger crowd gathering, he'd tried to make it over there to see it first-hand. Of course, there had been a *lot* of sexy scenes at Black Light

East, not that he'd given Spencer a single hint of what he was thinking as he'd left to get on the plane back here.

"What's it say?" Emma asked, her hair still damp from the shower as she sat down next to him with a mug of coffee.

"The members are very happy with Roulette," he answered, reaching over to tuck her hair behind her ear.

She smiled, rolling her eyes a little. "We knew that already. It's why we've done it four years in a row! What scenes stood out?"

"Well, someone used a latex outfit for a pretty hot scene using the stocks, and Elliott, who does demos at the club sometimes, got lucky and his sub spun *fire play*, so he got to set a flogger on fire."

"Someone set floggers on fire and I missed it?" Chase asked, his voice a sleepy drawl as he yawned in the doorway. He was wearing jeans and nothing else, his abs flexing as he stretched.

"Yeah, you did," Jaxson said, chuckling a bit. "But Elliott has done fire stuff before when we were on the East Coast."

"Not floggers," Chase grumped, pulling down a coffee mug to fill it.

"Why are you awake already, anyway?" he asked, turning to stare at Chase who had to be tired, but somehow managed to look particularly sexy with his hair still tousled from bed.

"Bed was empty," he muttered, dumping sugar into his mug. Walking toward the table, he waved his hand. "Keep going, what else happened at East?"

Glancing at his notepad, he flipped a few pages and felt the sadist in him purr. "One of the doms used a posture collar to do breath play, it was... hot."

Emma's eyes widened. "That sounds intense."

"It is," Chase answered from behind her, setting his coffee mug on the table before he laid his hand over her throat, gently squeezing. "But you trust us, don't you?"

"Of course," she squeaked, and Jaxson reached under the table to adjust his growing hard-on as he watched his subs together. Unfortunately, they needed to make decisions before the video call with the clubs.

"Sit down, Chase. You're distracting me."

"Yes, sir," he replied, kissing Emma on the top of her head before he took the chair to her left.

"So, who won?" Emma asked.

"I'm not sure yet. There are quite a few favorites here, and it doesn't seem like Maxine remembered to add them up." Scrolling through the document, he rubbed his temple, feeling the exhaustion like a spike straight through his skull. "Not that I can blame her, she sent this very late last night."

"Let me get my laptop so I can see if Madison sent the stuff from West." Chase stood up, walking toward the front door, and Emma leaned over to squeeze Jaxson's arm.

"You're both worn out, can't we just push this to tomorrow and crawl back in bed together?"

He groaned, wishing that they could, but the staff had already made plans to meet up for the big reveal at both clubs. Changing it now would just be more of a headache than the war had already been. Shaking his head, he picked up Emma's hand to kiss her fingers. "Unfortunately, no. But I love you for wanting to drag us back to bed."

Emma sighed and picked up his notebook to flip through it while he continued to read through the comments. Someone had done watersports, which had caught some attention. Another couple did fisting in the medical room, which had earned quite a few votes. He'd caught the scene on a couch where the big Russian had used a butt plug on his little submissive, spanking her, and then adding a vibrator to the mix until she'd come spectacularly.

It was a scene he planned on recreating with Emma. Maybe while she had Chase in her mouth.

Distracting.

"Got it," Chase said as he sat down at the table with the laptop already open in his hands. "Madison gave me the tallies in the email she sent."

"Why didn't Maxine—" Jaxson was halfway through the complaint when he switched back to the email and saw that she had, in fact, told him who the winners were with the associated vote count. He had just opened the attachment without bothering to read the entire email because he was too tired to think straight. "Nevermind, I have it."

"So, we have our winners?" Emma asked, sitting up straight in her chair with a big smile. "Tell me about them!"

"Elliott and his sub, Lovely Lisa, won the overall vote."

"With setting a flogger on fire, I'm not surprised," Chase said, and Jaxson shrugged as he went back to the transcribed comments.

"That was definitely part of it, but they got a lot of votes for a pretty wild CNC take-down scene that ended over a table in the bar." Jaxson shifted in the chair remembering how Lisa had caught his attention as she'd run, naked, through the crowd, with Elliott on her heels. "I got to see the end of that scene, and I have a feeling that swayed the vote more than the flashy fire display. Remember, most of the regulars have seen Elliott do fire demos, and many of the subs have had the chance to participate."

Chase looked distracted for a second, his coffee mug hovering in front of his mouth, and then he seemed to snap out of it with a chuckle. Taking a drink, he grinned. "Well, I have to say, I wish I'd had the chance to see that. It sounds hot."

"It was," Jaxson acknowledged. "But we had a lot of great scenes on the East Coast this year. Fisting in the medical suite, full-latex in the stocks — which included some face-fucking with a ring gag. A spanking scene that involved both a butt plug and a vibrator, quite a bit of anal, a watersports scene, and that posture collar with breath play." Skimming the document, he added, "And it seems like Mister M and Miss Payne were a close second in the votes."

"Which ones were they?" Emma asked.

"Latex suit and posture collar scenes," Jaxson answered, distracted by some of the comments as his hard-on grew uncomfortable. "Over-all, as much as it would begrudge me to satisfy either of our Dungeon Masters in this little war they invented, it's possible that the East Coast won."

"Hold on," Chase said, raising his hand as he leaned back in his chair. "You weren't even *at* the West Coast."

Chuckling, Jaxson crossed his arms and leaned back, mimicking Chase's posture. "Well, then, tell us who won at Black Light West."

"Pierce Montgomery and a sub who signed up as *Baby*." Chase clicked around the laptop for a few seconds, before continuing. "Tori Brewer is her real name."

"What did they *do*?" Emma asked, groaning. "Come on, I missed both events, the least you can do is paint a picture for me."

"Well, according to the DMs I chatted with, Pierce is known for being kind of an asshole. Into degradation, and the sub he spun was a Little… and then *she* spun humiliation."

Jaxson grinned, unable to hide it. "That sounds like a rough match-up."

"I thought so too, but when I stopped by she seemed to get pretty into it. He used a marker to write a bunch of words on her, like slut, fuckdoll, dirty girl, and did some pretty intense orgasm torture with her on his lap. Legs spread, draped over his thighs. The audience got a very nice view." Chase blew out a breath, shaking his head as he seemed to remember it. "And I'd be willing to bet that the facefuck scene they did was more intense than the one on the East Coast. He had her hands tied behind her back, gave her a ball to hold for a non-verbal yellow and had a local dom monitor it. Pierce was *rough* with her, but the girl didn't safe word out, even when he stayed in her throat for longer than I thought he would."

"Damn," Jaxson acknowledged, feeling a bit of jealousy at missing the scene. "Was she okay?"

"Apparently she loved it. Called herself his dirty little slut in front of the entire audience, and later in the night he put her on top of a wooden pony and used a violet wand while she tried to get herself off. According to Tyler, he ended up having to help her come, and they had sex on the pony, and the floor."

"I can see why they got the votes, but that doesn't really compare to—"

"Whoa," Chase interrupted. "That was just one couple, *and* Black Light West had three unique couples. A female domme and a male sub, a female domme and female sub, and then a male dom and a male sub. Did you guys have any diversity over on the East Coast this year?"

Jaxson felt his jaw clenching, feeling defensive until he remembered that they owned *both* clubs, and ultimately he didn't care who won. "We only had one domme with a male sub, so maybe we missed the mark on bringing in some different types of couples, but nothing you've described so far seems to top the scenes I saw."

"Okay." Chase grabbed a notebook from his bag, flipping it open. "We had a Daddy Dom and his sub spin pet play, and he turned her into the sexiest little kitten. Making her meow and beg for him to touch her and they had a crowd outside of the room when he fucked her while she was still wearing the tail plug. Karly Starr, the pornstar, was also there, and she spun pony play. Her dom locked her in the stocks in pony gear, whipped her ass for being late — which she deserved — and then fisted her. They had a good crowd watching her squirt."

"Of course Karly Starr had an audience, half the men there had probably seen one of her movies!" Jaxson huffed, not understanding why he suddenly wanted the East Coast to win. Maybe because he'd seen the participants first-hand?

"It was still hot. And they ended up doing breath play in the pool, and a spontaneous take-down scene outside of it. And we had a couple spin watersports, using the group showers." Chase flipped another page, snapping his fingers. "Oh! The guy that went by Tanner47 got paired with a new member named Quinn, and they spun ABDL. He definitely made it work for them, used a vibrator in her diaper and I heard a few audience members saying that their face-fuck was hot too."

Jaxson wanted to brush off the scenes Chase had listed, but he hadn't been there, and they did *sound* hot. Grumbling under his breath, he scrolled through the list of comments on the spreadsheet in front of him. "How on earth are we supposed to choose the winners when each of us only have half the information?"

Emma cleared her throat, pushing the lids of both of their laptops down with a sharp *clap*. "I'll choose."

"What?" Chase asked, looking at her like she'd lost her mind, and Jaxson wasn't far behind, but he could tell their sub wasn't going to back down.

"You two are going back to bed for a few hours. The meeting isn't until 2:30 this afternoon, and neither of you are going to make any sense by then if you don't get some sleep." Emma reached over, pulling Jaxson's laptop in front of her, and then she did the same to Chase's. "I've heard you both plead your cases, I've got the raw data, and I'm going to read the comments from the voting cards and make a decision on East versus West."

Jaxson felt a smile tugging at his lips, and then Chase laughed, leaning over to kiss their sub.

"Judge Emma to the rescue," Chase said.

"Absolutely," Jaxson agreed, standing up from the chair to steal a kiss of his own. "You're actually impartial to all of it, so your vote will be as fair as it can be. Such a good girl."

"Thank you," she answered, beaming a smile at them before she shooed them away. "Go sleep, I have to research."

"Don't get too sassy. I still have a lot of ideas for things to do with you when you're naughty," Jaxson warned, enjoying the pink flush to her cheeks as he turned and smacked Chase on the ass. "Same goes for you."

"Yes, sir," Chase said, still grinning, and Jaxson didn't have the energy to be annoyed.

"Let's get some sleep while Judge Emma makes her decision."

~

Emma

IT HAD TAKEN a couple of hours to read through all of the comments, and decipher her husbands' handwriting, but she'd made it through all the material and she felt pretty confident in her decision.

Whether or not the Dungeon Masters would like it would be a totally different issue.

"I feel more human," Jaxson said as he sat down next to her at the table. He smelled like his cologne and the tantalizing soap that both he and Chase used.

"I'm glad. I was worried about both of you this morning. This whole thing was just..." Emma let her voice trail off, trying not to be rude, but Jaxson caught her chin and turned her to face him.

"Finish your sentence." It was a command, that delicious edge to his voice that always turned her into melted butter.

"It was... stupid," she finished, already feeling guilty for using the word, but Jaxson smirked.

"I'm well-aware."

Surprised, she leaned back, her frustration building until she had to speak her mind. "If you knew this was stupid, then why did you let them do this? Why did you guys have to fly out to the clubs to referee their insane little war?"

Jaxson's eyebrows lifted a little, and she sighed.

"I'm sorry, sir."

"No, I'm glad you were honest about how you feel, and I can't say I wouldn't feel similar if I'd been the one stuck at home." Reaching over, Jaxson took her hand in his, squeezing it. "You know that I never want either of you to feel left out, and this situation put us in a place where no matter what we did, someone would be left out."

"Right," she whispered, and she couldn't deny that it would have sucked just as much to leave either of her men alone at the other club while she was with one of them. Even if it would have been more fun.

"Emma, listen to me." Jaxson waited until she met his gaze again before he continued. "I can assure you that it will *not* happen again, but this year it happened because I think their little pissing contest will help to get it out of their system. Hopefully it will help the staff at both clubs work together better, and next year we'll figure out a way to measure their success without breaking up our family for the sake of Roulette."

"I have some ideas for that," she said, and he smiled at her, leaning over to kiss her.

"I'm not surprised. You're brilliant."

Those words filled her with a buoyant energy that pushed away some of the lingering sadness at missing Roulette. "Thank you, sir."

"It's the truth," Jaxson said, squeezing her hand again.

"Are we live yet?" Chase asked as he walked into the room, still finishing the bottom buttons on his shirt. He had color back in his cheeks, and looked a lot better with more sleep, but she wouldn't be surprised if all of them weren't in bed soon after the twins were.

"Not yet," Jaxson answered, turning to look at Emma. "You ready to face them?"

"Ready as I'll ever be," she answered, smiling a bit as her men flanked her on either side. Leaning forward, she unpaused their end of the video chat and an explosion of noise crackled out of the speakers.

"They're live!" someone shouted from Black Light West, and both tables full of staff slowly settled. It was a lot of eyes looking at her, but Jaxson helped get the ball rolling.

"Hello everyone. This won't be a long call, but we did promise you that we'd give you the results today, so we're following through on that. Before we get to the results though, I'd like to acknowledge our Runway club managers, Maxine Torres from the East Coast and Madison Taylor from the West Coast, who stayed up until the early hours of the morning compiling the voting cards and the silent auction numbers that helped us make our decision."

The tables clapped politely on both sides of the country, and Madison and Maxine waved to the camera.

"Happy to help!" Madison called out.

"You owe me time off!" Maxine shouted, and everyone laughed.

"I'll take your suggestion under advisement," Jaxson answered, keeping his expression flat, which just made Maxine laugh again, and Emma couldn't bite back her smile.

She's never going to be afraid of you, Jax.

"One more thing before we announce the winners," Chase said, leaning further into the frame. "The three of us spent much of the morning discussing the various scenes we saw at both clubs, and one thing became clear. Whether it's the East or the West Coast, Black Light is *the* hottest BDSM club around, and all of you put on an incredible event, which gave us some fantastic memories."

Another loud round of cheers and shouts, several of the DMs on both coasts high fiving each other. Their camaraderie was endearing, and Emma felt a little less annoyed at the groups that had caused her stress as she watched them.

"That's true," Jaxson agreed, and Emma nodded along with his words. "I can assure you we won't forget it anytime soon, and neither will our attendees who raved about so many different couples in the comments section of their vote cards. Of course, the purpose of this little war was to identify the winners."

"Drumroll please," Chase requested, tapping the table in front of him, and a low rumble came from the speakers as the staff drummed their feet and their hands.

"On the East Coast, the winners were Master Elliott and Lovely Lisa, for their fire play scene and CNC scene!" Jaxson smiled as the East Coast staff exploded into conversation, talking about the scene and who had seen what. Waving his hand in front of the camera to draw their attention, he tried to quiet them down. "We still have the West Coast winners, guys. Calm down."

"That's right!" Chase said, leaning further into the frame again as he smiled at everyone. "On the West Coast, the winners were Pierce and Baby, for their humiliation scene, and violet wand scene!" Another raucous wave of sound came from the speakers, only this time it was the West Coast table cheering loudly and talking over each other.

Jaxson looked at her, and Emma took a deep breath, giving him a little nod. When the group had quieted once more, Emma sat up straight, looking between the two groups on the split-screen.

"So, I didn't get to attend either of the Roulette events this year, but I talked to both of my husbands today about everything they observed, and I read all of the notes from the voting cards, and we've made our decision for which coast won." Emma paused, feeling an inkling of guilt as she looked down at the notes she'd made. "Based on overall event performance, creativity with kinks, and a three percent lead on proceeds from the silent auction, the winners are... Black Light East!"

Both coasts erupted for different reasons. The East was cheering, several people high fiving, and Muscles actually lifted Spencer out of his seat to wrap him in a bear hug. On the West Coast they were busy shouting over each other with different arguments, bringing up different scenes from the night in rebuttal. The only one *not* yelling was Elijah, the Dungeon Master.

Emma lifted her hand into the frame and lifted one finger, then two, and just like a group of children they went silent on both sides before she got to three.

"Thank you," she said, smiling at the camera. "We're all extremely proud of both clubs, and while Black Light East will have the Roulette trophy for the next year, we will be choosing a different method of deciding the overall winner in the future, because my husbands and I don't plan on being separated for Roulette next year."

"That's understandable, Mrs. Cartwright-Davidson. We'll be happy to help with that during the next staff meeting. But, before you go, may I say something?" Elijah asked, standing up to move closer to the camera.

Emma glanced at Jaxson, and her dom squeezed her thigh under the table, before nodding slightly.

"Sure," Emma said, feeling awkward as the Dungeon Master asked *her* for permission.

"First, we're obviously disappointed, as you heard, but it's only because we had some truly spectacular participants this year who went above and beyond our expectations." Elijah turned to wave a hand at the staff who started speaking behind him. "Second, I'm man enough to respect when things don't go the way I expected, and I'd like to tell you congratulations, Spencer."

Spencer was still standing from Muscles' hug, and he moved closer to the camera to face Elijah. "Well, it sounds like you guys had a pretty good night out there on the West Coast too, old man." Coming from Spencer, that was almost a glowing compliment, and Emma grinned as the two men waved at each other from opposite coasts.

"We did, and while we won't have that trophy this year, you can bet we'll be coming for it even harder next year," Elijah said, and his staff cheered behind him, several of the DMs reaching over to slap him on the back.

"And we look forward to winning again," Spencer retorted, laughing as his staff cheered as well.

"That's it for this meeting, everyone. Have a good night, and thanks for making Roulette an epic event. I have a feeling it'll be even bigger next year." Jaxson waved a hand at the camera, before clicking the 'end call' button.

"You really think it can get bigger?" Chase asked, looking past her to their dom, and Emma turned to Jaxson too.

"Who knows?" Jaxson said, a sly smile spreading over his lips. "Anything can happen in a year."

THE END

THERE'S MORE TO DISCOVER IN THE WORLD OF BLACK LIGHT!

Black Light is the first series from Black Collar Press and the response has been fantastic, but we're not done yet. There are many more books to come from your favorite authors in the Romance genre! Including some continuations from the characters in Valentine Roulette, but we won't spoil anything…

If you're new to the world of Black Light, be sure to catch up with the books already released in the first two seasons of Black Light, so that you're ready when the next stand-alone BDSM fueled book is released! Keep in mind that all books in the series can be read as a standalone or in any order.

And be sure to join our private Facebook group, Black Light Central, where fans of the series get teasers, release updates, and enjoy winning prizes. If you are brave enough to become a member, you can find us at Black Light Central.

BLACK LIGHT SEASON ONE

Infamous Love by Livia Grant is the prequel that started it all! It explains how Jaxson, Chase, and Emma get together, fall in love, and fight to stand for their relationship against the forces that would keep them apart.

Black Light: Rocked by Livia Grant is Book 1 in the world of Black Light that begins on the opening night of the club, it follows a rockstar named Jonah "Cash" Carter and his love interest Samantha Stone. Misunderstandings and a dark history have turned this sweet, childhood romance into a dangerous situation – and when Cash and Samantha finally meet again there's only one thing on his mind: revenge.

Black Light: Exposed by Jennifer Bene is Book 2 in the world of Black Light. Thomas Hathaway and Maddie O'Neill would have never met if it weren't for the reporter opening at The Washington Post. But with her dreams on the line Maddie only has one focus: get the story, then get the job. When she lies her way into Black Light on Thomas' arm, everything seems perfect, except that she enjoys the belt and the man who wields it a little too much. Before time runs out Maddie will have to make a tough choice… to follow her dreams, or her heart.

Black Light: Valentine Roulette was the first boxset in the series where for the first time dominants and submissives came to the Black Light BDSM club to spin for their chance at a night of kinky fun, and maybe even love. With eight stories from eight USA Today and international bestselling authors, it's sure to heat up your Kindle! Featuring: Renee Rose, Livia Grant, Jennifer Bene, Maren Smith, Addison Cain, Lee Savino, Sophie Kisker, and Measha Stone.

Black Light: Suspended by Maggie Ryan is Book 4 in the world of Black Light. Charlize Fullerton is a tough DEA agent who has worked hard to prove herself, and when she meets Special Agent Dillon MacAllister on a joint task force to take down a drug ring sparks start to fly. When their mission ends he's sure he's lost his chance with her, until they run into each other at the Black Light BDSM club, and Dillon refuses to let her go a second time.

Black Light: Cuffed by Measha Stone is Book 5 in the world of Black Light. Sydney is a masochist that doesn't stick around for Doms who don't push her to the edge. Tate knows exactly what Sydney is after and he's intent on giving it to her, just not until she begs for it. One snag, there's a murderer in town and it's their job to make sure they get the right guy and keep him behind bars. But when the case starts to hit a little too close to home can Tate and Sydney work side by side without losing each other in the fray?

Black Light: Rescued by Livia Grant is Book 6 in the world of Black Light, and we're right back with Ryder and Khloe from Black Light: Valentine Roulette. Saying goodbye after Valentine Roulette had crushed them both, but Ryder Helms is a realist. He knows his CIA covert career will never allow him to be with a superstar like Khloe Monroe. But when things go sideways for both of them, it's not just their lives at risk, but their hearts as well.

BLACK LIGHT SEASON TWO

Black Light: Roulette Redux by eight talented authors was Book 7 and our second boxed set in the Black Light world. Our couples are back to their naughty shenanigans on Valentine's Day by being randomly paired and made to play out scenes decided by the turn of the wheel. Are you brave enough to roll?

Complicated Love by Livia Grant is the follow-up to the prequel, Infamous Love. It gives Black Light fans another look into the complicated lives of the trio, Jaxson, Emma, and Chase as they try to live their unconventional love in a sometimes uncompromising world. This book is a must read for MMF menage fans!

Black Light: Suspicion by Measha Stone is Book 8 in the world of Black Light. Measha is back with another fun dose of suspense and sexy BDSM play combined Sophie and Scott work together to solve crimes by day and burn up the sheets by night. When Sophie is in danger, there is little her Dom won't do to keep her safe, including warming her bottom when she needs it.

Black Light: Obsessed by Dani René is Book 9 in the Black Light world. Dani's first story in the series is also the first Black Light book set on the West Coast new club. He might just be a little obsessed with his new submissive, Roisin. Does he go too far?

Black Light: Fearless by Maren Smith is Book 10 in the Black Light world. The talented BDSM author, Maren, is very familiar to Black Light fans since she has had short stories in both Roulette boxes sets. In fact, fans of her short story Shameless will recognize the beloved characters in this full-length follow-up novel. This is a must read Black Light book!

Black Light: Possession by LK Shaw is book 11 and the final book of season two. It brings the action back to the East Coast and gives us a glimpse of another fantastic menage relationship set in the middle of danger and intrigue. It is the perfect ending to our second season as we move forward into season three with Celebrity Roulette.

BLACK LIGHT SEASON THREE

Black Light: Celebrity Roulette by eight talented authors is Book 12 and our third annual Valentine's Day boxed set in the Black Light world. New couples are back to their naughty shenanigans on Valentine's Day by being paired, this time with a celebrity auction, and made to play out scenes decided by the turn of the wheel. Come see how the celebrities play on the West Coast!

Black Light: Purged - A Black Light Short by Livia Grant is a bit unique in the Black Light world. It is a short glimpse into the lives of some of our beloved recurring characters, Khloe Monroe and Ryder Helms. It is a dark and realistic view into the lives of someone living with an eating disorder and how having someone who loves you in your corner can make all the difference in the world.

Black Light: Defended by Golden Angel is book 13 in the series. It takes us back to the East Coast for a delicious, and our first, full-length Daddy Dom book. If you've ever wanted to explore this unique kink, this is a fun introduction and you will love Kawan and Melody.

Black Light: Scandalized by Livia Grant is book 14 in the series. Scandalized breaks a lot of the rules when it comes to romance novels. It follows two couples, not one, and take on a controversial social topic by exploring sexual harassment in the #metoo movement times. This book is full of old favorite characters and is guaranteed to make you laugh out loud one minute and cry the next. Looking for a book that will stick with you for a long time after you finish reading it, this one fits the bill.

BLACK COLLAR PRESS

Black Collar Press is a small publishing house started by authors Livia Grant and Jennifer Bene in late 2016. The purpose was simple - to create a place where the erotic, kinky, and exciting worlds they love to explore could thrive and be joined by other like-minded authors.

If this is something that interests you, please go to the Black Collar Press website and read through the FAQs. If your questions are not answered there, please contact us directly at: blackcollarpress@gmail.com

WHERE TO FIND BLACK COLLAR PRESS:

- Website: http://www.blackcollarpress.com/
- Facebook: https://www.facebook.com/blackcollarpress/
- Twitter: https://twitter.com/BlackCollarPres
- Black Light East and West may be fictitious, but you can now join our very real Facebook Group for Black Light Fans - Black Light Central

GET A FREE BLACK LIGHT BOOK

Enjoy your trip to Black Light? There's a lot more sexy fun to be had. All of the books in the series can be read as standalone stories and can also be enjoyed in any reading order.

Get started with a FREE copy of **Black Light: Rocked** today. Your fun doesn't need to end yet!

Made in the USA
Columbia, SC
10 January 2021